TIDEWATER DYNASTY

The Lees of Stratford Hall

TIDEWATER DYNASTY

The Lees of Stratford Hall

NON INCAUTUS FUTURI

Carey Roberts and Rebecca Seely

A Harvest/HBJ Book
Harcourt Brace Jovanovich, Publishers
San Diego   New York   London

To Frances N. Shively,
with affection and great appreciation

Copyright © 1981 by Carey Roberts and Rebecca Seely

Library of Congress Cataloging in Publication Data

Roberts, Carey.
Tidewater dynasty.

(A Harvest/HBJ book)
Originally published: New York: Harcourt Brace
Jovanovich, 1981.
1. Lee family — Fiction. 2. Virginia — History —
Revolution, 1775–1783 — Fiction. 3. Virginia — History —
Colonial period, ca. 1600-1775 — Fiction. I. Seeley,
Rebecca. II. Title.
PS3568.02375T5   1983   813'.54   83-8388
ISBN 0-15-690336-9

Printed in the United States of America

First Harvest/HBJ edition 1983

B C D E F G H

Contents

Contents

Authors' Note

The Tidewater is both place and time, reality and myth. It is that low fertile part of Virginia through which four broad rivers wind inland from the Chesapeake Bay past somnolent, rich fields and leaf-shaded ravines, to be abruptly stemmed by rocky falls in the northern hills. Embraced and shaped by the James, the York, the Rappahannock, and the Potomac, the land forms a golden triangle that at its longest stretch measures about 160 miles north to south and 120 miles east to west.

The land known as the Tidewater is carved by the rivers into three narrow peninsulas. The southernmost lies between the James and the York; the second nestles between the York and the Rappahannock; the third, which is the wildest and most isolated, lies to the north between the Rappahannock and the Potomac rivers and is known as the Northern Neck.

The James, the York, the Rappahannock, and the Potomac are freshwater rivers, nourished in the north by mountain water sheds, but they are *also* tidal estuaries—powerful inland reaches of the Chesapeake Bay and the Atlantic Ocean beyond. Salty and deep, the four rivers have as their current the ebb and flow of the ocean tides. Into them flow tributaries with curious and sing-song Indian names—Matchotique, Mattaponi, Pamunkey, Wicomico, Coan, and Nomini—as well as countless streams, creeks, and runs.

These shorelines were long the home of the Algonquin tribes, who were held to this ground by its generous yield of fish, animals, and pelts. Before it was claimed by England, the Tidewater was briefly visited in the late sixteenth century by Spanish sailors exploring the North Atlantic coast. The Tidewater's time of greatness, however, began in the spring of 1607, when three small sailing ships, the *Susan Constant*, the *Discovery*, and the *Godspeed*, having braved the treacherous deeps of the Atlantic Ocean, entered the sheltering capes of the Chesapeake Bay and eventually anchored on a small island fifty miles above the mouth of the James River. Here, these English adventurers of the London Company made the first permanent English settlement in the Americas, which they christened Jamestown after their Stuart King.

The land was fair and bountiful, but the claiming of it proved perilous. The settlers clung tenaciously to this edge of the great dark continent until a hundred years of pestilence, starvation, and massacre had passed. Then, a beautiful golden period began to unfold in this Virginia Colony. A unique civilization flourished, producing a high-born race bound in a web of kinship. They were born to privilege and responsibility, prized their obligations to Church and State, and were always mindful of their ancient heritage and their rights as free Englishmen.

They lived as gentle courtiers in a beguiling but danger-filled wilderness. Theirs was a code blended of bold personal expectations and humanist ideals. Their influence would reach far beyond the Tidewater to affect indelibly the creation of a new nation and the course of the history of the world. Bound to one another by their love for the land, they were destined for greatness and determined to lead.

In *Tidewater Dynasty*, it is the authors' intent to lay before you the story of one distinctive family. We have based this book as fully as possible on the records, diaries, letters, and documents of the time, striving always for honesty and strict adherence to fact. Notes for authentic letters and words appear at the back of the book. Still, this book is a novel. No one knows the exact words spoken, the expressions on the faces or the thoughts in the hearts of these men and women. We have taken the known and lived with it. Every event, conversation, and relationship happened or *could* have happened. No real character has been artificially placed, no dialogue created, that is not compatible with the personality, vivid or shadowy, that came to life for us as we sought to re-create the story of the glorious, rebellious Lees of Stratford Hall.

ACKNOWLEDGMENTS

The authors would like to express their deepest appreciation to the following: Frances N. Shively, Secretary of the Society of the Lees of Virginia and Director of the Lee-Fendall House, a memorial to Light Horse Harry Lee, in Alexandria, whose support and encouragement were constant from beginning to end; Admiral Thomas E. Bass, Executive Director of the Robert E. Lee Memorial Association, Inc., and the staff of Stratford Hall, in particular to Mrs. Gerald Allard, whose hospitality was unfailingly gracious and whose assistance was invaluable; Margot C. J. Mabie, whose belief in the project and careful, professional editing made this book possible; Mrs. Leslie Cheek, Jr., Director for Virginia of the Robert E. Lee Memorial Association, who shared with us her historical expertise; Betsy E. Walsh, for her careful preparation of and assistance with the manuscript; Lynn Holland, without whose typing efforts we could not have met deadlines; Dan Seely and Cay Roberts, who stepped into the gap whenever needed; Estelle Lee and Gussie Washington, whose dependable support was much appreciated; Lindsay Fulcher of the London Museum, Christine Laude of the Benjamin Franklin Library, in Paris, and the staffs of the Lee-Fendall House and the Lloyd House, in Alexandria, and of the Virginia Historical Society, in Richmond, for their assistance; Mark Meagher, President of the Washington Post Corporation, for his encouragement and advice; Peter D. Olch, M.D., for generously sharing his library; and Peter and Jeremy FitzGerald, who provided a sylvan setting for work sessions.

Last, and wholeheartedly, the authors thank their families—their husbands, Bill Roberts and Earl Seely, who never doubted and always encouraged, and their children, Cliff, Chuck, Cay, and John Roberts, and Laura Seely Przewlocki, Dan and Elizabeth Seely, whose love sustained them.

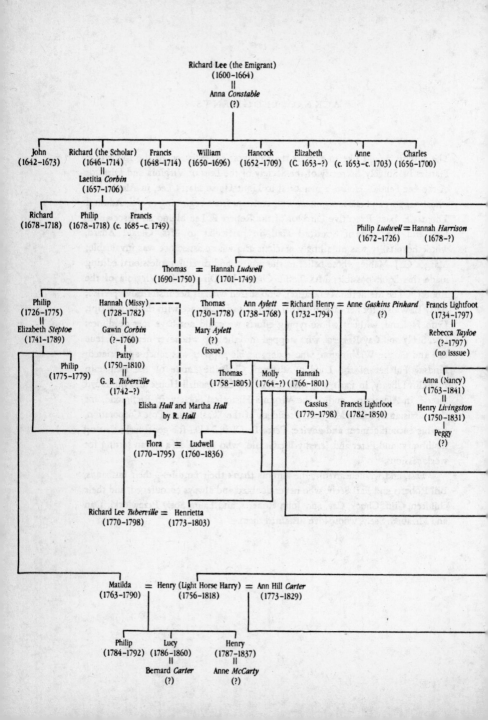

Richard **Lee** (the Emigrant)
(1600–1664)
॥
Anna *Constable*
(?)

John (1642–1673)	Richard (the Scholar) (1646–1714)	Francis (1648–1714)	William (1650–1696)	Hancock (1652–1709)	Elizabeth (C. 1653–?)	Anne (c. 1653–c. 1703)	Charles (1656–1700)

Richard (the Scholar) (1646–1714)
॥
Laetitia *Corbin*
(1657–1706)

Richard (1678–1718) Philip (1678–1718) Francis (c. 1685–c. 1749)

Philip *Ludwell* = Hannah *Harrison*
(1672–1726)   (1678–?)

Thomas = Hannah *Ludwell*
(1690–1750)   (1701–1749)

Philip (1726–1775)
॥
Elizabeth *Steptoe*
(1741–1789)

Philip (1775–1779)

Hannah (Missy) (1728–1782)
॥
Gawin *Corbin*
(?–1760)

Patty (1750–1810)
॥
G. R. *Tuberville*
(1742–?)

Elisha *Hall* and Martha *Hall*
by R. *Hall*

Thomas (1730–1778)
॥
Mary *Aylett*
(?)
(issue)

Thomas (1758–1805)

Molly (1764–?)

Hannah (1766–1801)

Ann *Aylett* = Richard Henry = Anne *Gaskins Pinkard*
(1738–1768)   (1732–1794)   (?)

Cassius (1779–1798)   Francis Lightfoot (1782–1850)

Francis Lightfoot (1734–1797)
॥
Rebecca *Tayloe*
(?–1797)
(no issue)

Anna (Nancy) (1763–1841)
॥
Henry *Livingston*
(1750–1831)

Peggy (?)

Flora = Ludwell
(1770–1795) (1760–1836)

Richard Lee *Tuberville* = Henrietta
(1770–1798)   (1773–1803)

Matilda = Henry (Light Horse Harry) = Ann Hill *Carter*
(1763–1790)   (1756–1818)   (1773–1829)

Philip (1784–1792)   Lucy (1786–1860)
॥
Bernard *Carter*
(?)

Henry (1787–1837)
॥
Anne *McCarty*
(?)

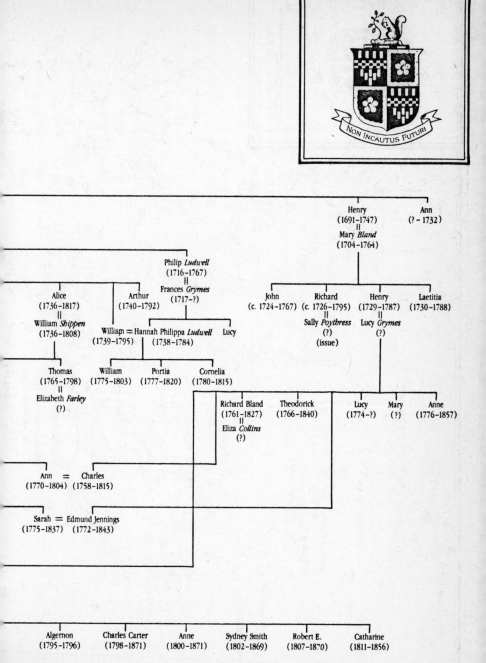

NON INCAUTUS FUTURI

Henry
(1691–1747)
=
Mary *Bland*
(1704–1764)

Ann
(? – 1732)

Philip *Ludwell*
(1716–1767)
=
Frances *Grymes*
(1717–?)

John
(c. 1724–1767)

Richard
(c. 1726–1795)
=
Sally *Poythress*
(?)
(issue)

Henry
(1729–1787)
=
Lucy *Grymes*
(?)

Laetitia
(1730–1788)

Alice
(1736–1817)
=
William *Shippen*
(1736–1808)

Arthur
(1740–1792)

William = Hannah Philippa *Ludwell*
(1739–1795)   (1738–1784)

Lucy

Thomas
(1765–1798)
=
Elizabeth *Farley*
(?)

William
(1775–1803)

Portia
(1777–1820)

Cornelia
(1780–1815)

Richard Bland
(1761–1827)
=
Eliza *Collins*
(?)

Theodorick
(1766–1840)

Lucy
(1774–?)

Mary
(?)

Anne
(1776–1857)

Ann   =   Charles
(1770–1804) (1758–1815)

Sarah = Edmund Jennings
(1775–1837)   (1772–1843)

Algernon
(1795–1796)

Charles Carter
(1798–1871)

Anne
(1800–1871)

Sydney Smith
(1802–1869)

Robert E.
(1807–1870)

Catharine
(1811–1856)

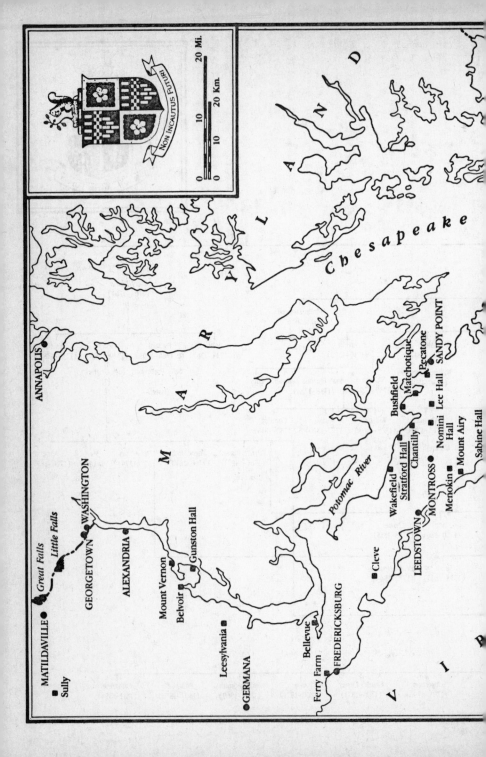

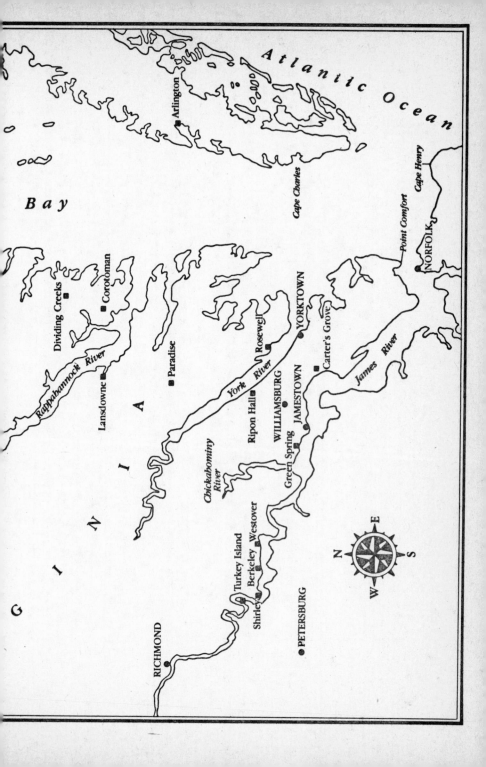

TIDEWATER DYNASTY

The Lees of Stratford Hall

Prologue

San Antonio, February 16, 1861

The colonel had lain for hours listening to the tramping of boots just below his hotel window. Twice as the night had worn on, he had risen to look out on the shadowy clusters of armed men who were patroling the narrow dirt streets and the plaza that fronted the Read House Hotel. Many of the younger soldiers wore strips of red flannel on their shoulders proclaiming their allegiance to the Lone Star flag that had today replaced the Stars and Stripes over the Alamo. Their spurs jingled loudly in the darkness, and their voices sounded jubilant, unafraid.

Unafraid of so momentous a step . . . unafraid of what lay ahead. The colonel could remember a night almost sixteen years before when he too had walked these same streets, filled with eager tension. He had been a captain then, a West Point–trained engineer, scheduled to depart under General Wool's command on the dawn for the Rio Grande. Two thousand men had marched out the next morning in pursuit of a defiant Mexican army led by Santa Anna, and he had been as filled with anticipation and self-confidence as the rest.

Later, that winter, he had almost been killed when a bullet grazed his breast at Vera Cruz. But that was long ago. He seldom thought of it now.

The February night was mild, tinged with the fragrance of the San Antonio River and the heavy scent of moss that even in winter draped the branches of the trees along its banks. It reminded him of Virginia when the night breezes came inland from the rivers of the Tidewater. After a time, he closed the window and went to stand by the rickety chiffonier, where a candle lighted earlier in the night was almost burned down to its wick. Trembling with emotion, he put his hands on either side of the looking-glass.

He was a modest man despite the fact that he had always been considered bracingly handsome, with a commanding air and the well-set shoulders of a horseman. He looked younger than his fifty-four years; his hair and mustache were dark and luxurious, just beginning to silver, and his fine features were enhanced by a patina of strength and experience.

The colonel came from an old Virginia family and the vibrant nobility of his forebears was reflected in his carriage and bearing. But this lineage had left its most favored mark in his face; it was as if the Creator had there assigned the best of bold and sweet features from his antecedents.

Tonight, the wavy glass reflected a face pale and hollow-eyed, marked by a line of sweat across the brow. He was a man who had never known fear in battle or given in to despair, even when there had been reason. He had never shirked a challenge or faltered from choosing the hard path if he thought it the right path. But now there was no right path. He had laid out the factors in his mind and gone over the argument a hundred times. Soon he must take a stand.

He blew out the candle and lay down on the rumpled bed thinking that perhaps he would hang up his sword, take his family to a safe place and plant corn, committing himself to neither side. More than anything he wanted to go home to the Virginia land from which he had sprung. He ached for the hot green fields and the shady pine forests that for generations had nurtured his family. Perhaps he could purchase Stratford Hall, the great fortresslike house that for well over a hundred years had dominated the cliffs of the Potomac River. It was the house in which he had been born. Often throughout the years his mind had turned to it, for its haunting image always sustained him.

The colonel cushioned his hands behind his head on the pillow. His engineer's mind compelled him to view life as a logical and orderly process, but he had within him also the soul of a poet, another portion of the legacy from his passionate Virginia forebears. It was his renaissance nature that caused him to sort out the complex threads of his heritage and order the stories, myths, and legends that were Stratford Hall's. He would plumb their intricacies for the values and the strength to resolve his own life.

Closing his eyes in the dark hotel bedroom, the colonel willed away the bitter laughter in the plaza below, the desperation of the hour. Somewhere in the past lay the answer he must find, accept, and live with through the harsh days to come. Somewhere in the monumental stories that had colored and shaped his life the answer lay hidden. He had only to go back and find it, go back to the beginning . . . to the land . . . and in the beginning the land was all that mattered.

To Reach the Cliffs

1718

The Tidewater, 1718

The young man stirred restlessly in the hot August afternoon, scoring the sand with an impatient square-toed boot, as he watched the languid sail of the approaching raft-ferry. Soon that rough barge would transport him across the swift-flowing Rappahannock River to that finger of Virginia known as the Northern Neck. He had made this journey more times than he could count, but never before had he felt such urgency to complete the three-day ride. From Williamsburg, the sleepy capital of the British colony of Virginia above the James River, he and his four-year-old gelding, Star, had been traveling northeast across the low-lying Tidewater country. Already they had ferried the deep, narrow channel of the York, and once across the Rappahannock, they would turn into dark, primal forests. Halfway up the Neck was his family's plantation, known by the Indian name of the creek that divided the meadows—Matchotique.

"By God's grace, man," he chided himself. "No need to be so confounded impatient. If I've waited five years, I can wait one more day. Tomorrow by this hour I will be delivered turf and twig." He savored the words, for in them lay the key to the first of his fierce-held dreams.

Of dreams he had a multitude, dreams of destiny and of dynasty, dreams that it would require all his talents and energies to bring to fruition, for, though born of a respected family that had garnered wealth and power in the New World, Tom Lee had inherited precious little of either. In custom, as in all other matters, the Royal Virginia Colony closely followed the homeland, and in this instance, the custom was primogeniture, whereby the eldest living son inherited the bulk of the land, wealth, and hereditary positions of power. Without land, younger sons, like Tom, tended to sink into oblivion. It was not a prospect that appealed to him, or one he would accept.

Tall, slim-hipped, and broad-shouldered, with a handsome, compelling mouth, Tom closely resembled his Lee grandfather save that he had his Corbin mother's intimate blue eyes and quick laugh. Indeed, the similarity to his audacious empire-building Lee grandfather extended beyond physical features to the vigor and intensity of his face, and the young man spoke with the same pleasant clipped accent that Richard Lee had carried to Virginia from Essex some eighty years before.

Now he, Thomas Lee, was about to lay claim to his future across the river, in the Northern Neck. It was beautiful and inviting land, but wild and unconquered compared to the more settled lands and estates along the James and York rivers, where the fields of tobacco and corn blanketed flat, rich lands, long ago claimed and patented and now neatly cordoned between stands of evergreens. With the opening of the Fairfax Proprietary, the Virginia land rush was now turning to the Northern Neck. This was premium land, a prize for the ambitious—and daring.

The afternoon stillness was suddenly rent by a pounding of horses' hoofs and the clamor of rumbling carriage wheels. Tom turned quickly to see approaching on the rutted, sun-baked road from Yorktown a dusty, ornate carriage with several brightly clad gentlemen riding alongside at an easy canter. Close behind, as usual on lonely inland roads, were two mounted servants carrying muskets. As the party neared, Tom recognized the green carriage to be that of Philip Ludwell, an influential planter of the James River basin, master of Green Spring plantation, and a powerful member of the elite twelve who made up the King's Council in Williamsburg.

Tom's face broke into a welcoming smile. He had known Councilor Ludwell all his life, for Tom's father had served with Ludwell on the council. Ludwell of Green Spring and Lee of Matchotique had inevitably allied themselves as loyalists and aristocrats on the majority of issues brought before the council. But it was not the sight of the crusty councilor that caused Tom's heart to soar; if the gentlemen were traveling on horseback, the carriage must surely contain ladies—Ludwell's wife, no doubt, and, more important, his green-eyed daughter, Hannah.

Resplendent in a light, flowing cape of olive-green that matched the plumes on his broad-brimmed black hat, Philip Ludwell spurred his horse into a gallop when he caught sight of Tom, then reined in with a theatrical flourish, raising a cascade of oyster shells and stones that settled at Tom's feet. "You rascal," the councilor greeted Tom in a loud cry, "I've not laid eyes on you in months! Dare you visit the James and not pay your respects to us at Green Spring? Not putting on airs since you've been to London, are you, young man?"

"Hardly, sir," Tom said as he looked up at the flushed face of the older man, marveling that his austere father and this blusterous, outspoken planter had been such close friends.

Councilor Ludwell rapped smartly on the side of the wooden phaeton as it pulled onto the landing beside them. "Look sharp, ladies," he called out. "See what I found washed up on the shores of the Rappahannock—none other than long Tom Lee. Thought he would elude us on his visit to Williamsburg, did he? Well, we've followed him halfway home!"

"What a pleasure to see you, Tom!" The councilor's wife poked her pretty, bonneted head out of the wide carriage window.

Tom bowed in affectionate greeting, his eyes eagerly combing the dark recesses behind her. There, in the shadows, was the very heart-shaped face he had been hoping to find!

"I was only in Williamsburg for a bit of a stay, madam," Tom tore his gaze from the girl to explain, "settling some business with my uncle Jennings. Were it not for an urgent personal matter, I most certainly would have called at Green Spring. Surely you know I consider your home the most gracious in its hospitality of all the plantations in the Tidewater. Indeed"—his eyes swept over Hannah—"some of my most pleasurable moments have been spent beneath its roof."

Green Spring had been built in the previous century, when Jamestown was the colony's capital. Known for its deliciously cold springwater and the lush gardens and fruit arbors on its terraced banks, Green Spring, once the home of the aristocratic royal governor William Berkeley, had been Virginia's most handsome and prestigious estate for seventy-five years. Now, just as then, the house was a hub of colonial political and social activity, its drawing rooms and library abuzz with convivial and momentous conversations. Tom had always been drawn to the glossy, luxuriant life at Green Spring, so unlike the atmosphere established by his own vinegary, retiring father, who had not relished house parties at Matchotique.

"Strange you didn't pass us on the road, Tom. But then, we've been moving slowly, stopping to visit with kith and kin. 'Tis a long journey out to this river, especially for the ladies. Would have come by water myself, but my good wife was afeared of it." The councilor glanced at his wife.

"My dear Mr. Ludwell," she reproved gently, "if we ladies were allowed to learn to swim, then we would have little reason to fear the water!" She put her hand over her eyes and shook her head. "Why, I dread even this ferry crossing."

"This barge is a sturdy vessel, dear lady." Tom could not resist smiling at Hannah as he spoke. Her mother's words reminded him of a hot summer's day at Green Spring eight years earlier when the then ten-year-old Hannah had appeared on the bank of the James, where Tom was cooling himself, and imperiously commanded that he teach her to swim. It had taken him the better part of the afternoon to convince her that, doing so, Tom might be permanently banished from the plantation. Only then did the impetuous little redhead relent. From Hannah's amused expression, Tom knew that she, too, had not forgotten the incident.

Now, under her appraising eye, Tom was suddenly and acutely conscious that his white mull cotton shirt was plastered to his back with sweat and a strand of black hair had worked loose from his queue. From Williamsburg he had ridden hard to Yorktown, where he had spent the night sandwiched between two burly fellows in an upstairs tavern chamber, forced by the lack of space to sleep chockablock. Having lingered to exchange talk with ship captains, he had left the port late this morning, avoiding the crowded "rolling road" down which hundreds of hogsheads of tobacco were being rolled to the crowded Yorktown harbor.

"If we missed each other on the road, it is because I crossed the salt flats by an old Indian trail," Tom explained to the councilor.

"You cannot plan to make Matchotique by nightfall, Tom. Where are you stopping to spend this night? At Corotoman?" Ludwell questioned.

Before Tom could reply, the shadow of a second rider fell between them. Tom looked up in surprise. The pleasure that he felt in the presence of the Ludwells ebbed, for towering above him on a hard-breathing stallion was the imposing figure of Ludwell's fellow councilor, Robert "King" Carter, whose plantation, Corotoman, lay a few miles inland on the opposite shore of the Rappahannock.

"Mr. Lee." Carter spoke in a gravelly and commanding tone. "It is good to see you."

There was a moment of strained silence as Tom struggled with his feelings, for he would have chosen to shun, at any cost, a meeting on this particular day with Carter, the most aggressive land baron in the New World. The two had locked horns in the past when Tom was serving as agent for the Fairfax Proprietary.

Hannah's pert voice broke the moment. "Look who we've come upon, Ben," she called out to yet another horseman cantering up to the party. "It's Tom Lee!" Benjamin Harrison IV, a student at William and Mary College in Williamsburg, was Hannah's first cousin. The young man, fair-haired and stocky, quickly dismounted and bowed to Tom, easing the tension with his quick chatter.

Pulling out a gold pocket watch, Robert Carter interrupted. "On your way home, are you, Lee? Well then, the ferry awaits. If you wish to visit further with my guests, the Ludwells and young Harrison, you will be obliged to join us for the night at Corotoman." Before Tom could respond, Carter turned away to speak with the boatman, and Councilor Ludwell ordered his coachman to draw the carriage onto the wide-boarded ferry, then led his mount onto the raft. Tom·had no choice but to follow reluctantly.

Struggling to control the anger surging through him, Tom positioned himself with Star on the opposite side of the swaying rectangular barge to provide ballast for the more corpulent councilors. He stared down into the deep-blue water, which danced against the side of the barge. What was there about Robert Carter that both angered and intrigued him? At forty-six, he possessed thousands of acres of rich Virginia farmland and a seat on the King's Council, but Robert Carter had not always been so imperious. As the younger of two sons, King Carter had inherited only a thousand Northern Neck acres, half of his father's books, and his dead mother's necklace. But when his older brother had died early without a male heir, he had assumed Corotoman. With that had come opportunity—opportunity Robert Carter had eagerly seized.

Tom eyed the stocky planter on the far side of the boat. Wealth and power well earned him the sobriquet "King." Used sometimes in awe and sometimes in derision, the term was always said with deference, for no man in Virginia dared cross King Carter. He was a commanding figure, pragmatic by nature, who appeared never to spend a moment in self-doubt. If Carter believed in a divine order, then he obviously placed himself near the top of the hierarchy.

At the thought of Carter's offhand, contemptuous invitation to stay at Corotoman, Tom felt heat rising in him. Considering what had passed between them, he had no qualms about refusing, although to do so would be a breach of Tidewater custom—in fact, an insult. By God, no! He would decline!

"Do you dream of some lovely London lady? Is she a fair-hair or a brunette who captured your heart?" said a teasing voice behind him.

Tom turned, his bright eyes creasing with laughter at the impudence of the remark. "I think I prefer auburn, particularly if the lady has green eyes to compliment," he countered.

She gave her head a shake, the silken hood falling back to reveal her dark red-gold hair. "I thought perhaps you had sailed to England to find an heiress to be your wife, which seems the quaint but common practice for many a young Virginia gentleman! And then," Hannah added, arching her brow slightly, "I decided you surely found one, for you have come so rarely to visit us at Green Spring in this year you've been home. Have you arranged a fair match?"

Tom resisted an urge to clasp in his arms this woman he had watched grow from a pampered, beloved child into the most challenging and attractive young lady in the colony. She was a petite girl, fine-boned, even fragile, but as erect and defiant as a Virginia cedar. Just eighteen, a full ten years younger than he, Hannah Ludwell was now clearly a woman.

"I wasn't daydreaming, my dear girl." He offered his arm as support against the swaying of the barge. "Only calculating how to tell Councilor Carter that I will spend this night under a pine in the woods of the Neck, as had been my original plan."

Hannah drew back as if scorched. "Is my presence so unappealing that you would choose a night with the wolves and the bears rather than with me?"

Tom captured her hand in his. "By God, Hannah, it is not that! I'm longing to spend time with you."

"You're not afraid of Councilor Carter, are you, Tom?" The girl's tone was incredulous. "I thought better of you."

He gave her a bitter smile. "There is no love lost between us, Hannah. Robert Carter considers the Northern Neck his own domain, and he allows no room for challengers."

The green-eyed girl pressed on. "But your grandfather was the first Englishman to settle in this Neck, the first to patent lands on the peninsula."

"Aye, but Carter's father was not far behind. The Neck was once known as Lee and Carter country, but my father was more interested in his books than in planting tobacco, and he bothered to add hardly a parcel to his holdings. Meanwhile, Robert Carter was adding tremendously to his. And now," Tom added ruefully, "the peninsula is referred to as Carter's Neck."

"Does that bother you so much?"

"Of course it does!" Tom's tone was low but adamant. "The only thing that matters is land, Hannah. It is the key to power and opportunity in this colony. Tobacco is our money crop, and since the leaf wears down the soil, one must have more and more land to cultivate. You know that!" Tom gripped the rough poling that served as a rail. "I have explored the Northern Neck as no one else has done. I have ridden into underbrush so fierce I had to hack my path through forests strung with vines as thick as a man's thigh. I've seen the woods give way to grassy meadows as fertile and promising as any in the Tidewater. I don't claim to want it all, Hannah, but I mean to have my share, and I'm not afraid to joust for it."

"Then joust for it, Tom," the girl said quickly, "but do stay this night at Corotoman. My cousin Ben has come to see Anne Carter. They were childhood playmates and he's come"—Hannah put her face close to Tom's to whisper—"to court her!"

Tom's senses reeled at the nearness of Hannah's cheek. He could smell sweet myrtle soap, a scent that always seemed to envelop her. What he would give for an evening by her side at Corotoman! He ached with longing, but there was an appointment to keep on the morrow. What's more, he was loath to accept Carter's peremptory invitation.

"We're across, Hannah," Ben called from where he stood by the carriage, "with nary a drop of water on your pretty red stocking."

"Were you afraid of the crossing, too?" Tom whispered. "I didn't think anything existed that frightened Hannah Ludwell! Perhaps I *should* have taught you to swim!"

With a laugh, Hannah turned back to the carriage, her skirts of soft Holland cotton swishing. Beneath white petticoats could be glimpsed a sheer red stocking and a small silk slipper. As the barge ground onto the north bank of the Rappahannock, she turned and cast him one last pleading look.

Tom hesitated, his hand on Star's bridle. Who could refuse the fascinating, provocative little Ludwell?

The dining room at Corotoman was not so fine as Tom had expected, although it was situated in the newest section of this old house, which had been added onto over the years in a rambling fashion. The daubed upper walls of the room were white-lined with oyster-shell plaster and hung with English paintings of hunt scenes. The wainscot and woodwork were a pleasing deep-blue. In the corner stood a walnut desk and writing table, their polished surfaces stacked with books and writing materials. Already moths fluttered around the flames of candelabra on serving chests and table, for the windows on the river side of the house were open to let in what few breezes stirred on this sultry August evening. The dinner hour of three in the afternoon, customary in the Tidewater, had long passed; but at Corotoman the meal had been held for the arrival of the master and his guests from Williamsburg.

In the glistening English looking-glass hung over the serving table, Tom could see reflected the entire dinner party. It made a pleasing picture, the bewigged gentlemen with lace at their throats and the ladies in imported silks, their deep décolletage—the latest English fashion—provocatively setting off glittering multicolored necklaces and the lines of their shoulders. The murmur of pleasant conversation all but drowned the faint evening song of the cicadas in the garden.

Sitting at the large round table beside his English-born second wife, Betty, King Carter toyed with his knife on the white linen tablecloth as he listened impassively to Philip Ludwell's heated presentation of his grievances against the colony's royal governor, Alexander Spotswood.

"Spotswood is a roaring snob!" the councilor, dashing in yellow silk and a brown curled wig, bellowed. "Daily he grows more haughty and unreasonable! Now he accuses the Assembly of a lack of devotion to England."

Tom smiled at the truculent squire's ever-patient wife. A Harrison before her marriage, she reflected that family's famed good nature as she listened tranquilly to her husband's ranting. Across from Tom sat Carter's second daughter, Judith, a solemn, scholarly girl, and her young husband, Mann Page, debonair in a scarlet coat with silver buttons—a "cavalier," thought Tom. Educated at Eton and Oxford, Page had inherited rich lands on the York River and now, at twenty-eight, sat on the King's Council, the highest honor in the colony.

Tom sighed. How easy to offer an heiress your love when you can offer her a future bright with security as well. In the looking-glass, he caught the reflection of Hannah, who sat beside him talking with great animation—to Ben Harrison, on her right. Where do I stand with Hannah, Tom wondered. How beautiful she looked tonight, her young swelling breasts rising from a dress of finely embroidered cotton. She eclipsed all the others at the table. True, she flirted with him, seemed always to seek him out, but there were distances between them in age, in wealth. Did he dream too much where she was concerned?

At his lingering glance she rippled her blue fan and whispered from behind it, "You looked to me like a fierce young hawk when we came upon you at the landing this afternoon, Tom Lee, and now you brood just like one!"

"A hawk? Fancy that!" he murmured in amusement. "Well, better a hawk than an owl who never betrays his thoughts—even when he is preparing to pounce." Tom looked meaningfully at his host.

"And that is certainly better than a noisy jay!" she whispered, indicating her father with a little toss of her head. "How often must we listen to the boring details of this feud between Spotswood and the council?"

"It isn't boring to the council or to the governor," Tom rejoined. "The issues over which they quarrel are only moderately important, but it is, in fact, a power struggle, my dear Hannah."

"There was once a time when the governor and my father got on terribly well," the girl mused. "When Spotswood first arrived from England eight years ago, my father held a great reception for him at Green Spring, and I remember thinking the new governor very handsome as he gallantly kissed all the ladies' hands."

"True, he has a strong, pleasing way about him—more so, I fear, with the ladies than with the gentlemen," Tom said with a laugh, "and he is a capable administrator. The trouble lies in his determination to reassert the Crown's power over the council. The councilors are as loyal to the King as the governor is. But they are also the Virginians with the largest stakes in the well-being of this colony, and it just happens that of late their own best interests are at odds with those of the Crown," he concluded with a smile.

Councilor Ludwell's voice rose to a crescendo. "And now, our royal governor writes to the Board of Trade asking for a purge of the council. He would have them replace me"—he patted his bright-coated chest for emphasis—"William Byrd, and my brother-in-law, James Blair. Spotswood *cannot* keep his nose to his own affairs. He has even interested himself in the management of the Anglican Church here, which is Commissary Blair's bailiwick. He dares call the three of us 'treacherous and unfaithful'!"

But more significant, thought Tom, Spotswood has not asked for Robert Carter's removal from the council. Despite his opposition to many of Spotswood's policies, Carter has managed to hold the royal governor's respect.

Tom watched the host in his severely styled white wig and blue silk waistcoat lift his goblet of red wine. Robert Carter was not ostentatious or given to show—"foppery," as he called it. This dinner table, prodigiously covered with well-prepared dishes including a great roast of veal, fricassee of chicken, fresh corn, and the finest imported wines and ale, was but an expression of King Carter's appreciation of superb cuisine. Except for a few silver serving pieces and an abundance of fine white linen, the table was set simply, with pewter service and candelabra.

Tom placed his knife and spoon across the top of the large dinner plate and stole another glance at Hannah. How lovely she was tonight, a filmy scarf trimmed with lace about her shoulders, her red-gold hair gleaming like satin.

"I've missed you . . . more than you know, Hannah," he whispered softly.

The girl looked at him intently. "Then why didn't you come to see me? I thought we were friends, you and I."

Tom drained his wineglass and set it down carefully. Friends . . . is that what she would call them? "I was in Williamsburg only for a day or so. Although my uncle has returned from England to actively take over the agency of the Northern Neck Proprietary, I still do the surveying and record the deeds. I came only to deliver records for his signature." He hesitated. "And to discuss some plans of my own. I didn't call on you, Hannah, because it is important that I be back at Matchotique by tomorrow. I have an important appointment on the cliffs to—"

A sudden stillness enveloped the room, and Tom was conscious that all eyes were now upon him. He could not, would not, go on.

Robert Carter's voice cut the silence. "Mr. Lee, if I might intrude upon your *tête-à-tête* with Miss Ludwell, I believe all would enjoy hearing of your recent trip to England." Folding his arms, Carter leaned back in his tall leather chair as though preparing to hear a plantation foreman's report. "I trust you found your eldest brother well. I wonder, does he have plans to develop the Matchotique plantation, perhaps to patent more lands in the proprietary?"

"I found my brother Richard well," Tom replied evenly. "Quite happily married . . . to an English heiress," he could not resist adding. "He appears content to act as a Virginia agent in partnership with my uncle Corbin in London. I cannot really speak to his future plans for Matchotique."

"And what of London, Tom?" Anne Carter, her fair hair pulled up in a mass of becoming curls, leaned forward to ask eagerly.

In his strong, measured voice, Tom gave his impressions of the vigor and gloss of London. He tried not to sound simplistic or ingenuous, for he knew that Carter, Page, and Ludwell had been educated there. And he kept to himself the repugnance he had felt at the crowding, poverty, and idleness of London.

The visit to London had indeed been an eye-opener for the impressionable, untraveled young Virginian. He had been readily absorbed in the bustling social life of Britain's capital city, for, in accent and appearance, he was like any well-born young Englishman. It had taken him only a short time to realize that the colony of Virginia was but a small piece in the puzzle that was the British empire. And for the first time he had rubbed shoulders with colonists from the New England colony. How different, how somber those Puritans were!

"I am particularly intrigued with the architecture of London." Mann Page's face sparked with interest. "Since the great fire, there has been some marvelous design. Do you like Inigo Jones's work?"

Architecture was a subject that fascinated Tom as well. "Aye, particularly the new St. James's Chapel designed by Christopher Wren, and the plans for Blenheim, the great country house being built for Marlborough."

Ben Harrison looked down the table at Tom. "A professor at the college said the house is not handsome at all, but, rather, cold and ugly."

"I've heard that criticism, but I consider the design strong," Tom asserted.

"But what of the court? Did you see the King?" Hannah asked, touching his arm.

"I regret to say I did." Tom's tone lightened. "William Byrd and I went to one of his open drawing rooms at Hampton Court, and a more dismal afternoon I have never spent! Those beruffled and bejeweled ladies and gentlemen, bored beyond measure, stared for hours from behind fans and eyeglasses at—" Tom hesitated and looked at his host—"you will permit me a candid observation—our most unappealing monarch, who, to be fair, seems to find the English no more attractive than we him."

Philip Ludwell broke in bluntly. "Is he truly as gross and difficult as I have been told?"

"From what I have learned from my son John's letters," Carter interrupted to answer, "the King is unquestionably too heavy of body, and as for being difficult, I cannot fathom why he did not learn our language when he has known for so long that he would inherit the English throne. That fact does not go in his favor."

"I heard that he has locked his queen away in a dungeon in Germany," Mrs. Ludwell put in, her expression wide-eyed. "I cannot believe that."

"From the gossip of London, that is apparently the case." Tom gave her a fond smile. "The King has accused his queen of . . . indiscretions, and for this has had her imprisoned. But I must say he suffers little by her absence, contenting himself with two German mistresses, one as thin as a Maypole, the other as fat as a sow. It is quite confusing," he added dryly. "The ladies of the court do not know whether it is fashionable this season to be stout or to be slender!"

Despite the peals of laughter, Philip Ludwell struck his fist in irritation. "How damn difficult to have this Hanoverian on the throne after the glory of the Stuarts."

"My son John, was he perfectly well?" Robert Carter was not to be deterred from his questioning.

Tom told of the walk he had taken in Kensington Garden one evening with Carter's oldest son, who was reading law at the Inns of Court. But he did not tell of the night he and John Carter had spent drinking arrack punch in Captain Isham Randolph's lodgings. Young Carter had cautioned Tom not to mention Randolph to his father, because Carter had had little use for the Randolphs of Turkey Island ever since the time old Henry Randolph stole the position of speaker of the House of Burgesses away from him, if only for a short while. Nor did Tom reveal that he found John Carter pompous and not particularly good company unless in his cups. He much preferred the bright, colorful Captain Isham Randolph, who knew everything about birds and animals and fish, and who boasted a spirited young English wife, to boot.

"And what of my friend Byrd? I would know everything.", Carter's flat, commanding voice flicked Tom on the raw.

"I found him restless, not in good spirits. He grieves for his wife," Tom answered quietly.

"Dear Lucy," Philip Ludwell murmured, then exclaimed, "By Jove, it's all to be attributed to that infernal Spotswood!"

Another of the Carters' dinner guests, Captain Posford, whose ship was being loaded at the Corotoman Wharf, looked puzzled.

"Colonel Byrd's Westover plantation lies on the James, next to Ben's

Berkeley," Ludwell began to explain, nodding toward Ben Harrison. "After a stormy row with Spotswood three years ago, Byrd sailed for England to plead his case and that of his fellow councilors before the Board of Trade. The next year, his wife, my niece Lucy, joined him in London, only to die of the pox a few months after she arrived. A fetching girl ... such a pity."

"It's no wonder Colonel Byrd is wretchedly unhappy," Mrs. Ludwell added with a sigh. "He has been plagued with misfortune. First, he and Lucy lost their baby son, the heir to Westover. Next came the trouble with Governor Spotswood, and finally the loss of Lucy." She shook her head sadly.

Ironic, thought Tom, that William Byrd II's misfortunes did not deter the charming but sensual Virginian from wenching his way through London or from spending his hours in the liveliest coffee houses of the city.

Almost as if he read Tom's thoughts, King Carter inquired of the latest coffee-house talk. The conversation was moving to heavy ground. Tom had liked best his evenings in Will's Coffee House on Bow Street, where poets and critics had talked of the blind poet Milton's *Paradise Lost* and the popular writers—Defoe, Swift, Addison, Steele, and Pope. But he knew the councilors wanted gossip of the Virginia coffee house in Threadneedle Street, where traders, sea captains, and Virginians in England for business or pleasure met to politic over tobacco and to exchange the latest of world and court gossip.

"Much of the talk you already know," Tom began. "The end of Queen Anne's War has altered England's position, and thereby ours in the colony. England may rule the waves and dominate world trade, but she will have her hands full with Bourbon monarchs on the thrones of both Spain and France. Undoubtedly these two will side against us in the shifting European balance of power."

There was a moment of silence as two retainers removed the serving dishes and stripped the linen cover. On the fresh white cloth beneath, they spread a variety of jellies and a creamy apricot pudding, and renewed the decanters of red wine and ale. Betty Carter deftly sliced and began to serve the nut-covered torte before her. "At long last, that wretched war with France is over," she said in her high, Herefordshire-accented voice.

Her husband added, "Thank God there are again markets for tobacco outside England and Holland! Since Queen Anne's War began, every Tidewater planter has been in debt to his London factor while our tobacco rotted in English warehouses. In many cases our factors all but own us."

"But England's not yet favorably disposed to colonial trade." Captain Posford threw down his napkin. "You must still send your tobacco to England to be resold by middlemen, and I am permitted to sail only to English ports. My cargo is more often than not in convoy with a man-of-war— ostensibly protecting us against pirates, but really preventing trade in other ports. And there is no use protesting to the King! If he doesn't care a twit for his subjects in England, he certainly doesn't for those in far-off America. Parliament and the Board of Trade, which governs the colonies, are Virginia's only hope."

"Aye, the power of the Parliament does grow. I heard a quip that speaks to that," Tom threw out. "It goes, 'France is ruled by kings, Spain by priests, England by gentlemen.' "

Amid the laughter Betty Carter rose, gathering her voluminous skirts and saying, "We will leave you to your brandy. Afterward, gentlemen, please join us in the drawing room."

"Where my cousin Hannah must sing for us," Ben Harrison added warmly.

"That would be a pleasure I have long missed," Tom whispered softly to her as he held her chair. But the girl gave only a quick toss of her head as she moved away from him.

All night, Tom tossed in his sleep, his dreams haunted by the memory of Hannah's sensuous voice. Two house servants came at dawn, in accordance with Betty Carter's instructions, one carrying his freshly laundered traveling clothes and freshly polished boots, the other, a china pitcher of hot water for shaving.

As he splashed away the night's sweat and lathered his face, Tom studied himself in the glass that hung over the shaving table. Now that he considered it, he did indeed look like a young hawk—a hawk that was soon to make his nest on the cliffs!

Footsteps outside his door and the murmur of voices told him that the big house was beginning to awake. He must leave quickly if he was to keep his meeting at the appointed hour. A sound like the popping of a wine cork suddenly caught Tom's ear. There—it snapped again, twice. He was reminded of the crackle of firecrackers on the Williamsburg green when the King's birthday was celebrated. Was it musket fire? My God, an Indian attack? No, it came from the direction of Carter's wharf. Pirates!

Tom dove for his boots and flung open the bedroom door. Once outside the great house, he found men from all parts of the plantation converging on the wharf. Moored at the dock were two sloops and a flat boat, part of Carter's inland flotilla used for transporting goods back and forth among his outlying plantations on the river. Dwarfing them was Captain Posford's schooner, the tall-master *Lion*. Tom grabbed a packet of musket powder and a long gun from the box a plantation foreman pried open, then dodged through the swirling confusion of men who were barricading the far end of the wharf with heavy tobacco barrels. He swung up the *Lion*'s loading planks and hurried to join the captain at the far rail. His nightshirt tucked hastily in his trousers, Posford was searching with his spyglass the long expanse of the creek and beyond it, the Rappahannock River, toward the bay.

"Pirates! Pirates in the river!" a seaman in the crow's nest above Tom's head shouted, his message echoed by the cries of men on the wharf. For a second, Tom caught a glimpse of sunlight glinting on the bow of a ship, a big sea-weathered lady, flying a flag of black, her nose pointed in the direction of Carter's Creek, the two big cannons in her bow aimed at the wharf.

Tom's breath caught in his throat. It wasn't the first time he had seen pirates. As a boy, he had once glimpsed the *Alexander*, Captain Kidd's sloop, anchored in a cove of the Potomac River. For some thirty-odd years, pirates, Spanish buccaneers, and French men-of-war had harassed the Virginia coastline. They were a swaggering lot who swooped down on isolated plantations to provision themselves at leisure or, when the opportunity arose, audaciously plundered ships in Chesapeake Bay or the Atlantic. But this was the first time Tom had looked down the barrel of a ship's loaded cannon.

The *Lion* swayed as seamen struggled to prime her one small gun, which, unfortunately, was pointed toward land.

"Heave to! Bring her around with ropes!" he called to the first mate. "These blunderbusses will do us little good if it comes to a hand-to-hand fight," the captain said. "I'd rather have my sword!"

As the ship slowly began to come about, Tom saw Robert Carter standing on the breakwater. Fully dressed, booted, and belted, Carter gestured calmly but authoritatively to his workers. The confusion on the docks melted away as barrels were rearranged under Carter's direction and two small shiny cannons, kept near the docks for just such attacks, were rolled into position. Other men took up positions on the creek's grassy edge.

"Here she comes, moving closer," a seaman called in a choked voice.

Tom could see movement aboard the pirate ship, but he could not make out the name on the bow. It might well be the *Queen Anne's Revenge*, the sloop of the feared Edward Teach, called "Blackbeard" for his bushy black beard, which he wore in gaudy bow-tied pigtails.

Behind Tom, the cannons roared. For a second, a stillness hung over the crowd as all eyes were riveted on the approaching ship.

"Ready again, fire!" Carter ordered coolly, and in a few seconds, the guns spoke again. Fired only as threats, for the pirate ship was still far away, the guns gave stern warning that the wharf was armed and would defend itself. Indeed, the pirate ship's speed slackened, and at the wide mouth of Carter's Creek, she came almost to a dead stop, then paused to fire one vengeful, ineffectual round of grapeshot in their direction, turned to catch the wind, and disappeared into the blue haze of the river.

Shouts of victory filled the air. Captain Posford slapped Tom heartily on the back, while Carter was surrounded by an entourage of enthusiastic young men—Ben Harrison, Mann Page, and Carter's three long-legged younger sons, Robin, Charles, and Landon. But the stern master was loath to waste time in idle talk. Soon he had directed his lookouts to watch that the marauders did not return and his other workers back to their duties. The crowd thinned quickly, and the house servants, who had been watching from a grassy knoll, turned back across the dewy grass to resume the more humdrum routines of the summer's day.

Captain Posford and Tom lingered on the *Lion*'s deck. "Can anyone wonder why he is called 'King'?" the captain asked, his voice full of respect.

Tom nodded. Carter did indeed cast a long shadow. Though only of medium height, with a muscular figure beginning to grow thick, the planter reflected a rare quality of command and a quick mind that instinctively knew what had to be done, then got it done.

"What capacity that man has!" The captain's smile creased his sunburned face. "He misses nothing! His 'people,' as he calls them, number in the hundreds, yet Carter knows each by name, the work he does best, the size of his shoes, and the ages of his children. I've seen villages in England not nearly so big—or so productive," Posford exclaimed as he surveyed Carter's empire. Before them were the wharf, boatyards, warehouses, and the wooden river store that served as a trading center for planters up and down the Rappahannock. Dominating the scene was the rambling, ungainly brick manor house in a nest of gardens, around which were clustered various dependencies: kitchen, schoolhouse, laundry, milk house, and the office where indentured clerks kept accounts for the main plantation and the forty-odd smaller plantations Carter held. Hidden from the big house by its encircling wall and gardens were cottages for white indentured servants, slave quarters, barns, and farm buildings; there were shops for the artisans, for wheelwrights and carpenters and joiners, for the millers and bricklayers who manufactured and repaired most of the articles used in this all but self-sustaining world.

"But it's all for naught without the land," Tom commented as the two men began to walk back to the house. "For the strength of this empire, the whole reason for its existence, lies in these green fields of tobacco that stretch out mile after mile, to infinity."

"Ah, tobacco!" the captain mused. "Virginia's gold, the fragrant leaf. It is King Carter's treasure—and mine as well," he added almost insolently.

When he had hastily packed his saddlebag, Tom asked that Star be brought around to the side entrance, then went belowstairs for a hurried breakfast. The women, girls, and younger children, having watched the morning's excitement from the second-story windows of the house, had returned to their rooms to dress, and Tom found only Betty Carter with the gentlemen in the dining room, dispensing tea to a young indentured girl who carried a china cup to each place. Cold ham, hot-battered eggs in a large blue Delft dish, ground-wheat bread and corn muffins with crocks of sweet butter and strawberry jam, and a large crystal bowl filled with stewed peaches were spread on the table.

"Damn impudent rogues!" Still in his shirt sleeves, Mann Page stood by the window, his thin face flushed with excitement. "They swoop down like vultures. One's life, much less one's cargo, isn't safe on land or sea any more! When Judith and I finish our manor house at Rosewell, I see we must post continuous lookouts on the York as you do on the Rappahannock," he said to his father-in-law.

Carter calmly drew on his pipe. "We colonists, particularly the Carolinians, bear some blame. We abetted the villains by trading with them in the past, purchasing their contraband because we could buy at lower prices than the Crown extends to us." He shook his head. "It is a most complicated picture."

Philip Ludwell seized the opportunity to scorn Alexander Spotswood again. "If our royal governor worried less about the power of his councilors and more about threats to their homes and property, the colony would be a damn sight better off!"

The councilor's sallow deep-cut face softened as Tom took his seat. Handsome lad, Ludwell reflected. He liked this young Lee, always had, but then Ludwells and Lees went back a long way together: Tom's grandfather, Richard the Emigrant, and Ludwell's own father had been councilors together when Jamestown was no more than an island fort in the river. Brave men they'd been, and loyal to their monarch—stood staunchly by Charles II when he was in exile during that upstart Cromwell's time. At Governor Berkeley's behest, Richard Lee had even sailed to Holland to entreat the Stuart monarch to make his home in Virginia. How different life would have been for this colony if he had accepted, mused Ludwell. King Charles had affectionately dubbed Virginia his "old dominion," and if he had come, the King would undoubtedly have lost his heart to Virginia. Then, the colony would have become his court, the capital of England! Ludwell sighed for the lost opportunity.

Posford, his plate heaped with breakfast, settled down in the black leather chair next to Ludwell's. "A nice bit of nonsense to start the morning," he grumbled, reaching for his tea. "Do you think it was Stede Bonnet, or that cursed devil Blackbeard? He's been harassing the Carolina coast all summer!"

Ludwell shrugged, exasperated. "Could well be Blackbeard. Of late, his men have had the audacity to recruit for those filthy voyages on the very streets of Williamsburg."

The captain looked down the table at Tom, then murmured quietly to Councilor Ludwell, "I've a liking for that young man, Lee. But I've felt a coolness sitting between him and Mr. Carter. Do you sense it?"

Ludwell eyed the sunburned, strongly built young man quietly eating his breakfast. "Their feud stems from the proprietary business," he confided to the captain. "Carter was the first land agent for Lady Fairfax in England, beginning in 1702, and as agent he surveyed, leased, and collected quitrents on her lands in the Northern Neck and beyond. The position was a lucrative one—very lucrative! He patented some thirteen thousand acres of fine land for his own use, another thousand acres for each of his four sons, plus a portion of all quitrents he collected. Losing the agency removed the advantage to choose the best land as he increased his holdings. Seven years ago," Ludwell went on to explain, "Lady Catherine Fairfax became dissatisfied with Carter's management of her lands. In this, Carter was abused, for he had been a good agent. But she imagined the land might be handled better and turned for advice to Thomas Corbin, who is an agent in London. He suggested that, if she wished to remove the agency from Carter, she might place it in the hands of his kinsman Edmund Jennings. It seemed an ideal choice at the time. Jennings was president-elect of the council and a man well liked by all. Thus Jennings received the position of agent, and since he was planning to be in London on business for several years, he appointed his nephew Tom as acting agent in his stead. Old Robert didn't like having anything taken away from him, even then." Ludwell cackled softly. "But in a way it was appropriate that young Lee serve as acting agent. His father, my friend Councilor Lee, was responsible for opening up that whole piece of Virginia territory for the Fairfaxes."

"How is that?" The captain cupped his hands around his teacup.

The voluble councilor quickly explained the story of the Northern Neck proprietary claim. "It all began in 1647 when Charles the Second generously —too generously—rewarded a handful of followers who followed him into exile by granting them titles to land in this part of the colony—not that he had the slightest notion what he was giving away!" The councilor rolled his eyes expressively. "Well, the planters who had already settled on the lower portion of the Neck—the Lees, Carters, Corbins, and Fitzhughs—immediately challenged the King's act of excessive generosity. The controversy lengthened into years and finally all the rights in the proprietary were, on a gamble, bought out by Sir Thomas Culpepper, who became governor of the colony—not that it did him a damn bit of good in collecting on his claim! Eventually it became the inheritance of his daughter Catherine and her husband, Lord Fairfax. Actually," Ludwell continued, slowly slicing his ham, "it is only a point of honor, you know. All the lands in Virginia technically belong to the King, anyway; and each landowner is only a renter whose quitrents are taxes paid to the Crown. Acknowledging the proprietary claim of Lady Fairfax meant only that new purchasers would pay quitrents to the Fairfax family instead of to the Crown."

"But Virginians are a stubborn lot, and the planters refused to recognize the Fairfax claim, eh?" the captain said, laughing.

"Precisely," Ludwell said with an emphatic nod, "which meant no land could be patented or farmed until the dispute was settled. Finally Tom's father made a compact with the Fairfaxes, which acknowledged the claim and thus broke the impasse. Soon after, all the Northern Neck planters fell into line. Now the Fairfax family was eager to reap the profits from hundreds of patents, which they hoped would be issued in this wilderness of Virginia. As you might have suspected, Robert Carter, the most vehement in opposing the Fairfax claim, was quick to take on the post of agent when it became available." Ludwell hooted in amusement. "And as I say, he did very well by the position."

"Then came Jennings and Tom?" The captain nodded to the other end of the table.

"Yes," Ludwell replied. "Tom worked like the very devil. It was his idea that each patent application be accompanied by a surveyor's plat, which did away with boundary confusion."

Captain Posford nodded with approval. "Did he patent any land for himself?"

"As far as I know, he did not. Perhaps he thought it improper while acting agent. More likely, he simply hadn't the cash. He doesn't have any means to speak of—a younger son, you know."

At the far end of the table, Tom had risen and was saying his goodbyes around the table.

Betty Carter teased him maternally. "My dear Mr. Lee, you must come again—particularly if you and your brother Harry weary of your womanless household and are in need of a good dinner and some female attention."

Robert Carter elaborated on his wife's remarks. "It is time you settled down and took yourself a little Northern Neck wife, Tom. Your friend Augustine Washington has done just that. I hear he is building himself a small house on Pope's Creek. Why not follow his lead, my boy? There is always a place in this world for one who works hard. I believe in the parable of the talents, Tom—I have lived by it all my life."

Tom's boots resounded sharply on the bare wooden floor as he strode from the room. A few minutes later he was fastening his saddlebags and swinging himself up on Star's back. "A little Northern Neck wife . . ." he muttered under his breath. By God, Carter had dismissed him as if he were a pup. The King will get a jolt, Tom promised himself, a hearty jolt, by damn!

"Master Lee . . ." A servant appeared suddenly at his knee and held up a slip of paper, folded twice: IN THE GRAPE ARBOR. H.

In a morning dress of white gingham, her auburn hair in a soft knot at the nape of her neck, Hannah Ludwell sat plucking nervously at a meandering vine. Glimpsing him in the boxwood alley from the drive, she hurried to meet him, the tiny tendrils flying from her skirts like wind-whirled snow.

"Would you have left, then? Would you not have said good-bye?" she cried out as he dismounted. Taking his arm she led him deeper into the shadows of the arbor. Then she began, suddenly gentle, "When I was a child, you would come to Green Spring with your father, or to our house in Williamsburg, and you would throw back your head and laugh at me."

"That was because you were such an independent, saucy little thing, saying the first thing that came into your mind, flying at my knees," he answered softly.

"You would take me up in your arms and twirl me about, Tom. You were the older brother I wanted and didn't have. And then, it seemed, we became true friends. You told me the dreams you had, the things you wanted to do. When you became agent for your uncle, you would ride into Williamsburg, all rugged and glowing, talking of the land, how big and deep and beautiful it was. You said, 'This colony stretches from the Virginia seas across great mountains to the golden island of California.' You told me how you loved the land and what it meant. You confided your dreams. I guess I always thought—foolish girl that I am—that I would be part of your life, that you thought me special."

"Special! My God!" Tom said quickly. "You are the dearest, the most . . ." He groped for the words. "Hannah, you are also the very beautiful, very wealthy daughter of one of the most influential men in the colony—his adored daughter. You could do a great deal better than to marry me. You could wed someone like John Carter, or Mann Page, landowners, educated men."

Hannah's small chin jutted out defiantly. "Perhaps I could, but I won't. I will marry whomever I choose. I shall marry a stronger, more important man than they are or ever will be."

"Hannah, the things you say." Tom gasped. "If you are foolish enough to mean I am that man, then you are, by some wild fancy of imagination, going against all odds." He leaned his hand against the arbor support. "Here is Ben Harrison at scarcely seventeen, well educated, master of Berkeley. And I, with only a local cleric's tutoring, an inheritance of a ragged cow pasture and a handful of plate . . . do I dare court you, the princess of the James?"

"You're a Lee, aren't you? You are like that grandfather of yours that I have heard about. He wasn't afraid to leave the James and fight the Indians in the wilderness of the Neck. He became a member of the King's Council, to stand up for what he believed. And your own father was a brilliant man, a scholar. You've got their blood." Hannah put her small fists on her hips. "I am in the habit of getting what I want, Tom Lee," she said indignantly.

"My God!" Tom threw back his head and laughed. "You are the damnedest girl!"

"Well, then, tell me what is going on in that head of yours," she said. "You go to England. You come home. Then, I hear you are the justice of the peace in Westmoreland County. The next thing I'll hear is that you are standing for the House of Burgesses. What of me? Am I to die an old maid on the vine?"

Tom's face grew serious, intent. He reached down and put his hands on her slender waist and drew her closer. Her eyes were luminous, her mouth tender, as he bent his head. "I still hold all the dreams I told you about. But I must have land before I ask for your hand. Only then will I have something worthy to offer you."

"I can wait as long as it takes, Tom"—her mouth, trembling beneath his, was caught by his kiss—"just as long as I know."

Tom's mind was awhirl. To think that Hannah loved him, believed in him, wanted him, would wait for him! It was a grace he had not imagined possible. He threw back his head and gave a whoop of pure joy.

Trotting down the narrow, cypress-lined drive from Corotoman, Tom and Star began their journey home. Hannah would be his one day! It was high time he married, time to hold a woman in his arms through the night. Not that he hadn't taken full and satisfactory advantage of opportunities in London. Quick memories flooding his mind made Tom grow hot in the cool morning air. Marriage, however, was something else. In the structured society of the Tidewater, marriage was an all-important consideration. The right alliances could make all the difference. A man wanted a properly bred woman with whom to build a promising future, and a dowry of substance was also an advantage. But if one truly fell in love with a daughter of wealth and could win her heart, that was rare good fortune.

Hannah was right. He was indeed like his adventurous grandfather Lee, a younger son who had chanced the hazardous voyage to Jamestown in

1636 and, shortly after his arrival, advantageously married a ward of the royal governor.

Two years later, Richard Lee claimed his first land in the New World. In those days one could buy the land with cash or—the more popular method—use the headrights system, by which fifty acres were given for each person one brought into the colony and an additional fifty acres for one's own "personal adventure." In 1642, Richard had received a patent of one thousand acres, awarded for himself, his wife, Anna, one manservant, and seventeen other settlers whom he had sponsored in Virginia.

The key to his grandfather's character lay in his decision not to settle on the hospitable, tree-lined banks of the James. He chose land, which he promptly called Paradise, on the north side of the York, where the river marries the Chesapeake.

Richard and Anna lived in their wilderness Paradise for less than two years; warned of an impending Indian attack, they narrowly escaped massacre by fleeing with their infant son back across the York in a small two-masted shallop.

But Richard the Emigrant had fallen in love with the wilds, and as soon as a tenuous peace was reached with the Indians, his gaze reached farther, beyond the Rappahannock toward the wilderness of the Northern Neck. There he patented land on Matchotique Creek and finally settled his family on another plantation, Dividing Creek, on the west Chesapeake Bay.

Having served as the colony's secretary, high sheriff, a member of the House of Burgesses, the colony's attorney general, and finally a member of the prestigious King's Council, Richard died in 1664. The best and largest portion of his sizable inheritance went to the oldest son, John, who had been educated as a physician in London. The rest he divided into small parcels for his younger children, leaving that original piece of Virginia land, Paradise, to his scholarly second son, Richard.

At a lofty ancient tulip poplar, Tom left the sandy road and followed a narrow path into a forest of pine, willow, and cottonwood. The morning sun, still climbing in the flat blue sky, was already hot. But the woods were cool, the forest aisle sheltered to the point of darkness by the trees and their entangling vines. The air hung pungent with the scent of sweet gum and mulberry leaves. How he loved these deep woods of the Neck, the quick glimpses of beaver dams and white-tailed deer. And the birds! Here were not only cardinals, blue jays, and small brown forest birds of all kinds, but also white swans, floating like graceful carvings on the quiet ponds, stalk-legged cranes appearing without warning from the tall swamp grass, wild turkeys, quail, and snow birds in the forest underbrush. An occasional whiff of brine reminded all passersby that the Tidewater rivers and the Chesapeake lay near. Though he had not seen a soul since leaving Corotoman, Tom sensed Indians of the Neck were silently about. Few in number and generally peaceful, living under treaty with the English, these tributary Indians were often harassed by the more hostile Sioux and Iroquois to the north, and there was continual trouble with the Catawbas in the Carolinas.

For this wild, untamed land Richard the Emigrant had been willing to risk everything. Tom's father, Richard the Scholar, had been of opposite nature, a quiet, contained man who was happiest when alone in the libraries and cathedrals of England. He had aspired to a life of holy orders, only to be abruptly ordered home by his father, who wanted his children to remain Virginians. As a second son, Richard had been left only Paradise, his father's first plot of one thousand acres. But when his older brother, John, died at age twenty-eight, suddenly struck down by the flux, as emphatic as the blow of a tomahawk or the bite of a deadly snake, Richard was forced by the ancient custom of primogeniture to assume the rights and obligations of the eldest son.

By all accounts, the firstborn, John Lee, had been a dashing, vibrant young man with a native intelligence honed by his training as a physician and with a love for the land he would inherit. As a bachelor, he had built the house on Matchotique Creek, a snug, handsome brick-and-timber house of one and a half stories, encircled by a palisade of brick with round lookouts at each of the four corners for protection against marauding Indians and wildcats.

Tom had known little of John Lee until his mother spoke wistfully of him, shortly before she died, some thirteen years ago. "I remember his coming to Pickatown, the wide meadow where families that lived along the Potomac met for picnics. Long black hair he had, and gray breeches. He rode a gray stallion with silver bells on its bridle. I don't think I'd ever seen such a vigorous and appealing young man."

Then John Lee, so full of promise, had suddenly died, leaving nothing behind—no child to bear his name, no record of his thoughts, not even a portrait to capture a semblance of his features.

Later, Laetitia Corbin of Pecatone had married Jack's quiet brother, Richard, who had come reluctantly from Paradise to fill his brother's obligations on the Matchotique Creek, to assume his brother's seat in the House of Burgesses in Jamestown, and to become colonel of the horse in the three county militias of the Northern Neck—Westmoreland, Northumberland, and Stafford. Later he would serve as Potomac naval officer and receiver of duties, and eventually, with the strictest devotion and commitment, albeit not enthusiasm, he would spend twenty years in the King's Council during a most turbulent age, when England was ruled by Charles I, Cromwell,

Charles II, James II, William and Mary, and Queen Anne. But he increasingly withdrew. Had Laetitia Corbin lost her heart to Jack Lee and forced herself to contentment as the wife of his younger brother? She had always shown a special tenderness for her fourth living son, Tom, the vital, dark-haired boy so unlike his father.

By mid-afternoon, as the russet brick walls of Matchotique rose before him, Tom felt a renewed surge of anticipation. A quick rest, a fresh horse, and he would be off to the cliffs. Pray God Sorrell was still waiting for him! Inside, the small house was carelessly kept, cluttered with guns, books, and all that accumulated around two bachelors. Tom threw down his saddlebags and rumpled jacket and with a pleasurable groan stretched himself out on the Turkey-work carpet.

"Where the devil have you been?" Harry Lee strode into the room a few minutes later. Dressed in pale deerskin breeches, Harry was flushed with color, his fair hair unkempt, in damp curls on his forehead. It was this younger brother to whom Tom was closest, although they differed subtly in nature, for Tom was patently driving and ambitious, while Harry was more serene, a less political young man. "Gus and I've been checking the wolf traps," Harry exclaimed. "Caught two good-sized ones, we did! When you did not arrive earlier in the day, I sent word to Mr. Sorrell that you had been delayed and asked if he would be so kind as to wait at The Cliffs' tenant house until we arrived. So what in God's name kept you?"

"Can you believe, I was at Corotoman! Robert Carter came upon me at the Rappahannock ferry. With him were the Ludwells—the councilor visiting to talk politics, and Hannah to see her friend, Anne. Carter insisted I stop the night."

"Forced to stay, were you?" Harry laughed. "How is that Anne Carter? Still a pretty maid?"

"Aye," Tom said, stretching his weary muscles. "I have it from Hannah that Anne is all but betrothed to young Ben Harrison."

Harry pulled off his muddy boots and looked at Tom with wry amusement. "A guest at Corotoman . . . I say, did Carter allow you to sleep in the house or were you bedded with the servants this time, too, as when we went to collect the Fairfax records? You know," Harry said, growing suddenly thoughtful, "if there are any two men in this colony more destined to rivalry than you and the great King Carter, I have yet to hear of them."

"Carter has yet to realize that," Tom replied with exasperation.

"You didn't tell him of your plans for The Cliffs? You could have, you know. The lands are yours already. Today's meeting is mere formality, Carter can do nothing to threaten your transaction."

"He asked no questions, and I thought it wise to offer no information—

although the King does seem to have a few suggestions for my future, nice neat little plans that he hopes will keep me in my place!"

Tom broke off as their neighbor Gus Washington, who had lingered to douse his face at the well, entered the room. Young Washington was a tall, strapping, fair-haired fellow whose word was as trusted as anyone's on the Neck.

"Upon my word, it is good to see you, Gus!" Tom exclaimed as he got to his feet. "And kind of you to work the traps with Harry while I was gone. Tell me, how fares that new son of yours?"

Gus's face was a wreath of wide smiles. "He's quite a lad, Tom. Blustery and bawling now, but I have great plans for my young Lawrence."

Fierce with ambition . . . Tom smiled. How similar were their stories. Their English grandfathers had made their marks in colonial politics and landholding and entrenched their families in the higher echelon of Tidewater society. But now Tom and Harry Lee and Gus Washington were perilously close to slipping between the threads and out of the golden web that closely bound the ruling upper class of Virginia society. By the rules of primogeniture, the eldest son became the squire, the rest yeomen, a fate all three were struggling to avoid.

Old Peg, a Negro house slave left to Harry on his father's death, brought in a tray with a rejuvenating meal of cold bluefish, cornbread, melon, and foaming tankards of cool ale from the root cellar. As the three ate hungrily, Gus asked about the talk in Williamsburg.

"It is what you would expect," Tom answered, then took a long drink from his tankard. "There is pleasure that tobacco prices are up, but anger at the Crown's tightening controls on illegal shipments to and from the West Indies. And the feud between Spotswood and the council continues unabated."

"And at Corotoman?" Harry asked.

"More of the same, especially with Councilor Ludwell there. Carter worries about worm infestation in this year's crop, for it could eliminate the extra margin of profit, and Ludwell is obsessed with Governor Spotswood!"

"Strange, isn't it," Harry pointed out. "When Alexander Spotswood first arrived in the colony he seemed so taken with Virginia and Virginians. Why, they say he slapped mosquitoes at his welcoming ball without missing a step of the minuet!"

"But now Spotswood is in the fire, at odds with the entire council! The last straw came when the Assembly boycotted an elegant dinner party the governor gave on the King's birthday, choosing to celebrate by themselves in the half-finished capitol!" Tom looked up, suddenly serious. "I stand with the Assembly against the governor on issues where local interests are involved, for that strikes at our ancient rights as free Englishmen. But I must say, Spotswood understands the Indian problem better than most Virginians! Our councilors have been too well soothed by the long peace with the local tributary tribes. They don't see the Indians as a problem the Crown must face as she extends her settlements westward. Yes, Spotswood knows the value of the Shenandoah Valley and knows how difficult it will be to win it from the redmen!"

"Spotswood, council, Assembly!" Gus thumped down his empty tankard and leaned back in his chair. "Thank God, politics aren't a love of mine. Oh, I'll do my duty, all right, as a gentleman in the militia. I rather like being a justice of the peace"—he smiled at the Lee brothers, who also sat on the Westmoreland County bench—"but I'll leave the Williamsburg maneuvering for you, Tom."

"The political life will be to his liking," Harry said, pointing his knife at Tom. "I'll warrant you, Gus, one day Tom Lee will sit in the House, and maybe even on the King's Council." For a moment, the prediction hung like a challenge in the air. Then Harry drew down his napkin, exclaiming, "Enough! We've important things to do, lads! Tom, it is time we were about our business—I should say, *your* business!"

Tom rose. "I have only to get the papers from the cherry-tree room."

John Lee had built the house with great thought to security. The brick wall was strong, the downstairs windows narrow, and beneath the stairwell was secreted a small closet made of the finest hard cherry, used solely for the storing of valuables. Tom took the brass key from his belt and in a few moments brought out a metal box, which he opened to reveal a bundle of papers tied with a silk string.

"Four years of effort lie here in my hand," he indicated. "Here is my original request concerning The Cliffs. Here is the survey, the plat, all the letters of correspondence. Ah, here . . . the receipt for its purchase, the deed from the Pope family for which I traveled to England, and Nathaniel Pope's letter of transfer for Thomas Sorrell."

"Pray, who will be mistress of The Cliffs?" Harry teased gently, as he put on his best waistcoat—"It is really my courting droggit, but today is a grand occasion," he explained to a wide-eyed Gus.

"Hot-blooded lad that you are, I've no doubt that you will be wedding and bedding long before I!" Tom retorted. "Why, look at Gus, younger than both of us and already with a wife, a son, and a house abuilding. We can't let him get too far ahead of us. Now can we?"

It was a still, breathless afternoon with long stretches of shade dappling the fields through which they rode. A sense of urgency and excitement was rising in Tom. Years before, as boys, he and Harry had ridden their ponies to The Cliffs—"discovered it," Tom liked to say. From the first this land had fired Tom's imagination. It was a beautiful, wild piece of land, not flat and sandy like much of the lower part of the Neck, but high and rich with verdant forests and dense underbrush, and bounded on the northeast by a palisaded promontory overlooking the freshes of the Potomac.

Emerging from the dark forest, the three riders drew side by side onto a wide plateau. Giving his brother a sly sideways glance, Harry asked, "You say you saw the lovely Hannah Ludwell at Corotoman?"

"Aye, I told you that."

"I like Hannah well enough," Harry went on, "perhaps I like her better than most. But if you are thinking seriously to court her, Tom, remember she is a fragile girl, used to finery and soft living."

"You need a strong mistress for living in the Neck," Gus asserted soberly. " 'Tis a hard life, a lonely life for any woman. Ask my Jane."

"But then"—Harry's fair face broke into a smile—"Hannah Ludwell is said to be a spirited lass."

Tom felt a tingle go through him as the remembered touch, scent, voice of Hannah filled his senses. "Aye, she's spirited," he agreed.

But Harry would not stop. "I dare say she is not so fiery as her cousins were." He referred to the nieces of Councilor Ludwell, Frances and Lucy Parke.

"I've heard of Frances," Gus said with a laugh. "They say she and John Custis have terrible rows and sometimes for days at a time talk to each other only through a servant who carries written messages to and fro. They unite only in affection for their little son, Daniel Parke Custis."

"And Lucy!" Harry exclaimed. "That little spitfire led Byrd a merry chase. But, dear brother, if you can't entice the fair Miss Ludwell, there are other heiresses to consider. What of Elizabeth Hill? One day she will inherit Shirley plantation. And she is but one of many flowers blooming in the Tidewater." Harry's voice was light with humor.

"I am well aware there are Randolphs and Fitzhughs and Beverlys abounding with daughters. And there is also a damsel named Mary Bland, at Jordan's Point. You haven't forgotten her, have you?"

Harry's face brightened in color. He spurred his horse forward, leaving Tom and Gus behind. "I'll fetch Sorrell from the tenant farm," he called out from the bluff.

"So you can give a fair measure of teasing but you can't take any yourself!" Tom called after him.

Picking their way through the dense underbrush, Tom and Gus moved onto the narrow precipice overlooking the Potomac. Tom drew in his breath. How he loved this water the Indians called "the River of Swans." He had explored it from its mouth to its fall line, and someday, Tom thought, he would have a wharf here as fine and busy as the one at Corotoman.

He turned to look across the wild ravine. What promise the land offered for tobacco and wheat and corn, good land for horses and livestock. And there in the center of this broad meadow a great manor house would one day rise, a strong house that would dominate the plantation, a setting for a dynasty.

"I envy you your purchase," Gus said, his gaze following Tom's. "This parcel might well have been mine. You know it was first patented in 1651 by my great-great-grandfather Pope. Had it passed to me, I'd certainly never have sold it. But then, I'm well content with the land I've got at Pope's Creek and my acres up the Potomac at Little Hunting Creek, the land the Indians call 'Epewasson.' Strange, isn't it, that was once a Lee patent, which lapsed for want of settlement or cultivation in the specified time, and then was patented by my grandfather."

"So turnabout is fair, is it not?" Tom said lightly, giving his friend an affectionate cuff.

Gus's blue eyes returned the warmth. "Wakefield, my house on Pope's Creek, is not big, you understand, and it won't be finished for another five, six years, but it is sturdy. And I am happy to have you as a neighbor."

"Here you are," called out Mr. Sorrell, climbing up the incline with Harry. "It is Mr. Thomas Lee, Gentleman! Have you brought the letter of transferral from Mr. Pope?" The clerk made a great show of reading the proffered document. "All seems to be in order. What will you be calling the place, Mr. Lee?"

Tom thought of the love his grandfather had for the land. He thought of the house in Stratford-Langton in Essex that his grandfather had sold so that his children could settle more comfortably in Virginia. He would call this place Stratford.

Handing Tom a spray of dogwood and trickling the soil from a clod of the rich reddish-brown Virginia earth into the young man's outstretched palm, Sorrell pronounced clearly, "On this, the ninth day of August 1718, I, Thomas Sorrell, being fully thereunto empowered, do give Thomas Lee, Esquire, full possession of this plantation by delivering him turf and twig on the same plantation in token of livery and seizure of the whole lands and appurtenance and possession of the same."

With a yelp of delight, Harry reached into his saddlebag for a leather pouch that held a quartet of silver cups and a bottle of sparkling red wine. "To celebrate, my lads!" he called out gaily.

But for a moment, Tom heard nothing, saw no one. Clenching the soil and bough in his fist, he looked toward the sun that flamed the trees to the west. The gaining of this land had been the dream of his boyhood, the passion of his manhood. Nothing else had mattered so much until today when he had finally held Hannah Ludwell in his arms. One day he would stand again in this meadow, her hand in his. He lifted his silver cup to the future.

So the Stratford story began. The purchase of the Cliffs plantation was only a first step; by living frugally at Matchotique with his brother, Tom Lee was in time able to amass additional lands farther north in the Fairfax Proprietary. Already a gentleman justice and militia colonel, he also took on the heavy responsibilities of naval officer and receiver of duties for the Crown along the Potomac River.

In 1720, the young planter gained a seat in the House of Burgesses. This lower house of Virginia's bicameral government was fashioned after England's House of Commons, while the upper house, the King's Council, was the equivalent of the House of Lords. To become a member of the House of Burgesses was a great accomplishment, for the assembly of Burgesses was select and boasted a proud heritage, dating back to July of 1619 in Jamestown, when the first legislative assembly gathered on New World soil.

Securely positioned, the enterprising young colonel approached Councilor Ludwell for his daughter Hannah's hand in marriage. Their wedding took place in May of 1722 at Green Spring plantation, and following a lavish week-long celebration, Tom took his bride back to Matchotique to set up housekeeping in the wilderness of the Potomac. From his stronghold at Corotoman, Robert Carter undoubtedly watched with interest the rise of the eaglet on the cliffs.

Where Eagles Nest

1729–1732

The Tidewater, 1729

The first days of 1729 brought a dusting of powdery snow over the Tidewater. The January air was bitter and still, and for a fortnight the sky above Matchotique remained the unbroken color of smoke.

Tom Lee woke at dawn one day near the end of the month to the sound of the cock crowing in the barnyard. For a moment he lingered to savor the warmth of the bedcovers, then moved quickly over the cold floorboards to stir alive the dim embers and crack the shutter for a look at the sky. A day clear and bright for a change, a good day to ride to Stratford and see how the work was progressing!

Behind him the rope-springed bed creaked. Hannah was observing him sleepily from beneath her soft white sleeping bonnet. She smiled, green eyes narrowing at the corners, and in less than a moment Tom was back under the down comforters, his nose deep in the warm hollow of her neck. "Would you mind if I abandon you today to go to Stratford?" he whispered in her ear.

"Just for this day?"

"I thought I would stay the night. I know"—he looked in amusement into her indignant eyes—"your cousin Ben Harrison arrives tomorrow with this chap Dabney from the London Board of Trade, who visits the naval officers along the rivers. By God's truth, I swear to be home by the dinner hour."

"Tom, please don't ride there alone." Hannah twined her arms around his neck. "Ask Harry to go with you. It worries me to have you travel alone with all the trouble we've had of late." There had been threats against Tom's life by servants he had caught stealing and, as a county magistrate, sent to stand trial in Williamsburg. Hannah touched his mouth with her finger. "And I fear those scalawag runaway sailors who waylay travelers. No one is safe on the highways, particularly you, Tom. Everyone in the Neck knows you don't hesitate to give a harsh sentence when this kind comes before you at court."

Lazily he untied her bonnet, and her bright auburn hair spilled out on the feather pillow like a halo around her face. "What will you do with yourself, Mistress Lee, while I'm away?" He planted light kisses on her nose and cheeks.

"Why, nothing at all, m'lord," she answered teasingly. "I've not a thing in mind except to manage this household and make ready for my guests."

He hushed her words with a long kiss, then said, "Dabney and Ben won't be staying at Matchotique. After dinner they will go on to Lee Hall to spend the night."

"But, Tom," Hannah protested, "Mary Bland has as much to do as I. She is big with child, too."

Tom ran his hand gently over his wife's curving belly beneath the warm blanket. "Mary Bland has more servants to help her."

Hannah sighed with pleasure at his caress. "Then, promise to return home in good time for dinner tomorrow, and I shall let you go quite peaceably!"

He pulled her closer against him, feeling the quick beating of her heart in her finely fashioned body. He never ceased to marvel at the happiness he had found in this marriage. Both Tom and his brother Harry had wed in the same year, Tom bringing his twenty-two-year-old bride to Matchotique, while Harry had provided for dark-eyed Mary Bland a new one-and-a-half-story frame dwelling on the land he had inherited nearby.

These six and a half years of marriage had not been easy for Hannah. Indeed, she had known tragedy: their firstborn had died in her arms, and she had lost both parents in the last two years. But her high spirits had in time returned, her eyes sparkled again with their green fire. Two healthy children filled the nursery now—two-year-old Philip and small Hannah, not quite one—and in a few months there would be another. All the while she managed their household with little staff, urging Tom to place as many workers as possible at Stratford to hurry its completion.

One day, Tom vowed, holding her close, he would make up to Hannah for all the hardships. Stratford Hall would be the first step. Hannah was as caught up as he in the planning of the new house. They had spent long hours selecting the features they liked best from all the buildings they had known or from drawings they had spread out and studied together. When finished, Stratford Hall would be like no house in the Tidewater—in the world, for that matter!

In less than three hours, Tom and Harry covered the twenty miles between Matchotique Creek and the high plateau on which Stratford Hall was rising.

Looking inland from the top of the river bluff, the brothers could clearly see in the bright January morning the red brick walls and tall chimneys above the broad ravined meadow, which, like a moat, separated the rising house from the surrounding forest and river bluff, a perfect barrier to danger.

"There, Harry, what do you think?" Tom asked proudly.

"By God's truth!" Harry stared in wonder. "I knew it was to be large and handsome, but I had no idea it would be so imposing. It is a castle, Tom!"

"Aye, I've even heard it called a fortress," Tom said, laughing.

Like the Capitol in Williamsburg, the house was laid in the shape of the letter *H*. On the main floor the crossbar of the *H* would serve as the great hall, in this regard echoing the plan of Green Spring. On the high basement level the crossbar area would serve as counting room and offices for a wharf. For tax purposes, the house was termed a one-story dwelling with a high English basement. Stone steps descended from the great hall on both the river and the land sides. At each end of the crossbar on both the main-floor and basement levels were four rooms, each with its own fireplace and windows on two sides. The four chimneys clustered at each end, their tops linked by arches, had at their center a floored area where lookouts could be stationed.

"Much remains to be done before we can move—perhaps a year or so of steady work," Tom said. "I've pledged my last shipments of tobacco for the finishings from England, tools and glass and hardware and a grinding stone for the mill house. Only the furnishings remain to be ordered. Every shilling of Hannah's dowry and every cent of profit from my tobacco crop is tied up in this house or set aside to pay quitrents in the north. But it is worth it!"

"More than worth it," Harry agreed. "I admire you for taking such great risks. As for Stratford Hall, it is going to be spectacular. And you've made a name for yourself already in the House of Burgesses, Tom. With our brother, Richard, dead these ten years, I think you are the Lee who should assume Father's place on the council—that is, King Carter permitting."

For a moment Harry studied his dark-haired brother, who had shed his boyish look and now was as lean and intent as a racehorse. Tom was spreading himself thin, risking all he had for a grand future. Harry turned his attention to the partially completed manor house in the distance. It took getting used to, this Stratford Hall, for it lacked the soft, graceful lines of the great houses now rising along the James. The walls of this wilderness manor house were forbidding, broken only by the pattern and texture of brick and the flaring stone staircases. Too mammoth to be shaded by trees, it rose up starkly, resolute and commanding on the still-rough field.

"How you and Hannah could have dreamed such a house staggers me! To draw these plans without benefit of an architect was one thing, but to succeed in building it...!"

Harry well realized what a prodigious undertaking this was from his own experience in building Lee Hall, a modest house by comparison. To begin with, slaves and indentured servants had to be settled on the land in a colony of cottages, barns, workshops, storerooms, and the like. Only then could land be cleared; lumber cut and seasoned; huge stones quarried and pulled up from the nearby pit; vast amounts of sand carried from the river and lime burned from the Chesapeake Bay oyster shells for plaster and mortar. Most laborious was the brickmaking. Tom had been at it almost eight years, and the end was not yet in sight.

Drawing closer, the brothers could see the gruff Scottish foreman, Wallace, overseeing a team of brickmakers at work in the courtyard. A team of mules drew the long horizontal boom in a circle around the press, rotating the wormscrew, which in turn compressed the dark-red clay inside, breaking it into lumps and forcing it to the bottom of the press, where it was fed out through a hole to be placed in wood molds. Hundreds of molded red blocks were now spread out in the courtyard sun to dry before being baked.

Catching sight of the two riders approaching from the riverfront, the foreman doffed his hat and walked to meet them at the edge of the field. "We had a feeling you'd be over, Colonel Lee, the weather breakin' like this," Wallace called out. "And Capt'n Lee, 'tis nice to see you again, sir.... Boy, come take the gentlemen's horses."

A small black child of ten or so took the reins from the men.

"You are Pru's boy, young Will, aren't you?" Tom looked down. "You've grown fast this year."

The boy nodded with pleasure at his master's words.

"Take the saddlebags to the office building, Will." Tom pulled the bags from his horse.

But Wallace put a hand out. "Ho, now, I'll have to unlock it, Colonel. I've got everything bolted up tight today."

"What is the problem?" Tom's dark brows narrowed.

" 'Tis a strange thing occurred last night. I was dozin' by the fire—
'twas after midnight, I'd say—dreaming of Glasgow and the River Tweed I
was, when the dogs began to bark somethin' fierce. 'A deer or wild boar, is it
now, Wallace?' I sez to meself." The Scottish foreman snorted in disgust.
"Ye never know in this godforsaken spot what's coming out the woods
next—not meaning to be disrespectful to your property, Colonel Lee, but
Virginia's not Scotland!"

"On with it, my good man," Tom pressed impatiently.

"Well, 'Just to be sure, Wallace,' I sez to meself, 'why don't ye send a
boy to check out the great house?' And that I did. Well, back comes the
darky, shakin' all over and eyes like saucers, cryin' out that he seen three
females—'three wenches,' he says—a-dancin' and peerin' around the big
house and the office building!"

"Wenches!" Harry scoffed.

"Aye, 'tis what he sez. Saw the gold of their earrings, he did, long hair
flyin' in the night, skirts they had on. And in the morning I found a hammer
and chisel missin'—took 'em, stole 'em away, they did."

"Mr. Wallace, had you been into the village for a nip last night?" Tom
asked coolly.

"Well, 'tis a fact I'd gone in the tavern for an ale or so, and, true, I
carried home a bottle of red, jus' to ward off the cold, but drunk? Nay, I was
not that, sir!"

"Did you give some of the drink to the boy?"

"I gave him a nip just for courage—just a nip, mind you—afore he
went to check, but not enough to have him seein' things that weren't thar.
Bodies were out there all right, pokin' about the big house and the office
building, dancin' in the moonlight, they were!"

"Can it be the Scottish are as daft as the Irish for dreaming?" Tom
wondered aloud as he and Harry walked slowly toward the brick press.

"I don't know." Harry looked concerned. "There is something downright unsettling about this. You should get to the bottom of it."

Tom shrugged impatiently. "There are more important things to think
about if this house is ever to be finished." Already he had stripped off his
gloves and was inspecting the sun-hardened clay bricks that had been
stacked to a height of twelve feet with eyes, or passages, between each row.
In the eyes, hickory fires had been burning steadily for several days, and
now some of the baked bricks were ready to be pulled out to cool.

One had only to look at the walls of the manor house to understand
why the brickmaking was of such importance to Tom. Much of the beauty of
Stratford Hall lay in its brickwork. At ground level, the walls of the English
basement were constructed of oversized bricks laid in Flemish bond design,

with stretchers alternating with glazed headers—bricks that had been placed close to the fire so that their salts and minerals had baked out, giving them a shiny surface. Above the basement level, the bricks were smaller, uniform in their rubbed red color. But where the chimneys began, the glazed headers were reintroduced. The brickwork was handsome, intricately done, just one example of Tom's desire to build an enduring as well as a beautiful house, unlike any other in the Tidewater.

" 'Tis a good fire we'll need this night, that is for certain," Harry said later, when the afternoon sun lay low in the sky, and the brothers sat on the steps of the completed office building to rest.

"Colonel Lee, beggin' your pardon, sir." Wallace approached with a look of concern on his weather-beaten face. "I've something curious to show ye. Was postin' a watch behind this here office like ye told me, when we came upon evidence of last night's intruders. Found footprints in the mud, we did, and signs that someone was trying to break in through the back windows."

"Isn't that where you store furniture and such for the big house?" Harry shot Tom a quick glance.

"Aye."

The two men pushed through the brush to the rear of the office building. Behind tightly boarded windows, the large back room contained articles that were intended to grace the great house one day—family portraits, rugs, and pieces of valuable English furniture left to Hannah from the Ludwell estate at Green Spring, as well as some of the books and furniture from Matchotique that belonged to Tom.

"Look here, if you will, sir." Wallace pointed to the bottoms of the shutters. "Someone's been jimmyin' at these, had 'em almost off, I dare say. Must a' been scared off by me dogs . . . or the boy I sent comin' upon 'em," he declared with a touch of self-righteousness.

"It would seem whoever it was knows a great deal about my affairs." Tom's tone was acerbic.

"I know who your wenches are!" Harry called out suddenly. He held aloft a dirty blue square of bedraggled cotton. "A seaman's scarf, caught in the briars! You know who dropped this, Tom? Most likely one of that pack of runaways from the *Elizabeth!* The boy thought them wenches because of their long hair, earrings, and wide leather breeches, which resemble ladies' skirts."

Tom looked at the filthy scarf in Harry's hand, then turned to Wallace. "Were there seamen in the tavern last night?"

"Aye, that there were. A passel of 'em comin' and goin', drinkin' like this colony was soon to run out of ale and carryin' on—braggin'—with the servin' wench. I heard one talkin' about waylayin' a traveler on his way up to Stafford County, and another claimin' he wasn't long out of Newgate prison—not that the servin' wench took any mind to them, much preferrin' the likes of a Scotsman, she does . . ." the foreman swaggered.

Harry grabbed Tom's arm. "No doubt the sailors have been consorting with those houseservants who robbed Matchotique earlier, listening to their complaints that you treated them harshly when you ordered them to Williamsburg."

"I'm a fair judge, Harry, just as you are."

"Yes, but you do not hesitate to deal out strong sentences, and they may look to take revenge." He indicated the brick mansion.

"I dare not risk this house," Tom groaned. "It matters too much to Hannah—and to me. As a justice of this county, I'll issue a warrant for the arrest of the sailors from the *Elizabeth*. This attempt to rob me is the final straw. I'll take no more."

"That is your only course, although they will have it in for you."

Tom looked determined. "I'll send notice to the sheriff. I'll direct Gus Washington to seize the sailors on my warrant."

The boy, Will West, had been dogging Tom's footsteps all day. "I'll take the message to Pope's Creek, Colonel Lee. I know the way! I know jus' how to get to Sheriff Washington's house."

Tom looked gently at the boy. "Nay, Will, I have better plans for you. Tell your ma I'm taking you to Matchotique with me. You could help your mistress in the house and with the children. Would you like that?"

Young Will leaped from one foot to the other with uncontained pleasure.

"Then fetch the little brown mare from the far field. You may ride her back," Tom added.

Harry looked at Tom, instinctively reading his thoughts. "We'd best head back," Harry said quietly.

"That we must." Tom's eyes lingered on the brick walls and gaping windows of the half-finished house. "Perhaps those rogues have left the Neck for good and we shall have no more trouble from them, no more trouble at all."

"Don't depend on it." Harry's eyes followed Tom's to the vulnerable mansion.

A carriage ride through the desolate Northern Neck woods was uncomfortable at any time of the year, but it seemed to Ben Harrison that his coach-and-six would never reach the haven of Matchotique on this cold, late-January day. Although as fine as any made, the Harrison carriage jostled rudely over the narrow frozen ruts of the trail that ran northwest from Corotoman. Ben gave his traveling companion, Jonathan Dabney, a reassuring smile, for the elderly man's face, under his gray-powdered wig and wide-brimmed black hat, looked wan, almost ill from fatigue. Still, Ben was not worried. The traveler from Britain displayed remarkable resurgences of energy, and never seemed to run out of pithy comments on what he had observed thus far in his visit to the royal colony.

Wrapped in his greatcoat and tucked under a traveling rug, Dabney was now inclining his head forward to be heard above the noise of the carriage wheels. "It is increasingly apparent, my dear Mr. Harrison, that your father-in-law, Robert Carter, rules Virginia!" He put up his gloved hand to ward off protest from Ben. "No, no, I was well aware of that before I came to Virginia, for his influence is known to all who deal with the colony. But now I have seen his empire with my own eyes. Carter is truly *king!*"

Ben threw back his head in laughter. "I can assure you, sir, there is no king for Virginians other than George the Second."

"His Majesty will be glad to hear it. But I was saying, my head reels with the scope and style of Carter's life—almost like that of a feudal lord. What is more, there is Carter's extraordinary political control. His actions as president of the King's Council go unquestioned. His eldest son, John, serves as the colony's secretary; his son-in-law, Mr. Page, sits with him as a member of the council—"

"He's not to be judged harshly on that," Ben put in quickly. "You see, we are quite an inbred society, all connected in one way or another through birth or marriage." He smiled engagingly. "We spend a great deal of our time sorting out cousins, their offspring, new houses, horses, land acquisitions, and such. We know each other well—at times perhaps too well!" He underscored the last remark with a raised eyebrow.

The carriage gave a great lurch at a pocket in the road and both men were thrown violently from their seats. Just as they regained their balance, a tree limb swept the top of the carriage, sending them to their knees again.

"This Northern Neck!" Ben said in exasperation. "It is too wild, too untamed for my taste, and far too dangerous."

Dabney looked up in alarm. "Dangerous! Pray, do you mean Indians?"

"Here, here, Mr. Dabney! Our driver and outriders are well armed!"

Ben pulled a glass bottle from the wicker basket near his feet and poured out two small glasses of brandy.

A spot of color returned to Dabney's cheeks as he sipped the spirits. "This wilderness house to which we travel, is it the home of Colonel Thomas Lee or of his brother, Captain Henry Lee?"

"To tell the truth, Matchotique belongs to neither," Ben explained. "As manor plantation of the Lee family, it passed to the oldest son, Richard, who has since died in England. Henry Lee lives close by at his plantation, Lee Hall, with his wife and small sons. Mary Bland Lee's mother was a Randolph. Perhaps you know Mary's uncle, Captain Isham Randolph?"

As Dabney shook his head, Ben continued, "Tom Lee rents Matchotique from his brother's widow in England. I hear the tariff is the modest sum of one peppercorn a year, due on Christmas Day!"

"She'll not earn much interest on that!" replied Dabney with a chuckle, then asked curiously, "Why does Thomas Lee have no home of his own?"

"Oh, but he builds a great house called Stratford Hall not far away on the cliffs above the Potomac River." Ben leaned forward to say confidingly, "They say it is a house like no other in the Tidewater—handsome, but austere and fortresslike, the house of a man who would be a king."

"What kind of man is Tom Lee, this dreamer, this empire builder? Your father-in-law does not seem taken by him."

Ben pressed his cold feet against the warming bricks on the carriage floor. "Tom comes from a fine Northern Neck family. When he was in his early twenties, he became surveyor and acting agent for the Fairfax Proprietary. He wrested the job away from my father-in-law, and *that* was the beginning of the feud between them."

Dabney was attentive. "Feud, pray tell?"

"A bitterness, shall we say, which has deepened over the years. My father-in-law is now again the Fairfax agent, and Tom complains that he follows a practice of omitting all worthless swampland on the plats of land he patents for himself but refuses to do the same for others. Although, to be fair," Ben rationalized, "there should be some reward for shouldering the responsibility of the proprietary! But Lee also strongly condemns my father-in-law's treatment of his uncle Edmund Jennings."

"Ah, Jennings, I knew him well when he resided in London," Dabney offered. "He was president of the King's Council . . . a well-respected man, I believe he was the son of a member of Parliament. In fact, wasn't he known for the fine strains of tobacco he grew at his estate, Ripon Hall?"

"He was, but no more," Ben replied. "Jennings was no businessman. He mismanaged the proprietary agency after he took it over from Tom Lee, who, I must say, had handled it competently. Then Jennings compounded his problems, got himself deeply in debt"—Ben flushed slightly—"largely to my father-in-law, who finally was forced to call the notes he held on Jennings's estate. Carter gave Ripon Hall to his son Charles, who also has the estate Cleve. Tom has never forgiven my father-in-law for humiliating Jennings so," Ben concluded.

"And what think you of Tom Lee?" Dabney asked gently.

"He's an enterprising man, albeit hardheaded." Ben shifted uncomfortably. "Tom has always had a rebellious streak."

"And now, how does this Tom Lee entertain himself?"

"Besides serving as the King's receiver of duties along the south side of the Potomac, he is a justice of the peace, a colonel in the militia, and representative for Westmoreland County in the House of Burgesses. He has ... how shall I say ... great vigor." Ben put his finger to his lips. "His wife, my cousin, Hannah Ludwell of Green Spring, is most ... estimable."

"Attractive, is she? I have found that Virginia claims more than a fair share of estimable ladies." Dabney's eyes twinkled.

Ben Harrison raised his almost empty glass to acknowledge the compliment. "Granted, Mr. Dabney, but Hannah Lee is a rose of rare perfume and beauty. Not without thorns, you understand—high-spirited and determined—but a rose indeed in the garden that is Virginia."

Elegant, was that the word? Dabney's eyes surveyed the party in the small whitewashed dining room of Matchotique.

The room was not particularly elegant, but his dinner companions most certainly were. Dabney observed Ben Harrison, tonight a dandy in ruffled cuffs and a braided waistcoat. The ruddy, laughing-eyed Captain Henry Lee, whom everyone called Harry, sat in proper attire, his serene, satin-gowned wife, Mary Bland, at his side. No, "elegant" was not the precise word. "Aristocratic"—that was it, most especially for the host and hostess, Colonel Thomas Lee and his lady.

These dinner companions, like all the colonials who had entertained him on this journey, were impressive. Charming of manner, they exhibited a streak of the stubborn and unpredictable, which made their company bracing. Perhaps Governor Gooch had the right approach: one must handle highly bred horses with a gentle touch.

The Lees were not as well endowed financially as some with whom he had stayed in the Tidewater. But they held themselves proudly, appearing to feel equal to the best England had to offer.

Curious, curious indeed. He considered the mistress of this house, Hannah Lee. Harrison dubbed her a rose, but she was certainly a hardier flower, for her chafed hands indicated she worked directly in the running of a plantation. Yet she was gowned in the latest style, and her table was set with the best spotless linen and fine silver serving pieces with the Lee mark of squirrel and acorn. The meal was outstanding—produced by one elderly woman and a lone black boy to serve her table.

"A delightful dinner, madam," Dabney complimented warmly. "Venison from your own forest, bluefish from your bay, and the trifle—superb!"

"Thank you," Hannah replied in her direct manner. "The trifle we call syllabub. 'Tis my sister-in-law's receipt." She inclined her auburn head in Mary Bland's direction.

Dabney glanced down the table. The talk, light and full of laughter, centered upon Councilor Byrd of Westover—"the Black Swan," Harry Lee called him—and his recent return to the colony with a new English wife, an elegant carriage to put her in, and a ship's hold of three thousand books for his library.

But unfathomable undercurrents played beneath the surface of the pleasant conversation. Young Ben Harrison, garrulous as could be in the carriage, was oddly distracted, eating scarcely a morsel. And something, evidently of a private nature, seemed to prey on Tom Lee.

Aware of Dabney's gaze, Tom cordially inquired, "And have you found our colony to your liking, Mr. Dabney?"

The Englishman wiped his mouth on the large white napkin and sighed with satisfaction. "That I have, Colonel Lee. In only a few months, I have developed what Ben Jonson called 'Virginia Fever.' Your grandfathers caught it when they came in search of gold—"

"And found tobacco," Harry finished sardonically.

"Gold in its own way, Captain Lee! It provides a most extraordinary way of living for you who plant it. I have been quite struck with your plantations—so like self-sufficient English villages."

"But with a curious difference, my dear sir." Tom caught Dabney's eye. "English villages are diversified, their economies and opportunities varied. Our plantations exist only for trade with England. We plant one major crop, tobacco, and it is not a subsistence crop. We cannot eat it! We must sell it, and thus contend with capricious decisions by the Board of Trade, often influenced to our detriment by your London merchants."

"You say we live well," Hannah put in, "but only the Virginians who own considerable land live well, Mr. Dabney."

The English visitor could not mask his surprise at this feminine incursion into the serious conversation.

"Considerable land, indeed," Tom said, glancing supportively at his wife. "Land is the sole reason one is either rich or poor in Virginia, Mr. Dabney. If a planter does not have vast acreage or the means to acquire it, he will remain poor, able to sell his produce only through the large planters who ship in volume and can bear the fluctuating prices set in London. Eventually the small farmer is forced to sell out. Thus, we have all but eliminated the yeoman class from the Tidewater. And since we've no towns of size—even Williamsburg and Yorktown are only villages—there are few prospects for advancement."

"And we've no industry in Virginia, since manufacturing is not allowed in the colonies by law!" Hannah said spiritedly.

"Those laws do not keep our New England colonies from engaging in clandestine manufacturing," Dabney retorted dryly.

"New England has no money crop to sell to the Mother Country as do we," Ben pointed out. "The sale of pitch, spars, and lumber was not able to support their expanding population. Smuggling thus became a trade in itself."

"So, each colony obeys or breaks the law to suit its own economic purpose," Dabney mused. "While those in New England engage in illegal manufacturing, many of you Virginians sell tobacco illicitly, circumventing both your factors and English taxes."

A slight coolness settled over the party. How haughty and proud these Virginians were!

"Ah, scuppernong wine from the grapes of Matchotique, my favorite," said Harry with a tone of anticipation as the serving boy brought a silver tray with crystal glasses and decanter from the sideboard.

Tom pushed back his chair and stood with raised glass, the candlelight reflecting the sheen of his satin jacket. "Ladies and gentlemen, may I offer a toast: To our King."

The answering "To the King" rippled throughout the room.

Ben Harrison then rose to his feet. "To our beloved majesty King George the Second, may he come to appreciate the true devotion of his Virginians."

"And may he come to appreciate the true *value* of his Virginians," Tom finished, his blue eyes inscrutable.

"I do not think we English are yet used to the idea of a German king sitting on the throne of England," Harry said frankly. "We shall, no doubt, always consider the House of Hanover as usurpers! We might have railed against the Tudors and the Stuarts, but at least they were our own, of English blood!"

"The Georges have Stuart blood, Harry. Was not George the First the German great-grandson of our James the First?" Mary Bland remonstrated.

"Aye, but it is not the same," Harry insisted stubbornly.

Jonathan Dabney sipped his wine. This Virginia innovation was a pleasant surprise, leaving a pungent sweet taste in his mouth, unlike the grainy cornbread, which had been served to him repeatedly during his tour. He grimaced at the thought of it.

"What is our new king like, Mr. Dabney? Does he differ at all from his father, George the First?" Mary Bland asked.

"Rather." Dabney smiled over his spectacles. "He speaks English, for one thing, and that is to both his and our benefit. Still and all, he is a German princeling at heart, irascible, stubborn, Teutonic."

"And Queen Caroline? She is much loved, is she not?"

"Respected—and it is a well-earned respect. Caroline of Ansbach is able and intelligent, quite an asset to the King, I believe. It is widely known that she and Sir Robert Walpole, chief minister in the House of Commons, have great influence on the King."

Harry took a nut between his thumb and finger and cracked it sharply. "More than influence, if one is to believe the Tory newspapers. They say, 'You may strut, dapper George/But 'twill all be in vain/We know 'tis Queen Caroline/Not you, that doth reign.' "

Jonathan Dabney could not resist joining in the laughter. Then he rose, holding high his wine glass. "May I propose a toast to our gracious and lovely hostess, who will soon, it is my understanding, become the mistress of a great new Tidewater house, Stratford Hall."

Hannah's smile grew luminous. She *is* like a superb English rose blooming in a wilderness, thought Dabney. She deserves a grand house to set her off.

A gentle knock sounded at the dining-room door, and Dabney saw the hesitant face of the indentured serving girl—"kids," they called them here in the colony.

"What is it, Elizabeth?" Hannah said from the table.

" 'Tis the babe, madam. She's been crying for most over an hour. Can't hush her atall."

"I shall come directly." Hannah rose, moving gracefully, though big with child, to say good-bye to her guests. Regally she held out her hand to Dabney. "Please come again to see us when you next travel to this colony. I hope you will then find us at Stratford Hall."

The older Englishman offered his arm as they left the table. "I wonder, do you not fear living in this desolate part of Virginia?"

"Heavens, no." Hannah looked up at him calmly. "I have my husband and servants for protection, and at Stratford, Augustine Washington and his family will be only some five miles away at Wakefield on Pope's Creek." She paused, then added in a challenging tone, "But I do resent the ruffians, the refuse of your English prisons, whom you send to us as indentures. They cause mischief and mayhem. I cannot think but that the Board of Trade might not somehow help."

Dabney saw Tom and Harry Lee exchanging quick glances. Was there something in this conversation about robbers that disturbed them . . . something of which Mistress Hannah was unaware?

"But, please, excuse me, sir. I must go abovestairs to my children,"

Hannah concluded with a deep curtsy. "May your journey home be a pleasant one."

"Madam, it has been a most memorable occasion." Dabney's bow was formal and gallant in return.

As the young women wrapped their shawls around their shoulders and left the dining room, Tom Lee bent over the table to extinguish the candles. It was then that Ben Harrison, his cheeks slightly mottled with color, put a hand on his arm. "Tom, if I might speak with you for a few minutes in the library, there are some urgencies of business I would discuss. They concern your lands to the north at the Little Falls of the Potomac."

Such a difficult, headstrong baby, this little girl. Hannah shook her head wearily, allowing the cradle to rock gently to a rest, then lingered a moment to be certain the whimpering would not begin again. At less than a year, little Hannah—"Missy," as Tom affectionately called her—was her father's darling. Reluctantly, Hannah admitted to herself that her baby daughter possessed a nature quite similar to her own. When hungry, she already banged the table imperiously with her pewter spoon or, if thwarted, emptied a cup of milk over her wispy curls. Tom only laughed. She was, he claimed, a high-spirited young colt demanding her head.

Hannah paused to tuck the covers around the slight body of her sleeping son, Philip. This child was a love, a prince if there ever was one. She bent to kiss his forehead lightly, then walked quickly down the chilly hall to the master bedroom, where Elizabeth was turning down the covers of the bed.

"She is a handful sometimes, that little one," Hannah sighed as she began to twist off her rings. "Help me with the buttons of this dress, will you, child. My back is aching like the very mischief!" When she had slipped into her loose, long-sleeved white nightgown, she stepped on the stool and, with a sigh of relief, sank into the high bed, finding pleasure in the warmth of the heated bricks that Elizabeth had placed beneath the heavy comforter.

Hannah lit the tall myrtleberry candle on the bed stand and took up a quill pen and drawing pad. For a few moments she sketched silently, then appraised her work carefully. "Come, Elizabeth, see what I have done! It is a design for the fireplace back in the nursery at Stratford."

The girl turned from folding Hannah's yellow dress into the clothes press and came slowly to the bedside. " 'Tis very nice, madam. Angels, ain't they?"

"Cherubs, Elizabeth, to watch over my cherubs—" She looked up suddenly with concern at the indentured girl's face. "What is the matter? Not homesick still?"

"Just a wee bit, madam"—the girl sniffled—"and I can't say why.

You've been quite kind to me. Only 'tis lonely here, not atall like England . . . not that there is anyone there at home in Devon waitin' for me!" She caressed a quaint pin on her kerchief. "This brooch is all I have left of me mum."

"And it *is* lovely. You must cherish it always." Hannah held the girl's hand tight. "Go to bed now, Elizabeth. Your tears will soon pass. You need your rest, for Missy will have you up at the break of day."

"Go to bed, Elizabeth," Tom's voice echoed from the doorway. "Sleep well."

When the girl's candle had disappeared down the hall, Tom stripped off his waistcoat, tossed it on the chair, and lay down across the bed beside Hannah.

"What do you think, love?" She showed him the drawing of the cherubs.

"The nursery at Stratford . . ." Tom sighed with pleasure.

Hannah smiled radiantly. "I once promised you a dynasty, did I not?"

"Aye, you did." Tom stared up at the ceiling. "And I promised you a great many things. A fine house of your own, seasons at Williamsburg . . ."

"Which in time you shall provide. I have no doubt of you, my darling."

Tom rolled over on his side, his finger tracing the soft outline of her chin. "But I worry sometimes, Hannah, that you are not strong enough for this life. 'Tis lonely on this Northern Neck, and there are dangers for which one cannot prepare. . . ." He sighed, deciding to keep his fears to himself. "Perhaps you should have married a cavalier—one educated at the Inns of Court, whose lands lie along the quiet James."

"Thomas, how could you?" Hannah drew back against her pillow in mock horror. "You sound like that odious Mr. Dabney. For, despite his compliments, I cannot think he understands or appreciates Virginians. He condescends to us!"

Tom nodded. "If his viewpoint reflects that of the Board of Trade, or that of the Parliament—or even that of the King—then someday, I think, there will be a reckoning, for we are not an outpost of imperial Rome. We are Englishmen, and deserving of fair consideration."

Hannah snuggled deeper under the comforter. "I was quite intrigued by my cousin Ben tonight! As a child, I was always a bit sorry for him, you know. He seemed a shy, lonely boy, growing up out at Berkeley. Oh, he was wealthy enough, but it was a quiet, unkempt sort of place after his father died. Then Ben reached his majority and married Anne Carter, built a fine new house—with the help of Carter money, of course." She dimpled. "And now, he's so social. Mary Bland was saying that she couldn't believe he would travel all the way out to the Neck in the dead of winter just to see us."

"Ben's call was more than social," Tom answered bluntly. "He came as emissary from his father-in-law, carrying a cajoling letter in Carter's own hand, full of sweet words and compliments."

"Ah, now I see!" Hannah nodded thoughtfully. "Before dinner Ben mentioned to me the possibility of your selling at a good price some land at the Little Falls. Is that what Carter wants?"

"Aye, the Carters have discovered what appears to be a large copper deposit in the upper reaches of the Fairfax Proprietary. They have formed a mining company and hope to cut a road to the Little Falls in order to transport the ore downstream for shipment to England. The only navigable sites at the falls lie on my land."

"What did you say?"

"I told him that my land was not for sale. It is prime land, Hannah, for Virginia fast expands beyond the Tidewater, and someday a town, perhaps even a city, will rise at the fall line of the Potomac. It is an ideal site, and I mean for the Lees to be a part of it! Now that we've the money to finish Stratford Hall, there is no need to sell. What's more, there is principle involved. Robert Carter thinks he can buy anything." Tom put the drawing pad and pen on the night table. "Lee land is not for sale, not even for the 'King's' ransom."

"What did Ben say to *that?*"

"That my answer would not be acceptable." Tom laughed cynically.

Hannah slid lower into the pillow. "What a marvel! And with my cousin Ben as emissary!" She rose up suddenly on one elbow. "Was I so 'evident' in my yellow tonight, Tom? I feel so cumbersome, and Ben is such a gossip. He'll go back to the James and tell everyone that I've lost my looks out here in the wilds, that I've turned into nothing but a brood mare!" Hannah's green eyes glinted with indignation.

"If he does, then he shall be a liar!" Chuckling, Tom bent and kissed her, then rose from the bed. "I'll bank the fires and lock up your silver-plate."

It was cold belowstairs, the fire dying on the hearth as Tom wrapped the silver candlesticks and serving dishes in green baize and stored them away in the cherry-tree room. He opened the metal safekeeping box on the shelf and for a moment stared reassuringly at his leather money pouch. Coinage was hard to come by in the colony. To have it was a security, for tobacco's worth rose and fell and could not be counted on to hold steady value. He closed and, with his key, securely locked the door, remembering how Hannah's dowry of six hundred pounds—a sum left to her by her Harrison and Ludwell grandfathers—had quickly disappeared in the drain of new house expenses. For a long time, Tom stood staring into the dying embers of the fire, thinking of the mysterious happenings at Stratford. Perhaps he and Hannah were now too vulnerable.

Will West could not sleep. Wrapped in his blanket, the boy burrowed deeply into the pile of sweet-smelling hay until only his small black face was exposed. From his corner of the Matchotique barn, which smelled of dried apples and leather and, best of all, horses, he fixed his eye on the little mare that Master Tom had let him ride back from Stratford. She was his! Well, not really, but he could pretend. She was the only thing he ever felt like he owned, and he had already named her Little Flower. He missed his ma something awful but it was good to be here. Now he had important things to do every day, like keep the master's boots polished, carry the hot dishes from the kitchen to the big house, and, most important, help with little Philip and the baby. He liked it especially when Master Tom put his hand on his shoulder and said he was a fine boy, as he did tonight when Captain Lee and his lady and the two gentlemen were getting in their carriage and Will had held the burning pine knot high so they could see where to step.

As Will's dark lashes began to droop sleepily on his cheeks, he heard Little Flower move with a bump in her stall. There it was again. What was that noise? Will sat up quickly in the straw and threw back the blanket. In his stocking feet, he ran to the horse's stall.

For a moment he heard only the pounding of his own heart, then again the strange sounds—someone was running past the stable door! Will threw back the wide swinging door, then stumbled out into the chilling darkness. He could see the big house's reassuring outline, solid and secure in the dark night. Beyond the brick wall, the trees swayed and rustled in the cold breeze. "Maybe 'twasn't anything," he murmured. " 'Jes a deer—" Then, without warning, the boy was struck from behind and sank to the ground.

"That'll learn ye, meddlin' brat," said a menacing voice above him.

Another voice spoke roughly. "Did ye get everything?"

"Aye, we've lightened Colonel Lee's purse considerably and left him a warming present to remember us by!"

Moments later, dazed and bewildered, Will struggled to his knees. Was that candlelight coming from the big house? No, it was much brighter! Flames leaped in the fanlight over the front door and in the parlor windows.

Terrified, the boy stumbled in his stocking feet toward the house. "Master Tom," he called out frantically, "it's a fire, it's a fire! Miss Hannah, wake up!"

In the big upstairs bedroom, Tom lay sound asleep. He did not feel Hannah stirring beside him, coughing slightly. Neither heard the boy's cries.

"Your house is afire! Master Tom, Miss Hannah, wake up!"

Seizing a thick vine of honeysuckle that climbed toward the bedchamber windows, Will tested its strength, then climbed hand over hand, seeking precarious toeholds. As he struggled past the downstairs window, he could feel the scorching heat and smell the smoke seeping from the shutters. Finally his fingertips touched the rough edge of roof overhanging the first floor. Will lunged to pull himself up, but the vine parted from the wall, and, finding nothing to grasp but air, he tumbled with a fearful cry back to the hard ground.

Tom was tossing restlessly. Dreaming his baby daughter was crying from somewhere far off, he suddenly started awake, his eyes wide open. "Dear God, no!" Hurriedly he pulled Hannah to her feet. "Fire, Hannah! Steady, now." He gasped, taking her by the hand.

The children's room was so thick with smoke that Tom could not see, but he could hear the quiet sobs of his son and the choked screams of the baby. As he groped to reach them, he called to Elizabeth, who was stirring on her narrow cot. "Up quickly, lass . . . don't be afraid . . . help me get the children out."

Blindly fighting through the smoke, Tom smashed open the bedroom window. One arm cradling Missy, he guided Hannah, who clutched Philip's small hand, onto the narrow sloping roof. Close behind followed Elizabeth. "Me brooch," she sobbed. "I forgot me brooch."

"You must jump." Tom firmly pushed Hannah toward the edge of the roof. He heard her draw in a sharp gasp of air. "Close your eyes and jump," he ordered. "Will is there, he'll help you."

Tom felt her hand reluctantly slip from his, and Hannah and Philip hurtled toward the hard frozen earth.

The flames were beginning to billow out toward the stable buildings. "Get the horses out!" he hollered to the hands gathering below.

"You're next, Elizabeth." He turned back to help the girl, but she had disappeared. "The little fool!" he murmured between clenched teeth. He called down to one of the men in the yard, "I am going to throw the baby. Can you catch her? By God, you must catch her!" He tore the little girl's clutching arms from around his neck and held her small, arching form over the side of the roof, then opened his hands. Unable to look, Tom turned and, shielding his face with his arm, crawled back into the house after Elizabeth.

News of the Lees' tragic fire at Matchotique carried quickly. The calamity was discussed in the great houses along the James, the York, the Rappahannock, and the Potomac rivers, with sorrow, even with tears—for they were all family, as Anne Carter Harrison said plaintively.

At Corotoman, Robert Carter studied an account of the Northern Neck fire in the *Maryland Gazette*, which Robin had carried home from Annapolis:

> Last Wednesday night. Col. Thomas Lee's fine house in Virginia was burnt, his office, barns and outhouses, his plate, cash to the sum of ten thousand lbs., papers and everything entirely lost.
>
> His lady and child were forced to be thrown out of a window and he himself hardly escaped the flames, being much scorched. A white girl of about twelve years old (a servant) perished in the fire. It is said that Col. Lee's loss is not less than £50,000.

For a long time, the old man stared from his bedroom window at the drizzling afternoon rain. "Funky, foggy weather," he muttered. Despite their differences, he certainly never wished such calamity to befall young Colonel Lee. He liked, even admired the man, for Lee reminded him of himself, perhaps more than any of his own sons. Tom Lee would survive this, Carter told himself. He closed his eyes. . . . "God's will be done!" he intoned, slowly twisting the diamond ring on his finger. Of course, the loss of the cashbox at Matchotique might mean a change in Colonel Lee's resistance to selling his land at the Little Falls. Robert Carter limped to his desk to pen a note of condolence.

Beyond the "King's" bedroom, in Corotoman's parlor, a pale Ben Harrison described the disaster to his brothers-in-law, Robin and Landon. "Burned to the ground. Only bits and pieces left . . . not a stick of furniture. By the time we reached Matchotique, the house was a solid wall of fire. We managed to rescue the horses and livestock before the stable and barn caught."

"At least Tom and his family were saved," said Landon.

"Aye, but Hannah lies desperately ill, near to death, they say. . . . Lord, help her." Tears welled in Ben's eyes. He turned his back on the brothers and leaned his arms on the mantel.

"No, no, I can't see." Hannah was tossing her head from side to side, her hands feebly flailing the hangings of the tall canopy bed.

Mary Bland hurried to dampen the corner of a linen cloth in the china bowl on the washstand and gently wipe Hannah's brow. "You are dreaming again, Hannah. You are at Lee Hall and everything is all right."

Moaning, Hannah turned her face to the wall, tears welling in her eyes. "I keep dreaming of Matchotique and the smoke and the terrible heat. All I remember is falling, falling. . . ."

Mary Bland smoothed Hannah's hair and brow. "You must forget about the fire, Hannah. You must grow strong again."

"I've lost the baby, poor Elizabeth is dead, Matchotique is gone, and . . ."

Mary Bland broke in. "Dear Hannah, you must stop this! Tom and the children have quite recovered from their ordeal. Only you, my dear, mend too slowly." Mary Bland bent her dark head close to Hannah's and whispered pleadingly, "Please, try to be your old self again. You were ever the dauntless one, Hannah, picking up your skirts to climb fences, always riding faster than the wind, dancing till dawn at balls and frolics. You were never afraid of a challenge. Now you *must* get well—for Tom, for your children."

But Hannah did not answer; she lay still as if sleeping. For a moment, Mary Bland watched the slight rise and fall of the blanket, then slipped from the stool and went quietly down the narrow curving staircase to the main floor.

Sprawled in the deepest sitting room chair, his booted legs outstretched on the red Turkey carpet, Gus Washington listened impassively as Harry reported on the case against the sailors of the ship *Elizabeth*.

"As you know, Gus, they came before the court for examination early last month." Harry paced back and forth the length of the room. "But those who testified against them were not considered men of enough character to have their word taken as sufficient evidence to send the seamen to Williamsburg for trial. As a slave, young Will West cannot give testimony, and besides, his report was confused at best. In good conscience, the bench could find them guilty only of vile and abusive speech against Tom, and mutiny. We fined them fifty shillings each." Harry shook his head bitterly. "A light punishment."

Gus stared at Tom, who stood quietly by the window. "And what of the future?"

Tom shrugged wearily as if he had no interest in the subject. "Last week, Hannah birthed and lost a son." Tom's eyes were dark with pain. "A well-shaped baby who never drew a breath. Even without the consideration of Hannah's health, our situation is perilous, Gus. The blackhearts took everything of value—our money as well as silverplate. There is nothing left. I've no cash to work with." He paused, his voice showing the strain of his feelings. "I am considering Carter's offer to buy my land at the Little Falls."

"Would that be so intolerable?" Mary Bland asked comfortingly. "You still have other land holdings in the north."

"If only someone other than Carter wished to buy that land," Tom said hotly. "This Neck, this colony, is too big for one man to hold such power. Oh, I accept his words of sympathy upon my 'dismal calamity,' for I believe he means them. He, too, has suffered from ruffians and thieves, but . . ."

"You are too proud, Tom," Harry said gently. "Stay here with us at Lee Hall and rebuild a temporary house on the grounds of Matchotique."

Mary Bland sighed. "Surely that is the best idea."

"*The best?*" Hannah Lee stood framed in the doorway, pale but erect in her blue dressing gown, auburn hair flowing over her shoulders. "Sell our land to Carter, Tom? Put off our move to Stratford? Live in another temporary house? How can you say any of that is the best?"

Tom moved quickly to his wife and helped her to the couch.

"How can we give up our hopes and dreams?" She held on to his hand tightly. "We will go on to Stratford, Tom. We can live in the office building, for it is cozy and sound, and one day we shall finish the great house just as we planned. I will not have another baby born any place but Stratford!"

"It will be years before we can complete the manor house," Tom protested. "It would be very difficult. I cannot have you—"

His words were interrupted by the babble of children. Small Philip Lee stood with his cousins in the doorway, his long curling hair framing a slender, aristocratic face. Behind the children, Will West hovered with Missy braced on his hip. "I tried to stop 'em, sir, but Master Philip wanted to see his mother."

" 'Tis all right, Will. Come here, son."

Hannah leaned forward, her green eyes intense, and whispered to Tom fiercely, "Stratford Hall is Philip's legacy. I would have him grow up there, to see from the beginning the tobacco mellowing in the fields, to feel the sunshine of its days, to smell the honeysuckle of its nights, to see the great house come to life. I would have him know the joys—and, yes, the struggle—of Stratford's first days. Indeed, I demand it, Tom!"

For the first time in weeks, Tom laughed. "Hannah Lee, you are impossible. And somehow, by God, you'll *have* the impossible."

The Tidewater, 1730

Williamsburg was exquisitely beautiful that May, spangled with the pink and white of dogwood, its neat fenced gardens green with boxwood and herbs. It had been the center of power of the Virginia Colony for some thirty years, since the government had moved inland from the mosquito-infested Jamestown settlement. Finally, it was becoming a handsome capital city, with a bustling market place, a bowling green, a playhouse theater—the New World's first—an arsenal, and the prison house.

When the General Assembly sat in the spring and fall, Williamsburg became a beehive of outdoor fairs, balls, parties, and small intimate get-togethers. Like the gathering of a private club, the sittings offered opportunities to renew old friendships to its members, whose plantations dotted the river-laced Tidewater.

". . . A dinner at Berkeley to celebrate your well-deserved good fortune." Ben and Anne Harrison's invitation referred to the recent bounty of three hundred pounds ordered delivered to Tom Lee from the royal purse.

"A gift from Queen Caroline in recognition of your family's suffering in the discharge of your duties as a justice in Her Majesty's court," Governor Gooch had announced as he ceremoniously presented the purse to Tom in the House of Burgesses.

" 'Tis only a pittance and in no way offsets our loss, but we appreciate Her Majesty's gesture," Tom explained to Anne as they strolled in her renowned rose garden before dinner.

"You must remember every bit of news to take home to Hannah," Ben called out as he poured Tom a cooling rum drink on the shaded terrace overlooking the James. "Tell her our former governor, Alexander Spotswood, builds a fine house in the north at Germana. I hear he brought back a ship's cargohold full of nightingales to be released at the falls of the Rappahannock in hopes he can fill the American skies with English music! And tell her that the brilliant John Randolph is now home from England. . . . I always thought my dear cousin Hannah might choose him to wed, you know," Ben teased Tom with a twinkle in his eye.

Tom smiled in amusement. "Have you heard any news of his brother, my friend Captain Isham Randolph?"

"He's gone to sea again." Ben shook his head. "Randolph quickly tires of the lavish and comfortable life he leads at his plantation Dungeness."

Anne Harrison fluttered her fan mischievously. "There is a shocking rumor that Captain Randolph's Irish overseer is romancing one of the Randolph nieces of Tuckahoe, Tom! Will Byrd says one must never underestimate the Hibernian charm, though I have never really cared for the Irish myself."

The Harrisons and Tom were joined on the terrace by William Byrd of Westover, the Harrisons' adjoining neighbor. The saturninely elegant Black Swan had come through the woods with his dark-haired English wife and his exquisite daughter, Evelyn.

At dinner, when Tom complimented him on his daughter's piquant beauty, Byrd whispered, "She is twenty-three and refuses all her Virginia swains! Quite a stubborn, antick virgin." He rolled his eyes. "My Evelyn lost her heart to someone I deemed unsuitable when she was sixteen, just a slip of a girl, but I thought her too young to know her own mind. It happened in England in 1723, the year when she was presented at the court of George the First. By the way," he added, putting his hand on Tom's arm, "do you know what the King said when he saw my Evelyn? He asked, 'Are there many other as beautiful birds in my forests of America?' "

Byrd's laughter at the King's play on words was as amused as Tom's. Evelyn Byrd, who obviously had heard the story many times before, threw her father a disdainful look across the table.

Tom fell to his dinner, thinking how William Byrd, now fifty-six, had mellowed from the arrogant, passionate cavalier who for many years had lived for nothing but London gossip and female conquests. Byrd tended his vineyards, experimented in horticulture and iron-ore mining, and was now rebuilding Westover into a sumptuous home. And at last he had obtained his greatest wish—a son and namesake, William Byrd III, born two years ago.

A disciplined man, the slender Byrd refused all but the main course of soft-shell crab, for by habit he ate only one dish at a meal, preferring to indulge in conversation rather than rich food.

"It is my opinion, gentlemen, that the Mother Country must eventually let us do our own pig-iron manufacturing as well as mine the ore," he declared when the three men retired after dinner to enjoy their clay pipes and brandy in sheltered wooden chairs placed near the banks of the James. "We cannot be a single-product colony forever. By God, the Scotch and Irish pour into the Shenandoah Valley. They can't all grow tobacco! If the English have to consume all our tobacco output, they will begin to resemble chimneys—every household will need a sweep to clean the soot from Virginia smoke!"

"The Shenandoah settlers must first survive the rampaging Indians," Tom pointed out. "The treaty Spotswood gained in 1722 is weak. Something must be done if England is to conquer the Americas. We all know the colonies of Nouveau Français expand widely throughout the interior, while we English strengthen our colonies only along the Atlantic Sea. We sorely need more inland cities and towns of size." Tom gestured emphatically. "True, there is the settlement of Fredericksburg and your new city of Petersburg..." he said to Byrd. "I am pleased to hear of your plan to raise a town on your land at the fall line of the James."

"A good site for English commerce!" Byrd's eye sparkled with enthusiasm. "It is the very dividing point between civilization and the untouched, savage forests. My father and his uncle before him maintained a trading post for trafficking with the Algonquins, Sioux, Catawbas, and Cherokee. I plan to call my promising town Richmond," Byrd added, "for the terrain resembles Richmond on the Thames."

"We sorely need a port city on the Potomac," Tom continued. "I could well picture one close to the lands near the Little Falls."

"But as you point out, Tom, first the Indians must be dealt with," said

Ben Harrison with a shiver. "I still fear their presence, even in the safety of the dear old James. We have an escape tunnel from this house to the river just in case. . . ." His voice trailed off as a clap of thunder crashed the stillness of the summer night. "Perhaps we should move inside, gentlemen," he suggested nervously. "I fear a thunderstorm is coming—perhaps lightning as well."

But Councilor Byrd was caught up in the conversation. "Were you aware, Tom, that I recently served on a long and difficult mission to adjudicate the border between Virginia and the colony of North Carolina? We encountered ferocious redmen armed with muskets. . . ."

"Sold to them by the French, no doubt," said Ben, rising to his feet, "but still better than the deadly silence of bow and arrow."

"Well, I tell you," Byrd continued jocularly, "those Carolinian settlers differ greatly from Virginians—more 'primitive,' shall we say. . . . Buxom ladies who are not afeared to fight mountain lions with their bare hands, and bearded fellows who delighted in the delicacy of 'bear's foot'! Personally," Byrd's voice rolled expressively, "I was a bit put off by the fact that it so resembled a human foot—heels, toes, and all!" With that, a crack of lightning dispatched the men to the safety of the great house.

"Here, love . . ." Tom turned from unpacking his saddlebags and handed a parcel to Hannah. "Anne Harrison sent you these rose clippings from her garden." He looked with sudden alarm at his wife's face. "Are you all right, Hannah?" Immediately upon his return, she had told him all that had transpired while he was away. She had confessed with delight that she thought she was with child again. Now she told of Gus Washington's arrival home from a year in England at the end of May, only to learn of his wife's death last November. "All these months, Tom," she said, her voice quivering, "he did not even know that Jane was dead! He is quite crushed and broken over it. I feel so badly for him."

In late December, in the makeshift bedroom of the plantation office-cottage, Hannah with great ease gave birth to another son—a calm, brown-eyed baby whom she named Thomas Ludwell. "But the next child I bear will be born under Stratford's roof!" Hannah told Tom emphatically. "I will not be put off!"

The Tidewater, 1731

Life in the colony and the contentious situation with Mother England seemed soothed by the leadership of the diplomatic and affable Governor

Gooch and Robert Carter, the able president of the council. The aging King Carter's political concerns were, however, secondary to his personal problems, for 1731 brought great sadness into his life—the death of his son-in-law, Mann Page, at Rosewell on the York River. Tom wrote a sincere and heartfelt note of condolence. "Births and deaths," he commented to Hannah in the early summer as he watched her rocking baby Thomas by the open door of the office, "seem to be the benchmarks of life."

"You aren't forgetting marriage, are you?" She smiled, reminding him that Gus Washington had in recent months taken himself a new wife.

"I know little about his bride," said Tom, "only that her name is Mary Ball, a local girl of twenty-three years—something of an old maid not to be already married. Lasses wed young on the Neck!"

"Still and all," Hannah insisted, "at least she's brought a woman's touch to Gus's lonely little house at Pope's Creek."

The Tidewater, 1732

Finally, on a cold, windy morning in January 1732, Tom moved his family into the great house. It was done without ceremony, for the house was not finished. But the four rooms of the east wing were complete enough.

"Ah, we occupy this house just in time," said Hannah with a tired sigh, for she was again big with child. "I promised you that my next baby would be born beneath Stratford's roof!"

"My God, you're not ready to drop this foal already, are you?" Tom gave her an anxious look as he tucked her into the tall bed in the spacious master bedroom. "Do you think it will come soon?"

"Very soon." Hannah's eyes were bright with anticipation.

She had taken five-year-old Philip into the bed beside her. "By morning you will have a new little brother or sister," she said in a reassuring voice.

The child looked at her intently. "But, Mother, I'd rather not."

Laughing, Tom scooped the boy up—" 'Tis much too late to tell your mother that!"—and carried Philip high on his shoulders toward the nursery, where Missy was playing before the fire with a pile of Philip's blocks. A smile brightened the four-year-old girl's face as she looked up at him.

Tom went down on one knee, an arm around each of the children. "One day, when you look in this fireplace, you will see angels, for your mother has designed a fireplace back. One day we will send home to England to have it forged—just for your nursery."

"Why do you always say 'home to England,' Father?" Philip asked, imperiously sweeping the blocks out of Missy's reach. "Why don't you say 'home to Virginia'?"

Tom laughed. "Because we are English and our king is in England. In truth, Philip, we have two homes, Virginia and England. But come now, 'tis time you were in bed, in Virginia!"

At dawn, Hannah lay in the high canopied bed with her newborn son nestled in the blankets beside her.

"Shh, shh," she whispered, "he sleeps."

"Another fine son . . . You do me proud, madam." Tom looked adoringly at Hannah. "He must bear the name of two strong men, my grandfather and my favorite brother, Richard Henry Lee."

"A magnificent place you've carved out for yourself here on the cliffs," Gus said one day the next August as he walked with Tom on the river side of the house. He had come from Wakefield with his wife and their six-month-old son to visit at Stratford. "I know it hasn't been easy, but you've done it all, and without a compromise. You didn't even have to sell land to Carter."

"The irony of it is that the Carters' copper mine near the Little Falls proved a false start. The struggle over my land was for naught." Tom shook his head. "But tell me, do things go well with you, Gus?" Tom thought his friend seemed tired. "Are your sons at school in England well?"

"Aye, but I don't seem to get much ahead." He put his hands deep in the pockets of his breeches. "Sometimes I think I might move my family up to the Epewasson site on the Little Hunting Creek. Mary is not all that happy at Wakefield, another woman's house and all that. What's more, we've all had a lot of dysentery and must frequently take the bark. The land at Epewasson is higher than at Pope's Creek, and I feel there may be something invigorating about a fresh start. I don't know." He shrugged and gave Tom a warm, crooked smile. "But you, my friend, you seem to have your life well under control."

Tom stared out at the vista of blue river in the far distance. "Plans, anyway. There is so much to do, gardens and orchards to put in. One day, Gus, I hope to build a wharf. Then even the largest trading vessels can sail directly here by the Potomac, just as they reach Corotoman by the Rappahannock."

"You sit on important committees in the House of Burgesses, Tom. Perhaps you'll sit on the King's Council one day?"

Tom's eyes narrowed. "As long as King Carter holds tight the reins of power, you can be assured that Tom Lee will not be allowed that seat. Even if Gooch should push my appointment in London, Carter would surely block it."

Gus shrugged. "Not for me the push and shove of Williamsburg and

London politics . . . I'll stay right here on the Potomac, thank you!" Big, ruddy Washington looked suddenly toward the shade of a large oak tree at one corner of the lawn where the wives and small children were picnicking.

Hannah had spread out a soft rug under the tree, and the two babies lay in the dappled shade beside their mothers. "Thirty days apart . . ." murmured Hannah, "and they are much alike . . . fair, sturdy boys. Your George has an unusually wide, handsome brow, my dear."

Mary fell silent. There was a tentative quality about Gus's new wife that Hannah could not define. Mary wore a dark skirt, not of the latest fashion, and a simple white blouse. Her brown hair was tightly rolled in a bun at the nape of her neck, and a strand had slipped loose and hung down her back. Her best feature was her eyes, a pleasant gray, but she kept them cast down and rarely met Hannah's steady gaze. "Aye, George is a good baby," she said finally, "but 'tis confining, having a child. Even with the servants, I feel I must be at home. . . . There is so much to the caring of him, and then there's the cooking for Gus and little Jane. Before the baby, I used to ride for hours every day. I do miss that."

"You rode your horse alone, in the woods?" Hannah's tone was incredulous.

"And still do, when I can get away." For the first time, the girl showed some animation. "I can take care of myself. Once a black bear came at me, rose up on his hind legs and came straight away at me."

"What in the name of God did you do, Mary?"

"Reared the horse back and slashed the bear one with my crop," she said proudly. "Teach him to come after me!"

What a curious girl Mary was! Hannah watched Tom and Gus crossing the lawn to join them. Tom looked dashing in his red jacket and well-cut breeches. He was better looking now, more distinguished than when she had married him. She watched him throw Missy into the air, her skirts flying. If only he wouldn't do that. Little girls shouldn't be treated so roughly—it made them bold and boyish, like Mary Washington.

Hannah, rising as the servant brought out the teaboard, saw Harry Lee ride into the courtyard. "Is everything well at Lee Hall?" she called out anxiously.

"Well as can be." Harry bowed his greetings to Mary Washington and turned with a look of expectancy toward Tom and Gus. "I couldn't wait. I had to ride over myself and tell you the news! But perhaps you've already heard—"

"Heard what?" Tom broke in.

"You'll be receiving a letter from the governor soon enough, but I've just come from Landon Carter at Sabine Hall, so I know it's true." Harry's cheeks flushed with the import of his news. "Seems his father took ill a week ago." He paused. "The 'King' has died at Corotoman."

For a moment, Tom stood silent. Then: "I'm most sorry to hear that. Robert Carter was a man I respected; difficult, but a man of vision, and in that he enlightened my life." He spoke with obvious sincerity. "I shall mourn his passing."

"Aye, but there is more . . ." Harry went on excitedly. "You, Tom Lee, have been chosen to fill his place on the King's Council. Now you have your chance to turn this colony in the way you would have it go."

Tom looked at Hannah, who leaned against the gnarled trunk of an elm tree, her curving mouth parted in a smile. It was not a smile of surprise or even of congratulations. It was a smile that said, "There! You see, just as I long ago told you in the grape arbor . . . I knew you were destined to great things. And this is only the beginning."

Ironic, mused the colonel, that it was by the death of his old enemy, Robert Carter, that Tom Lee gained a coveted spot at the council table. While many planters were called from their prosperous tobacco plantations in the Tidewater to serve in the House of Burgesses, only a privileged few sat on the King's Council. It was the most prestigious honor a colonial-born Englishman could attain, for the Royal Governor was by tradition an envoy direct from the court. In addition to their legislative and administrative duties, the twelve councilors also sat as the highest court in the colony.

Virginia was fast becoming a center of erratic but surprising scholarship, of high ambition and amazing conviviality. By the time Tom Lee became a member of the council, in 1732, Virginia had already fashioned a complex, distinctive culture. In the languid, water-seamed wilderness of the Chesapeake, a sturdy strain of transplanted English seemed determined to recreate the best England had to offer. Yet the human spirit was sorely tested by physical adversity, for despite their silks and satins, these admirable adventurers contended valiantly with all manner of daily discomforts: boils, pus and pox, aching teeth, red eyes, the itch, the flux, and pleurisy.

Still, the farsighted Tom Lee dared to dream enormous dreams for his household of children and for an expanding Virginia.

Building the Dream

1742–1743

The Tidewater, 1742

Fifteen-year-old Missy Lee had been dreading this day for weeks—in fact, ever since the party was planned and the invitations sent. It was to be a tremendous frolic, an all-day, all-night celebration . . . the finest affair ever given in the ten years the Lees had been at Stratford Hall. Mamma said it would be marvelous fun. Well, it might be marvelous fun for everyone else, Missy thought with a sigh of despair, but not for her. For her it was going to be just horrid!

There would be horse racing in the morning. Missy sniffed indignantly: that was for boys only! And dancing in the ballroom until all hours of the night, which might appeal to some people! She thought with disdain of her female cousins and friends forever giggling under their parasols.

From her bedroom window on the ground floor of the great house, Missy could see the long cypress-board tables erected by the plantation carpenters for the noon dinner to be served on the river-side lawn of the house. It was scarcely seven in the morning, yet a dozen servants were already carrying wicker baskets filled with crisp table linens, polished cutlery, sparkling glass, and china to be inspected by the mistress of the house before the tables were laid.

Hannah Lee, in a yellow morning dress and a dainty lace cap, stood beneath a tree scrutinizing the preparations. One thing was certain: everything would be perfect, for her mother's standards were the highest—sometimes so high the archangels themselves couldn't please her, Missy thought with a mixture of admiration and resentment.

The girl watched Hannah unclasp the brass key ring at her waist and hand two metal keys to Will West, the only person trusted to dole out provisions from the plantation's larders. That her mother was a good economist who managed this great plantation house with both skill and charm Missy hadn't the slightest question. But in truth, it was terribly difficult to be her daughter!

With a start of delight Missy caught sight of her father dismounting beneath the trees at the side of the yard. He had most likely been down to the wharf, for two schooners from England were loading at Stratford Landing. Missy started to rap on the bull's-eye glass to catch her father's attention, but she stopped short, for her mother was hurrying across the dewy grass toward him.

She watched her parents embrace and turn, arm in arm, to survey their great house and the tables set beneath the fresh budding trees. The house party, which would draw dozens of guests from every corner of the Tidewater, was to be an anniversary celebration. Twenty years ago this May, Tom and Hannah Lee had been wed in the magnificent flower-filled drawing room at Green Spring.

What an eternity twenty years seemed! Yet her parents were still vibrantly young and full of ambition. How wonderful to be so sure of yourself, knowing exactly what you wanted from life and feeling confident you could gain it!

The mingled scent of baked smoked ham, slab bacon, and fresh-baked batter bread wafted from the dining room down the stairway to the lower floor, where the bedchambers were located. Missy wrinkled her nose distastefully; she never ate very much in the morning. And at this moment there was nothing she wanted less than breakfast, for she would be forced to make polite conversation with the guests who had stayed the night at Stratford. She winced at the idea of making small talk with formidable Governor Gooch and his lady from Williamsburg, or of contending with her noisy Harrison cousins from Berkeley. She did not even want to talk to her adored uncle, Philip Ludwell, who had arrived last night from Green Spring with his wife, Frances. Though not much older than Missy, Frances seemed a million years older because she was married and the mother of four-year-old Hannah Philippa.

Missy's hazel eyes swept the sun-washed bedroom usually shared with her six-year-old sister, Alice, but this morning filled with various girl cousins —three dark-haired Harrisons and ten-year-old Lucy Grymes, the younger sister of Uncle Phil's wife, Frances.

"Actually we are double cousins," Lucy had told Missy with an engaging smile; Frances and Lucy Grymes were granddaughters of Missy's great-uncle, the late Edmund Jennings.

It doesn't matter if we are all cousins a hundred times over, I'm not a bit like any of those feather-headed little gooses, Missy decided as she jerked on her riding boots beneath her oldest calico skirt. No matter how she—or her mother—tried, she would never be like them. Never would she have the doll-like looks of Lucy Grymes or the dark, lush charm of the budding Bette Harrison. Not that she really wanted to! She had outgrown dolls, and certainly she wasn't one bit ready to get married! She had things to see and do!

She took a cypress twig from the cup on the washstand and gave her even white teeth a quick polish, then ran a comb through her straight wheat-colored hair. With scarcely a farewell glance at the chattering nightgowned girls, Missy unbolted the brass lock on the door that gave onto the courtyard and stepped into the sunlight.

Oh, it was a lovely morning. The haze had already burned off, and the Potomac lay like pale-blue satin ribbon on the horizon. She stood for a moment with her face upturned, absorbing the gentle warmth of the April sun and savoring the familiar scent of boxwood mingled with the fragrances of flowering fruit trees in the orchard beyond the privet hedge.

"Missy Lee, how come you out in this sun without a parasol or a bonnet on yo' head!" Will West shook his head in amused exasperation as the slender, boyish Missy approached. "And in yo' old clothes on such a fine occasion. Don't let yo' mamma see."

Missy tossed her head as if to throw off Will's words as well.

He looked appraisingly at the girl. "You not ailing this morning, are you, chile? You look right peaked. Have you had yo' breakfast? There's fresh shad roe, yo' favorite!"

Missy turned her eyes and stared into the distance. "I don't want any breakfast. Truth is, Will," she said with a sigh, "I don't really know what it is I want."

"You feeling restless again. Yo' pa letting you stay in the schoolhouse with yo' brothers—I heard tell too much book larning's not good for girls . . . burst they little heads wide open."

Despite her misery, Missy joined him in laughter.

"Well, I got things to be doing this morning. Can't be standing here talking the whole day away." He threw her a sympathetic smile.

Missy's long-legged stride kept pace with the quick-moving young black man's as he headed down the sloping lawn to the arch of trees sheltering the brick springhouse. Now in his early twenties, Will West was an integral part of life at Stratford. He served as Councilor Lee's personal servant, occasionally accompanying his master on the twice-yearly visits to Williamsburg, but more important, Will oversaw the Stratford house staff. With a Scottish schoolmaster, Mr. Currie, in command of the schoolhouse, and reliable

Annie in charge of the younger children, he had given up his daily responsibilities for the Lee children. But Missy knew that he was someone she could always depend on.

With a long hooked pole Will pulled earthen crocks of corn relish, watermelon rind pickles, and apple butter from the cold waters of the springhouse and, with two crocks on his shoulders, set off through the fragrant herb gardens to the square brick kitchen house.

"Perhaps, as I think about it, I could just eat a biscuit," Missy allowed as the aromas of the kitchen reached her nostrils.

"This kitchen too busy to be waiting on you," Will remonstrated gently, but he thrust a platter of biscuits slathered with fresh butter into Missy's hand.

She clambered above to the loft, there to eat while watching the three busy cooks and their two helpers, their faces shiny with perspiration, struggling to prepare the noon banquet.

After days of cooking, their preparations were now coming to fruition. An ox was browning to a final golden crisp on the spit over the seven-foot-wide fireplace, the handle rotated patiently by a battery of young black boys. Fresh Potomac flounder was baking in Bordeaux wine, and in black iron pots, swamp terrapin simmered in beef stock laced with rum. Huge piles of oysters and clam fritters were ready to be deep-fried and smothered in wine sauce. Casseroles of baked celery with delectable imported almonds that had just arrived by ship, along with spices from the Indies, had been assembled. One of the cooks, her skillful hand flashing, prepared fresh spring asparagus, beets, and peas. A dozen lemon cakes, like a galaxy of frosted suns, cooled on the shaded windowsills. Luscious blancmange and crunchy marzipan were ready for dessert. But best of all were the beaten biscuits. Nothing could surpass a good, crisp, melt-in-the-mouth biscuit, big enough for only two tasty bites. No matter if one had them every day; biscuits were still the best food in the world!

"Where you be going, Missy Lee?" Will West called as she slipped out the kitchen door, but Missy pretended she did not hear and ran across the back lawn toward her father's orchard. She could see that guests were beginning to arrive at the circular drive on the west side of the house. There were the Tayloes of Mount Airy, the Ayletts, and the McCarties from Longwood; and just dismounting from their handsome carriage were her aunt Mary Bland and uncle Harry Lee. Their attractive blond teen-age sons, who had followed on horseback, were heading toward the stables to join the young men gathering for the race.

Missy slipped into the long brick stable through the side entrance and moved toward the laughter in the sun-filled paddock. There, a dozen young men, most in their teens or early twenties, were grooming their horses, assisted by servants, each dressed in the bright livery of the family he attended. The air was thick with excitement and tension, for Tom Lee had put up a purse of fifty Spanish gold pistoles, a magnificent sum.

"When you take the first jump, by the catalpa tree, swing hard to the left by the run to take the hedge," young Ben Harrison V, in a crimson silk riding jacket, asserted.

That's foolish! Missy had to bite her lip to keep from calling out. You should swing wide to let your horse build momentum to take the hedges. Oh, if only I could ride the point-to-point. Charmer and I, we'd show them how to ride a good race!

A gentle hand touched her shoulder. "Thought I might find you in here," Will West murmured gently. "No use wishing you could ride this mornin' with them young gentlemen, Missy Lee. You got to grow up now and learn to ack like a lady, not trundle trash." He stood for a moment looking quietly at the girl's set face and lowered lashes. "Your ma is asking where you be. Yo' place is out on the front lawn greeting the guests with yo' ma and pa. Now you go up to the house and put on your bes' dress and do your hair up—and don't forget your parasol."

In the courtyard Tom and Hannah Lee were welcoming their guests to Stratford Hall. It was not often that such a crowd of Tidewater families gathered so far from Williamsburg, and Tom recognized it as an honor and a compliment that so many had traveled so far for the day's festivities. His eyes moved with anticipation across the bright sun-dappled lawn that ran toward an avenue of oaks and cedars. In the meadows beyond, the point-to-point race would take place. The final quarter mile of the course, which Tom had personally laid out, would bring the riders up the long avenue of trees right to the gates of the forecourt lawn, where he would award the gold pistoles to the winner.

The spacious court, bounded by the great house, the office building, and the kitchen house, created a spectacular stage for the brightly attired crowd. Most of the gentlemen wore the latest English style of well-fitted knee breeches with silk stockings of a lighter shade. Their bright colors complimented the long swishing skirts and soft capes of the ladies, whose morning dresses were edged with lace at the wrists and neck. Many of the guests stood or sat in a sweep of skirts and bent knees on Turkey rugs spread upon the grass; others strolled about, stopping here and there to form clusters of laughter-filled conversation. In and out among them, children played tag and other spirited games. Everywhere there were small Harrisons underfoot. "Confound it," Tom muttered, "how many children have Anne and Benjamin Harrison had?" It was ten at last count—two more than even he and Hannah could boast!

Tom turned toward the far end of the lawn, where Governor Gooch was deep in conversation with some of the racers.

"I say, it's quite different from a steeplechase at home," Tom heard the governor remark with a sweep of his hand. "In England, one can see across the green rolling meadows from one steeple to another, while your point-to-point must go through timber and over rough fields—much more challenging."

"I think it will be a splendid race," young Philip Lee declared proudly. "The Neck is noted for its fine racehorses, your honor."

Eighteen-year-old Ben Harrison V slapped his palm with his glove. "Fine by country standards," he challenged, "but not by James River standards."

"By any standards," Philip sputtered. "I would wager that Northern Neck horses are the fastest in the entire Tidewater! Have you not heard of Smoker, who won his Northern Neck owner four thousand pounds of tobacco? Or Young Fire? Or Hartley's Campbell?"

Tom interrupted the exchange. "There are fine thoroughbreds in this Neck as well as throughout the Tidewater, sound horses of good wind. But the only competition that counts today takes place here at Stratford. Now, then"—Tom gave Philip's black mare a slap on the rump—"be off with you."

"Fine young men, full of competitive spirit," the governor declared as the boys moved toward the starting line. "Your Philip is an exceptional lad, as is young Harrison. Virginia can expect great leadership from them, for as Lorenzo de Medici said . . . 'The rich must have the state.' It is a responsibility these boys will one day bear."

As the two men crossed the crowded lawns, William Gooch put his hand on Tom's arm. "What a pleasure it is to be here at Stratford—in the wilds, so to speak!" The governor looked admiringly at the massive red brick house. "Stratford Hall looks nothing at all like Rosewell or Westover or Green Spring. No, it is unique, a house that aptly fits the wilderness of the Northern Neck and at the same time reflects its impressive builder and his family. With eight children, you have nothing less than a dynasty. You must be most content."

Hannah poked Tom's arm. "Thomas, where is Missy? I sent Will West to fetch her over an hour ago."

"No doubt she is around." Tom clasped Hannah's slim fingers into his hand while he scanned the throng of spectators. Of all their children, Missy was, at least to his mind, the most lovable—and, he must admit, the most often in trouble. Philip, while inclined to arrogance, could be consummately charming; he was his mother's favored child. At twelve, Thomas was a laughing-eyed, merry boy who tended not to be around when trouble was afoot. Ten-year-old Richard Henry was a quick lad, asking innumerable questions and puzzling over their solutions behind clear gray eyes. Eight-year-old Francis Lightfoot was a born diplomat, and handsome to boot. The younger girl, six-year-old Alice, was a gentle soul and her mother's darling, always pleased to be dressed in the daintiest of frocks with her hair fashioned in long blond curls down her back. As for the two little boys, still babes in the nursery, it was too early to know other than that two-year-old Arthur was fair and noisy and three-year-old William was dark and placid. But of them all, it was Missy over whom Hannah stewed.

Tom caught sight of Will West passing through the crowd with a silver tray of brandies and ale for the dozen men who had gathered close to the starting line at the far end of the lawn.

"Where the devil is that daughter of mine, Will?"

"I found her, Master Tom. I tole her to change her clothes and get her parasol."

A warm voice broke across Tom's shoulder. "Councilor Lee, my, but you are looking well." Gus Washington stood at Tom's elbow, a hesitant smile on his lips.

"Gus! It has been a long time—too long." Tom clasped the other man's hand heartily. They had seen little of each other since 1735, when Gus had abruptly moved his family forty miles upriver on the Potomac to the Epewasson site at the Little Hunting Creek. It was a beautiful but isolated spot, yet still some thirty miles away from the Principio Iron Works, which Gus managed. So three years later the Washingtons had moved again, that time to a farm on the Rappahannock River across from the new town of Fredericksburg and closer to Gus's business venture. Despite years of hard work, his fortunes had improved only slightly, though he and Mary now had four more children besides the boy George, who had been born the same harsh winter as Richard Henry.

"My Mary, unfortunately, had to remain at Ferry Farm with the younger children. But I was pleased to bring my second son, Austin, who is this past month returned from school in England, and young George."

"I am sure it pleases you to have Austin home from England again after all these years," Tom said warmly.

Gus's thin face flushed with pride. "We are staying this week at my old house on Pope's Creek, which Austin remembers well from his childhood. In time, I may settle him on that piece of land, to run the mill I set up there or try his hand at farming."

"And what have you heard from your oldest, Lawrence?" Tom inquired cautiously, for twenty-five-year-old Lawrence, the apple of Gus Washington's eye, was serving in the British Navy in the war with Spain. The conflict might be joshed about as the War of Jenkins's Ear but it was a serious international conflict. In the beginning hopes had been bright that the Spaniards could be run out of Florida quickly and the Spanish West Indies liberated for trade. England's American colonies had enthusiastically furnished three thousand troops for the cause. Young Lawrence Washington, fresh from his studies in London, had received one of four captaincies from Governor Gooch and was sent to command a contingent of the Virginia troops, composed mainly of ex-convicts.

The expedition had proved disastrous, for Vice Admiral Edward Vernon chose to attack Cartagena, Spain's strongest fortified city in the Central Americas. While his ships had got into the harbor, his land attack on the citadel had been thrown back with heavy losses.

"We've no news from Lawrence, no letter in months," Gus replied disconsolately.

His words were interrupted by the sharp crack of a pistol; the race was about to begin! The course, a well-laid-out run with its challenging hurdles of brush and fence, made Tom yearn to ride with the leather-booted young men. At Philip's request, it was to be a maiden run: no horse or rider who had won a similar competition before was permitted to enter, thus eliminating most of the older men. A dozen horses pranced nervously behind the starting line. Most of the riders Tom could recognize, but one strange chap, a slender youth at the end, his hat pulled low over his forehead, he could not immediately identify. Was that perhaps young Byrd of Westover?

The gun sounded again and the riders were off. "It would be hard to place a safe wager," Austin Washington, a massive young man who resembled his father, said with a grin. "Excellent riders on fine big mounts. The importation of English thoroughbreds has really strengthened our Virginia stock."

As the horses disappeared into the woods, Tom turned back to the spectators on the lawn. Where the devil in this crowd was his Missy? Shading his eyes, Tom studied rows of pretty girls decorating the curving stone steps of the great house, their pastel skirts spread about them like the petals of spring flowers.

In the turnabout at the side of the house, Tom came upon Richard Henry and young George Washington climbing into the branches of a tree. "We are hiding from Francis Lightfoot," the slender red-haired Richard Henry called down mischievously.

"If you lads see Missy, tell her I am looking for her," Tom instructed.

Cries of excitement indicated that the riders had rounded the second point at the far end of the long drive.

"I couldn't make out who holds the lead," exclaimed Harry as Tom joined him on the lawn. "Upon my word, they were flying like the wind." Harry's eyes were shining with excitement.

"You could take the best of them any day," Tom teased, for at fifty, Harry Lee sat as taut and quick in the saddle as he had in his youth.

"Aye, that I could," Harry rejoined, "and you as well. There is not a son of ours that can beat us on horseback yet."

Now the first riders appeared on their final lap down the long avenue of oaks toward the finish line. Four led the pack, among them Philip Lee, who gave his horse the whip all the way. A crimson color on one horse revealed young Ben Harrison as another contender, with Henry Lee, Harry's third son, close behind. But the slender rider on the black horse was taking the lead.

Tom pushed his way through the crowd until he stood only a few feet from the finish line as the riders pounded down the lane. It was nip and tuck between Philip and the unknown boy on the black horse. And then they were across the finish, the black horse winning by half a length. Philip Lee had lost! The young man pulled his horse up with a jerk and hurled his crop in disgust across the road as the other horses came thundering up the drive.

"Who is it?" William Gooch asked. "I can't make him out."

From under the brim of an old riding hat glowed the triumphant face of Missy Lee.

"I would see you in my study immediately, Philip," Tom had said in a firm voice as the midday feast came to a leisurely end and the boy was attempting to slip away unobserved in a party of young Harrisons.

"Actually, I deserved first place," the boy muttered to himself angrily as he waited in the library for his father. "Missy is but a girl and didn't qualify to compete." Fifty beautiful gold pistoles . . . Philip ached at his loss and even more at the humiliation of having been bested by his sister.

The young man turned quickly as his father strode into the room and firmly closed the heavy paneled door behind him. "I say, Father, your party is turning out quite nicely," Philip said in an ingratiating tone.

"If this affair is going well, Philip, it is certainly not because of you." Tom paused, indicating that Philip should sit. "Your petulance and ungracious actions at the finish line this morning were embarrassing to me." Tom crossed his arms on his chest and leaned on the corner of his desk. "Do you know what attributes mark a gentleman, Philip?"

"I think I do, Father." The boy's face flushed, partly in shame and partly in suppressed anger. "I would say, sir, they are those qualities held up by Aristotle—fortitude, temperance, prudence, and justice."

Tom nodded coolly. "But would you not add liberality and courtesy? Courtesy is not a veneer of affection but swells from within and is instinctive and natural." Tom's voice softened slightly. "My father once told me this story, Philip: An old nurse of King James the First begged the King to make her son a gentleman. 'A gentleman I could *never* make him, though I could proclaim him a lord,' the King replied. I believe you are fast becoming a young lord, but I fear that you have not yet become a gentleman."

Philip stood up. "I stand corrected for my behavior, Father. I offer my apologies." His voice was rigid, a vein pulsing in his temple.

"Then you are excused." Tom watched the boy stalk toward the closed door. "Philip, remember that you carry the outer signs of a gentleman—grace of body, dignity of bearing, polished speech—but they will serve you only if you are a gentleman within your heart as well."

Tom settled into the depths of the leather chair. By God, it was a challenge to raise one's children properly. First Missy and that absurd, if admittedly admirable, exhibition this morning, then Philip throwing his whip and sulking over losing the race.

"I say, my dear Colonel Lee." William Byrd leaned, arms folded, against the half-open library door, fingering an ivory gaming counter. "The ladies are at rest before the dancing begins, and I have stolen a moment from the gaming table to look at your renowned library. But," he paused courteously, "I do not mean to disturb your thoughts."

"Come in, sir, you by no means disturb me." Tom ushered the older man into his well-appointed study. "Indeed, I was merely thinking what a challenge as well as a pleasure one's children are."

"True words, my dear Tom, true words indeed. You know, I have not yet got over the loss of my daughter Evelyn, who left the world for eternity five years ago." Byrd sighed. "You recall what a beauty she was, an ethereal sort of girl. But she simply pined away and died of a broken heart . . . or so Anne Harrison claims. Her memory haunts me yet." The older councilor turned suddenly, his dark eyes searching Tom's face. "Do you believe that the spirits of the departed can return to walk this earth?" He put his hand on Tom's arm. "Anne Harrison, my Evelyn's closest friend, claims that she often sees Evelyn's form, clothed in white, strolling the rose garden at Berkeley at the spot near the river where our properties meet. The spirit hovers at the bench where Anne and Evelyn would sit for hours to work their embroidery, but never speaks," Byrd continued softly, "just strolls the garden and fades into the moonlight. Tom, I believe Anne Harrison, for she is levelheaded and not given to fantasies. I've not seen Evelyn's ghost myself, yet . . ." Byrd's voice trailed off.

"I share your puzzlement." Tom shook his head. "But at least you have other children to console you, particularly a fine handsome son who will succeed you at Westover."

Byrd's face brightened. "Indeed I have. Billy thinks himself something of a prince, with a doting mamma and a houseful of older sisters to fuss over him. I tell you, Tom, my daughters have made Westover a lively house these past two years, with much courting and merriment under its roof. First young Daniel Parke Custis of Arlington on the Eastern Shore came acourting Annie. But his father and I could not agree on the terms of the marriage —John Custis is quite the old devil, a fact of which I am most well aware since we were brothers-in-law through my first marriage. I truly believe time has made him even more obstreperous. How Frances has endured him all these years is more than I can imagine!" Byrd's eyes twinkled. "Have you heard the latest tidbit in their stormy marriage? No? Well, once, when they were traveling in their carriage, Custis in a fit of anger drove the horses right into the Chesapeake Bay. When Frances asked where he was going, he replied 'To hell, madam.' And she retorted, 'Well, then, drive on. It is preferable to Arlington!' "

Tom threw back his head in laughter. "Perhaps it is just as well that your Annie does not have old John Custis for a father-in-law."

"Quite true," Byrd said with a sniff. "Young Daniel now courts Martha Dandridge. And my Annie is unquestionably better suited to Charles Carter of Cleve, whom she married the previous year, quite shortly after her sister Maria wed his brother Landon Carter during the Christmas season. Indeed, my dear Tom, I could not be more pleased than to have my two daughters married to the sons of my old friend Robert Carter. I have sorely missed him."

William Byrd was scrutinizing the leather-bound books on the closet shelves of Tom's library. "My young Billy will soon sail to England for his formal education, although"—William Byrd looked directly at Tom—"it is not the Inns of Court alone that shape a man. I am aware, sir, that you had little formal schooling, and yet my admiration for you as a gentleman of learning and ability is unbounded."

Tom bowed his head to acknowledge the compliment. "To be candid, there was a time I was sorely uncomfortable with my lack of formal schooling. Over the years I have read deeply. Yet I must admit that even now I am only tolerably adept in Hebrew, Greek, and Latin, all of which are second nature to you."

"That matters little," Byrd protested. "It is your opinion that I have grown to respect, Tom." Byrd began to pace. "How do classical languages help solve the problems that face our colony? Governor Gooch, for all his good nature and abilities, lacks the depth and strengths of our old friend and onetime adversary, Alexander Spotswood. Our council president, Commissary Blair, at eighty-eight years, is now so in his dotage that it is all he can do to set his wig straight, much less to marshal the ideas within his head! No, Tom, it is you who must lead us decisively into the future."

"You flatter me, sir," Tom said with a nod. "I do confess I am concerned about the French. They are the force to be feared in these Americas. Despite England's botching of this foolish war, the Spaniards are not yet guileful or strong enough to threaten Virginia, especially with Oglethorpe's new colony of Georgia buffering to the south. We Virginians must look to the west, where our opportunities for expansion lie. Our greatest obstacle is posed by the French, who vie with us to own the Ohio and Mississippi river valleys. And the devil of it is that the Indians welcome the French, for they see them only as traders, trappers, and explorers—not as settlers."

"Ah, the redmen! You have put your finger precisely upon the prime issue." Byrd settled down on the damask couch. "Parliament cannot comprehend the complexity of Virginia's problems if they do not take the powerful Indians seriously. It is they who will determine if England, France, or Spain is to gain control of this continent. The French use the redmen more astutely than we," he went on. "With the aid of the Iroquois and the other Indian nations, they will eventually seize the passes of the Alleghenies, thereby stopping all English migration west. Perhaps in time they will drive us right back into the sea! They test us now by inciting Indian skirmishes in the Shenandoah Valley."

"The settlers of the Shenandoah will not easily be run out. They are a sturdy lot," countered Tom. "Having fled religious persecution in Europe and Indian massacres in New York and Pennsylvania, these settlers will cling fiercely to their small, hard-won farms. They have nowhere else to turn."

Byrd sniffed slightly. "You call these Scotch, Irish, and Germans a sturdy lot. But among them are Mennonites, Presbyterians, Quakers, and other freethinkers. I cannot say they add much to Virginia. Why, they pour into our colony like the Goths and Vandals of old!"

Tom laughed. "Well, no matter what you think of their religion and their manners, the Protestant settlers of the Shenandoah have thrown in their lot with England. Indeed, sir, they are our forward thrust, the outriders of our English empire."

Byrd rose, stretching gracefully. "Well, dear fellow, let us leave these weighty matters until the council meets later this month. I, for one, want only pleasure today—horse racing, the gaming table, and conversation with beautiful women, three attractions that, God willing, I shall never outgrow."

As the sensual Byrd disappeared down the west wing toward the card games in the gentlemen's sitting room, Tom opened the doors of the great hall to check that all was ready for the dancing that would begin shortly. The afternoon sun made honey-gold squares on the floors, and through the open windows drifted the scent of the flowering peach trees and the laughter of children playing honeypots on the front lawn.

At the far end of the room, Richard Henry and Francis Lightfoot, scrubbed, brushed, and dressed in their satin waistcoats and buckled slippers, stood contemplating the large crystal bowl of applejack punch Will had placed on the side table for the evening festivities.

"No, Frank, you are not supposed to!" Richard Henry admonished his younger brother as Francis Lightfoot greedily dipped a cup into the golden liquid and took a hearty swallow.

"Mmm, that is certainly fine." The smaller boy choked slightly at the fiery taste, then sighed his satisfaction. "I am just going to have one more glass."

"Well, then," Richard Henry wavered, "I shall have some, too! But no one must know."

"In particular, I wouldn't let your mother know," Tom cautioned, laughter in his voice.

The boys leaped as though stung by bees.

"We didn't see you, Father," Richard Henry stammered.

"That is obvious." The councilor tousled their heads affectionately as he went off to dress.

An hour later, distinguished in his blue camlet coat faced with red and trimmed with silver braid, Tom stood with Hannah in the great hall welcoming the dancers. The children's dances had already commenced. "What rascals," said Tom as Richard Henry and Francis Lightfoot joined the other children following the steps of the dancing master Tom had imported from Williamsburg.

Hannah put her hand on his arm. "I declare, I believe the dancing lessons they fought so fiercely have taken, after all."

"You do make handsome children, madam," he complimented. "Just look at your younger daughter."

Alice Lee had taken her place on the floor and was curtsying gracefully. She wore a long embroidered skirt and a tight-fitting cap of soft white Holland linen stitched with pastel flowers to match the colors in her dress. Her wavy blond hair was cut in long bangs across her forehead and hung down to her waist in back from beneath the curve of the cap. From her maternal grandmother, Alice had inherited delicate patrician features. Like most of the Harrison women, she seemed destined to be a beauty.

Across the room Gus Washington was encouraging his son George to join the other children on the floor. Despite his unfamiliarity with the intricate steps, the boy moved well, and soon he and the graceful little Lucy Grymes were dancing a minuet.

The dances ended in a flurry of exaggerated curtsies, and the children ran from the room to their supper. Ben Harrison held out a gloved hand to Hannah and said over her head to Tom, "May I claim the pleasure of dancing with your beautiful bride?"

Tom smiled as Hannah swept away in her cousin's arms. On this special night, Hannah wore a gown of pale creamy silk embroidered all over with rows of tiny amber beads, her red-gold hair fastened in a caul of amber silk. Even now, after twenty years of marriage and eight children, there was no woman in Virginia that appealed to Tom as did his spirited wife.

Through a covey of white-shouldered ladies he spied Anne Harrison moving toward the dance floor on the arm of Governor Gooch; the governor was splendidly dressed and fashionably painted, down to his beauty mark.

Tom turned and bowed low over the hand of his brother's wife. "Will you honor me with this dance, Mary Bland?"

"With great pleasure." She took his arm. "What a success your party is. And because it is such a lovely party, you must promise me something, my dear Tom."

Tom looked down at his dark-eyed sister-in-law with affection. "I will promise you anything within my power," he answered warmly.

"You must not be harsh with your Missy over taking part in the race this morning. I realize it was unseemly. But there is much that is good and fine in your daughter, and you both must be patient with her. She will mature with time." Mary Bland's eyes widened suddenly. "In fact, look behind you, Tom, and you will see what I mean."

Tom gave Mary Bland a whirl that allowed him a view of the dance floor. Missy had joined the dancers for a gavotte on the arm of one of her Corbin cousins, twenty-two-year-old Gawin. The solemn, thickset man had had the recent good fortune to inherit Pecatone plantation from their mutual uncle, the London merchant Thomas Corbin.

"I cannot decide which are more difficult to raise, sons or daughters," Tom later told Ben Harrison; they were sitting over supper in the candlelit dining room.

"Why, sons, to be sure," Ben answered quickly. "Daughters have only to be beautiful and chaste until we have wedded them off. But our sons are our destiny." Ben took a long sip of wine. "I say"—his face brightened—"your musicians are calling a Sir Roger de Coverley. I do believe the little repast has replenished my strength sufficiently for me to accept that challenge. I wager that I can outdance you, Tom Lee, even on the night of your anniversary."

From all over the sprawling house, from the parlors and card tables and supper tables, people came back to the great hall to watch or—if they were quick-footed and game—to participate in the vigorous dance. A Sir Roger de Coverley was a contest as much in endurance as in grace. Without touching so much as his partner's hand, each gentleman used his movements alone to lead his lady around the room in a series of quick steps. The dance soon exhausted its participants, and as dancers flagged, others waiting on the sidelines would move in to take their places.

Governor Gooch often described the Sir Roger de Coverley as a "Virginia Reel," and tonight, despite his severe leg injury from the Spanish War Expedition, he was eager to participate. Already he had claimed Hannah Lee as his partner and was leading her onto the dance floor.

"Your good husband has challenged me, my dear," Tom said as he claimed Anne Harrison. "It is a dance to the death, so be prepared, for I shall give you a good whirl."

Anne Harrison, her fair hair now streaked with silver, was still a pretty woman. She lifted her chin to the challenge. "Do not forget I am a Harrison by marriage, dear Tom, but a Carter by blood! I cannot bear to be bested. Dance away!"

Tom lost himself to the music and the swirl of skirts and the exhilaration of the dance. Austin Washington passed by him with pretty Anne Aylett, close by the nimble-footed William Byrd with Mary Bland Lee. The music slowed and quickened, and an hour and innumerable partners passed by without breaking Tom's step, until only a flushed Ben Harrison, dancing now with Hannah Lee, and Tom with Mary Bland, remained in the competition.

"Time to change partners!" Tom called, and with a swift movement, Hannah and Mary Bland switched places.

"My dear lady," Tom bantered between quick breaths, "your cheeks are aglow, your green eyes sparkle. I think I could lose my heart to you if I dared."

Holding her skirts with one hand, Hannah moved close enough to tease, "You are too bold, sir. I am a woman much in love with my husband!"

With a surge of relief, Tom saw that Ben Harrison had thrown up his hands in graceful defeat and was leaving the floor. The spectators burst into applause, and as the music rose to its final crescendo, Tom took Hannah on one last triumphal whirl around the floor. "A most fortunate man, your husband," he whispered in her ear, "to find you in his bed this night!"

From the platform formed by the cluster of four chimneys on the west wing of the house, Missy watched her parents' entourage depart for Williamsburg and the spring sitting of the King's Council. As the caravan of carriage (containing her mother, Richard Henry, and Francis Lightfoot), pack horses, and mounted servants reached the far end of the drive, her father, who rode beside the phaeton, gave a final salute to the girl.

Missy offered a disconsolate wave in return. Not that she wanted to go with them to Williamsburg. To be in the capital "in season" meant endless social calls, afternoon dinners, and evening balls. Missy remembered the recent anniversary party at Stratford Hall. Thank heavens, she'd not had to dance very much. In fact, no one had asked her but her cousin Gawin Corbin. He wasn't much like the rest of the young men—"the young bucks," her father called them. Gawin never tried to tease or order her about. He was quiet, and quite nice—and to be perfectly honest, boring. "Just boring, boring, boring!"

With a sigh, she moved to the other side of the chimney pavilion and looked toward the Potomac River. It was her favorite view in the whole world, for it was always changing, never quite the same. Sometimes the waters were blue and serene—as blue, Mamma said, as Francis Lightfoot's eyes. Other times the river was mist-covered, or tossed by the winds until its waters foamed like beaten egg whites. But her greatest delight was the occasional sight of sails upon the waters. One day she had spied a British man-of-war patroling the river against French and Spanish privateers, but most of the traffic was trading schooners on their way to upriver plantation wharfs.

This Potomac River is the highway to the world, her father said, to England, or indeed, if one were brave enough, to India!

"In-ja," Missy rolled the word on her tongue. It brought to mind all manner of lovely, exotic things of which the sea captains who frequently dined at Stratford Hall hinted. Someday, she mused, she would journey to Russia, where there were frosted palaces and endless snow, or to Austria, which had no king but a queen whose name was Maria Theresa. How wonderful, Missy thought, to wake up one morning and find oneself a queen.

"I am the queen. I can do anything I want!" she cried out as she ran down the winding stairs from the tower. "Don't dare to stop me or I'll chop off your head!"

That evening the rain began. The babies, William and Arthur, were fretful, so Missy stayed with Annie in the nursery and helped with their supper. Little Alice looked pale and sad-eyed as she lay on the braided rug wrapped in the bedraggled comforter she favored, clutching a wooden-headed doll.

"Don't be sad, pet," Missy entreated softly as she stroked Alice's fine silky hair. "Mamma will bring you a marvelous present from the shops in Williamsburg." Missy nuzzled her nose against Alice's pale cheek. "Shall we go to the barnyard to see the new baby chicks tomorrow?"

The little girl nodded balefully, tears glistening in her eyes, and slept that night with her small fingers clasped in Missy's.

By morning the rain had turned into a steady sullen drizzle, and Alice was still listless. Missy clomped noisily in her wooden clogs down the stairs to the girls' bedroom and took from its hiding place the Chinese lacquer box with its cache of gold pistoles. Her mother had given her this box with the scene of a winsome Oriental girl swinging in a beautiful garden on its square flat cover. Once it had held English chocolates; now it held her prize money. Carefully, Missy pulled off the cover of the box and folded back a layer of silk—to reveal only a pile of smooth creek stones! Philip had done it! Of course it was Philip, that scoundrel! And there was no way she would ever be able to prove that he had taken them.

In the parlor of Henry Wetherburn's Tavern in Williamsburg, Tom Lee sat with Ben Harrison and Captain Isham Randolph over pewter tankards of ale. Around their table, boisterous brocade- and silk-clad planters, many having just arrived in town from outlying plantations, greeted one another loudly.

"Williamsburg is becoming a little London," Tom commented over the din. "Why, I remember when Spotswood straightened the Duke of Gloucester Street from a winding cowpath."

"I prefer Williamsburg to London these days—no court intrigue and more vitality," Randolph offered. "I say, Tom, have you met the young man who has wed my daughter Jane? I would like him to know you." Peter Jefferson, an enterprising young surveyor and planter from the new county of Albemarle, and Isham's nephew, William Randolph, master of Tuckahoe, had worked their way to the table from the back of the tavern.

Tom turned his attention to the brawny Jefferson. "I have heard, sir, that you are attempting to map the Shenandoah Valley. How challenging!"

"It is marvelously beautiful land, Councilor," Peter Jefferson began enthusiastically. "Why, the valley is one long prairie, unbroken for miles, rich in game. And there are great forests and—"

William Randolph interrupted. "We both hope to patent land in the valley, the council willing."

"Considering you are Randolphs, by blood or marriage, you should have no trouble getting your way with the council," Ben Harrison said archly.

Since the Shenandoah Valley was recognized as a new and important source of land by the planters at the top of the political hierarchy, land grants to those outside the golden web were rare. Just recently the council had rejected out of hand a petition for twelve thousand acres from one planter, reasoning that, since the petitioner was not known to any of the council, his request was too grand for someone so obscure.

Isham Randolph snapped his fingers for the barman to bring more ale, but Peter Jefferson shook his head regretfully. "Not for me, thank you. I would be waterlogged if forced to down another drop." He laughed. "William sold me a tract of land in exchange for the biggest bowl of Henry Wetherburn's famous arrack punch. It was so big that he almost drowned in it! Thus the purchaser was forced to help the seller complete the deal!"

Later, as Tom and Ben Harrison made their way down the crowded dirt side paths of the Duke of Gloucester Street, Ben confided, "I admire young Peter Jefferson. He is not a man born to wealth, but his mind is good and he is ambitious. Perhaps he'll even add charm to that pompous Randolph clan!"

The following morning Tom traveled with his sons through the lowland woods to the old capital of Jamestown. The horses' hoofs, like falling stones, clattered on the wooden bridge spanning the pitch-and-tar swamps bordering the land side of the old settlement. Tom had been to Jamestown many times, but never did he approach the site without a feeling of wonder and pride.

Richard Henry and Francis Lightfoot scampered down from the carriage, running toward the river's edge to the overgrown piazza that had once been the center of the fort. This city, previously the heart of the colony, was now all but abandoned, the ivy-encased bones of its old buildings bared to the sun and sea breezes. Only a scattering of inhabited houses, a tavern, and a few shops remained. Tom followed his boys to the waterfront, where the remains of the old log-palisaded fort lay half submerged in the dark waters of the James.

"The fort is like Atlantis, fallen back into the sea," Richard Henry cried in amazement. "Jamestown is so old and tumbledown."

"Tumbledown it is," Tom agreed, "but certainly not so old as you think—that is, compared to the ruins Mr. Currie has told you about. But Jamestown is more important than you could ever imagine, lads. On an April day in 1607—just think, one hundred and thirty-five years ago—the first Englishmen anchored in this narrow channel and stepped ashore to claim the land for England and James the First."

"Was my great-grandfather Lee on that ship?" asked Francis Lightfoot.

"No." Tom snapped the stem of a cat-o'-nine-tails growing near the tree-shaded waters. "He did not come for another thirty years."

"Why did they come at all, Father? Why didn't they just stay at home?"

"This new land held golden promise for England. She was then, lads, not an empire but an island kingdom, her cities overcrowded with dispossessed country people. What's more, England was warring for control of the seas with her great rival Spain, who was already colonizing in South America and Mexico. From this Tidewater outpost, England hoped to build a base against the Spanish. Through its waterways she hoped to find a passage to the spices and riches of the Orient. In its forests she was certain she would discover gold as well as find needed timber, pitch, and tar to build ships. And remember, as Spain was carrying Catholicism to the New World, so it was the obligation of England to bring our Anglican Church here. The first attempt to colonize on the shores of Carolina had failed. And now, King James approved two colonial business ventures—the New England Company was to settle the northern part of North America, the Virginia Company, the southern part, of the English claim. Picture, if you will, the Virginia Company's three small ships, *Susan Constant*, *Godspeed*, and *Discovery*, setting sail across the sea on this brave adventure."

"Did they have to go?" Francis Lightfoot broke in with a shiver. "Did the King make them go?"

"No," Tom answered gently, "they chose to go, a party of forty seamen and one hundred and five adventurers, more than half of them gentlemen." Tom paused, thinking of the incongruity of those gentlemen explorers, in ruffs and doublets with pointed garters on their knee breeches and silver buckles on their shoes. He could picture the pallid faces, their soft gentlemen's palms and unmuscled bodies so unfit for the adversity that lay ahead!

"After a long, exhausting voyage, they sailed between the capes and entered the Chesapeake Bay, to be welcomed by the smells of honeysuckle and wild grape—and by Indians." Tom smiled. "A party of warriors, creeping like bears with bows in their mouths, came close and wounded one of the Englishmen with an arrow, but other Indians were friendly. One day the *werowance*, or chief, of the Rappahannock tribe greeted them on the beach, his body painted crimson, his face stained blue and sprinkled with silver. He delighted them by playing a reed flute.

"They explored the coves and the mouths of the four great rivers of the bay before choosing to sail up this river, the James. Sixty miles upstream, they came upon this little island connected to the mainland by a narrow strip of land, which could be easily defended. So they built a log fort." The two boys leaned over Tom's shoulder as he outlined the fort's design in the sand with a stick. "The fort was triangular in shape, and in each of the three corners was a bulwark in the shape of a half-moon, in which stout English guns from the ships were placed."

"Did they love Virginia, Father?"

Tom put his hand on Francis Lightfoot's head. "I wish I could say they did, but their first three years were plagued by malaria, starvation, and massacres."

"Why did the Indians kill them?" Richard Henry asked indignantly.

"This was the Indians' land, my son. Don't forget, Powhatan's confederacy of forty Algonquin tribes had lived along these rivers for centuries."

"I don't like the Indians, they are dirty and they steal things." Richard Henry folded his arms across his chest.

"You are unfair," Tom reproved. "The Algonquins were once a proud, strong race. Read the accounts of Captain John Smith. He found the natives a handsome people, dressed in the skins of wild beasts, their bodies intricately painted and adorned with chains of copper which they wound around their necks and arms and looped through holes they had pierced in their ears. One warrior even looped a yard-long green-and-yellow snake through his earlobe! The snake was his pet and would coil around his neck and kiss his lips."

Richard Henry shivered. "How did Captain John Smith learn so much about them?"

"Because he was brave and curious, not afraid to take risks, wandering deep into the forest and sailing his shallop up each of the four great rivers."

"I shall be an explorer and do brave things," Richard Henry declared, his small face resolute.

"No doubt you will. But remember, you must always be fair and fight only for what is right."

Afterward, as his two sons explored the riverbank, Tom considered the harsher realities of the story. One day he would tell them how the first settlement foundered in part because the settlers disdained physical labor, squandering their resources on the search for gold.

Only six hundred of the eighteen hundred who had put out from England in those first years survived to 1618. Unused to the wilderness, they ignored the game of the forest and fought bitterly over a dwindling supply of food. One unfortunate who was caught stealing oatmeal had needles driven through his tongue and was chained to a tree until he starved. Another murdered and ate his pregnant wife; when discovered, he was hung by his thumbs with weights on his feet until he confessed, then slowly burned to death.

He would tell the boys how the tide of fortune had slowly turned. The mother lode was to be not gold but tobacco. Shortly after the "starving time," John Rolfe improved the Indian strain of tobacco by planting Oronoco seeds, a sweet, rich variety from the West Indies. In 1617, the first tobacco fleets sailed from Virginia with a cargo of twenty thousand pounds. The English and Dutch smokers couldn't get enough of the aromatic weed.

Until this time, the Virginia Company had reaped no profit from its

venture and desperately needed labor to develop the new industry. To encourage immigrants, the company offered land. Between 1619 and 1622
came over twenty-five hundred settlers—sons of gentry but also destitute
children, paupers, felons, and impoverished laborers, most destined to serve
in the colony as indentured workers for four or more years. There was a
Dutch ship containing twenty blacks to be sold as slaves, as well as an English ship with one hundred young women to be wives for the bachelor
settlers. Soon twenty or more small tobacco-growing settlements dotted the
James River banks, but Jamestown, its fort still the colony's hub, was the
settlers' haven.

The uneasy peace between the Tidewater tribes and the English settlers
had been delicately cemented by the marriage of Powhatan's daughter,
Pocahontas, to the planter John Rolfe. But following her death in London
and then the death of her father, Opechanchanough allowed his warriors to
vent their long-suppressed hostility. On Good Friday of 1622, Indians visited outlying houses scattered on the riverbank with turkey, fish, deer, and
furs to sell. Unarmed and apparently in good humor, they sat down to
breakfast with the unwary settlers. Suddenly, as if moving to a silent inner
signal, they slaughtered their hosts—men, women, and children—with the
settlers' own tools and weapons. At the end of the massacre, nearly one-
third of the white population of Virginia lay dead.

Jamestown was saved from destruction by a Christian Indian who
warned of the impending attack. The massacre gave the settlers an excuse to
seize the Indians' land, but it dealt a cruel blow to the Virginia Company. In
1624, King James dissolved the company and made it a royal colony.

In the end, Virginia's gold, the tobacco leaf, pulled the venture through.
In 1625 frail Virginia paid revenues to royal coffers surpassing those from
any other colony, from the Antilles to the Orient.

That evening, in a candlelit bedroom of Green Spring, where the Lees
were staying with Hannah's brother, Philip Ludwell, Tom told his wife of
the history lesson as he helped do up the pearl buttons on the back of her
low-cut evening gown.

"You didn't tell them only about the riffraff, did you? You did tell them
about the loyalists from the court of Charles the First, and the highborn
ladies, the cavaliers, and the sons of the gentry who came after Virginia became a royal colony? That is their real heritage, Thomas, the Lees, the Ludwells, the Harrisons, the Corbins. That's the part of the story I like."

Tom nuzzled her soft white shoulder. "They will hear all that often
enough, my dear, for it is the part everyone loves. But I want them to know

all of it. I fear sometimes our children know too little of anxiety or heart-break."

Later, whenever Will West recalled that wet April night when they had searched so desperately for Missy, a cold chill would settle in his heart. He had not worried when the girl missed her dinner, for she had done that often to ride Charmer. Then he and Annie had been so absorbed with Alice, who had begun to run a fever, that it was not until late afternoon that Missy's note was discovered in the molding of the nightstand looking-glass.

Clutching the scribbled paper, Will stared at the lacquered box with its pathetic treasure of stones. "I'll ask Master Thomas to read this, but I knows already jus' what it say."

Mr. Currie, Philip, and Thomas set out on horseback to search through the wet gloom of the heavy April dusk. But they found no trace of Missy.

"Perhaps she's just gone to Lee Hall or to the Ayletts'," Thomas suggested.

"No." Philip's face looked unusually white. "She's too proud for that. It was only a joke, you know."

Will stared impassively at Philip. For a long time, he had been waiting to see the young heir of Stratford Hall mature and grow, but it had not happened. "I ain't jus' worried about Missy," Will murmured. "I'se worried bad about Miss Alice. She burning up with the fever."

Thomas's brown eyes showed alarm. "Have you given her the bark?"

Will snorted. "Course I has. But none gives it like Missy."

"Oh, God," Philip groaned.

"Go on to bed," Will told the boys firmly, "there ain't nothing more you can do tonight."

Mr. Currie stayed behind. "Will, should we perhaps send a messenger to Williamsburg to fetch Colonel Lee?"

"What, and worry the colonel half to death? 'Sides, what'll we tell him—that his elder daughter done run away and his littlest girl is burning up with the fever? No, let's just see what the morrow brings."

"You have been a slave of Colonel Lee's for a long time, haven't you, Will?" The tutor looked at the black man intently.

"I belong to him, and he belong to me, all my life," the young man answered. "All my life he has put things that mattered to him in my hands— his children, his valuables, his house. When I wanted to marry a gal from Mr. Aylett's plantation, Colonel Lee bought her—said he'd pay whatever Mr. Aylett wanted. We bear a bond between us, him and me."

"Well, then, I trust your judgment." The tutor reluctantly took his candle and returned to the schoolhouse.

Will stared out into the darkness of the rainy night. How he wished he could find that girl, not just for her own sake but for Alice's as well. For all Missy Lee's lack of grown-up airs, there wasn't anything she couldn't do, from binding a book to mending a broken cup when it was in a million pieces. And, more important, there was no one better at mixing herbs for curing.

As he opened the window, Will felt the wet rain pelt his face, and a tang of fresh drifting salt breeze, up from the river, assaulted his nostrils. Where was it Missy always talked about going? Around the world on a sailing ship! On lightning feet, Will was down the stairs to the boys' dormitory. "You coming with me, Master Philip. Right now. I got an idea where that sister of yours done gone to!"

The ground was muddy and wet beneath their feet as they ran through the meadow and into the woods toward the landing. "I can't go so fast. Slow down, Will," Philip gasped.

"Pick up yo' feet, Master Philip, it's yo fault she done run away at all. Least you can do is help find her."

Branches lashed their faces as the young men half slid down the sloping ravine toward the landing, where two sloops were moored close together at the wide wooden dock.

"Ahoy," Philip called out to the watch who was leaning over the side of the *Betsy*. "I am coming aboard to see your captain."

On the dark wharf, Will waited impatiently. He eyed the *Carter* swinging quietly at her moorings at the far end of the dock. If Missy is down here, she's aboard that dark empty one. In a moment he stood on the swaying deck, then he swung down an open hatch into the dark hold, which reeked of tobacco mingled with fish. He could not make out even his hand in front of his face. He'd have to find a light. Suddenly, there was a slight rustling.

"Missy?" he whispered tentatively. "It's me, Will." Silence. His anxious words tumbled out. "If that be you, Missy Lee, listen to me. I know what Master Philip did. It was a bad thing, but he say he is sorry. He say he is goin' to give the coins back. Now, Missy, listen to me. Listen to Will. You can't do this. You gonna break yo' pa's heart, girl, upset him so bad he won't be able to think straight. You gotta come home."

A silence hung in the dank air. "Missy, I'm telling you, you gotta come home right now. We needs you. Your little sister is bad sick, and yo the only one who knows how to mix that bark just right. Yo the only one who knows how to bring down a fever. Yo gotta come back and save Miss Alice."

When Tom and Hannah returned from Williamsburg, they heard about Alice's illness, how truly sick she had been, and how Missy had bathed her sister's slight body in cooling herb baths, given her artfully concocted medicinal drinks, and sat by her side for hours.

Tom had looked inquiringly at Will. "There is more to this account than you are telling. I know about Philip taking her purse, but there is still more."

"All's well that ends well, Master Tom. I've heard you say that before, and that is all there is to that story." Will's expression was serene, but in his heart he scorned Master Philip. That boy wasn't one bit sorry. He was just lucky things turned out the way they did. A young girl out there at sea with them sailors . . . Will shook his head.

The Tidewater, 1743

"It's such a frightful journey, Tom." Hannah explained why she was not going with him to the Spring Assembly. "The bouncing of that carriage makes my bones ache for weeks, and just about the time I am fully back together, why, it's time to return to Stratford! Besides"—she smiled ruefully as she brushed out her long hair in the morning sunlight—"I do believe my children need me here more than you do in Williamsburg. When we are there, your head is full of politics, land grants, Indian problems, what have you! Why, I am fair neglected most of the time!"

"What man could possibly neglect Hannah Lee?" Tom ran his fingers through her hair. "What if we sailed to Williamsburg, so as not to bruise your delicate bones?"

"And be seasick and scared half out of my wits for four days going and four days returning? No, my love, I shall stay at Stratford, but you might bring me some kid slippers and a new hat—a straw skimmer or a Ranelagh mobcap."

"It won't be the same without you," Tom said as he looked out on the new grove of imported English boxwood beyond the ha-ha wall. "I don't really want to leave Stratford either, Hannah. I am torn between the council and the Neck. When I am at one place I worry constantly about the other."

Hannah came up behind him and put her arms around his waist. "Well, don't worry about Stratford this time. We shall manage."

He took her in his arms. "Do be kind to Missy; I don't feel she is really happy. I am concerned about her."

As he sat in the council chamber, Tom listened with only half an ear, his mind still back at Stratford Hall. There were still so many things he wanted to do, new varieties of trees that he would like to introduce into his orchards, improvements he wanted to make to the property. But his thoughts lingered most on his children, on the haughty fire that was so quick to ignite in Philip, the rebellion that he believed was not yet dead in Missy's heart, the gentleness of Thomas, and the extraordinary fair-minded reasoning abilities possessed by young Richard Henry. The charm and poise of Francis Lightfoot and Alice were remarkable. As for the babies—what kind of men would they become someday?

The dullness of the spring session was abruptly stemmed by the arrival of Captain Lawrence Washington, home from his long, disappointing assignment with the British Navy. The tall, narrow-shouldered militia officer had come to Williamsburg to accept the appointment of adjutant general of the colony, succeeding Isham Randolph, who had died earlier that spring. "Of all the Randolphs, he was the one I most preferred," William Byrd had confided to Tom. "He brought my Evelyn, then ten years old, to England after Lucy died. Arrived safe and sound with only a case of the itch, she did."

After the brief ceremony, Tom took off his heavy white wig and left it on the brocade-covered table while he accompanied Lawrence out into the hallway. "Your father will be much pleased to hear of this new position," he complimented.

Lawrence looked up, pain in his eyes. "I am sorry to tell you that I have just received word from Austin that our father is dead. It was sudden—gout of the stomach." Lawrence took a deep breath. "My brother says he did not suffer much, thank the Lord."

A week later in the council chamber, Byrd noticed the mourning ring Tom wore on his left hand. "I little realized you and Augustine Washington were close friends," he said in his soft, intimate voice. "Your lives and stations were quite diverse."

Tom looked beyond the councilor to the tree-shaded Duke of Gloucester Street. "Aye, diverse but somehow intertwined, almost as though the hand of the Almighty were involved!"

Byrd leaned forward to whisper dramatically. "The hand of God works in other ways! It's rumored in the taverns that Governor Gooch will lay before the council a letter from the governor of Pennsylvania, asking if Virginia desires to meet with the chiefs of the Six Indian Nations along with commissioners from Pennsylvania and Maryland. The Indian interpreter, Conrad Weiser, will arrange such a meeting so that we may discuss purchasing from the savages the lands of the Shenandoah."

Tom was intrigued with Byrd's news. If the chiefs of the Six Nations could be negotiated with at one sitting—as Spotswood had done at Albany in 1722—the English might win the valley lands and solve the frontier problem with the French.

Tom's face broke into a half smile. "It is equally the hand of Robert Carter working beyond the grave."

"How so?" Byrd's dark eyebrows rose in curiosity.

"Carter was one of the first planters to see the possibilities in the Shenandoah. Reappointed agent for the Fairfax Proprietary, he patented large plots in the Shenandoah for his sons. Why, in 1724 alone, he patented ninety thousand acres, and Governor Gooch backed him, saying that patenting such large plots would give stability to the valley."

"Of course!" William Byrd nodded. "And to lay claim Carter had to insist the Shenandoah Valley was part of the original Fairfax Proprietary. The original patent read that the proprietary lay east of the heads of navigation of the Potomac and Rappahannock rivers." Byrd locked his fingers in contemplation. "Indeed, the question still is, does one consider the heads of navigation to be the forks of the Rappahannock or, as Carter claimed, the headsprings of the river, which rise far beyond the mountains west of the Shenandoah Valley?"

"A mere difference of two million acres or five million acres?" Tom reminded him in amusement. "The British Board of Trade has yet to render its verdict, but I'll wager that Carter's claim will be upheld!"

"But"—Byrd leaned forward intently in his chair—"whether it be the proprietor's or the Crown's territory, it is imperative the lands be patented and settled by the *English*, before the French move in! To seal our claim, we must have the valley deeded to us once and for all by the Six Nations."

Stratford Hall shimmered in the summer moonlight as Tom left his horse with a stableboy and climbed the stone steps. Hannah was asleep, one slender arm flung out across his pillow. He stood quietly, looking hungrily at her face, before moving to pull off his high leather boots and strip off the tight buff breeches. She woke when he touched her and came into his arms with ready passion. "I've missed you! Oh, I've missed you," she murmured before his lips closed off her words.

Later, when they lay content in each other's arms, he told her about the Indian conference.

Hannah shivered. "I would not fancy a meeting with the *sachem* and the painted warriors of the Six Nations! What if they grow angry and slaughter those sent to negotiate?"

"The Indians take great pride in honorable negotiations, my love." He closed his hand around hers. "This conference in Pennsylvania offers the chance to bind the wounds from recent frontier skirmishes and to secure once and for all the lands England claims as hers. We have already named our representatives to go to Lancaster." He hesitated. "One is William Beverly of Blanfield."

Hannah rose up on one elbow and looked at him indignantly. "What you are really telling me, Tom, is that you are going to be the other!"

There can be no question this odyssey north to Pennsylvania had a powerful impact on Councilor Thomas Lee, who, with the exception of his 1716 journey to England, had never left Virginia. On a bright April morning in 1744, he departed from the Stratford wharf with his son Philip and a party of "fine flaming gentlemen," as one account described them. The curious gathered with the well-wishers to watch the bright, billowing sails of the yacht *Margaret* as she cast off, amid the boom of cannons, for Annapolis.

In the Maryland capital, parties and levees were given for the Virginians, where it is said that Philip danced each night with the town belles until three in the morning before the Virginia and Maryland representatives moved on to Philadelphia and, joined by the Pennsylvania delegates, due west toward the farming community of Lancaster.

From the mountains of the north the warriors of the Six Nations descended in ceremonial procession, their copper bodies glistening with a heavy sweat that reflected the strands of shiny beads adorning their dress. Their *sachem*, or chiefs, strode in front, followed obediently by women and children on horseback.

They met to parley in the Lancaster town hall, and the clinking of glasses was soon punctuated by the noisy "*huzzas*" of the Indians. The redmen's intermediary, Pennsylvania-German Conrad Weiser, wise in the ways and languages of Indians, informed the commissioners that the warriors were angered because they were served rum in small French glasses instead of in large English glasses! Eager to accommodate, the commissioners had enormous tumblers rushed to the hall. By the final day of the conference, the Indians had expressed satisfaction with the mirrors, trinkets, and four hundred pounds of sterling that the commissioners offered in exchange for title to the lands west of the mountains to the banks of the Ohio.

The colonel recollected reading, as a schoolboy, an account of the Lancaster meeting published by the enterprising Philadelphian Benjamin Franklin. What he remembered most clearly was the fable the Iroquis *sachem* Cassatenaga told. The Dutch came across the big sea, he said, and offered their friendship to the Indians with a strong rope so that the Indians might tie their ships to our shores. But when the English came, they said the Dutch rope was not good. The English would use a rope of silver that would not rot or break. Cassatenaga told the hushed gathering of councilors and warriors, "We Indians take your rope as a bond of brothers in friendship, and we give to you our lands that lie where the great fire in the sky goes to sleep and our word to be your friends."

It is sad that these Indians, so innocent and unworldly, and the commissioners, elated over having obtained title to the land, could not realize that this meeting was the first act in the scenario for the fierce war that would break the English colonies from the Mother Country, causing an irrevocable schism in the British empire.

As the Twig Is Bent

1748–1750

The Tidewater, 1748

"A head start, yes, but not half the distance! There is no sport in that!" Missy's clear voice cut Tom Lee's reverie one crisp February morning as he looked toward the high cliffs west of Stratford Hall.

Laughing at her indignation, Tom gave his new imported thoroughbred, still skittish, a reassuring pat. "Easy, Star." Each of his favorite horses had been named Star after the first horse he had ever owned, the bay mare with a blaze on her forehead given him by his father when he was sixteen. This was the fourth to bear the name.

Horses . . . children . . . accomplishments—so many ways for a man to measure the years of his life. More and more, Tom had come to think in terms of this Virginia land, measuring time by the calendar of the land, the darkening of the hills to blacks and browns and grays in autumn, the greening of the lowlands in the spring. How he loved Virginia!

Tom spurred Star after the girl, who was disappearing into the dark stand of trees. By God, it was a beautiful day! Not quite mid-February, there was still a hoarfrost on the ground, but a feeling of fresh life already filled the air. This morning he had caught the flash of a red-headed woodpecker in one of the mossy-cupped oaks he had brought back from Philadelphia four years before. It was hard to believe it had been so long since his return with the Indian Treaty for the colony and assorted seedling Pennsylvania trees for his gardens. He had worried that the delicate weeping willows would not survive, yet now, in the late winter of 1748, it seemed they had all taken root—his trees, his fortunes, and, most important, his family. His two youngest sons had come through the perilous period of babyhood and were sturdy lads of eight and nine. His one loss had been his brother, Harry, who died a year earlier. It seemed to Tom a part of himself had died also.

Glimpsing Missy's blue cloak through the trees, Tom urged his mare forward. Missy would have to earn her victory in this race to the landing.

"I won!" Missy claimed triumphantly on the cliff's edge overlooking the mill and Stratford Landing. "I had you by half a length."

"I was beguiled by the morning," Tom defended himself. "Did you see the shadbush in the ravine?"

"And the red maple spattered in the forest. I delight in the first signs of spring just as much as you!" The young woman turned her smiling hazel eyes on him.

How he loved to see her like this, full of natural beauty, her fair hair tumbling loose from its bun and falling about the shoulders of her padded pelisse cape. "Twenty years old—she's an old maid," Hannah fretted in private. "Whatever shall become of her?"

"Look, Father." Missy pointed at the raft of ducks on the shoreline beneath the cliff.

Tom followed her gaze to see the wintering pintails and mallards and, more important, the flocks of gulls diving for their breakfast. "When the ice floes have broken, spring is truly on its way."

Tom looked anxiously up the glittering Potomac. Lawrence Washington's letter had said that if the river was clear of ice, he would come from Mount Vernon by water; if not, by land. Either way, he planned to reach Stratford by noon. The letter had reiterated that Lawrence looked forward with great enthusiasm to further discussion of Tom's ideas, proposed last fall in Williamsburg.

For his part, Tom was eager to see his venture launched. The Treaty of Lancaster, signed in the summer of 1744, had been the first step. That purchase of lands from the Six Nations had, in one stroke, validated England's claim to the Shenandoah Valley and the Ohio basin. And in early 1743, the Privy Council had voted in favor of Lord Thomas Fairfax's claim to additional western lands. His title to quitrents for some five to six million acres—God knows how much, for the land was still to be surveyed—had been recognized *in toto*. Through his nephew and agent, Councilor William Fairfax, the proprietor was pushing for stronger, faster colonization of the west. A few squatters had already settled beyond the valley; others were seeking to move over and beyond the Alleghenies, but there were neither towns nor forts to protect them against the cunning French and the inconstant Indians.

Tom had proposed to friends that they form the Ohio Company and petition the Privy Council in London to grant five hundred thousand acres along the Ohio River. The company would, like the proprietary, get quitrents on that land in exchange for settling some one hundred families there over the next seven years. A garrison to protect the settlers would also serve as a trading post for English goods and the fabulous animal pelts so coveted abroad.

Only thirty-year-old Lawrence Washington had avidly pursued the matter of the Ohio Company. Already a member of the House of Burgesses, Lawrence was just beginning to make his mark, farming at Little Hunting Creek on the upper Potomac lands that he called now Mount Vernon after his commander, Edward Vernon. Lawrence had made a most advantageous marriage to Nancy Fairfax, the daughter of William Fairfax, whose gracious red brick manor house, Belvoir, lay a few miles downriver from Mount Vernon. Perhaps conversations with his land-rich in-laws had whetted young Washington's interest.

"I was just thinking that Lawrence Washington would have been a good husband for you, my love," he teased Missy, who wrinkled her nose at the idea.

"Really?" she asked. "I was thinking how nice it would be to sail with Richard Henry when he leaves for school in England."

"I know you would like that, but what would you do? With whom would you stay? It wouldn't be safe or seemly to loose you on the streets of London."

"I've heard it all before from Mother." The girl shrugged, then changed the subject. "I don't see a sign of your guests on the water. Shall we head back?"

"Let's go the long way," said Tom. "I want to speak with the blacksmith." He knew she would enjoy that. Nothing about running the plantation escaped Missy, particularly when it concerned the horses or the land.

As they rode on through the cluster of cabins that housed the indentured servants, Tom heard the jeering sounds of laughter and catcalls from the nearby slave quarters.

"It's probably some of the slave younglings having a go at each other," he said to Missy, urging Star among the narrow buildings and into the clearing. There crouched Richard Henry, his third son. Jacket tossed carelessly on the ground, his shirt sleeves rolled above his elbows, the young, slender Lee was countering the heavy, low thrust made by a stocky slave boy with an awkward uppercut to the jaw.

"Damnation!" Tom's oath reverberated like a pistol shot. Richard Henry, of all people, Richard Henry! To strike a servant or a slave in anger was never acceptable, but to engage in a common brawl was unforgivable.

Richard Henry was the last person Tom would have expected to see in such a situation, for the boy was calm, given to wry humor and occasional cutting remarks, but never to physical violence.

Tom's hand tightened on his crop—with effort he restrained himself from lashing both boys. "I command you to stop immediately."

The antagonists drew back, and Tom saw his son's face, already flushed from the fight, grow crimson with embarrassment as he caught sight of his father.

"I would see you at the house," Tom ordered his son curtly, then abruptly spurred and wheeled his horse toward the big house, Missy following closely behind.

"There had better be a good explanation for your exhibition in the slave quarters." Tom greeted the boy tersely in his study. "Whatever could Juno have done to provoke you to give such vent to your temper? No matter what it was, there is no excuse for your behavior. Lees do not roll in the dust like drunken sailors engaged in a tavern brawl."

Richard Henry swallowed hard. "It wasn't anything Juno did. I asked him to fight. In fact, I paid him a gold coin for going a round with me."

"What?" Tom was incredulous.

"Well, Philip and Thomas write that bullies at the English schools taunt the colonials, particularly the Virginians." The boy stammered slightly. "I hate to fight, Father, but I thought it best to prepare myself. So I asked Juno to box." Richard Henry's earnest white face broke into a small smile. "I held my own, too, Father! I'll do all right if I'm pushed to it."

Tom let out a sigh. "By Jove, you are a pistol," he conceded. "But you put Juno in an uncomfortable position. It was not appropriate."

"Father," Missy called as she tapped on the heavy study door, "a carriage is coming up the drive."

From the window Tom saw an open equipage approaching, and in it he could make out the genial face and narrow sloping shoulders of Lawrence Washington. Beside him sat his younger brother Austin, who had taken over Wakefield on Pope's Creek. Opposite him sat another man, whom Tom did not recognize, and beside *him* yet another of Gus Washington's boys, young George.

Richard Henry was jubilant. "I haven't seen George in a year at least."

"My dear councilor!" Lawrence Washington, the first to step down from the carriage in the gravel turnaround, made a respectful bow to Tom. "My brothers you know, sir, and may I present my brother-in-law, George William Fairfax. He is much interested in your Ohio Company, so I took the liberty of bringing him along."

"Delighted that you could join us, Mr. Fairfax. My wife's brother, Philip Ludwell of Green Spring, will be with us, and I have invited Gawin Corbin of Pecatone, who has also expressed interest."

As the men disappeared inside the house, Richard Henry gave his friend a hearty embrace. "You are looking splendid!"

"Aye. Things go well enough with me." As always George spoke in a strong, unhurried manner. "I hear you are soon to leave for school."

"Wakefield Academy in Yorkshire," Richard Henry proudly admitted. "And I hope someday to read law at the Inner Temple in London, like my older brothers. Let's go to the schoolhouse. The new tutor, Mr. Craige, has taken the younger boys down to the landing to count bushels and barrels. We'll have the place to ourselves."

Inside the schoolhouse, Richard Henry stirred the fire with a poker. "The last time we met, you were talking about joining the English Navy."

"It was Lawrence's idea, he being a navy man." George swelled with obvious admiration for his older half-brother. "He thought it a good career for me, but my mother was dead set against it." He paused. "So now I am working, as a surveyor! I came across my father's surveying compass and tried running the lines of Ferry Farm. Then I got a few odd jobs—got paid for them, too!—sometimes in tobacco, but sometimes in cash."

"But are you a real surveyor?" Richard Henry looked dubious.

"I've passed the standards. Now I need experience, for I plan one day to be a county surveyor, or at least a surveyor's deputy. You know, I've just been offered the most amazing assignment," he said with a blush of candor. "Earlier this month I went up to visit Mount Vernon. It's a beautiful spot, and Lawrence has built a beautiful house—not as monumental as Stratford, of course, but quite handsome."

"Well, what is this offer that has you so intrigued?" Richard Henry urged George on.

"I went with Lawrence and Nancy to call at Belvoir, when Lord Fairfax, the old proprietor himself, was visiting. Quite a strange fellow—wears ragged clothes about, hates women, and lives for the hunt." George rolled his eyes. "He wants the proprietary surveyed, so a team has been set up, and I have been invited to be a member!"

"Lucky bloke, I do envy you!" Richard Henry exclaimed.

"A veteran surveyor will take charge of the party along with Nancy's brother, George William Fairfax, who came with us today. I will go as an assistant!" George's blue eyes were bright. "I have never been into the Shenandoah—for a fact, I've never been outside the Tidewater."

"How wonderful!" Richard Henry stared into the fire. He did envy George, although he knew that his opportunity to study in England was by all measure the more advantageous. With little education or inherited land, George's fortunes would depend solely on how he used his wits.

"We must go in to dinner." Richard Henry stood up and stretched. "I must warn you. It will be hard to keep your mind on the talk of trails, surveys, patents, and settlements once you catch sight of a certain lovely face at the table."

"Whose might that be?"

"Do you remember Lucy Grymes? She's come visiting with my uncle Phil, and she'll quite take your breath away!"

"Well, I shall give you strong competition for her favor," George challenged.

"You are not the only one. Mark my words: my cousin Henry Lee will come cantering into the yard some time this afternoon. Oh, he'll say he has just come over to do some shooting, but it will be the Lowland Beauty he has come to see, you watch!"

Talk was as Richard Henry had predicted. While dining on a great roast of beef, served by Hannah from the red-and-white marble table at one side of the pleasant dining room, the visitors from upriver joined Tom, Philip Ludwell, and Gawin Corbin in a lively discussion of the proposed Ohio Company.

"I have been in contact with the London merchant John Hanbury, who is most dedicated to the prospect," said Tom. "Of course, his profits will be enormous if the fur trade can be established. He has offered to present our petition to court."

"Well, count on Austin and me as founding partners of this enterprise," Lawrence declared firmly.

"And I'm in as well," George William Fairfax said. "In fact, I feel certain Lawrence and I can induce Carlyle to support the venture."

"Yes," Lawrence murmured thoughtfully. "I believe he is just that farsighted." He turned to Tom. "We speak of Colonel John Carlyle, sir, a Scotsman descended from the royal Bruces, or so he tells me! Married to another of George William's sisters, and a good businessman—in fact, he is already a partner in our efforts to incorporate a port city on the Potomac south of the Great Falls. We plan to call it Alexandria. Yes," Lawrence said emphatically, "I feel certain we can count on Carlyle's participation."

"And you, Phil?" Tom asked.

The young master of Green Spring placed his knife and fork neatly across his plate. "I am with you in spirit, my dear Tom, but as for becoming an active partner, do let me think about it. You know I like to muse on things before I take action."

Tom suppressed a smile. He was deeply fond of Hannah's younger brother, whose gentleness and kindness were without limit, even if he lacked the dash and spirit of his father. Tom pushed back his chair, encouraged about the prospects for the Ohio Company. His eyes moved down the table to the broad-shouldered sixteen-year-old George. A puzzle, that one. Not as engaging or as quick to speak as his older step-brothers, but then, he hadn't had their advantages, either. What a stroke of luck that Lawrence Washington had married into the land-rich Fairfax family. With all the surveying they would have, young George could make a comfortable niche for himself!

"Did you see how silly Richard Henry and that tall young Washington behaved at dinner?" Missy later asked her mother scornfully. "Both absolutely mooning over that saucy little minx Lucy, first one whispering into her ear, then the other! And she was just as bad. Did you notice the funny way she has of putting her hand over her mouth when she giggles?"

Hannah looked at her elder daughter reproachfully. "I didn't see anything silly about it. That is just the way most young people act."

"Well, I've never acted like that," Missy retorted hotly, "and no coltish lad with berry-red cheeks is going to whisper in my ear!"

"No, because you only scoff and toss your head at them." Hannah's tone softened. "Not that several young men haven't tried, but you put them off in every way."

"Oh, bother! I've stuck my finger!" Missy threw down her embroidery and went to the window. "Now, would you believe Henry Lee is here again? He has all the instincts of a male dog when there is a bitch in season."

"Missy Lee!" Hannah gasped.

"You know as well as I that he has come to see Lucy Grymes," Missy retorted.

"Courting and falling in love are very natural parts of life—very nice parts, in fact," Hannah said gently.

"Did you love Father very much when you married him, Mother?"

"I had loved him for a long time—to be sure, I had set my cap for him. But I was fortunate. Most girls marry with only a fond, affectionate feeling for the man their families have accepted for them. Then if they are blessed, deep feelings of love gradually grow."

Missy stared out at the long fingers of afternoon shade that lay across the wide lawn, a curious sadness welling up within her. "Then what is the satisfaction in marriage?"

"There are many satisfactions. Companionship, if not always love, and children. And these, Missy, do not underestimate these." Missy saw her mother's fingers go to the basket on one wrist filled with the tiny keys to her escritoire, sewing table, and linen press. The ring at her waist held the larger keys. Each day, accompanied by Will, she doled out the day's rations of meats from the smokehouse, flour, butter, sugar, molasses, and lard from the storeroom, and spirits for sauces from the cellar. Next she proceeded to the weaving room on the lower floor of the big house to talk with the housekeeper about house linens and the clothing in various stages of preparation for the people of the plantation. And, of course, she nursed the sick, both in the big house and in the servant and slave quarters. She supervised the gardens, arranged the flowers, and saw that the chickens were fed, the fires laid, the bread kneaded, the beds made, and the house kept clean and aired. Missy sighed; she'd never be a match for her mother. Even when sitting here in the parlor, Hannah always had a piece of sewing in her hand.

"I think it's time you married," Hannah said firmly. "Take, for example, a fine man like George William Fairfax—now don't wrinkle your nose! His wife will be mistress of quite a domain."

"He is too handsome, too charming . . . too English!" Missy leaned her elbows on the windowsill. "Anyway, it's rumored he is quite taken with Sally Cary."

"Well, consider your cousin Gawin Corbin. He isn't particularly handsome or charming, if those qualities offend! In fact he is rather quiet, and he would love to court you, my darling." Hannah looked at Missy. "He needs someone just like you. Pecatone has been neglected for too long. Gawin needs a strong wife to help him make it the profitable plantation it once was."

For a long moment, Missy said nothing. Then she asked in a low voice, "But would Gawin Corbin accept help with the orchards and the fields and the stables?"

"I think he would welcome it!" Hannah was emphatic. "Pecatone might be just the challenge you are looking for."

Missy sighed, then watched her breath frost the windowpane. With a hesitant finger she drew a crooked heart in the misted glass and wiped clean its center, through which she could see her father walking in the orchard with his guests.

Tom took Lawrence Washington's arm. "Well, then, it is all settled. I shall pursue the plans for the Ohio Company in Williamsburg this spring. We need twenty backers before our proposal can be presented to the King." Tom paused. "I have a few in mind whom I am eager to approach."

"I envy George Washington," Richard Henry said to his father as the Lee carriage swayed and rumbled through the heavy underbrush of the Northern Neck on its journey to Williamsburg. "He is off on a glorious adventure with Mr. George William Fairfax. They are riding toward the Occoquan River, then northwest into the wilderness to meet the rest of the surveying party at Ashby's Bent, which lies between the Occoquan River and the crest of the Blue Ridge Mountains. Doesn't it sound glorious?"

Tom had caught the wistfulness in his son's voice. "A trip west will undoubtedly prove valuable for George, for each man must learn and profit from his experiences. But don't forget that you, too, are setting out on a glorious adventure."

"Oh, I realize that!" Richard Henry's voice grew excited. "There are so many places I've read about that I want to see, both in England and on the Continent. Nothing interests me so much as history and government. It's endlessly fascinating!"

"What do you know of England and where she stands today?" Tom was curious to hear his son's view of the current world situation.

"All I know is what I hear in your study, what I read in the *Virginia Gazette*, and what Mr. Craige has told me," the boy replied, beaming.

The British hostilities with Spain, known originally as the War of Jenkins's Ear, had widened into a conflict with France, for the Bourbon rulers of Spain and France were linked by a family compact. That conflict had been further complicated when Frederick the Great of Prussia had seized Silesia from the Hapsburg Queen, Maria Theresa of Austria. A brief war had developed, in which Prussia and France lined up on one side against England and Austria on the other.

"I would like to have seen King George leading our English troops at Dettingen," Richard Henry exclaimed, "but I guess the fighting is over. The treaty of peace being drawn up at Aix-la-Chapelle is supposed to last forever."

"I doubt if any treaty will curb the rivalry between England and France on this American continent." Tom smiled at his son. "You admire our Hanoverian for his courage, do you? I suspect your grandfather Lee would have taken the side of the young Stuart Pretender when he tried to wrest the throne from George the Second. My father was intensely loyal to the House of Stuart, you know."

Tom was referring to the 1745 challenge to the English throne by Charles Edward Stuart, the Catholic son of James II, whose hopes for regaining the English crown were shattered by the forces of the bloody Duke of Cumberland, the son of George II. "Yes," Tom continued, "my father was very loyal to the Stuarts, as I have been loyal to the House of Hanover. Loyalty is a complex thing," Tom mused, "most admirable when based on a well-reasoned commitment."

"Well-reasoned?"

"What is right for one man in his time may not be right for another in his. The Stuarts stood for absolute monarchy, which my father supported. I agree with John Locke, who said men are by nature free, submitting to government not because they acknowledge any divine right but because they find it convenient to do so." Tom narrowed his eyes as he stared from the carriage window into the April sunshine. "I think a man must be very certain of what he believes before he goes back on a loyalty once pledged. It is not a step to be taken lightly, but there are times when it might be right and necessary. After all, circumstances have a way of changing."

And the men who control circumstances also change, Tom thought a week later as he surveyed the faces of those sitting around the oval council table. These twelve councilors, the principal gentlemen of the colony, could be swayed by the head of the council alone. He considered the council presidents he had known: his father-in-law, Philip Ludwell; the driving King Carter; old Commissary James Blair; the farsighted and erudite William Byrd of Westover; and now John Robinson.

With Byrd's death, shortly after Tom had returned from the Lancaster meeting, the council had been taken over by the Robinson faction, which included the Randolphs and their allies. Tom was not a member of the Robinson coterie, so he moved cautiously in presenting his plans for the Ohio Company. But the general reception to the idea was guarded. Even Governor William Gooch was not particularly encouraging when Tom called at his offices at the palace.

"I am bone weary, Tom," he complained gloomily. "I cannot tell you how I still suffer from the wounds I got at Cartagena, and I begin to think it is time to retire and return to England. To be frank, I have little interest in joining your Ohio Company." The old governor got up from his chair and hobbled painfully to the window. "You know, I was created a baronet by the King two years ago," he said with gentle pride. "More and more I dream of English hillsides and the bells of Westminster. No, Tom, the only land I yearn for lies home in England. What an experience awaits your young Richard Henry!"

In the weeks that followed, Tom realized how much he missed his thoughtful third son. In Richard Henry, Tom had found a mind, interests, and spirit well matched to his own, so, it was to Richard Henry that Tom wrote about his frustrating search for partners to back the Ohio Company. "Only one of my fellow councilors is willing to commit himself to the financial obligations. But Lawrence and I have complete confidence that the venture will be realized in time. Tomorrow I shall leave Green Spring and travel up the James to Berkeley and Westover in hopes that their young masters will join the venture."

The next morning dawned clear and sparkling. From the high covered porch, Tom started down the steep staircase to the yard, where the Ludwells' shy ten-year-old daughter, Hannah Philippa, threw corn to a flock of cackling geese. At the gate a Ludwell servant waited with Star.

What memories Green Spring held for him. The plantation was not ostentatious and ambitious as it had been in Governor Berkeley's heyday, when, besides tobacco and sustenance crops, Berkeley had made experimental plantings of rice, indigo, hemp, and flax, as well as introduced groves of mulberry trees, which he hoped would be the beginning of a silk industry. Now the plantation was less prosperous, the land worn from years of heavy planting. But the manor house was as gracious as ever, its airy, high-ceilinged rooms still filled with the finest Stuart furniture and glass, silver, and porcelain.

When he reached the dusty roadway, Tom turned onto a narrow path that would take him to the Chickahominy River ferry. Once across that brisk, slender tributary of the James, he would move up through the flatlands to Berkeley, some twenty miles north on the James. Swamp willows framed his last glimpse of the great three-story brick-and-timber Green Spring. After Berkeley's original house burned, around 1660, this larger, more lavish house had been built upon the original foundations. The mansion symbolized the beginning of the bold and brilliant times that brought to the fore the Lees and the Ludwells, Carters, Harrisons, and Byrds ninety years before. Little wonder it was the part of Virginia's story that Hannah Ludwell Lee loved best!

Sustained by tobacco, the Virginia Colony had overcome the brutal Indian massacre of 1622 and soon had a stable population and a thriving economy based on the jovial weed. In 1639, Charles I formally recognized the House of Burgesses, an assembly of freemen that had been meeting off and on in Jamestown since its settlement. That had been, Tom realized, a most important step in establishing the principle that Virginia would be self-governing. Of course, it would have a royal governor and a council appointed in London, but it guaranteed a representative assembly to be chosen by men of the colony.

On an April day in 1642, a new governor, thirty-four-year-old William Berkeley, a member of the King's Privy Chamber, and the brother of a lord, arrived in Jamestown. He was charmed by the bustling little river-island capital surrounded by shimmering, slumbrous swamps and vine-festooned trees. Already the tobacco fields covered the sloping banks of the James.

When the long-smoldering civil war broke out in England and Charles I was beheaded, in 1649, William Berkeley led the Virginia Assembly in proclaiming loyalty to the exiled Charles II and condemning Oliver Cromwell and his Puritan followers. More important to the future of Virginia, the persuasive Berkeley encouraged the King's supporters to seek asylum in Virginia.

So the cavaliers came! At first a few, then a stream of the loyalists poured into the colony, travel-worn but still resplendent in velvet cloaks, lace collars, and long curls that fell to their shoulders beneath feather-plumed hats.

Richard Lee the Emigrant had been farsighted enough to come to Virginia in 1636, before the civil war erupted, but there was no question where his loyalties lay, and in 1649 Berkeley appointed him to the prestigious post of secretary of the colony.

This commonwealth period was surprisingly productive, for tobacco prices were high and the Cromwellian government, immersed in their own affairs, ignored Virginia. With the governor in seclusion at Green Spring, the House of Burgesses took up the reins of the government. For the first time since the colony's founding, these hard-working yeomen and middle-ranking planters were in control of their own destiny.

Meanwhile the cavaliers swarmed to Green Spring! Highly personable and charming, these exiles had a strong appreciation of country-gentry life, its gallant code of fairness and manners. But more significant was their sybaritic notion that life is more than just hard work. Life was silver dram cups, coats of arms, Oriental tapestries, horses and hounds, and dances with lovely ladies by candlelight.

In 1660 Cromwell was dead. The Restoration of the plump, charming Charles II was a glamorous period for London, bringing new theater, fashion, and gaiety. But for Virginia, it was a period of dismay. This Stuart King treated the colony as his own personal property, his "old dominion." He saw Virginia as a cluster of jewels from which he could break off bits to reward his friends. The Northern Neck Proprietary was but one example. He also began enforcing old laws, particularly the Navigation Acts, which required that all tobacco go only to English ports in English boats.

The small planters of the colony had had a taste of power, and they were not about to accede to the wishes of the restored governor and his council. Moreover, the unpopularity of the Navigation Acts was exacerbated by floods and hurricanes, which played havoc with the tobacco crop.

And the Indians were again on the rampage. Without first obtaining the governor's approval, a charismatic young planter, Nathaniel Bacon, led an expedition against the warring Indians. Although well aware that most Virginia frontiersmen supported Bacon's Rebellion, Berkeley charged Nathaniel Bacon with treason and suspended him from the council.

Nonetheless, the rebel army moved against the friendly Pamunkey Indians, then marched to Green Spring for a feast at the absent governor's table, and then to Jamestown, which they torched and burned to the ground. On retreat, Nathaniel Bacon became desperately ill and died of the bloody flux, a sordid and terrible end for the defiant rebel.

Tom could recall his father's quoting an epitaph that had circulated among Berkeley's supporters:

> *Bacon's dead.*
> *I am sorry at my heart*
> *That lice and flux should act*
> *The hangman's part.*

Within a few weeks the governor had captured Bacon's chief aides and hanged at least twenty of the rebels. When he learned of the harsh punishments, Charles II said, "the old fool [Berkeley] has killed more people in that naked country than I have done for the murder of my father." Never again after Bacon's Rebellion would a royal governor have absolute power over the colony.

Through it all, Green Spring had endured. Berkeley's widow, a dashing and beautiful young woman whom the aging bachelor had wed late in life, married Councilor Philip Ludwell in 1680, but nonetheless insisted on being called "my lady Frances Berkeley." She was the grande dame of the colony, giving lavish balls as though still the governor's wife. Green Spring had passed to Hannah's father and was now the domain of Philip Ludwell III, her brother, and would one day belong to his daughters, Hannah Philippa and Lucy.

Green Spring's glory was a part of Tom's own heritage. His father, Richard the Scholar, had stood firmly by Berkeley when the colony was split by Bacon's Rebellion. He had been captured by Bacon's army and for several weeks imprisoned by the rebels—an experience that had embittered and scarred him. Perhaps Bacon's followers, those yeomen farmers, were only rabble—"rogues" and "dogs," Berkeley had called them. Ironically, it was the courage and audacity of those small farmers and frontiersmen that Tom was now counting on. They would, by God, hold the Ohio basin for England.

"Young William Byrd the Third and Ben Harrison the Fifth are not like their fathers, not at all," Tom reported brusquely to Hannah and Missy on his first day home. "Oh, they were gracious enough—in fact, too gracious. They think only of grand clothes, fast horses, dancing, and good drink." There was a note of resentment, even anger, in Tom's voice.

"Don't forget they are only lads in their early twenties," Hannah soothed, "no older than our Philip."

Tom shrugged and dropped the subject. He felt too good being again at Stratford to argue with his beloved lady about anything. Long rays of sunlight lay across the shiny walnut table, burnishing the centerpiece bowl filled with fresh strawberries and raspberries and casting a beam on the glass that protected the portrait of good Queen Caroline. The young children had already eaten their dinner in the schoolhouse with Mr. Craige, so Hannah and Missy were his only companions at this dinner of squirrel-and-vegetable-laced Brunswick stew.

Tom sipped a cool draft of ale. "I stayed in the guesthouse at Berkeley." He nodded at Hannah. "The small building Anne used to call the bachelor house. It was most agreeable, for the main house was chock-full of Harrisons—young Ben and his new bride; his sister, Bette; and her husband, Peyton Randolph. Quite a house party! One day we drove to Westover in the pony cart to play cricket. Billy Byrd and Peyton Randolph are so recently returned from school in England that they know little of our colony and the great opportunities that lie here. In fact," Tom said, breaking off a piece of bread and spreading it lavishly with blackberry jam, "they are so alike—Byrd, Harrison, and Randolph—all big, strapping, handsome fellows, well-educated, charming rascals, and all three newly married." He paused. "I met Byrd's young wife, Eliza Carter of Shirley plantation—you recall, the daughter of John Carter and the heiress Elizabeth Hill. Eliza seems a shy young thing, perhaps a bit overwhelmed by the pace of life at Westover."

"That makes three of William Byrd's children who married children or, in this case, a grandchild, of King Carter. That would have pleased Byrd mightily," Hannah said.

"Aye," Tom agreed. "I visited the Black Swan's grave in the garden at Westover. He lies in a grove of sweet-smelling boxwood surrounded by the flowers and fruit he so loved, a fitting repose for a fellow so elegant and charming. I say," Tom's voice grew firmer, "he has left his son quite a fortune, Hannah. It amounts to nearly two hundred thousand acres throughout the Tidewater and the Shenandoah. In addition, he gets much livestock, the mills at the falls near Richmond, and a great many slaves. He is much better off than young Ben Harrison."

"How is that?" Missy asked, curious.

"Ben left his eldest son the six plantations that compose Berkeley and much stock and equipment, not to mention the manor house itself. But then he divided the bulk of his estate and most of his outlying lands among his other four sons. In trying to be equitable, he has left young Ben in an insecure position—not that the boy realizes this yet," Tom added with asperity. "He, like Billy Byrd, is more engrossed in racehorses and the quality of his latest shipment of Madeira wine!"

"How did they receive your idea for the Ohio Company?" Missy inquired.

"My dear, all were entirely gracious and flattering to me as a councilor and as an old friend of their fathers'. But they have no interest in the Ohio Company. To be frank, I detected evasiveness on the part of Peyton Randolph. He may have ideas of his own to rival mine." Tom threw down his knife. "But it matters little. Lawrence and I have finally found our twenty partners for the Ohio Company. We are applying immediately to King George the Second for a grant. We didn't need young Byrd or Harrison and their fortunes after all!"

Hannah rose from the table, fanning herself with a languid, almost melancholy motion. "I wish I had gone with you, Tom; I would so have liked to see Berkeley again."

Tom pushed back his chair and went to put his arm around her. "There was no pleasure, Hannah, without Ben or Anne there. I could hardly bear looking up at the window."

Hannah knew exactly what he referred to. Four years ago, on a hot summer day, Ben had been playing dominoes with his younger children in the cool grass on one of the upper terraces above the river. When a sudden thunderstorm came upon them, he had shepherded the children into the house, noticing as he did an open window on an upper floor of the red brick house. He rushed up to close it, one small daughter clinging to his leg, another in his arms. A bolt of lightning and the life-loving Ben Harrison, along with his two little girls, was killed instantly. Rocked by her triple loss, Anne Harrison had died shortly afterward.

"But their lives were good and they left fine children to take their place in the world. It is all one can ask, the best one can ask." Hannah stirred in Tom's arm. "We have been waiting for you to come home. Missy has something she wants to tell you, something I believe you will be delighted to hear."

Missy blushed. "If you give your blessing, Father, I will become the mistress of Pecatone."

For a moment, Tom stared at the girl, then his face broke into a smile that mirrored delight and disbelief. "How wonderful! But are you sure that is what you want, my love? Of course, you know I will consent, but only if ... Do you truly love Gawin, Missy?"

"Of course I love him, Father." The girl turned to the window. "He is your kinsman. How could I not love him?"

Tom wrapped Missy in his arms. "Then I give you my blessing, my darling. A most distinguished family! Why, there were Corbins on the lists of Battle Abbey. And to have you marry into my mother's family ties you that much closer to me."

Missy pulled from his arms and looked directly in his eyes. "That is what I wanted to hear. I shall tell Gawin that he may speak with you."

"Are you pleased, Hannah?" Tom asked his smiling wife.

But before Hannah could respond, Missy retorted with a soft smile, "Now what do you think, Father? You'd almost think it had been her idea."

A great calmness settled over Missy. Her father was pleased with her decision, and when she thought deeply about it, she told herself she was terribly fortunate. The more she got to know Gawin, the more hours she spent walking in the orchard beside him or talking with him in the quiet of her father's study on hushed summer afternoons, the more she realized that her mother had been right: Gawin was not only much in love with her, but also pleased with her interest in refurbishing and developing the once proud Pecatone.

He was not humorous or easy with words, but then, she herself had little use for repartee. They were more like two young business partners, comfortable in each other's company, relying upon each other's strengths.

In the dry, dusty days of August drought, Missy rode with her father as he made his daily rounds of the Stratford plantation.

"We need the rain badly," Tom murmured as they passed over dry ice pond beds and brown, reedy swamp grass. He looked at the sky. "It is the sickly season now. There is ague and fever in the quarters, half my work force is ill."

Later that day, Missy went out to the lowland fields to gather meadow calamus. "Called wormwood, to be cut into small pieces, mixed with rue and camomile in jugs of spring water," she explained that night to Will West. "Give a glass of it at dawn and bedtime to anyone in the quarters who has the fever."

"I think yo' ma feels poorly." Will worriedly shook his head. "She don't say nothing, but she's touchy today, and her eyes don't look quite right."

Missy quickly sought out her mother. Touching Hannah's brow, the girl drew a breath of dismay. "You burn with the fever."

For four long days, Missy hardly left the bedside, allowing only Will to prepare Hannah's food—"chicken broth skimmed clear of fat and laced with molasses to give her strength," she explained to Tom, who hovered anxiously around his wife's bed.

On the fourth evening, Missy admitted defeat. "I have tried everything, but I simply can't bring her fever down."

Tom looked at her pale, anxious face. "I hear a doctor has settled near

Sabine Hall. I'll send for him, Missy." He put his arm about her as distant thunder rumbled in the darkening sky. At last the drought was over.

Missy wearily pushed the hair out of her eyes. "I don't want mother bled," she stipulated, "but yes, send for the doctor, and pray that he arrives in time to help."

The rains had been falling an interminable time before they heard the welcome sound of horses' hoofs in the lane.

Dr. Richard Hall was young and rangy. His dark-brown hair, dampened by the long wet ride, had been hastily reclamped in a careless queue, and drops of moisture glistened on his brow and in the sunburned creases of his neck. With skillful fingers, he felt the texture of Hannah's skin and took her pulse. "Have you been able to give her an emetic?"

"Yes," said Missy, "twenty-five grains of ipecacuanha, and I have dosed her with the bark. It is malaria, isn't it?"

For a moment their eyes met, hers intense, bright with concern in the candleshine; his dark, steady, analyzing. "Probably." He threw back the summer blanket, took one of Hannah's white slender feet to feel its flexibility and the texture of the skin.

"Your nursing is excellent. She's got a fair degree of strength and she's not dehydrated," he said quietly. "I have brought with me two pounds of the best Jesuits' powdered bark. Have it mixed, and we will give her two cups of it now mixed with rhubarb."

"You won't bleed her?" the girl said anxiously.

For a moment their eyes met again. "No, I won't bleed her," he said. "There is no need."

It was a long night. The young doctor sat by Hannah's bed, rarely looking up except to answer Tom's occasional questions. Yes, he was from the Neck. He had attended the College of William and Mary and then served as an apprentice, first to an apothecary and then to a physician in Yorktown. No, he was not married—no time for that.

Missy found Richard Hall's presence unsettling. She was torn between the comfort he offered and a strange agitation that rose in her. Never had she had such a feeling and, despite herself, she could not resist covertly watching him. He had rolled up his sleeves, and the soft hairs on his brown, muscular arms gleamed golden in the candlelight.

Dawn was breaking over the treetops when he looked up and gave her a quick, almost joyous smile. "Her fever has broken at last. I believe she is over the worst."

Missy went to the window and threw back the shutter to reveal a sky streaked with gold and purple and lavender. "Thank you, God," she whispered.

"You are very skillful." Richard Hall now stood beside her at the window. "In fact," he said softly, "I think you are exceptional."

Behind them, Hannah stirred, looking up at Tom as he bent over her. "I shall be fine," she murmured, "just fine, I promise, in time for the wedding."

"The wedding?" Richard Hall looked inquiringly at Missy.

For a moment, she could barely breathe. Then she answered, her voice a bit louder than she meant it to be, "I am to be married in the middle of September."

Later, as months went by, it seemed to Missy Lee Corbin that those days of August 1748, when she had ridden out upon the land in the early morning with her father, were the last serene, uncomplicated days of her life. The simple afternoon ceremony that had bound her to Gawin Corbin, if marred by the almost luminous frailty of Hannah Lee, was also made beautiful by the delight both her mother and father took in the marriage. And it was a good marriage! Gawin was everything she had expected him to be: kind and undemanding and pleased to have her involved in the management of Pecatone. Perhaps in time she would feel less chilled when his hands were on her.

What was unexpected was how much she would grow to love Pecatone. She poured her energies and passion into it, rising early to ride out upon the land with Gawin, returning to meet with the carpenters and so-called undertakers who were restoring portions of the massive brick manor house. In the evenings she wrestled with the ledger books and the records in the plantation office. The energies Missy poured into Pecatone's restoration and the clearing of its neglected fields were more than made up for by the strength she drew from it, a strength that sustained her through the bleak January of 1749, when her mother died.

The Tidewater, 1749

Only Missy was able to offer Tom any sort of comfort in the painful weeks that followed the burial of Hannah Lee in the family graveyard at Burnt House Fields. Day after day, he would ride over from Stratford to walk with her along the water's edge or sit by the fire in the parlor at Pecatone, talking of Hannah and their life together. How remarkable, thought Missy, that anyone could love another that much.

It was not until July, when Governor Gooch announced the awarding of two hundred thousand acres from King George to the Ohio Company, that Tom was roused. "Our tract lies between the Monongahela and Kanawha Rivers, and in time we shall expand to the north, but first we will build a fort, then a trading post, to draw the Indians," Tom told Missy.

But there was some unexpected competition. Gooch also announced another allotment of eight hundred thousand acres to John Robinson's Loyal Company. Missy was relieved to see how revitalized her father was. As to her own emotions, she could not explain them. It was almost as if there were a fever raging within her that only the building of Pecatone could soothe.

"Gawin claims you're working too hard, that you exhaust yourself," her father cautioned.

"Ah, but look!" With a sweep of her arm, Missy indicated the flourishing orchards and overflowing gardens.

"But you must be careful now that you carry a child," he admonished.

"Loving Pecatone keeps me happy, Father. Isn't that important?"

Tom observed her tanned face, the healthy lines of her lithe, young body. "Aye," he conceded. "Love it, then, but in moderation. You have your husband—and soon a child—to consider as well."

The first of September, an urgent summons came from Williamsburg. Acting Governor John Robinson had fallen ill and died. Council President John Custis of Arlington, also ailing, was leaving office. "Thomas Lee, Esquire, next of the Council, was invited to come down to Williamsburg with all convenient speed and appoint a Council to swear him into the execution of his office immediately." Tom would be president of the council, acting governor, and commander in chief of His Majesty's colony!

The colony never had a more handsome, more distinguished, more amiable governor than Tom Lee, Missy thought as she stood by her father in early September at his first official reception, in the gold-papered salon of the elegant Governor's Palace in Williamsburg. At fifty-nine, Tom moved with the grace of a much younger man, the vigor and warmth of his personality charming each citizen, each Burgessman and lady and shopkeeper who passed through the upstairs drawing room to shake his hand. But it was an ungodly hot day; Missy felt the perspiration beading up. As their carriage had rolled through the palace gates marked by the stone lion and unicorn, she had noted the British flag hung limply in the still air and, even now, with the aid of cooling drinks and half-drawn blinds, she was sweltering in this crowded room. So many faces, so many voices. She found herself looking among them, searching . . . hoping to see . . . No, there was no one she was hoping to see.

"I would much rather stay in Williamsburg with you, Father," said Francis Lightfoot a few days later as the Lee carriage prepared to return to the Neck.

"To be honest, Frank," Tom looked the boy directly in the eyes, "I have need of you at Stratford. In my absence, and with your older brothers abroad, you must be in charge, and fortify your brothers and sister."

"I'll not let you down, Father." Frank's sensitive mouth tightened decisively.

An Indian summer lay upon the Tidewater, and President Lee returned bone weary each evening to Green Spring, which Philip Ludwell had put at his disposal, since the palace was undergoing repairs. Tom's head reeled with proposals, requests, and ideas of what he wished to pursue. He was responsible for all judicial, civil, and military appointments as well as awarding land grants. He forged ahead with plans to strengthen Virginia's borders by erecting a new battery and lighthouse near the southern capes of the colony and restoring the far-flung forts in the mountains.

Mount Vernon, 1749

In mid-November, Tom journeyed north to Mount Vernon to visit Lawrence Washington. The crackling red and yellow leaves swirling about his horse's hoofs, he crossed the Rappahannock and traveled north toward the Virginia hills. It was good to be back in this familiar land he had explored and mapped as agent for the proprietary, but Tom was shocked by his friend's appearance. Earlier, he had been distressed at Lawrence's inability to shake a persistent cough, and it now seemed Lawrence's condition had deteriorated. The young planter kept his handkerchief constantly in his hand to stifle frequent spells of coughing. But his enthusiasm for the Ohio Company waxed as strong as ever. "Since Conrad Weiser reports that the western Indians distrust our plans to build a fort, I feel the Indian trading post should be our most immediate project. To capture the fur trade, we must build a warehouse here on the Potomac, then send west those English goods the Indians desire."

All this Tom poured out in letters to Richard Henry: "I found Captain Washington in good spirits, but quite miserable health, and his wife, Nancy, appears frail as well. Young George appears to be the healthiest member of the family and is held in great affection by Mr. Washington. We dined one evening at Belvoir. Its new mistress, Sally Cary Fairfax, is a handsome, fine-spirited young lady who delights in teasing George, who is still not given to small talk. Yet George has matured greatly since becoming a county surveyor. For one thing, he carries a purse full of doubloons and pistoles earned from his surveying and takes great pride in making small loans to his brothers, cousins, and friends, which he records quite neatly in his ledger book."

The Tidewater, 1750

At the November 5 session of the King's Council, Tom announced news from the Indian intermediary Conrad Weiser confirming that the Six Nations of Indians had joined the French in the Ohio. But the French claim to the Mississippi and the western lands was not valid, Tom told himself. In time the lands would be settled for England, and then the Ohio Company must prosper! It must, if he was to conserve a respectable estate for Philip and still have lands for his other sons. Exhausted and sick, he left for Stratford Hall.

Missy came to Stratford Hall as soon as she heard that he had returned. She left her baby daughter, Patty, with Gawin, who was supervising the hanging of the tobacco leaves in the barns of Pecatone. Her heart sank when she saw her father's condition. "We must send for Richard Hall," she told Francis Lightfoot.

But by the time the young doctor arrived, Tom had lost consciousness. "We can only wait. I will stay with you." Hall took Missy's cold hands in his and chafed them gently. "There's nothing more I can do."

Her eyes filled with tears. "There is no need for you to remain. I'll manage." Reluctantly she pulled her hand away from the warmth of his.

"I want to stay. You need someone with you."

Tom died in the early hours of the fourth day of his illness, with Richard Hall and Missy at his bedside. They buried him at Burnt House Fields following to the letter the instructions he had left with his will. His coffin had been placed between that of his mother, Laetitia Corbin Lee, and that of his wife, Hannah, the bricks on the side next to Hannah Lee removed by Will's own hands so that his master could lie as close as possible to the wife he had loved so much in life. It was the last thing he had asked Will to do.

Mary Bland came from Lee Hall with her sons to care for the household in the sad days that followed. "You must stand by these poor orphaned children," she told Will. "They depend upon you . . . just as their master did."

"I always do my best, Miss Mary."

"Everything will be better as soon as Philip and Thomas arrive home from England," Mary Bland went on soothingly. "Philip has a strong, decisive nature. At least he won't duck his responsibilities."

Will West nodded, but he was uncertain in his heart. He had not seen

Philip Lee in the five years since the boys set out for London, and he could only pray that time and education had changed the new master of Stratford Hall. No, Philip won't shirk his duties; I dare say he'll relish the power, Will thought to himself.

A great man dies. Influenced by him, shaped by him, his children must carry on, yet they have their own destinies to follow and fulfill—the colonel still remembered the pain he had felt at the age of eleven when his own father, a man much loved and respected, died. So too it must have been for the young of Stratford Hall.

When Thomas Lee, Council President and Acting Governor of the Colony of Virginia—indeed, he was to become the first native-born governor, but he died before news of his appointment by George II reached the shores of Virginia—died on November 14, 1750, in his sixtieth year, the mantle of family authority came to rest on the shoulders of the twenty-four-year-old bachelor Philip Lee. This young man, a curious and mercurial mixture of his Lee, Corbin, Ludwell, and Harrison ancestry, was now the master of Stratford, responsible for its lands and its future and charged with the upbringing and education of his younger brothers and ten-year-old sister. The family had a strong heritage and the support of the Lee clan, particularly the cousins at Lee Hall. But, the colonel thought, it must have been with some anxiety that the third Stratford son, the introspective Richard Henry, prepared to return from his years abroad, well educated and ambitious, but uncertain of the path he would follow.

The Ripening Years

1751–1759

The Tidewater, 1751

The young man, his chiseled face arresting in its intensity, had been standing on the quarterdeck of the high-masted schooner H.M.S. *Grace of London* for almost an hour, ever since the hoarse cry "Land ho! Land ahead!" brought him bounding from below. Now the leadsman was sounding bottom from the taffrail as the ship moved into the coastal waters, which had lost the murky dark grayness of the deep Atlantic and were slashed with color and occasional pieces of pale-green seaweed.

In the unusually cool June morning air, he pulled his light cape closer around him. Not for the world would he miss seeing Virginia take shape before him.

His eyes, an enigmatic blue flecked with gray, had been fixed on the horizon. For a long time only a mistily smudged outline, it had darkened and widened in the bright sunlight, to reveal finally a thin line of white, bounding surf and, beyond, golden sand overshadowed by the black silhouette of forest.

Home, by God, finally home! Richard Henry Lee, at nineteen, had been away for three years. With a surge of pleasure, he caught sight of Fort Wool on the tip of Point Comfort and the wide breach in the shore where the Atlantic Ocean reached inland between Cape Charles and Cape Henry to become the Chesapeake Bay. The shores of America appeared serene and untouched after the teeming confusion of London, Glasgow, and Amsterdam. He marveled at the clean, windswept outline of the Virginia beaches, wide and golden with hillocks of sea oats shimmering in the sun. Close behind, oaks and scrub pines bent landward, as if beckoning him home, home to arrogant, elegant, self-absorbed Virginia.

"How marvelous it looks!" His cabinmate, Rob Carter, had joined him on the quarterdeck. The robust grandson of King Carter was already dressed for landing in a blue silk coat with an ornate lace collar, new English boots, and the latest short curly white-powdered wig. It struck Richard Henry that a taste for fashionable attire and a curious interest in the Evangelist John Wesley were about all that Rob Carter had absorbed in his two-year tour of England and the Continent.

The young Virginians had come upon each other by accident on the docks of Plymouth before boarding the *Grace of London,* which was heavy with merchandise for Virginia planters. Packed in trunks below deck were satins and laces from London's best shops. For elegant dining there were crested silverplate, sets of delicate china, and fragile crystal to hold the contents of the cases of fine wines and brandies, also below. For the plantation masters she carried huntsmen's saddles, tools, guns, and even an upholstered coach with some family's coat of arms emblazoned on the doors. Fine Georgian furniture, pewter, paper, and gunpowder were on the bill of lading. To satisfy the cultural and educational ambitions of the colonials, there were spinets, harpsichords, and books of all kinds, classical and popular.

As the two young men had lain in their hammocks, lulled by the dark choppy swells and the ship's bells chiming the half hour, Rob Carter had talked of nothing but Virginia. He reminisced about his schooldays at the College of William and Mary and discussed his plans for Nomini Hall. Born only a few miles apart on the Northern Neck, the two had scarcely known each other; after his father's death, Rob had lived with his uncles, then with his stepfather, in distant reaches of the Tidewater. Now they would again be neighbors, for Rob would soon take over Nomini, the plantation built in 1731 by his father, Robin Carter.

Three years was a long time to be away, and Richard Henry knew he was not the boy who had sailed from Yorktown that April day in 1748. Wakefield Academy had proved difficult for one accustomed to the warmth and hospitality of Stratford Hall. He had been teased unmerçifully by the other boys, particularly about his Virginia accent, with its broadened *a* and softened *r*, a habit he tried to overcome as he adjusted to the rigors of an English boys' school. Eventually he had grown to love the old Roman-built city in which Wakefield was situated, immersing himself in his studies, learning to read and converse quite ably in Greek and Latin. As a final triumph, he managed to lose his dread of the Reverend Wilson, the difficult and demanding Vicar of Wakefield.

But now what did the future hold? As a third son, he had a limited inheritance in land, but not one sufficient to make him a large planter, and in truth, he wasn't interested in that. During his travels these past few months, his passion for politics and government had hit him with full force.

He had observed the rancor the Treaty of Aix-la-Chapelle had evoked; George II was not a monarch who sat easily on this throne. The uprising of the Stuart Pretender's followers still lingered in the King's mind, despite the fact that Bonnie Prince Charlie's supporters had been roundly defeated. George II now fawned over Maria Theresa of Austria, anxious to confirm alliances with Austria and Russia that would guarantee the security of his beloved Hanover. Gossip in Vienna hinted that Maria Theresa was less than enchanted with her alliance with England and was warming toward France. This in turn could provoke the crafty Frederick II to align Prussia with England.

Richard Henry's head swam with impressions of Europe, the baroque charm of St. Mark's Square in Vienna, the sparkling canals of Amsterdam, the pervasive influence of France, which permeated Europe with the glittering power and style of Versailles. He was captivated by talk of the French King's mistress, Madame de Pompadour, the delicate, romantic new style of painting created by Chardin and Watteau, and the lively salons of Paris.

They moved slowly upriver, passing the myriad inlets and creeks that flowed inland to the Northern Neck plantations. "There's Pecatone, the house my sister Missy and her husband have refurbished!" Richard Henry cried excitedly as the great brick-and-timbered mansion appeared. An hour later, as the ship headed directly toward the Stratford wharf, Richard Henry scanned the crowded docks, waiting for the blur of white and black forms to enlarge into familiar faces.

"By Jove!" he exclaimed. Could that wiry lad jumping up and down on the landing be Arthur? Beside him stood the darker William, solid and shy-eyed at eleven, and poking his head between the two youngest Lee brothers was their best friend, Nat, Will West's boy.

"We saw you first, Richard Henry," Arthur yelled proudly. "William and Nat and I were fishin' when we saw your ship coming up the river. We ran and rang the bell till everybody came! Except Philip. He's gone to Colonel Tayloe's auction to buy a horse, but he'll be back this afternoon."

"Are you Rob Carter?" Alice asked, disentangling herself from Richard Henry's embrace.

"I am, m'lady." Rob gave her a courtly bow.

"Your uncle Landon Carter is here to fetch you. He waits at the house," she continued shyly.

"Frank and Thomas wanted to meet you," Arthur whispered, "but they had to be polite and wait with Councilor Carter, who didn't want to ride to the docks in the pony cart—probably thought it wasn't dignified enough." The youngest Lee giggled at the thought of the imperious Landon Carter bumping down the steep road in a cart.

"How did he know we were due this afternoon?" a puzzled Rob asked as they walked up the sandy shore.

"You were sighted off Sandy Point, and a messenger rode to Sabine Hall posthaste to carry the news," explained William, always a good source for information about his godfather, Landon Carter.

Once inside the manor house, Richard Henry and Rob stopped in the gentlemen's parlor by the west door. "What do you plan to do now that you're home?" Rob Carter asked as he toweled his face.

Richard Henry, his toilet complete, turned from the deep recessed window. "I'm not quite certain, except someday I would like to stand for the House of Burgesses."

"Ah," said Rob quickly, "that's just what I have on my mind! I'll wager you five pistoles that I sit in the Assembly before you!"

"Only if my credit is good," Richard Henry said, laughing. "I've not received my inheritance from my father's estate, so I've no cash to put up."

"Your name is your credit," Rob said warmly.

The young men proceeded down the passage to join Frank and Thomas Lee and Landon Carter for a welcoming brandy in the library. Then Rob and his uncle rose to leave. "I must get Rob to Sabine; we've a grand celebration planned," Colonel Carter explained.

When the Carter phaeton had disappeared down the lane toward Landon Carter's Rappahannock River plantation, Richard Henry turned from the doorway and strode through the house, his hungry eyes sweeping each room. Everything and everyone at Stratford looked the same, yet different.

Francis Lightfoot, for example. He had never been apart from his brother for a single night until he had gone to England, and the bond between them went deep. Now eighteen, Frank was extraordinarily handsome, slender and tightly built, with his father's coal-black hair and startling blue eyes, still warm as ever. But there was a new tautness about his mouth.

Something was amiss at Stratford Hall. Richard Henry sensed it in William's downcast gaze and in Arthur's quick, nervous gestures. He had felt it in Will West's smothering embrace at dockside.

But the greatest change had fallen over Alice. When he left, she had been a laughing-eyed little girl, doted on by all, especially by their mother, who had delighted in curling her long blond hair with an ivory comb. Now her hair fell carelessly, and though there was still great natural beauty in her face, it seemed wan and solemn.

Entertained by stories and anecdotes of Richard Henry's European adventures, the family was finishing the last course of dinner when a door at the far end of the house slammed and the forceful click of boot heels reverberated down the hall.

Alice's face turned ashen as Richard Henry rose to greet his eldest brother, the dark-eyed autocratic master of Stratford Hall. For a long moment the brothers eyed each other. Then with a roar of pleasure, Philip threw open his arms in welcome.

"You were always his favorite," Francis Lightfoot told Richard Henry later in the privacy of the library. "No"—Frank held up his hand—"it is all right. Perhaps your presence will have a good effect on him."

"It's really been so bad, then?"

"Bad is hardly the word. How can I explain what he's like?" Frank peered restlessly around the room until his eyes settled on a portrait of Thomas Lee done by a limner who had passed through Westmoreland County some ten years earlier. It captured both the likeness and the character of its subject.

"Where our father was strong, kind, caring," Frank began in measured words, "Philip is arrogant, cruel, and insensitive. He browbeats William, humiliates Arthur, ignores Alice, and always he plays the brutal master with the servants. He doesn't browbeat me—I won't allow it. But obviously he has the upper hand and the power." Frank broke off. "I have been hoping that you would stand by me."

Richard Henry asked gently, "Has Thomas been no help?"

Frank snorted. "Thomas kowtows to Philip. He says things like 'Don't come down so hard on them, Philip,' or, 'That was a bit unfair,' but that is all. Anyway," Frank added sardonically, "Thomas is in love with one of the Aylett girls, and that takes up most of his attention."

"And Missy has been no help, either, I suppose—too far away to do much good," Richard Henry mused.

Frank nodded. "That, and she is consumed with the affairs of Pecatone. She and Philip have never got on well, so anything she said would probably just make matters worse. But you, you are another story. He'll listen if you handle him right. We all live such a wretched existence that you must see if you can't make life more bearable. The main problem is that Philip hasn't even begun to settle Father's will," Frank continued. "None of us can claim our inheritance until that is done, and believe me, he is in no hurry. So, we all remain firmly under Philip's thumb at Stratford, having to beg for everything, while he plays lord of the manor."

Later, in the soft dusk of the June evening, Richard Henry lit a candle and wandered the rooms of the house. He stood for a long time in the great hall, looking at the large oval portrait of his mother, painted by the same hand that had painted his father. In her late thirties, serious in expression, one long back curl brought around to rest on her shoulder, the woman in the painting hardly suggested the sparkling, shining-eyed, truly beautiful lady he remembered.

He ran his hand over the surface of the piano-forte, almost able to hear the music she had drawn from it. What a multitude of bright, triumphal events had taken place in this elegant ballroom—christenings, balls, dances, Missy's wedding. Would there ever again be happy moments here?

It seemed to Richard Henry he must now serve as crossbar of the Lee family—the middle child who holds his father's sons together.

Richard Henry's presence seemed to bring an uneasy peace to Stratford Hall in the months that followed. Philip grew surprisingly jovial, and at Christmas gave generous presents. Then, at dinner, just as the flaming plum pudding was served, he hurled his cannonball.

"I have come to a decision," the master of Stratford Hall announced in his commanding voice, sweeping the dinner table with penetrating eyes. "It is my duty to educate and prepare William and Arthur so they can make their way in this world, and I have done much hard thinking about their future occupations. A family agent will eventually be needed in England to broker Lee tobacco. I have decided that William is to be prepared as that agent." He looked sternly at the pensive, dark-browed William. "You will leave the classroom immediately and learn the business of this plantation. As for Arthur"—he turned to the fine-featured younger boy—"I plan to send you to Eton . . . eventually to become a physican."

"But I don't—"

"My decisions will not be disputed," Philip shouted.

With a strangled cry, Arthur pushed back his chair and ran from the dining room.

"Give him credit. At least Phil is thinking of their future," Richard Henry told Frank as the two rode to the west glade to hunt quail later that day. "And he has not chosen badly for them. It was more his manner, the way he did it, than what he said."

"You are far too charitable. Phil is despicable!"

"We must be reasonable. We have little choice so long as Philip controls our money. I dare say battles remain to be fought with him."

Despite the problems with his oldest brother, Richard Henry was delighted to be back at Stratford. There was no denying it took some adjusting. He had come from crowded, exciting European cities. Here in the quiet Virginia countryside, everything stood out in bold relief—the apples in their silver bowl serene on the dining-room table, the rain plaintive on Stratford's roof and windowpanes. How silent Stratford was, without the city sounds of carriage wheels, street urchins, bells. He enjoyed hearing the faint, melodic slave songs in the evening, glimpsing Arthur, William, and Nat West as they trudged across the plantation's horizon, plumbing the subtle changes in Alice. What he could not understand was his restlessness, his sense of purposelessness.

The Tidewater, 1752

"You're planning to leave for Williamsburg at daybreak?" Frank looked up from the saddle strap he was mending by the fire. "You couldn't pay me to go anywhere with Phil! Don't count on anything but a cold, unpleasant ride with a rude, officious companion."

Richard Henry thought ruefully of Frank's words after five days of slogging through mud and rain-swollen creeks and crossing rivers on tossing ferries that threatened to capsize at any moment. His face was chapped, his fingers numb to the bone, and there was little rest between the cold, damp sheets of the vile country hostelries where they had spent their nights. In those taverns Richard Henry saw Philip at his hot-tempered worst, haughtily demanding attention and respect—once with a raised crop—from the harassed tavern keepers. Only when he caught sight of the red brick Wren Building of the College of William and Mary and glimpsed the cheerful candlelight streaming from the windows of the houses and shops of Williamsburg, did Richard Henry's spirits rise. Their destination, Green Spring, lay ten miles beyond the capital.

That afternoon, bathed and dressed for dinner, Richard Henry came up from one of the guest houses that spread like sheltering wings from the great house to join the party in the library. Philip be damned! The stimulation of this lively company, talk of politics and gossip mingled with the swish of ladies' skirts, the warmth of the fire, and the glow of the red wine, gave him an unusual sense of well-being.

"A great man, your father." The paunchy new governor, Robert Dinwiddie, sympathetically pressed Richard Henry's hand. "A man of extraordinary vision—a pity he died before learning the King had chosen him Virginia's first native-born governor. England needs this caliber of leadership in her most favored colony. I hope you will follow in his footsteps."

Philip, dashing in a scarlet coat piped with gold braid, moved to Richard Henry's side just in time to catch the governor's last sentence. He bowed over the governor's ring. "That, sir, is surely my intent."

"How are affairs at Stratford?" Phil Ludwell inquired of Richard Henry at the dinner table. "I worry about the young ones, particularly Alice. Calamities are hard to bear when one is young."

"Calamities are hard to bear at any age, particularly when expensive," the heavy-set William Byrd III interjected sardonically before Richard Henry could reply. "Did you hear of our fire at Westover?" Will bent his dark head close. "It began with an accident, a bloody foolish accident!" Byrd obviously relished retelling the dramatic tale; there was more than a hint of the Black Swan's engaging charm in the son's delivery. "It was two and a half years ago, on an August night that was hot, tinder-dry. Actually, it had been a glorious day, for we had christened a new son that afternoon, and the house was overflowing with guests. Hardly had we retired for the night when shouts of 'Fire! Fire!' rang from above us! The housekeeper had turned her back as she brewed lotion over a brazier on the third floor, and the curtains, swept by a breeze, touched the coals. Soon the entire third floor was ablaze."

"How did you ever put the fire out before the house was destroyed?" asked Richard Henry, fascinated by the account.

"A water line, my lad, what else?" Will rolled his slanting Byrd-blue eyes heavenward. "My overseer organized a human chain of guests and servants and slaves that ran from the river right into the house, and bucket after leather bucket was passed up through the night until we had soaked the second floor and flooded the first. By dawn, the fire was out, but what a soggy, scorched mess. Cost me an enormous sum to refurbish—in fact, we are still at it! I am now resolved to have only the finest for my Westover."

Extravagant, flamboyant though he might be, Byrd was now being modest. The story was that, after he shepherded his wife, Eliza, with their newborn son and their guests to the lawn, he realized that his wife's two young brothers, Charles and Edward Carter of Shirley, were not accounted for, and courageously dashed up to the third floor and led them out as the roof began to collapse.

Richard Henry's eye, moving down the table, was caught by the glistening white shoulder of the fetching blond Lucy Grymes, who was flirting with one of the Randolphs. Cousin Henry Lee had better keep his eye on this one if he intends to wed her, he thought, amused and envious.

"I attempt a most difficult and perplexing task." Governor Dinwiddie commanded everyone's attention. "A strange divergence of viewpoints exists between the Englishmen on this side of the Atlantic and those on the other. As your governor, I find myself right in the middle! Virginians do not wish to see themselves as they are—servants of King George the Second. They wish to make their own rules. My instructions, which I receive from the Crown, will I fear be looked on by the Assembly merely as 'guidelines' to be altered or, more likely, ignored."

"No subjects are more loyal than Virginians!" the young lawyer Peyton Randolph returned hotly.

"Loyal to the King, I grant you, but not to the principles of the empire," Dinwiddie faltered.

Richard Henry understood what Dinwiddie was aiming at, unpleasant though the accusation was. British imperial theory rested upon the premise that all major nations compete for precious metals and goods and a favorable balance of trade while maintaining economic self-sufficiency. The colonies, as producers of raw materials and as purchasers of the Mother Country's finished goods, were thus important to England's overall economic health, but they were seen for the most part only as strategic outposts existing solely for the benefit of the Mother Country, their inhabitants mere menials in the service of England. God knows, he had gotten a stomachful of that haughty attitude while at school in England! But, in truth, as Virginia grew more self-sufficient materially, her ties to the Mother Country were reduced to those of trade, tradition, and loyalty to the King.

"Our governor makes a valid point." All eyes were now riveted on Richard Henry. "England's Glorious Revolution of 1688 established the supremacy of the legislature over the Crown. We Virginians have an assembly—our own small Parliament, if you will—so we do not see the necessity to deal with the Parliament in England, which does not understand our needs. Yet the same revolution bound the Crown to the houses of government. Though we might wish otherwise, they move as one. Still, it seems Parliament has the louder voice in the partnership." Turning to Dinwiddie, Richard Henry concluded, "If Virginians look on your instructions simply as guidelines, sir, it is because our assembly ought to have the right to make all decisions relating to our daily life, except those about trade and war."

Later Philip took Richard Henry aside. "Oh, but you were clever at dinner, expounding on political theory as if you were the president of the council himself," he sneered. "Remember that you are not in any position to deliver such weighty speeches to your betters. Why, you are still a schoolboy, wet behind the ears. At least wait until you are a member of the House of Burgesses."

"Thank you for your advice," Richard Henry shot back. "I intend to run for the Assembly at the first opportunity—perhaps even against you!"

Eager to escape Philip's overbearing presence, Richard Henry accepted the governor's invitation to visit in Williamsburg. The next day he walked with nostalgia the muddy streets of the capital, marveling at the new shops and houses added since his last visit three and a half years before. He passed the mapmakers and explorers Peter Jefferson and Joshua Fry wrapped in their greatcoats, as they headed for Raleigh's Tavern. If he were less shy, he would congratulate them on the new map of the colony, which the governor had described the night before as "superb."

Idly Richard Henry was making his way up the Duke of Gloucester Street toward the new Capitol, which was to replace the one destroyed by fire, when a tall figure caught his eye. There was something about the breadth of the shoulders, the cut of the head, that he recognized instantly. "George Washington!" he called out.

When George turned, Richard Henry saw with shock deep circles under his friend's eyes and a face ravaged by what had to be a recent bout with the pox. "By God, George, what brings you to Williamsburg in the coldest, wettest part of the winter?" Richard Henry all but stammered the words.

Washington's eyes lit up with pleasure. He clasped Richard Henry's outstretched hand gratefully. "Am I pleased to see that red head of yours!" George's cheek twitched slightly. "Actually, I am just off a ship, thirty-six miserable days from Barbados. I carry dispatches to Governor Dinwiddie from my brother Lawrence."

"Splendid! As it happens, I'm at the governor's house myself. But how is Lawrence?" Richard Henry asked. "Father wrote last year that he suffers from a vexing coughing ailment."

George shook his head in despair. "Lawrence is worse. His physicians suggested a change in climate, and my brother, not wanting to subject Nancy and their baby, Jenny, to the long sea voyage, took me along instead. Barbados was lush and beautiful enough, but then I got the pox." He indicated the ugly scabs on his face in sad apology.

The two young men had begun to walk through the misty winter rain. "I am truly concerned about Lawrence." George's voice broke slightly. "He simply must get well, for Nancy and the baby and . . . well, we all depend on him."

"I know what you are feeling." Richard Henry sensed a familiar knot forming in his own throat as he thought of his father, who had given such reassurance and stability to the family at Stratford.

Robert Dinwiddie and his family were living in a temporary house on the Palace Green while the Governor's Palace underwent extensive renovations. After dinner, Richard Henry withdrew with his host and George to the governor's study.

"Very interesting, your brother's letters concerning the Ohio Company," the governor said to Washington. Then he turned to Richard Henry.

"I will discuss the subject openly, since George and I are members and you are a son of the company's past president. But I must insist that you keep all that I say to you quite privy.

"As you both know, the Treaty of Aix-la-Chapelle calmed Europe, but the rivalry over our western territories continues unabated. The French have grown more aggressive and now move down from Canada to reassert their claims to the Ohio Valley. Your father's death was a tremendous loss to the Ohio Company, Richard Henry, a loss in prestige, political leverage at the Capitol, and momentum. But," Dinwiddie said, turning to George, "even hampered by poor health, your brother Lawrence has been infinitely resourceful as the company's new president. He and the treasurer, George Mason, have given the company new life."

"But I gather, sir, there are problems besides the French?" Richard Henry suggested.

"A myriad of problems," Dinwiddie acknowledged. "For one, those treacherous Indians can never be depended upon. For another, Pennsylvania contends that the lands at the fork of the Ohio are not ours, but theirs. They have a reasonable case; the lands in Virginia's charter of 1609 and Pennsylvania's charter of 1681 somewhat overlap. But we'll win that simply by settling the land first with Virginians, even new Virginians!"

"You mean Scottish, Irish, and Germans?" Richard Henry asked.

"Whatever," Dinwiddie replied with a wave of his hand.

"It would appear, sir, given your own loyalty to the Ohio Company, that your problem is right here in the capital," Richard Henry responded.

"You are sharp indeed, young man. Yes, the King's attorney, Peyton Randolph, is an ardent supporter of our rival, the Loyal Company. It's a sticky wicket, I tell you." Dinwiddie puffed angrily on his clay pipe.

As he rode back to Green Spring in the cold afternoon gloom, Richard Henry's mind turned over the governor's candid remarks. Land speculation and fur trade little interested him. What he did find fascinating was the contrasting characters and the juxtaposition of ideas—for example, the governor with his merchant's mind, pitted against those wily Randolphs! Then there was Uncle Phil Ludwell, who had inherited power and a seat on the King's Council that he did not wish to use, opposed to clever Will Byrd III, who, like Philip Lee, would one day inherit that same power. Both would delight in exploiting it to further their own interests!

Richard Henry spurred his horse down the mired road. As for himself, if he could just win a seat in the House of Burgesses! He could not help contrasting himself to George Washington, who at least had a profession. Being a surveyor well suited George; he was interested not in the political realm but in the practical—things that could be charted and measured.

The Tidewater, 1754

Although the Neck was blanketed with a thick cover of snow, the Lees of Stratford Hall journeyed to Wakefield, Austin Washington's plantation on Pope's Creek, on the day after Christmas in 1754.

Fragrant with the aromas of goose and chestnuts roasting on the fire, the frame farmhouse bustled with guests, including Anne Washington's pretty young Aylett stepsisters. Richard Henry was still stamping the snow from his boots on the wooden porch when he caught sight of George standing by the mantel. He smiled with anticipation. It had been almost three years, and they had much to catch up on. His own life was lashed to the strained activity at Stratford Hall, but his friend had been in the thick of events almost constantly.

As Governor Dinwiddie had predicted, the French were moving into the Ohio Valley, and had penetrated halfway from Lake Erie to the western ridge of the Alleghenies by the summer of 1753. Dinwiddie frantically begged for permission to build forts along the Ohio. George II ordered a warning notice sent to the French in the Ohio, a communiqué the colony's new adjutant, Major George Washington, volunteered to deliver.

When George's journal of the mission was published in the *Virginia Gazette*, Richard Henry read it avidly. Accompanied by the veteran woodsman Christopher Gist, Washington had ridden northwest into the wintry Ohio wilderness, crossing high mountains and traversing the rough country of the Youghiogheny Valley, through the sleet-glazed forests and icy streams of the Ohio basin to Fort Le Boeuf, which lay within fifteen miles of Lake Erie.

Dinwiddie's letter, setting out the British demand for the peaceful departure of the French from English soil, was presented to the fort's commander. "One of his officers replied that the country belonged to the French," Washington wrote, "that it was their absolute design to take possession of the Ohio, and by G—— they would do it."

Unsuccessful, Washington and Gist returned to Williamsburg early in January 1754. "But if I know George," Frank had said, "he has returned with a head full of figures, the precise number of French soldiers, the exact dimensions of their forts, down to how many canoes and muskets they possess."

Richard Henry knew only the barest outline of what had happened next. Commissioned a breveted lieutenant colonel, George had been dispatched to Alexandria to raise and train three hundred soldiers to march under Joshua Fry to the garrisoned storehouse of the Ohio Company at the fork of the Ohio and the Monongahela rivers.

Tragically, Joshua Frye had fallen from his horse and died on the march west, so at twenty-two Washington had become the little army's senior field officer—"Led it straight to disaster," Uncle Phil reported from Williamsburg.

George had discovered with dismay that the French had built a strong fortification at the fork of the Ohio, Fort Duquesne. Cautiously he positioned his troops at Little Meadows and built a palisaded stockade, Fort Necessity. Should he attack Duquesne or wait for the French assault? What followed was a war of nerves heightened by small confrontations, then a savage battle with the French and their Indian allies in which Fort Necessity fell. Not only had George lost a hundred men, he had also surrendered the only British outpost west of the Alleghenies.

"I have heard it said that Colonel Washington journeyed the entire one hundred and sixty miles to Williamsburg in utter silence," Uncle Phil had written. "He arrived and found himself in some disgrace. Some say he was rash, others that he had suffered from inexperience and poor judgment. He and Governor Dinwiddie are no longer on the best of terms, but young Washington is Fairfax's protégé, and that sustains him."

"By Jove, you are a hero!" Richard Henry now gave his friend's hand a hard, affectionate grasp. Despite his recent ordeal, George looked stronger and leaner than three years before. The pockmarks had faded, leaving only faint scars on his face, now so tan after months out of doors that his eyes blazed a startling shade of blue.

"Hardly a hero!" George's smile flickered.

"But you are—even the King knows you by name. I read that he laughed when told your remark: 'I heard the bullets whistle and, believe me, there is something charming in the sound.' "

George smiled wryly. "And the King's reply to that was, 'He would not say so, if he had been used to hear many.' Actually, I have just resigned my commission," George announced brusquely, staring into the fire. "Not that I don't like the militia . . . My inclinations are strongly bent to arms." He hesitated. "But you, old buck, I've not heard a word of you or from you!"

"I wish I had some interesting adventures to tell. I am horribly restless, yet I feel compelled to stay on at Stratford."

"Why?" With the iron tongs George was lifting a crackling chestnut from the roaster. "I thought you talked of studying law. Why don't you go down to Williamsburg for a while?"

Richard Henry looked about to be sure no one was near. "We've been having a hellish time. Philip keeps cracking his whip over the rest of us. Now we are like a tinderbox ready to explode! Frank went to court and had his guardianship changed to our cousin Henry Lee, thinking it might give him better leverage to fight for his inheritance. God, what a pitched battle Phil put up over that! We were forced to stand by Frank or be smashed by Philip. At this point Frank, Alice, William, and Arthur are also under Henry's guardianship. We all, including Thomas and myself, have brought complaints against Phil in the Westmoreland courts. It's one damned mess! But by God, George," Richard Henry apologized, "I didn't mean to bend your ear so with my problems. You've had bad enough times yourself!"

"That is all changed." George stood very still, his hands shoved into his pockets. "I told you, I have given up my commission. I'm not a quitter, but it was just one thing after another. First the loss of Fort Necessity, for which I was the scapegoat." George reddened. "You see, I was forced to surrender during a blinding midnight rain, with an interpreter who hardly spoke French. When I got to Williamsburg I was told I had unknowingly admitted to assassinating a French patrol party! Then, Governor Dinwiddie tried to badger me to go back and fight the French, but it is a hopeless prospect, for they have every advantage in men and supplies. The crowning blow," George continued in a steely voice, "is that all colonial regiments are now to be commanded by officers not above the rank of captain. I would be dropped from a colonel to a captain, and lose the King's commission in the bargain. Every half-pay English officer would outrank me! No!" George continued with emotion. "I devote my energies to Mount Vernon."

Lawrence Washington had died in July 1752, soon after returning from his exhausting and futile visit to Barbados. Six months later his widow, Nancy, had married Richard Henry's cousin George Lee, of Mount Pleasant. "Did you know," George went on proudly, "I have arranged to rent Mount Vernon from Nancy's husband? We signed the lease two weeks ago . . . fifteen pounds of tobacco a year—a stiff price, I warrant, but it is what I really want."

Richard Henry nodded. George had succeeded his brother as adjutant of the colony. And now to rent Mount Vernon! George seemed strangely driven to pick up the unfinished pieces of his dead brother's life.

George's tone lightened. "I have already settled in—in fact, I've even given a card party! Sally Fairfax has come over any number of times, bringing her housekeeper from Belvoir to help me get the place in order. Sally pities my bachelor state, so she's been helping me decide just what I need to order from England."

It seemed to Richard Henry that George's voice carried an unusual note of pleasure. "There must be a lady in your life, dear fellow," Richard Henry teased. "Is she a Carter, a Beverly . . . ah, perhaps the youngest Fairfax? Now that you have a house, I should think it is high time that you find a wife to keep your fires bright and your bed warm! Then you would not need to run Sally Fairfax back and forth from Belvoir."

George laughed. "Actually, I seem to spend most of my time now with married folk. George William and Sally are my closest friends, and I frequently see the Carlyles in Alexandria. We play a bit of cards, dance, talk. I am quite content."

But it seemed to Richard Henry that George made the last remark too casually.

As the guests began to move toward the dining room for dinner, Richard Henry saw Francis Lightfoot, charming rogue, standing in the candlelit arch talking with Annie Aylett, the younger of Anne Aylett Washington's stepsisters. A lovely, fresh-faced little thing she was: why, her waist looked so small, he could put his hands around it with ease. In fact, he longed to! Trust Frank to have singled her out.

"I choose Miss Annie Aylett as my dinner partner," Richard Henry summoned his courage to challenge.

"Too late!" Frank grinned broadly. "I have already asked her. She has the face of an angel and would break my heart if she dined beside anyone else tonight!"

The Tidewater, 1755

One day in mid-February 1755, Philip returned home from a trip to Williamsburg and thrust a newspaper into Richard Henry's hand. "There! Go fight the French and be a hero like your friend George! Major General Edward Braddock and His Majesty's Coldstream Guards have descended upon Williamsburg, with two more regiments to follow. Virginia militia are invited—indeed, expected—to join Braddock when his forces march against Fort Duquesne this spring. Here is your chance, my boy—if you have the stomach for combat!"

Washington's defeat at Fort Necessity had finally galvanized the British. The Duke of Cumberland, the aggressive warrior son of George II, had proposed a grand design to eliminate the French from the American continent once and for all. English forces would attack Fort Duquesne as well as the lake forts Crown Point and Niagara, and Fort Acadia in Canada. The Earl of Halifax worried that a standard European baggage train equipped with caissons, gun carriages, loaded supply wagons, and four twelve-pound cannons could not negotiate the forest and mountain paths to reach the Ohio. But his objections were overruled.

"Yes, I know what you're thinking." Philip anticipated Richard Henry's response. "I am commander in chief of Westmoreland's militia, but the idea of marching off to fight Indians and chase the Frenchmen doesn't appeal to me one whit. If you would like to call up the regiment in my place and do the honors, be my guest."

Phil's sarcasm couldn't dull the excitement rising in Richard Henry. Here was a chance to stem his restlessness, to push his world beyond the boundaries of Stratford Hall, to get his life under way.

Given the fervor of the moment, it was not difficult to raise a unit of the Westmoreland militia. Within two weeks, Richard Henry had recruited a corps of over a dozen young men from the premier families of the county— Blands, Tayloes, Wormeleys, Corbins, and Ayletts. Richard Hall joined as their physician. But cousin Henry was the only other Lee who could be induced to join. Even Francis Lightfoot put off his brother's pleas. "I am with you in spirit, but I was really not cut out to be a soldier."

Equipped from their families' private stores, mounted on their own horses, and led by Captain Richard Henry Lee, the enthusiastic if not overly disciplined band set out on a windy March morning for Alexandria, the departure point for Braddock's westward push.

Mount Vernon, 1755

"I never would have thought it," George Washington said when the spirited contingent arrived at Mount Vernon on April 1. "Richard Henry Lee, you are the very last man I would have expected to enlist! Do you realize how physically punishing our expedition is going to be?"

"I am quite prepared," Richard Henry said a bit defensively. "I gather, since you refer to 'our' expedition, you have changed your mind about the military?"

"With some reluctance," George admitted. "I hate leaving Mount Vernon without a manager, but I badly want to go."

"What unit will you command?" Richard Henry pressed.

"I told you I wouldn't accept a militia command, and I haven't. Braddock has offered me a place as a volunteer aide on his staff. If I can get my affairs in order here at Mount Vernon, I shall give my services free."

What a clever compromise, Richard Henry thought. George, once a colonel, would not have to settle for a militia captaincy and would be in a more powerful position as a respected aide, part of the "family," eating at the general's table.

George led Richard Henry into the simply furnished drawing room, where several clusters of people were taking tea and biscuits. Most wore riding clothes, and, judging from the panting of George's favorite hound, who lay on the hearth, the party had just returned from a morning of fox hunting.

"So you and your Westmoreland companions offer your services to General Braddock, do you, sir?" Sally Fairfax's confident eyes, slightly challenging, searched Richard Henry's face. "If you have the courage and the ability of our friend Mr. Washington, I am certain you will do well."

Sally was a tall, willowy girl with dancing dark eyes and an intriguing smile, an intimate smile that hinted you and she shared a secret. Richard Henry could not help liking her.

Amazing, thought Richard Henry, how full of confidence George seemed with the wealthy Fairfaxes and their friends! Intrigued, he watched as the broad-shouldered host helped Sally remove her green beaver riding hat; for a moment it seemed as if George were charged with lightning.

Behind the tea table stood a young man who chose to observe the stylish group from a vantage point above his teacup.

Richard Henry extended his hand. "You're George Mason of Gunston Hall, downriver. Our fathers were friends years ago. You are treasurer of the Ohio Company, are you not?"

The dark-browed Mason nodded sardonically. "A company whose land you are about to offer your services to defend."

Richard Henry stiffened. "I can't say I envision my involvement quite that way. I would never qualify as a mercenary. Count it an act of remembrance to my father and his dream of settling the western frontier—though, to tell the truth, I hadn't thought of it as an effort solely in behalf of the company."

Mason shrugged. "Have you had the opportunity to meet General Braddock or any of his officers yet?"

Richard Henry shook his head. "Not yet!"

"He is a difficult bastard. I chanced to meet him at Carlyle's house. He and his 'family,' as he calls his top aides"—Mason smiled slightly—"they have been cordially welcomed in the city and given the finest accommodations and entertainment. But neither he nor his officers seem in the slightest appreciative or even congenial. They complain about out dense forests and the rolling Virginia hills, which seem formidable to them in contrast to Ireland, where they have recently been stationed."

"Good God, these tiny coastline hills are nothing compared to the Shenandoah and the Allegheny mountains they are about to cross!"

George Mason took another long sip of tea. "It was only my impression. Braddock has not been well since he arrived in Alexandria. Maybe his surly manner can be laid to that, though I did overhear one of his haughty officers comment that dining in a sweltering Virginia house, served by half-naked blacks, made him think he was dining in Dante's inferno!"

That evening, as the company made their pallets in the straw of the Mount Vernon barn, Richard Henry said to his cousin, "I wonder about Braddock and what lies ahead."

"And I was dwelling on what lies behind." Henry had recently won the hand of Lucy Grymes and was building a manor house, Leesylvania, on property his father had willed him south of Mount Vernon; his older brother, the voluble, good-natured bachelor Squire Richard, had inherited Lee Hall. "Still, I wanted to come. It is my duty," Henry reasoned. "I hear an advance party of Braddock's men already builds a base camp, called Cumberland, at the Ohio Company's Potomac River storehouse on Will's Creek. No doubt we shall be stationed there for several weeks for training before marching west." Henry yawned. "It's exciting, but I miss my Lucy and home."

On the other side of Richard Henry, Richard Hall suddenly spoke. "I wouldn't be here at all if I had a wife at home—someone I loved."

"Why aren't you yet tethered, Richard?" Henry asked curiously. "You're a good-looking chap, and while our fortunes rise and fall with the price of tobacco, you always have a steady supply of customers!"

Richard Hall returned the salvo. "Aye, Henry, yet many of my patrons have limited means. As to my bachelor state, my hours would make a tavern wench blanch. The wife for me must be a strong, independent woman. So far I've met only one that fills my bill of sale, and she's already taken." His voice grew soft. "I think I find myself in somewhat the same situation as your friend George!"

"What situation?" Richard Henry was mystified.

"Haven't you noticed him around Mrs. Fairfax—Sally, I believe she's called? There's a man infatuated if ever I've seen one. Totally smitten in an affair of the heart that's destined to be unrequited—unless, of course, they choose to defy society. But only kings and lords can get by with that." Richard Hall's voice grew sleepy. "Defy society?" he repeated slowly. "I would not be above that if the woman I love were that much in love with me."

George appeared at dawn at the barn door. "My mother arrived quite unexpectedly late last evening from Ferry Farm, intent on dissuading me from this campaign." He attempted a smile. "I shall hear her out, but the madam can be quite fierce! Here"—he handed Richard Henry a note— "would you be kind enough to carry this to the general's aide-de-camp, Robert Orme? Despite the madam's objections, I am accepting Braddock's offer."

Alexandria, 1755

In high spirits, Richard Henry and his friends packed up their gear for the morning's trek into the port of Alexandria—where they arrived just in time. At the edge of the shallow waters north of the docks, General Braddock and his aides were just boarding small boats to be rowed out to the *Centurion*, which lay at anchor in the river.

Richard Henry was painfully self-conscious as he marched with his contingent down the dock, for every eye was upon them. The general, a stocky, gray-haired, strong-chinned man, watched for a moment, then stepped into the boat and ordered the sailors to push off.

Richard Henry faltered, torn between outrage and embarrassment. On an abrupt signal from the commodore, a tall man with kind eyes standing at the far end of another boat, a seaman pulled his rowboat back ashore. Mustering his courage, Richard Henry moved quickly to explain his mission as Commodore Keppel stepped ashore.

"Come aboard with us, Mr. Lee," the commodore invited him courteously. "The general has a meeting aboard the *Centurion* shortly, but I am certain he will have a few moments for you afterward."

An hour later Braddock sent for Richard Henry. "Be about your business, sir!" he ordered crisply, "for I've no time to waste."

Bristling at Braddock's curtness, Richard Henry proceeded to offer his unit's services to Braddock.

The general immediately shook his head. "By God, man, I've no place for provincials untrained in warfare! If you colonials were competent, there'd be no reason to call us in from the seas to expel the French. You're at best an inefficient lot with no discipline and little organization." Braddock rose, ending their meeting. "Take that motley bunch back to their farms and alehouses. That's what you're suited for. It's obvious you must leave your defense to British soldiers!"

Admiral Keppel gave Richard Henry a sympathetic pat on the shoulder as the shattered young Virginian started down the rope ladder of the *Centurion*. "It may be just as well," he called after him. "Who knows, you might have got a bullet in your belly."

Preferable, Richard Henry gritted his teeth, to the prospect of telling his men of Braddock's rejection.

The Tidewater, 1755

For days afterward, days that blended into months, whenever Richard Henry allowed himself the pain of remembering that meeting with the harsh, mocking Edward Braddock, he was consumed with anger and resentment. He had been prepared to give his life for England, only to be ridiculed as a provincial, a clod, because he had nothing to offer but blind loyalty. What was it his father had said about committed loyalty, reasoned loyalty?

"You aren't destined to be a soldier," Francis Lightfoot offered philosophically. "Leave that to George and pursue what you do best."

"What?" Richard Henry asked sharply. "What do I do best?"

Frank's blue eyes were amused. "Well, you do *think* rather well. In fact, you think and write very well."

Despite his anguish, Richard Henry followed with high interest George's involvement in Braddock's expedition, depending on Austin Washington at Wakefield for much of his information. "Our youngest brother, Jack, is managing Mount Vernon for George, so he was able to ride with Braddock to Fort Cumberland at the end of April," Austin reported. "George says the general is overwhelmed and disheartened by the complications of dealing with the colonists. The Quakers don't want to fight, and the Swiss and German farmers have no British spirit or loyalty. They offered to sell their grain to his army at inflated prices but refused to furnish the wagons necessary for the campaign. A newspaper chap named Ben Franklin was dispatched by the Pennsylvania Proprietary to persuade the Lancaster County farmers to offer their wagons to the expedition—offer, George writes, or have them taken by force! Franklin posted handbills in German and English all over western Pennsylvania. Quite an effective advertisement it was!"

Richard Henry smiled. "I read in the *Pennsylvania Gazette* that when Franklin warned him about the cunning and brilliant attack skills of the Indians, Braddock said the Indians may, indeed, be a formidable enemy to the colonials, but not to the King's regular and disciplined troops."

But the boast was an empty one. In early July thirteen hundred Englishmen were ambushed and hacked to pieces by eight hundred Frenchmen and Indians in full battle dress, and the haughty Braddock was among those who fell.

"Thank God, George survived the disaster," Richard Henry told Austin. "More than survived! I hear he was the savior: weak from dysentery, he had himself strapped into his saddle and charged into the thick of fire.

Four bullets in his hat and jacket, and yet emerged unharmed . . . by damn, that George is lucky!"

"I told you," said Philip when he heard the tragic account, "a disaster from beginning to end. Fortune smiled when Braddock turned you down—a little more wanly on George, but at least he survived."

In September, the exhausted remnants of the British troops left for England, and Governor Dinwiddie was allowed to commission George Washington as a colonel and commander of all Virginia militia.

"Now Washington really has his hands full!" Francis Lightfoot exclaimed as he read the announcement of George's assignment in the *Virginia Gazette.* "Four hundred miles of Virginia frontier to defend, and a road Braddock carved from the Ohio to Alexandria for the French to march down whenever they please. The western Indians are falling over one another to join the French now that the English have been so roundly defeated. I fear our friend George has jumped from the thicket into the brier patch."

Richard Henry read the article more dispassionately. It wasn't that he didn't care, but at last his own life was taking on direction. Even Britain's formal declaration of war on France in February 1756 served only as a pale backdrop for the more immediate world he was beginning to create for himself.

The Tidewater, 1756

In April 1756 the Lees again dined with the Washingtons at Wakefield, and Richard Henry found himself gazing across the table into the captivating black eyes of that sprig of a girl, Annie Aylett. She had always fascinated him, and it was not just her appealing beauty: she had a way of looking him over that reduced him to tremors.

In the course of their game of Break the Pope's Neck, with Phil as the Pope and Richard Henry as a friar, he found himself clasping Annie in his arms as she ran in mock fear from the Pope's judgment. "How old are you, Annie?" he whispered urgently.

"Eighteen," she whispered back, "quite old enough!"

The Tidewater, 1757

They were married on a December morning in 1757. It was a small, elegant wedding held at Hominy Hall, the Northern Neck home of Colonel James

Steptoe, whom Annie's mother had married after the death of William Aylett. Following the ceremony, Richard Henry brought Annie to Stratford
Hall.

"You must live with me," Phil declared engagingly. "Indeed, I can't do
without you. The house is empty, with Thomas now married to Annie's sister
Mary and living in Stafford County and Francis Lightfoot settled on his lands
in Loudoun County."

The idea of moving to the lands he had inherited in Prince William
County held no appeal for Richard Henry. All he desired were Annie, whose
innocent pleasure in the intimacies of their marriage bed had captivated him,
his books in the library at Stratford Hall, and, with the help of God and the
Westmoreland voters, a seat in the Virginia House of Burgesses. Annie, thank
God, was agreeable to the arrangement.

She was, in fact, the most agreeable human being he had ever met,
going about her duties at Stratford Hall with light, quick steps, meeting him
in the halls and watching him across the table with laughing eyes. She
understood him instinctively. They did not really need to talk.

"I promise someday to build you a house of your own," he said, giving
her an impulsive kiss on the nape of her neck. "Philip has offered to lease
me some land below the cliffs."

But all thoughts of that were temporarily driven from his head, for the
new governor, Francis Fauquier, had called for an election for the House of
Burgesses. Philip Lee, now known as "Colonel Phil," had recently been ele-
vated from the Assembly to a seat on the King's Council; the incumbent
burgessman, Austin Washington, was ill and unable to stand for re-election,
so Richard Henry Lee was elected delegate from Westmoreland County.

The Tidewater, 1758

On September 14, 1758, Richard Henry, along with Richard Lee of Lee Hall,
Francis Lightfoot representing Loudoun County, Thomas, from Stafford
County, and Henry Lee, from Prince William County, all elected to terms in
the Assembly, swore their oaths of allegiance to the King.

"Come!" said Landon Carter as the ceremony closed, "let us repair to
the Apollo Room at the Raleigh for a drink to celebrate your first term as
burgesses and"—Carter's face grew grim—"commiserate about our defeats
in the Ohio."

Reports were starting to filter into Williamsburg that the most recent
British campaign against Fort Duquesne was failing. This assault was the re-

sult of a change of policy at Whitehall. The new prime minister, William Pitt, weary of the humiliating defeats in Europe, had committed all of England's force to winning the war with France on the American continent: General James Abercrombie was dispatched to the New York lakes to take Fort Ticonderoga; Sir Jeffrey Amherst was to attack the French fortress of Louisbourg in Nova Scotia; and General John Forbes and four thousand British regulars were sent to Virginia to take Fort Duquesne. There, a flying column of eight hundred British and colonial troops had been ambushed, and many prisoners were taken. Those British regulars who escaped owed their lives, it was said, to the guerrilla skills of the Virginia regiments, who knew how to fight on the Indians' terms. Nonetheless, English disdain for colonial commanders, like George Washington of the First Virginia Regiment and Will Byrd of the Second Virginia, continued unabated.

Much as Richard Henry had dreamed of being a part of the House, of taking a seat on the brown wooden benches of the Assembly Hall, and concerned as he was by the war against France in the west, he could not keep his mind on either. In early November he broke away and rode for Stratford.

Just in time. On a misty November night, after ten hours of arduous labor, Annie gave birth to a son. "My dearest Annie, my dearest Mrs. Lee..." was all he could say.

Later, when he thought back to that eventful autumn, it was that night that he remembered with the greatest clarity and pleasure. The excitement of Williamsburg faded with the recollection of Annie looking up at him with her tired shining eyes, the warmth of the baby in his arms, and the singing in celebration that drifted from the slave quarters to the big house.

In mid-December, Francis Lightfoot bent admiringly over his nephew's cradle. "A handsome lad, little Thomas, like all Lee men," he complimented, looking up at Richard Henry. "By the way, have you heard George Washington's smashing news? He arrived in Williamsburg just before I left. It seems after our first disastrous attack on Duquesne the situation changed abruptly."

As George had outlined it to Frank, the Iroquois, impressed by the valor of the English forces at the Great Lakes, decided abruptly to renew their alliance with the British. Word was sent to the Delawares, the mainstay of the French at Fort Duquesne, to slip away, leaving the stockade undermanned and vulnerable.

Thus the French had been forced to burn and abandon their fort at the fork of the Ohio, leaving only charred chimneys and smoking ruins. Immediately, the British erected Fort Pitt, named after Prime Minister William Pitt, on the same site. "Colonel William Byrd will remain as the resident commander. As for George, he is resigning and going back to Mount Vernon, this time for good!" Frank announced. "He plans to marry Martha Custis at the first of the year and will join you as a burgess at the spring session."

"That's marvelous news!" Richard Henry was astounded. "Leave it to him to marry the wealthiest widow in the colony. Daniel Parke Custis left his widow well off, and her monies and lands could transform Mount Vernon into the estate George wants it to be. And a burgessman, to boot! How did he get elected so quickly?"

"Fairfax influence," Frank replied quickly. "George has an uncanny knack for coming out all right in desperate situations, have you noticed?"

The Tidewater, 1759

Richard Henry had his first opportunity to meet Washington's new bride at the spring session of the Assembly, in February of 1759. He found her to be a delightful woman in her late twenties, perhaps a few months older than George. Small-boned, she was dressed in the latest fashion, a fawn-colored gown with soft box pleats that fell from her neck and ended in a long train, her hair powdered and adorned with tiny pearls. While Martha did not have the flair of George's Potomac friends, she was, Richard Henry observed, nonetheless charming, accustomed to the deference accorded the Custis clan. Her confidence seemed contagious, for George appeared unusually tranquil and happy in his marriage.

"There! I've won all your counters, even your ivory fish!" Annie cried triumphantly as she scooped up the gambling chips. On this languid October afternoon, Annie, Frank, and Richard Henry were playing loo in the parlor.

"Bested by a pretty lady!" Frank put down his tarot cards. "I think I shall retire to a fishing pole at the millpond!"

He had hardly spoken when nineteen-year-old Arthur Lee burst through the side door of Stratford Hall, calling in a strong, clear English accent for all to come greet him.

How different he was! Slim, blond, and bright-eyed, he fairly brimmed with vitality. And how English these years at Eton had made him. Richard Henry threw his arms around Arthur in a welcoming bear hug.

"I couldn't resist the chance to come home on Landon Carter's ship bound from Bristol to Sabine Hall," he explained. "I know it is expensive, but I missed you all so very much!" Even Colonel Phil offered no chastisement but inquired only when he would return to Europe to begin his medical studies.

"I am not really certain that medicine is the right choice for me," Arthur confessed. "I would much prefer to read law as you did, Phil. I believe politics is my bent."

"We have enough bookish, political men in this family. You haven't one acre of land to support you, my lad, and no prospects! Do you intend to drain my purse forever? You will return to England to study medicine."

"Come with us to Williamsburg for the fall Assembly. The whole family is going," Richard Henry consoled. "You can talk with Richard Hall, who has moved there. I am certain he will encourage you about medicine."

"Can Nat West come, too?" Arthur begged. "I haven't seen him in so long. He can valet William and me."

"England has done wonders for you, Arthur. I think it a good idea for William also to come with me when I move there next spring," Uncle Phil said with enthusiasm. "I plan to rent a large house in London and would welcome the addition of a young man in my household. And Arthur is to consider it his second home when he has time away from his medical studies."

Richard Henry saw Arthur grimace slightly. He turned to Richard Hall, who had been invited to dine with the Lees at Green Spring. "What would you say to encourage a young man to pursue a career in medicine, Dr. Hall?"

The young doctor looked probingly at Arthur. "I would not want to encourage him unless he had a love for the healing arts, an interest in biology, and a very strong stomach."

"The interest in biology I hold," Arthur admitted, "but then, many things hold my interest. How the devil am I to know which one I like best?"

Phil Lee tightened his fist on the carved arm of his chair. "I won't tolerate any more talk about it. I have decided that you will study medicine," he roared, "and you will study medicine! As for William's going along"—he looked at the dark-haired boy, who bit his lip nervously—"I don't think the time is ripe. At the moment I need him in Virginia more than in London!"

Diplomatically Uncle Phil changed the subject. "It would appear, gentlemen, that the war in the Ohio is winding down. You've heard General Montcalm lost the French garrison at Quebec. Despite the staggering costs of the war, there is a great mood of expectation in the council."

"To be sure, I've also felt a rising vigor and assertiveness in the House during the year I've been a member," Richard Henry stated. "I've decided it flows from our new burgesses from the new western counties. They are rugged planters, common farmers, not part of our ruling families, whose interests bind all the other burgesses. Their fresh ideas intrigue me."

In early November, Richard Henry was asked to present an important measure before the House. Just holding the paper in his hand made him tense, and the idea of speaking to the Assembly brought blood pounding to his head.

"You don't have to," Thomas said. "Say you are indisposed, that you suffer from the toothache. Landon Carter will do it for you."

The resolution proposed a heavy duty on the importation of slaves into Virginia. Richard Henry strongly supported the bill, for he believed slavery to be a vile and ugly practice. There was much opposition, for the bill flew in the face of Virginia's agrarian economy, which was based on high-volume production and cheap labor. Moreover, this resolution would price slaves beyond the means of the small farmers in the west, greatly increasing the value of slaves already owned by the big planters, with whom the western farmers vied. It posed a wrenching dilemma.

He returned to Green Spring in a thoughtful mood. "Don't let anyone bother me, Annie," he said, going into the study. "I need some time to think this problem out."

In the 1400's, Africans had been brought into the Indies by the Spanish to work their gold mines. For more than two centuries, the prosperous slave trade was the bulwark of European empires, as Portuguese, Dutch, French, and English men-of-war competed to transport slaves to the labor-hungry Spanish colonies in the New World.

The North American slave trade had followed shortly afterward, when New England ship captains discovered a lucrative triangular trade: rum from New England to be bartered for slaves in Africa, which were exchanged for sugar and molasses in the Indies, which were then transported back to New England and used to manufacture more rum. Imperceptibly, and then with a rush, the number of human chattels in Britain's North America grew, until in 1710 over forty thousand slaves populated the colonies. Now, Richard Henry thought with chagrin, there are ten times that many, and they are concentrated in Virginia. It was the accepted practice, the way of life, and yet not many men, outside of the profit-hungry traders, professed to like the system. Richard Henry could remember his father talking to William Byrd's father about the subject a long time ago at Stratford. While Tom Lee had seemed accepting of the practice, the Black Swan of Westover had grown red in the face: "Our scourge, our disgrace and sorrow," he had stormed. He had lavishly praised an edict of the new colony of Georgia that sought to exclude slavery and liquor from its boundaries. But the edict could not be sustained, for the white indentured English servants could not withstand the devastatingly hot southern fields. Governor Gooch had been another who openly despised the institution, claiming it a disservice to white as well as black, for it made white masters disdain physical work and look down on those who labored with their hands.

Slavery had in time served to draw a dramatic line between those who were free and those who were not. It underscored the fact that freedom was a privilege not to be taken lightly. But, Richard Henry wondered, was freedom a privilege? Was it not perhaps a right?

The subject weighed on his mind throughout the afternoon and evening as he labored to translate his thoughts into words. Suddenly William and Arthur burst into the study, their eyes blazing. "You must do something, Richard Henry," Arthur cried. "Phil is planning to sell Nat West to Colonel Tayloe!"

"What the devil do you mean?"

"We were at the bowling green having some sport this afternoon and Nat was with us," William began; Arthur could only sputter. "Colonel Tayloe and Phil rode by. Colonel Tayloe apparently remarked on what a strong, well-built buck Nat is, so Phil offered to sell him. To sell Nat! He's Will's son! It would kill Will. He was born at Stratford and he's part of us."

"Where is Phil now?" Richard Henry asked quietly.

An hour later Richard Henry pulled up his lathered horse on the Palace Green. Faint sounds of music emanated from the governor's house. Francis Fauquier was noted for his after-dinner musicales, and invitations to attend them were considered an honor.

Richard Henry quickly mounted the cleated stone steps and was admitted by one of the governor's red-coated British soldiers. "Please tell Colonel Philip Lee that his brother waits. It is very important."

For ten minutes Richard Henry cooled his heels in the walnut-paneled anteroom. Finally Phil Lee, in a velvet jacket and embroidered waistcoat, appeared in the doorway, obviously irritated. "What the devil do you want?"

"Is it true that you plan to sell Nat West to Colonel Tayloe?"

"Of course it is true! Tayloe has offered a good price." Phil folded his arms across his chest. "Anyway, if Arthur is soon to leave and William is eventually to go to England as well, what difference does it make if their old playmate gets sold?"

For a moment Richard Henry stood in stunned silence. "Can you think how Will would feel if you sold his son? If you insist, then let me buy him from you!" he said.

Phil laughed. "With what? Stratford money to buy a Stratford slave?"

Gradually he began to chafe under Richard Henry's unyielding gaze. "All right, then," he said condescendingly, "we'll toss a pistole to decide the matter. Heads, my slave will be sold; tails, I'll tell John Tayloe I have decided to keep him." He drew a gold coin from his pocket.

Later, as he rode back to Green Spring with the jubilant Arthur and William, words and phrases raced through Richard Henry's mind. He stirred the library fire and took up a freshly sharpened quill to complete his speech. How despicable that a man's fate could hang on the toss of a gold coin.

The next day, dressed in a brown silk jacket with his best lace at throat and cuffs, Richard Henry rose in the House of Burgesses to make his first presentation. He looked up at the speaker, whose bewigged head was dramatically framed by the circular window above. His eyes swept the assembled burgesses. George Washington watched him with an interested expression in his eyes; George Mason, now the delegate from Fairfax County, hid his mouth behind his fingers, but his eyes were curious and inquisitive; the gazes of Thomas and Francis Lightfoot and his cousins Henry and Richard, always supportive, buoyed him.

He took a deep breath and clenched his sweaty hands. He had practiced this speech twice before the mirror and once for Annie and his uncle Phil. Though not long, it reverberated with all his feeling about the horrors of slavery.

He began hesitantly; then with growing confidence he boldly compared Virginia with its neighboring colonies. Settled later than Virginia, all had nonetheless outstripped her in cities and commerce. He compared Virginia to Greece and Rome, where some of the greatest ancient upheavals were caused by the insurrections of slaves. He concluded by pointing out that civil slavery had been abolished in Europe. "Let us who profess the same religion, practice its precepts; and by agreeing to this duty, convince the world that we know and practice our true interests, and that we pay a proper regard to the dictates of justice and humanity."

A frightening silence filled the room. Then a smattering of applause led by the Lee coterie broke forth.

"By Jove, you shocked them! There were indeed some startled faces in the Assembly," Francis Lightfoot crowed over dinner later in Raleigh's Tavern. "Your arguments are so logical they cannot be countered. But remember, men do not always like to hear unpleasant truths, particularly when their pocketbooks are affected. You've probably made some enemies with your stand!"

"Richard Henry Lee! Richard Henry Lee!" A voice called over the tavern din. Richard Hall was pushing his way through the crowd. Something was amiss. Richard Henry jumped to his feet. Was Annie or the baby ill at Green Spring?

Richard Hall held a white envelope, its seal broken. "It is from your sister Missy. Gawin Corbin has been hurt."

Surely it must have shocked Richard Henry, engrossed as he was in the intricacies of his long-awaited political career and the joys of his growing family, to see tragedy strike where it was not expected. Of them all, Missy Lee Corbin's life had seemed the most settled, the most predictable. And yet it was she who was to be tested. Upon reflection, it seemed to the colonel that Missy embodied that rare grace, that strength of spirit, that marks, when moments of crisis and decision are faced, the extraordinary personality.

The Torch Is Lit

1759–1766

The Tidewater, 1759

"The master done fallen, fallen off his horse!"

For a moment Missy stared numbly at the orchard boy, who stood in the afternoon dusk gasping for his breath, his eyes huge with fright.

"My God . . . dear God!" She sensed at once it was not an ordinary fall, the kind every rider takes now and then. Grabbing her shawl, she ran out of the office. "Have the wagon brought around from the barn, the small one; hurry, now." she ordered. "And get blankets from the tack room, and a flat board."

Gawin's horse was wandering aimlessly in the yard. Missy seized his bridle and, bundling her petticoats, mounted with a leg up from the stable boy and spurred in the direction of the low field, which was being cleared for planting. Although it looked like an open meadow, it was a morass of tree stumps and tough, snakelike roots that had been left until the spring thaw would allow them to be dug out. Gawin knew that! Whatever possessed him to ride across that field?

Having tethered the horse to a tree, Missy began picking her way across the rubbled meadow. There, in the diminishing light of dusk, her husband lay looking up at her with a glazed expression.

"Gawin," she cried, "can you speak? Please, say you are all right!" But she knew he couldn't, and an overwhelming terror seized her.

"Gawin had been ill with the flux all fall," she told Richard Henry later. "He'd get better, only to sicken again with the fever and shakes and the passing of green bile. But he tired of staying in the house. I knew he was weak. Why didn't I stop him?" Missy moaned.

"Don't blame yourself," Richard Henry said gently.

"After dinner that afternoon Gawin asked me if I wouldn't like to go down to the tobacco barns and then maybe take a look at the wheat." She continued, staring mournfully into the distance. "But I had things to do in the office. So he went alone." She shivered suddenly. "As soon as I found him, I could tell. . . ."

Two bleak December weeks had passed with no change. Gawin lay in the main bedroom of Pecatone, conscious and showing little pain, yet unable to move a single muscle below his shoulders with the exception of his right arm and hand, and those only slightly.

Now Richard Henry studied Missy as she stirred the sitting-room fire. There was great strength in his sister. All her once unbridled passion was now channeled into the management of Pecatone and her love for Patty— not that she wasn't a good wife to Gawin, but Missy was hardly a romantic. His own Annie would never be able to hold up so well in the face of misfortune. Far more dependent than Missy, pliant and gentle-natured, Annie curled like a soft ball against him at night. Her fingers were small and soft when they touched his face, his neck, his chest.

He was jolted from his thoughts when Richard Hall entered the sitting room. The doctor's face was troubled, his eyes discouraged. There was obviously no good news. Richard Hall needed taking care of himself, Richard Henry mused. The young doctor's boots were worn and a button was missing from his jacket. A quiet, outdoors sort of chap, Hall was widely respected for his extensive knowledge of medicinal herbs and preparations, as well as his skill at treatment. He had been part of their lives for a long time, certainly all through the eight years since Richard Henry's return from England, until a year ago, when Hall had abruptly moved down to Williamsburg. Probably looking for a good match, Richard Henry concluded. What Hall needed was a little land-rich heiress, someone like the widow Custis, whom George Washington had swept up.

"I am discouraged about Gawin's chest." Hall sat down wearily in a rush-seated chair and stretched out his legs by the fire. "The flux is back upon him. His lungs are filling up with liquid, and he's not got the strength to cough it up."

"Will his muscles ever recover?" Missy asked in a low voice.

Richard Hall's eyes moved slowly about the comfortable room, then rested squarely on Missy. "I told you from the first, dear lady, your husband's neck appears to be broken. I fear he will never regain the use of his limbs."

Stratford Hall rose secure and beautiful in the soft sun-splintered light of the winter evening as Richard Henry's one-chair carriage returned home.

"Do you really think that it is proper for Hall to stay at Pecatone?" Phil asked, greeting Richard Henry as he ascended the west steps.

"Can you think of a more appropriate place for a doctor to stay than in a house where a man lies dying?" retorted Richard Henry impatiently. "But to set your mind at ease, Phil, he is not living in the big house. Missy has had the schoolhouse prepared for him."

"Does Gawin know that he is dying?" asked Frank, who had delayed his return to Loudoun County because of this crisis.

"He knows," said Richard Henry. "We haven't talked about it specifically, but he told me he had his will drawn up this fall. Phil and I are to stand as guardians for Patty."

At Pecatone, life seemed suspended in one long excruciating moment for Missy. All her days and nights were spent ministering to Gawin, for Patty was staying at Stratford. She forgot entirely about the Christmas season until Richard Hall reminded her it was Boxing Day and rum and coins must be given to the servants and slaves. "I'll do it for you," he offered. Before he left the house, he put potatoes to roast in the sitting-room fire; an hour later he returned with a black cauldron of hashed pork, hot from the kitchen house. "I've a special bottle of French brandy out in the schoolhouse. You'll feel better if you drink it with me."

Missy shook her head. "I don't drink spirits," she said faintly.

"I prescribe it for you." He poured two generous glasses, which they drank silently before he went to check again on Gawin. When he returned, Missy was standing in the window embrasure of the sitting room, her forehead pressed against the cold, dark glass, which reflected the shining tears in her eyes. He came close and took her hand.

"It won't be long, Hannah," he said quietly, using her given name for the first time. "In a few hours, a few days at most, Gawin will die. When it is over, I plan to leave Pecatone."

At her stricken look, he smiled reassuringly. "Just for a while. If it is your wish, I shall come back to you. And when I do, I will stay forever."

She could not take her eyes off his face. "It is not right for you to pledge . . ."

"Not right to pledge my love while your husband is still alive?" His voice was hoarse. "I pledged it to you even before you had a husband. I gave my heart to you the night we first met at Stratford." With a soft sigh he pulled her gently to him. "But we shall speak no more about it. I tell you this now only to give you strength. So that when I go away, you will know I am coming back."

"No, Richard," she whispered fiercely, turning her face away so that his lips grazed only the corner of her mouth and burned instead across her cheek. I've felt that kiss before, she realized with wonder, a million times I have felt that kiss in my dreams.

The Tidewater, 1760

A week later, Missy stood in a circle of friends, family, and servants as Gawin's body was lowered into the ground. The glare of the January sun reflecting on the polished wooden casket brought tears to her eyes, or was it sorrow in Gawin's death? In many ways, theirs had been a good marriage. There had been no expectations—at least none on her part—that had gone unfulfilled. They had shared the joy of Patty's birth and of Pecatone's regained strength. But there had been no real intimacy, no shared rapture in each other. Almost reluctantly, she allowed herself to look at Richard Hall standing in a cluster of close friends on the other side of the grave, her eyes playing over the familiar cleft of his chin, his tan face and intense eyes. Could she dare let herself believe? Would God be so kind as to let her have his love?

"I can only believe," Colonel Phil told Missy one morning a week later, "that your husband thought you loved Pecatone enough to . . ."

Missy paced about the parlor at Pecatone, her eyes blazing with anger. "Enough to be a widow forever! What a horrid thing to do to me! I simply can't live that way—can't and won't!"

Richard Henry looked toward Richard Hall, who leaned on the back of a wing chair, a look of resignation on his face. "Tell her, Hall, there isn't anything she can do about it. Gawin's will clearly states that Pecatone is Missy's property only as long as she does not marry again. When Patty is twenty-one, the estate is to be divided between them. However," he said after a pause, "if Missy chooses to marry, Pecatone goes immediately to Patty."

"But Patty is only a child," stormed Missy. "She doesn't know what Pecatone means, what one has to do for it. And if it becomes hers and she dies without heirs, then . . ."

"Then the estate reverts to Gawin's family," Richard Henry finished for her. "It is not really that unusual a will, although I would never do that to Annie." He looked sympathetically at Richard Hall, who had left the Northern Neck the afternoon of the funeral, returning only yesterday. Last night Hall and Missy had journeyed to Stratford Hall and confided to Richard Henry and Colonel Phil their love and their plans to marry after a decent interval. But Gawin's will, read this morning, provided an unexpected complication.

Richard Hall now spoke in strong, measured words. "I shan't let you give up Pecatone for me, Missy. I know how hard you have worked to rebuild it. I cannot ask you to give it all up. I have very little to offer, my dearest, only a poor country doctor's income and my love."

"Your love is all I want, all I need," Missy said softly. She whirled on her brothers. "It is not fair! Just because I am a woman, have I no legal rights, none at all?"

Colonel Phil shook his head. "None, my dear, not under the laws of this colony."

Missy's hazel eyes shone bright as she turned to Richard Henry. "Well, then, change the law. You sit in the House. You worry about the freedom of the slaves. They're nearly as free as I am, all of us chattels! But I won't submit easily. There must be a solution, and I'll find it. You can be assured of that. I mean to have both Richard and Pecatone!"

"It is the old Missy, ever the hellion," Richard Henry told Frank. The Lee brothers were staying at Green Spring for the spring Assembly season and were catching up on family news as they dressed for dinner in the bedchamber.

Frank shook his head admiringly. "I confess I'm glad to hear her spirit has returned. I've rather missed her presence in all our family wrangles."

"I haven't told Colonel Phil yet, but Hall has moved back into the schoolhouse at Pecatone until the matter can be resolved. It doesn't look proper, of course, but they are aching to marry. I don't know if it is possible for her to have both marriage and the estate. Hall doesn't give a hoot about the inheritance, but he knows the land means a great deal to Missy. She's never made any bones about that," Richard Henry said.

Frank stretched out on the bed, pillowing his head on his hands. "Hall's living at Pecatone will no doubt offend Colonel Phil's sensibilities when he learns of it."

"He will be damnably outraged, especially since he is thinking of taking the giant step of matrimony himself. Lord knows, he wouldn't want gossip about the good family name."

Frank sat bolt upright. "Phil getting married? You must be joshing. What lady draws breath who would put up with Phil for more than an hour?"

Richard Henry snorted. "You can say that because you know him too well. Look at our Phil objectively. At thirty-four, he is rich as Midas, a member of the King's Council, dashing, well dressed, assertive—and, since he looks a great deal like you, you must admit that he is inordinately handsome!"

Frank's quick laugh acknowledged the compliment. With his extraordinary looks and vivid coloring, he was a charmer who enjoyed the pleasure of escorting one pretty belle after another to the balls and parties of each season, though his seduction inevitably stopped with kisses stolen behind the opulent draperies of Williamsburg and Tidewater mansions.

"Well, who the deuce can she be?" Frank asked curiously.

Richard Henry sat down on the end of Frank's bed. "He's gone quite mad for his ward, Miss Elizabeth Steptoe, and if she'd have him, he would marry her tomorrow."

Frank's blue eyes narrowed as the news registered. Elizabeth Steptoe was a younger half-sister of Richard Henry's Annie and Thomas's Mary. Upon her father's death, Colonel Phil Lee, neighbor and brother-in-law through the marriage of the Aylett daughters to Lee sons, had become Elizabeth's guardian. Now he hoped to be more.

"But she's only seventeen! She's a pretty enough minx, with her heart-shaped face and long swan neck. I have often noticed her at Stratford when she visited Annie and thought to myself, There is a delicious little creature, but she is a baby!" Frank was almost indignant. "For myself, I like sophisticated ladies, not bright-eyed kittens who smell of nursery milk!"

"Well, this kitten has tamed the lion in his lair. Phil is a different person around her," Richard Henry chortled. "Now we must see if she will have him."

"Oh, she'll have him," Frank said cynically. "What Colonel Phil wants, Colonel Phil gets, or haven't you noticed?"

When Frank had gone, leaving before his brother had finished dressing, Richard Henry studied himself critically in the looking-glass. For certain he had not inherited the dark, dashing looks of Francis Lightfoot, Phil, Thomas, and William. No, he and Arthur were the changelings . . . both fair and "different," as Arthur put it. But whereas Arthur had delicate features with great light-blue eyes beneath silky blond hair, Richard Henry seemed all cheekbone, nose, and eyes. His thick russet hair grew back from a high brow, beneath which penetrating eyes overset an aquiline nose. Well, Annie thought him attractive, and that was enough.

London, 1760

"How I love the bells pealing and crowds cheering!" Arthur Lee exulted as
he burst into the Cecil Street house, off the Strand, where Uncle Phil and his
two daughters lived. "Though they're for the coronation of our new king,
George the Third, they might also be to welcome me back to England!"
Arthur's patrician face was aglow.

"Are you really so glad to have left Virginia behind?" Philip Ludwell
asked his nephew. A year earlier, the widower Ludwell had resigned his seat
on the King's Council and moved to England, for a change of scene and to
introduce his daughters, Hannah Philippa and Lucy, to London society.

"I don't miss Virginia a whit." Arthur thrust his hands in his pockets
and roamed the handsomely decorated sitting room. "Oh, Uncle," he said,
"you've done it all so well! A few Green Spring pieces blended with all this
magnificent new furniture—most admirable! There is a *feeling* about London, isn't there? Doesn't it just thin your blood?"

The genial Phil Ludwell smiled indulgently. There was an incandescent,
even childlike quality in his favorite nephew that was enormously appealing.

"Well, I'll admit London does seem to have a special quality these
days. It is because our new king, so unlike his grandfather, is popular with
his subjects."

On October 25, 1760, the aging monarch had suddenly dropped dead
in his dressing room. George II had to his last breath looked upon the nation
he ruled with scornful lack of interest. Despite his bravery in battle and his
shrewdness in finally and firmly establishing England as the dominant world
power, he was little mourned. His subjects considered him too mean, too
German, and too condescending of all that was British.

"The thing the English like best about the old King's grandson and heir
is that he is *not* like his father or his grandfather," Phil Ludwell said.
"George the Third is truly English, by upbringing and inclination. Though
he is young and anxious to please, he is also pious and diligent," Uncle Phil
told Arthur. "From what I hear, he is rather comely in appearance, a huge,
tall man, as yet unmarried. You shall see, Arthur, London talks of little else
but George the Third, and always with great admiration. There has not been
so much fervor over a coronation since Charles the Second was restored a
hundred years ago. But tell me now of Virginia. Charming though London
is, I always long for word of home. And when your cousins Hannah Philippa
and Lucy return from shopping, they shall besiege you for news!"

Arthur leaned on the back of a chair. "You've heard, of course, the splendid news that Montreal, that last bastion of New France, fell in September. More dismaying and more important to Virginia, the Indians are again on the warpath in the Shenandoah and on the southwestern border, which Will Byrd as commander of Fort Pitt must attempt to deal with—as if he hadn't enough worries!" At his uncle's raised eyebrow, Arthur continued, "Colonel Byrd's wife, Eliza, was tragically killed early this fall when a tall mahogany high chest fell on her as she was reaching into one of the uppermost drawers."

"Poor sweet Eliza . . . a Carter of Shirley!" Phil Ludwell shook his head. "And what of the Stratford family, Arthur?"

"All well." For a moment emotions churned through Arthur. He had hated leaving William and Alice behind, but then Colonel Phil was so engrossed with his fiancée, Elizabeth Steptoe, he was not bearing down as hard as usual. "Oh, I say, there is some news!" Arthur's face broke into a grin. "In October Richard Henry and Annie had a second son, named him Ludwell . . . bit of red hair and all that!"

A week later, Arthur penned a letter home to Richard Henry: "Uncle Phil and I took supper at Clifton's Eating House in Butcher Row, where I have met a great number of literary and artistic figures, including the fashionable portrait painter Sir Joshua Reynolds and the writer, Samuel Johnson."

What excitement he had felt! He dipped his quill in ink and continued:

Last night I was in company with Mr. Johnson, author of the English Dictionary. His outward appearance is very droll and uncouth. The too assiduous cultivation of his mind seems to have caused a very great neglect of his body; but for this his friends are very amply rewarded in the enjoyment of a mind most eloquently polished, enlightened and refined; possessed as he is of an inexhaustible fund of remarks, a copious flow of words, expressions strong, nervous, pathetic and exalted; add to this an acquaintance with almost any subject that can be proposed; an intelligent mind cannot fail of receiving the most agreeable information and entertainment in his conversation. He proposes soon to publish a new edition of Shakespeare, a work which he says has employed him many years.

Arthur closed his eyes, remembering the evening. The heady conversation had been full of references to the new King, whom Johnson claimed would be a patron of the arts, and to Johnson's friends, the actor David Garrick and the poet Oliver Goldsmith. Some of the party had later adjourned to a private room in the Turk's Head Coffee House in the Strand for brandy, where Dr. Johnson inquired about Arthur's plans to pursue a medical education. He suggested the University of Edinburgh, pointing out that the study of medicine at Oxford or Cambridge would require seven years, whereas the same could be accomplished in two or three at Edinburgh, the Scots being a thriftier people, Johnson contended.

Richard Henry, an admirer of Johnson, would be interested in that tidbit, but it would be the political news he would crave: about the new monarch and the court. Arthur took up his pen:

The general grief occasioned by this melancholy event [death of Geo. II] was soon allayed by the welcome succession of his grandson, Geo. 3rd. Never did a king ascend a throne with a more universal applause. Each heart and voice was for him, and every tongue was busied in his praise. A perfect harmony subsists between his ministers, at the head of whom Mr. Pitt still holds foremost place in worth and eminence. The young King has committed but one error since his succession; instead of permitting the Ladies who come to Court to kiss his hand, he salutes them himself. Pleased with the Royal touch, they flock in such numbers to his Court, that he is like to suffer for his gallantry in being kissed to death—an effectual way this to win the hearts of ladies and consequently of the men. For who can help loving *such* a polite, genteel, good-natured young King?

The Tidewater, 1761

Weeks later, when Richard Henry had read Arthur's letter aloud at dinner in Stratford's dining room, he looked up to add, "And I would gather from Uncle Phil's letter, which arrived by the same ship, that Arthur has decided to take Samuel Johnson's advice and go to Edinburgh for his studies."

Colonel Phil stared with annoyance across the table. "Why the deuce does Arthur write you instead of me? Who put forth the money for his medical education? Am I not the one who paid some five hundred pounds for his schooling at Eton? You would think there would be some gratitude, some word of acknowledgment, from that insolent pup!"

"I am sure he is grateful, but he is excited," Richard Henry soothed. "I say, Phil, why don't you ride with me this afternoon to see how our house is progressing?" He winked at Annie. They were building a house on a fine high spot in a wooded glade three miles east of the big house, closer to the Potomac. Their sanctuary, their "nest in the trees," was to be named Chantilly after the magnificent château built by the Prince of Condé near Paris. Their

Chantilly, however, would be only a comfortable wooden house tucked among the poplars.

"Missy and Dr. Hall are riding over later," Richard Henry continued. "You've not seen either of them in a while."

Phil stood up abruptly. "Nor do I wish to! I do not approve of his living at Pecatone. I know you say he lives in the old schoolhouse and keeps busy with his medicine and herbs. But there is gossip, and I will not tolerate scandal. Either Missy should marry Hall and give up her rights or, if she wishes to keep her plantation, she should send him packing. She can't have it both ways."

Edinburgh, 1761

Now settled in a "cold little room" near the University of Edinburgh, Arthur was most certainly not enjoying the spring. "If one can éven call this windy, gray, depressing season in Scotland, Spring!" he wrote to Richard Henry in May 1761.

I know that you thought Edinburgh charming when you visited years ago. But it was your good fortune that you did not have to dwell in one of these crowded old houses that line every dismal, evil, stinking narrow street for mile after mile. The dreary places boast no cellars, or yards, and no necessary houses! The common practice is to throw the filth and slop from the windows at night, and carts come round in the early hours of the morning to shovel it up. I cannot tell you with what trepidation I go out each evening!

To be fair, I find my medical lectures most interesting. Dr. Alex Munroe is providing me an excellent background in anatomy with the aid of the cadavers of paupers destined for the city graves, which are instead brought into our lecture theater. While a gruesome, evil-smelling practice and morally questioned by some, it proves a tremendous aid to learning human anatomy. You will be pleased to know that I have made some good friends in Edinburgh.

Indeed, there were several delightful English chaps with whom he often ate his midday meal and whom he joined at night for ale and a game of draughts. But one fellow student, a truly brilliant young Philadelphian, had become his closest friend.

Not only is William Shippen, Jr., well born, but he is also very wealthy. His great-grandfather amassed a fortune in the mercantile business and was William Penn's first mayor of Philadelphia. Shippen's grandfather was also prominent in politics in the province of Pennsylvania, and his father is an

eminent physician. Will studied under his father in Philadelphia and later served
a year with the famed surgeons William and John Hunter in London. He is a
boon companion bursting with ideas and plans for improving the medical
education of doctors in the colonies when he returns to Philadelphia next year.
He talks of little else.

On the first sunny day in late May, Arthur and Will Shippen skipped
their lectures and climbed the steep slopes of Mound and Lawnmarket
streets to reach the gray stone castle that dominated the city from its bed of
massive rocks.

"What a glorious day," Arthur exulted. "I swear it is the first time in
months that my bones have been halfway warm."

"Your Virginia blood is not thick enough," Will joked. "You should
have grown up in Philadelphia and suffered a few chilblains and frozen toes
to prepare you for the Scottish winters." Will hoisted himself onto a low
wall. "By the way, Father writes that my cousin Mary Willing has this past
January married a Colonel William Byrd of Westover, a widower with several children. Do you know him?"

"Yes, of course," said Arthur. "His father and mine were very close
friends."

Will Shippen snorted. "I should have known! You first Virginia families are thick as molasses."

"No more than Philadelphians!"

"There is a difference." Will gazed into the distance. "There is something exotic and different about you Virginians. You stand out bolder than
life. Take, for example, this Colonel Byrd, whom Father writes is striking in
appearance and compelling in conversation, and acts like an English lord.
Virginians truly are our colonial aristocrats."

"If your father thinks Will Byrd lordly, you should have known *his*
father, the Black Swan of Westover! He was considered knowledgeable on
every subject under the sun—from agriculture to history—and each day he
rose at dawn to read an hour of Greek or Latin. What's more, it is said he
could charm the skirts off every lady whose hand he kissed."

"What do you suppose produced so interesting a breed as Virginians?"
Shippen regarded Arthur from beneath half-closed eyelids. "It is intriguing
to me how different the several colonies are. For example, our New England
brethren are a breed of shopkeepers and fishermen confined by their Puritan origins. Then the New Yorkers, those thrifty Dutchmen, are dour as the
devil but astute traders and merchants—"

"It's hard to say. We Virginians," Arthur broke in, "regard the South
Carolinians as indolent rice growers, only slightly below, at least geographi-

cally, the North Carolinians, who are nothing but hunters! Between us we have the Marylanders, who are a little of everything, yet not a great deal of anything—at best, a nondescript bunch! Finally, you Pennsylvanians. Would you say peace-loving Quakers or hard-minded Germans to be the most fitting description?"

"My family isn't Quaker," Will said, growing serious, "but to be sure, all Philadelphians are influenced by the liberal and thoughtful Society of Friends. They are not in any way colorful but lend a steadying hand to Pennyslvania."

Arthur looked out at the glittering Firth of Forth and, in the far distance, the faint coast of Fife and the Ochils. "You see, Will, it is land, the abundance or lack of it, that distinguishes each colony. The New Englanders are town people. Their family plots have been divided for their sons so many times that they must all become shopkeepers, or 'yeomen farmers,' as we call them in Virginia. It is said that there are many wandering poor in New England—just as in Edinburgh. Now, in Virginia, two factors determine our style of living. Land is our first obsession. And there it lies, acre after acre of it, with more waiting beyond the mountains. The other factor is slavery." Arthur's mouth tightened on the word. "By God, Will—and I say it as a true Virginian—it is the most horrible, the most abominable of institutions."

"It has existed since the beginning of man," Will commented soberly.

"I know, but slavery based on race is new with this century. For Englishmen to engage in it is peculiarly repugnant. We pride ourselves on our *rights* under the law. We are freemen, not the King's galley slaves! To fill our labor needs by owning another human being, my God! At least with indentured servants it is the labor that is sold, not the man himself!"

"I have heard many a justification for slavery, however," Will pressed.

"Oh, it is easy enough for slave owners to bandy about excuses like, The african is an infidel, or, The african is not able to take care of himself, in which there lies some truth, for they have no common language or skills. Yet, I can only believe that my poor Virginia will suffer the more because of slavery."

Shippen studied Arthur's slim, intense face. "Perhaps that will be your challenge in life, to rid Virginia of slavery. If I am to be so bold as to introduce the idea of a medical school's using cadavers to the prim and proper souls of Philadelphia, then surely you can put your sword to the villain slavery."

Arthur sighed. "If you only understood Virginia! Each plantation is an empire, its master and mistress a kind of lord and lady. There are no towns on the order of Philadelphia, only Williamsburg, which all but belongs to the governor and the Assembly. Most important, we have no middle class, only those who have everything—lands, wealth, power, freedom—and those who have little or nothing. In particular, no freedom. Perhaps it is why Virginians consider freedom so dear, for it is the great separator."

"Tell me," Will said as he slipped down from the wall and they began to walk on, "what is the latest news from your family? Lord, are you an interesting crew! What of the autocratic Colonel Phil? Has your elder sister been able to keep her plantation? What of the ambitious Richard Henry, the dashing Francis Lightfoot, and, most particularly, the fair, gentle Alice, the sleeping princess of the Potomac?"

"Come with me to London next week," Arthur invited, "and meet the princess herself. Uncle Phil wrote that William and Alice have just appeared on his doorstep, like two birds who flew the Atlantic with the aid of wings. I know nothing more, except that I am invited down at my earliest convenience to visit. And I'm sure you'll be welcome!"

London, 1761

For several lovely, breathless weeks, Alice Lee had been living in England. From the wide French doors of the Ludwell house she now looked down on Cecil Street, marveling at the fascinating vista, handsome brick houses in front of which passed an endless parade of fashionably dressed gentlemen with elegant ladies on their arms.

"You cannot imagine the charm of a busy street for one who has spent a lifetime watching a river flow!" she told Uncle Phil with a burst of laughter. And it is I who have been changed by it, she thought. Brought back to life, forever altered. She put her fingers to the cascade of curls that fell from an ivory clasp at the back of her head. Her cousin had arranged her hair in this new fashion and insisted Alice discard her simple colonial frocks for some silk gowns of her own. "You and I are exactly the same size! Not everyone boasts a sixteen-inch waist, my dear," Hannah Philippa confided.

Alice put her hands around her waist. Through the silk of her dress she could feel the whalebone stays, "a pair of bodies," Hannah Philippa called them, which not only made her small waist still smaller, but also pushed up her bosom quite wickedly! Was it vain and awful to care so about one's looks? Was it a sin to enjoy all this so frightfully much? If only life could always be full of beautiful things and laughter and love.

With a cry of delight, she flew from the French doors to embrace Arthur, whose excited, boyish voice had just invaded the drawing room. "We've been waiting for hours," she exclaimed, then broke off with a gasp, for behind Arthur stood the handsomest person she had ever laid eyes on. Of medium height, with laughing yet confident dark eyes, clear white skin, and a smile dazzlingly warm, Will Shippen bent low over Alice's hand.

Later, when they were all settled in the bright drawing room, its crewel-draped windows and French doors open to the June afternoon, Arthur begged for an explanation. "How the devil did you two get away from Phil? And what are your plans?"

Sitting in a nest of hoop skirts on the sofa next to Hannah Philippa, Alice could not suppress her glee. "You are the one who put the idea in my head," she said with a toss of her curls. "Then William made it possible. He had laid aside all his earnings from the landing store, which paid our passage. In exchange, I have signed over all rights to my inheritance from Father—not that William will ever get it," she added indignantly.

"That doesn't matter." William's voice was quiet. "What does matter is that we have escaped Colonel Phil. As for what we are going to do, I don't know . . . travel a bit, as long as our money lasts." A look of confusion came over William's face.

"But how the deuce did you actually get away from Phil and Stratford?" Arthur persisted.

"Quite audaciously," said Alice, her eyes shining. "Philip was planning his wedding to Elizabeth Steptoe, and so for days had hardly paid the two of us any mind. Following the ceremony, there were festivities all afternoon, with people coming and going. That's when we left."

William carried on. "I had arranged for Nat West to meet us at the millhouse between Chantilly and Stratford, with our trunks in the wagon. We slipped away, leaving behind conflicting stories about going to Pecatone or Wakefield. Actually, we spent the night at Sabine Hall, where a tobacco schooner was scheduled to sail at dawn. Landon Carter helped us, albeit unwittingly, for he had no idea we were escaping. I only hope Nat didn't get into any trouble with Phil. We tried to make it look as if he were an innocent party."

"One thing is certain," Alice said firmly. "I shall never return to America. I have fallen in love with London and I shall stay forever, even if I have to take in sewing to earn my living!"

Will Shippen put his head back against the chair cushion with an amused sigh. Imagine this fragile, beguiling creature managing on her own. Absurd.

Arthur wrote to Richard Henry a week later,

Alice charms everyone she meets. She is indescribably more beautiful than I ever remembered her. And I have never known her to be so buoyant. William appears a bit melancholy and unsure of himself. It is understandable. He needs some time on his own. If there is any way you can persuade Colonel Phil to send them, or me, for that matter, any extra cash, it would be most welcome.

There is no real political news. Our new King, who, it seems, has hopes to *rule* his empire as well as reign over it, is going against the Whigs in Parliament, who have dominated palace and profits since 1714. He gives more and more power to his old Scottish tutor, Lord Bute, to whom he is devoted. This appears to spell the end of William Pitt's influence. Pity.

Will Shippen and I visited the House of Commons yesterday to dine with Ben Franklin, the agent for the province of Pennsylvania. He is a remarkable gentleman . . . canny, manipulative, yet utterly charming. He tells us the Crown is desperate for money to fund its newly expanded empire. Also, there are heavy expenses from the late American war, as they prefer to call it here. As you may have heard, there is fear in the inner circles that the Americans, who are considered a prickly, obstinate breed by some, might band together and break off from the empire. Ben Franklin has written a pamphlet to reassure the powers that such a bonding of the colonies would be improbable, impossible, and inconceivable. He claims the provinces, colonies, and commonwealths that make up British America are far too diverse to be unified. He pointed out that we cannot even unite to meet the Indian problems! The British for the most part think we are only greedy profiteers who force England to protect our land speculations, oblivious of the best interests of the empire!

London, 1762

William struggled to adjust his silk cravat. "You'd best hurry or you'll be late for the theater, Arthur."

"Confound the theater!" Arthur cried with disgust. "All I've done this year is accompany my love-stricken friend Will Shippen to London every other weekend so that we can escort Alice to a dinner or a ball or a performance at Drury Lane. I'm damn worn out!"

"How hardhearted you sound, Arthur. Haven't you ever been in love?" William threw him a mocking glance.

"Of course I have been in love! I am in love at least twice a month, but I don't let it upset my life!" Arthur stormed out of the room. "I won't go to the theater tonight, even if it is Mallet's *Elvira*."

The theater party did not allow Arthur's pique to disturb them. Phil Ludwell sat between his daughters in the box, William at the side of Hannah

Philippa. Will Shippen and Alice Lee chose the two chairs well in the back of the box.

"You won't be able to see back there in the shadows," William teased.

"But then, those sitting in stalls can't see me weep if the play is sad," Alice rejoined spiritedly.

"They are in love," William whispered to Hannah Philippa. He could not fathom his cousin's expression, which again and again during their stay in London struck him as both tantalizing and unnerving. Two years older than he, Hannah Philippa was subdued, yet pretty, with a fine figure. She was also quite self-confident. Perhaps that was to be expected in heiresses.

In the shadows, Alice felt Will Shippen's fingers twine with hers. "Say yes, my darling Alice. Please, please. Say yes!" he implored.

"But I've no dowry, Will. . . ."

He squeezed her fingers tightly. "You need no dowry; I have more than we shall ever need. Marry me and I shall build you a fine house and get you every pretty dress your heart desires, with kid slippers to match. We shall love each other forever and ever and ever, I promise."

"Shh." William looked over his shoulder. "Talk of love tomorrow," he whispered, "but watch the play tonight!"

"I never thought I would be willing to go back to America," Alice told Hannah Philippa the next day as they were dressing for an afternoon boat ride to the Vauxhall pleasure park. "I have so loved this year in London with you and Lucy and Uncle Phil. If I thought of going anywhere, it would be Italy or the south of France. When William and I left Stratford Hall, almost a year ago, we said we would *never* go where Colonel Phil could touch us."

Hannah Philippa's calm, searching eyes met Alice's in the mirror. "But now your brother is almost out of money and you have fallen in love."

"Madly, desperately, completely!" Alice smiled, her fair cheeks coloring to rose.

"Will Shippen is very persuasive." The dark-haired Ludwell girl put down the ivory comb and looked at her younger cousin. "He is also handsome and charming and, I've no doubt, brilliant. He suits you, Alice."

"Somehow I don't think you really like him," Alice faltered.

"Of course I do," Hannah Philippa reassured her quickly. "Will Shippen is very sure of himself. He pleases so competently. Somehow I am more comfortable with those who are less certain that life is controllable."

Alice stood up, smoothing the silk hem of her skirt. " 'Life is what you make it to be,' my Will says."

"If that is true, my dear Alice," Hannah Philippa said quietly, "I am

certain your Dr. Shippen will make it very beautiful for you." She smiled
and put her arms around her cousin. "I myself suspect that the fates decide
our destinies."

The Tidewater, 1762

Spring has never been quite this lush, Missy thought, or perhaps I have
just never experienced spring so deeply before. The soil between my fingers,
the scent of the wakening garden; no, I have never been so affected. She was
walking with Patty up from the beach just as the sun was setting behind
Pecatone. In a wicker basket over one arm she carried a mass of blossoms,
their sweet redolence suffusing the soft air around them.

"Where is Dr. Hall, Mamma?" Patty asked suddenly. "It seems he is
always away."

"He's gone to Sandy Point to treat some slave children who have the
fever." She patted the child. "There's a lot of ague and fever about."

"I do like Dr. Hall, Mamma." Patty turned her face up to Missy. "I like
to go down to see him in the schoolhouse when Plato takes him his breakfast. Sometimes he carves things for me with his hunting knife." She fished in
the pocket of her apron. "He made this little boat. . . . It is an Indian canoe
to sail on the creek. Sometimes I put a flower in it and pretend an Indian
maid is sailing on the river."

They passed the darkened schoolhouse. Come back soon, Richard,
Missy thought longingly, I miss you, I need you.

That evening, when Patty had gone to bed, Missy sat quietly on the
steps of the manor house, her hands folded around her knees, listening to the
chorus of peepers along the margins of the creek and the light summer
breeze in the leaves of the tall Virginia oaks surrounding the house.

"What are you thinking, Hannah Corbin?" Richard Hall stood in the
grass looking up at her.

"Oh, you startled me!" Hannah laughed. "My mind was wandering."
She moved her skirt so that he could join her on the step. "No, to be honest,
I was thinking of you, wanting you to come home." She loved the warmth of
his shoulder against her arm, the good rich scent of his body, sun and sweat
and leather. She put her hand out to brush the thick brown curls that fell
over his brow and felt his unease. "What is the matter, Richard?"

"I've something to tell you, Hannah. I don't know how to do it." His
voice was pained and muffled.

She felt a rising panic.

"I must go away—no, hear me out. It is the only way. God knows I love you, Hannah. More than anything in this world, I want you to be my wife." His tone was firm, steely, resolved. "But I love you too much to take you away from Pecatone. You would never be the same if I did that to you. The memory of this land would hang like a shadow between us."

"But I love you, Richard." Missy's voice was only a whisper. "I would willingly go."

"I know you would, my love, but that is your heart speaking, not your head. You need Pecatone as much as it needs you." He stood up, looming over her in the fast-gathering darkness. "And I can't stay here any longer, wanting you as badly as I do. I have to leave, and the sooner the better for both of us."

He turned quickly and ran down the steps, leaving her in the shadows. Inside the house, her fingers trembled as she tried to light a candle. Damn you, Gawin! Hot tears filled her eyes as she bent over the washbowl, her cheeks burning as if she had the fever. The water felt cool, calming to her face, her neck, and her breasts, but her hands would not stop trembling. She could not brush out her hair.

Missy blew out the candle and sat listening to the faint sound of the rain caressing the leaves of the tall beech outside her window. She would not let him go! She didn't give a fig for anyone but Richard Hall and Patty. What had she been waiting for? With quick fingers, Missy wrapped a silk shawl over her long white nightdress and ran barefoot through the hall and out of the house, down the wooden steps and across the velvety wet grass toward the darkened schoolhouse.

"Hannah! My God, what the devil are you doing here?" Still in his breeches and shirt, he was standing in the open door of the schoolhouse, staring out into the darkness.

"Richard, oh, Richard," she sobbed, "please don't leave."

She felt his mouth on her hair, her temple, hungrily tracing the curve of her neck. "You've got rain on your hair, my darling . . . rain on your cheek," he murmured.

He pulled her into the shelter of the building. "I was watching your window." His voice was husky with emotion. "I always watch your window before I go to bed at night. You must return to the house. It's not proper. I—"

She stopped his words with her mouth, pressing herself against him, curving into him until he almost cried out with desire. The shawl fell from her shoulders to the dirt floor, and as his hands moved down her back, she felt the awareness come over him that she had nothing on but the sheer night shift, that she had come to him, that she wanted him, now, tonight.

He lifted her in his arms and took her to his bed. Oh, the joy of his weight on her breasts, the heat and insistence of his mouth, his cheek against hers. Perhaps it was better for the waiting, better for all the longing.

He was not gentle with her the first time. The desire was so strong that he could not wait, and he took her fiercely, whispering her name over and over.

In the darkness of midnight, he made love to her again, slowly and lovingly, with tender gentle hands and mouth and body. They slept, then woke together and lay intertwined, watching the dawn break over the pale-gold river.

"To leave you now is harder," he said, "not easier."

"Richard, there is no reason for you to leave." Missy was quite sure of her words. "I am proud for the world to know that you love me and that I love you. I want you to move into Pecatone. I want us to live together freely, bound only by our love."

"But your family? Colonel Phil would be outraged."

"Phil can go to the devil!" Missy sat up in bed, pulling up the covers over her breasts. "I haven't the slightest qualm about what anyone thinks or says. Have you?" she challenged indignantly.

In response, Richard pulled her down to him, wound his hands in her hair, and guided her head down to kiss her lips ardently. "I'll never leave you, my darling," he said finally. "Let anyone who condemns us be damned!"

Missy laid her cheek against his chest and closed her eyes. As though a dam inside her had broken, she was flooded with peace and happiness. "I think for the first time now I am about to live my life exactly as I want to." She leaned up on one elbow and looked down at him. "It is absolutely intoxicating!"

The changed relationship between Missy and Richard Hall was not immediately perceived by the families at Stratford Hall, Chantilly, Wakefield, or the other neighboring plantations.

William was the first to notice. He had reluctantly returned to Virginia in the fall of 1762 when Colonel Phil insisted he was needed to straighten out some problems concerning the plantation, "which was a lie, of course," William told Richard Henry indignantly. "Other than the fact that Phil spends a fortune on Stratford, adding outbuildings, expanding the wharf, buying furnishings for the house and new horses for his stables, he has no real problems. He just needs me to keep his books and transactions in order, and he wanted to avoid sending me the funds he still owes." William gripped the arm of his chair. "He is hard as steel, unfeeling through and through. He'll never change!"

"Except where his Elizabeth is concerned," Richard Henry replied.

"Nonsense," William scoffed. "He only likes to buy Elizabeth lovely things and bring her to Williamsburg for the season to show her off. And now that she is with child, his unbearable ego will only swell—if that is possible!" William's face suddenly softened. "I wish you could have attended Alice's wedding at St. Mary Le Strand in London. Now, that is a true match of love."

"I like the way you describe her young doctor. Coming from a strong, respected family, dedicated to his profession—William Shippen will make a sound husband," noted Richard Henry.

"Aye, but more than that . . ." William struggled for the right words. "They are so alike. Why, the moment they walk into a room, every eye turns their way, for they are extraordinarily beautiful and full of life. I declare, I have never met a man so amiable and full of charm. But more important, he loves Alice deeply. Oh, the marvelous plans they have—for his practice, a big house of their own, a prominent place in Philadelphia society, children. They want it all. Shippen hopes to reshape the training of physicians in the colonies to include lectures in anatomy. Imagine such bold innovation from this Pennsylvanian."

"So long as Alice is happy I am well satisfied, even if Shippen is not a Virginian," Richard Henry said candidly.

"She is happy, I assure you of that. But strangely enough, her radiance cannot hold a candle to Missy's." William smiled knowingly at his brother.

"Missy's? I haven't noticed anything new about Missy, least of all contentment. For a fact, I thought she was having a hard time deciding between her heavenly love for the good doctor and her earthly claim to Pecatone."

"You haven't looked closely of late. She is no longer struggling. I would venture that she has captured them both."

"What do you mean?" Richard Henry was genuinely puzzled.

"My sharp eyes tell me Hall is no longer pining away in the schoolhouse, but is sharing Missy's life quite comfortably in the big house."

"I'll be damned." Richard Henry rubbed his jaw thoughtfully. "Well, if you're right, good for Missy! Only thank God, Phil hasn't noticed. He'd probably try to kill Hall or at least run him out of Westmoreland County."

"And you say Phil doesn't realize that they are lovers openly living together?" Frank almost choked on his ale. "There will surely be hell to pay when he does!"

Richard Henry had just enlightened Frank on the delicate situation at Pecatone. William, who had joined his brothers for baked shad at Christiana Campbell's Tavern, nodded agreement. "I think we should tread softly.

The truth is, they aren't bothering anyone. They rarely entertain, so few know. Hall has his medical practice, and Missy the plantation. They are, how shall I put it, rugged individualists, both of them."

"Shh . . ." Richard Henry caught sight of a party of fellow burgesses just entering the room and determinedly making their way toward the Lee table.

"Aha!" Ben Harrison cried in his jovial manner. "The Lees are holding court! If the entire clan were present, brothers, cousins, and so forth, there would be no room for anyone else in the tavern! Mrs. Campbell could well survive by appointment to Lees only!"

Laughing warmly, Richard Henry motioned Ben and his companions, Henry Lee and George Washington, to join the table.

"Devilish business this morning, what!" His silver dress sword clanked against the wooden chair as Ben settled himself in a Windsor chair beside Frank Lightfoot. "Governor Fauquier was none too pleased with his rebellious Assembly!"

Short of gold and silver coinage, the Virginia Assembly had several years earlier issued paper currency to pay its militia and meet the sundry expenses of the French and Indian War. They did this reluctantly, for the Massachusetts Colony had defaulted on its creditors after doing so. Recently, the London merchants, acting through the Board of Trade, had protested the volume of paper money, £750,000, issued by Virginia. Caught in the middle, the usually genial Governor Fauquier opened the Fall Assembly in a taciturn mood, ordering the paper recalled if the treasury held insufficient silver to secure the notes.

This morning, the burgesses had reported that the treasury could indeed cover the paper. Moreover, the House would resist any attempt by the governor and Council to declare the paper money not legal tender in payment of sterling debts. Displeased with the independent tone adopted by the House, Governor Fauquier in a fit of pique dissolved the Assembly.

"Hot-tempered devil, this Fauquier," Henry Lee muttered. "Does he think we are a gang of field slaves to be sent packing at his whim?"

"Suits me just as well," Ben Harrison snorted. "I have my fall planting, not to mention other interests"—he grinned as he rose—"beginning with the cock fights in Yorktown this afternoon!"

When Ben had departed, George Washington pulled his chair closer, a look of excitement playing across his face. "My friends, as our Assembly business has been abruptly concluded, I have another project to present." He laid a broad hand on the red checkered tablecloth. "I speak of land, gentlemen, land in the west!"

"Oh, the Ohio Company?" asked Frank resignedly.

Washington shook his head. "No. George Mason tells me that company is mired in problems. As you know, one of our members, George Mercer, is now in London to represent us before the King and explain that because of the war with France we were unable to fulfill the conditions of our original grant. No"—George pulled a hand-drawn map from his pocket—"the land I now have in mind lies south of the Ohio Company claim. I suggest we form a new company and petition the Crown for a grant of two and a half million acres. See here." He pointed to the neat, meticulous document drawn almost to scale. "From the juncture of the Ohio and the Mississippi rivers east to the Wabash River and then south to Tennessee."

"Two and a half million acres!" Frank repeated slowly.

"Aye, Frank, think of it! If fifty subscribers joined the company, each would hold as his share fifty thousand acres."

Richard Henry studied Washington's enthusiastic face. George was becoming so certain of himself, arriving in Williamsburg in a handsome coach and six. Shows what a little money in a man's pocket will do! What's more, since the deaths of Lawrence's widow, Nancy, her young daughter, and second husband, George Lee, Mount Vernon had become George's legal property. George was not a political man, but he was practical, and honorable. And, by God, he'd always had a head for numbers! Richard Henry bent his head to study the map.

"The Indians present a problem, do they not?" Henry Lee raised the issue quietly. "All spring, there has been trouble up and down the Ohio. The Indians have taken all English forts north of the Potomac and the Ohio except for Forts Niagara, Detroit, and Pitt. I've heard a war council was held last month of the Ottawa and Chippewa warriors. Chief Pontiac is sounding the war cry to besiege all remaining English forts." Henry shook his head. "I think the situation is too volatile for any land company to prosper."

"But, Henry," Frank said with rising eagerness, "if we Virginians don't move, then Pennsylvanians and New Yorkers will."

"As I see it," George said calmly, "backers of this Mississippi Company would have twelve years to settle the land, and the King would have to protect the territory with royal troops during that period."

"Well, count me in!" said Frank.

"Me, too." Richard Henry could not resist the lure, for he and Frank had not been included in the Ohio Company. "If the future of the New World lies to the west, as Father insisted, then I want to be part of it!" Richard Henry caught George's eye. "Perhaps William, a proven accountant, could handle the business transactions."

George eyed the solidly built, sober William for a moment, then said,

"I have no objection. And he should be paid a fee . . . perhaps five percent of all monies collected from the members."

"Arthur might be willing to serve as our London agent," Frank threw in.

Now George laughed. "I had in mind keeping the membership to subscribers from the Northern Neck and Maryland, but it would appear that Lees and Washingtons alone will make up the body of stockholders."

"Colonel Washington has ambitions to be a major planter, does he not?" William inquired when only the four Lees were lingering at the table for coffee.

"This Mississippi Company sounds far too good, too easy," Henry sighed. "Something will go wrong, just watch."

"Henry is probably right. The Indians will be the problem this time," William speculated.

The Tidewater, 1763

William's speculation proved prophetic, for Pontiac and his warriors were bent on keeping the English out of the west. Fierce bands of Indians, ravaged by smallpox yet determined to reclaim their lands, roamed among the settlements along the Pennsylvania, Maryland, and Virginia border.

By the Treaty of Paris signed in February of 1763, England had acquired all of French Canada and the North American lands east of the Mississippi. But this new territory was proving a heavy responsibility to the financially strained empire. The following October, the Crown sought to calm the restless frontier and exert control over the land-grabbing colonies by drawing a line along the chain of the Appalachians deeding all western lands back to the Indian nations.

The English were forbidden to settle, claim, or remain on lands lying west of the sources of the rivers flowing into the Atlantic. All efforts and dreams were for the moment wiped away. The coveted, long-fought-over Transappalachian country, with its rich Ohio basin, was once again Indian territory.

"A blow, though perhaps not a fatal one, for undoubtedly this ban on settlement is only temporary, but it is definitely a setback to the Ohio Company and our plans for a Mississippi Company," Richard Henry commiserated with Frank. "England is trying to win time to strengthen the empire before expanding west."

"And time to replenish her coffers," added Frank with a toss of his dark head. "The war in the Ohio has left a public debt more burdensome than any in England's history. Uncle Phil writes from London that Whitehall now struggles simultaneously with three concerns in her colonies: first, the western lands, with the complications of fur trade, competing land speculation, and Indian problems; second, the need to plug holes in the Trade and Navigation Acts, from which tax revenue leaks; and third, how to make the colonies more lucrative for the Mother Country!"

The Tidewater, 1764

The hedges were fast beginning to bronze, the sourwood leaves to flame, when Colonel Phil sent down a messenger inviting the Chantilly Lees for dinner at Stratford.

"You go on without me," Annie urged. "With Thomas and Frank both visiting Stratford, the talk will be nothing but politics. I prefer to stay here with the baby."

Richard Henry gazed at his six-week-old daughter in Annie's arms. "This is the season for girls! Last year Alice produced a daughter in Philadelphia, then Phil became the father of little Matilda, and now we have a Tidewater belle of our own."

"Not entirely a season for girls, my dear. Do not overlook Missy's new son at Pecatone," Annie reminded him.

Richard Henry almost winced. Phil's anger had been predictably explosive when he discovered not only that Missy and Richard Hall were quite content to "live in sin," as he phrased it, but also that not even the birth of a strapping boy, Elisha Hall Corbin, had induced them to marry.

"Yes, the talk tonight will undoubtedly dwell on politics," Richard Henry said as he slipped on his brocade vest. "Parliament's new methods for raising revenues are on everyone's mind and tongue. The New Englanders rail against the Sugar Act, a revision of the Molasses Act, which they have been happily ignoring for the past quarter century."

Annie rocked Molly gently as Richard Henry continued. "I can hardly believe this new Stamp Tax. Everything formally written or printed, from marriage licenses to playing cards, to be stamped by a royal agent! Why, if it passes the Parliament, England will bleed us dry." Richard Henry eyed himself in the large gilt-edged looking-glass. "Whitehall seems to want it both ways, Annie. On one hand they hold to the mercantile theory. But on the other hand, they claim the war in North America was fought strictly in behalf of the colonials, that we must pay the expenses ourselves. How shall it be?" Richard Henry looked indignantly at his wife. "Are we a part of the family or are we stepchildren of the empire, considered to belong only when convenient?"

"My pocketbook does not relish the Stamp Tax expense any more than yours," Colonel Phil insisted at dinner. "But as a councilor, the King's representative, I am well aware that the Crown drastically needs the revenue."

"I am every bit as fast bound an Englishman as you, Phil," Thomas answered, dark eyes flashing, "but, as John Locke pointed out, property is inseparable from life and liberty. Under the parliamentary system, no one can be deprived of it except by his express consent or that of his elected representatives. And where, may I ask, are *our* elected representatives in Parliament?"

"There are many reasons why we are not represented in Parliament, Thomas," Phil replied with condescension. "The expense is too great, and the physical distance involved would soon put an emotional distance as well between us and our representatives."

"Besides which," reasoned William, who was spooning mashed turnips onto his plate, "we colonials could never expect to be a majority in the House of Commons."

Francis Lightfoot leaned forward, the flickering candles highlighting his handsome features. "I would agree with you to a point, Phil. But consider this. The colonial assemblies are the parliaments of each colony. It is only right that they, and they alone, levy taxes in America."

"The tax load on the King's subjects in England is twenty-six shillings a head, while in the colonies it runs generally one shilling or less," Phil scoffed. "Do you think that each of the colonial assemblies will make a voluntary contribution to the Mother Country? Unlikely." He looked at Richard Henry. "English arms and English lives rid us of the French at great cost in blood and coin. How can you be so ungrateful? Can you think of a more equitable tax? No, you cannot!" Phil answered his own question. "Grenville asked the Pennsylvania agent, Franklin, if he could think of a better way to gain revenue," Phil went on. "And *he* could not."

"We throw away our liberty if we comply with this taxation," Thomas insisted stubbornly.

"Come now, Thomas." Phil refreshed his brother's wineglass. "Grenville promises that every Stamp Act agent will be a colonial, and all revenues spent in America. I fail to see what liberties we lose. You will come round in time to see that England has our best interests at heart," Phil said genially.

"Think of Parliament as a universal legislature with the constitutional right to impose any kind of tax in any part of our king's domain."

"That I will not accept," Richard Henry said, grimacing. "But I will give fair consideration to whether I should support the taxes, albeit grudgingly."

Late that fall, Richard Henry rose in the House of Burgesses to suggest that the burgesses write directly to the King about the issue and at the same time address a protest to the House of Lords and the House of Commons. The motion passed immediately, and a committee was named to draft the letters, headed by the colony's attorney, Peyton Randolph, with Richard Henry Lee, Landon Carter, and the lawyer, George Wythe, among its members.

"The letters are not overly strong," Phil grudgingly conceded, "but they carry a tone of asserting a right rather than asking the King's approval. Other than that I have no problem with them."

The Tidewater, 1765

Three weeks after returning to Chantilly from the spring 1765 session, Richard Henry received a thick letter sealed with a splash of red wax.

"Sir," Rob Carter had written,

Knowing of your great devotion to this colony, I must tell you of a remarkable occurrence at the Capitol shortly after you departed Williamsburg. I was not present in the House of Burgesses, though I have this account on several authorities, but its aftermath I can relate from personal observation. On the 26th of May, most business completed, the chamber was almost empty, only some thirty-nine of the one hundred and sixteen members present, with Speaker Robinson presiding. George Johnson of Fairfax rose to move that the House go into a Committee of the Whole to consider the steps to be taken in consequence of the resolutions of the House of Commons charging certain Stamp duties in the Colonies and Plantations in America.

Just the day before, Virginians learned that the House of Commons had started the parliamentary procedure for passing the Stamp Act proposed a year ago by Grenville—and this despite the protests and arguments put forth by the colonial assemblies. Rumors fly that the new tax will be stiff and quite inclusive.

At any rate, Johnson's motion was seconded by a new member of the House of Burgesses, Mr. Patrick Henry of Louisa County. It was carried, and the speaker left the chair and sat as committee chairman. Johnson again rose, then deferred to Mr. Henry, who submitted a most extraordinary series of resolutions. I have enclosed them for your perusal.

They speak for themselves but there is more. This fledgling burgess, only nine days a member, apparently rose to his feet, his notes scrawled on a blank sheet of paper torn from an old law book, and offered the resolutions in a manner and voice so compelling that the members sitting on the bench were spellbound. Henry is a controversial figure . . . at twenty-nine years, an all but self-educated lawyer and storekeeper. This son of a Scotsman is tall and thin, a bit of a bumpkin in dress but like a Greek orator when he rises to his feet. (Peyton Randolph and Robert Carter Nicholas, who examined him several years ago for the bar, said his law knowledge was incomplete but his manner of presentation and his way with words so extraordinary that they were compelled to pass him.)

As Richard Henry turned the page of the letter, the enclosed copy of Patrick Henry's resolutions fluttered out. "Resolved," they began, "That the first Adventurers and settlers of this his Majesties Colony and Dominion brought with them and transmitted to their Posterity and all other his Majesties Subjects since inhabiting in this his Majesties said Colony, all the Privileges, Franchises, and Immunities that have at any Time been held, enjoyed, & possessed by the People of Great Britain."

Richard Henry quickly read through the first four resolutions, but it was the fifth and last that was the most startling: "*Resolved therefore*, That the General Assembly of this Colony have the only and sole exclusive right and power to lay taxes and impositions upon the inhabitants of this colony, and that every Attempt to vest such Power in any person or persons whatsoever, other than the General Assembly Aforesaid, has a manifest Tendency to destroy British as well as American Freedom."

He's thrown down the gauntlet, Richard Henry thought with a sense of rising excitement as he returned to Rob Carter's letter.

It was the fifth resolution that caused the stir, for it went far beyond the assertion of the right of self-taxation and laid down the dictum that neither King nor Parliament have any right at all to impose taxes of any sort on the colonies. Members of the Assembly rose to argue the point and, as if roused by their debate to a tempered passion, Mr. Henry waxed most eloquent, ending his remarks with a sweeping, defiant gesture of his fist and the words, "Tarquin and Caesar had each his Brutus, Charles the First his Cromwell, and George the Third . . ."

Speaker Robinson interrupted sharply with a cry of "Treason!" At which point, Henry is said to have finished his sentence: "may profit by their example! If *this* be treason, make the most of it!"

The House was in an uproar. Mr. Henry immediately apologized to the Speaker and vowed his loyalty to our monarch, even to the last drop of his blood. But the mood was set, the words spoken. The resolutions were passed—the fifth, however by only a single vote. Peyton Randolph was so enraged at its passage that he was heard to murmur as he left the chamber, "By God, I would have given five hundred guineas for a single vote!"

On the following day, Mr. Henry was not present in the hall, for he had law cases in Hanover, and the House, still thin in rank but calmer in mood, was led by Mr. Attorney Randolph to expunge the fifth resolution. In my opinion, the first four are strong enough, the fifth is obviously gunpowder.

The point is, my dear friend, that the newspapers in New York, Philadelphia, and Boston are already publishing our resolutions, including the fifth. What problems this will cause I can only surmise, but many of us—George Wythe, Edmund Pendleton, Will Byrd, etc.—strongly feel that no matter what we thought of Henry's ideas, his method of presentation and the hotheaded words were most ill advised. Governor Fauquier is so distraught that he dissolved the House immediately, without even a word of thanks!

Oh, to have been there! Richard Henry despaired at his own early departure from Williamsburg. Perhaps Patrick Henry's words were said with too much zeal, but he had hit the nail on the head: self-taxation is the rock and sinew of freedom, the heartbeat of English rights, as expounded in John Locke's justification of the Glorious Revolution of 1688!

Rob's letter concluded:

The main account of Henry's speech was given me by a student who watched from the doorway—Thomas Jefferson, Peyton Randolph's cousin and the son of Peter Jefferson of Albemarle County. A young man of about twenty, he plays the cello and violin in Governor Fauquier's weekly musicale, of which I am, as you know, a member. I have come to admire young Jefferson, and I believe his account to be factual.

Patrick Henry's words and the passing of his resolutions by the Virginia Assembly to boycott English goods were the spark to ignite the tinder throughout the colonies. In late August, the newspapers blared that an effigy of the Massachusetts stamp distributor had been strung up from an elm tree on Boston's High Street. Later, several thousand gathered around the tree, marched to the stamp office, and burned it to the ground. Two weeks later, the mob marched on the residence of the chief justice of the colony, destroying the house and all its handsome furnishings. A secret military organization, the Sons of Liberty, was formed, with chapters spreading quickly to other colonies to oppose the Stamp Act violently, with actions as well as words.

Colonel Phil returned to Stratford from a council sitting in Williamsburg in late October. "The capital is full of strife and discord. I could not believe the disorder," he fumed. "Poor George Mercer. As our stamp distributor for Virginia, he arrived in Williamsburg with the stamps and was met by an angry mob. I swear, he would have been physically harmed if Fauquier had not taken him by the arm and led him safely through the crowd."

Richard Henry flushed, for he had been a prime participant in just such a denigration of Mercer here at home, in Montross.

Visiting his uncle in London, Arthur wrote disconcerting letters:

I understand all the colonies are protesting. Mock funerals and coffins for Liberty seem to be the most popular form. I visited the Mitre Street Tavern yesterday and picked up all the choicest gossip. There is much discord, of course, among the powers in Parliament, with Lords Bute, Grenville, Pitt, and Rockingham all jockeying for position. They are each harassed by *The North Briton*, a wonderfully astute scandal rag that takes shots at every one of them. It is edited by John Wilkes, a member of the House of Commons, who, along with Edmund Burke and the elder Pitt, has much sympathy for the Americans and urges repeal of the act. The London merchants, angry over the loss of trade with the colonies, back Wilkes heartily. Our poor king is ill . . . no one knows quite what or how . . . headaches, fevers. Despair, I believe, is the most likely diagnosis.

Richard Henry told Annie, "Our great ship Britannia, I fear, is leaking. . . ."

The Tidewater, 1766

As was his custom, Landon Carter was hosting a New Year's houseparty at Sabine Hall. Richard Henry and Annie did not plan to stay for the full three days, for she was again pregnant. But they crossed the Neck to spend a day there, eager to see their many friends among the sixty-odd guests, whom the Carters would bed down in every nook and cranny of the rambling estate overlooking the Rappahannock.

Bayberry candles flickered hospitably in all the manor house's windows, beckoning those arriving by carriage across the dry, frozen roads of the Neck or by barge along the bitter reaches of the river.

"Twenty-eight fires blaze in this house today," Colonel Carter's son, Robert Wormeley Carter, called across the hall as he greeted them cordially.

"We'll keep the cart and oxen busy all day just delivering cords to fuel them!"

Richard Henry looked about him with anticipation. Gathered here was the Northern Neck version of a Scottish clan, and the sense of belonging to this tightly knit, high-spirited society brought a glow of pleasure to his face. He caught his reflection in the tall looking-glass over the pier table in the hall. Above a new silk coat of pale gray, his narrow, strong-featured face looked both keen and content today. The thick red-brown hair was unwigged and brushed back from his high forehead to hang in a fashionable narrow sack at the back of his neck. He handed Annie's cape to the doorman and, giving his wife's elbow a squeeze, directed her toward their host.

"Ah, the Chantilly Lees! We have a grand contingency of your family this year!" The master of Sabine Hall ebulliently greeted them. "A covey of Lees has already arrived, including your cousins Squire Richard of Lee Hall and Henry of Leesylvania."

The drawing room buzzed with talk of tobacco, of the recent droughts that had sent prices spiraling up but limited the overall yield considerably. There was gossip about neighbors and horses and activities in Williamsburg, but talk of the Stamp Act rippled through all conversations.

The caustic but hospitable Landon Carter pointed to the silver trays of glasses of wine being passed by liveried waiters. "We're serving the last Madeira from my private stock, got it before the damn oppressive Stamp Act and Sugar Bill were passed. My boycott will be as complete as possible. Because I, for one, will not submit lightly to this injustice. I tell you, sir, I'll buy only the necessities. Frugal times will soon be upon us."

Richard Henry looked at the planter with renewed respect. He had never known his father, "King" Carter, but the son was a complex and contradictory man, just as his father was said to have been. He had enormous wealth, yet was thrifty—to the point of stinginess, some said. He took special interest in his godson, William Lee, and his orphaned nephews, Rob of Nomini and Charles of Shirley. Yet he got on badly with his own children, and the Sabine household was rife with animosity. Politically active, he had taken a strong stand against the Stamp Act, speaking out, almost before any other burgess, on the subject.

The ladies had gone into dinner first, following Tidewater custom, when George and Martha Washington arrived in the company of his brother Jack, whose plantation, Bushfield, lay slightly to the east of Stratford Hall. Richard Henry observed that George had come a long way from the shy bumpkin he once was. Now he moved gracefully, a polished fox-hunter and gentleman farmer comfortable in silk clothes and silver-buckled shoes. The Fairfax family had first encouraged that in George, Richard Henry mused, and his marriage, enhanced by Martha's money, had brought out the final buffing of confidence and self-assurance.

The dancing was to begin at dusk, and by four o'clock the violins and French horns were noisily warming up in the ballroom. Richard Henry settled Annie on the sofa with a glass of lemon punch. "If you will excuse me, my dear, Colonel Carter has invited several of us to join him in the study for a brief chat." He gave her a reassuring smile. "I shall be back to lead you in a gig before you miss me atall."

On his way down the hall, Richard Henry felt his brother Thomas touch his arm. "You know, I have been thinking back to October, when we hanged George Mercer's effigy in Montross. We should plan something of that nature again. What think you?"

Thomas was referring to the mock trial Richard Henry had staged on court day at Montross. The street was crowded with fairgoers when a hangman's cart containing two straw dummies had mysteriously rolled down in front of Westmoreland Court House. One effigy was of George Grenville, the hated prime minister, and the other was the Virginia Stamp Tax distributor, George Mercer. Surrounded by a company of mock bailiffs and executioners, Richard Henry, dressed as a chaplain, had appeared to hear the stamp collector's alleged confession that he had loved gold above patriotism! The dummy of Mercer was then mounted backward on a horse, whipped, cropped about the ears, and, to the cheers of the onlookers, branded, hanged, and burned.

Richard Henry reddened. He knew he had been somewhat carried away by the growing anti-tax fervor. "I question whether demonstrations like that do any real good," he replied as they entered the study door.

"But it gives the people a way for their indignation to out," Thomas insisted.

"Boycotting all goods from England that bear a revenue stamp is our most effective way," George Washington interjected. "The British pocketbook will be our most persuasive target."

"But this boycott and our agreement not to buy stamps are equally disastrous for Virginians. No ships can clear our docks, no debts can be collected, no legal business transacted." Richard Henry paused. "It will be effective only if *all* stand together. I think we must form a Northern Neck association to enforce the boycott strictly."

"Like the Sons of Liberty?" Washington questioned.

Richard Henry nodded, fired by the prospect.

"It seems, gentlemen, you are discussing the very subject I had in mind when I asked you to join me in this room!" The master of Sabine Hall entered the study quickly and motioned for his son to close the door. "It seems that a local merchant and shipowner of Hobb's Hole named Archibald Ritchie has declared his intention to break the boycott and clear his wheat-laden ship for a voyage to the West Indies. Obviously a Tory! He is willing to buy stamps in the face of the Virginia Assembly's resolutions to boycott them. If merchants begin to yield, then our boycott will be a farce!"

Thomas looked quickly at Richard Henry. "I believe the time is ripe for your . . . association. A call on Mr. Ritchie is imperative."

Robert Wormeley Carter's face was taut with excitement. "And our call had best have sharp teeth to convince Ritchie of the error of his ways. I suggest we ride armed, not just for effect but for self-protection. Emotions are ragged over this issue! I think it well to expect retaliation from the Tories."

"And those who hold profits above honor," George added quietly.

Richard Henry had begun to pace up and down the room. "If we can round up all the local men who feel strongly about the matter, we'll put together a party of patriots that will impress Mr. Ritchie."

"Or scare the very devil out of him," Thomas finished.

"It is a chance to do more than simply appeal to or threaten the merchant Ritchie." Landon Carter was looking directly at Richard Henry. "What is needed is a strong action that will have far-reaching effects!"

"An action that reaches across the Atlantic into the very bowels of Parliament, an action that shows Virginians as Englishmen to be taken seriously . . ." Richard Henry's mind was racing. "Our first step must be to rouse to action our fellow patriots on the Neck!"

"You walk close to treason," Colonel Phil fairly spat as he strode into Richard Henry's study, brandishing a copy of the circular his brother had recently sent throughout the Neck. Phil's face was white with anger. "It was bad enough when you led the locals in hanging George Mercer in effigy at the court—yes, I heard about that—but no, by damn, you must go on, to the detriment of your own reputation, not to mention mine." He crumpled the circular and flung it into the fireplace.

"If you choose not to join us, Phil, that is your own concern," Richard Henry replied coolly. "I respect your position on the council. But remember that while you are *appointed* by the Crown, I am *elected* by the people. I must stand for their rights as free Englishmen—and my own."

At Leedstown in two days' time! Richard Henry stared at the note from his brother Thomas: "We propose to be in Leedstown on the afternoon of the twenty-seventh inst., where we expect to meet those who will come from your way. It is proposed that all who have swords or pistols will ride with them, and those who choose, a firelock. This will be a fine opportunity to effect the scheme of an association, and I would be glad if you would think of a plan."

Leedstown, a shipping port on the Rappahannock, lay directly across the Neck from Stratford. How many would gather there, he could not guess.

Richard Henry slept fitfully throughout the night, waking frequently to the echo of Colonel Phil's last angry shout: "Lees are the King's most loyal subjects! It has been so since the first Lee touched foot on Virginia! If you must do something foolish, please disguise yourself. I am ill-resolved to spend the next year trying to save you from the hangman's noose."

But what was the value of taking a stand without publicly acknowledging commitment to it? So far, the colonial letters and protests to Parliament had been done in the name of assemblies or through anonymous associations and stealthy mob actions.

In the early dawn, he rose from bed, moving carefully so as not to wake Annie. He stirred the fire to life in his study and sharpened his quill. He would write a statement of his thoughts and then present it to the men who gathered at Leedstown, signing it before their eyes. Would they join him and affix their names as well?

"Where are you going?" Annie asked nervously as he buttoned his leather hunting jacket in the early afternoon of February 27. At his grave look she went on quickly, "No, don't tell me. Please be careful, my dearest."

Richard Henry pulled her into his arms. "If Phil should come looking for me, tell him I have gone to Pecatone to visit Missy. Say nothing more to anyone."

Over a hundred tense-faced but exultant colonials crowded Bray's Church, which sat high on a windswept hill overlooking the Rappahannock River. Richard Henry could not believe so many men had gathered. Overcoming his reluctance to speak publicly, Thomas Lee made the first proposal: "We must call on Ritchie at Hobb's Hole. Bring him back to the courthouse in town; there, with his hat off, he'll read this apology." Thomas waved a paper aloft. "He must promise not to use stamped paper until the Assembly permits it! If he refuses, we'll strip him to the waist, tie him to the back of a cart, and carry him to the pillory to stand for an hour!"

Bray's Church resounded with shouts of "Aye!" as the men accepted Thomas's proposal.

"What if Ritchie refuses and says he will obtain the stamps and sail with his cargo?" someone called out.

"Then," said Richard Henry, rising, "by God, he will be forcibly restrained."

He paused dramatically, then said, "I propose we go a step further. I have drawn up a list of resolves. Addressed to the King. I submit that we agree upon them as a group, then step forward, one by one, and sign our names."

He felt the fear that swept the cold, crowded church.

"Read them, Mr. Lee. Let us hear your resolves," someone called out.

Richard Henry loosened his jacket, grasped a candle like a torch in one hand, and leaned over the communion rail. If he was ever to be eloquent, it must be now! He proposed his resolves with emotion, the words flowing with passion and commitment, his burnished red head vivid in the candle glow.

Richard Henry read in the clear, strong, and harmonious voice for which he was now well known: "Roused by danger and alarmed at attempts foreign and domestic to reduce the people of this country to a state of abject and detestable slavery . . ." His resolves declared the allegiance and obedience of the signers to the King and to the law insofar as was consistent with the preservation of constitutional rights and liberty. But they went on to pronounce that every effort would be made to prevent the execution of the Stamp Act in Virginia and to declare that any who abetted the act would be "the most dangerous Enemy of the Community, and we will go to any Extremity not only to prevent the Success of such Attempts but to stigmatize and punish the offender." The signers of the resolves bound themselves together in protection of their lives and property. The statement ended, "In testimony of the good faith with which we resolve to execute this association, we have this 27th day of February, 1766, in Virginia, put our Hands and seals hereto."

When he had finished, his cousin Henry moved boldly to his side. "We will be recognized, then, as rebels in defiance of the Crown," Henry said slowly. "I have ridden down from Leesylvania because I believe stern action is necessary. My cousin's words convince me that if our actions are correct, we must not fear to stand by them. I will sign my name beside his."

Richard Henry's boots and spurs sounded resolutely as he strode down the center aisle. He laid out the paper, a pen, and an inkwell on the vestry table. Within a hushed, watchful circle of his kinsmen, friends, and neighbors, he signed in a bold scrawl. The rest quickly formed a line. Thomas stood near the front, with the two youngest Washington brothers, Samuel and Charles, close behind, and then Francis Lightfoot and William, their cousins Henry, Richard, and John Lee, Landon Carter's son, Robert Wormeley Carter, and John Augustine Washington.

Francis Lightfoot signed his name, then moved close to Richard Henry, his cheeks pale from the cold of the unheated church. "It's done. We are all now bound to each other . . . one way or another."

Was the signing of their names to the Westmoreland Resolves an act that directed the younger Lees down a path from which there was no turning back? Was this night at Leedstown a decision point? It would seem so, the colonel decided. As Virginians and free Englishmen, they were determined to demand their rights from their sovereign and, most important, honor demanded that they sign their names to their words.

From Dark

1766–1769

The Tidewater, 1766

Behind the long leafy grove of beeches, the afternoon sun, just beginning to sink, laid dappled slashes of green across the wide back lawn of Stratford Hall. The mansion sometimes appeared formidable beneath its high-pitched gray roof, like a bastion, the tall chimney watchtowers anchoring it to the meadow like the turrets of some ancient fortress. Today, in the shimmering July haze, it looked only handsome and sheltering, the brickwork softened by the light of the sun to dull rose shot through with streaks of bronze and purple.

It never ceases to amaze me, William Lee reflected, that every hand-molded brick was inspected by Father before the masons set it in place some thirty-five years ago. Lying beneath a dogwood tree in the orchard behind the stables, William drank in the familiar fragrance of the gardens, the blue English larkspur trembling in the river breezes, the insect staccato. If only Stratford Hall were mine, he thought, instead of that damn Phil's! He looked quickly at Frank, napping in the shade beside him. He would not want anyone to see him looking at the great house with his unvarnished longing.

Four months had passed since that February night when he and Frank had galloped across the Neck in the chilling rain to join Thomas, Richard Henry, and the others who had gathered at Leedstown. Not that the meeting had any real effect, William thought with a sigh. Unknown to the men who had daringly signed what were now known as the Westmoreland Resolves, the detested Stamp Act had been repealed in London several weeks earlier; it was not until May, when the *Lord Baltimore* docked in New York, that they heard the welcome news.

Still, we took a courageous step, William thought, savoring the memory of that night at Leedstown and the following day at Hobb's Hole, when they forced Ritchie to sign a pledge not to purchase the stamps. And in a way, they had also been rebelling against Colonel Phil and his high-handed, imperious ways, for Phil, with his position on the council, did in a manner represent the British government.

"May I join you two good-for-nothing loafers?" Arthur dropped down in the grass beside them with a sigh, his hair curled in damp wisps around his sunburned face. "I've been fishing with Richard Henry and his boys. Didn't catch a thing myself, although they were landing fish left and right! I am simply not cut out to be an angler," Arthur volunteered, looking at William in mock distress.

"Don't worry, old boy, you'll soon enough be a distinguished practitioner of medicine in Williamsburg, with everyone bowing and scraping to the eminent Dr. Lee of Edinburgh. That should suit you well enough," William teased gently.

Arthur lay back, stretching lazily. "Williamsburg is not London. However, it will have to do. I suppose I can at least keep an eye on the Assembly."

William marveled at his younger brother's self-assurance. Three weeks before, the twenty-five-year-old had returned from London with his medical degree and a head full of opinions and advice that he was not hesitant to express. He had done outstandingly well in Edinburgh, walking off with top honors in his medical class. The renowned Benjamin Franklin, always looking for bright young colonials to encourage, had sponsored him for membership in London's prestigious Royal Scientific Society. Arthur had lingered in Europe until the first of May, when his paper on the medicinal values of Peruvian Bark in the treatment of malaria had been read and accepted by the society. Then, bright with triumph, he had sailed for Virginia.

William could not deny a twinge of envy, for Arthur's future as a respected physician in Williamsburg was assured. No doubt he'd marry a James River beauty and be the toast of the Tidewater. William considered his own lot; he had no real prospects whatsoever. True, he had the Mississippi Company account to manage, but for the time being the speculative land venture was hopelessly mired in British politics. He sighed.

"Why all these sighs, William?" Francis Lightfoot's voice broke William's thoughts. "They disturb this lazy Sunday and my nap!"

"I'm sorry." William's voice was apologetic. "I was thinking about my . . . future, or lack thereof."

Frank rose up on one elbow. "Your trouble is that you sell yourself short, William. You've gained valuable experience working for Phil. You manage his lands, make all the purchases for his outlying plantations—in short, you've made him quite prosperous. Now do the same for yourself! Your experience would serve you in good stead as a Virginia tobacco merchant in London. Then, if you wish to hold lands, come home and marry an heiress! As for myself"—he grinned broadly—"I prefer to have nothing that encumbers my freedom!"

"You can't mean to remain a bachelor all your life," Arthur protested. "You'll break the heart of every lady in Virginia."

The slamming of a door reverberated through the quiet orchard, and the three looked to see Colonel Phil, Rob Carter of Nomini Hall, and John Tayloe of Mount Airy on the steep steps that led down from the great hall to the back lawn.

"Phil appears to be in a good mood," Frank observed. "But then, he is happiest when he can show off his family, his plantation, his new stallion, whatever. It doesn't matter, he just likes being admired."

Supporting his brown-haired three-year-old daughter, Matilda, on one broad shoulder, Phil could be seen gesturing toward the impressive brick stables, in which there were now stalls for the sixty or more horses wearing his racing colors. His latest and finest import was a black stallion, "the swiftest horse England could provide, Eclipse excepted," Phil proudly asserted. Dotteral, the crown jewel of Stratford's stable, was already earning a tidy sum for Phil, who advertised his availability at stud for "six pounds the season or thirty-six shillings the leap." With this horse Phil would soon make Stratford the finest stud farm in the Tidewater.

"No doubt Phil would like us to join him now to pay homage to Dotteral at the paddock gate?" Arthur rose with a groan.

"I've admired that damn horse enough!" said Frank, and he picked up a calf-bound volume of Voltaire's works lying in the grass.

He turned to his marker as his younger brothers made their way through the fruit trees toward the stables. A bit of admiration for the handsome Dotteral was perhaps not too much to ask in exchange for the hospitality of Stratford Hall. Frank felt a twinge of remorse at his own indolence. On the other hand, they had all paid more than their pound of flesh to Philip and owed him nothing. Why, William and Arthur had still not collected the inheritances from their father's will! It was all the more galling when one considered how freely Phil spent money. He and his stylish Elizabeth had filled the house with magnificent imported furnishings, and the coach house held a shiny new carriage with the Lee crest, the squirrel and acorn, emblazoned on its door. And to think of all those horses!

Stratford Hall had never been more prosperous than now. Still, to his mind, Stratford Hall had never shone more brightly than when his father was its master. Though the furnishings had been simpler and the gardens less formal, each day had been a small gem. Carefree days were spent splashing in the millpond, fishing in the Potomac, running the calves and colts with Nat, and riding their ponies to the cliffs in search of pirates. Throughout those halcyon times, the strong presence of their father was ever watching over and guiding them. It was a pity that William and Arthur had been so young when he died. They had had no opportunity to draw on his strength.

Frank brushed a cloud of gnats from his eyes. It was hard to keep his mind on Voltaire when he was so pleasantly lulled by the sounds of the plantation at rest. Sundays, the slaves were free to work on their wooden houses, fish, or tend their small garden patches, and, as they went about their activities, the sound of banjos and ballators and melodic voices floated in the air.

Suddenly Frank put down his book. Another voice, an enchanting girl's voice, humming with one of the slave songs, lured him to his feet, then to the brick wall by the dogwood trees. Beyond it, he beheld a child of twelve or so dancing by herself with a sort of grave simplicity.

"Bravo!" he said, clapping his hands when the girl curtsied to an unseen partner. "You've learned your dancing lessons well!"

Startled, she whirled and stared at him.

Now, who the devil is she? Frank wondered. A Steptoe, an Aylett, or a Washington? Ah, he recognized the high, rounded brow and the deep-set violet eyes. She was a Tayloe of Mount Airy, of course, one of Colonel John's eight daughters.

"You shouldn't have been peeking. I was practicing," she reproached in a distinctive low-pitched voice.

"You must forgive me, but you are very good—graceful as a fawn. Come," he beckoned, "tell me your name." Frank swung himself over the faded red brick wall, noticing as he did that a quick look of disappointment crossed the child's face.

"Well, I know who you are, Frank Lee! Don't you remember me at all?" She smoothed out her skirt and hesitantly moved closer to where he sat, swinging his feet idly. "And I stood right beside you." She smiled reproachfully.

"Come here, little goose!" Frank reached out to help the girl settle herself beside him on the wall. "You are quite wrong to think I'd forgotten you, quite wrong indeed. You stood beside me in the great hall here at Stratford when Matilda was christened three years ago. You are a little Tayloe!"

Clearly pleased, she began to swing her feet in imitation of Frank.

"Now, let me see, Miss Tayloe, you were just a tiny thing then—nine, ten years old—still wearing sewed-on sunbonnets!" he said with a laugh. "I remember well!"

What a lovely day that had been! Phil, obviously enthralled with his little heiress, had beamed as he held the winsome Matilda, to be christened in the heirloom dress made by Hannah Lee that every Lee baby had worn. All day, family and friends had come in to view the little princess of Stratford Hall. Squire Richard had come from Lee Hall; Henry and Lucy Lee and their family from Leesylvania; Carters from Sabine and Nomini; Washingtons from Wakefield and Bushfield; and Tayloes from Mount Airy. Even Missy and Richard Hall had ridden over with Patty and their own two babies. It was the first time in many years the Lee family had all been so lighthearted together.

Frank's attention returned to the girl beside him on the wall. "Ah, my dear Miss Tayloe, you were just a little girl then," he said with a smile. "However, I see you are now an elegant young lady, learning to dance. Before you know it, you will be all grown up." Frank took her hand and measured her palm against his, her small fingers as delicate as thistledown against his hand. "One of these days you will be dressed in a beautiful gown, twirling around at a great ball, perhaps the King's Birthday Ball at the palace, and you will spy me on the sidelines and say to yourself, 'Good grief, there is old Mr. Lee. I suppose I should be kind and give him a dance.'"

Her eyes fastened on him intently as she gravely considered his words. Gently, but firmly, she pulled her hand from his and folded her hands neatly in her lap. "No," she replied, "I shall say, 'There is dear Mr. Lee. I should like to dance every dance with him.'"

Frank threw back his head in laughter. What a darling, a rosebud about to bloom! How lucky the fellow who would one day capture this spirited little prize.

The girl slipped from the wall and turned toward him, color rising in her face. "You mustn't laugh, Mr. Lee! I have it in mind to marry you—when I grow up, that is!" Then, blushing at her bold words, she turned and ran up the garden path.

"Wait, my little darling!" he called after her. "Don't run off, at least not until you tell me when we're to wed!"

But she was gone, disappearing like an apparition into the beauty of the rose garden.

"Well, I'll be damned," Frank murmured; then, drawing a deep breath, he collected his book from the grass beneath the dogwood and strode up to the big house.

Elizabeth Steptoe Lee kept Stratford Hall bustling with people. Inevitably, one found Ayletts, Steptoes, Washingtons, and Lee cousins swarming throughout the great hall or the parlors, but this afternoon, the main floor was strangely empty. Frank peered into the alcove parlor and the adjoining dining room, where the cover for cold supper had already been laid. Across the hall, the master bedroom and Matilda's nursery were as empty as the great hall. Wandering down the west wing, Frank found Richard Henry reading in the study. "Where the devil has everyone gone?" Frank inquired from the doorway.

Richard Henry peered over the top of his newspaper. "I can't really say. I believe the ladies have gone up to the towers to catch the river breezes, and another party's gone riding. Looking for anyone in particular?"

"Have you seen John Tayloe about?"

"Probably gone riding with Philip," Richard said distractedly.

"What keeps you from the party?" Frank asked.

Richard Henry handed Frank the *Virginia Gazette* he had been reading. "This."

Frank's eyes quickly came to rest on a letter signed by "An Enemy to Hypocrisy." The letter pointed out that Richard Henry Lee, who had so fiercely condemned George Mercer for acting as Virginia's stamp distributor during the brief life of the act, had himself once applied for that same position. It suggested that Lee's attacks on Mercer stemmed from envy.

"My God," Frank gasped.

"Applying for that position was an impulsive act, ill thought out, and why I did it, I don't even know!" Richard Henry snapped. He began to pace about the study. "It is true, Frank. In November of '64, before the implications of the Stamp Act were understood, I did submit my name for the position of stamp collector. Our kinsman Richard Corbin pointed out that the position would offer me financial reward and power in the colony. Since Corbin had considerable power to influence the appointment, and with Phil's encouragement, I was persuaded." He turned to Frank, anguish in his face. "I was too damned ambitious! But in truth, as soon as I thought through the implications of the Stamp Act, I withdrew my name. Frank, you know my actions in behalf of the act's repeal came from my heart. There was no malice intended by our charade. Poor George Mercer simply stood for something we all honestly opposed."

Frank fell quiet, remembering that October day in 1765 when the effigies of Grenville and Mercer had been hanged in the Montross square fronting the Westmoreland Court House. Richard Henry had played a leading role. Animated by the spirit of the day, his foxlike face had been aglow with excitement. Richard Henry had even dressed his servants in "Jack Wilkes" costumes—cocked hats, flaming red coats, and shiny high boots!

"Frank, you know my charade was not meant personally against George Mercer. For a fact, I think him to be a most amiable chap. He is George Mason's cousin and he fought hard for the Ohio Company when he served as agent in London."

"This letter is outrageous, probably written by Mercer's father or his brother the burgess from Hampshire County. But its contents will alienate some who read it, Richard Henry, and you had better be prepared for that."

Richard Henry had to agree. "It will also please others, who would like to see me taken down a peg."

That night, following the supper of cold fricasseed chicken, yellow squash, and muskmelon with pound cake, the beeswax tapers were lit in the great hall for a musicale. Colonel Phil, who had inherited his mother's musical ability, sat at the piano-forte, while Rob Carter, master of a number of instruments, played the guitar; one of the young Tayloes had her flute, and Annie Lee was called on to play the harpsichord. Voices began to drift across the evening air, singing the English country ballads they all knew so well. Then Annie Lee sang "Greensleeves."

For a time, Frank stood beside the piano-forte watching the candlelight flicker on the faces of the singers. There were at least thirty, including children of all ages, who sat in the open doorway or played on the stone steps as twilight settled over the Potomac. House servants had gathered to listen in the east-hall doorway, joining in with their low, melodic voices when a familiar hymn was sung.

Frank took small Matilda, who was beginning to fret, and led her out on the south steps, the thick risers still warm from the departed sun. The little girl nestled sleepily against his chest while he put his head down to breathe in the clean, sweet scent of her hair.

"Nothing, absolutely nothing compares to a family Sunday in Virginia," Arthur said as he joined them on the steps. "A part of the liturgy of our peculiar Virginia religion, I believe."

"Religion?"

"Of course! My school friends from the northern colonies tell me that they—Congregationalists, Quakers, what have you—go to church to hear the sermon, to repent, and to pray. We go to church to thank the Almighty we are Virginians and to see which of our friends we would like to invite home for dinner!"

Frank chuckled, then fell silent as the strains of "I Gave My Love a Cherry" drifted out into the night air. Across the darkening lawn children dashed about gaily to catch fireflies in their cupped hands.

"Who is that pretty child in the white dress?" Frank asked.

"Oh, the little Tayloe? They call her Becky," Arthur offered. "She is her father's very heart, for they almost lost her to the fevers when she was small. In fact, she still is quite a frail little thing. Rather enchanting, isn't she? Some day she might make a nice wife for brother Thomas's boy. They are near each other in age, I believe."

The next November, Richard Henry set out for Williamsburg with reserved expectations. Shortly after reading the letter from "An Enemy of Hypocrisy," he had posted a response to the *Gazette* explaining that he had impulsively applied for the position of distributor without knowledge of what the Stamp Act was about, and when more was known, he had realized the injustice of the act and had withdrawn his application, then fought vigorously against the act. When no other letter appeared after the publication of his explanation, Richard Henry's fears of continued controversy began to abate.

A buoyant feeling marked the Assembly, a sense of relief over the repeal of the Stamp Act; the planters' confidence was clouded only by tight credit, the misfortunes of a poor tobacco season, and Parliament's confusing clamp on expansion to the west.

Colonel Phil chose to spend the season in Uncle Phil Ludwell's handsome brick townhouse on the Duke of Gloucester Street, but Richard Henry and Francis Lightfoot decided to lodge with Arthur, who had rented a comfortable house in town. He had recently bought on credit a fashionable coach with two high-stepping horses, and announced himself "open in the business of medicine." Already patients were flocking to his front-room dispensary.

"I know I'm going to be successful," he said with a rueful sigh the first night Richard Henry and Frank were in town, "but in truth, medicine bores me stiff! Nothing but itches and aches and pukes and pains from morning to night. Thank God, the Assembly is in session to dispel my ennui."

Richard Henry's eyes met Frank's over the table. In the candlelight, their youngest brother looked like a petulant fawn.

"Perhaps you should consider Philadelphia!" Frank suggested. "Will Shippen would surely take you in as a partner, or at least help you set up, and Philadelphia society might prove more lively. It's a larger city, more like London."

"Will Shippen is more dedicated to medicine than I will ever be!" Arthur exclaimed. "Not only does he offer instruction in midwifery, an arcane and delicate subject suitable only for old women and witches, but his anatomy lectures at Pennsylvania Hospital have rather shattered the nerves of the older physicians of Philadelphia. To tell the truth, I've not enough interest in medicine to join our good brother-in-law."

"Allow yourself a year or so," Richard Henry suggested. "Perhaps it would help if you found yourself a damsel to wed."

"Why do people always say that? If that is all one needs, than a visit to a brothel whenever one is in low spirits should be sufficient! Is it a panacea —two spoonfuls of marriage and you'll feel better by morning?" Arthur threw down his napkin. "If companionship and affection solve one's problems, why are you still a bachelor, Frank?"

Frank's laugh was easy. "My few needs are better solved by the charms of numerous ladies. I have yet to find one for whom I would be willing to give up all the others!"

The Tidewater, 1767

In May, the magnetic, powerful treasurer and speaker of the House, John Robinson II had died at his estate on the Mattaphony River. Thus the burgesses' first order of business was to fill his positions. Robinson had been so admired, even loved, that Governor Fauquier had until now disregarded the Crown's instructions to separate the position of speaker from that of treasurer. Robert Carter Nicholas, who was serving as temporary treasurer, was formally elected to that position. It was not unrealistic to think that Richard Henry had a good shot at Robinson's other post, speaker of the House.

Indeed, it was one he longed to fill. With the backing of numerous Lees and other stalwart supporters, he had a fair chance of being elected speaker if things fell his way, and new rumors that Robinson had mismanaged the accounts, as Richard Henry had long claimed, just might work to his favor.

Richard Henry had been first to raise the issue when two years ago he had called for a House investigation of Robinson's books. What a howl that had brought from Robinson's supporters! But a committee had been formed and a modest investigation attempted, which reported the treasurer's books in good order. Now, however, Robert Carter Nicholas was hinting that there were indeed irregularities in the books, that they were proving delinquent for a vast, as yet undetermined sum. "Mr. Attorney," as the impressive lawyer Peyton Randolph was known, was nominated for speaker by Archibald Cary.

"I think," Frank whispered, "we should move slowly with your nomination. Let us test the wind."

Richard Henry rose from the bench to extol the qualifications of Richard Bland. He thought very highly of the fifty-six-year-old Bland, who had won notice as a liberal thinker and pamphleteer in the struggle against the Stamp Act. In praising Bland, Richard Henry hoped to assert his position of leadership in the House and remind the moderate and liberal delegates that they had previously spoken of nominating him for speaker. Perhaps his words would set them thinking. But the bait was not taken, and to Richard Henry's disappointment, the learned forty-five-year-old Peyton Randolph was elected to the post.

"What is this I hear about you and George Mercer?" George Washington asked Richard Henry when they met at a dinner party at Rob Carter's townhouse that evening. "**I have** heard talk all the way from Fredericksburg to the taverns here in Williamsburg to the effect that the Mercers have sworn to bring you down for disparaging one of their family."

Stunned, Richard Henry could not reply. So that had been one of the forces playing against him! He smarted with embarrassment over that immoderate pageant in Montross. True, similar protests had taken place all over Virginia and in other colonies, and he could easily defend himself—if only he hadn't applied for the stamp-distributor position!

Rob Carter, a genial and expansive host, raised the first toast to the King, which was followed by a second and a third. "There was *never*," he said with emphasis, "the slightest question of our loyalty to the sovereign in our protests of the Stamp Act."

"Never!" echoed the table.

"One would almost think," Arthur whispered wryly, "that the King had been on America's side all the time!"

Richard Henry held up his glass. "I propose a toast to the great William Pitt, Earl of Chatham; and to Lord Camden, who stood by America in its hour of need; to the Earl of Shelburne; to John Wilkes; to all those in the House of Lords and the House of Commons who spoke for us. To our friends!"

"Hear, hear!" Glasses were raised and drained.

"I was in the House of Commons when Pitt delivered his splendid oration in our behalf," Arthur announced to the table with typical candor. "He was magnificent! He said he *rejoiced* that we resisted the tax. And I can tell you firsthand, gentlemen, Lord Shelburne is a most brilliant young man. He told me that he believes Parliament should encourage western expansion and then improve the collection of quitrents to raise revenues—thus avoiding new American taxes."

"New American taxes?" The words reverberated around the table.

"I grant you, the repeal of the Stamp Act was a major concession, but don't forget the accompanying Declaratory Act, which proclaims Parliament's authority to make laws to bind the colonies and people of America as subjects of the Crown," Arthur reminded.

"But the wording of the Declaratory Act is vague."

"Vague enough," Arthur broke in on Rob Carter, "to allow for future taxation."

"You are asking for trouble with that interpretation, Arthur." Colonel Phil spoke impatiently from the far end of the long oval table. "Not even Patrick Henry or that Massachusetts rabble-rouser Sam Adams has said a word against the rider to the Stamp Act's repeal." He looked around the table. "I apologize for my outspoken younger brother. He may have some fine English political connections, but he lacks the experience of age."

To break the long, awkward pause, George Washington started to speak of his crops. He spoke confidently, his words as usual slow and measured. "I have given up planting tobacco, gentlemen, at least on my northern Potomac lands. We sweat blood over the leaf from the spring planting through autumn curing, then have no control over prices. I think it too dear a labor for so small a profit." Washington pounded his fist on the table. "Wheat is a much more substantial and dependable crop...."

Despite Arthur's sociability after dinner, Richard Henry knew by the brightness of his eyes and his assiduous avoidance of Phil that his youngest brother was seething with anger. But not until Rob Carter's front door closed behind the three Lees did Arthur turn on Phil.

"By God's grace, I won't have you humiliate me like that! How dare you speak so in front of others, you bastard?" Arthur blocked his oldest brother's path on the steps, his voice aquiver with rage.

Richard Henry put his hand on the young man's arm and addressed Phil directly. "Arthur's right, Phil. You were tactless. Arthur may be hasty in his concern over the Declaratory Act, but—"

"I don't give a tinker's damn about your opinion," Phil shot back at Richard Henry. "You are taking yourself awfully seriously these days, what with your burning of effigies and those treasonous Westmoreland Resolves— all of which were totally ineffectual! You know as well as I that the Stamp Act was repealed because Grenville's government fell and there was too much pressure from London merchants who did not want trade with America jeopardized. Your dramatic and foolish shenanigans had nothing to do with it!"

With a rough hand, Phil pushed Arthur from his path; then his dark eyes met Richard Henry's squarely. "Another thing, my dear brother," he said in a hard, sarcastic tone, "if you are wondering about the coolness you are feeling in the Assembly, let me enlighten you. When John Robinson's accounts are finally squared away, you will probably be proved right. Robinson was a generous man, a man who stood by his friends to save them and our economy from ruination. Your attack on him, though fair, will therefore not be appreciated." He threw one parting shot. "You are far too esoteric,

Richard Henry, and you as well, Arthur. You are not practical men who deal with economic realities. And you think I attack you when in truth I defend you!"

Philadelphia, 1767

The long investigation into Robinson's tangled books bore out Phil's angry speculation to an extent that few had imagined. Ten years of heavy taxes and war on the western frontier, years of short tobacco crops and tight credit abroad, had caused many of the colony's leading planters to suffer, some drawing close to bankruptcy. Virginia law required that paper money issued by the colony be burned when returned in payment of taxes. Robinson had instead privately loaned one hundred thousand pounds in treasury bills that should have been retired as well as thirty thousand pounds of his own to the beleaguered planters. Nearly all was loaned to his James and York river friends and supporters.

"So Robinson decided to play king, manipulating the funds of the colony as he wished." Arthur was telling Alice the story of the scandal as they sipped their tea in the high-ceilinged drawing room of Shippen House. "Planter after planter was revealed to be in debt to Robinson or to the Treasury, from William Byrd of Westover, who leads the list at ten thousand pounds, to Ben Harrison, near the bottom with a small loan of one hundred fifty pounds."

"That would never have happened in Father's time," Alice responded with dismay.

"To be fair, John Robinson faced a difficult decision," William quickly added. "By burning the paper money, he would bankrupt his friends. He chose instead to save them."

Alice rose, teacup in hand, and wandered to one of the tall, luxuriously draped windows. "I wonder what any of us would do in such a circumstance. You know, after Eliza's death, Colonel Byrd married my Will's first cousin, Mary. I had always thought the Byrds quite well-to-do, for indeed they keep a winter house here that is lively with children and friends. I had heard that Colonel Byrd is an immoderate gambler, but to think he could have borrowed so much!" Alice's fair brow furrowed.

"Well the furor is settling down, but there are problems closer to home," Arthur said glumly.

Alice started, her porcelain face reflecting concern. "Is someone ill at home? Do you bring me bad news?"

"Oh, no, everyone is well enough. Colonel Phil is thriving," he said almost bitterly, "and Stratford Hall has never looked better. I think I would resent Phil's good fortunes more were I not so fond of Elizabeth and Matilda."

"Well, how about Missy and Thomas?" Alice prodded.

Arthur laughed reassuringly. "Thomas has quit the House of Burgesses, claiming it takes too much time from his family and Bellevue. And Missy is as well as ever, independent lady that she is. She now infuriates Phil by refusing to attend the Anglican church and calls herself a New Light Baptist. Phil has to hold his tongue in public, for Rob Carter of Nomini also proclaims this new religion."

"How like Missy to follow her own thinking. She is so persevering." Alice clapped her hands.

"No more than you," William said gallantly. "You have made your own happiness, just as Missy has."

He and Arthur had arrived only a few hours earlier and had not yet talked to Will Shippen, but it was apparent that their friend was doing well. He had built a house for Alice in the fashionable Court End section of Philadelphia. It was an aristocratic three-and-a-half-story house of red and black brick, dazzling both outside and inside, with gleaming marble steps and elegant appointments. The Shippen children, four-year-old Nancy and her younger brother, Thomas, were dark-eyed, captivating children. Arthur had particularly lost his heart to Nancy. He had danced her about and held her on his knee, reluctantly giving her up only when it was time for her to return to the nursery.

"You seem to thrive in Philadelphia, my dear Alice." Arthur thought her more lovely than ever and awash with confidence.

"Our City of Brotherly Love is not so beautiful as Virginia, but far more handsome! And while life in Virginia is comfortable, here it is far more exciting!" Alice laughed lightly, adding in explanation, "I have been much spoiled by the Shippen kin, who live all around us. Why, Will's cousin Judge Shippen has his home right down Locust Street and across from us. Uncle and Aunt Willing have built a row of lovely stone houses for their grown children, one of whom, Mary, relays a great deal of Virginia news. It is she who is married to our Colonel Byrd, you know."

"Philadelphia is indeed a very appealing city," Arthur agreed. "It surpasses Williamsburg in almost every way. One being that it is a truly great port."

"About the only thing I don't fancy is the weather," Alice continued. "It is not at all like Virginia, or even London. Here the elements change quite unexpectedly from sweltering heat to sudden storms. And the winters are miserably windy and cold. In my opinion, though I cannot get Will to agree or disagree, such changes weaken one's resistance to the flux, fevers, and smallpox. Of course, Philadelphians compound the problem with their strange custom of keeping windows open constantly when the weather is mild. The mosquitoes fly in quite fiercely, and the racket of coaches and drays clattering over the cobblestones simply drives one mad!" She looked nostalgic. "It is not one bit like sleeping in the quiet country at Stratford Hall."

William nodded. In his brief ride through the city this morning on his way to Shippen House, he had been surprised by Philadelphia's size and the orderliness and sparkle of clapboard and brick houses along cobblestone streets. The faint reek of slop in the gutters was the only jarring note in the lovely setting that Alice had fashioned for herself.

"But, Arthur"—Alice turned to her youngest brother, who sat moodily in his chair contemplating the toes of his boot—"you intimated that something is amiss at home. Is that what has caused you to accept our longstanding invitation? Have you some news about Richard Henry or Frank?"

Arthur hesitated. "Politically, Richard Henry has had some disappointments this year, but he is well enough, and Frank goes his merry way without a care in the world! The problem lies with William and me." Arthur shook his blond head. "It has been a wretched year for both of us, and for cheer and good advice we have come to you and Will."

"How delightful!" Alice dimpled. "We shall have marvelous parties and long talks together. Indeed, I shall introduce you to some young Philadelphia beauties. They do not flirt so beguilingly or dance so gracefully as Virginia ladies, but they are, in general, more learned, and they speak their minds most candidly. I rather think you will both be challenged and charmed."

Their attention was diverted by Will Shippen's arrival home for dinner. The handsome doctor greeted his Virginia in-laws and immediately led them to the dining room, where he uncorked one of his best bottles of wine.

"A toast: to our happy memories in England!" Will lifted his glass high. "To London and the day I first set eyes on Alice Lee, and to her brothers, who are now my kinsmen as well as friends!"

"Oh, I'll drink to those memories," Arthur said longingly. "What pageantry! I remember the procession for George the Third's coronation, the royal carriages, the Horse Guard, and those crowds. . . ."

"I remember how beautiful his new Queen was in her tiara of diamonds," Alice sighed ecstatically.

William Shippen looked at his wife lovingly across the table. "You are the beautiful one. Charlotte of Mecklenburg was very regal, even glowing, but she was not nearly so beautiful as the girl on my arm!"

"By the way, Will, what ever has become of John Morgan, that fellow who watched the procession with us?" Arthur was referring to a dapper classmate from the University of Edinburgh. "As I recall, you two had great plans to start a medical school in the colonies."

"The medical school is under way," Will replied. "In fact, my dear fellow, we now have ten students. Morgan lectures in physics, and I do the honors in anatomy and surgery. We even have a course in midwifery. I have set up a temporary lodging house for indigent women for their lying-in. I am convinced that every physician should deliver at least one infant before his medical education is complete."

Arthur grimaced. "A charming idea! But I am enormously glad it was not part of my preparatory work. I am far more interested, Will, in your surgery and anatomy lectures. And where, if I may be so indiscreet, do you find your cadavers?"

"Arthur, really, old lad, must you ask such questions at the dinner table?" William Lee raised his hand in protest.

"From Potter's Field, not from any church graveyard, I promise you that," Will answered quickly. "My soul, ever since I began there has been the most terrible fear that I shall rob some family grave in the dark of night. Why, a night watch has even been posted in St. Mary's graveyard next door. Sometimes I think I am fighting uphill all the way."

"And John Morgan, has he been no help?"

"Dr. Morgan has not played fair with Will," Alice burst in. "Morgan returned from his European travels last year and presented the scheme for a medical school to the trustees of the Pennsylvania Hospital as if it were all solely his own idea! He hardly made mention of Will, though they collaborated on the plan while at Edinburgh." Alice's face flamed with indignation.

"Well," Will said soothingly, "the medical school is under way, and that is all that matters." But his face revealed that the affair rubbed him.

After dinner, Will showed Arthur the anatomy lecture room he had set up in the yard of his physician father's house on Fourth Street. "Aha, this is the charnel house, I presume!" Arthur teased.

"Do not jest," Will reproved spiritedly. "As I tell my students, 'The butcher is author of many discoveries.' He must be taken seriously!"

Alice and William remained in the Shippen House gardens. Shaded by weeping willows, the small townhouse yard was a mass of sweet-smelling jasmine and guilder roses. Alice sat in the swing and pulled in her skirts to allow William room to join her. In his dark eyes she could discern hints of pain. But then, there had always been pain. It saddened her that this strong, silent brother, who had shared her misfortunes, financed her flight to London, and stood witness at her wedding to Will Shippen, had not yet found happiness.

"I think, William," she said thoughtfully, "that you must try again to break away from Stratford Hall. It doesn't really matter what you do. You must break Phil's hold over you!"

"I think you are right," William said with a crooked smile. "I came to visit you and Will to see if you might have some suggestions."

"And why did Arthur come?" Alice asked gently. "What are his problems?"

"You won't believe what a bramble patch he has got himself into this year! It would be funny if it weren't so painful. When the accusations against Richard Henry by the Mercer family worsened this spring, Arthur, thin-skinned and hot-tempered as he is, challenged Mercer's brother to a duel. It was the talk of Williamsburg, only it never came off! Arthur swears they had arranged to meet with pistols in a field outside Williamsburg at five in the morning, while Mercer insisted that the time had been set for six and they were to meet with swords on the road to the racetrack near Yorktown."

"My Lord, what happened then?" Alice could not take in this absurd picture.

"Mercer and his rowdy friends burned an effigy of Arthur one night, then Arthur took a swing at Mercer when they bumped into each other in a coffee house the next day—and received a black eye for his trouble. The whole thing ended in a kind of draw, but Arthur's reputation was somewhat damaged. His practice fell off badly—not that he gives a damn."

"Then what does he care about?"

"As far as I can see, politics, and only politics. He wrote an essay about colonial currency for the *Gazette*, but, the Lees being much out of favor these days in Williamsburg, the paper refused to print it. They had published another piece Arthur wrote earlier in the spring that aroused much controversy. Once burned, you know."

"Arthur has always been prolific with his pen and vocal with his opinions," Alice commented. "What was the earlier piece about?"

"A letter to the Assembly in support of a bill to tax slave traders in the colonies and to use the revenue to retire paper currency. Angry ripples went through the Tidewater because of it. People feared that literate slaves might read Arthur's opinion that insurrection by the slave population was possible, and attempt it!"

Alice gave the swing a gentle push with one silk-slippered foot. "So, Arthur felt it better to get out of Williamsburg for a while. I can understand that! Well, you are both welcome to stay at Shippen House as long as you like."

The sound of hasty footsteps broke the tranquillity of the garden. Arthur and Will Shippen rushed through the gate. "My father just received this letter off a schooner from Boston," Will said hotly, throwing a thick envelope into William's lap. "Read it! Just read that! Parliament again moves to tax the colonies. According to my father's correspondent in London, last month they passed the Townshend Duties. We're to pay tax on all imported glass, paper, paint, lead, even on the East India Company's tea!"

"I can't believe Parliament can be so thickheaded," William said incredulously. "Surely they understood, when they repealed the Stamp Act, that we will not stand to be taxed except by our elected representatives." He stared down at the letter, then began to read it aloud. " 'You will recall, my dear Dr. Shippen, that Mr. Pitt, Earl of Chatham, fell ill shortly after taking over the government last fall. His successor, the young Duke of Grafton, is an amiable chap but unfortunately not strong enough to lead His Majesty's government. The Chancellor of the Exchequer, Charles Townshend, took advantage of his weakness to introduce a bill this May in yet another effort to draw revenue from the colonies. I wish, my friend, that you had been present on the eighth of May, when Townshend rose in the Commons to deliver his speech. Although witty and well spoken, it was filled with lies. Townshend (known as "Champagne Charlie") taunted our former Prime Minister Grenville over the repeal of his Stamp Act. Grenville then replied, "You are cowards, you are afraid of the Americans, you dare not tax America!" Townshend retorted, "Fear? Cowards? Dare not tax America? *I* dare tax America!" Grenville jeered, "I wish to God I could see it!" And Townshend declared, "You will, you will!" ' "

William looked up in amazement at Arthur and Will Shippen. Arthur's face was crimson. "So, by God, Townshend rammed his act through the Parliament. Now they have done it, they've pushed us to the edge!"

Leesylvania, 1767

"Arthur is the angriest of us all. Why, I dare say he took the Townshend Duties almost personally!" Richard Henry related to his cousin Henry Lee at Leesylvania as the fall of 1767 ripened into November. "He persuaded William to cut short their visit to the Shippens' so he could return to Williamsburg to rally a response. You've not yet received a letter from him concerning the subject?" Richard Henry asked, incredulous.

"No, I've not received a letter from Arthur." Henry chuckled. "To be honest, I am glad Governor Fauquier declined to call the Assembly this fall. I realize that he is hoping tempers will cool before we reconvene in the spring; however, I am curious to see how the other colonies respond to this dastardly action by Parliament. What's more, I am delighted to avoid the long weeks in Williamsburg. It's such a shame to miss a good hunting season."

Richard Henry looked with affection at his cousin. Like his brother, Squire Richard of Lee Hall, Henry Lee was faithful in his attendance at the House of Burgesses, but neither took an active role. They rarely addressed the House and were in no way firebrands, as he and Francis Lightfoot had been dubbed.

"I am not at all sure I understand this talk about the distinction between 'external' and 'internal' taxation," Lucy said as she poured dishes of tea.

"It was the Pennsylvania agent, Ben Franklin, who most unfortunately raised that point during the Stamp Act debates," Henry explained. "He said there was a sharp distinction between 'external' taxes, such as customs duties on goods entering the colonies, and 'internal' taxes, such as those on legal documents. He maintained that 'external' taxes are proper but 'internal' taxes are not. Townshend has now turned that distinction to his own advantage."

"To be fair to Mr. Franklin," Richard Henry added, "he later moved off that position. According to Arthur, no one has been more persuasive in behalf of the colonies before Parliament in recent years than Ben Franklin of Pennsylvania."

"Perhaps," Henry ventured, "the duties imposed by the Townshend Act are of lesser concern than is the administrative 'reorganization' that Parliament has adopted at Townshend's suggestion."

"You are on the mark there!" Richard Henry responded with heat. "But I'll wager that the northern colonies will feel this step the most. They will be the first to protest. To control smuggling, these custom commissioners are now empowered to use those damn writs of assistance—search warrants, if you will. Parliament has even gone so far as to allow the admiralty courts to try cases without a jury in order to snuff out the New England smuggling trade," Richard Henry continued.

"It seems they're making a strong effort to tighten the holes in their trading system—caused in part by their own lax collection of customs duties," Henry commented wryly.

"True! Another disturbing aspect of this legislation," Richard Henry continued, "is that the funds they wring from us will be used to pay our royal officials and judges, making those gentlemen independent of our assemblies for their salaries and beholden to the Mother Country instead."

"I think," said Lucy, "that the King could at least have sent a royal commission to talk with us about the best way to raise monies in the colonies."

Richard Henry nodded emphatically. "Arthur's friends in England write that our colonial agents were not even consulted before the new taxation plan and 'reorganization' were put into effect."

"Well, there's nothing to be done about any of this until the Assembly can meet and discuss the affair." Henry rose and stretched. "I propose we set our minds to duck hunting instead."

A small hunting party left Henry's comfortable wooden country house well before the sun rose the next day. "Looks to be a clear morning," Henry crowed exuberantly over a cup of steaming coffee, cold ham, and cornbread set out in the kitchen house. "A good covey of mallards and ringtails were sighted in the west marsh yesterday. Come, let's not dally."

Richard Henry followed Henry's two eager boys, eleven-year-old Henry (nicknamed Harry) and his younger brother, Charles, into the courtyard. "I should have brought Thomas and Ludwell along," he murmured to Nat West, who was oiling their guns.

Nat flashed him a smile. "Well, *we* going to enjoy it anyway!"

The party left the house yard, Henry's pinto leading the way, and turned into the fields, the last rider dismounting to pull closed the wooden gates behind them. Already there was a light frost on the ground. Richard Henry reached into the pocket of his leather jerkin for his gloves. The cold early morning air felt good on his face, jolting him awake.

"Do you like hunting as much as I do, Uncle Richard Henry?" Young Harry Lee had urged his mare up beside him. "I think I like to shoot better than anything!"

"Aye, I like the sport, lad," Richard Henry answered, sizing up the boy. Harry Lee was a handsome young fellow, broad-shouldered, quick-witted, as quick in the saddle as he was of mind. It was said that he was becoming the finest young horseman in the neck, winning nearly every race he entered. Henry and Lucy adored their first-born son, and he was indeed a boy of whom they could be proud. Young Harry Lee of Leesylvania was a lad of exceptional confidence and ability. Everyone had noted it, George Washington more than once.

The day was growing brighter, trees and rocks taking shape. As the horses splashed through the fords, Richard Henry could make out the red plumage of the low-growing sumac that bordered the creek.

The brisk morning dispelled all thoughts of politics and problems, leaving only the sheer pleasure of living and the anticipation of sport. He prided himself on being a good shot. He had a keen eye and a steady hand. It was something his father had taught him long ago in the marshes and hollows around Stratford.

"We'd best tie the horses here," said Henry. "From this point on, the land is very swampy as we approach the Potomac."

While the horses were being tethered, the muskets and bags of powder were handed out. Richard Henry took his gun and rubbed it affectionately. It was a long flintlock rifle—a "backwoodsman gun," Frank called it—that he had traded for in Williamsburg the year before. It had a longer barrel and was a great deal more accurate than the usual English muskets.

"I sho' glad the snakes done retired to winter quarters," Nat volunteered as they mucked their way through the swamp, mud gushing and sucking against their boots. "Dey de only thing what bothers me about this here hunting."

Henry held up his hand. "Shh . . . Look there! Swans in open water on the other side of the marsh," he said softly.

Richard Henry removed his gloves and hurriedly pulled a paper packet of gunpowder from his pocket, bit off the top of the packet, and poured the powder down the barrel, tamping it down with the ramrod.

"There must be six of them at least," whispered Nat.

"But there is no good shot from here," young Charles moaned. "They've all moved into the brush."

It was true; the opportune moment had passed. Richard Henry lowered his gun.

"Follow me," Henry instructed quickly. "Careful now, it looks like mudgut . . . very treacherous. Step only where I step."

Cautiously, Henry began moving out across the dark reedy swamp, then glanced back encouragingly. "It will be worth it. There is a natural blind on the other side." He paused suddenly. "Let me test this next stretch."

Richard Henry saw almost immediately that Henry was in trouble. As he had moved out upon the muddy ground, his boots sank and were enveloped rapidly with an eerie smoothness. After another step or two, it was obvious that the sands and mud were less substantial than they appeared. Henry was up to his knees in the swamp.

"Turn back, father," Harry warned anxiously.

With a cry of frantic desperation, Henry called over his shoulder, "Stay where you are! It is sinking sand!"

"Can you make it? Can you make it back?" Richard Henry asked urgently.

"I am trying, by God, I am trying! But whenever I move, I sink deeper."

"A rope, Nat!" But the rope had been left with the horses. Richard Henry pulled off his jacket while Henry's servant ran back to the thicket. "Catch hold of the sleeve." Richard swung the jacket out over the murky swamp water, but the sleeve fell far short of Henry's fingers.

"I don't think it's strong enough anyway," he groaned.

"Don't move any more, Henry. For God's sake, every time you move, you—"

Henry Lee was now almost waist-deep in the swamp, the horror of his dilemma etched in his face.

Richard Henry looked about desperately. Quickly he pointed the barrel skyward and pulled the trigger to clear it of powder. The flints sparked but there was no gunfire. He pulled back the flintlock and fired again. It was the same.

A look at Henry told him there was no time to waste. Richard Henry got down on his knees, the rifle in his left hand, and began to crawl cautiously out upon the mudgut. For a foot, two feet, the ground held, but ahead it seemed to give way under his hands.

He extended the rifle, holding it by the long barrel, until Henry's fingers closed around its carved stock. "I am going to pull you back, Henry. Just let yourself be dragged. Nat, grab my feet."

Slowly, with all his strength, Richard Henry began to pull back on the rifle barrel with both hands; it was working, Henry was moving toward them.

"Just a few more feet, Richard Henry. Keep on pulling! I am almost clear." Henry's pant legs and boots, soaked and stained with mud, were coming free of the swamp.

"One more pull," Richard Henry gasped. Suddenly the gun slipped in his hand, its flintlock grazing a stone near the water's edge. He heard the explosion and felt the searing pain, like a hot iron branding his left hand, as Henry lunged past him onto dry ground.

"His fingers done been shot off!" cried Nat. "He bleedin' bad."

Stunned, Richard Henry held out the gushing hand, clasping it at the wrist with his other hand.

For a moment, everyone was frozen, staring in horror at the blood pouring from the wounded hand. "Give me his jacket and get me a stick," young Harry Lee ordered. With quick, sure movements, the boy tied the sleeve of the leather hunting jacket around Richard Henry's wrist.

Numbly Richard Henry watched the boy slide the stick under his sleeve and twist it. The fabric tightening around his wrist was the last thing he felt before he fell unconscious.

The local doctor examined Richard Henry's shattered left hand. "He's lost the four fingers from the knuckles down. I'm not sure if we can keep him from developing infection, perhaps losing the whole hand . . . or even his life. I can prescribe no other treatment than heating the steel and searing the stumps. Fill him with brandy. The more he has, the less he'll feel."

The Tidewater, 1768

In January, Arthur came up from Williamsburg with a new salve for Richard Henry's slow-healing knuckles. "I got this from the apothecary shop in Williamsburg, the Unicorn's Horn. It is the latest thing from Europe for burns. You'd be a lot better off if you wouldn't smoke, you know. What a vile habit!"

Arthur perched on the foot of the daybed in the Chantilly parlor where Richard Henry lay resting, a clay pipe in his good hand, and related all the news from Williamsburg. "Fauquier is ill, and I have no word whether there is to be a spring session of the Assembly. There is, of course, much talk about the Townshend Duties." Arthur drew a newspaper from his pocket and shook it open in front of Richard Henry's eyes. "Have you seen the remarkable essays in the *Pennsylvania Chronicle?* This is the fifth in the series, by a Philadelphia lawyer, John Dickinson, entitled 'Letters from a Farmer in Pennsylvania.' "

"No, I've not read any of them." Richard Henry put down his pipe to take the newspaper. "I'm eager to learn what a Philadelphia lawyer has to say about our present situation."

Arthur's face flushed with excitement. "He has a great deal to say, and what's more, he is not afraid to say it! He condemns the recent acts of the British legislature in straightforward, yet respectful tones. He also addresses the Quartering Act—you know, the one requiring local authorities to provide quarters for the King's troops and furnish free supplies, including beer or rum. Well, the New York Assembly agreed to provide for eleven hundred men but balked at the free drink. For that, the New York Assembly is to be suspended by the British. Dickinson says that all Americans should protest in behalf of New York."

Richard Henry scanned the article carefully. "What is the news from the other colonies?"

"They name liberty trees and sing protest songs as far north as Boston and south to Charleston. All the newspapers are filled with articles roundly denouncing the British. Just listen." Arthur took back the paper and read aloud: " 'Let us behave like dutiful children, who have received unmerited blows from a beloved parent. Let us complain to our parent; but let our complaints speak at the same time the language of affliction and veneration.' I think Dickinson is too gentle, far too appeasing."

"And what would you say?"

"That we petition for relief, not as dutiful children but as equal Englishmen who are owed our rights."

Richard Henry's gray-blue eyes searched Arthur's. "Why, then, don't you let it be known that a sterner message needs to be sent?"

"That is all you had to say and Arthur dashed for quill and paper," Frank teased three months later when Arthur's first letters, signed "Monitor," were published by Rind's *Virginia Gazette* in Williamsburg. Frank had come down to Stratford and Chantilly on his way to Williamsburg for the spring 1768 sitting. Governor Fauquier had died on the first of March, and Council President Blair had called the Assembly. "As usual, Arthur managed to work his arguments against slavery into his message. He is quite eloquent!" Frank declared with a laugh.

"I am proud of his words, Frank," said Richard Henry. "Rebellious as they sound, they call for a posture the British cannot ignore."

Frank nodded his agreement to Richard Henry, who stood beside him in the fresh sunshine of the April morning. How pale his brother looked, his wounded hand still swathed in linen bandages. "I will miss your company in Williamsburg. With Thomas no longer in the House and with you absenting yourself this session, I feel a weighty responsibility as the only Lee brother in the Assembly."

"Don't forget Phil."

"But we don't count him, do we?" Frank replied wryly, as he walked toward his waiting horse.

Yet Phil was not to be counted out completely, Frank found out a month later when, surprisingly, Phil voted with the council to back the House of Burgesses' address to Parliament protesting the Townshend Duties.

"I completely agree with John Dickinson's call to colonial legislatures for resolutions and petitions," Colonel Phil said as he and Frank rumbled in Phil's carriage on their way to Berkeley for a weekend house party at the close of the session. "But I find Arthur's 'Monitor' letters most offensive. They are far too emotional, and what is this idea of his about asking Parliament for a 'Magna Charta Americana'?"

"He thinks of it as a bill of rights, so to speak," Frank explained. "But I must agree with you, that would be pressing Parliament a bit much."

As the blue-and-white carriage left the King's Highway and turned into

Ben Harrison's private forest of ash, oak, and holly laced with dogwood, Frank felt his expectations rising. The scent of boxwood and the soft air had put him in the mood for dancing and romance. He whistled under his breath at the thought of this promising weekend. William Byrd would come over from Westover and Charles Carter down from Shirley, and each boasted pretty daughters. Then there were Carys and Blands and Randolphs. Like a child dreaming of sweetmeats, Frank ticked off the luscious possibilities for the weekend.

Already carriages were unloading in the oval turnaround on the land side of the Georgian brick manor house. Servants dressed in the Berkeley livery stood ready to carry in the visitors' baggage; dogs yapped their welcome; and from the dependencies that lined the turnaround, aproned black women, babies in their arms and big-eyed children at their knees, watched the handsome guests arrive.

Phil and Francis Lightfoot descended from their carriage just as Speaker Peyton Randolph and his wife, Bette, stepped down from theirs. The Randolphs were childless, but traveling with them was Peyton's cousin, the tall red-haired Thomas Jefferson, who had just begun to practice law in Williamsburg. Also with them was Speaker Randolph's brother, John, who had succeeded Peyton as attorney general of the colony, and his son Edmund.

The Randolphs were staying in the manor house since Bette Randolph was Ben Harrison's sister and therefore "family." Phil and Frank were taken to the comfortable red brick "bachelor" house to the left of the main house.

"This will be a glossy crowd," said Phil as they dressed for the evening. "I just saw the Tayloes, and John Page from Rosewell."

Frank appraised himself in the mirror. He rather liked this newest style of forgoing a wig and powdering one's own hair, or letting it go natural and simply brushing it back, the ends captured in an eelskin or a silk bag at the back of the neck. At thirty-four, he had not a trace of gray in his raven-black hair. In that respect he was like his father, whose dark head had only a few strands of silver when he was in his fifties.

Frank arranged the spotless linen at his neck and wrists and set out with Phil along the brick walk toward the great house, where sounds of music already floated on the blossom-scented air.

Their host greeted them genially just inside the door. "Ah, Colonel Lee and 'Loudoun' Lee, I am most delighted to have your company."

"And we are gratified to be included, dear cousin." Phil made a courtly bow to Harrison, a huge bear of a man who stood well over six feet and was most substantial in girth.

Though an active member of the Assembly, Ben took even greater interest in the business and pleasures of plantation life. He was especially proud of Berkeley, which was decorated with fine oil paintings and elegant furniture, the equal of any in the New World. Now he was at his most expansive. "You will find dinner spread in the dining room, gaming has begun in the parlor, and, as you see, the dancing is already under way— amazing, as the evening is so young! A portent that we shall have a rousing time before this night is over!"

Phil moved toward the parlor with Ben and John Randolph, but Frank stopped short. One of the dancers, tiny and graceful, her brown hair caught up in a soft knot held with a rose, had whirled past him, her white embroidered skirts floating gracefully in her wake. He was transfixed by her luminous eyes. Surely they had met before. But he could not remember having ever shared a dance with her, and such a beautiful creature one would not forget. She was perfection! He could not tear his eyes from her . . . the rounded breasts, the soft lift of her chin as she turned in the dance.

"I say, Frank." Phil tried to catch his attention. "There is talk in the parlor that you should hear. Frank, are you listening?"

Reluctantly, Frank followed his brother into the parlor and accepted a glass of wine. By God, his hand was shaking! Who the devil was she?

"Listen, Frank." Phil shook his arm. "Will Byrd and I make the exact same point about the Townshend protests."

Frank forced himself to concentrate.

"While it is all well and good to protest the Townshend Duties," Byrd was saying, "we are still hard put to find a solid legal argument against them, for we freely acknowledge Parliament's power to regulate the empire's commerce. Nor can we deny that many of the new regulations are designed to enforce old laws already on the books and long accepted. We can hardly dispute such laws now, even if we did not always abide by them in the past. It is indeed a dilemma that lowers the spirit." He stopped to take a sip from the crystal glass in his hand. "But at least these spirits are fine!" He raised his glass, Berkeley's fine blend of corn liquor gleaming amber in the light.

"I would hope," Phil said optimistically, "that by appealing directly to the King we might find a solution—"

"You know what Arthur says to that," Frank broke in. "We would be complaining to the front legs of a steed about its back legs. Now that Lord North has succeeded Townshend as Chancellor of the Exchequer, it is his faction of the Whig party, known as 'the King's friends,' who hold the power in Parliament."

With that, Frank excused himself to return to the hall. But the mysterious dancer was no longer there. Nor was she in the dining room, where guests were filling their plates from silver and china platters of aromatic ragouts, fricassees, finely marbled roast, and whole broiled fish, artichokes, sweet potato soufflé dotted with black walnuts, sweets, fruit marzipan, and, wonder of wonders, strawberry ice.

Undeterred, he wandered through the crowded rooms on the main floor of the house, stopping to converse with friends or kiss the hands of the pretty belles, all the while his deep-blue eyes sweeping each room. Had he imagined her? What the deuce had happened to her?

From the doorway he could see couples wandering arm in arm along the terraced gardens that led down to the river. Below the gardens, the waters of the James glittered as the golden sun plummeted in the sky, then suddenly met the water. There was an emerald flash—and it was gone! Frank stopped for a moment, mesmerized. In his entire life, he had seen that flash only one time before, when he and Richard Henry had journeyed to Jamestown with their father.

Berkeley's Hundred had been one of the first settlements built outside the confines and protection of the Jamestown fort. Its settlers from the ship *The Margaret* had been brutally murdered in the Indian massacre of 1622, and its lands eventually purchased by the second Ben Harrison. Frank sauntered down the steps and stood beneath one of the oaks that sheltered the house, his eyes following its trunk to the window where the present master's father had been struck by lightning with his little daughters in his arms. And somewhere there was a carving, a heart with a *B* and an *A* inside it, chiseled by that same Ben Harrison when he built this house for his new bride, Anne Carter Harrison. Following the path toward the kitchen house, he located the touching symbol of love on the side of the house right above his head.

"There is dear Mr. Lee," a soft voice wafted behind him. "I should like to dance every dance with him tonight. . . ."

Behind him, wrapped in a filmy blue shawl, her eyes dancing with triumph, was the very girl he had been so desperately searching for.

Frank turned, his arms folded across his chest. "I should have known it was you. Turn around for me, Becky Tayloe. You are all grown up. I can't believe it."

"So I am!" She pirouetted triumphantly beneath his outstretched hand, then looked up at him suddenly with a provocative gleam in her eyes. "Indeed, I have grown up . . . for you."

The hunter was now the hunted. Caught slightly off-balance, Frank took a step back. She moved closer, undaunted. "Would you now like to claim the dance I promised you two years ago at Stratford?"

Frank swept the girl into his arms and brushed satiny strands of hair at her temple with his lips.

Later they walked in the moonlight on the middle terrace. "How old are you?" He kissed her nose lightly.

"I am sixteen, well, almost sixteen." She stood on tiptoe, her mouth seeking his, foreclosing the question.

"Oh, God," he groaned. He pulled her into his arms. "Can this really be happening? Have you really grown up so quickly?" Untwining her arms from about his neck, he led her to a wooden bench shielded by a tangle of vines bordering the ladies winter garden where herbal aromas suffused the soft river breezes.

"The sweet, sweet smell of last year's lavender." Becky breathed in deeply. "Did you know these five terraces from house to river were laid expressly for Anne Harrison?" Becky asked.

He pulled her close, stroking her rounded arms, the soft curve of her shoulder. "Let us not talk of trifles. This may seem precipitous, Miss Tayloe, but I am compelled to tell you that I have fallen desperately in love with you and want to marry you. I am more sure of that than of anything in my life. Does this shock you? Perhaps you are too young as yet to know your own mind."

A delicate finger against his lips stanched his words. "I have known my own mind since I was eleven years old and stood beside you at the christening of Matilda Lee. I fell in love with you that day, my dear Frank, and I have loved you steadfastly ever since. Nothing, nothing will ever change my mind." She pulled back suddenly and looked at him with mock chagrin. "I am not really *that* young. Girls of thirteen get married. Why, there was Ann Fitzhugh at Eagle's Nest long ago, and that was a most happy marriage!" She paused, growing serious. "To be sure, my father will object. He may present some difficulties."

Frank awoke in the early hours of the dawn, tossing in his bed, reliving every romantic moment of the evening just past. It was Becky Tayloe that he held, longed for, needed. He could still smell the faint odor of violets that had been in her perfume. Before breakfast, he sought out Councilor John Tayloe, who strolled on the upper terrace near the house.

"I know what's on your mind, Frank. I saw it in your face when you came into the house with my Becky on your arm last night." John Tayloe's face was drawn. "I saw it in her eyes, too. You just can't ask this of me, Frank. You are nearly twenty years older than she. You would take her far away from Mount Airy to your farm in Loudoun County, and I would not see her often. Becky is very precious to me, Frank. She is such a delicate girl. It would break my heart if . . ."

Frank was silent as the older man trembled beside him. It was true that

Becky Tayloe was as fragile as a spring flower. Did he have the right to take her away from the opulent Mount Airy plantation to be the mistress of his simple farm in the isolation of Loudoun County?

"Just give her time." Tayloe put his hand on Frank's arm. "Let Becky grow up at home for a year or two; then, perhaps, we shall see."

Later, as they gathered for the morning hunt, Becky appeared with the rest of the women to send the riders off. Frank dismounted and came quickly across the grass. Through wide slits in her silk sun mask, her violet eyes searched out his. "Father told me of your talk this morning. Two years is an eternity. You must fight for me, Frank," she whispered urgently.

London, 1768

A miserable November rain pelted the back garden of the small, fashionable house on London's Cecil Street. In the drawing room, William was explaining the complications of Frank's new love affair to his cousin Hannah Philippa, who sat in an armchair by the fire listening intently.

"Frank has courted all the Northern Neck girls in turn. Suddenly, little Rebecca just grew up in the twinkling of an eye."

"She's hardly grown up at fifteen, William." Hannah Philippa's dark eyes were fastened on his face. "Your brother Frank has loved many times before. He may change his mind—indeed, he has a fickle heart—or, for a turnabout, she might!"

"This time it is different." William stared into the fire. "I spent a week with Frank before Arthur and I sailed, and I assure you he is entirely smitten by this little creature. The Great Lover means to have her even if he has to wait several years."

"You sound envious." Hannah Philippa surveyed William's strong, brooding profile in the firelight. "Have you never been in love yourself, William?"

He paused, then stared at her. "Love? I am not certain I even know what the word means. I am far more comfortable with you, dear cousin, than with any other woman I have ever known. If I had prospects to offer a woman, perhaps . . ."

When Arthur had impulsively given up his Williamsburg medical practice to return to London and study law, William had taken the opportunity to travel with him. The two now lodged in Arthur's rooms at Middle Temple, and William had made application to merchant with the East India Tea Company. "I care little where they send me," William had told Arthur moodily. "Any damn place in the British empire will do."

From the ground floor of the tall narrow townhouse, the pealing of the front doorbell shattered the quiet of the drawing room. Hannah Philippa's eyes danced with amusement. "Something about the impatience of that bell tells me Arthur is here. He has a way of ringing it so insistently."

Footsteps pounded on the stairs; Arthur burst into the drawing room. He pulled off his leather gloves and handed them to the footman, who followed behind, already burdened with cape, tricorner hat, and silver-headed walking stick.

"I say, you two make a cozy picture. Exchanging secrets, are you? Have you a spot of sherry for a freezing relation, Hannah Philippa? I've trudged through the foulest of muck on the Strand!"

With a rustle of taffeta, Hannah Philippa fetched the crystal decanter from a side table. "Why, Arthur Lee, a Bond Street dandy, striding through the muddy, rutted main streets of the city—what an image! Sit down, dear boy, and tell us what mischief you are up to! You are clearly bursting with something!"

Arthur's countenance was, as usual, utterly transparent. "Today the *London Gazetteer* has published an essay of mine that is quite smashing, if I do say so myself. Moreover, publishing in the *Gazetteer* means having the piece reprinted in every colonial newspaper! And I've another that they've promised to print in a week or so—it, too, is on the subject of the alarming events taking place in Massachusetts."

Arthur now stood with his back to the fire. "I contend in these essays that there is a conspiracy afoot, that the Massachusetts royal governor, the British ministry at Whitehall, and their new band of henchmen, the customs collectors, plot to keep Boston in such disorder that rioting will be inevitable—and therefore, justify—aye, even invite—outright repression. Why, look what happened there last June. A wealthy young merchant named John Hancock, one of the chief contributors to the Sons of Liberty, was falsely charged with smuggling Madeira on his sloop, *The Liberty*. A Boston mob, roused at the instigation of Sam Adams, rescued Hancock and his vessel, in the process badly harassing the royal customs officials. Then the governor dissolved the Massachusetts Assembly and called troops down from Nova Scotia to restore order."

"I think you're on to it," William nodded. "I've heard Lord North told Parliament that America should be prostrate at their feet before they even deign to listen to her complaints. God, it would appear we've no friends at all in London!"

Arthur smiled in exultation. "There you are wrong. We've the Whig opposition leader, Lord Shelburne, small though his following may be, and don't forget—even more important—John Wilkes is in our corner! I am on my way to prison to dine with him today."

"Dine with John Wilkes at the King's Bench Prison, will you?" William could not help giving Hannah Philippa a sidelong glance. "A fitting place for two firebrands to plot rebellion!"

"That devil Wilkes," as King George III was wont to call him, had defied every political combination that had governed Britain during the past five years. A notorious lover and rakehell, he had acquired a reputation for his support of the rebellious American colonies. In 1763 Wilkes had forfeited his seat in Parliament, fleeing to Paris to escape arrest for libeling the King and his Scottish advisers in the forty-fifth issue of his scurrilous newspaper, the *North Briton*. He had returned to London some ten months ago, and won a seat in Parliament the very next month, his bravado, quick wit, and personal charm capturing the hearts of the people of London and Middlesex County. Even now he was still the popular hero of the city.

Wilkes voluntarily surrendered to a London court in April and, convicted of the long-standing charges, was incarcerated at the King's Bench Prison, across the Thames in Surrey. In the comfortable apartment to which he was assigned there, he received both unrestricted guests and hordes of gifts from sympathetic friends in all parts of the empire. The South Carolina Assembly voted fifteen hundred pounds to pay Wilkes's debts, and Maryland and Virginia had sent him large containers of tobacco, and Jamaica, exotic pineapples. The Boston Sons of Liberty had shipped two enormous turtles, one weighing forty-five pounds (Wilkes's slogan was forty-five), the other forty-seven pounds. "That makes ninety-two pounds, which equals Massachusetts's patriotic number," Arthur had explained to his Ludwell cousins. Wilkes's constituents may have elected him an alderman, but the House of Commons stubbornly refused to seat him on the bench in St. Stephen's Chapel as the elected representative from the County of Middlesex.

"And that intolerable situation, an outright violation of English common law," Arthur pointed out as he rose to depart to dine at King's Bench, "brings up a major question of import to us all. Does not an Englishman, whether from Middlesex or America, lose his sacred rights when he is taxed by any other than his *elected* officials?"

"I do rather worry about him," Hannah Philippa commented as he dashed out. "The radical element in this city is like a whirlwind, quick to swirl one up and then throw one down."

"You needn't worry about Arthur. While he consorts with the likes of Wilkes, he also keeps company with poets and philosophers whose sensibilities are as sharp as his own. Arthur's angelic appearance belies a nerve as steady as any general's."

Hannah Philippa held William rapt in her gaze. "You give Arthur all the glory. Your sentiments are as strong and incisive as his, yet you hesitate to speak out. I'm never certain what lies in your heart. . . ."

William stared back into her eyes. Why Hannah Philippa had not yet married, he had often wondered. She was not an extraordinary beauty, but her looks were serenely pleasing, and she moved with delicate grace. This quiet young woman, now thirty, had always been close to her father, and her sorrow over Phil Ludwell's death the previous year made her in some ways even more self-contained. She would probably sail home to Virginia soon, William realized, and claim her legacy, of which Green Spring was a major portion. He turned away almost bitterly, leaving Hannah Philippa standing alone by the fire.

The Tidewater, 1768

In early December, Francis Lightfoot set out from his farm in Loudoun County for the Christmas holidays at Stratford and Chantilly. His coach was loaded with gifts—fine brandy and books for his brothers, imported silk shawls for the ladies, and toys and sweetmeats for his nieces and nephews. Carefully wrapped in silk and secreted deep in his trunk was a velvet box containing a delicate cameo brooch and garnet ring. He would personally deliver that box to Mount Airy the week before Christmas. Whether he would be allowed to call on Becky or not, his gift would be waiting for her on Christmas morning.

He had spoken briefly with John Tayloe while in Williamsburg in October for the short session called to herald the arrival of a new royal governor, but they had skirted the subject of Frank's suit for the fair Rebecca.

"She remains at Mount Airy with a cough," Councilor Tayloe had commented tersely to Frank's inquiry. "I thought it best not to subject her to traveling." Despite his anxiety, Frank had not pressed the issue.

Traveling across the Neck, Frank thought about the new governor. Richard Henry would be curious to know more about Baron de Botetourt, the first royal personage to be sent to govern Virginia since Berkeley.

The sixty-gun man-of-war *Rippon* had dropped anchor on October 25 in Hampton Roads, and the next evening Botetourt arrived in Williamsburg, where torches and bonfires illuminated the streets in his honor. Amid the gawking crowds lining the Duke of Gloucester Street, Frank had watched the governor and his welcoming committee, the King's Council, House Speaker Peyton Randolph, Attorney General John Randolph, and Treasurer Robert Carter Nicholas walk the mud road from the Capitol to a waiting banquet at the Raleigh Tavern.

Almost immediately rumors began circulating that Botetourt had been instructed to call this Fall Assembly solely to dissolve it; and if a newly elected Assembly still persisted in its protests against the Townshend Duties in the spring, he had orders to dissolve it again and suspend any councilors who sided with the burgesses. Frank was eager to hear what Richard Henry thought about this.

A light December snow was falling as Frank's one-horse carriage turned off the King's Highway down the two-mile drive into Stratford. Should he stop and pay his regards before driving on to Chantilly? It would soothe Phil, he concluded, and he turned his horse toward the great house.

"Thank God, you've come, Frank! I have terrible news." Phil put his arm around his younger brother's shoulder and drew him quickly into the dimly lit hall. "It is Richard Henry's Annie," he continued hoarsely. "She died this morning of the pleurisy. Our brother is stunned beyond belief." Phil's face was white with anguish. "She was truly a lovely lady. We all loved her."

"Everyone at Chantilly had been sick with the dry heaves and coughing," a tearful Elizabeth Lee explained in the alcove parlor. "Richard Hall diagnosed Annie, Thomas, and Ludwell as all having severe pleurisy. He gave them the most up-to-date treatment, tartar emetic, and the following day they were bled and given butterfly weed." Her voice broke. "The boys responded immediately, but Annie grew only weaker. Then, this morning at daybreak, she died in Richard Henry's arms."

Phil embraced his distraught wife and looked pleadingly at Frank. "Perhaps you can help him."

It was almost midnight when Frank's coach reached Chantilly. A single candle flickered in the chilly front room, where a handful of embers sparkled wanly in the fireplace.

"She's gone, Frank," Richard Henry whispered, his face pale as death and his eyes glazed as if he were filled with the fever. "One minute she was alive, then she was gone before . . . Frank, you make a mistake to wait. Go now to John Tayloe and plead your suit. Happiness is so fleeting that, if you find it, you must seize every moment."

Four days later, Frank arrived at Mount Airy. Becky rushed to greet him in a swirl of red velvet skirts as he stamped the snow from his boots in the front hall of the great stone house. "I knew you'd come!" she cried.

Paying no attention to either the servant or Becky's little sisters, who had followed her into the hall, Frank swept her into his arms. "I swear I shall not leave without a date for our wedding!"

Becky's face flooded with joy. "Father is in the library. Go to him now, Frank. Make him understand!"

"By Jove, it's Loudoun Lee, is it? What a surprise on a cold December day!" Colonel John Tayloe slammed shut his book. His words were hospitable as he welcomed Frank into his library, but his manner was guarded.

"No, Frank! I say no!" He interrupted before Frank could get out more than a few words. "There is no family I would rather see Becky marry into than yours, but I cannot let her go at sixteen." The colonel shook his head adamantly. "She is still a delicate creature. She should remain at home a little longer." His expression was set. "When I am certain that she knows her mind, I will reconsider."

Frank faced him squarely, hands thrust in his pockets. "Becky knows her mind, John. If I were not totally certain of it, I would not press my suit so strongly. Yes, she is young and fragile; I mean to cherish and protect her just as you do." Frank's tone grew insistent. "You must agree to our marriage, or . . ."

"Or what?" The older man folded his arms defiantly across his chest. "You know, Frank, that Becky cannot wed without my consent. No argument of yours can alter the fact!"

" 'Or what?' you asked, Father." Becky's husky voice filled the silence. "Or, the fact is, you will break my heart."

The two men were transfixed as the small brunette approached them from the shadows of the doorway.

"You *must* give your consent, Father. I have loved Frank Lee all my life—as long as I can remember." Her eyes suddenly brimming with tears, she put her hand on Colonel Tayloe's arm. "Please, if you wish me to be happy, you must say yes."

Colonel Tayloe wavered. This slip of a girl had always been the daughter closest to his heart. He looked pleadingly at Frank. "I cannot bear the thought of Becky's being taken so far away from all she knows and loves. Would you accept as a wedding gift, instead of a dowry of money, some thousand acres of land here on the Rappahannock, with a house designed by you both to be raised at my expense?"

Frank looked down at Becky's luminous face as she stood in the curve of his arm. "Would that be to your liking, my love?"

At her nod, he held out his hand to John Tayloe. "Then it is agreed. I shall lease out my house and lands in Loudoun and resettle here on the Rappahannock." His arm tightened around Becky's slim waist. "Ours shall be a house filled with love and gentleness and honor, sir. I assure you."

The Tidewater, 1769

The marriage took place at Mount Airy in the second week of March. In an embroidered dress of pale-blue tucked silk edged with lace, Becky Tayloe said her vows to Francis Lightfoot Lee.

"I have never seen a more radiant bride," Missy Corbin whispered.

"Or a more ardent bridegroom," Richard Hall replied. "True love shows a face that cannot be disguised."

"Nor should it be disguised, but nurtured for an even greater bloom," she said firmly, lacing her fingers with his.

Richard Henry stood beside them and completed the thought in a quiet steady voice. "And appreciated always, for the rare grace it brings into our lives." He shook his head and turned away.

A rich black wedding cake studded with dried fruit and soaked with brandy dominated the mahogany serving table of the dining room. Colonel Tayloe had set forth his finest Madeira for the wedding celebration and had called up the dancing master from Williamsburg.

During a lull in the afternoon's festivities, Frank sought out Richard Henry and found him in the Tayloe dining room, studying the gilt-framed paintings of English racehorses that hung above the Chippendale serving table. For a moment Frank hesitated, not quite certain whether Richard Henry was really looking at the paintings.

"Please do not think that in my joy today I am unaware of the sadness in your heart," Frank said gently.

Richard Henry turned away, struggling to control his emotions. "Nor must you think, Frank, that in my sadness I do not rejoice in your marriage. I wish the greatest happiness and health for you both."

Frank poured out two glasses from the heavy glass decanter on the side table. "I am glad you have been re-elected to the Assembly this spring, Richard Henry, and am sorry I cannot join you. This year I must settle Loudoun Farm and build a house for Becky. It is a pledge I made to Colonel Tayloe. But you must keep me informed, for our problems with Parliament must be settled for once and all!"

Botetourt had dissolved the Assembly! Richard Henry stumbled out of the red brick Capitol, shocked at this abrupt ending to a session that had started so auspiciously.

"An interesting fellow, this Botetourt," Benjamin Harrison had murmured as the burgesses trooped downstairs after taking their oaths of office in the paneled council chamber. "You know, he left a bit of romantic scandal behind in London—that, plus losing his fortune speculating in an unincorporated brass company. Our good king has saved both his reputation and his financial livelihood by granting him this governorship."

Reassembled in Burgess Hall, the House members in short order had re-elected Peyton Randolph speaker. Thomas Jefferson, a new and eager young burgess, had been allowed to compose the traditional response to the governor's welcome, a response that Robert Carter Nicholas had shaken his head over, rewriting several sentences he thought not quite elaborate or wordy enough. Botetourt received the kind words with a smile, then formally opened the session.

A few days later, the burgesses voted to bypass the governor and send a petition directly to King George concerning the Townshend Duties.

"This will bring down Botetourt's wrath," Henry Lee had predicted, "just wait and see. He will not tolerate our going over his head."

Indeed, within the hour Botetourt's chariot rolled posthaste from the Governor's Palace, and the clerk of the General Assembly strode down the aisle of the House chamber calling out, "Mr. Speaker, the governor commands your immediate attendance."

Waiting in his chair of state behind the oval table in the upper chamber was the grave-faced governor. "Mr. Speaker and Gentlemen of the House of Burgesses." Botetourt, in a plain suit of crimson silk, looked grimly at the men who stood two and three deep around the paneled chamber walls. ". . . You have made it my duty to dissolve you; and you are dissolved accordingly."

In stunned silence, they now streamed from the Capitol. George Washington nudged Richard Henry. "Our meeting is not yet over," he said quietly. "We are to reconvene in the Apollo Room of the Raleigh immediately."

When the clamor in the front room of the popular tavern had quieted, George Washington rose to present a plan of action drafted by his Potomac neighbor George Mason. Haltingly, George proposed a voluntary association that would bind its signers to practice frugality, and he enumerated a long list of English goods signers would refrain from importing until the Townshend Duties were repealed.

It may have been written by Mason, but it was based on a sentiment Richard Henry had often heard George Washington expound: action over oratory. The curtailment of merchant trade would, just as it had with the Stamp Act, provide leverage. The next morning, after ninety-four burgesses signed the nonimportation agreement in the Raleigh Tavern, they called for glasses: "To the King! To the Queen and the royal family! To Lord Botetourt and to prosperity in Virginia!" At the last, George raised his eyebrow at Richard Henry.

When the glasses were again refilled, Randolph called for a final toast: "To a speedy and lasting union between Great Britain and her colonies!"

"In truth, we are standing by our brothers in the northern colonies," the burly Peyton Randolph said later, over dinner in the King's Arms. "Abiding by this nonimportation agreement will be harder for Virginians than for those in Massachusetts and in New York; they have their own manufacturing to support their economy, but we shall simply have to do without."

"Which," said George under his breath to Richard Henry, "will do a world of good for some of our planters, who sink deeply into debt from much good living. Wools instead of silks will become honorable apparel."

Honorable, but not preferable to Virginians, thought Richard Henry. They were seated at a round table with Squire Richard of Lee Hall and Henry Lee of Leesylvania. With Henry was thirteen-year-old Harry, who seemed entranced by these momentous events. The boy's shirt was of the finest lawn, and the silver buckles on his shoes gleamed. Even the young in Virginia were used to the good life. No, it would not be easy for Virginians to forgo luxuries, or anything else. But, by God, they would if they had to!

George bent to catch a remark young Harry was making. "Aye, sir," the boy was saying, "my brother Charles and I shall be off to the College of New Jersey at Princeton at the end of the summer. Dr. Shippen in Philadelphia recommends the college highly—I believe his family were founders—and Mr. Madison of Orange County has a son who is in his second year at Princeton. He also speaks highly of the institution."

"Have you a thought of a future profession, lad?" Richard Henry asked this boy who had once saved his life.

"I have, sir. I lean toward law."

Henry Lee stretched across the table to put in, "Arthur writes to suggest that Harry eventually join him in London."

"I say, Richard Henry." George Washington turned suddenly. "Has William got his assignment with the East India Company? I would be curious to know where he has been sent. To the Indies or Calcutta?"

For the first time since his arrival in Williamsburg, Richard Henry's face broke into a wide smile. "Interesting you ask of William! I found a most remarkable message waiting for me when I arrived in Williamsburg. It appears that William, on the very eve of sailing for India, decided instead to embark on the sea of matrimony. He writes that he has wed our cousin, Hannah Philippa Ludwell, at St. Clement Danes Church in London!"

Will West was later to confide to his son, Nat, that Richard Henry had spoken with some amusement of Frank Lee, who was so enchanted with his violet-eyed young wife that he could rarely be induced from the banks of the Rappahannock, where they were building a house on Menokin Creek.

The colonel suspected that Richard Henry had been a little envious, and that he must also have been somewhat taken aback by William's unexpected marriage in London. Certainly he wished his younger brother every happiness, but he had not come to expect impulsive romantic actions from one who was generally so unsure of himself and lacking in bold gestures.

He might have expected to hear of a dramatic alliance by Arthur. But it appeared from the youngest Lee's correspondence that, for the time, Arthur was so enamored of his law studies at the Middle Temple and his involvement in the turbulent political milieu of London that he had no time to think of matrimony.

Through the Rising Light

1773–1775

London, 1773

Between William Lee and his dark-eyed Hannah Philippa ran a bond so deep that it sometimes seemed to William each knew what the other was thinking. So happy was he in his marriage that it terrified him when he occasionally woke in the night from dreaming that these four years were only a figment of his imagination.

"It is only a two-year assignment," Arthur had reassured him that February day in '69 when word arrived from East India House that he was to sail in a fortnight for Bombay. "Then, you can decide whether you want to stay on in the East, come back to London, or return to Virginia. Perhaps you will lose your soul to India, become a nabob!"

"Or, more likely, end up in the Black Hole of Calcutta," William had retorted morosely.

His Ludwell cousins had received the news with apparent enthusiasm. "How wonderful for you, William!" exclaimed the younger Lucy as she clasped him affectionately around the waist.

"It should be such a great adventure," Hannah Philippa's eyes had turned black with emotion. "I've no doubt about your abilities, my dear cousin. You will do splendidly in the mercantile trade. Lucy and I shall correspond, of course," she had said, turning abruptly to the window.

And in fact, this assignment was just what he had been hoping for, so why, he wondered, was he so miserable.

"I hope you will think of us occasionally," Hannah Philippa finished.

Then he had wanted only to leave London as soon as possible. He had walked for hours, stopping in a jeweler's near Fleet Street to buy a French antique locket, which he had wrapped in black velvet and sent without a message to Hannah Philippa. Since her father's death in 1767, she was wealthy enough to buy a hundred lockets if she chose, and it would mean little to her, but he could not resist the gesture.

On the evening before the Indiaman *Princess of Wales* was to sail from Plymouth, William had dispiritedly gone above deck for air. Black pools of rainwater glittered on the long, shadowy wharf, and the quiet was broken only by the rumble of a carriage. He had watched it materialize from the dark, narrow lane and turn with a clatter of horses' hoofs toward the dock, where, in the pale light of the winter moon, it had suddenly become recognizable.

The Ludwell coach-and-four had pulled to a halt when William ran down the gangplank. "Does Miss Hannah Philippa ride inside?" he asked, hardly daring to breathe.

"Aye, Mr. Lee." The coachman, down from his high seat, was already lighting a torch. "We drove all day with hardly a stop, she being afraid we'd miss your sailing."

When William opened the carriage door, he saw Hannah Philippa just waking. Her little bonnet, a pelisse of green silk, framed a face that seemed all eyes and hesitant, trembling lips.

For a moment, William had stood gazing at her, then climbed in to take her in his arms. Desperately she had clung to him. "I knew you loved me, William, but you wouldn't say it and I wasn't sure you knew it yourself." Her words were a velvet whisper in the darkness.

"But you cannot love me," he had protested almost bitterly. "I am not good—"

Hannah's gloved fingers came up to trace the firm features of his face. "Not good enough?" She remonstrated. "You are strong where I am weak, brave where I am cowardly. You are the only person that I can talk with, laugh with, be myself with! You, William, are the only person in the world who gives my life meaning."

"I've nothing to offer you, no land—not even the inheritance left me by my father. You are an heiress."

"William, you are a Ludwell as well as a Lee. Is it not right that we share the legacy of our grandfather—that is, unless you don't love me. . . . I am your first cousin, after all."

He stopped her words with a kiss. "You are blood of my blood, the love of my life!" he murmured harshly. "If you will come to me as wife, then I shall take you proudly as wife!"

"Then you will not sail for India?"

"Let us find your coachman, my darling, to help collect my belongings. I've only to write a few notes resigning my position and we shall set off for London tonight." He paused. "Hannah Philippa, you are certain? You were so self-contained when I called to say good-bye. What changed your mind?"

"The locket," she said with a smile, "and the words engraved inside. I realized then that you did love me, and I wasn't afraid to let you know that I loved you also."

"What words?" William stumbled.

"In French . . . 'You are my heart,' engraved inside the locket," she said almost impatiently.

Venus had intervened for him. William had taken her chin in his hand and lifted her face. "My darling, they are the truest words ever."

On March 7, 1769, William and Hannah Philippa had exchanged their vows in the handsome dark-paneled church of St. Clement Danes on the Strand.

Even now, four year later, he could hardly believe his good fortune. Marriage with Hannah Philippa meant not only personal happiness but material advantages as well. His wife was rich in land, having inherited Green Spring and more than seven thousand acres on the James River, as well as several houses and lots in Williamsburg, a stable of thoroughbreds, and 164 slaves. Lucy having moved into the home of her guardian, Peter Paradise, an old family friend, he and Hannah Philippa had acquired a fashionable new home at 33 Tower Hill, overlooking the great Tower of London. The mansion had been handsomely appointed, from the office and counting rooms on the ground floor up to the drawing-room level and the bedrooms above. Even the houseboy was dressed in elegant livery, marked with an *L* for Lee and Ludwell. Now only the wavering fortunes of his new business clouded their happiness.

In the fall of 1769, determined to strengthen the family fortunes, William had gone into partnership with the respected merchant and colonial agent for the Massachusetts Bay Company, Dennys De Berdt, and a young American merchant, Stephen Sayre. As the major investor in De Berdt, Lee and Sayre, William purchased a new 180-ton ship, which Arthur insisted he christen the *Liberty* in honor of John Wilkes's popular slogan.

De Berdt's untimely death in April 1770 had thrown all the financial responsibility for the venture on William's shoulders, and with tobacco prices depressed, he was just holding on. If only he could win the support of more Virginia tobacco planters to fill the *Liberty's* cargohold.

He had, however, made many friends and now felt comfortable on the Virginia Walk of the Royal Exchange. He had joined the Haberdashers, one of the more influential of the guilds. Through this association he had become a freeman of the City of London, with the right to vote for the lord mayor, the sheriffs, and officers of the City, who were not appointed by the King, as elsewhere in England, but, rather, chosen from the all-powerful guilds and elected by the freeholders, a right jealously guarded by Londoners. It was, William had noted, as if London were all but a self-governing colony like Virginia.

"I say, William, are you daydreaming?" Arthur called over the tea table. "You've not been listening to a word I've been saying!"

"Not true. I've heard you telling Hannah Philippa about the Bach concert last night at Covent Garden. And then you asked if I would dine tonight with you and John Wilkes."

"Well, what's your answer?"

"I was mulling it over in my mind. I don't like forsaking the pleasure of my heart's companion for an evening, albeit rousing, with the Society of the Bill of Rights!"

Arthur gave his sister-in-law one of his engaging smiles. "I well understand your dilemma, but we need you tonight, William, really we do! Hannah Philippa I'm sure understands."

The young woman handed Arthur his tea with an amused sigh. "I understand only that you have an irresistible way of talking William and me—everyone, in fact—into doing whatever you would have us do!"

Arthur gave a laugh of delight and dropped a cube of sugar into his tea. At thirty-three, this youngest Lee had shed his brash and boyish impulsiveness. In its place was an even more winning sort of charm, polished and persuasive.

In addition to his studies at the Middle Temple, he worked as a law clerk and as assistant agent for Massachusetts. Upon De Berdt's death, Samuel Adams had suggested Arthur as the colony's permanent agent, but repeal of the Townshend Acts in early 1770 had divided the Massachusetts Colony, and Adams's influence was not enough. Moreover, Arthur's youth and recognized radicalism worked to his disadvantage, and thus the moderate Benjamin Franklin, already representing Georgia and New Jersey, was chosen agent for the Bay Colony. As Franklin's assistant, the young Lee monitored Parliament for the Massachusetts Assembly.

Under the penname "Junius Americanus," Arthur had circulated through the coffee houses a series of spirited essays that had been instrumental in replacing the colonial secretary, Lord Hillsborough, with Lord Dartmouth, a more reasonable man. But since Parliament's repeal of the Townshend Duties, anger against the Mother Country had quieted, and there was little for Arthur to do. True, there was still a small tax on tea, which the moderates in the colonial assemblies pooh-poohed, claiming it was trifling.

"No matter how trifling, a tax by Parliament is unjustifiable," Arthur had written Sam Adams. "Parliament capitulated on the Townshend Duties on the grounds that they were anti-commercial, but Parliament has still not relinquished its *right* to tax the colonies. The remaining tax on tea is their way of flaunting this power."

The strident voices in the colonial newspapers were now quiet, and the nonimportation agreements among the colonies were shelved. Indeed, British trading ships clogged New World harbors, and the colonies were enjoying the greatest prosperity in memory.

So Arthur's energies of late had been turned to local London politics. When the rabble-rousing John Wilkes had walked out of King's Bench Prison in April of 1770, to the welcoming cries of scores of supporters, he immediately set about organizing the Society of the Bill of Rights, a political party, to do battle with the King and Parliament over the rights of the City. Arthur Lee was now John Wilkes's chief aide and spokesman. The burning issue at the moment was freedom for the city printers to publish Parliamentary debates in their newspapers, a right prohibited by a resolution of the House of Commons. "A free press is at stake," he wrote Richard Henry. "There are precedents to be set that concern the colonies."

"So, William, it is imperative that you dine with Wilkes and me tonight," Arthur implored. "Midsummer election day approaches, and I am intent upon seeing that both City sheriffs elected are from our party. You hold great sway with the Haberdasher Guild and the City merchants. I desperately need your help."

Hannah Philippa put her hand on her young brother-in-law's arm. "First, we have something that you ought to know."

"Well, what the devil is it?" Arthur asked impatiently.

William's eyes met Hannah Philippa's. "We are considering returning to Virginia."

"By God, you can't! The Society—Virginia—needs you here in London!"

William countered his brother's indignation. "There is Green Spring to consider, Arthur. The plantation is sorely in need of management, and we can picture ourselves quite happily settled there. This tobacco business is precarious at best; far too often the *Liberty* sails from the Chesapeake only half full. Richard Henry and Frank give me all their business; Thomas does what he can; but Colonel Phil and Landon Carter, whom I counted on, give me very little. They have long-standing ties with another agent, which they cannot or will not break. Actually, it is Colonel Phil's advice that I return to Virginia."

"You would place weight on Phil's advice?" Arthur exploded.

William shook his head. "I cannot disprove the arguments he makes in favor of our return. The Mississippi Company, like the Ohio Company, is hopelessly stalemated, since King George is resolved to keep a wilderness barrier between the colonies and the Indians. What's more, we both long for the sweet life in Virginia. Surely you can understand that."

"No! I don't understand it. Nor could I bear living in Virginia as long as its economy is supported by slave labor!" Arthur shot back hotly.

William's face tightened. "You know as well as I that strenuous efforts have been made by the House of Burgesses to reduce slave trade in the colony. Richard Henry drafted an address to the King last year requesting an end to the importation of slaves. What more would you ask? That planters give up their livelihood for the sake of principle? That they immediately free their slaves, which would mean a great financial loss to them and probable starvation for the slaves as well?"

"Oh, William, if you love Virginia, then you must see that she needs you here." Arthur's eyes were pleading. "Things are quiet now, but the tax issue will rear its head again, and when it does, you must be here to fight in her behalf. Think on it. At least come to dinner and hear what Wilkes has to say."

"All right," William relented. "To make you happy, I shall join you and "Liberty John" at dinner. But do not take this as a promise that we shall stay in London. I agree the tax issue is not resolved, and I, too, have a great foreboding that trouble lies ahead. For a fact, I have been thinking of advising Richard Henry to remove his boys from St. Bee's and get them back to America. Ludwell tells me there is great animosity against him at school—his father is known as 'that radical from Virginia.' Perhaps the boys would be happier in Dr. Witherspoon's College of New Jersey at Princeton, where our cousin Henry's boys study. There they would be less affected by the strife with the Mother Country."

Arthur grinned. "Judging by Harry's letters from Princeton, nothing in our struggle for justice escapes him. Don't you know that whippersnapper is the most ardent patriot of us all!"

The Tidewater, 1773

In August of 1773, Harry Lee graduated with honors from the College at Princeton and returned to his home at Leesylvania in Virginia. At seventeen, he was a high-spirited, idealistic young man not entirely certain just what road he should follow.

Richard Henry Lee at Chantilly privately advised his cousin Henry to reconsider allowing Harry to study law in London at this time. "There is political trouble in the City and that, combined with the stress between

Virginia and the Mother Country, would make it, in my opinion, a place unfavorable for one so young and fine-tuned—particularly since the tensions brought on by the *Gaspee* affair," he warned.

The incident to which he alluded had occurred in June of 1772, when the revenue cutter *Gaspee*, employed by the British to enforce anti-smuggling laws in Narragansett Bay, Rhode Island, had run aground on a sandbar while chasing a smuggler's ship. A party of local patriots had promptly burned the cutter at the water's edge. It was the British efforts to arrest the culprits and send them directly to England, rather than allow them to stand trial in Rhode Island, that had set off new colonial protests.

In Virginia, Richard Henry and Frank Lee met secretly at the Raleigh Tavern with fellow burgesses Patrick Henry and Dabney Carr, who had brought along his brother-in-law, Thomas Jefferson. The next day Carr presented their resolution to the House. It called for a Committee of Correspondence to be set up to communicate with the other colonies—a unique and exciting idea, agreed the burgesses, who promptly passed the resolution.

Tensions between the colonies and England were further exacerbated by the remaining Townshend Duty on tea. In May of 1773, Parliament had moved to relieve the financial distress of the East India Company by rescinding all other taxes on tea sent to the American colonies, leaving only the token Townshend Duty of three pence a pound. The act also allowed the company to sell directly to the colonies instead of through middlemen, which in turn made the East India Company prices lower than those charged by other colonial merchants and smugglers. It had not taken the astute colonists long to realize that to buy East India Company tea implicitly acknowledged the Townshend Duty. Colonial newspapers referred to "illegal monopoly," and there were spirited protests throughout the colonies in December 1773, when the tea-bearing ships arrived in the four major colonial ports— Charleston, Philadelphia, New York, and Boston.

But Boston's response had been the most dramatic. On the night of December 16, a group disguised as Mohawk Indians and Negroes boarded the British ships in Boston Harbor and dumped all the tea, 342 chests of it, into the sea. Sam Adams, unquestionably an instigator and participant, had written all the particulars of the evening to Richard Henry.

As the new year of 1774 dawned, a great deal now lay at stake.

The Tidewater, 1774

What a marvelous day! Richard Henry breathed in the crisp February air. He squeezed the mittened hand of his little Molly as he stood with George

Washington beside the frozen millpond that lay between Stratford and Chantilly, laughing at the family and friends who glided and stumbled about on iceskates sent by Alice and Will Shippen from Philadelphia.

"Father!" Molly gave his hand a little tug. "Let's skate!"

Richard Henry shook his head. "They are an awfully boisterous lot, my darling. Give them a few more minutes to get their sea legs, and then we shall give it a try!"

George's eyes followed the agile movements of Harry Lee, who shouted and reached out to tag his cousin George Lee, of Mount Pleasant—a touch that sent the other lad sprawling. "I've always been fond of that Harry. He has a manliness about him that I wish my stepson would emulate."

Richard Henry looked up. "I understand Jacky Custis has recently married?"

"Aye." George's expression was set. "I thought him too young and unsettled, but he would have it so! I must say his bride is a lovely lass—Miss Nelly Calvert of Maryland." He smiled slightly. "Her presence at Mount Vernon does help to heal the pain of losing my stepdaughter Patsy." Martha Washington had taken the death of her frail seventeen-year-old daughter very hard.

"Now that Jacky has married, there will undoubtedly be grandchildren soon to fill your lady's arms," Richard Henry consoled. "As for Harry Lee, he is indeed a topping lad, graduated with laurels. He had hoped to sail for London this spring to study law, but the City heaves with political convulsions and Arthur advises caution."

"I heard just this morning at Stratford that Arthur has been appointed colonial agent for Massachusetts." George's eyes flashed with admiration. "And also that William is now a sheriff of the City of London! They have made their mark and are Virginians of whom we can be proud."

"Aye. But already they are under great pressure, I am afraid. Arthur thrives on it; William endures it." Richard Henry shook his head as he watched the graceful skating strokes of his niece, the pink-cheeked, laughing Matilda, as the child skimmed over the ice after one of Rob Carter's daughters. "The Tea Party, warranted though it was in my opinion, has put the colonial agents in London in a most difficult position. Just after the dumping of the tea, Arthur and Ben Franklin presented the Massachusetts Assembly's request to remove Governor Hutchinson from office. But the lords of the Privy Council were so angry over the destruction of the tea that they termed the petition against Hutchinson scandalous and groundless. And more ominous, the lords verbally attacked Franklin as he stood in the cockpit before them. Poor Franklin was called a thief, incendiary, and assassin. He has been forced to resign in disgrace. It is through this unpleasant scenario that Arthur has become colonial agent for Massachusetts."

"What's to become of Franklin? He is nearing seventy years, is he not?" George asked.

"Georgia and New Jersey have dismissed him as their agent, and he has lost his position as postmaster. The old man is despondent, of course. Thank God, Franklin has at least moved from a posture of conciliation to one nearer Arthur's own stand. I think Arthur little respected Franklin before, because he never supported America's loyal friend John Wilkes, but Franklin's position seems to be toughening, although even yet he urges restitution for the tea!"

Washington folded his arms across his chest. "It's not an unreasonable idea," he said slowly. "The property was destroyed, so it should be paid for. In fact, your brother Frank shares that opinion."

"I disagree with you both!" Richard Henry flared. "The British don't want payment. They only wish to see us grovel. Boston's action was courageous and must be supported! In my opinion the Tory ministers will not retaliate against Boston if we let it be known that the other colonies stand beside her. Unity is the answer. I understand from my brothers in London that even the simple act of inviting the other colonies to engage in correspondence with Virginia was looked on with great significance by the King."

"Please, Father, can we skate now?"

Richard Henry set Molly on the ice. "All right, love, but keep hold of my hand. If you'll excuse me, sir," he called back to George, "we can continue at dinner."

George waved them off. "If dancing and cards do not divert us. The charm of a fair lady has been known to draw even you away from politics—especially now that you've succumbed to Cupid's arrow!"

Richard Henry could not help smiling as he sailed onto the ice. In truth, no one enjoyed a dance or the light repartee of a dinner party more than the tall, engaging Colonel Washington, for sparkling eyes and the flutter of a fan always seemed to bring out the lighthearted side of George's personality. But his words were particularly appropriate for Richard Henry.

It had begun in Williamsburg at the close of the Assembly five years before, when Annie had been dead not quite six months. Colonel Phil had urged him to stay over for a party at the Governor's Palace. But Richard Henry had declined. "I must get home to the children. Nat and I will leave at once by horse. I'll leave Nero and Jeb to accompany you in the carriage."

Once he was on the road, his restlessness ebbed. The hours passed quickly as they made good time toward the Yorktown ferry, and only once was the quiet of the May morning broken, when a small coach came too suddenly around a curve in the road and bore down upon them, the driver cracking the whip viciously over the team's backs.

"He gonna rile them horses if he keeps that up," Nat West grumbled at the coach rocked past them.

When they stopped for dinner in the White Horse Tavern in Yorktown, the same coach, a vehicle neither recognized, stood in the side yard. "Ain't nobody worth knowing, let his driver treat horses like that," Nat muttered as he dismounted. Just then Anne Gaskins Pinkard emerged from the inn. She was the daughter of Colonel Thomas Gaskins of Northumberland County, and the widow of his fellow burgess Thomas Pinkard.

The small-boned woman, perhaps in her early thirties, acknowledged Richard Henry's bow with a slight nod of her head, then disappeared into the carriage. Anne Pinkard had often been at dinner parties and balls he had attended, and he had always considered her particularly attractive, her self-containment a foil for the appealing sparkle in her eyes.

As he turned to hold open the tavern door for her sister, it crossed his mind to warn the ladies that their driver seemed dangerously harsh with the whip, but a loud commotion distracted his attention. A tavern dog sniffing about the coach had spooked the horses, which reared and snorted in alarm. With a snarl of anger the impatient coachman flashed his whip, but instead of subduing the horses, the lash sent the team surging forward. The coach, its door swinging open, lurched after the horses.

"Dear God!" Richard Henry leaped toward his horse, followed by Nat. The coach and its frightened team were already careening out of the turnaround in front of the tavern and onto the dusty road.

Some forty yards down the rutted road, Richard Henry drew abreast of the carriage and reached out to grab for the swinging door. With a quick jump he pulled himself inside as Nat seized the horses' leads. His cry of "Whoa! Whoa there!" came floating back to them. As abruptly as they had taken off, the horses came to a halt, but as they did, the coach rolled over on its side in the ditch.

Even now, Richard Henry marveled that no one had been killed. Bruised and shaken, they had returned to the White Horse Tavern, where a shallow cut above Anne's eye had been treated. Then, after tethering their mounts behind, Richard Henry rode in the carriage with the sisters while Nat sat above, keeping a sharp eye on the errant driver.

Anne Pinkard had decided to visit the Gaskins family in Northumberland on short notice, so the team and its driver had been rented without references in Williamsburg. "The driver would not listen to our admonitions to go light with the whip. He said he knew his own horses." Anne's cheeks flushed with color. "We shall never be able to thank you and your man enough, and I do insist that we deliver you home to Chantilly. Your shoulder is too sorely bruised for you to be comfortable on horseback."

How was it, Richard Henry wondered, that the familiar Tidewater could seem so new, that a bumpy carriage ride could be so enjoyable. After five days of spirited teasing, conversation, shared meals and confidences, of watching Anne Pinkard fall asleep across from him in the narrow confines of the vehicle, he felt they had discovered a special intimacy with each other.

When they reached Chantilly late in the evening, Richard Henry knew as he watched Anne's face that she was touched by his four young children, two sturdy boys and shy, wistful baby girls, who clung to her skirts before being led off to bed by their nurse.

"Need a mother, those little ones do," murmured Anne's solicitous older sister over the light supper Richard Henry had ordered in the parlor. "You must turn your thoughts to marrying again, Colonel Lee—hard though it will be for you, from what you've told us of your dear wife, it is your Christian duty to those poor little waifs!"

"She means well," Anne apologized later as they sat on the veranda in the deep, peaceful quiet of the evening. "Just doing a bit of matchmaking— her favorite pastime!"

Richard Henry stood up suddenly, his hands thrust into his pockets, and stared off in the darkness. "She was only saying what is on my mind," he said quietly.

"That you need a mother for your children?" She had risen to stand beside him.

"I need you, Anne!" The words escaped before he could restrain them. "I need you now, desperately."

She had understood, shared his need, and she had come into his arms with quick passion that night in the summer darkness. But it took several weeks of persuasive wooing to win Anne Pinkard. So consumed with love was he that not even George Washington, who had stopped by Chantilly in June, had been able to turn his attention to politics or, for that matter, to any subject but Anne.

Finally, in mid-June, she had accepted his proposal. "It is not because your children need a mother," she said firmly, eyes full of quiet laughter. "And *not* because I am grateful that you saved my life. Do you not realize, Richard Henry Lee, that I love *you*?"

They married quietly a week later, and their first daughter, born in December 1770, was a visible and perfect expression of the passion that had surged in that spring of 1769.

• • •

The spring Assembly of '74 was momentous. "We were convened on the fifth of May," Richard Henry later wrote to William in London:

Governor Dunmore would have preferred to avoid calling a session, but he needed the Assembly to settle our boundary dispute with Pennsylvania. There was much discussion of the events in the port cities—particularly the tea escapade in Boston. As the governor's lady is newly arrived in the colony, numerous parties and balls were held to greet her (a handsome lady she is, but Ben Harrison is convinced that the governor's heart belongs to another—only James River gossip, of course!), and there was much conviviality.

A quick arrival from London brought us the tyrannic Boston Port Bill. To close the port of Boston until the Bostonians pay for the tea destroyed in December is unspeakably vengeful! In the fear that debate in the House would result in Dunmore's dissolving the Assembly, and that 'older wiser heads' would stanch all protest, a secret meeting was arranged. Present were Patrick Henry, as aflame with anger now as he had been over the Stamp Act, Tom Jefferson of Albemarle County, Frank, myself, and George Mason, who was fortuitously in Williamsburg on private business. We devised a strategy to delay discussion of the Boston issue until the final days of the Assembly, so that nothing would be lost if we were dissolved.

Accordingly, we waited until the twenty-fourth of May, then, with Robert Carter Nicholas acting as spokesman, proposed that the first day of June (which we understand to be the day commerce is to stop in the port of Boston) be set aside for fasting, humiliation, and prayer in Virginia. The idea was approved by the Assembly with little argument!

As you might anticipate, we were dissolved by the governor two days later and, as we had done in '69, adjourned to the Apollo Room of the Raleigh. There was much violent debate! We 'radicals' (P. Henry, G. Mason, R. C. Nicholas, Frank, and I), wanting to forbid exports to Britain as well as imports, were talked down by the moderates (P. Randolph, Carter Braxton, E. Pendleton), reinforced by a delegation of local merchants.

I strongly denounced the Boston Port Bill and urged that a meeting be called immediately with deputies from other colonies to consider the means of securing the rights of colonials under our British Constitution. Our Committee of Correspondence was instructed to communicate with its counterparts in the various colonies on the expediency of such an intercontinental meeting. A circular letter was written and sent out by post on the twenty-eighth of June.

Through this all there had been great calmness of spirit. George Washington, a great friend of the governor's, continued to dine with him throughout the month and reports Dunmore is for the moment quite philosophic about our activities.

Our actions may well cause you problems in London. You might point out to your friends that we are aware of and grateful for the support given us by the sterling Edmund Burke and John Wilkes, as well as the London merchants who openly deplore the punitive steps taken by Parliament. It was with these merchants in mind that we refrained from voting a complete boycott of English goods, concentrating only on those of the East India Company except spices and saltpetre.

Your many friends in Williamsburg have asked after you. Ben Harrison has a new son, named William Henry. My love and warmest thoughts to you, our beloved cousin Hannah Philippa, and to my sons when next you see them. I was distressed to hear that Arthur's extremist writings have put his life in danger this winter and hope that he has taken Wilkes's advice and retired to France for a few months. For God's sake, take care that neither of you lands in the Tower of London! I remain, with great affection,

your brother,

Richard Henry Lee

Post Script: The day of fasting and humiliation went splendidly. Peyton Randolph led the procession down the Duke of Gloucester Street and there was much praying in all the churches. Also, since returning home, I have received word that the other colonies are in accord with us on such an intercolonial convention. Speaker Randolph has set August 1 for a Virginia convention to meet in Williamsburg to elect delegates.

Philadelphia, 1774

"Suppressed excitement, anxious excitement! I hear it in every conversation and see it reflected in every face. Don't you?" Alice Shippen asked her husband as they dressed for dinner at Shippen House.

Will Shippen turned to look at Alice's flushed cheeks and glistening eyes. "I certainly can see it in your face!" he teased. "But what I sense most in our city, I am afraid, is apprehension. No one is quite sure what this Continental Congress will bring about, or what kind of fellows the representatives will be."

"But it *is* wonderful!" Alice protested. "I heard the delegate from Massachusetts, the plump one, John Adams, who breakfasted with us earlier, say he thought this would be a gathering of the greatest men on this continent. Of course, Will, he didn't mean *all* the greatest, because you are not a delegate...."

Will smiled at his wife's loyalty. "I am quite content to be a doctor, love, not a politician. As for Mr. Adams's remark, while I agree with it, many—particularly our peace-loving Quakers—are less certain. There is an unknown quality about this group. The delegates know little of one another, and there is fear that the meeting will be swayed by the hotheads, who will further alienate us from our King and perhaps lead us to civil war."

"Fiddlesticks!" Alice bent over her jewel cask and chose a string of amber beads to compliment her dress. "Richard Henry predicts this congress will pass petitions powerful enough to convince the King to redress our grievances." She patted into place the fashionable new high roll in her honey-blond hair. "It is almost dinnertime, and I do wish they would return! I am so anxious every day to hear how the session went!"

At Will and Alice's insistence, Shippen House had become the home of the Virginia delegation. Four members, Peyton Randolph, Richard Bland, Benjamin Harrison, and Richard Henry Lee, had arrived on Friday. Three other members, George Washington, Edmund Pendleton, and Patrick Henry, had appeared on Sunday to find the Locust Street house bustling with callers and full of notes of welcome and letters of invitation to dinner by prominent Philadelphians.

How impressive the Virginia delegation looked, thought Alice with satisfaction. There was something in the way the Virginians moved and carried themselves. It was not just their physical stature, although all seven were tall, imposing men; they had an all but royal aura of authority, accented by their rich dress and sleek, spirited horses.

"Noblemen," Will Shippen commented with wry admiration. "I have always said that Virginians are a breed apart. They move among us lesser mortals with the air of noblesse oblige while quoting Vergil, Locke, and Cicero."

"They don't mean to appear above others," protested Alice. "But they are substantial planters, used to deference. Indeed, I thought John Adams was noticeably impressed by them."

"Are not we all?" Will laughed affectionately. "For one thing, they have such commitment. Ben Harrison said he would have come on foot rather than miss this meeting! And they're quite well organized, for they come with good ideas and better instructions from their Assembly—'their country,' as they say—than most of the delegates. I assure you, my dear Alice, your admiration for the Virginia delegation is widespread."

Later that evening, sitting among friends at supper, Alice delighted in the familiar inflections and cadences of Virginia accents as the delegates exchanged pungent observations on the first three days of the convention. When they had assembled on Monday morning at City Tavern, the fifty-five delegates, representing every colony but Georgia, were told that the Pennsylvania Assembly had voted the use of their State House for the meeting. The Carpenters' Guild had also offered to lend their handsome new hall to the Congress. It was a long, paneled meeting hall with smaller rooms for committee meetings and, in between, a passage for caucusing. "Carpenters' Hall is the clear favorite, for it places us at arm's length from partisan government," Richard Henry commented.

That Peyton Randolph had been chosen president of the Congress was not a surprise to Alice. Tall, heavy, and affably commanding, Randolph was a born leader. Even now, sitting at her dinner table, he gave her such a nod of affirmation after tasting the consommé that she felt supremely complimented.

Alice caught Richard Henry's eye and gave him a quick smile. How distinguished he had become. It was clear to Alice as she observed her brother across the table that he had undergone subtle changes since she had seen him last. He was far more burnished. Dramatic—that was the word. His thick plume of red hair topped a high, sunburned forehead, steady deepset gray-blue eyes, craggy face. . . . And he was so much more confident! Even the black silk handkerchief wrapped about the mutilated fingers of his left hand was impressive, rather like a black eye patch.

"Which of the delegates do you find most congenial?" Will was asking Richard Henry.

The Virginian paused. "Outside of my friends at this table, I would say without hesitation the Adams cousins from Massachusetts. Through Arthur's persistence in encouraging our correspondence, Samuel Adams and I are already friends of a sort, and upon meeting him and conversing with him and the younger cousin John, I find we have a great deal in common. Samuel is less affluent, a rabble-rouser, a man who is one part Puritan and three parts Republican. John is the more learned—more cultivated, if you will—but their thinking is alike."

"You do not perceive the Adamses to be immoderate in their views?" Ben Harrison asked with a sniff of displeasure. "I sense that they prefer to work through persuasion, 'out of committee,' so to speak, while, frankly, I prefer that all business be conducted on the floor, where strategies are open. We Virginians have been raised to follow strict parliamentary style, and I for one do not approve of their behind-the-scenes maneuvering. Their radical views are suspect, and if they are not careful, they may push this convention in the opposite direction!"

Alice knew that her husband agreed. She had heard Will remark earlier that Samuel Adams impressed him as a rough-cut conniver.

Alice's quick eye swept the table. Ben Harrison, handsome, heavyset, slightly petulent in expression, sat beside his brother-in-law, Peyton Randolph. To his other side sat George Washington, dressed in his blue-and-buff Virginia militia uniform ("a symbol, my dear Alice, that we are prepared, and capable of bearing arms"). Randolph was lordly, Harrison swaggering, Bland was reserved, and Pendleton, although handsome and an eloquent speaker, seemed somewhat remote and scholarly. She eyed Patrick Henry, deep in conversation at the far end of the table. There was something fascinatingly theatrical about him with his dark, unpowdered hair, black eyebrows, and carelessly cut dove-gray suit. Haunting, Patrick Henry was haunting. Was it true, she wondered, that his wife had gone raving mad and had to be forcibly confined to her chambers.

But it was Colonel Washington whom she liked most. He did not talk very much, but he carried himself magnificently, steady in both gaze and movements. She marveled at his large, fine-boned hands and the way he listened to a point of conversation as if giving it his undivided attention. Moreover, there was great gentleness and courtesy in the man. On the day of his arrival he had taken the time to talk for almost an hour with the Shippen children, eleven-year-old Nancy and nine-year-old Thomas.

"Alice," Will addressed her across the table, "in the discussion earlier this week on whether each colony should have a single vote or votes proportioned to their population, our guest Patrick Henry was said to be most eloquent."

Richard Henry urged his friend on. "Do repeat your words, Mr. Henry. My sister and her husband did not have the opportunity to hear you."

"I would not be so bold, or so tiresome, as to repeat it," Patrick Henry said to Alice with a vivid smile, "especially since my oratory was not convincing. It was my opinion that the heavily peopled colonies such as Virginia should have the larger vote, but it was decided that each colony should have one vote only in this congress!"

"But the words you used," Richard Henry persisted, "they were quite moving!"

Patrick Henry stared above Alice's head as if in a trance. "I think the words to which you refer were the last ones." His voice rose, warm and compelling. "The distinctions between Virginians, Pennsylvanians, New Yorkers, and New Englanders are no more. I am not a Virginian, but an American."

All sat spellbound. Alice shivered as she took in the implications of Henry's remark.

"We are all Americans, but nonetheless we delegates are a strangely mixed lot," Richard Henry commented to Samuel Adams later. "As your cousin John has said more than once, 'We differ in politics, religion, economics, and interests.' It is little wonder that we cannot seem to settle our mutual business."

Adams gave a fleeting smile. "More of value is accomplished at these lavish Philadelphia dinner parties than emerges from Carpenters' Hall, I regret to say."

Richard Henry chuckled. A gray-haired man with a powerful presence despite his palsied hand, Samuel Adams was of the merchant class and not comfortable in the silk-and-satin salons of Philadelphia. Moreover, he suffered from a delicate stomach and was forced to content himself with bread and milk at the rich banquets given in the delegates' honor.

Richard Henry, however, had thoroughly enjoyed each and every one of the social affairs. His second evening in Philadelphia, he and Ben Harrison had accompanied Will Shippen to the home of delegate Thomas Mifflin, a wealthy Pennsylvania merchant. There they met the dapper Rutledge brothers from South Carolina, the eminent Dr. Witherspoon of the College of New Jersey at Princeton, and John Adams.

Following this high evening of toasts and spirited conversation, dissipated by nervous exhaustion and throbbing temples, Richard Henry had felt too sapped even to attend the opening session of the Convention. Since then, he had resolved to keep both his emotions and his appetite for good brandy under better control.

Turning his attention from spirits to food, Richard Henry had thoroughly relished the parties that had followed, especially a recent dinner at Chief Justice Chew's elegant townhouse, which he described in a letter to Anne:

We dined on turtle among other things and a profusion of sweetmeats, flummery, floating islands, and a marvelous dessert of almonds, pears, raisins, and peaches. Ben Harrison claims the ladies of Philadelphia are stiff and lacking in grace. He offers a reward for every pretty face that we may pass, and I must admit I have not seen one with your sprightly charm, my dear Anne.

Pretty faces aside, of all the delegates the one I like best is Samuel Adams. He is a tough, no-nonsense man who doggedly presses the Massachusetts case. The occupation of Boston by British troops under General Thomas Gage is a fact that Adams will not allow us to forget. More than once he has said, "I left a port city empty of commerce, ringed with warships. Lobsterbacks tramp our streets, tents are pitched on the Boston Common, The Royal Welch Fusiliers on Fort Hill. The tension in our city is unbearable."

I find myself one of the few delegates totally sympathetic to Boston.

As the weeks of the session wore on, it was apparent that he and the Adams cousins had formed a distinct coalition in the Convention. It was their contention that this congress must demand repeal of the bill that closed the Boston Port and of the act that dissolved the Massachusetts House of Representatives. Equally intolerable, they maintained, was the Quebec Act, which extended the borders of Quebec down to the Ohio River—obviously a sop to the French Catholics, but a deathblow to Virginia's plans to expand westward.

A more conciliatory group was led by Joseph Galloway of Pennsylvania, James Duane and John Jay of New York, and the Rutledge brothers, John and Edward, of South Carolina. In the middle hung the vast majority of delegates, including Ben Harrison and George Washington, Caesar Rodney of Delaware, and John Dickinson of Pennsylvania.

Beset by indecision, mutual distrust, and lack of direction, the convention could come to no agreement on the next step to take until an incident in Boston spurred them to action.

In mid-September a silversmith named Paul Revere galloped into Philadelphia with the alarming news that the towns around Boston had declared the Intolerable Acts unconstitutional and void. They were urging the citizens of the Massachusetts Colony to arm and declare themselves a free state until the Acts were repealed. Massachusetts had moved to stand alone on the brink of war.

The word "treason" was privately uttered more than once as the delegates bristled at the news from the north. Richard Henry advocated that the Congress endorse the strong stand taken by the Massachusetts towns, while Galloway and his conservative faction pressed for reorganizing relations between Britain and her colonies. They suggested the King appoint a president-general for the colonies, to preside over a Grand Council chosen by the colonial assemblies. Laws for the colonies would have to pass both this council and the Parliament.

Richard Henry led the opposition to Galloway's plan, declaring it more restrictive to the individual colonies than the present structure. Moreover, Virginia's delegation was not empowered to change the structure of her government without instructions from the voters.

In early October, Massachusetts's stand was bravely yet nervously endorsed by the Convention, an act Galloway termed "a declaration of war against Great Britain."

Five weeks had passed, and the autumn leaves were beginning to drop from the trees. There had been successes and failures for the Virginia delegation. Richard Henry had succeeded in pushing through the Convention a unified version of Virginia's Non-Importation Act, which, it was hoped, would put heavy pressure on the British. Threatened with severe economic loss, the powerful London merchants would help wear down the King. But to the chagrin of the delegation, addresses to the King and the people of Great Britain, drafted and presented to the congress by Richard Henry Lee and Patrick Henry, fell on unreceptive ears. "There was a tad too much oratory in both presentations and a great deal of accusation," Will Shippen confided to Alice. Rewritten by committee, they now showed the conciliatory hand of John Dickinson and were finally approved.

The Virginians, too long away from their plantation affairs, were eager to start the long ride home. Peyton Randolph had already left, called home by Governor Dunmore, and Ben Harrison was loudly grumbling that he had business to attend to back home. The majority of the Virginia delegation departed Philadelphia on October 23, the day after the session concluded with a resolution to meet again the next May if the colonial grievances had not been remedied. George Washington and Richard Henry Lee, with power of attorney from the other delegates, remained behind to sign the petition to the King for Virginia.

On their last evening in Philadelphia, Richard Henry and George walked in the Shippen garden with Alice and Will. Earlier that day the two Virginians had gone shopping with Alice for gifts to take home with them. George purchased a pocketbook for Martha, a sedan chair for his mother, and a new sword chain for himself. Richard Henry had found a shawl of the softest wool for Anne, sweets for the children, and the five-volume set of David Hume's *History of England* for Colonel Phil.

George seemed particularly elated. "This has been a most extraordinary session! True, there have been long days, but we have not sat in the Virginia House of Burgesses for fifteen years without growing hardened to such things."

Richard Henry nodded. It had been a successful session, a meeting of sensible Englishmen set on ironing out their differences with their King. And if they had succeeded in making their position clear, as he firmly believed they had, then surely reconciliation, on constitutional principles, would be offered by spring.

There was much the delegates could take pride in. They had agreed on a Declaration of Rights, reiterating the principle that Americans were entitled to all the liberties of Englishmen, and they took the first wobbly steps toward unity with their Non-Importation/Exportation Association and their endorsement of Massachusetts's stand against tyranny. Richard Henry was highly satisfied with the role he had played; he had served on six of the Convention's nine committees, chairing three. Some delegates whispered he was a puppet of the controversial Adams cousins, that they pulled the strings while he served as their front. But the accusations did not worry him. He had found common viewpoints with the Adams party, and he was no man's pawn, his interests being his own and Virginia's.

He put his arms around his sister and brother-in-law. They had done much to make the stay in Philadelphia comfortable and productive for the Virginians. If ever there were two successful people, it was the Shippens. Will was eminent in the colonial world of medicine, while Alice made their home beautiful, reflecting her exquisite taste and hospitality. What's more, it was obvious that after twelve years of marriage their love for each other had only deepened.

London, 1774

Extraordinary! Arthur thought as he and William traveled back to London from Bowood, Lord Shelburne's country estate near Bristol. On this gray December afternoon, even William's usually somber face had a faint glow.

"So, we have won Lord Chatham as well as Shelburne firmly to our side. I think, my dear William, that the tide is beginning to turn, and Mother England is preparing to admit her errors and welcome her colonies back to the bosom of the empire!"

William scoffed. "I would hardly say the tide is turning, but there are some promising signs, I warrant you that." He flexed his gloved hands for warmth under the woolen lap rug.

Arthur gave his brother a quick glance. William always had been cautious. There was no question that things were looking up. In the two months since he had returned from Paris he had witnessed a groundswell of support for the colonists' cause.

An urgent letter from John Wilkes had insisted Arthur was badly needed in London. George III had called a general election, obviously wishing to have Parliament in session when he responded to the petitions from the Continental Congress. Though John Wilkes was elected lord mayor of London and the Whigs won a few new seats in the House of Commons, their efforts to bring down Lord North and his Tory coalition failed.

When the anticipated petitions from the Continental Congress arrived in London, Arthur, along with William Bollan and Benjamin Franklin, who was lingering in London, were the only colonials willing to present them to the Court of St. James. Lord Dartmouth later told them the King had received the petitions graciously and would lay them before the houses of Parliament.

But Dartmouth's words were only meant to soothe. When the King had sent the petitions to Parliament, they were buried at the bottom of a great pile of lesser papers on America, the King thus showing his contempt for the efforts of the Philadelphia congress.

The City of London was in turmoil over the colonial question. Merchants and radical city politicians talked of little else. Now the renowned William Pitt, Lord Chatham, had spoken out, expressing his complete satisfaction with the proceedings in Philadelphia. The day after Christmas, Pitt had told Franklin that the American Congress had acted "with so much temper, moderation and wisdom, that I thought it the most honorable assembly of statesmen since those of the ancient Greeks and Romans . . ."

But could the ailing, egocentric, mercurial Pitt pull together the splinters of opposition and offer a plan of conciliation that would be acceptable to the King, the entrenched North ministry, Parliament, and the American colonies? If anyone could, thought Arthur, it would be the farsighted Pitt.

The meeting at Bowood had been for the purpose of strategy: the London forces supporting the colonies must be unified. Arthur himself would attend to the popular press in London, and William, the dominant radical Whig merchant in the City as well as one of the City's two well-respected sheriffs, would start a pro-American petition among the merchants and other guild members. But in the end, it would all depend on Pitt. Had he enough power in Parliament to offset Lord North's coalition and, more important, neutralize North's anti-American influence on the King?

"Come in to dinner with us, Arthur. Hannah Philippa will be displeased if you don't!" William insisted as the carriage drew up in front of 33 Tower Hill.

"Tell your darling wife not to be angry. Actually, I have a dinner engagement with another of her fair sex."

As William climbed down from the carriage, Arthur called after him, "Tell her that I shall be displeased if she doesn't deliver me a niece! I should prefer one as spirited as Phil's Matilda, as enchanting as Alice's Nancy, and as sweet as Richard Henry's Molly. . . . I don't care what she's like, as long as it is a girl!"

"I shall tell her that she must not disappoint you," William called over his shoulder, his face bright with joy.

Arthur had never known William to be happier. True, his tobacco business was only marginally successful despite all the poor fellow's efforts. But the Ludwell fortune kept the wolf from the door, and William was proving to be a popular sheriff of London, showing an unusual aptitude for politics. His was a powerful position; the responsibility for the peace of the City lay in the hands of its two sheriffs, who served writs, impaneled juries, collected fines for the Royal Exchequer, and administered the two City prisons. The sheriffs were present at every public hanging, dressed in black and seated on horseback, carrying white rods to symbolize their authority.

Arthur stared out the carriage window at the dark streets of London. Had there been a time when William and Hannah Philippa had seriously considered returning to Virginia? They never spoke of it now. If anything, William was ambitious to gain further power in the City. Perhaps he would run again for the House of Commons or for the post of alderman, a position that would then be his for life. That would be another coup for the pro-American faction of the City. And now to be a father. Hannah Philippa was thirty-eight, rather old to be bearing a first child, but God knows it would make William happy!

Arthur stretched his cramped legs. He was the only one of the family not wed. But he had so much to do, so much that was pressing. There would be time later for marriage, he thought, as the coach carried him into the black London night.

"Our good friend the Earl of Chatham visits Benjamin Franklin!" One of Arthur's political friends had stopped by his chambers on a Sunday afternoon to share the startling news that Pitt's coach was seen waiting in front of Franklin's home on Craven Street. "What an overt show of support for your American cause! With all this talk about civil war, our dear Chatham has also come to be reassured, no doubt, that it is *only* talk. Drawing-room gossip has it that you Americans are actually seeking independence."

Arthur shook his head ruefully. "People should not talk about it so much. It will fix the idea in our heads!"

On January 20, Franklin accompanied Pitt to the Lords' Chamber, where the English elder statesman moved that British troops be withdrawn from Boston as a first step toward settling the dispute.

Franklin wearily told Arthur about it the next day at the Virginia Coffee House. He looks tired, thought Arthur, and, like Pitt, very old. "William Pitt reminded me of an old Roman senator," Franklin confessed admiringly. "I brought you a copy of his speech. Listen." Franklin adjusted his spectacles. " 'What is our right to persist in such cruel and vindictive measures against that loyal and respectable people?' " Franklin looked at Arthur with a smile. "He *was* magnificent, I say, claiming that we have been abused, misrepresented, and traduced in Parliament in a most atrocious manner. Considering that, he states we Americans have behaved admirably. The Duke of Richmond took our part as well. He warned his fellow peers that 'no people can ever be made to submit to a form of government they say they will not receive!' "

"And?"

"Unfortunately, Pitt's motion to remove the troops from Boston was *not* passed, but he returns to Parliament on the first of February to present his plan for conciliation with the colonies. I shall be with him. I am hopeful, my dear Lee, hopeful, is all I can say."

Pitt's presentation was superb, thought Arthur as he watched from the gallery. He courageously called for repeal of the Intolerable Acts, the Quebec Act, *and* the tea duty. His plan specified that Boston be set free and the Continental Congress recognized as a legal body, competent to grant money for imperial defense. Parliamentary control would continue over trade and navigation and must be recognized by the Americans as the supreme legislative authority and power. And there would be no taxation without representation! It seemed a reasonable compromise for everyone; it saved face for the Mother Country while conceding every practical point the Continental Congress had raised.

Arthur waited expectantly. Pitt's forceful speech had to sway them to the side of the Americans!

But his hopes were crushed. "The tide is turning, but not in a favorable direction," Arthur reported bitterly to William and Hannah Philippa. "Pitt said both sides are simply waiting for the signal to engage in a martial contest, that ruin and destruction will be the consequence to both. By God, it's all so foolish!"

William was grave. "It may also be the destruction of our family, Arthur. This will set Lee against Lee if Phil stays with the Crown. In his own way, he is as loyal a Virginian as any of us, but what will he do if we come to civil war?"

Arthur's eyes clouded. "I have a strange foreboding that if it comes to that, it will not be a civil war but a war for independence."

The Tidewater, 1775

A very light snow had fallen at Stratford, silently blanketing the meadows, deep ravines, and glades. Now the trees stood out in stark relief against the somber sky as Richard Henry and Frank trudged up the wide stone steps of the great house. The funeral was over. They had stayed at the grave until the last spadeful of dirt had been packed in place. Both were surprised at the depth of emotion that filled them.

On February 21, 1775, Philip Ludwell Lee, master of Stratford Hall, had died quite suddenly of nervous pleurisy. He had returned from his offices at Stratford Landing flushed and breathing hard after a gallop through the woods—"in good spirits," Will West had related later. "He call for a glass of brandy and went down the hall to his study. I find him at his desk slumped over like he asleep . . . still wearing his cape and gloves. I shook him, I call Nero, and we lay him on the sofa. I sent for Dr. Hall, but 'fore he get here, Colonel Phil be dead."

To compound the tragedy, Elizabeth Steptoe Lee was already days overdue with her third child. But she had comforted her young daughters, Matilda and the small Flora, and quickly sent notes to her brothers-in-law who lived nearby. First to Thomas at Bellevue, who would, by their father's will, inherit Stratford if Colonel Phil had no male heir; then to Richard Henry at Chantilly and to Frank at Menokin on the Rappahannock. For the past several years, Missy and Richard Hall had been living in distant Richmond County, but fortuitously they were visiting Missy's daughter Patty and her husband, who were now managing Pecatone.

The family had gathered, stunned and shaken. "God knows, Phil could play the devil," Frank told Richard Henry on the morning of the funeral, "but there were qualities in him we could be proud of."

"Strange, isn't it? He was always good to Elizabeth and adored Matilda," Richard Henry agreed quietly. "It was as if all the gentleness in him was coaxed out by them."

Despite the raging weather, many of Phil Lee's friends and fellow planters in the Neck braved the snow to stand by the grave and watch his coffin be lowered into the earth. The burial was made even more poignant by the absence of Elizabeth Lee, who had waked this morning in labor. Matilda had gone to the graveside with Richard Henry, Anne, and their children. Five-year-old Flora had been sheltered in her uncle Frank's arms until, frightened by the strangeness of the cold winter ceremony, she had begun to cry uncontrollably and had been taken home by Will West.

"Three days he has been dead, and I still can't believe it," said Richard Henry wearily as the brothers took off their heavy cloaks and frozen boots before the fire in the gentlemen's receiving room. Then they walked down the long passage toward the great hall. There would be callers all day. Already several carriages waited in the turnaround at the side of the house, and voices, muted and soft, filtered from the large salon.

Anne met her husband and gently took his arm. "My dear, you will be pleased to know that just an hour ago Elizabeth delivered a son, a healthy boy."

Richard Henry pressed her hand, unable to answer.

"Rejoice for Phil now in the birth of his son, the new master of Stratford Hall." Frank put his arm around his brother's shoulders.

The reassuring scent of coffee wafted from the dining room. Even for an event such as this, they would not break the Association's boycott of tea; despite his loyalist stance, Phil had honored the Non-Importation/Exportation Act.

"The governor is being notified," Thomas said quietly as Richard Henry joined him in the receiving line. "Robert Carter says he knows Dunmore thought highly of Phil. He and the council will wish to pay their respects . . . and there are messages coming in from all kinds of people and places."

Landon Carter had arrived with the party from Mount Airy. "I cannot tell you how distressed we were to hear . . ." The gray-haired planter's words brought a sudden rush of tears into Richard Henry's eyes. Taking the older man's arm, he moved away from the line to the window looking out on the river now hidden by fog. The snow-laden back meadow stretched out to the sky itself.

"Beautiful, isn't it, that view in wintertime?" Landon Carter's voice was subdued. "I used to come here in your father's time and marvel at what a grand estate he had made in this wilderness. Your father was much like my own." The man's voice had grown dreamy. "They were both strong men, younger sons who dared to dream big dreams, and they accomplished much that was good in their lifetimes. They dealt with their world as . . . as bravely and courageously as they could, as now we struggle to deal with ours! What would they have thought of a Virginia that quarreled with its King?" Carter asked bitterly. "What would they have thought of their King's revoking Virginia's right to settle her own western lands, of Parliament imposing taxes upon free Englishmen? Our fathers were proud men."

"I wish," Richard Henry said gently, "that you were attending the Convention as well. Your thoughts are always wise and valuable." Richard Henry knew that Landon Carter, another proud man, smarted because he had not been chosen to attend the Convention in Philadelphia last fall, resenting the fact that his speeches and pamphlets, among the first to protest the Stamp Act, had been overshadowed by the oratory of Patrick Henry.

Carter smiled wanly. "I shall wait to express my opinions at the next sitting of the Assembly—that is, if Governor Dunmore ever sees fit to call one. Twice he has set a date and twice he has changed it."

"He cannot decide whether he wishes to hear what happened at the meeting in Philadelphia last fall or not," Richard Henry joked. "But to be fair, he has been much absorbed with the Ohio Valley war with the Shawnees. Now that Chief Cornstalk and his warriors have been roundly defeated, he should breathe easier—although there's still our border dispute with Pennsylvania, not to mention the King's refusal to allow any settlement of our western lands. Poor Dunmore . . ." Richard Henry shook his head. "The colonial secretary in London no doubt reports that he is handling Virginia badly. Loyalists like Will Byrd advise him to stay calm, while all around him he sees reasons for alarm: the local counties arming and training their independent militia; and the strong speeches of radicals, as he most certainly terms the likes of you and me."

"Did you read in the *Virginia Gazette* of Lord Dartmouth's circular letter to the colonial governors informing them the Crown has now forbidden exportation of gunpowder and arms to the colonies?" Landon Carter broke in.

"Aye," Richard Henry said with a nod, "everyone waits to see what will happen next. I continue to hope that the wise and good voices that speak out, in England as well as on this side of the Atlantic, will compel Parliament to redress our grievances. Yet the sands of time are running fast. We will soon reach a point when no reconciliation will be possible."

"What of William? Arthur? What is their opinion?"

"*They* are still hopeful. Certainly they pour themselves into the fight for reconciliation."

"What about young Harry Lee's plans to join them in London and study law?"

"Twice he has booked passage and twice changed his mind."

As if aware that Richard Henry and Landon Carter were discussing him, Harry Lee crossed the room toward them. He wore a sash of mourning, and his unpowdered blond hair was pulled back severely. He bowed, then said to Richard Henry, "I am greatly distressed, sir, over the death of your brother. I have long admired Colonel Phil as a planter, a horseman, and a Virginian."

"Your words are comforting, Harry." Richard Henry put his arm around him. "Philip Lee served Virginia as he thought best, and I have little doubt he would have stood by her with utmost loyalty no matter what lay in her future."

"I hear you have decided not to sail for England, lad?" Landon Carter put in. "I think back with the greatest pleasure over my years in London as a young man. If you've the opportunity, I urge you to take it."

The young man's dark eyes were troubled. "I am torn, sir. I have great interest in the law as well as in literature, but I feel my calling would more naturally be the military. Yet, in these times, how could I—"

"Consider a commission in His Majesty's forces?" Landon Carter finished abruptly. "You simply could not! I understand that Will Byrd's son, Otway, wants desperately to leave his ship, the *Fowery*, which is anchored in Annapolis. His father has said he will disown him if he does."

"If it comes down to a choice, I would stand with Virginia," Harry said quietly. "While I am an Englishman, I am first and foremost bound to Virginia's soil."

London, 1775

Arthur could not recall times more turbulent. He woke every morning eager for what the new day would bring, his nerves still tingling with the excitement of the day before. Never had he felt more alive. He was in love . . . with life, with the colonists' cause, with London, but most of all with a pretty French girl, Nicole, to whom the French playwright Beaumarchais had introduced him.

As Arthur turned over in his narrow bed in his rooms in Middle Temple, he could hear the bells of Westminster enlivening the warm Sunday morning. At noon he would call a waterman to ferry him up the Thames to Tower Hill, to dine with William and Hannah Philippa, who were so enraptured with their son, William Ludwell, that they hardly knew the hour.

On March 7, he and William had been part of the noisy crowd of London merchants and friends of the colonies who publicly burned a copy of the King's Address to Parliament, which declared the Bostonians to be in rebellion. A week later they had joined a crowd of enraged London merchants who were presenting a protest to the House of Lords.

William, who had helped draft the merchants' protest, was growing pessimistic. "Waste paper! That is all these protests are! No matter how well reasoned, they fall on deaf ears," he had exclaimed hotly to Arthur.

Still, they had tried one more time. Fifty thousand cheering Londoners thronged the streets and cheered from windows and rooftops as Lord Mayor John Wilkes led the black-robed City officials, High Sheriff William Lee among them, from the City of London to the Court of St. James to deliver the strongest protest yet to the King. The Londoners demanded not only the repeal of all coercive legislation but also the immediate dismissal of Lord North and his ministers. Arthur knew the protest by heart, for he had composed it.

What a strange monarch, this tall, awkward, earnest George III. One almost felt sorry for him, for he seemed to try so hard to control, to deal with the situation. "Be a king, George!" his mother was supposed to have advised him. And by God, the man tried. But he followed all the wrong advice. He had reacted to the protest of the London crowds by saying that he was displeased to have subjects who encouraged the rebellious disposition now existing in some of his colonies in North America.

Arthur stretched lazily. As the colony's agent, he now handled Massachusetts's business. But what a sorry kettle of fish that was! Boston lay under martial law, no commerce allowed. Something had to give. In Boston General Gage was now reported to feel more captive than captor. Rumor had it that he, too, advocated repeal of the Intolerable Acts. Certainly the King must realize that the empire's best interests would be served by conciliation! If only he weren't so proud—or was it his Hanoverian stubbornness?

Meanwhile, the City rocked with gossip and dissension, and frivolity. In mid-April, Arthur had attended John Wilkes's glittering Easter Ball in the Egyptian Hall at the Mayor's Mansion House. The evening had been a spectacular success, a magic night of minuets, allemands, cotillions, with Arthur leading out all the loveliest London ladies in graceful commanding sweeps of the floor.

Wrapped in a dressing gown, Arthur now took a cup of coffee out to the garden. Beyond the iron fence he could hear the footsteps of passersby on their way to church. At the end of the small enclosed garden, the waters of the Thames lapped against the green bank.

These years in London had been the best of his life. Law fascinated him, the political scene excited him. The ambience of London, with its theaters, opera, and bustling social life, could not be found at home. And, through the Royal Society, he rubbed shoulders with the brightest minds in London. How ironic that he should love this city so and yet be willing to endanger the relationship that he, a colonist, had with it. He was now thirty-five years old, at home anywhere in the world. He was a Lee of Virginia, a physician and barrister, a writer, a thinker. Where fate would carry him he could not imagine.

"I wonder what transpired this spring in Williamsburg, and whether the recent convention in Richmond went off well," Arthur remarked to William and Hannah Philippa later that afternoon.

Smiling, William pulled open a drawer. "I've two letters to show you. Both arrived just yesterday."

He took two thick white envelopes from the secretary. "Listen to what Richard Henry writes about the Second Virginia Convention in March." After scanning the page, he began to read: " ' Twas convened by our indefatigable Speaker Randolph at St. John's Church in Richmond, a city I had not visited in years, and the comparison with the larger, more cosmopolitan Philadelphia was much in my mind. The church is situated on a hill, small in size but suitable to our purposes (although our ample Ben Harrison complained that he could hardly fit himself in one of the narrow pews!). As you will recall, Richmond was initially an Indian trading post for the Byrd family, and the present Will Byrd's father developed the city by selling the plots through a lottery. It is serene and charming, with a handsome dockyard, but it is not in any way as bustling as Philadelphia, nor are its taverns adequate for such a company of visitors.

" 'Our main business was to elect delegates to the Second Continental Congress, which is to meet this May in Philadelphia. The seven original delegates, Peyton Randolph, Edmund Pendleton, Patrick Henry, George Washington, Benjamin Harrison, Richard Bland, and I, were again chosen, with Thomas Jefferson, the young burgess from Albemarle, as an alternate.

" 'The other business of note was a heated discussion over whether the Virginia counties should put themselves in a posture of defense. George Washington spoke to us on this point, for he and George Mason are quite involved in organizing the Fairfax County militia. Some wished to delay such action until we had heard the King's response to the petitions of our First Continental Congress, but in the end the motion to arm ourselves carried sixty-five to sixty!' "

William skimmed down a few lines. "Here, Arthur, this is the part I wanted you to hear! He finishes, 'We were subjected to a riveting piece of oratory by Patrick Henry, whose words left us stunned and silent with emotion. "Gentlemen may cry peace, peace, but there is no peace. The war is actually begun! The next gale that sweeps the north will bring to our ears the clash of resounding arms. Our brethren are already in the field! Why stand we here idle? What is it the gentlemen wish? What would they have? Is life so dear, or peace so sweet, as to be purchased at the price of chains and slavery? Forbid it, almighty God! I know not what course others may take; but as for me ... give me liberty or give me death!" ' "

Arthur whistled. "Those are strong words. Patrick Henry's speech against the Stamp Act served as gunpowder for that revolt. I wonder if these will spark another. The man is a radical with words."

Hannah Philippa looked up from her knitting with a quiet smile. "Father used to say that *no one* spoke with more grace and style in the House of Burgesses than your brother Richard Henry. I think our Virginia delegation to Philadelphia is fortunate to have both your brother and Mr. Henry in it."

Arthur went over to give his sister-in-law a kiss on the cheek. "I also think the colony of Virginia is fortunate to have the services of William Lee and his lady in London, my dear."

Hannah Philippa's eyes sparkled. She was enormously proud of her husband's recent election as an alderman of London. It was a prestigious position, and the victory of Virginia-born William Lee, an anti-ministry merchant, underscored the City of London's support for the colonial cause.

"When will you be sworn in?" Arthur asked his brother.

"In June," said William, removing the second letter from the drawer, "in a ceremony of pomp and ancient ritual, our dear lord mayor assures me." He grimaced.

"Don't look like that! You shall love it, you know you shall. Your little son will be the child of a famous personage. I shall carry him around on a silken pillow!"

"Stop teasing!" Hannah Philippa said. "Now read him the other letter, William." She looked at Arthur. "It comes from Will Shippen and is of great interest."

"Here!" William held it out to Arthur. "Take it home to your chambers and read it for yourself."

"The golden Shippens . . ." Arthur put the letter in his pocket. "Does Will express himself on the widening rift with the Mother Country?"

"Never in a personal sense," William said thoughtfully. "Will is very tactful. One doesn't always know exactly what he thinks. Certainly he is a patriot, but the word 'independence' has never appeared in any of his letters. He does say Philadelphia is waiting expectantly for the Second Continental Convention to meet, but that is all."

" 'Independence' is a dangerous word," Arthur remarked, "a treasonous word. Every time I look upon the green that fronts your house, I am reminded that only thirty years ago young Scottish lords lost their heads on that very spot for their part in the Jacobite Rebellion. I quite like my head where it is!"

That evening, Arthur read Will Shippen's letter as he awaited the arrival of a supper guest. The charming Nicole was due at seven. His servant would set out cold chicken and champagne and, after lighting the candles, absent himself for the evening. It had all the markings of a very enjoyable night.

Will Shippen's letters had always been a pleasure, literate, newsy, and full of affection. Aristocrats by nature, the Shippens of Philadelphia, like the Byrds of Westover, had always been staunch Tories. Yet Will was tolerant of his wife's family's republicanism, never condemning the radical activities of Richard Henry, Frank, William, and Arthur as a betrayal of class. How difficult for Will, Arthur thought, if it should come to a choice of loyalties.

A light knock at his chamber door banished all political thoughts from Arthur's mind for the rest of the evening. The voluptuous Nicole was as enchanting as he remembered her. In London for a few months, she would soon be returning to Paris, where she belonged to the glittering court of the twenty-one-year old French King, Louis XVI, and his queen, Marie Antoinette.

As shadows fell over the Thames, the French girl regaled him with stories of life at the French court. How charming she was, how quick of wit and dazzling—how explicit! There was something delightful about the way the French could use the coarsest descriptions and make them sound quite natural, not at all improper!

"Louis Seize is much in love with his little Austrian Queen and quite true to her," she confided. "His only other passion is hunting, I am afraid." She sighed, obviously dismayed by the King's amazing virtue.

Arthur laughed with delight. "Give him time, my dear. He has been married only a few years; a king less than one year. When he does decide to expand his romantic horizons, there shall be lists of lovely ladies waiting, and if he is anything like his grandfather, you shall have to wait your turn to share his bed!" Arthur slipped a grape in the girl's ripe red mouth. "My friend John Wilkes told me he once dined in Paris with twelve gentlemen, eleven of whom declared they should think it their pleasure and duty to surrender their wives to the King if he desired!"

"To attract the King's favor is a problem, no question," Nicole mused. "Then one must have the intellectual abilities of a Madame de Pompadour or the charm of a DuBarry to remain in favor."

Arthur leaned forward and stroked her arm gently. "Tell me of your interesting friend Beaumarchais and his strange mission in England."

With a giggle of suppressed laughter, Nicole snuggled closer. "First, do you realize the background of the witty and elegant 'de Beaumarchais'? He was born the son of a watchmaker, but, with high ambitions and an advantageous marriage, he found himself a member of old Louis Quinze's household, first as an officer of the Pantry, one of those haughty, insignificant gentlemen who each day put the King's meat on the table, then as a music master to the royal princesses. After that, he rose to be an honorary royal secretary!"

"Plus a playwright of renown," Arthur contributed.

The girl nodded enthusiastically. "*Oui*, is not *The Barber of Seville* marvelous? I have seen it a dozen times!"

"Then what?" persisted Arthur.

"Well, then he undertook a secret mission for the old King as a way of winning back royal favor, from which he had apparently fallen at that time. He set out for London to pay off a journalist who was blackmailing Madame DuBarry, threatening to publish a thinly described biography of her called *The Secret Memoirs of a Public Woman*. Beaumarchais accomplished the job most admirably. He paid off the journalist and personally burned all three thousand copies of the offending memoirs in the furnace of a friend's house here in London."

Arthur nodded knowingly. "So since then he has been recognized in the French court as a good man for private missions and a touch of espionage."

"*Oui!* He is here now to meet with the Chevalier d'Eon, a Frenchman living in London, who was one of Louis Quinze's . . . how do you say . . ."

"Spies," Arthur put in promptly.

"Well, let us just say that the charming and elegant d'Eon was quick to report what he heard and saw at the English court to his own King in France. Now the old King is dead, d'Eon has been hinting that he has some secret papers of Louis Quinze that the English would like to have, and that therefore he would like to be reimbursed for them adequately by the French court. Well"—the girl's almond eyes opened wide—"when Beaumarchais arrived in London and was introduced to the old spy at the home of your mayor, Mr. Wilkes, he found the chevalier was addressed as the 'chevalière' and was a most handsome lady in coiffe, diamonds, and silken petticoats. Yet this is apparently a *recent* metamorphosis. She was always a *he* until now!"

Arthur roared with laughter.

Nicole leaned forward. "Beaumarchais does not know whether to challenge *him* to a duel, if it is indeed a he, or have a love affair with *her*. It is most perplexing, *n'est-ce pas?*"

"Well, that is the gallant Beaumarchais's affair," Arthur said as he refilled the girl's champagne glass. "We have our own little affair to consider, do we not?"

It was not yet morning when Nicole, hearing the pounding on the door, nudged Arthur. "Is that your man wishing to come in?" she asked sleepily.

"He has his own key." Arthur groaned and sat up with a yawn. "Who the deuce can it be at this hour!"

"An important message from America," a hoarse voice sounded from the other side of the door as Arthur struggled with the lock.

A ship's boy, still in his leather skirt and cap, held out a fat missive to Arthur.

"It is about the shooting, sir," prompted the boy. "There was a dreadful battle in Massachusetts, and you are the first man to receive word in all England! We are off a fast schooner in ballast from Salem, Massachusetts, and Capt'n Derby was told to deliver this immediately. My captain says it is very important, sir, that you hear the news before anyone else in England."

Stunned, Arthur scanned the letter from Sam Adams. It seemed a British infantry force had been sent out from Boston by General Gage on April 18 to seize the powder stores in the village of Lexington, some ten miles northwest of Boston. The military party was met early the next morning by a line of minutemen, who, having been warned of the approaching Redcoats, were waiting on the village common. From behind a stone wall a musket was fired, and a battle had ensued. Eight Massachusetts farmers fell.

The British then marched on to Concord, looking for a fight. Two Americans and three British regulars were killed there. The Redcoats retreated toward Boston, their column sniped at all along the route. By the time the soldiers had reached the safety of Boston, seventy were lost from the ranks.

All Arthur's senses seized on the image. The polished, regimented soldiers, the proud farmers, the challenge in the hostile air, then those first shots! "My God, it's happened," he murmured, leaning in dismay against the doorframe. "War has begun."

Word of the bloodshed at Lexington and Concord on April 19, 1775 seems to have taken almost as long to reach the backwaters of Virginia by postrider as it did to reach London by fast ship. Unaware of that altercation, Richard Henry Lee rode leisurely northward in the last days of April toward Philadelphia and a second sitting of the Continental Congress. His fellow delegate, George Washington, had suggested that Richard Henry come by way of Mount Vernon so that they could make the journey together. Thus Richard Henry traveled up the Northern Neck with his elder brother Thomas and their friend Charles Carter of Cleve, both having business to attend to in Alexandria.

It was a memorable spring—one, no doubt, Richard Henry Lee never forgot. In the next weeks and months, events, small and large, merged to create a momentum that could not be stopped. Yet, the colonel thought, if someone had told Richard Henry as he rode through the peaceful calm of the Neck that in little over a year the colonial bond with Mother England would be totally rent, he would have no doubt been incredulous.

The Valiant Band

1775–1776

Leesylvania, 1775

The May sun was high overhead, already heavy and warm on the riders' shoulders as Richard Henry Lee, his brother Thomas, and Charles Carter started up the pleached road to Henry Lee's estate.

"Halloo. Welcome to Leesylvania!" a slim young boy called out disarmingly as he trotted down the dirt lane toward them. Henry's third son, thirteen-year-old Richard Bland, greeted each man singly, then turned his pony to escort them to the fieldstone farmhouse. "Colonel Lee, my father says you plan to go on to Philadelphia for the Continental Congress. I wish I were going with you!"

Richard Henry smiled at the unbridled enthusiasm of the dark-eyed boy, who made him think longingly of his own sons, Thomas and Ludwell, far away in England at St. Bee's School.

"I say, have you no servants or additional horses with you?" Richard Bland asked curiously.

"They travel directly to Philadelphia while I stop at Mount Vernon to join Colonel Washington, a fellow member of the Congress," Richard Henry explained. "Has your brother Charles returned yet from Princeton?"

"Charles is still at school—" Richard Bland's words were interrupted by a battle cry from a glade to their left.

"What the devil?" Charles Carter gasped in alarm.

"That is Harry!" Richard Bland announced.

Richard Henry turned in his saddle in time to see Henry and Lucy's eldest son flash through some distant trees. Thrusting and slicing at imaginary adversaries, Harry Lee rode at full gallop straight for the target and with one quick thrust ran his saber through its small black-ringed center.

Richard Henry whistled in admiration. "Take a look at that fellow! You'd think he had been training in the military for years."

"He's a marvel, isn't he, sir?" the boy beside him boasted proudly. "His saber tip is weighted with a bit of heavy metal to make it all the more difficult." Richard Bland sighed. "No one around these parts will duel with him any more, because he always wins!"

Mount Vernon, 1775

"That lad reminds me of a young Greek warrior," Richard Henry commented to his friend George Washington at Mount Vernon that evening. "Perhaps a bit too idealistic—he quoted Locke and the antiroyalist philosophies of Algernon Sidney all through dinner today. Still and all . . ."

"You don't need to convince me of Harry Lee's merits," George answered quickly. "He is the son I might have had—indeed, would have wanted to have," George said wistfully; then he broke into a grin. "Actually, young Harry came to Mount Vernon for a visit last week in the company of that rascally soldier, General Charles Lee. What an eccentric, foul-mouthed fellow he is—no relation to you, thank God—but knowledgeable as the devil about soldiering! The two talked of nothing but the merits of the cavalry all night!"

The May evening was unseasonably hot, and the two men lingered for a few moments on the front lawn of Washington's white frame manor house to catch the gentle, cooling breezes from the Potomac. The Lee brothers and their Carter companion had left Leesylvania after dinner and at nightfall had finally come upon the broad wheat fields of Mount Vernon, where George Washington, riding through the lilac dust of evening with his houseguest, Horatio Gates, had met them.

George's face was sober as he handed his broad-rimmed planter's hat and crop to a servant. "By the way, how does our friend Charles speak about the new Convention?" George was acutely aware that the master of Cleve was as loyal to the King as his father, King Carter, had been, and, like many Virginians, was disturbed that events might get out of hand in Philadelphia.

"It is hard for him to accept the differences that have arisen between England and Virginia," Richard Henry answered quietly. "I have promised him that no one in our delegation will present a motion or sign his hand to a document without instructions from Virginia. I think he is reassured."

George ushered Richard Henry toward the candlelit front parlor where Thomas, Charles Carter, and the gray-haired Gates were already helping themselves to the supper Martha had ordered for the travelers.

Hungry and thirsty after the long ride, Richard Henry surveyed the rich black-bean soup and the veal croquettes. He took a tankard of cold cider from a black-coated servant, drained it to the bottom, and allowed it to be refilled.

What a handsome room this parlor was! He remembered the way George had looked years ago as he stood here with his Fairfax and Carlyle friends. Then the house his beloved half-brother Lawrence built had been modestly furnished. Now it was done up quite elegantly. Richard Henry leaned back in the comfortable brocade chair. Mount Vernon was a prosperous plantation, its manor house much improved and enlarged. The scaffolding at the south end of the mansion was for a new library, George had explained modestly. It was obvious that George was content in his marriage. There had probably been nothing to the rumor of his romantic interest in Sally Fairfax, although George had told Richard Henry in Philadelphia last fall that he still corresponded with George William and Sally Fairfax, who now lived permanently in England. It had been George who had closed their house and arranged for the sale of the Belvoir furniture. "I purchased a few pieces myself," he had told Richard Henry quietly with a sort of finality in his voice, "pieces that had special meaning for me."

George closed the parlor door and sat down in a straight chair by the desk, his long, tightly breeched legs stretched out before him. "Gentlemen, I have been waiting impatiently for your arrival. Mr. Gates is aware of what has recently transpired, but it is my understanding that you are not. Let me bring you up to date."

The planter leaned forward, elbows on his knees, and spoke in his slow, deliberate voice. "I shall try to begin at the beginning." He paused, almost awkwardly. "I was dismayed when I received the startling news last month that Lord Dunmore has voided the land claims awarded to the Ohio war veterans, and I immediately dispatched a letter to the governor appealing that decision. I was stunned by this reversal of policy, for Lord Dunmore and I had held long discussions on that point. There are many veterans of the war in the Ohio, men who risked their lives in battle against the French and the Indians, who will be sorely betrayed by this reversal."

Including George himself, thought Richard Henry. The master of Mount Vernon's claim was for over twenty-three thousand acres.

George went on in a more dispassionate tone. "The governor's answer, terse and quite unfriendly, contended that the veterans' patents are null and void because of a 'technical point.'"

"I see a hint of reprisal and blackmail in this action," Richard Henry broke in.

"Agreed." George nodded. "But an even more disturbing letter arrived from Hugh Mercer of Fredericksburg. He had just got the news from Williamsburg of the removal of the gunpowder from the colony's magazine by the Royal Marines." George's eyes blazed in anger. "You have heard the story, perhaps? The gunpowder was carted away in the dead of night without anyone's knowledge. It was the governor's doing, of course. Mercer suggested that our county militia march to Williamsburg to demand the powder's return."

"Don't forget that we have just come from Leesylvania, where we learned Mercer also alerted the militia at Dumfries," Charles Carter, agitated, interrupted. "The raid was a dastardly act, done in stealth—wagons with greased wheels pulled by horses with padded shoes in the dead of night! Henry Lee and his son were preparing to go, halted only by your message to hold off until you send further notice. I am in agreement that Governor Dunmore's action in removing the powder was inexcusable, but cool heads are needed. I commend your restraint."

George gave a scoffing laugh. "It was not so much my cool head or restraint as the advice of Speaker Randolph, who sent word that the militias should not march. The governor, obviously fearing for his own safety, posted warnings that should any harm come to him or his affairs, he would proclaim liberty to all slaves and reduce Williamsburg to ashes."

The burly Horatio Gates, a former British soldier from the days of Braddock's campaign, swore softly. "That threat alone would have had me boiling enough to set out with musket and powder for Williamsburg!"

"Patrick Henry did just that," George said quietly. "He rode immediately for the capital with a company of militia from Louisa County. And I must say his actions were more effective than all the calm words of Speaker Randolph and Mr. Nicholas. Hearing that Henry and his militamen were approaching, Dunmore quickly produced compensation for the powder. Henry's march was halted ten miles from Williamsburg by the Assembly peacemakers! Carter Braxton of King and Queen County arranged with his father-in-law, Richard Corbin, receiver general of the King's quitrents, to pay for the powder." George rose to his feet abruptly, wiping the sweat from his brow with a white silk handkerchief. "Dunmore has issued a proclamation declaring Patrick Henry an outlaw and threatening punishment to any who aid him."

Richard Henry shook his head slowly. "A hundred years ago it was Nathaniel Bacon, and now it is Patrick Henry who is branded outlaw!"

"I wonder if my services won't be needed here in the colony in the weeks to come more than in Philadelphia," George mused. As the recognized military expert of the colony, he would be expected to organize any military actions in Virginia. "On the other hand," George reversed hotly, "there is Massachusetts!"

"Massachusetts?" Richard Henry echoed in surprise.

George reached to his desk and took up a creased issue of a newspaper. "I dare say you haven't seen this, for it arrived only yesterday."

It was a copy of the *Maryland Gazette* postmarked Annapolis, April 27, 1775. Richard Henry quickly noticed the article George had marked with his pen, then read the tragic account aloud to the other men. On April 19, two days before Dunmore's seizure of the powder in the Williamsburg magazine, a British infantry force had appeared in Lexington to take over military stores belonging to the colonial companies there. The mission had failed because of the stout defense put up by the local villagers, some of whom were slaughtered by the Redcoats.

"Those Redcoats would have failed in Virginia as well if we, too, had been warned in time," muttered Gates.

Thomas looked at his brother. "Now that men have died at Lexington and Concord, the situation is fraught with peril."

Richard Henry's eyes moved to George. "The ramifications of this Massachusetts affair will certainly reach Virginia. I think you have no choice, my friend, but to come with me to Philadelphia."

Philadelphia, 1775

When the Washington coach—an imposing green chariot pulled by sturdy parade grays which he had purchased from Governor Botetourt several years before—arrived in Baltimore, Maryland militia companies thronged the town square to greet him. "They are ardent but inexperienced, yet these Marylanders are hot to set off for Boston!" George explained to Richard Henry, who traveled with him. "Unfortunately, I spot only a few seasoned soldiers among them." He shook his head and confided, "The latest word from Boston is that farmers and militiamen from the countryside have seized the promontories overlooking the city. They have dug themselves in and plan to stay as long as the British are barricaded there. Now others flock to join them from all over New England."

Though he had been a planter and fox hunter for the past ten years, George's true arena was the military. Indeed, his face grew animated at the very mention of battle. "I still have some reservations about leaving Virginia.

There is wheat to be harvested, problems to be solved with my tenants, decisions hanging fire with Dunmore." He gave Richard Henry a wry look. "But then, you are not much concerned with your fields or your investments. You've a one-furrow mind—did you know that?" His mouth tightened resolutely. "Still and all, if I can serve Virginia best in Philadelphia, then Philadelphia it will be." He pulled back the Venetian blind for a last look at the crowd before the carriage pulled away. "I told Martha to expect me back in six weeks," George said with a sigh, "by July first at the very latest."

Five hundred spirited horsemen gave the Washington chariot a rousing cheer as it entered the outskirts of Philadelphia. Fast-happening events had caused an unlikely bonding of the colonies. It seemed they must turn the King and Parliament to their liking . . . or else.

"Or else what?" Richard Henry asked Ben Harrison that night over dinner at the home of Joseph Reed, a Philadelphia trader and merchant. "Are we ready to take up arms, go to war to win our rights? Certainly there can be no question of accommodation on our part."

"None," Harrison said, in complete agreement. "But I do not think it will come to war—it must not, for there is too much at stake for all of us." He pounded one heavy fist into the palm of his other hand. "Such a bloody shame we can't sit down over glasses of ale and simply talk this all out. They say King George is a good sort, likes his dogs and a bit of farming. By God, I swear I could explain our position so that he would completely understand it. Why don't they send a bargaining party over to listen to us . . . damn them all!"

"Quite right, Mr. Harrison," thirty-eight-year-old Silas Deane, a delegate from Connecticut, interjected. "There the King sits in the splendor of St. James's Palace, influenced and dominated by his friends." Deane looked around the table, holding each man's eye. "He has a restless dependency in Ireland, a sullen one in Scotland, and what does he do? Refuses to settle his differences with his most satisfactory and productive subjects three thousand miles away!"

Silas Deane illustrated his point well. There was, however, something about the man that Richard Henry did not trust. He was too much the dandy, the merchant, for his taste.

As the clock struck ten the next morning, the Second Continental Congress came to order. This time the delegates of twelve colonies, Georgia again absent, chose as their meeting place not Carpenters' Hall but the red brick Pennsylvania State House at Fifth and Chestnut Streets. Again voted president of the assembly, Peyton Randolph settled his massive frame in a chair on a low dais by the newly placed stand of British colors.

"All the same faces," Richard Henry informed the Shippens a few days later. "Samuel and John Adams and John Hancock from Massachusetts, Philip Schuyler and a trio of Livingstons from New York, the Rutledges, Gadsden, and Middleton from South Carolina, Caesar Rodney from Delaware, and Silas Deane and Roger Sherman from Connecticut." He smiled. "Your prudent farmer John Dickinson again represents Pennsylvania, along with the reactionary Galloway and Robert Morris."

"What do you think of our addition to the Pennsylvania delegation?" Will Shippen asked, a glint in his eyes.

"Ben Franklin? Cynical and pessimistic though he may be, he is knowledgeable and gives us the benefit of the years he has spent in London dealing with North's ministry."

Franklin, now in his seventieth year, had landed at the Philadelphia harbor five days before the proceedings opened and had already expressed his discouragement and lack of optimism for future negotiations. "Franklin says if the passion and eloquence of Edmund Burke speaking in the House of Commons, and the mass of written petitions and appeals from both sides of the Atlantic, have not taken effect, he can't imagine what more could move the King or the Parliament."

"And what is the overall spirit of the Assembly?" Dr. Shippen asked.

Richard Henry hesitated. "Much personal good will flows, for we are now old friends, but there is disagreement as to what course this convention should take. John Adams came with a plan of action, he and his cousin obviously hoping to wed the cause of this Convention to the cause of Massachusetts. It is my personal feeling," he said, leaning forward intently, "that the men of Massachusetts hope to countermand further efforts at conciliation and would like to establish a national army with a *generalissimo* elected by this Convention."

Doctor Shippen sat back in his chair. "Is war inevitable?"

"It is, in their opinion. But many disagree, looking on the New Englanders as troublemakers who would embroil us all in their local problems."

"What is your own opinion?"

Richard Henry's gaze was steady. "Arthur and William write from London that we must stand together or fall separately. It would seem that war is inevitable."

For this session, Peyton Randolph, Ben Harrison, and George Washington shared the rent of a small, comfortable house in the north of Philadelphia. At around half past three each day, when the meeting adjourned, the three Virginians would join Richard Henry and Delegates Chase of Maryland, Alsop of New York, and Rodney and Read of Delaware for dinner at the City Tavern. "Kidney pie," Ben Harrison allowed grumpily, "is the one dish I have found here that compares with dishes prepared in Virginia."

But when the party met on May 19, they were still too stunned by news from New England even to notice what they were eating. Peyton Randolph had been roused from bed the night before by a rider bearing news of a strange, almost ludicrous victory by the Vermont militiamen nine days earlier. A daring frontiersman named Ethan Allen led comrades he had dubbed the Green Mountain Boys on a successful raid against the British troops at Fort Ticonderoga in New York, capturing sixty pieces of artillery.

When Randolph delivered that thunderbolt to the Convention, the delegates had cheered.

"Walked right up to the door of the garrison before break of dawn, roused the commander, and ordered him to come forth, which he did, his breeches in his hand." George could not resist telling the story again. " 'In whose authority?' asked the British commander. 'In the name of the great Jehovah and the Continental Congress,' says Allen!"

"John Adams says a colonel in the Massachusetts militia, Benedict Arnold, was setting up plans for just such a raid when he heard that Allen and his boys were already en route," Richard Henry added. "Arnold hurried to join them, then led the attack on Crown Point later that day."

"Regardless of who deserves the credit for the raid," George stated emphatically, "the result has been to open a route to Canada and to put in our hands sixty pieces of badly needed artillery."

" 'Our' hands, Colonel Washington?" Ben Harrison asked quickly. "Have we come to that point?"

George did not answer but took a long drink from his glass, his eyes masked by the tankard.

Ten days later, Richard Henry wrote to Anne at Chantilly:

How I wish you were with me, my dear love. If there is a next time, believe me, I shall insist that you accompany me to Philadelphia, for while my head is here, my heart remains steadfastly with you in Virginia.

Perhaps you have heard, Governor Dunmore at last calls a meeting of the Assembly for June 1. Naturally, Speaker Peyton Randolph must attend. He left Philadelphia today. (It is my understanding that Mr. Jefferson will take his place.) All of the Virginia delegation are torn between remaining at this convention and returning to Williamsburg. We have concluded that it is in the best interest of all that we stay here, but I have sent a letter of opinions and suggestions to Frank, who will be present in the House of Burgesses, representing Richmond County.

I cannot write that we accomplish a great deal here in Philadelphia. We did this very day, however, send an appeal to Canada inviting that province to join in our stand. And if they do not? It is the feeling of the most zealous among us that they must be allowed no choice. Samuel Adams remains my closest confidant, and we are together in our beliefs. He is an odd fellow, clever, shrewd, certainly a manipulator when given the chance. This time he is nicely dressed, for a change, in clothes bought for him by friends in Boston! But he is not popular with the majority of the delegates. His cousin, John, is quite different, an equally brilliant mind, amiable but quick to make judgments. He is admired but is far too egotistical to suit the popular mood.

Alice and her family send their love to Chantilly. Daughter Nancy is quite a lovely girl of twelve. She makes me think of Molly.

The hour is late and my hand shakes with weariness. I must close, but know, my dear Anne, that my heart is filled with love for you, my mind with the sweetest memories of hours we have spent in each other's company. I remain, until we meet again, your devoted   Richard Henry Lee

P.S. An amusing spectacle: Upon Peyton Randolph's removal from the Convention, Mr. John Hancock, a dapper gentleman of Boston, was chosen president. He pretends great modesty and hesitated to take his presidential seat, whereupon the burly and impatient Ben Harrison bodily lifted Hancock and sat him firmly in his chair!

On the hazy warm morning of June 14, Richard Henry walked to the State House, drawn by the familiar white wooden belfry with its handsome clock. His spirits lifted as he strode the clean, neat streets of America's largest city. God knows he had no reason to be lighthearted. The news from London was discouraging, the Convention seemed stalemated. Yet he had never felt more clearheaded.

He had waked early and lain in his tree-shaded bedroom at Shippen House wondering whether the colonies would face economic and political collapse if the situation became so desperate that ties with the Mother Country were severed. Independence! The very thought had sent a spurt of exhilaration and anxiety through him.

A Whig, he had also been branded a "revolutionist" at this Convention, admired by some, disliked by others. His mind *did* run in a liberal direction, toward the eventual prospect of an equitable mass distribution of land, the abolition of slavery, the separation of church and state, but in truth he was a conservative. There were certain natural laws that transcended man-made laws. Man did not have to be coerced by his own government. Man-made law should be as benevolent as natural law.

In truth, these Philadelphia delegates hardly seemed the "renegade band" of outlaws that Arthur wrote they were termed in London. In general, they were a distinguished, well-dressed group—wigged or powdered, always freshly shaved and resplendent in fine frocks and choice linen. In fact, it was the preparation of their toilette that often made delegates less than punctual.

Samuel Adams was waiting for him on the State House steps. "We need your support today," he said urgently. "The time is right."

Richard Henry nodded grimly. It had been generally agreed by the Congress that the growing "army" around Boston must be supported. Gunpowder, saltpetre, flour, had already begun to flow in from the various colonies, albeit erratically. Yet all actions seemed to occur in a zigzag of confusion and vacillation. While on June 3 one committee of the Congress was instructed to prepare another polite petition to the Crown, a second committee was set up to find ways to borrow six thousand pounds to purchase needed gunpowder. On June 12, they had passed a motion that July 20 be observed as a day of fasting, when all colonists were to pray to God to remove "our present calamities . . . to bless our rightful Sovereign King George the Third and to inspire him with the wisdom to discern and pursue the true interest of all his subjects . . ." Two days later, the Congress authorized the raising of ten companies of expert riflemen from Pennsylvania, Maryland, and Virginia to march to Boston. Once there, they were to be employed as light infantry under the command of a chief officer in that army.

Who should the chief officer be? That was the question now hanging in the air this June morning.

Some favored Artemas Ward, a Massachusetts man now in command of the colonists dug in around Boston. Others spoke of Israel Putnam, a New England hero. The odd and eccentric Charles Lee had been mentioned more than once, and even Horatio Gates had been put förth as a candidate. But it was the opinion of Samuel Adams and his cousin, John, that George Washington should have the position.

Richard Henry took his place in the chamber. He had no illusions as to why the Adamses wanted George. He was, after all, the most experienced of the available younger military men, and he had in the Convention committees shown great familiarity with military matters. But his appointment would also bind Virginia to Massachusetts, and where Virginia went, the other colonies would follow. Very pragmatic.

And I am as pragmatic as they, thought Richard Henry. Virginia—her interests, her rights—must be considered first. These would be obtained only

by a united stand, as William and Arthur urged. And who should lead a
united stand but a Virginian?

He watched Ben Harrison and George Washington, big, impressive
men, stride into the whitewashed chamber. As always, George wore the red,
blue, and buff uniform of the Ohio campaign. The uniform suggested that he
might enjoy being chosen for the command, though in private he seemed
reluctant even to discuss the possibility. There was no question that such a
nomination would put an enormous personal burden on Washington. He
would also be risking much of the prosperity he had worked so hard to
create at Mount Vernon.

The rest of the Virginia delegation strongly disapproved of appointing
George commander, knowing that it would commit the colony to Massachu-
setts. "We must ask ourselves, Is it in Virginia's best interest?" Edmund
Pendleton had argued last night at dinner. "I cannot imagine it is in Colonel
Washington's."

Hancock took up the silver mace and called the session to order. The
doors of the chamber were closed to onlookers as John Adams rose to his
feet. The small, round-faced lawyer was well respected, though viewed as an
extremist, for he was already an outspoken advocate of separation from
Great Britain. Adams was speaking now on behalf of the Massachusetts
Provincial Congress in Boston. Swift support was needed, he argued. Should
its little makeshift army disband because of lack of unity, the calling of
another army would be practically impossible. Parliament would have
triumphed! Now was the time to show the patriots gathered on the Boston
hilltops that all of British North America was behind them. This Philadelphia Congress must take over the army at Boston and place the troops
already gathered there under the direction of a man appointed by the Congress.

There was one man who came immediately to mind, John Adams said
in his mellow Bostonian accent. Perhaps this was not the time to nominate
that individual formally, but it was the time to point out to the gathered
assemblage his attributes.

Richard Henry saw John Hancock flush slightly and straighten his
shoulders. Did the wealthy Boston merchant think that Adams was referring
to him?

The gentleman in question was a man of integrity, Adams explained, of
demonstrated skill and experience, a man of independent fortune. He would
unite the effort of the colonies more completely than—

"He is talking about George, obviously," Ben Harrison whispered
under his breath.

"And George knows it," Henry muttered in response.

The tall Virginian in his conspicuous uniform rose self-consciously to his feet. With a look of utter dismay, he bolted from the room to the adjoining library.

"God save him," muttered Patrick Henry.

"Colonel Washington accepted Congress's assignment with manly dignity but considerable anxiety," Richard Henry said a week later over breakfast at Shippen House to Thomas Jefferson, who had just arrived to take the seat of Peyton Randolph. "Few men know Washington as well as I. Believe me when I tell you that he is mindful of the honor, for his election was unanimous. But he is keenly aware of his own limitations and desperate situation. He has already departed for Boston with members of his newly elected staff."

The lean, sandy-haired Jefferson took a sip from his coffee cup as he listened impassively to the account.

"Fearful that there might be those who think he took the position for the pay Congress attached to it, he waived the five-hundred-dollar salary, saying he will accept payment only for his expenses." Richard Henry smiled. "My friend George is a proud man, very proud."

"And, I must say, very apprehensive," Patrick Henry added emphatically. "He said to me with great emotion, 'Remember, Mr. Henry, what I now tell you: from the day I enter upon the command of the American armies, I date my fall, and the ruin of my reputation.' His situation is a most difficult one. Mark my words."

Thomas Jefferson's slate-blue eyes were coolly sympathetic. "I am no military man," he said quietly. "I can hardly fathom his situation. The Congress gave him no opportunity to put his affairs in order at home?"

"There was no time! Every day brings a worsening of our position." Richard Henry responded brusquely to the detachment in Jefferson's tone.

Then, with a twinge of remorse, he went on more softly. "I realize that you are still tired from your unexpected journey, Mr. Jefferson. We do appreciate your joining us this morning, for we are most anxious to know the news of the Assembly in Williamsburg."

"I've a great deal to convey." Jefferson pushed aside his plate and rested his elbows on the table. "Most of it is predictable. My cousin, Speaker Randolph, was met in Williamsburg on May 29 by a detachment of Williamsburg volunteer militia, who escorted him into the city with a great deal of cheering and loud huzzahs. Accordingly, he opened the session of the House of Burgesses on the first day of June to consider the Conciliatory Resolution offered by Lord North."

"Conciliatory, hah! Damned bit of impertinence, that resolution!" Patrick Henry broke in, "aimed only at causing division among the colonies!"

Richard Henry smiled sympathetically at his friend's impatient rage. It was true the resolution was sheer fakery. It conceded little, although on first reading it sounded reasonable. By its terms, Parliament agreed not to levy taxes for revenue within a colony's border if that colony's assembly contributed satisfactorily toward expenses of common defense of the empire and provided for support of its own civil and judicial officers.

Jefferson nodded to Patrick Henry. "It is a change in the form of oppression, but it does not lighten our burdens. Mr. Randolph was aware of the similar sentiments of this convention and anxious that Virginia should be the first colony to reject the resolution. It is my belief that he feared Mr. Nicholas would undertake to sway the House into agreement, and therefore pressed me to undertake an answer. I did so, and it passed the House more or less intact." A slight smile played on Jefferson's face. "I have brought a copy to you."

"Did the governor respond?" Richard Henry asked.

"He fled Williamsburg," said Thomas Jefferson flatly.

"What!" Will Shippen and Patrick Henry spoke as one.

Jefferson nodded. "There was a trivial incident at the powder magazine during the first week in June. Some young boys were injured, and the Assembly suspected a trap set by the British troops. A committee, which included your brother Francis Lightfoot, investigated, and after much discussion, the keys to the magazine were turned over to the Assembly. I can't imagine why this small incident should have prompted it, but on the night of June 8, the governor, accompanied by his wife and children and a few of his staff, stole out of Williamsburg and boarded the *Fowery*."

"Stole?" echoed Richard Henry, incredulous.

"In the dead of night! It quite astounded the Assembly. A committee visited His Lordship aboard the ship. Your brother Frank was again among those who went, as was the governor's friend Will Byrd. The governor was assured that if he and his family returned to the palace, no harm would come to them. But they refused."

"What was the governor's response to your answer to North's Conciliatory Resolution?" Richard Henry inquired.

"Short and straightforward. He sent us this message: 'Gentlemen of the House of Burgesses— It is with real concern I can discover nothing in your address that I think manifests the smallest inclination to, or will be productive of, a reconciliation with the Mother Country.—Dunmore.'"

"My God." Will Shippen leaned back in his chair. "And he remains aboard the *Fowery*, does he? Mr. Jefferson, what is the reaction of Mr. Byrd to this? You know, Will Byrd is my cousin Mary's husband."

Jefferson paused. "I am sorry to tell you, sir, that Will Byrd is sorely distressed. But he remains Tory—loyal to his king, to his governor, and to

Virginia. The division between his own sons reflects the problems we face. His eldest, Thomas Taylor Byrd, a captain in the British Army, welcomed the governor aboard the *Fowery*. His second son, Otway, who held a commission in the Royal Navy, had already jumped ship in order to fight for the patriots' cause."

"Imagine," Patrick Henry marveled. "It was only this past January, scarcely six months ago, that we danced, by the governor's invitation, at the Queen's Birthday Ball in the palace. Dunmore brought out his new infant daughter, who had just that day been christened Virginia. There is a momentum, a destiny that is moving us too swiftly toward—"

Ben Harrison, a late arrival, now loomed in the doorway, tense and breathless. "There is news," he cried, "news from Boston . . . a terrible battle. Seems the British decided to take one of the hills of the city—Breed Hill, I think it is called. They eventually won it"—he looked up with a glimmer of satisfaction—"but at a terrible price. At the cost of fifteen hundred British troops, half of the regiment who stormed the hill. Accounts say General Gage had little idea the patriots would prove so stout-hearted!"

London, 1775

Arthur Lee was existing in a whirlwind of contradictions. As a colonial agent, he bent all his efforts toward conciliation; yet everything seemed to be moving irrevocably toward a break between the colonies and England. He felt knocked around like a croquet ball!

The slender Virginia agent had just ascended the red-carpeted staircase of the lord mayor's mansion in London and now waited in the doorway of the drawing room, watching his brother William already deep in conversation with his tobacco partner, Stephen Sayre, at the other end of the room. Ah, there was that rogue Beaumarchais! His company would add a gloss of lighthearted pleasure to the evening.

"My dear Dr. Lee." John Wilkes, urbane and polished, took Arthur's arm affectionately. "How well you look tonight. Did I not see you at the Garrick play last Thursday evening, with a lovely fair-haired young lady, all bedecked in pearls, on your arm?"

"You did, sir, although I don't believe I had the good fortune to notice you."

"No wonder!" Wilkes led Arthur toward a cluster of men at the hearth. "It seemed to me you had eyes only for your companion."

Arthur nodded ruefully. "Single-mindedness is one of my chief characteristics."

John Wilkes threw back his powdered head in laughter. By the charm of his personality Wilkes still held London in his palm. Just two days earlier, as lord mayor of the City, he had read Richard Henry's letter of thanks for their support on behalf of the Continental Congress to a great cheering crowd of London freeholders gathered in the Guild Hall. "Victory to America!" they had chanted in response. "Resurrection to the British Constitution!"

Not that cheering or petitions from either side of the Atlantic—or anything else, for that matter—accomplished much! Arthur accepted a glass of port and gazed appreciatively at a handsome rococo rendition of graceful nymphs on the far wall.

He knew from several sources that the Second Continental Congress had labored long on their Declaration of the Causes of Taking Up Arms. Rutledge of South Carolina had first drawn it up, Richard Henry had worked on it. Thomas Jefferson had also done a draft, but his was too strong for the peaceable Mr. Dickinson of Pennsylvania, whose viewpoint had to be indulged. An entirely new statement was prepared, along with a second petition, pleading for the monarch's intervention in the stalemate between the colonies and Lord North's government. The petition had been sent to London in the hands of the Pennsylvanian Richard Penn, who, together with Arthur, had presented it to the colonial secretary. Three weeks ago, on September 1, Lord Dartmouth had called them in to say that the King had dismissed the petition. Another opportunity for reconciliation wasted by a vengeful monarch and his proud Tory majority in Parliament!

"Greatest empire in the world . . ." Arthur's ear caught snatches of conversation by the window, and a sad lump rose in his throat. Of course it was. Britain was the greatest empire since Rome had extended her provinces throughout the Western world. And Virginia, the pride of England's colonies in America, the richest and most populous colony, should be part of her glory.

"I say, Dr. Lee," one of the Wilkesites drew Arthur into the conversation, "tell us the latest from your Philadelphia convention. What is the mood that you sense from your correspondence?"

The others, all interested friends, fell silent. John Wilkes had no one to his private parties who was not pro-America and against this "fratricidal division," as he scathingly termed it.

"The Congress has recessed for a few weeks, August being the sickly season in Philadelphia," Arthur began. "As for their common feeling, I cannot say that they have any. They are Whigs for the most part, gentlemen of education and means who strongly resist any unconstitutional act of Parliament. That is all they have in common!"

"But the American Congress has taken two actions of note," he continued. "First, they rejected the monarch's Conciliatory Resolution. Thomas Jefferson drafted their letter, which is why the wording resembled the rejecting letter from Virginia, which he also drafted. Second, when King George declared Massachusetts in rebellion, all the other colonies voted to stand by her." Arthur would not add that there were a few delegates—the Adamses of Massachusetts, his brother Richard Henry, Gadsden of South Carolina, and the aging Ben Franklin—who already talked of forging a confederation of independent colonies.

"It is my opinion," John Wilkes said with vehemence and a twinge of bitterness, "that our American colonies are all but lost to us. War already scorches the American continent at Lexington and Concord, brought on by the intemperate actions of the British troops—as Dr. Lee has so graphically laid out for us in his newspaper articles, which not only prod our sense of justice but also inflame those of us in London who deplore Lord North's excesses." He paused, lowering his voice slightly. "George the Third must not forget that the crown was once removed from the head of an English monarch over the issue of constitutional freedom—not only the crown from the head, but the head from the shoulders! It could happen again."

Wilkes's words were treasonous if quoted out of context. Perhaps, thought Arthur, the clever Beaumarchais, who listened intently, his expression veiled, was shocked. Such a remark uttered in Paris would send one quickly to the Bastille.

At supper later that evening, Wilkes asked Arthur to give those around the table a description of the new commander in chief, George Washington. "Tell us the news of your ragbone army of patriots who skirmish with the British in Massachusetts."

Arthur caught William's warning glance. The brothers were acutely aware that a recent letter from Washington had been full of anguish and disillusionment. The new American commander in chief had left Philadelphia in a din of cheering farewells, but in Cambridge, Massachusetts, he found only confusion, factionalism, fewer than fifty cannons, and very little military organization or dependable army stores of any kind.

Arthur searched for words carefully. "I have always found George Washington to be a man of rare common sense and judgment. William and I have known him all our lives, and we place infinite trust in him."

William broke in with calculated intensity. "The major thrust of the colonial military effort at the moment is directed toward Canada. A newly appointed New York general, Philip Schuyler, is currently en route to Montreal."

"Quebec is also targeted for seizure," Arthur put in. "Benedict Arnold, a Massachusetts militia officer who was instrumental in taking Ticonderoga and Crown Point, plans to lead an expedition toward that city. I also heard from my brother Frank in Williamsburg that Dan Morgan, a bold Virginia frontiersman, led his crack militia rifle corps north to Boston in early August. Perhaps he will struggle farther north with Arnold." He flushed lightly with pride. "It would be quite an advantage to Arnold."

The table fell silent. How ironic, thought Arthur with a shake of his head, to be pleasantly sitting over pheasant and burgundy while men were at this very moment marching with muskets on their shoulders through the dark forests of the American wilderness.

"I have been seeking to express privately to you, sir, the interest of my King in your cause," Beaumarchais confided to Arthur in the mansion's vestibule at the party's close. "France watches the struggles of the English colonies with much sympathy. My dear Mr. Lee, you appear to have great confidence in your General Washington's abilities to lead a diverse army of colonials against the entire British Army."

"Every confidence, my dear sir," Arthur said firmly. "Does George the Third think we can be put down like his Scottish Highlanders? They lived close at hand, whereas a wide sea separates England and America. Can the King afford to put soldiers in ships that are old and rotten? His Royal Navy has deteriorated and his seamen grown incompetent under the neglectful eye of the Lord of Sandwich. If there is to be a war, sir, we have the advantage."

Arthur accepted his evening cape from the footman and walked beside the small, dapper Frenchman out into the night fog.

No matter what private doubts he held about the abilities of the American Army, it was crucial to present an attitude of optimism. Arthur helped the Frenchman into the carriage. "I wonder, my dear Beaumarchais, if you would care to dine with me and my brother William tomorrow evening. I think it is important that we discuss the possibilities of a French-American friendship in depth."

Beaumarchais stared at Arthur from the darkness of the carriage interior. "You intrigue me, Dr. Lee. I am equally impressed with the power and respect your brother William has gained as sheriff and alderman of London. Now, more and more, I hear the name Richard Henry Lee—your brother in America, I presume?"

Arthur nodded.

"You are of a family of strong men, are you not? Partisans of that new political quality of life you call liberty?"

Arthur rested his hand on the carriage window. "We are Englishmen proud of our heritage and jealous of our constitutional rights. As Virginians, we are the keystone of the empire, my dear Count. We will have no less than we are due."

A smile quivered beneath the Frenchman's mustache. "It is my opinion that no man could better explain to me—and through me to the foreign minister—the advantages we French might find in lending the cause of 'frantic liberty' our support. I shall look forward to dining with you and your brother tomorrow night." He rested his hand beside Arthur's on the window frame. "How fascinating," he mused. "Three sons of Virginia so ardent for the same cause."

Arthur's face broke into a broad smile. "Not three—five! My brother Thomas is one of eleven recently elected to a 'committee of safety' to direct the defense and protection of the colony now that the royal governor has fled Williamsburg. And"—Arthur stepped back from the carriage and threw his black silk cloak over his shoulder—"that same convention dispatches another of my brothers, Francis Lightfoot, to Philadelphia to take his place beside Richard Henry in the Second Continental Convention. We are a band of brothers ardent in our devotion to Virginia!"

Beaumarchais raised a hand in parting as the carriage rumbled off in the September night. A thread, Arthur realized with excitement, albeit a fragile one, had been established with Louis XVI's court. If it were to come to an out-and-out war, the aid of France or Spain would be essential. His head reeling with the possibilities introduced by this brief interchange, Arthur summoned a linkman to lead him by torchlight down Fleet Street to the haven of his rooms at the Middle Temple.

Philadelphia, 1775

The skies over Philadelphia had turned from a windswept gray to a sullen lead in the course of just an hour. At least so it seemed to Becky Tayloe Lee as she nuzzled her chin into the fur collar of her new roquelaure cape and pushed her small hands deeper into her muff. Perhaps it would snow! A deep, heavy snowfall that would blanket the streets and frost the housetops. She had never seen a snowfall that did much more than lie like powdered sugar on a cream puff. The prospect of an all-enveloping snowfall was intriguing, delicious.

"Come on, my darling. You are daydreaming." Francis Lightfoot took the bulky box from the dressmaker, who stood at the door, and gently ushered Becky into the phaeton waiting at the curb.

"I was thinking of snow," she said dreamily as Frank tucked the lap robe around her and motioned the driver to move on. "Picture Philadelphia in the winter, copper sleigh bells jingling on the horses' bridles as they trot under trees beautifully laden with white from heaven. Picture you and me sitting by a cozy fire in our bedroom at Shippen House, drinking warm chocolate. Oh, Frank, I do adore warm chocolate!" She sighed with pleasure.

Frank broke into delighted laughter. Bringing Becky to Philadelphia had been like escorting Cinderella to the ball. Her joy had brought a constant sparkle to her eyes and kept her cheeks so flushed that he could barely keep his eyes—or his hands—from her.

"I am glad that Philadelphia pleases you so, my dearest, and I only hope the winter will be as romantic and charming as you picture it. To be truthful, I have heard Philadelphia winters are quite brutal."

"Well, I don't believe it. Our winter shall be wonderful, just as this fall has been," she said, snuggling close to him.

Frank looked down at her adoringly. They had left Menokin in early September, as soon as word had reached the Rappahannock that he had been chosen to fill the seat of the ailing Richard Bland at the Continental Congress. Becky had been like an eager child from the first day of the journey, her eyes riveted to the carriage window as the mellow September hills of Maryland, Delaware, and finally Pennsylvania rolled into view.

Frank and Becky had never before visited Alice and her husband, but no one could have won their affection more quickly than Will. "Kissing me so heartily he knocked off my skimmer!" Becky had remarked with a throaty little laugh when they were settling in one of the comfortable upstairs bedrooms. Frank had peered admiringly into the large, sunny master bedroom, and into those on the third floor that belonged to the Shippen children. Thomas was already at boarding school, but Nancy Shippen, a dark-eyed slip of a girl, had given him a shy hug. "She is quite different from her cousin Matilda at Stratford," Frank had told Becky as they dressed for dinner. "So tiny and very delicate, while well-formed Matilda is already attracting admirers!"

"They are both almost thirteen . . . hardly children," Becky had reminded him with a smile as she brushed her hair at the dressing table. Frank had taken the brush from her hand and run it down the long, satiny ripple of hair that fell from her chignon. "Now that you are a married lady, twenty-three years old, I don't quite know what to do with you," he had murmured. How beautiful she was in her white peignoir, his wife, his darling, his child!

He dropped the brush and slipped his hands beneath the heavy tresses to touch her slender neck. "Are you tired from the journey, my love? Would you like to lie down?"

Becky's eyes in the mirror had flickered to the high posted bed behind them. "I am not a bit tired," she had said in her distinctive low voice. "But I could be induced to bed."

As the carriage continued down the cobblestone street, Frank sighed with deep satisfaction at the memory.

Becky shook his hand gently, "Francis Lightfoot, what thoughts have carried you so far away?"

"I'm thinking of the reception tonight and how lovely you shall look in your new gown." He patted the box on the seat beside her.

The reception was to honor Martha Washington and her party, who were on their way to Boston. Originally there was to have been a ball, but the Tory ladies of Philadelphia would not support it, and Sam Adams, who frowned upon such frivolity, had been instrumental in calling off the gala. The Virginians were incensed. Ben Harrison in particular was furious at the slight to Lady Washington and had dressed Adams down in no uncertain terms. Tonight's reception was to be a compromise.

"I think Lady Washington is very brave to spend the winter with her husband," said Becky. "Why, she has never even been away from Virginia before, and Boston is such a long distance." She looked up at him from under the brim of her hood. "But I quite understand, for I would travel anywhere to be with you."

Frank squeezed her hand. "The general thought the hostilities would certainly end by Christmas and he would be at home, but, sadly, it is not to be. He has settled down for the winter in Cambridge. At least he will have his wife and young Custis with him."

It was growing dark, and candles flickered softly in the windows of the sedate, handsome houses they passed. Frank had to admit this bustling, energetic city fascinated him. Water pumps stood on every corner, and thanks to good Dr. Franklin, lightning rods decorated the rooftops. The cobblestone streets, baptized with logically ordered names of trees and numbers, ran straight. He had to give these Pennsylvanians high marks for modern, well-planned living.

The Continental Congress was less artfully drawn, a juxtaposition of abundant pride, jealousy, factions, and secrecy. The delegates had been so well described by Richard Henry that Frank could have picked them out at first sight. The Congress president, John Hancock, with his handsome, peevish face; solemn, gray-haired Livingston of New York; the droll Scottish educator Dr. Witherspoon of New Jersey; the Irish John Carroll of Maryland; and the elegant, dandified South Carolinians, well born and young— the oldest, Middleton, being only thirty-four.

At least that part had been predictable. What had not been was Peyton Randolph's sudden death last month here in Philadelphia. The erudite, commanding Randolph had been a powerful force in Virginia: king's attorney for many years, speaker of the house, and leader of their Continental

Congress delegation. Tom Jefferson was his cousin and Ben Harrison his brother-in-law, but all suffered his loss dearly.

Who now would the Virginia convention send to take Peyton Randolph's seat? A conservative, most likely. Frank stared out into the gathering dusk. The Virginia convention would no doubt debate the choice hotly. Richard Henry, Thomas Jefferson, the lawyer George Wythe, and Frank himself were seen as radicals, extremists who, if given their head, might lead the colony right off the precipice of the empire. Holding on more tightly to the coattails of the Mother Country were the moderates, Ben Harrison and Thomas Nelson. The deep resentment many Virginia planters felt toward Richard Henry for forcing the Robinson disclosures persisted. No doubt the Assembly would send another conservative—perhaps Robert Carter Nicholas or Carter Braxton, both grandsons of King Carter.

The reception for Colonel Washington's lady was held at the home of Joseph Reed, a merchant and now a member of Washington's staff, who had put together a small guest list so as not to overwhelm the wife of his commander in chief.

Not that Martha Washington would be overwhelmed by the King of England himself, Becky thought with amusement as she was drawn into a warm embrace by the guest of honor. Lady Washington was not in the least bit worldly or pretentious, Becky marveled, and she was so graceful and serene that she seemed more a beacon of strength than someone in need of protection. She was what she was—a gentle patrician lady, the competent mistress of a large plantation now on her way to join her husband, no matter where or what the circumstances. She would be traveling north in the morning accompanied by a small party of military aides, servants, Jack Custis, his wife, Nelly, and the portly wife of General Horatio Gates, who was also to join her husband in Cambridge.

"You are the prettiest lady here tonight," Frank whispered in Becky's ear as they moved from the receiving line. "Blue becomes you."

Becky blushed as she smoothed out the front of her graceful wool gown and looked down appreciatively at the tips of her blue kid slippers. Their fashionable Louis heels made her feel quite chic and graceful.

Accepting a glass of wine from Frank, Becky waited for Alice and Will Shippen, who were greeting Martha Washington. She wanted to show them something her sharp eyes had spotted. Mr. Reed had hung a portrait of George III upside down in the corner of the room. It was a popular fad. Alice and Will would be amused by that!

Becky had been drawn to the Shippens at once. Frank had told her stories of Alice's difficulties under the heavy hand of Colonel Phil, but if those hard times had left a mark, it was only in Alice's quickness to display her feelings. Frank had heard rumors that Will was sorely disappointed that his rival, Dr. John Morgan, was chosen director-general of hospitals for the Continental Army by the Congress, but Alice had said that Will had turned down the position. If Will felt any disappointment, it was not evident in his smiling face.

"My dear Mrs. Lee." Becky turned with a start to find herself looking directly into the brown eyes of John Adams.

"Did I startle you?" His expression was half proud, half shy. "I was thinking how nice it is that you have been able to accompany your husband to Philadelphia. My Abigail waits for me at our home in Braintree, outside Boston; she would so enjoy being here. But then, there are the children and . . ." he shrugged apologetically. "Actually, I was noticing your bracelet."

Becky held up her wrist so that the small, plump man could look more closely. She noted that he did not say "admiring" but "noticing." Frank had told her how the New Englanders were quite puritanical about silks, laces, and ornamentation.

"It is a very personal bracelet, Mr. Adams," she explained. "As you can see, the baubles on it are portraits of people I love or admire. This miniature is of Francis Lightfoot, and this one is of my father. That is one of my sisters, and this one is . . ."

His face broadened into a smile. "That one I recognize as a likeness of our gracious monarch, George the Third."

"Do you think, sir, a day will come when I shall have to remove that particular portrait from my bracelet?"

He would not be drawn in. "I have never known anyone to wear a likeness of the King," he said noncommittally, "except perhaps as a cameo or brooch."

"Oh, it was long the custom among the cavaliers in Virginia," Becky rejoined spiritedly. "My grandmother had a locket with a likeness of King Charles the First, which I thought most wonderful when I was a child, for it had three transparencies that slid into it: one of the King wearing his crown, the next without, and the third beheaded and all bloody, his poor head clutched by the hair in the executioner's fist!"

John Adams stared at her, transfixed. "Amazing," was all he could murmur. "Most amazing, dear lady." With a little bow, he melted away.

It was dreadful to enjoy shocking people so, but how intoxicating! Giggling, Becky tucked her wine glass into a niche. She liked John Adams. Frank said he was despised by Galloway and the most conservative elements of the Congress, but she thought him friendly and almost naïve.

Pulling Becky close, Francis Lightfoot spoke heatedly to Ben Harrison and Richard Henry. "Thank God, the Congress has voted to fill Washington's requests for supplies! It is bad enough to face well-trained forces with only a passel of ragtag militia units. They must have medicine, gunpowder, clothing."

Ben Harrison agreed. The subject was close to his heart, for he had recently returned from an official visit to Cambridge made with Benjamin Franklin and Thomas Lynch of South Carolina. "We found Washington angry, as frustrated and depressed by the Congress's inaction concerning supplies as he is with the British. He told us the size of the army must be increased from fifteen thousand to twenty thousand men, and he needs a dependable flow of supplies. But most important, General Washington insists his power to unify and lead the various colonial units must be strengthened by Congress!" Ben looked restlessly around the crowded room. "He faces formidable odds. Five regiments from Ireland are newly arrived in the port of Boston. It is rumored the King even tries to borrow troops from Catherine of Russia."

"At least news from Canada sounds good," Richard Henry said half-heartedly.

Becky glanced quickly at her tall brother-in-law. He seemed pale, and she noted the thread of desperation in his voice.

"That is, if rumors can be taken as good news," Frank remarked quietly. "If indeed Benedict Arnold is in possession of Quebec and Montgomery has Montreal, we hold the most valuable part of Canada. Pray God it is true."

"So, we've won Canada and almost lost Virginia," Richard Henry answered grimly.

Becky shivered. After sending his family back to England, Lord Dunmore had remained on his warship and assembled a flotilla of British and loyalists' boats, which were now harassing plantations throughout the Tidewater. Even Mount Vernon was rumored to be threatened. At the present, Dunmore was said to be occupying Norfolk. Becky and Frank had friends in that little seaport at the mouth of the James. She did not like to think about it.

"Virginians will never give way," she said bravely. "Our militias will surely drive them out."

"Drive them out . . ." Richard Henry repeated slowly. "Do you realize we are talking about our royal governor and British troops, which for two hundred years have been entrenched as our defenders and protectors? When they go, the whole civil government of Virginia will be in chaos."

The noise in the room was giving Richard Henry a headache. He hadn't particularly wanted to attend this party, for he wasn't fond of Joseph Reed, who was, in his opinion, supercilious. But his respect and affection for his friend George's wife had brought him out. He had always liked the small,

indomitable lady of Mount Vernon; she reminded him of Anne. Lord knows
he yearned to be at Chantilly. His affairs were sorely neglected. William's
tobacco ship had to be loaded, and, more important, Anne was again pregnant. The baby was due in a few days now. Would he be home in time?

In the two months he'd been in Philadelphia, the thought of leaving had
crossed Richard Henry's mind more than once. Yet so much lay at stake,
and there had been small victories to sweeten the sacrifice of staying. True,
he had not yet convinced the Congress to close the royal custom houses and
throw open the ports of the colonies to ships from all nations. The conservatives in Congress bitterly opposed so bold a step. But the Lee-Adams faction
had been able to carry a motion to allow American privateers to intercept
vessels laden with arms for the English troops. Already the English brig
Nancy had been captured, which delighted Washington, for it added two
thousand muskets and bayonets, a supply of flints, tons of musket balls, and
an impressive mortar to his pitiful store of armaments.

A few more days, Richard Henry promised himself. He would go home
as soon as he could, perhaps in a few weeks at most.

The Tidewater, 1776

Looking back, Richard Henry would remember that winter as the hardest he
had ever known. His seventh child, Sarah, had been born in his absence, and
he had only two weeks at Chantilly before the Virginia Convention began.
Arriving in Williamsburg in mid-January, he found bad news on every
side.

Virginia faced acute shortages of all kinds. Woodford's Virginia forces,
reinforced by militia from North Carolina, had finally defeated Dunmore's
squadron and the loyalists who were occupying Norfolk, but as Dunmore's
British fleet fell back to the Potomac, they destroyed half the town with their
cannons. The small port of Norfolk lay in ruins.

The news from the north was equally grim. The American assault on
Quebec, led by Richard Montgomery and Benedict Arnold, had failed. Montgomery lay dead and Dan Morgan, with many of his Virginia riflemen,
captured. The British now held Canada firmly as a launching point from
which to invade the northern colonies and isolate General Washington and
his army in Massachusetts.

The final blow was a letter from Arthur that awaited him at the Ludwell townhouse; in late December the King and Parliament passed an act
prohibiting all trade and intercourse with the thirteen colonies and authoriz-
ing the seizure of American ships at sea. "There had been every chance for
reconciliation this fall," Arthur had begun:

Edmund Burke submitted a proposal to that effect to the House of Commons in mid-November, but it was rejected by a two-to-one vote. The Dean of Gloucester, the economist Adam Smith, even Secretary of War Lord Barrington, have urged that all British troops be withdrawn from America, but to no avail.

I must further warn you that Russia is proving sympathetic, and it is said in London that the King has turned to his kinsmen and friends, the despotic rulers of the little states of Germany, Hesse Kassel in particular. For a price, they will supply some thirty thousand soldiers for service in the British Army.

As for myself, I have been busy mounting the defense of my friend Stephen Sayre, who was unjustly accused of high treason. Do not worry about me! There is no truth to the rumor that I was committed to Newgate for corresponding with rebels, although my mail to and from America was for a time intercepted. I discussed the matter heatedly with Lord Germain, who has taken Dartmouth's place as the new colonial secretary, and finally my letters have been released to me.

Despite his words, Arthur was in grave danger. There was no question of that. In late November the Continental Congress appointed a Committee of Secret Correspondence, whose first official letter had asked Arthur to function as an agent on their behalf. Of course he would accept—he was already functioning in that role! But Richard Henry knew it was a dangerous assignment that, if discovered, carried a hanging penalty.

The only bright spot Richard Henry found in Williamsburg was the amazing pamphlet *Common Sense*, printed in the *Virginia Gazette*. It was written by an Englishman, Thomas Paine, a protégé of Ben Franklin's recently arrived in America. Richard Henry brought copies of it when he returned unexpectedly to the Neck in February. Elizabeth Lee had written that Anne was still running a fever at Chantilly, this despite the almost two months that had passed since the baby's birth.

"But to my relief, she was up, dressed, and resolutely about her daily life when I arrived," Richard Henry told Landon Carter a week later. He had ridden over impulsively to show the explosive pamphlet to the master of Sabine Hall.

The old planter shook his head wearily. "Fever, agues, shakes, worms —the daily lot of man and of woman. I delight with you, sir, that Mrs. Lee has been able to conquer the fever...." He looked down at the clippings in his hand.

"As for Mr. Paine's *Common Sense*, I do not understand your enthusiasm for it ... or that of your brother Frank, who sent me a copy of the pamphlet from Philadelphia, where he says it is the subject of every man's conversation. I, for one, do not like to be coerced into a position of independence."

"You cannot deny it is well written," Richard Henry argued. "For too long we have separated in our minds the King from his Parliament, forgiving one while branding the other as despotic. Paine does away with that distinction. He calls George the Third 'the Royal Brute of Britain.' But forget his emotional words," Richard Henry urged. "I think his most important point is that we shall never win the support of France and Spain so long as we are subjects of Great Britain. And as struggling provinces, we must have that support to stand erect. There it is in a nutshell!"

Landon Carter grumbled dispiritedly and looked down again at the newspaper clippings. "I want what is best for Virginia," he said doggedly.

"We all do." Richard Henry was adamant. "This colony needs to set up a constitutional government, open our ports to world trade, and declare ourselves independent of Great Britain so that we are ready to form alliances where and with whom we wish."

"Did you persuade the Virginia Convention of that?"

"Anne's illness called me home before I was satisfied that I had made the points thoroughly, but I have laid the groundwork."

"Is it, then, to be thirteen provinces?" asked the older man. Landon Carter, like his brother, Charles of Cleve, and his nephew Rob Carter of Nomini, habitually expressed fear that hot and hasty action might bring more trouble to the embattled colony than she already had.

"Thirteen independent provinces bound by some sort of confederation only for purposes of trade and defense," Richard Henry agreed. "First, Virginia must think long and hard about the government she will fashion if she is to stand as an independent state. Last fall, on my way to Philadelphia, I stopped at Gunston Hall to meet with George Mason. He is a student of constitutional government and his ideas are as sound and true as any I have heard. I only pray that he will lend himself to shaping Virginia's new government." Richard Henry saw Carter's face flush slightly. "And you, too, of course, my dear friend. You have long been an eloquent and thoughtful actor on the stage of this colony. Your guidance is needed."

"I would give Virginia my life, sir, as my father would have done before me," the old planter answered with pride.

Philadelphia, 1776

"He looks drawn and intense, but with a determination I have never seen in him before," Frank commented to Becky in mid-March, when Richard Henry had returned to Philadelphia.

"It is determination alone that has brought him back," Becky agreed anxiously. "Tom Jefferson remains in Virginia, pleading the bad health of his wife and his own recurrent headaches. Richard Henry could do the same but no, he—"

"He is hell-bent to see this through, to see the colonies free and independent of Great Britain," Frank finished for her.

Becky looked at her husband warily. Not all the delegates shared the Lee brothers' approval of Paine's pamphlet, *Common Sense*, and of the growing movement toward independence. In particular, the representatives of Pennsylvania, New York, New Jersey, and Maryland were, as Frank put it, "not yet ripe for plucking from the parent tree."

But now there seemed to be no turning back. George Washington had broken the long stalemate at Boston. Strengthened by cannons and mortars from Ticonderoga, which his enterprising general Henry Knox had managed to transport by sled to Boston, Washington had moved quickly to Dorchester Heights, a site south of the city. Intimidated, the British General William Howe, who had relieved General Gage, evacuated Boston suddenly on March 17, leaving the city to the rowdy, high-spirited American Army. Before the last British sail had dropped below the horizon, Washington sent word to the Congress that the main part of his army was marching toward New York City, which he believed to be Howe's destination.

Finally, on March 23, the Congress issued letters of marque to permit the outfitting of American privateers to prey on British shipping. Ben Harrison chaired the committee that drew up the list of grievances justifying this drastic action. "But I think he does it with reluctance," Richard Henry told Frank. "Ben does everything he should, but always for pragmatic reasons alone. In my opinion, he is not convinced that our independence will improve his commercial endeavors, and he resents my leadership in the movement for it. He is barely civil to me."

"To me as well," Frank said cheerfully. "But, then, were we good farmers with piles of bills for last year's imports and granaries and barns bursting with wheat and tobacco we could not sell, we might be sullen as well."

On April 6, American ports finally were declared open to ships of all nations except Great Britain. At last Richard Henry and Frank could turn their attention to the Fifth Virginia Convention, which was to meet in Williamsburg in early May. They were determined that Virginia be the first colony to move for independence.

"You are the senior member of this delegation, Richard Henry, and you must arrange leave for yourself," Frank urged. "Harrison, Jefferson, too, will bluster that they think it unfair that you go while the rest of us stay in Philadelphia, but there are times when one must pull rank! Go home."

Even Carter Braxton, the Virginia delegate who replaced Randolph and opposed an immediate stand for independence, set forth ideas for establishing a governing machine in Virginia. He recommended a governor and council to serve for life. Richard Henry flung the proposal across the room when he read it. "Full of aristocratic drivel! We might as well have George the Third!"

The Tidewater, 1776

He was late in arriving in Williamsburg, hot and dusty after the long ride from Pennsylvania. Quietly, Richard Henry took his place in the back of Convention Hall, catching as he did the eye of Patrick Henry, who was seated near the front. Richard Henry gave his dark-haired theatrical friend a nod of encouragement.

What an imposing gathering! His heart swelled with pride and affection as he recognized face after face of the 128 delegates. Though there were some with whom he disagreed, he had enormous respect for them—all men who knew their law and their politics. The distinguished and silver-tongued Edmund Pendleton served as president, with Robert Carter Nicholas at his side. He saw his brother Thomas immersed in conversation with the older statesman Richard Bland. The slight young James Madison, a friend of young Harry Lee of Leesylvania, had just taken his seat. Near him sat twenty-three-year-old Edmund Randolph, who was serving as an alternate for George Wythe. Richard Henry wondered if the young man had heard from his loyalist father. John Randolph, who had succeeded his brother Peyton as the colony's attorney general, had after long and painful consideration come to the conclusion that he could not "stand with the Whigs against my King," and sailed back to England in the fall of 1775. Edmund, a member of George Washington's staff in Cambridge, chose to remain behind.

The convention followed the parliamentary rules that had guided the House of Burgesses for a hundred years. On May 14, it dissolved into a committee of the whole to discuss the general state of the colony. Meriwether Smith then offered a resolution proposing they draw up a new government for Virginia, but shied away from mentioning the general American move for independence.

Patrick Henry approached Richard Henry, who was chafing with impatience. "Tom Nelson will present my motion for independence shortly," he whispered.

"Why Nelson?" Richard Henry looked perplexed.

"I want the words to stand on their own," Henry told Richard Henry.
I do not want anyone swayed by my oratory! Look, Nelson signals to be
recognized now!"

Nelson's words calling for a Virginia free of all allegiance to the Crown
drew an immediate outcry from the conservatives in the hall. Oddly enough,
it was Edmund Pendleton who finally produced a moderate resolution
agreeable to all. Embodying most of Patrick Henry's points, it shared the
responsibility for independence with the other colonies. Virginia might go
first, but she would not stand alone. Pendleton's resolution called for the
Virginia delegates at Philadelphia to "declare the United Colonies free and
independent states, absolved from all allegiance to, or dependence upon, the
Crown or Parliament of Great Britain," and authorized "whatever measures
may be thought proper and necessary by the Congress for forming foreign
alliances, and a confederation of the colonies." It was unanimously passed,
and shortly thereafter a cannon began firing, and the British flag was hauled
down from the Capitol.

Richard Henry joined his brother Thomas, Patrick Henry, and George
Mason at the Raleigh Tavern to celebrate. "You will return to Philadelphia
on a mission of great importance, my dear Richard Henry!" Thomas exulted.

Patrick Henry raised his glass in triumph. "Our resolution shall warm
the cockles of George Washington's heart!"

"Which leaves us," George Mason said almost testily, "myself in particular, with the monumental task of supplying Virginia a new form of
government." He now headed the committee to prepare both the Virginia
Declaration of Rights and a plan of government for the independent state.

Richard Henry had visited Gunston Hall often enough to know that
Mason was passionately concerned that the preservation of civil liberties be
the fundamental element in any form of new government. Richard Henry
trusted the planter's judgment, yet he yearned to participate in forming a
new government for Virginia. "I am divided between my desire to be here
and my commitment to be in Philadelphia," he told Thomas with chagrin.

"Why not have Ben Harrison or even Frank present the resolution for
independence in Philadelphia?" Thomas suggested.

Richard Henry gave a half smile as he gazed at his companions in the
flickering candlelight. "I shall ride for Philadelphia on the morrow, present
the resolution for independence, and be back in Williamsburg by mid-June.
If a man can put himself in two spots at the same time, then I shall be that
man!"

He did not tell them of the letter in his pocket from Arthur. Working through his friend the playwright Beaumarchais, Arthur had persuaded France's foreign minister, the Count of Vergennes, to give the colonies one million livrès under the guise of a private mercantile transaction. Only independence would put them in the position to accept it. And Richard Henry was resolved that it would be he himself who presented the motion.

Philadelphia, 1776

Every eye in the Congress was focused on the gentleman from Virginia, Richard Henry Lee. He stood with great calm, leaning forward slightly as he waited for John Hancock to acknowledge his request to speak.

The Virginia delegation was of one mind on this day. Frequently split by dissension in the past, Francis Lightfoot Lee, George Wythe, Ben Harrison, Carter Braxton, and Thomas Jefferson now waited expectantly for Hancock to recognize their delegate.

Richard Henry glanced down at the instructions he had carried from Williamsburg. Carefully he adjusted the black silk scarf more tightly around the maimed fingers of his left hand. Four nights earlier, over dinner with George Washington in Philadelphia, Richard Henry had sensed his friend's guarded relief when told this step was finally being proposed.

"Never since I took command of this army have I entertained any real hope of accommodation with England," he told Richard Henry privately. "Your resolution delights me."

John Hancock's clear Boston accent cut through the low buzz of voices in the room. "Gentlemen, I now call on the distinguished gentleman from Virginia, Mr. Richard Henry Lee."

He did not have to read the words, for they were indelibly etched in his memory.

"Resolved, that these United Colonies are, and of a right ought to be, free and independent States, that they are absolved from all allegiance to the British Crown, and that all political connection between them and the State of Great Britain is, and ought to be, totally dissolved.

"That it is expedient forthwith to take the most effectual measures for forming foreign Alliances.

"That a plan of confederation be prepared and transmitted to the respective Colonies for their consideration and approbation."

Philadelphia was enveloped in late-summer heat. "Even so, it is for the moment the most exciting city in the world," Anne Lee of Chantilly said, fanning herself vigorously. "I'm so glad Richard Henry persuaded me to accompany him. Though the heat certainly does penetrate here more than in Virginia."

"But you will get used to it in time as I have, my dear." Becky sighed agreeably. "Alice says after a few years it becomes tolerable."

They sat in the shady garden behind Shippen House with tall glasses of lemonade. Alice, who had been with them a few moments before, had crossed the piazza to look in on her new baby.

"Alice looks worn," Anne said. "Bearing a baby in the summer is difficult, I can tell you. But she'll feel better in the fall."

"It's the baby's crying, not the heat, that wearies poor Alice. Anne, he is not a healthy baby," Becky said. "He does not seem to gain. It would help if Dr. Shippen were not gone so much. But now that he directs a flying camp hospital for General Washington, he is rarely home."

The bells of the Catholic church next door tolled melodically. "Have you told me all the news of Virginia? Isn't there at least a scrap more?" Becky asked longingly, pushing the swing to and fro with one slippered foot.

Anne wrinkled her nose with exasperation. "I've told you about everybody at least twice! Now that Dunmore and his ruffian sailors have given up terrorizing the Potomac and sailed for New York, life is almost dull!"

"What of the Byrds at Westover? Alice is so very fond of Mary Byrd and grieves at the situation they now find themselves in."

Anne plucked a leaf from the stem of mint in her glass. "They say Will Byrd is very low in spirits and confines himself to Westover. I gather his debts are large, and he feels abandoned by his friends now that he sides with the British!"

"The Shippens face similar problems," Becky confided in a soft voice. "Will's family is by tradition Tory. His cousin Judge Edward Shippen is quite outspokenly against the Congress and their declaration, which does make it hard for Will. You remember them, the family with the pretty daughters—the fair-haired one named Peggy, who was visiting Nancy when—"

Voices at the garden gate interrupted. Richard Henry and Frank were returning home early from the daily session of the Congress, accompanied by the tall, sandy-haired Jefferson.

Becky ran to meet Frank, giving him such an enthusiastic welcome that she saw Mr. Jefferson redden. She gave him a sympathetic smile. Frank had told her that Jefferson was anxious to retire to Virginia, for his wife was quite ill. Moreover, he was downhearted that it was George Mason's draft for a state constitution and not his own that had been passed by the Virginia

Convention. While he had drafted the Declaration of Independence for the Congress in Philadelphia, he evidently considered the authorship of Virginia's Constitution to hold the greater honor.

John Adams had confided to her one night at dinner just how Jefferson had been chosen to write the declaration. Adams had candidly admitted there was a feeling in both the Massachusetts and the Pennsylvania delegations that Virginia should, for political reasons, take the lead with that document. But Richard Henry was already serving on the Committee of Confederation, and it was thought neither convenient nor politic that the same person write both. Since Francis Lightfoot and Ben Harrison were not given to writing, it thus fell to Jefferson, who was known for his skill with words; his *Summary View of the Rights of British America*, written in '74, had been judged radical but extraordinary. Jefferson had labored on the independence document for seventeen stifling days in his airless rented room.

The men spoke of it now, congratulating the young lawyer for a superb job. "An eloquent prologue, combining a measure of Locke with a dash of Mason," Frank praised.

"I was most distressed that Congress cut out the antislavery portions," Richard Henry interjected. "John Adams claims they were some of the best."

"But the South Carolinians, as well as some of our fellow Virginians, would not hear of that! Perhaps they would have listened longer if the river breezes had been blowing the other way," Frank teased.

Becky could hardly suppress a giggle. As the declaration was being debated, a swarm of flies from a nearby livery stable had enlivened and shortened the discussion in the high-ceilinged chamber.

On July 2, the Congress had acted on Richard Henry's resolution for independence made on June 4. By July 4, the vote was unanimous. Becky recalled all the stories—how the cancer-racked Caesar Rodney had ridden through a night of thunder and rain to break the Delaware deadlock, how Ben Harrison had murmured to the slight Elbridge Gerry of Massachusetts that Harrison, being heavy, would have an easy time when they came to be hanged, whereas Gerry would no doubt swing in the breeze for half an hour, and how John Hancock had signed his name so large that it could be read from across the chamber.

Becky shook her head to dispel her wandering thoughts. The conversation now turned to war and the disastrous news from New York. "We are no match for the Redcoats in lines of battle," Richard Henry said grimly. "Were it not for the northeaster, which slowed the British landing on Staten Island, Washington would never have been able to pull his troops to safety across the East River!"

Jefferson shrugged slightly. He seemed impatient to be off. He was not, Becky recalled Frank's remarking, much interested in war.

After he had gone, Anne commented, "What a strange young man, that Jefferson. When he addresses me, I always feel he is looking somewhere past my left ear."

"Some of the Randolphs are like that," Becky reminded her. "I forgive him his manner, for I know he is much devoted to his ailing wife. In fact, he told me he has bought her some gifts today as well as new guitar strings for the musicales they enjoy at Monticello."

Richard Henry looked cynically at Frank. "Now Tom Jefferson plans to turn all his attention to Virginia and setting up its government. He has no interest in politics beyond its borders. How well I understand his sentiments."

"Mark my words, Jefferson has in mind to wrest the governorship from Patrick Henry. I have a feeling," Frank forecast, "Patrick Henry and Thomas Jefferson will soon be locked in a fierce struggle."

Frank put his hand on his brother's arm. "It seems we Lees are destined to remain in the larger arena, at least until this war is over." He smiled. "And I know another Lee who chafes to join the fray: young Harry of Leesylvania!"

Frank's prophecy that the volatile Patrick Henry and the scholarly Thomas Jefferson would vie for control of Virginia politics proved on the mark. As Patrick Henry struggled with his duties as the wartime governor of the newly created state, Thomas Jefferson deftly pursued and won control of Virginia's House of Delegates.

Meanwhile the four Stratford brothers, who were as devoted to Virginia as Patrick Henry and Thomas Jefferson, were compelled to remain on the wider stage of continental and European involvement. In September 1776, New York town fell to a British sea invasion and Washington's unsettled forces retreated north, only to be defeated in a stormy battle at White Plains. Within a few weeks, Howe had captured two American strongholds on the Hudson—Fort Washington and Fort Lee—causing Washington to suffer grievous losses.

Howe's British and Hessian troops then set out in leisurely pursuit of Washington's army. By early December, it was apparent that Washington's army was fast dissolving from desertions, sickness, and lack of organization, that he would soon lose the Jerseys as well as New York. A nervous Congress, with Richard Henry and Francis Lightfoot in attendance, fled Philadelphia for the safer haven of Baltimore.

Now events called to the fore yet another Lee, one who had been impatiently waiting in the wings. No words fell more sweetly on Harry Lee's ears than the news that the commander in chief, George Washington, had called for all available horse units to join the army.

Early in 1777, Patrick Henry released all mounted militia units ready and able to ride to Washington's assistance. Theodorick Bland's three groups of light dragoons headed north at once. Thus, on the eve of his twenty-first birthday, young Captain Lee left his home in Prince William County and, with a regiment of hard-riding cavalrymen he had hand-picked for his Third Troop, set out for the American army's winter encampment at Morristown.

To the Perfect Day

1777–1779

Philadelphia, 1777

"Oh, no!" the broad-shouldered young cavalryman groaned in alarm. Pale January sunlight streaming through the uncurtained window of the Philadelphia Bettering House, a temporary hospital of the Continental Army, highlighted the apprehension in the captain's vivid brown eyes. "I would rather take on a dozen British lobsterbacks than face that scalpel in your hand!"

Wiping the wicked-looking knife on the sleeve of his blue wool frock coat, Will Shippen chuckled. "Come, now. Why are the bravest soldiers reduced to jelly when confronted with a simple smallpox inoculation? Small girls face it with nary a quiver."

Shippen settled the wan Harry Lee in a straight-back chair. A handsome son of a gun! The doctor marveled at the well-built young man in his blue wool jacket and tight-fitting white breeches. In one hand he held his white leather helmet with a feather plume. Around his shoulders was thrown a blue cape lined in buff-colored silk, and a long-handled knife was tucked into calf-high boots.

Now Will helped him remove the close-fitting tunic and roll back the sleeve of his soft white linen shirt. With quick, sure movements, the Philadelphia doctor, now director of military medical services west of the Hudson, steadied Harry's muscular arm on the table and made two deep incisions on the inner arm just below the bend of the elbow. Talking all the while in a strong, brisk voice, he dipped a wooden probe into a jar of fluid on the table and introduced the probe into the cuts.

"As soon as this smallpox inoculation is set, Harry, you and your troops can ride on to Morristown. I must say, you're in splendid shape, quite fit and strong. How long has it been since I saw you last? As I recall, it was your graduation four years ago from the College of Princeton. Quite dashing you looked, decked out in gold lace. . . . There!" With a flourish, Shippen tossed the probe into the bowl on the table. "You are now infected with the live disease, and in a few days you should be running a slight fever and have a few pustules."

Color was slowly returning to Harry's face. "Actually it wasn't so bad," he murmured, pressing the cotton cloth Shippen handed him against the small bloody wounds. "You were very gentle, sir, and most skillful."

"God knows, I should be," Shippen replied. "I've done a thousand inoculations at least, including your cousin Frank and his Becky and Lady Washington. Now that General Washington is asking that all soldiers who have not had the pox be inoculated, I'll no doubt do a thousand more in short order!" The doctor tried to keep a serious expression as he teased. "We'll just hope your inoculation takes, Harry, so we don't have to do this over again!"

He had in fact been delighted to see the young man stride into his office. It was only by chance that Will had been on duty at the Philadelphia hospital today. When Washington and his depleted army had hastily retreated across the Delaware, in early December 1776, flying hospitals had been set up in Allentown, Bethlehem, and Philadelphia, and Will spent most of his time traveling among them, struggling to direct the care of the sick and wounded now flooding in.

Gingerly Harry rolled down his sleeve. "Now that this little ordeal is done with, I must relay my family's special love and affection to you and your family."

There was a particularly strong tie between the Shippens and the Lees of Leesylvania, a bond that had formed when Alice, in her childhood, turned to her older cousin Henry as her protector, and ultimately as her legal guardian, in the fierce struggle with Colonel Phil.

"My wife would dearly like to see you, Harry, before you go on to Morristown," Will Shippen urged. "Perhaps you could join her in Bethlehem for your inoculation period. You see, we've closed Shippen House temporarily and I've established my patients and headquarters in the Moravian hospital in Bethlehem. The situation in Philadelphia is grave." He shook his head. "These are terrible times, terrible times, with the British headed for Philadelphia and Congress fled to Maryland. Everyone's lives are upset by the horrors of war, lad. Philadelphia is fast becoming a charnel house."

Harry nodded grimly. He had been overwhelmed as he rode through the city earlier that day by the sight of sick and wounded men and the wagons stacked with bodies and coffins headed for open-pit graves at the edge of the city.

"The dead are as much victims of smallpox and disease as of battle," Shippen railed. "I am appalled by the conditions of the military hospitals established under John Morgan. They are filthy, Harry, the men suffering from hunger and the lack of surgeons and supplies! We will soon remedy that! I submitted to General Washington a plan for reorganizing the military hospitals." The Philadelphian broke off abruptly. There was no use ranting about John Morgan. Rumor had it he had already been relieved as director of Military Medical Services.

"But, Harry . . ." Will Shippen returned to their previous subject. "I am quite serious when I invite you and your friends to Bethlehem. It would mean a great deal to Alice. She's not been well these past months—at least, not in spirit. Since our baby died last fall, she's been terribly despondent. Your presence might relieve her melancholy."

"I am sorry to hear of her low spirits," Harry answered, adding, with his natural candor, "You know, sir, I have always considered Alice Lee Shippen the most beautiful woman I have ever seen."

"I have always thought so, too!" Will Shippen put his arm affectionately around the younger man's shoulder as they walked down the hospital corridor. "Although I am compelled to warn you"—his voice sobered—"hers is now a fragile beauty. She grieves constantly for her dead baby, her home, and her children away at school. Young Thomas is at the Forest of Needwood Academy in Maryland, and Nancy attends Miss Rodgers's School for Girls, near Trenton. I felt it safer for them to be away than with us in Philadelphia or Bethlehem. . . . Our lives are too uncertain. In fact," Will went on in a confidential tone, "I would appreciate it if you would prevail upon Alice to visit Stratford Hall for a few months."

"I shall be most happy to encourage her if that is your wish." Harry hesitated. "But I must warn you that this war has also touched Virginia. Have you heard the tragic news of Colonel Byrd?"

Will glanced quickly at the young man walking beside him. "What of Byrd, Harry?"

"I learned just before I left Virginia that he has killed himself."

Will Shippen stopped, stunned by the news.

Harry shook his head. "I can hardly believe it myself. He apparently woke before dawn on the first day of January, and, without disturbing Mary or his children, he dressed and went out to his armory, where he took down a dueling pistol, rammed it rod and bullet, and shot himself directly in the head. I believe, sir, the news of Washington's victory at Trenton brought home to him that, as a Tory, he was now sadly out of step in Virginia."

"Mother of God! William Byrd of Westover . . . !" Will's face went white with horror. "So many pressures . . ."

Harry reached out a comforting hand. "I know you were fond of him. I'm sorry to bear such a sad report."

"What a tragedy for my cousin Mary. Everyone seems to be a victim," Will continued in a distracted voice. "This hospital is overflowing with wounded from the battles in New York, the march across Jersey, and our successful attacks on Trenton and Princeton."

"Well, thank God, we've had victories at last," Harry said with ardor as they came into the sunlit square at the front of the hospital. "Tell me about Trenton, sir. If only I could have been there!"

Will Shippen shivered at the onslaught of frigid air. He snapped his fingers for his servants to bring around his carriage.

"It was a desperate gamble. After his defeat in the stormy battle at White Plains and Howe's capture of Fort Washington and Fort Lee, I believe General Washington was reconciled that the war was pretty well played out; his troops were ill and deserting in droves, enlistments to run out soon. Do you know, Howe and his British and Hessian troops were so confident they would overtake their quarry that the British buglers were wont to play the fox hunter's cry of 'tally ho' whenever they caught sight of the hapless rebels! But Washington felt it was worth one final bold stroke, so on Christmas night he took his army back across the Delaware. They surprised the Hessians encamped at Trenton, who, sleepy and full of goose and wine, could not rally themselves. And within the week he had swept down upon Princeton to check six British regiments under the Earl of Cornwallis that had barracked in your old college before attempting to retake Trenton." Shippen's face showed a glimmer of a smile. "They are not major victories, Harry, but they have for the moment saved Washington his army and the rest of us our necks. Enough men re-enlisted for another year, so it is not over yet!"

Will Shippen hesitated before stepping into his conveyance. "The important thing is, Harry, we have won back part of the Jerseys, and rumor has it that the British are withdrawing to New York town for the winter." He grimaced slightly. "I know Washington's army is exhausted. All of us now struggle to keep our soldiers alive in the frozen woods around Morristown."

"And the commander in chief?" Harry's eyes blazed sharply. "He is well?"

"Indomitable, though depressed at times. They say that at about four in the morning, as he stealthily marched his army on the frozen river toward Trenton, word arrived that General Sullivan's unit had discovered their guns and powder completely soaked. Not even one small arm was fit for the attack. Washington sent back this order: 'Tell Sullivan to use the bayonet. I am determined to take Trenton!' "

"And take it he did!" Harry crowed exultantly.

Will Shippen settled himself in his carriage and pulled up the lap robe. "You will see all for yourself soon enough, lad. As for now"—he paused— "we shall be expecting you and your friends later today in Bethlehem. I've a letter you will enjoy reading—just arrived by schooner from your cousin Arthur Lee. Perhaps you already know, he has been chosen one of three commissioners to represent the American Congress to the Court of Versailles."

Paris, 1777

What a curious triumvirate we make, Arthur thought to himself. He and his fellow commissioners were dining in the pleasant white-washed dining room at the Hôtel Hamburg in Paris.

Four months earlier, in September of 1776, the American Congress had chosen as its first commission to the French court Silas Deane, Benjamin Franklin, and Tom Jefferson. The third had declined to serve. ("Too engrossed in Virginia politics," Richard Henry had written his brothers, "and his wife is too fragile for living abroad.") Thus the southern slot fell to Arthur Lee, who hurriedly crossed the Channel to join the commission in its temporary quarters at this small hotel on the Rue Jacob, on the Left Bank.

He surveyed the suave, fashionably dressed Silas Deane, a Connecticut merchant and one of Franklin's numerous protégés. In Paris since the previous summer, Deane had been sent by the Congress to help encourage the flow of arms and munitions to the colonies. He and his personal secretary, Dr. Bancroft, blamed their failure on the fact that the French considered the colonies' breach with England to be only temporary. Arthur wrinkled his nose disdainfully as he considered the strange Dr. Bancroft. A medical doctor like himself, the haughty, English-trained Edward Bancroft exhibited a mind well versed in both poisons and politics. The shadowy secretary seemed careful to keep Arthur at arm's length.

True, both Deane and Bancroft had learned to speak tolerable Parisian French and became quite intimate with the influential, including the French foreign minister, Vergennes, and Arthur's friend Beaumarchais, but they had yet to charm the French court or rouse the populace to back the united colonies. No doubt this would soon be offset by the talents of the commissioner from Pennsylvania, Dr. Franklin. Arthur watched the senior commissioner rise from his chair to return the bows of a gentleman and a lady across the dining room. Franklin was amazingly popular with the French—royalty, diplomats, and commoners alike.

Dressed always in brown Quaker garb, a little fur cap perched on his wispy hair, the engaging Franklin would peer over his spectacles and toss off some witty remark that never failed to melt the stiffest gathering. The man was amazingly resourceful, Arthur concluded, quick of mind and tongue, engaging, but much too complacent and disorganized. He seemed unconcerned that the affairs of this Paris legation—private affairs that involved trade and munitions—were open knowledge almost from the moment they were negotiated. Nor did Franklin seem much bothered by the overt graft and corruption in the buying of supplies for the American Army.

Arthur had always prided himself on his intuition, yet, though in Paris for over a month, he had not plumbed his complex fellow commissioners.

Franklin's voice rent the silence. "Dr. Lee, you have not eaten your delicious apple flan, thereby violating two of my maxims in one fell swoop! The first is 'Waste not, want not,' and the second is 'An apple a day keeps the doctor away.'"

Silas Deane chuckled loudly to show his appreciation of Franklin's wit.

"You brood, Dr. Lee. Did your meal not agree with you?" Franklin gave Arthur a pleasant smile across the table.

"No, no." Hastily, Arthur turned his attention to his dessert, motioning for the waiter to refill his coffee cup. "I was just thinking, sir, of your fine accomplishment in diplomacy." During the previous week Franklin had met with the Count de Vergennes to offer to transfer the bulk of American trade from England to France, this in exchange for ships, arms, supplies, and a gift of cash. The offer was unacceptable, for Louis XVI was ill-prepared to recognize American independence and ignite war with England. But after negotiations, the French government, while still officially remaining neutral, agreed under the cover of private business to make a loan of two million livres, with another million coming from the government importing agency! In addition, they would allow American privateers and naval vessels to use French ports.

Ben Franklin was beaming. "I have long contended that a virgin state should preserve the virgin character and not go courting alliances, but we cannot help rejoicing in this offer of assistance from our friends!"

Nor help being dismayed, Arthur thought grimly, that the British ambassador in Paris, Lord Stormont, somehow learned within hours of the French offer and its acceptance!

"You will be off for Madrid shortly, will you not, Mr. Lee? I think it one of the world's loveliest cities." Although Silas Deane spoke casually,

Arthur knew that he was delighted Franklin had asked the Virginian rather than himself to make the arduous trip to seek aid from Spain's Bourbon king.

"I leave early next month and travel by way of Nantes and Bordeaux."

There was a pregnant pause at the mention of Nantes. William Lee, whose situation in London had become untenable since the Declaration of Independence was signed last summer, had sought appointment as the commercial agent representing the united colonies in the important French shipping city of Nantes. Deane, however, had not waited for Congress's decision, but obsequiously appointed Ben Franklin's nephew, Jonathan Williams, to the post.

Flushing slightly with annoyance at Arthur's pointed reference to Nantes, Deane returned to an earlier subject, the charm and gaiety of the French court. "Louis Bourbon and his little blond Queen, Marie Antoinette, fascinate me," the American was saying. "There is an innocence about them—oh, no, I am not misled, for I am aware of the amours and intrigue at court, but any pair who play shepherd and shepherdess at Versailles and quote Rousseau are, in my opinion, rather charming."

"A shepherdess with pearls and rubies sewed on her skirt!" Arthur commented sardonically, "while all the authentic shepherds are starving in the countryside!"

While the mission to Madrid was moderately successful, the trip itself was decidedly uncomfortable. In his report to Richard Henry, Arthur wrote:

I traveled by way of Nantes and Bordeaux and, at Bayonne, hired a carriage for the crossing of the Pyrenees . . . dreadful accommodations all the way, vile freezing chambers, straw mattresses crawling with vermin. And then, almost halfway to Madrid, arriving in Burgos, I found the Spanish foreign minister waiting in a fever of anxiety to intercept me. He begged that I not proceed, for he felt it would bring on diplomatic troubles with England.

We dined together. I pleaded for Spain's recognition of our independence. I told him of our military victories and Howe's humiliation in New Jersey, of the proven abilities of our General Washington. Out of it, I got a promise of more aid—all to be arranged secretly, of course, for the Europeans are terrified of offending England, although they hold no love for her. Indeed, when they realize that we are determined to *win* our independence (not just to *declare* it!), I am convinced they will delight in and profit from England's difficulties, for she has thwarted the ambitious Bourbons in the past and been less than sympathetic with the states of Central and Eastern Europe.

Back in Paris in early April, Arthur briefed a delighted Franklin, who listened intently without missing one bite of his enormous breakfast ("Frugality not being my main virtue," he told Arthur with a twinkle in his eye).

The American embassy was now comfortably established in Passy, a suburb of Paris, in the east wing of the Hôtel Valentinois. Arthur found it entirely acceptable—"handsome, in fact," he wrote to William and Hannah Philippa in London:

A large, private mansion set in a spacious formal garden, it has two wings projecting from the main building, each ending in a belvedere supported by Tuscan columns. The central part of the mansion is occupied by M. Roy de Chaumont, a prosperous, if unscrupulous, merchant who is one of Dr. Franklin's many friends. He loans us the left wing of the embassy free of charge (at least free of *obvious* charge!). There is a fine view of the Seine and large airy chambers, with a competent staff. I had just settled in nicely when Mr. Franklin asked me to attempt a mission to Berlin. Reluctantly, I have accepted.

In addition to our senior ambassador, Mr. Franklin, who has with him his two grandsons—an illegitimate lad of seventeen, William Temple, who works as his grandfather's secretary, and Benjamin Franklin Bache, aged seven, who is enrolled in the village school—we have Silas Deane, his secretary, Mr. Bancroft, and another secretary Deane has recently added to his staff, a truly strange, rough Englishman named Carmichael.

I cannot for the life of me fathom why we employ all these secretaries, for Mr. Deane can never come up with any accounts, vouchers, or bills of ladings for the supplies shipped to America, purchased or donated. My personal opinion is that Mr. Deane is far too involved in his own business affairs, which I fear are mingled with the business affairs of this embassy! I hinted broadly of all this to Mr. Franklin, who pats me on the head like a small boy and tells me not to trouble myself over such matters and that all is well. I doubt if you will hear from me again for several weeks, for I am soon off to Berlin.

Exhausted, Arthur returned to the Hôtel Valentinois from a disappointing journey through the German states to find William waiting for him on the hotel steps, excitement and tension evident in his dark eyes. "Finally, I've got the co-agency appointment to Nantes. I must be on my way, but I've been waiting in Paris to talk to you—to warn you! No, don't send your things up," he cautioned as Arthur directed his manservants to attend to the luggage. "Mr. Deane claims they were running short of space in the embassy, and he's ordered your belongings stored. It is the decision of Mr. Deane, with Mr. Franklin's blessings, that you are obliged to live elsewhere!"

"But I have rooms!" Arthur was bewildered. "They were decorated for me before I left for Germany. What do you mean, 'live elsewhere'?"

William put a restraining hand on his arm. "I am sure Deane will have some good excuse, but the truth is, you are to be isolated. I believe Deane considers you too dangerous to stay under the same roof, Arthur. I am quite certain your suspicions about the good Mr. Deane are correct; he is not a man to be trusted."

"What have you learned?" Arthur asked, his anger rising.

"A number of things. First, Deane has known for months that Congress had officially appointed me co-agent for the American states at Nantes, but he neglected to send word until just recently, and then I think most reluctantly, for when I arrived in Paris he told me to wait and not go on to Nantes until the Commission papers arrived. Just yesterday I learned he has had those papers in his possession for weeks! Affairs are being incredibly mismanaged at Nantes, and Deane knows it. He obviously does not want me poking into the handling of cargo heading for the colonies, or supervising the sales of prizes taken by American privateers."

"By God's truth," Arthur flared, "I cannot believe this!"

"I tell you, there is more to all this than meets the eye," said William. "Friends in London assure me that not a paper passes through this American embassy but a copy of it arrives on a desk in Whitehall a few days later. Why, when the young Marquis de Lafayette commissioned a ship to take himself to America, the English knew of it far in advance of General Washington!"

"You realize what you imply, William? That someone in the embassy is a British spy! Deane, Bancroft, Carmichael . . . perhaps more than one!"

Arthur voiced the Lee brothers' suspicions when he next met with Franklin to report on the German mission, but his accusations were shrugged off. Benjamin Franklin, socially the toast of Paris, was more than weighed down with his load of writing, meetings with French officials, and correspondence with the Continental Congress. "I do not seek trouble in my own embassy, Mr. Lee," he replied curtly. "Problems seem quite abundant without deliberately cultivating them."

"Franklin thinks I am mad," Arthur confided despondently to William. "I am certain Deane has turned him against me by intimating I am addled. What's more, Count de Vergennes and my old friend Beaumarchais have been turned against me. They will not so much as receive me when I call."

William looked up from a letter he was writing to Hannah Philippa in London. "I think you must apply yourself to proving that someone is engaged in spying, or 'espionage,' as the French put it, for the British. That is the only way you can regain your credibility." He glanced down at his letter. "I only wish I could remain in Paris long enough to be of help to you, but I must meet Hannah Philippa and the children in Nantes at the end of the month."

Despite his anxiety, Arthur smiled broadly. "Give your dear lady my love, and tell her I look forward to seeing her and little William Ludwell. Also tell her I am pleased she has delivered me a niece. I am quite partial to little girls, and have no doubt that Portia will win my heart."

It took three weeks for Arthur to find a suitable house, and when he did, it was in the Parisian suburb of Chaillot, some three miles from Passy. Every day he called at the Hôtel Valentinois, but inevitably Mr. Franklin was busy, either dining out, in conference, or at his desk.

In frustration Arthur roamed the streets of Paris, attending the glittering opera and the Follies by night, his morning hours idled away in sidewalk cafés, his afternoons in the darkened chambers of indolent Parisian ladies who were as charmed as they were charming. But Paris was not London. He longed for his stimulating friends, and he missed with an almost physical pain the vigor and the predictability of the City. It seemed to Arthur that everyone in Paris was either desperately poor—and dangerous and sullen, to boot—or terribly rich, unaware of the angry poor, who seemed to him exhausted by the expense of the decadent French court. It was with real pleasure that, at Richard Henry's request, he sent for his teen-aged nephews, Thomas and Ludwell, to come and stay with him in the house in Chaillot. Life had grown intolerable for the boys at St. Bee's. "They call my father a traitor," Ludwell said hotly. "The other boys say his head will hang from a gatepost one day!"

Arthur winced at his nephew's words, recalling the rotting head of one of the Scottish rebels that as late as the 1760's had stared down from the entrance to Old London Bridge, a grim reminder to all of the punishment for rebelling against the King.

As the summer wore on, Arthur became more and more convinced that the British had indeed infiltrated the American embassy. Everything began to fit together like a patchwork quilt. The previous summer, when Edward Bancroft visited London, Arthur and William had been surprised and dismayed to see the doctor dining with known members of the British Secret Service. When so apprised, Deane had been righteously indignant that his secretary was in any way suspected of improper action. The implication was clear: Silas Deane, proper Connecticut merchant, and Massachusetts-born Dr. Bancroft were both British spies. Probably Carmichael as well. But how could Arthur prove it when Benjamin Franklin considered him some kind of crank?

Arthur felt like a bumblebee caught in a web, but who was the spider?

The Tidewater, 1777

1777 had not been a very good year, reflected Richard Henry Lee moodily. In fact, it had been a damnably difficult year! Nonetheless, Christmas was greeted joyously at Stratford Hall, "despite lack of money, tobacco rotting on our wharves, and our exhaustion in nerve and body," Richard Henry said to his brother Thomas. "Yours in particular!"

"Just tired and getting old," Thomas responded ruefully.

But it was more than that, Richard Henry realized as he later watched his brother from across the room. Thomas's face had the flush of constant fever, and he had recently been forced to excuse himself from an important Assembly committee that was revising the laws of Virginia.

But, then, it had been an exhausting year for everyone. Scarcely had the Congress resettled itself in Philadelphia when General Howe and his Redcoats had swarmed down on the city, forcing the Congress—at least a diehard twenty or so of the delegates—to flee to York, where they hammered out the Articles of Confederation under most difficult circumstances.

The Articles were basically a series of compromises. A national Congress of representatives from the thirteen independent and sovereign states would have the right to wage war, make peace, and control foreign affairs, though the Congress would not be empowered to enforce their measures or to tax or regulate commerce. That would all depend on the mutual good will of the ratifying states. He sighed with some satisfaction, for the Articles were in large part his handiwork. They and a military victory at Saratoga in October, which took some of the sting out of the loss of Philadelphia, were the only good things to come out of 1777!

"You are very serious, my dear, and it *is* Christmas." Anne hugged him gently as she passed a tray of ginger cakes and lemon crackers.

Yes, it *was* Christmas, and how beautiful Stratford Hall looked, decked with wreaths of evergreens and sprays of holly, with bayberry candles in the windows. The great hall resounded with voices. Matilda Lee, a slender, glowing brunette of fourteen, was playing the harpsichord and singing just as her grandmother Hannah had. Richard Henry drank in the faces of the young, particularly his own daughters, bright-eyed thirteen-year-old Molly, Hannah, petite Anne, whom they called Nancy, gentle Henrietta, and little Sarah, not quite two.

The Washingtons of Bushfield and the boisterous Lees of Leesylvania had joined the festivities, and now the dining-room door was thrown open to reveal a feast of wild turkey stuffed with oysters, pickled peaches, candied yams, and beaten biscuits that could have come only from the kitchen at Stratford.

Memories of childhood crowded in upon him today. He recalled a party here years ago when he and Frank had dipped into the grownups' punch. He could picture Alice as she gravely followed the dancing master across the floor. He gazed across the room at his sister, still beautiful, though taut with pain and unhappiness in her exile from Philadelphia.

Will Shippen, who had replaced John Morgan as director of the Continental Army's medical services, was now at the battlefront, and with the children in school, Alice seemed very alone here at Stratford. Away from Will, she seemed confused and easily frightened.

"I worry about her, too," Henry murmured to him. "Alice is not strong enough to withstand turmoil. I understand Will is coming under fire—there is discontent with his management of the medical division. As many are dying in the hospitals as out, from what I hear," he said under his breath.

"It is not a position that I would wish on anyone—lack of supplies, lack of surgeons," Richard Henry said shortly. "Don't forget that John Morgan, who now attacks him vehemently, was much criticized himself, and Benjamin Rush has never been a friend of Will's!"

Henry shrugged. "Believe me, I do not criticize. But for the grace of God, my own Harry could be lying in one of Shippen's hospitals right this moment—he may be, for all I know."

"Most unlikely," Richard Henry reassured him. "From what I hear, your daring Light Horse Harry is protected by angels!"

Since their arrival in Morristown the winter before, Harry Lee and his troop of dragoons had quickly won a reputation for fearlessness and skill in scouting, raiding, and foraging enemy supplies. The young horsemen of the Third, now promoted to the First Troop, had taken to the saddle this autumn, as soon as word came that the British were landing near the Chesapeake, intent upon taking Philadelphia. Relying on surprise, daring, and superb horsemanship, they swooped down to overpower three full troops of British soldiers. The dragoons seemed omnipresent, fighting doggedly in battle, constantly deployed as couriers, scouts, and raiders, serving as General Washington's bodyguards, and, with Dan Morgan's Virginia rifles, harassing the British supply routes from New York to Philadelphia.

"Harry is with George Washington at a place called Valley Forge this winter," Henry said with evident concern. "His mother worries, for we hear the army is desperately ragged and lacking in supplies. You don't think he goes hungry, do you? I couldn't bear that!"

"Not so long as the British have a morsel left he can steal," said Richard Henry.

Valley Forge, 1778

Nothing in Harry Lee's life had ever prepared him for the cruel winter at Valley Forge. He had seen men hungry and cold, but this was incredible. Freezing weather compounded the specter of countless men dying of dysentery and typhus. What clothes the soldiers had were suitable only for summer, and most walked barefoot. Washington lamented that one could track his army by the blood of their feet. The bigger problem was food. There was never enough except "fire cake," flour mixed with water and baked on a griddle. Morale was terrible, shot through with apathy and despair.

At least Harry's Virginia First Troop still had boots. Now reduced by illness to forty-seven men, their once splendid uniforms shabby, the young Virginia horsemen were still the readiest cavalry unit in the Continental Army. With Washington's encouragement, Harry turned all the strength and nerve left in the First Troop toward procuring food for the starving army. Some six miles from the main encampment, in a stone farmhouse the troop laughingly called the Spread Eagle Tavern, they pored over maps of the overland supply routes between Howe in Philadelphia and his New York town base, then, aided at times by a few venturesome Iroquois braves, they began to "go fishing."

By mid-winter, an enraged General Howe had decided to close down the troublesome Lee "Tavern." He sent out a full regiment of cavalrymen under command of the daring Banastre Tarleton, with orders to take Harry Lee, dead or alive. At daybreak the scarlet-coated troopers overpowered a lookout patrol and appeared at the "Tavern" just as the others were finishing their breakfast. Seeing the flash of British uniforms through the window, Harry knew it was too late to escape. Doors were barricaded and men quickly stationed at the windows.

With eight men, not even enough to man each window, and surrounded by two hundred Redcoats, Harry feared his famous Lee luck was about to run out. Tarleton was hoarsely demanding unconditional surrender, "or," he shouted, "we shall burn down the house around you!"

"Only a fool would try to burn a stone farmhouse!" Harry shouted back, then rallied his men. "Stand and fight with me! It will be to your credit."

Rounds of gunfire assaulted the walls of the farmhouse, but Lee's men refrained from returning fire until the Redcoats had moved closer. "Now fire at will!" Harry ordered, and British soldiers fell like hailstones in the farmyard. Another wave of Redcoats surged forward, and once more the Virginia sharpshooters waited until they were sure of the aim, then fired into their midst.

The British fell back toward the barn at the rear of the house.

"Those damn lobsterbacks are after our horses," someone cried.

Harry's mind raced to devise a ploy. "Make them think reinforcements are on the way," he instructed a lieutenant, William Lindsay, who crept to an upstairs window and began to call out loudly as if encouraging a regiment of approaching soldiers where to fire.

As quickly as they could reload, the Virginians peppered the barn area with a strong spray of gunshot, and the cowed British melted into the trees.

That night at Valley Forge, rum and brandy wine were dispensed. For the first time in weeks men laughed and sang in celebration around the smoky campfires. The tattered young men of the First, who walked with a jaunty air and wore hats bedecked with grimy feathers, were the darlings of the frail American Army, and their young leader, now widely known as Light Horse Harry, was regarded with admiration and affection.

But it was a handwritten note of congratulations from George Washington that Harry treasured most, and when Alexander Hamilton, Washington's senior aide-de-camp, told him of the general's desire that Harry join his "family" as an aide-de-camp and liaison with cavalry units, the young man was torn by conflicting emotions. It was an enormous honor, but to give up the field, to keep his sword sheathed and sit behind a desk . . . Finally, he penned a letter declining the position. The warm note he received from the general in the early morning reassured him that the decision had not lessened the bond between them. At the general's request, Harry was promoted by Congress to the rank of major and with his men transferred from the militia to the Continental Army. At twenty-two, Major Lee was given command of a special unit designed by Washington, the "Partisan Force of Cavalry," which consisted of his own First plus the Second Troop consisting of trained frontier horsemen.

Harry could sense a difference in the soldiers who had withstood the devastating winter of hardship at Valley Forge. Their ranks had taken on new discipline, for in February one of the foreign soldiers of fortune, a stocky red-cheeked German who called himself Baron Friedrich von Steuben, had begun to instruct the men in the elementary military skills they lacked. Dressed in a tattered coat fashioned from a blanket, von Steuben struggled to hone the ragged units by establishing military regulations and personally supervising the drilling twelve hours a day.

Nathaniel Greene, a stocky, handsome Rhode Islander who was, in

Harry's opinion, one of Washington's best generals, had taken over from Mifflin the thankless job of quartermaster. Gradually, more food, clothing, and ammunition appeared in camp, and the valley took on the appearance of a proper military encampment.

The Tidewater, 1778

Richard Henry's plans to leave in early March 1778 for the national Congress were abruptly halted. Thomas was dying at Bellevue.

"It reassures me to have you here," Thomas murmured to his brother as he drifted out of an uneasy sleep. "It makes me think of the old days when we were children at Stratford Hall. How different we all are. . . ."

"But we're all Lees," Richard Henry said softly, "and all rebels."

"All Lees, but not all rebels," Thomas corrected. "You, Frank, Arthur —Missy, too—are the real rebels. William and I, we're reluctant ones. Gentle Alice, not at all a rebel. Ironic, isn't it, that Phil, harsh and determined, would probably have remained loyal?" He turned his head restlessly on the pillow. "Forgive my rambling. Tell me, what do you hear from Arthur and William?"

Richard Henry removed the most recent letter from his pocket and smoothed the sheets of paper. "Arthur writes that he and my sons are well and that they send their love to all. He says William found the accounts in Nantes in terrible shape and with relief set off for Berlin, where he is to serve as the commissioner for the United States—that is, if the Germans will receive him."

Richard Henry pulled his chair closer to his brother's bed, for Arthur's letter was long:

It is heartwarming to see how much the French people have come to love America and our ideals. Those who have read our Virginia Declaration of Rights think it monumental! The affection of the French government is pragmatic, of course, for our revolt saps the strength of the British. But to the intelligentsia, with their talk of a "reasonable" society, nature, and liberty, we are a marvelous experiment. They are fascinated by our "Cincinnatus" Washington and his volunteer army of patriotic republicans! When the British took Philadelphia, someone said to Dr. Franklin, "Howe has captured Philadelphia," and he responded, "Ah, no, Philadelphia has captured Howe!"

I cannot impress deeply enough how Burgoyne's surrender at Saratoga last October has altered French policy. That fox Franklin immediately took advantage of the victory by suggesting to Vergennes that the British might now seek a reconciliation, which the Congress would accept. Indeed, in early February Vergennes signed two treaties with the United States pledging help on most liberal terms, and he must have felt very clever when Lord North proposed his Conciliatory Resolution, which Parliament passed in mid-February. If it had been offered before the French so heavily supported us, it might well have been favorably received in America, for it answered every demand we proposed. On the night the treaties were signed, the curiosity of a man in my employ was piqued when Dr. Bancroft suddenly and inexplicably slipped away from a private celebration at the Hôtel Valentinois. My man followed him to the gardens of the Tuileries. The grand palace was itself all aglitter, but Bancroft did not approach its doors. He got down from his coach and sauntered down one of the formal paths, then appeared to be digging around the base of an acacia tree. When Bancroft left the garden, my man discovered in the soft ground a glass bottle which the doctor had buried. He pulled a paper out of the bottle, but it was perfectly blank! He examined it on both sides, then carefully replaced it in the bottle and reburied it. The following morning when he reported the incident, I sped with him to the gardens. Alas, the bottle was gone. So, again, I have no proof of conspiracy.

"I wonder if they thought of disappearing ink," Thomas suggested weakly.

"Well," Richard Henry said, putting aside the letter, "Deane is at last being recalled by the Congress—not because of Arthur's spy charges but to answer for his slovenly accounts. He also commissioned foreign officers for our army. The poor fellows—unemployed soldiers of fortune mostly—keep descending upon the Congress like locusts with contracts signed by Deane." Richard Henry could not help chuckling. "He promised a French officer named Courdray a commission as a major general with command of the entire American artillery. Washington was furious! He said that if his own man, Henry Knox, was displaced, the service would be 'unhinged.' At any rate," Richard Henry went on with a sigh, "Congress finally decided Deane had exceeded his authority and wants an accounting. I was nominated to replace him in Paris, but I could not see my brood so far from Virginia. John Adams will go instead."

"Better he than you," Thomas said.

"Actually, I ache to stay in Virginia. How I envy men like Mason and Jefferson, who can devote their time to shaping Virginia's position." Richard Henry's fingers drummed restlessly on the arm of the chair. "When I was in Williamsburg last month, Jefferson, Mason, and I dined at the Governor's Palace with Patrick Henry, who is greatly concerned about the terrible reports of hunger and hardship at the army's winter camp at Valley Forge. He talked all night about ways to help General Washington and strengthen Virginia's navy and militia—quite a contrast to Mason and Jefferson. They are dreamers, interested in land and liberties but not much inclined to strategies of war. At the moment they are caught up in George Rogers Clark's efforts to gain support from the Virginia Assembly in fighting the Indians in our new county of Kentucky. Mason and Jefferson fear land-hungry Pennsylvania will step in if Virginia does not. They are most effective when the problem pertains to government or expansion—Virginia's in particular. They are not militarily minded."

"Nor, I believe, are you," Thomas said gently, "even though you have spent most of the winter organizing the Westmoreland militia."

"Well," Richard Henry said despondently, "someone has to think about it if we are to win the war with England. But what a thankless job soldiering is. I was appalled at the vitriolic attacks on Washington when he lost Philadelphia to Howe last fall. What with his victory at Saratoga, even I was guilty of wondering if Gates might prove a stronger leader, but I have concluded George will prove himself if given time. Meanwhile, many men—patriots whose names would surprise you—make sweet profit off the war."

"Still," Thomas pressed, "your talents should not be squandered on military problems."

"Oh, I agree," Richard Henry responded. "I would much rather apply what few talents I have to Virginia's problems. You have no idea how much influence Jefferson has gained in the House of Delegates. Enough, I believe, so that he will soon control the legislature. He even pushes a bill through that separates the Church of England from the state."

Thomas laughed softly. "As a practicing Baptist, Missy Corbin will take pleasure in that."

"No," Richard Henry scoffed, "she will be satisfied only when she is allowed to cast her own vote on election day. She sends me a steady stream of letters ranting that widows should be excused from paying taxes until such time as they are allowed to vote!"

"The same old Missy," Thomas said softly. "I marvel at her."

Leesylvania, 1778

In the early spring of 1778, after an arduous winter of raids on Clinton's supply lines, Harry Lee was ordered home to Virginia.

"I don't understand!" the young major had protested when Alexander Hamilton delivered the orders. "Have I angered him?"

"Not at all," Hamilton had soothed. "General Washington is concerned that you haven't had a day's rest since you arrived at Morristown over a year ago. You can use the time to recruit men and horses for your new legion, but you are to go home to Virginia for three weeks. He says he only wishes he could go with you!"

"Harry has changed," Lucy exclaimed to her husband when her eldest son returned to Leesylvania. "He left us quoting poets. War to him was only in books, the stories of Alexander and Caesar and Hannibal. Now he is . . ."

"Part of its grim reality, part of a war that historians will someday write of. Harry's a man now, Lucy," her husband consoled her.

"He eats everything in sight!" Lucy sighed. "And when he's not eating, he sleeps like the dead. And when he's not eating or sleeping, he cleans and polishes his guns."

Henry nodded. He had seen his son totally absorbed in adjusting the hairspring triggers on a new brace of pistols, but he could not rouse his interest in much else. Dutifully Harry had toured the plantation, examining the well-kept ledger books and politely admiring the new colts of Leesylvania's bay mare, Famous. But the only thing that caused his dark eyes to blaze was news from the battlefields.

"Why, everytime I turn around he has sent a servant off to Alexandria for a newspaper," Harry complained to Lucy.

"Worse"—Lucy arched her brow—"he pays barely any heed to the young ladies who visit Leesylvania. He quickly bows over their hands and exchanges short banter, then excuses himself to see about new uniforms, or returns to polishing those confounded guns."

Henry looked at his family sitting around the dinner table. His chicks were growing up. Charles and Richard Bland, the younger boys, Theodorick and Edmund Jennings, and his little daughters, Lucy and Mary and the baby Anne—what a fine, handsome brood he and Lucy had. But no one was quite like Harry! His handsome good looks were compliments of Lucy, with a dash of Lee swagger. His scholarly mind was a legacy of Richard Lee the Second; his daring, that of the first Richard, who had landed at Jamestown and pushed into the wilderness beyond the James. Henry raised his wineglass in a private salute and a prayer that God would protect his firstborn. If only Harry didn't go off half cocked and get himself killed before this bloody war was finished!

When the news reached Leesylvania that the British had evacuated Philadelphia and the city had been reoccupied by the Americans, Harry hurried to complete his local military business so that he could rejoin his troops. With Charles as companion, he rode down the Neck to search out new horses for his legion. From General Washington he had a list of requirements for suitable cavalry horses. They should be at least a quarter blooded, neither under five years nor over twelve, and stand fourteen and one-half hands. Bays were preferred; pacing horses and mares were to be avoided.

"There's Nomini, Mount Airy, and Sabine," suggested the genial Squire Richard at Lee Hall, "but you should begin your search at Stratford Hall. Elizabeth Lee has sold off much of the stock, being somewhat short of cash, like all of us, but a few fine mounts still remain in the stables." Then he added, with a twinkle in his eye, "There may also be some fine fillies up in the great house who would prove of interest."

The Tidewater, 1778

"Indeed, I am most curious to see the Divine Matilda," Charles bantered as the brothers cantered across the spring hillside toward the big house, "the most beautiful young lady in Virginia, they say! You know, Harry, when we were small, I thought Stratford Hall was St. James's Palace, Colonel Phil was a king, and Matilda a royal princess. Strange that young Flora isn't like her sister," Charles mused. "Such an ugly duckling. Of course, Flora isn't doted on and decked out like *la belle* Matilda."

Harry did not admit to curiosity. The last time he had seen her, Matilda was thirteen and already a budding beauty. No doubt she had become spoiled.

As the big manor house rose into view, Harry pulled up on the reins of his horse. My God, it was magnificent, commanding the broad meadow like a fortress, softened only by the surround of gardens and trees. Though the red brick stables had some empty stalls, there were still a number of thoroughbreds. While Charles went to find the foreman, Harry began evaluating the horses.

"What do you look for in our stable, Harry Lee?" a bright, authoritative voice called from the paddock doorway.

Harry wheeled about, for a moment disconcerted. "I'm looking for horses for General Washington," he stammered. Charles was right! Matilda Lee had indeed grown up. At fifteen, she was tall and lithe, and breathtakingly lovely.

He gave her his best military bow, the solid click of his heels resounding in the dark stable. "I rather fancy the big gray fellow in the far stall."

A wisp of brown curl showed beneath Matilda's English riding hat. "I admire your taste, for he's my favorite, too." She called impetuously to the stableboy. "Saddle Dancer for me, Ned. I shall ride him this morning."

"He looks spirited." Harry took her arm as they walked out to the paddock. "Can you handle him?"

She pulled away and looked at him, bright-eyed, from under the brim of her hat. "Handle him? My dear Harry, I have grown up in the saddle. I've never seen a stallion I couldn't handle."

Harry tried to keep up with her as they rode to the cliffs. By God, she was a horsewoman! Molly Lee of Chantilly followed, riding sedately between Charles and William Washington of Bushfield, one of General Washington's nephews, who was courting. But Matilda or Molly, Harry couldn't tell.

A week later Harry was back at Stratford, this time alone. "I came to ride with you," he told Matilda, who was dressed in a pale-colored dress with a lace collar and forget-me-nots worked on the skirt.

"It will only take me a moment to change and have Cook fix us a picnic lunch," she said quickly. "Would you like to ride to Burnt House Fields, Harry? I've a yen to go there and see the old graves. We can pay respect to our ancestors. Do things like this ever cross your mind?"

The family graves . . . Harry walked with Matilda among the moss-covered stones. "Richard Lee of Matchotique and his wife Laetitia Corbin Lee . . . our great-grandparents," Matilda murmured. "I often wonder in what ways we are like them."

Harry's eyes swept the enclosure. "I only know that at times I feel a current surging within me, a feeling that I am a part of all that ever was. Perhaps the past is living still, Matilda, in you and me."

Remounted, the cousins rode nearer the Potomac River, where they spread their picnic in a leafy grove.

Matilda leaned back against an oak. "Tell me what the war is like."

"I can't." He shook his head slowly. "You would have to be there to understand. But I can tell you about the men I admire. Henry Knox is one. He is big, strong, and kindhearted. Though just a few years older than I, he is the general in charge of all army artillery. The laugh is, he was a bookseller in Boston before the war, and all he knew about guns he had learned from books! And there is Alexander Hamilton, and the quartermaster, Nathaniel Greene, whom you would consider decidedly romantic in looks." Harry sank down on one elbow. "But General Washington is the most admirable man in all of America. He is always honorable and fair, even when frustrated beyond measure with frictions and problems. Once a letter written by one of his aides, Thomas Read, to the scoundrel Charles Lee fell by accident into the general's hands. It was a terrible letter, castigating Washington. Hamilton told me the general sealed it up and sent it on with a polite note saying he was sorry he had inadvertently read it."

Harry reached for another chicken leg from the wicker basket. "When the officers' ladies come to join their husbands in winter camp, the general wins every heart. He dances with the ladies for hours on end. Lord, how that man likes to dance!"

"You make it all sound rather enjoyable." Matilda plucked a round pink clover and twirled it.

"I am telling you only about our few bright moments. To be honest, the ladies were brave to risk coming, for during the past winter at Valley Forge I wondered why General Howe did not simply move in and take us. It would have been so easy!"

"Why did he not?" Matilda asked, her eyes intent on his face.

"Most say that he was not so inclined, for he was the toast of society and caught up in a warm love affair in Philadelphia. But I think there was more to it than that!" Harry rolled onto his back and gazed at the bright spring sky. "Howe is a brilliant general, a good fighting man. Yet consider this: he did not choose to overtake Washington in New York, attack him at Morristown or Valley Forge, or follow up at Brandywine. Howe is a Whig, a moderate, and in my opinion didn't really believe in this war. He wanted to frighten us, chastise us, but he was not after blood. Once he realized that we Americans were bound to fight to the end for our independence, he immediately resigned. This spring he left for England."

"A gentleman, then?"

"Aye, a gentleman! I don't know that the same holds true for his successor, Sir Henry Clinton, who seems much more practical and cold-blooded. I believe he decided to evacuate Philadelphia because he did not see any military advantage in occupying it, the city being predominantly Tory."

Matilda took out a flask of lemonade. "Well, my aunt Alice was certainly delighted to hear the British were leaving, so she could return home to Philadelphia! She says that Shippen House will soon be open again, and then she plans to bring my cousin Nancy from school to stay."

"I remember Nancy," said Harry. "She's quite tiny and very gentle. She's just your age, sixteen. How is she?"

"Pretty," Matilda teased, "pretty as a picture! I wager you thought so, too!"

"She's no prettier than you," Harry said evenly, but he couldn't help admiring the way the sun dappled Matilda's brown hair and outlined her smooth patrician profile.

"Nancy writes me the most exciting letters." Matilda pretended she hadn't heard the compliment. "One was about her cousin Peggy Shippen, who fell in love with a handsome British captain, John André, during the occupation. And now that the British have left, Peggy is being wooed by

General Benedict Arnold, whom Washington has appointed as the new military commander of the city."

The story annoyed Harry. While the British held Philadelphia, the city turned out to entertain Howe's elegant British officers as the Americans starved at Valley Forge. He bit his lip and made no comment.

Matilda, her cheeks flushed with the excitement of such romances, went on. "My cousin Nancy is being courted also, by Colonel Harry Livingston, one of Benedict Arnold's New York friends. I can't say she sounds thrilled about it. She writes that she dreams of falling in love." Matilda's voice faltered slightly at the last words.

"What kind of man could you love, Matilda Lee?" Harry turned to stare at her.

"A man who is kind, I suppose," she said quietly, "one I can admire and trust. Oh, I don't really know! I'm not about to fall in love and I don't think Nancy is ready, either!"

Harry laughed gently. "I'm not about to fall in love myself, but when I do, I think I will fall in love with someone exactly like you."

Matilda tossed an acorn at him. "You will forget me, Harry Lee. You will go back to war and fall in love with a Yankee girl from the Jerseys, or have a whirlwind romance with a fashionable Philadelphia belle. What is Benedict Arnold like?" she asked suddenly. "Is he dashing? Is he handsome?"

"All you ladies are enamoured with the romantic images of military heroes." Harry feigned exasperation. "Who am I to say who is dashing and handsome, dear girl? For an old man of thirty-seven he is all right, although he limps badly from his war wounds. A widower who was, I believe, a druggist in Connecticut before the war, he is in my opinion one of our finest soldiers, yet he has not always received the credit he deserves, and he broods over it. To be frank, it was Arnold who won the battle at Saratoga, yet Horatio Gates got all the glory. All is not fair in love or war, you see! He was passed over by the Congress for major general a year or so ago, and he almost resigned until General Washington talked him out of it."

"Well, he sounds rather romantic," said Matilda, getting to her knees and brushing her skirt, "even more so than Nathaniel Greene! Come, Harry." She began to arrange her riding hat. "Let's ride down to the riverbank!"

Romance was forgotten, was it? What would she think, Harry wondered, if he chanced a kiss when they parted. Would she consider it cousinly affection? He untied her mount and suddenly, with two strong hands, lifted her gently into the saddle. Surprised, she teasingly flicked the leather loops of her crop across his cheek.

Philadelphia, 1779

Philadelphia was not the same any more since the Congress had returned after the evacuation of the British last summer. Everything seemed subtly different. Francis Lightfoot Lee stood beside his wife and looked about the handsome drawing room of Shippen House. On the surface this room full of laughing people, congressmen and their wives, wealthy Philadelphians, a few diplomats from the new French legation down the street, made a familiar scene. Yet it was not the same. Frank looked down at the gleaming head of his wife, whose small hand had just slipped into the curve of his elbow. What innocents he and Becky had been when they first came here in 1775, three and a half years ago. Had the intrigue and politicking been there earlier? Probably so, but they had been too naïve to see it.

Frank bowed to the city's military commander, General Benedict Arnold, who stood across the room in front of the mantel. He and his new Philadelphia wife created an interesting picture: Arnold, trim in his well-tailored uniform, ruffles at his neck, a diamond ring glittering on the hand that gripped his cane; his fashionably dressed young Peggy, with her powdered blond hair piled high and ornamented with pearls. Theirs had been the surprise marriage of the year. Scarcely had Arnold settled himself in Philadelphia before he began to court the pretty Peggy Shippen. And, by Jove, he had won her hand!

Beneath Benedict Arnold's conviviality tonight, Frank knew, there was bitter resentment. The Council of Pennsylvania had recently brought charges that he was building a fortune through his power in the city and that he was soft on the local Tories. But, then, his in-laws, the Edward Shippens, were loyalists, were they not?

Arnold wasn't the only one in that position, Frank thought wearily. Take Will Shippen, for example. On the one hand he was lauded for his unstinting work as the director of the military medical services. On the other, he was accused by John Morgan, and now by Benjamin Rush as well, of running disastrously inefficient hospitals, where men were crowded together on dirty straw without adequate care while Shippen turned a tidy profit selling medicines and wines supplied to him by the Congress. Was there any truth of that? Probably not. Morgan and Rush carried their own personal vendetta.

"Look, Frank, Missy looks so nice tonight!" Becky was whispering.

Hannah Lee Corbin was visiting the Shippens in Philadelphia, making a rare trip outside Virginia. For the first time this evening a smile hovered around Frank's lips as Missy firmly refused the wine forbidden by her Baptist faith.

"Why are you so jovial?" Richard Henry stood at his elbow. "I am hard put to discover a thing to make one smile." Richard Henry had just arrived in Philadelphia from Chantilly, weary, with legs and feet aching from his infernal rheumatism. "I can't get this damn Silas Deane mess out of my mind—the treachery and deceit of the man!"

Frank remained silent. What was there to say that hadn't already been said? Silas Deane had appeared before the Congress in the fall of 1778, without account books or records to support his defense but full of accusations against the Lees. Thus, the Congress soon fell into two factions: pro-Deane and pro-Lee. That Benjamin Franklin was known to be on Deane's side did little to help the Lees!

Already the affair had taken its first victim, and a tragically innocent one at that. Thomas Paine, the author of *Common Sense* and secretary to the Committee of Foreign Affairs, rushed into print defending Arthur by citing Lee's coup in arranging the first aid from France through his friend Beaumarchais. That aid, coming under the guise of a business arrangement, was not entirely legal, for the United States had not yet declared independence. The pro-Deane members of Congress professed great moral outrage. They charged Paine with improper use of his official position to gain access to confidential documents, and he was censured and removed from office. On December 5, Deane had published a long address in the *Pennsylvania Packet* in which he took personal credit for diplomatic achievements in France, bitterly attacked the Congress, and excoriated both Arthur and William Lee. He charged Arthur with having lost the confidence of the French court and William with putting personal considerations before his services as a commissioner! Frank immediately penned a brief rejoinder in the *Packet* asking its readers not to judge his absent brothers until they could present their cases.

Arthur, still in Paris waiting to present his credentials to the court of Madrid, wrote that he wished to be recalled to America to report to the Congress. It seemed this was a distinct possibility. The Committee of Foreign Affairs, realizing that suspicions and animosities over the controversy were wrecking the Foreign Service, would no doubt recall Arthur and William before the year was out.

"Sometimes when I think of our younger brothers," Richard Henry said quietly, "I wonder if they haven't sacrificed too much to the cause of liberty. William was almost certain to have been elected lord mayor of London after Wilkes. And Arthur, no doubt, would have won a seat in Parliament—or even a Cabinet post if Lord Shelburne is able to form a govern-

ment. They went against their private interests for what they believed in."
He shrugged.

"Try not to be disheartened," Becky consoled. "The war goes slowly for
everyone."

"Ah, I do have one bright spot of news," Richard Henry announced.
"I had a letter from Patrick Henry. George Rogers Clark managed an outstanding victory in the western part of our state, with fewer than two hundred
men. He has rescued the counties of Kentucky and Illinois from the British."

"How I wish I were in Williamsburg to toast the victory," Frank said
enviously. "Now that we have Articles of Confederation that Virginia can
live with, I am thinking of emulating Ben Harrison and retiring to Virginia.
I've had a stomachful of Philadelphia politics."

Becky clapped her hands with delight. "We are going home, then?"

"Yes, my dear, it's time we were back at Menokin," Frank said with a
smile.

"I, too, am weary of all this troublesome business in Philadelphia!
Perhaps it is now time for the Lees to take their places in the Virginia Assembly," Richard Henry concluded. "We shall go home, Frank. The time has
come."

Richard Henry's eyes rested on pretty Nancy Shippen, who had put on
a blue dress for the party tonight and was helping her mother pour tea. He
smiled, for he had detected that Nancy was involved in a little love triangle.
All evening the ruddy Colonel Henry Beekman Livingston had tried to capture Nancy's attention, which was, it seemed, held by the French ambassador's
young aide-de-camp, Louis Guillaume Otto. The Frenchman was as smooth
and gallant as Livingston was rough-edged and lecherous, but there was little
question which of the two suitors her father preferred, for Will Shippen
made certain that Nancy was seated beside Colonel Livingston at supper.
After all, Livingston was heir to a great New York fortune, and Will Shippen
had always been a practical man.

Perhaps his own Molly was now being courted! Richard Henry
frowned. By God, it *was* high time he returned to Virginia. Anne was expecting a new baby in the late summer, and he was staying home to watch this
child grow up!

New York, 1779

As the months came and went, Light Horse Harry Lee could not shake
Matilda out of his thoughts.

Closing his eyes, he could see her willowy body gracefully leaning with her horse as she took a fence. He had seen no woman, and few men, who held a seat as she did. What a glorious picture she made, shaking her long chestnut locks carelessly as she removed her riding hat and turned to him with a dazzling smile.

Harry eagerly combed the letters from Leesylvania for word of his pretty cousin at Stratford Hall. His father kept him up with all the news about Virginia. In May 1779, some eighteen hundred British soldiers had descended on Portsmouth, then burned the supply depot at Suffolk. Though of little military value, this action had terrified the civilian population and inflicted a staggering loss to the Virginia treasury. There was also the announcement that Richard Henry and Francis Lightfoot had resigned from the Continental Congress and had taken seats in the House of Delegates in Williamsburg. Anne Lee had given birth to a fine healthy boy, Cassius, at Chantilly. Thomas Jefferson had been elected governor of Virginia, and Ben Harrison speaker of the House. But the big news was that the capital would be moving to Richmond, a safer site than Williamsburg and more accessible to the burgeoning western counties. Henry Lee's letters to his son contained no mention of Matilda Lee.

In mid-July, Harry and the Partisans took part in the surprise attack on the British fort at Stony Point, New York. During the early summer scouting raids, Harry had reported heightened British activity at the rugged hilltop fort on the Hudson River.

An offensive against Stony Point was risky, but Harry's intelligence reports deemed it feasible. The American Army was growing stronger every day and badly needed victories to sustain its momentum. When George Washington asked General "Mad" Anthony Wayne from Pennsylvania if he would lead the assault, the loyal Wayne replied, "I would attack Hell if you planned it."

Security was crucial, and Harry was particularly disturbed that some American deserter might leak the news of the impending attack to the British. He wrote to Washington suggesting that desertion might be discouraged if culprits were hanged immediately and their decapitated heads sent around the camps of the light infantry.

Before the general could reply that he endorsed executions under the circumstances but *not* the cutting off of heads, Harry had made just such a move, ordering a deserter hanged and decapitated. The young cavalry leader accepted his commander-in-chief's remonstrance dutifully. He would try to be less hotheaded in the future!

The mission was carried out, and Wayne's clear-cut victory brightened the spirits of the army and the war-stressed thirteen states. But Harry and the Partisans did not have the opportunity to participate fully, for the rocky slope of Stony Point was too difficult for horses' hoofs. If the cavalry were overlooked by Congress for their part in the Stony Point victory, George Washington's praise for their intelligence work made up for the omission. The general added yet another troop to Harry Lee's command, making the Partisans the largest body of cavalry in the Continental Army.

His next grand enterprise was to be an assault against the British post at Paulus Hook, a sturdy, well-fortified log stockade securely situated on a small isthmus between the Hudson and Hackensack rivers. The fort was manned by a full regiment of British regulars, and a short distance away another ten thousand Redcoats hovered in the shadows of Manhattan Island. The Paulus Hook·fort appeared impregnable. General Washington had a mixed reaction to the idea, but finally authorized Harry to lead the attack.

Under the cover of the moonless August night, he led out his cavalry units and a reluctant corps of foot soldiers, their hats marked by identifying cockades. Taken by surprise, the British were quickly overrun by the Americans' bold bayonet charge. Hurriedly Harry and his men scoured the interior for the key to the powder and ammunition magazine. When they could not find it, they attempted to batter down the heavy doors, but to no avail; following Washington's order, the Partisans left—without the powder, but with nearly four hundred prisoners. They had pulled off a clear-cut victory against the greatest odds.

Harry was soon inundated with letters of praise. Washington personally sent his congratulations, as did Anthony Wayne, Nathaniel Greene, and Henry Knox. His spirits soared, only to be dashed when he opened a communiqué a few days later. Incredibly, he was to be court-martialed.

"General Washington and I are as dismayed as you." Alexander Hamilton was all sympathy. "Of course, it's nothing but jealousy! You are different from the rest. You drink from a silver cup, Harry. There is more than one who has taken notice of the personal servants whose saddlebags carry your monogrammed silver, china plates, and linen napkins. . . . You and the Partisans are the elite, the cavalry swooping down on the enemy in your fine uniforms with plumes in your hats. Moreover, you ride the best horses they've ever laid eyes on!"

"By God, we pay for those items out of our own pockets," Harry retorted hotly. "It's no one's business but our own if we choose to dine at night, even around a campfire, in the manner to which we have been accustomed."

"True," Hamilton concurred, "but remember you serve with New Englanders, Pennsylvanians, and the like, men who've not experienced such amenities. Enough of my lecture!" He put his hand on Harry's arm. "I speak from my own opinion, of course, but I believe Washington would resign if you were dishonorably discharged."

When his case came before the board, most of the charges were quickly disproved or explained. He had not lingered to burn the enemies' stores or fortifications because of Washington's instructions. Yes, his retreat had been disorganized, but unforeseen obstacles had made his original plan unworkable, and after all, the retreat had been successful. The charges dwindled down to one crucial one: Lee had been given the appointment in an "irregular manner" and had subsequently acted in a fashion unbecoming to an officer and a gentleman.

The reviewing board listened solemnly as Major Clarke testified. The envious infantry major, assigned to the strike, had been quick to recognize that if the assault were successful, the commanding officer would win a bounty of laurels. On the evening before the raid he asked Lee when he had received his commission, for those with seniority took precedence. Clarke contended that Harry had lied. His eyes steely, fixed on the wall ahead, Harry replied gravely that he had been so absorbed in the battle plans that he had been inattentive and given the wrong date, but that he had no intent to deceive a fellow officer.

It was completely understandable to those who sat in judgment that Harry Lee could not, would not, in good conscience allow another to take his place at the last minute. After all, George Washington had personally given him the command. The verdict was returned amid whoops of joy from Lee's Partisans. At the same time word arrived that the Congress had sent their congratulations for "the remarkable prudence, address and bravery displayed." A special congressional medal of gold was to be struck in honor of Lee's courage.

The Tidewater, 1779

The war for independence was subtly shifting as the British campaign, stalemated in the north, turned south. The slowdown in the northern campaign was intensified by the Christmas 1779 lull, so General Washington again ordered Harry Lee home to Virginia. This time he did not object.

"Where are you going?" his mother had protested when he stopped at Leesylvania just long enough to receive a hero's welcome from his family and don a fresh uniform.

He had whirled her around affectionately. "I am going courting, madam. I am in the mood to dance with a pretty girl under a twist of mistletoe!"

The great brick house seemed to gleam like a ruby on the brown fields.

Harry took off his plumed hat and waved it above his head, then stood in his stirrups and shouted as he came up the tulip poplar–lined lane, for he had caught sight of a slender figure waiting in the high chimney tower. Wrapped in her velvet cloak, Matilda Lee waved her lace scarf in return. Never had she seen anyone who looked quite so glorious as Harry Lee as he galloped toward Stratford Hall with the bright winter sun shining on his golden head.

No doubt Harry did not realize he was falling in love with his cousin during that brief visit to Stratford, the colonel reflected. The young man was filled with the glory of soldiering. And Matilda was distracted by the death of her four-year-old brother, Philip, who earlier in the fall had chased a butterfly through the doors of the great hall and tumbled tragically down the steep stone stairs.

By the spring of 1780, the storm center of the Revolutionary War had centered on the vast expanse of the south. London merchants had long urged the British military to concentrate on capturing the more vulnerable southern states, for their agrarian products were more valuable to the Mother Country. Georgia, overwhelmed by a massive invasion of its port city of Savannah, had fallen to the British in the autumn of 1779. In May 1780, Charleston, South Carolina was overrun. Later that summer, Washington ordered a change in the command of the southern army, recalling General Horatio Gates and offering the post to the thirty-nine-year-old Rhode Island General Nathaniel Greene. The new southern commander was pleased to learn that the recently promoted Lieutenant Colonel Harry Lee and his famed legion would be under his command.

But Colonel Lee had one final mission to attempt for Washington before heading south. In September 1780, Benedict Arnold had betrayed his command and his country. The defection had been brewing for over a year since a court-martial had found Arnold guilty of misconduct as a military commandant of Philadelphia. General Washington sympathized with the thirty-eight-year-old Arnold, who had been an outstanding battlefield commander; despite the court-martial, Washington awarded Arnold the prestigious command of the strategic post at West Point.

The groundwork for Arnold's treason was laid by Peggy Shippen Arnold's former admirer, the dashing John André, Clinton's adjutant general in New York. But André was caught with papers outlining the plan to betray West

Point secreted in his boot. Reading an early dispatch of André's capture, a frightened Arnold climbed from a window of his house at West Point and ordered his oarsmen to row him to the British ship anchored in the bay. Peggy, who feigned hysterics before Washington and Hamilton, was allowed to join her husband in New York.

On Washington's orders, Harry made a desperate attempt to kidnap Arnold from British headquarters in New York, a mission that would have succeeded had Arnold not moved to different quarters on the evening before the attempt.

Harry and his legion of cavalry and light-infantrymen appeared at General Greene's headquarters on the rain-swollen banks of the Pee Dee River in South Carolina in December 1780. It was the beginning of nine months of intense military actions that honed Harry Lee's skills as a military strategist and highlighted his enormous abilities to lead and influence the men over whom he served. Down the Pee Dee into the fever-ridden marshes the legion rode to join the Swamp Fox, Francis Marion, in his hideout on Snow Island. There could be no more incongruous pair than the bearded, dour Marion, who, among other eccentricities, drank several drams of vinegar daily, and the ruddy, graceful Virginia colonel. Marion's ragtag crew of hardened guerrillas, some wielding swords forged from saw blades, must have contrasted starkly with Lee's legion, for during his visit home the previous winter, Harry had dipped again into the Leesylvania purse to refurbish his men with fine new horses and uniforms.

Together, the legion and the followers of the Swamp Fox joined forces to harass the chain of British posts stretching across South Carolina. But it was the seasoned rifleman Dan Morgan who managed the first major encounter of the 1781 southern campaign. Morgan and his corps of professional Maryland and Virginia continentals, augmented by local militia, went against the brutal Tarleton in a bloody battle at Cowpens in January.

Morgan scattered one hundred and fifty of his best marksmen in the front line, with the unseasoned Carolina militiamen behind them. On higher ground to the rear were the professional soldiers, with the cavalry as reserve. The sharpshooters were told to hide behind bushes and trees until the enemy was within one hundred feet, then to take careful aim and fire. After two volleys, these sharpshooters could withdraw with honor while the militia covered their retreat. The militia had only to fire one or two rounds and they too could fall to the rear. His imaginative plan of firing in ranks succeeded, for when the smoke cleared, Tarleton was vanquished, having lost nine-tenths of his men and a shade off his terrifying reputation.

The British commander, Lord Cornwallis, now set the main force of his army in pursuit of Morgan, who was retreating north toward the Dan River. Calling for Lee to join him, Nathaniel Greene rode north to take over the command from Morgan, who had fallen ill. Wildly the ragged southern army raced across the sandy pine-covered plains for the safety of the Dan, while behind them the British doggedly narrowed the distance.

Assigned to bring up the rear, Lee's legion played a savage and desperate game of cat and mouse with the vanguard of the Redcoats, deftly slowing their pursuit. For a grueling twenty-four hours, the men of the legion never left their saddles, going without food or rest until Greene's army was safely across the river. With only minutes to spare, Lee's horsemen boarded the last barges and escaped across the Dan into Virginia.

After only a brief rest, the southern army, Harry and the legion in the forefront, recrossed the Dan to confront Cornwallis at Guilford Court House. It was a brilliant, bold move on Greene's part, for though his own army was exhausted, Cornwallis's forces were more so, their ranks riddled with sickness. The British troops had found little food or shelter in a hostile North Carolina, nor were they accustomed to marching in full gear at the pace set by the retreating rebel army.

Lee and his legion played a vital role in this bloody battle, which was to be as hard-fought as any of the Revolutionary War. While the Continental Army suffered a technical defeat at Guilford Court House, it was in fact a victory, for Cornwallis lost many officers and over a quarter of his troops.

All that long difficult summer, under a burning malarial sun, the legion rode alongside Andrew Pickens and Francis Marion in raid after raid on the British garrisons—Fort Watson, Fort Granby, Forte Motte, and Fort Cornwallis. In September, Lee's legion stood with Greene in a fierce battle at Eutaw Springs against a superior force under British Colonel Alexander Stuart. While the Americans could never seem to claim a clear win, with every battle the British were forced to withdraw from the offensive until, by September 1781, they held only Charleston and Savannah.

Greene now considered his situation. So long as he was undermanned and lacking the supplies a bankrupt Congress could not provide, there was no hope of retaking those key cities. But the circumstances of the war had taken a surprising turn, for as Greene moved south after Guilford Court House, Lord Cornwallis had ventured north into Virginia. His army was in an impossible position at Yorktown, surrounded on land by the strongest American force yet to assemble and blocked by the newly arrived French fleet of twenty-eight ships and three transports under Comte de Grasse.

The tide was turning. Greene sat down at his field desk to outline for Washington the situation in the Carolinas and to beg for men, equipment, and gunnery to recapture Savannah and Charleston. He chose as his special courier that young soldier whom he knew held a special niche in Washington's affections. Burned tawny by the Carolina sun, a thin, battle-taut Colonel Harry Lee headed north to Yorktown in the first days of October 1781.

Perihelion

1781–1790

The Tidewater, 1781

Harry could hardly believe the sight that confronted him at Yorktown; the peaceful port had become a British garrison. Behind well-fortified earthworks and redoubts, more than seven thousand British soldiers were entrenched in the narrow streets and brick-and-timber houses of the sloping hillside town. As he looked down from a high bluff, Harry drew in a breath of pleased astonishment. The Redcoats were sandwiched between the York River on one side and a vast encampment of French and American military forces. Men and horses, cannons and howitzers, were strewn across the landscape, sunlight glinting on artillery and bayonets, wind-snapped standards and divisional flags flashing above the brown field tents. "Powerfully different from what we left on the Santee, eh?"

His companion, Captain John Rudolph, shook his head wearily. "I had got so I thought war was little more than sleeping on wet ground, eating Injun corn, and drinking brackish water while some Redcoat or loyalist waited in the brush to bushwhack me!"

Harry's eye swept the colorful spread of French sails far out on the Chesapeake Bay. "By God," he murmured, "we've surely got Cornwallis surrounded. There!" He pointed beyond the neck where the York River narrowed between Yorktown and Gloucester Point. The French fleet, headed by its flagship, the massive *Ville de Paris*, lay at anchor beyond the river's mouth. "They'll hold off any reinforcements Sir Henry Clinton might dispatch from New York."

"Not to mention cut any attempt to escape by sea—if that's what Cornwallis has in mind," the captain agreed.

"We'd best move on," Harry said. "Somewhere in that vast valley of military splendor, Rudolph, is General Washington. We must deliver General Greene's messages."

Harry could feel his hands trembling on the reins as he picked his way through the congested American lines. It was partly the effects of the fever, which, along with stomach grippes, had tormented him all the way up through the Carolinas. But it was also the keen anticipation he felt for this reunion with George Washington, whom he had not seen since he took his legion south a year before to fight with Greene.

"Colonel Harry Lee! Is it really you?" Alexander Hamilton was standing outside Washington's headquarters. "Damned if you are not still alive!" There was a glint of laughter in Hamilton's voice. "Still alive!" was a talisman greeting between these two soldiers since 1777, when they were sent by General Washington to destroy a British-held mill on the Schuykill River. Their party of calvary and infantry was within fifty yards of the mill when the British turned on them, muskets blazing. Hamilton withdrew his men by boat, while Lee, not wanting to lose his horses, mounted his men two to a horse and made a run for it. They parted, each certain that the other was doomed to capture or death. Harry outran the Redcoats and sent a message to General Washington expressing his concern for Hamilton. As Washington was reading the note, Hamilton straggled into headquarters, lamenting the fate of Harry Lee, much to Washington's amusement. The two young soldiers were thus bonded, and never tired of this greeting, their private joke.

Hamilton enveloped Harry in a bear hug. "God, you are nothing but sinew and bone, Harry, and you are shivering! Are you all right?"

Harry brushed away the questions with a quick shrug. "I haven't eaten since yesterday, and I've ridden hard. Where is General Washington?"

"He's with Rochambeau and Lafayette on the far side of camp. How pleased he will be to see you! But first, let me find you a tent and something to eat."

Gratefully, Harry let himself and Rudolph be taken in hand. He was tired, every joint aching . . . probably a touch of the malaria that had plagued the legion all summer.

"I must tell you how impressed the general is with you, and the efforts of Greene and Morgan as well," Hamilton said as the two officers dug into dishes of hot stew and loaves of freshly baked bread. "In many ways it is the Southern Campaign that has led us to this moment. The Marquis de Lafayette is unquestionably high in General Washington's favor, but even Lafayette does not outshine Greene and Lee."

Had there been a trace of discontent in his friend's voice, Harry wondered as he watched him pace back and forth in the confines of the field tent.

Alexander Hamilton had been a student at King's College in New York at the outbreak of the hostilities and had joined the New York militia, where his quick mind and skill with words had eventually brought him to Washington's attention. Like Harry, Hamilton had been fanatically loyal to the Virginia commander in chief. Something now obviously preyed on his mind.

"And what of you, my friend?" Harry probed gently. "It has always been my impression that Washington could not get along without your able self at his side. But then I heard you resigned as his aide-de-camp?"

Hamilton stopped his pacing and stared at Harry. "The general and I have indeed had our differences of late, but I'd rather not go into it. I believe I have served him well, and feel somewhat ill-used. I offered my services as a soldier and ended up a scribe, and there is no glory in wielding a quill pen, I assure you! You were right to turn this position down, Harry. You've become a hero and I am—"

"Still alive." Harry pushed back his dish with a grin. "Both of us are still alive, and we've both served where we were needed."

"I guess I needed to spill my feelings." Hamilton smiled sheepishly. "Oh, I say, did you know my Betsy expects a child in December?"

Sighing theatrically, Harry offered his congratulations. "Now, see what you've done! Why, I've not even captured a wife, and you are about to become a father. You may envy me my battle laurels, Colonel Hamilton, but, believe me, I envy you your marital state!"

During the previous year, Hamilton had made an advantageous match with the daughter of the wealthy General Philip Schuyler of Albany. "Marriage is marvelous, Harry, truly it is." Hamilton took his seat at the camp table. "Every year since the war began, it has made such a difference when the ladies arrive in winter camp. Lady Washington brought dignity and warmth to Morristown and Valley Forge. Do you recall the sight of her walking among the sick and wounded, dispensing comfort and hot soup, her shawl held fast by a thistle? Lucy Knox, with her jolly humor, is a proper foil for Henry's boldness; and you know firsthand the charm of Kitty Greene!"

Indeed Harry did. He had never seen such a beautiful, ardent love as that between the stocky, handsome Rhode Islander Greene and his enchanting Kitty. Every year she had come, baggage and babies, to join her husband for the winter encampments, brightening the gloom with her beauty and lightheartedness. Even Washington was beguiled; he danced with her one night for four hours straight.

"Do prepare to dine tonight with General Washington, Harry," Hamilton continued, "for he will be anxious to hear your reports. Furthermore, you'll get an inkling of what he anticipates at Yorktown. If we succeed, God willing, an extraordinary victory shall be ours."

"With all the excitement, General Washington has not yet had time to draft a response to Greene's request," Harry explained to Frank and Becky two weeks later when he stopped overnight at Menokin on his way to Leesylvania for a ten-day furlough. "These past weeks have been unbelievable—a spectacle such as I have never witnessed before!"

"Do try to tell us," Becky urged, her piquant face aglow with excitement.

"When I dined with General Washington on my first night at Yorktown, and again the following," Harry began slowly, "he told me of his frustrating year, with Clinton's fifteen thousand troops occupying New York and with mutinies in the Pennsylvania and New Jersey lines. It is a wonder the general held up, for as recently as this past June he had only five thousand troops he could depend on. What unbelievable endurance! Then, with Count de Grasse's navy in the bay, French troops to bolster the power of the Continentals, the ebullient Lafayette and Rochambeau at either elbow, and Cornwallis trapped like an old lion on the banks of the York, the war finally fell in place for him."

"Tell us what happened," Frank pressed.

"Cornwallis abandoned his outer redoubts and pulled back his line to hole up in the town proper—I think he was still confident Clinton would reach him by sea with reinforcements. But Washington immediately began his siege. With the French hammering from one side, the Americans could dig their entrenchments on the other. By the seventh of October, those trenches were manned and the orders sent out to storm the inner redoubts."

"What did you do, Harry?" Becky's eyes were fastened on his face.

Harry's mouth tightened. "Hamilton reminded me that I am chief of cavalry in the Southern Department, and that taking even a temporary assignment might be viewed as an insult to my commander, Nathaniel Greene ... something that neither General Washington nor I would wish."

"And so you could only watch." Frank's eyes were sympathetic; he knew how the young man must have ached to take part in the great encounter at Yorktown.

"Yes. I watched with His Excellency, General Washington, and Generals Lincoln and Knox from a spot close to the front, and I swear I shall never forget it! The very ground beneath our feet trembled from the pounding of the artillery and the bombshells exploding above our heads—in the dusk they resembled meteors with brilliant, blazing tails. .."

"How truly spectacular!" breathed Becky.

"And devastating." Harry closed his eyes, the picture vivid in his mind. "The British Army struggled like a captured beast trying to work itself free. At the end, Yorktown lay in a shambles, with hardly a house standing. Even then the British were unwilling to recognize our American victory! They approached the surrender field with their eyes firmly fixed on the French contingency, and then attempted to present the sword of surrender to Rochambeau, who directed them toward Washington."

"It was George's finest hour." Frank thrust his hands in his pockets.

Harry nodded, remembering Washington's face as the British regiments, their colors cased and their drummers beating a mournful royal march, moved into the circle formed by French hussars to lay down their muskets in a great mountain of wood and steel. "And now Washington must turn his attention to eliminating Clinton in the north and aiding Greene's efforts to free Savannah and Charleston in the south."

"With Yorktown satisfactorily concluded, Virginians can sleep safe in their beds again," Frank said with a sigh of relief. "We've suffered a hard time, Harry, with Cornwallis moving up from the south and that devil Banastre Tarleton slashing his way through our countryside. But even more terrifying, Benedict Arnold sailed up the James with his British warships last winter—bold as life! Right up to Richmond he came, chasing Governor Jefferson and the Assembly into the Shenandoahs to save their necks! Then the marauders descended upon the James River plantations. His twenty-seven ships, both men-of-war and brigs, anchored at Westover with bagpipes shrieking. Our turncoat Benedict Arnold was the first on the dock, splendid in his brand-new scarlet-and-gold British uniform."

"Poor Mary Byrd! As though she hasn't suffered enough, after her husband's sorry end!" broke in Becky. "Now, here comes her cousin Peggy's husband to call. Actually, the British didn't harm Westover, but they marched next door to Berkeley, which the Harrisons had hastily abandoned, and piled all those lovely family portraits in the front yard and lit a bonfire with them! Can you believe that? The vandals!"

In a quiet bedroom under the eaves at Menokin, Harry tossed and turned in the darkness. Even beneath the weight of three blankets he shivered, and the perspiration on his brow was as cold as the icy waters of the Dan in February. Night images haunted him—the tired whiskered faces of his men as they plodded through the dark forest beside the muddy Savannah River; his little bugler Gillies, brutally massacred in the road by Tarleton's green-coated dragoons; the nights and days when every sense was needed to survive, yet a heavy weariness lay like iron on one's limbs and eyelids; and, over and over, the spectacle at Yorktown seen from the sidelines. No one had even been aware of his role in the Yorktown victory, that it was he, Harry Lee, who had suggested to Greene that Cornwallis be craftily lured north into Virginia, like a fox lured into the circle for the kill.

Why was his name not included with that of Francis Marion's on the honors list sent to Washington following the battle of Eutaw Springs? Could it be that Greene had not wished him to receive the praise he had earned? Yet many gossiped that he was Greene's pet, as well as Washington's. He threw back his blanket, the fever searing his body.

Harry was up as soon as the dawn touched the treetops along the Menokin Creek. Freshly dressed and booted, he leaned out the window to look over the plantation, peaceful on this Indian summer morning. As Harry reflected on the devotion of Frank and Becky Lee, he envied them their contentment in this beautiful house above the "Quick Rising Waters," as the Indians called the Rappahannock. He envied their beautiful partnership, their delight in each other. With a surge of joy, he suddenly thought of Stratford Hall. He had dreamed of Matilda Lee so many times this past year in the high hills above the Santee. Now he desperately wanted to see her.

"That," said Becky as she watched his departure from the open front door, "is a most extraordinary young man! Sometimes he is so jaunty and cocksure that I want to thrash him, but most times I just want to hug him. He is so deliciously appealing, fascinating to talk with, and yet so very kind."

Frank threw his wife a sideways glance and said with mock ferocity, "There is to be no hugging between you and Harry Lee. Why, there is less than three years between you and him!" Frank watched Harry disappear over the hill in the shimmering morning sun. "He is an idealist, my love, he asks too much of himself. All his life he has been the best, striving always to do his best. Therefore, he is shocked by those human traits—jealousy, greed, laziness—that are the earmark of ordinary men. What did Harry say was drummed as the British soldiers surrendered at Yorktown . . . 'The world turned upside down'? I think Harry's world is somewhat like that; he has fought so hard, so fiercely, and soon there will be no more battles to fight. He is too green to have known such glory."

Matilda Lee let her russet-brown hair tumble onto her shoulders and smiled with delight at herself in the tall bedroom mirror at Stratford.

On autumn days like this, time seemed eternal—sweet-smelling, ripe with endless promise. The trees were glazed with a special golden light, turning the sourwoods a glowing red and the sugar maples and hickories a lovely hue of yellow. Matilda moved forward to examine herself more closely. Last night Harry Lee had said her eyes were green, flecked with yellow and touched with blue around the edges. How extraordinary that he should notice so precisely!

"Matilda!" Her younger, dark-browed sister, Flora, stood in the bedroom doorway. "You can't mean to be seen with your hair hanging down like a schoolgirl! It looks dreadful that way, absolutely dreadful!"

"No, it doesn't." Matilda gave her profile a side glance in the mirror. "Actually it looks rather charming, like an Indian princess. All I need is a headband and feathers!"

"You act so giddy since Harry Lee arrived. I do believe you are infatuated with him, just like every other girl in Virginia. Why, every friend you have has just happened to come calling, only to find—quite by accident, of course—that the charming Colonel Lee is visiting. Once here, they linger on, paying not one bit of attention to us, just hanging on his every word!" With a sigh of disgust Flora threw herself down, hoop skirt and all, on the canopied bed she and Matilda shared.

Matilda turned back to the dressing table and, picking up a silver brush, began giving her thick hair vigorous strokes. How exasperating Flora could be! No wonder she wasn't especially popular. "I say, Flora darling, let's ask Mamma if we may have a dance Saturday night. We shall call it a victory ball in honor of Yorktown, and we'll invite everyone for miles around—the Washingtons, and the Carters from Nomini and Sabine, and Uncle Richard Henry's brood from Chantilly, and—"

Flora stopped her with a frown. "Do whatever you want, Matilda. Parties don't interest me one bit!"

"What a marvelous idea!" Matilda pulled up her brown hair in a careless knot on top of her head, covered it with a gauzy cap, and hurriedly slipped into a morning dress of blue lawn. Where was Mother? Surely she would say yes. She always seemed to say yes these days, because she was happy again for the first time since losing Father and poor little Phil. This past September, Elizabeth Lee had married a kind, thoughtful Maryland gentleman, Philip Fendall, who had brought a new sparkle to her face.

"An outdoor ball? But Matilda, my dear, it is almost November!" Elizabeth Lee Fendall sat writing letters in the small room that had once been the nursery.

"But see how lovely and mild it is outside, Mother." Matilda clasped her hands. "And the harvest moon will be full by tomorrow night! Do say yes! We can send out riders with the invitations this morning. Why, there is nothing more fun than a spur-of-the-moment party!"

Elizabeth smiled at the animation in her daughter's face. Matilda had always been a pretty child, but in the past few years she had grown truly lovely. What was it the local swains called her ... the Divine Matilda.

"Do you think our houseguest would enjoy a ball?" Mrs. Fendall asked solicitously. "After five years at war, Harry perhaps might prefer peace and quiet to frivolity."

Sitting on the rug in front of the small nursery fireplace, Matilda gazed at the cherubs on the firewall. "I'm certain he'll say yes." She leaned over to kiss her mother's hand. "You know what? Today I love everything—you, this house, my angels. I think they protect us and Stratford Hall." With a quick, graceful movement, she rose and was gone from the room.

Matilda found Harry walking at the end of the orchard beside Will West's slow-moving hay wagon.

"If a little dancing can tire me out, then I'll be of no use to Greene when I return to the Santee," he said when she told him of her mother's comment. He lifted her suddenly onto the back of the wagon. "Give us a ride, Will!" he called as he clambered up beside her.

"I'm goin' out to the far pasture, out to the big barn. You don't want to walk back from there," Will said skeptically as he looked back at them from his perch. "Not Miss Matilda in them little shoes."

"I shall carry Miss Matilda back to the house, if need be!" Harry said with a broad grin.

"Such foolishness," Will grumbled, clucking the horses into a faster walk.

"This *is* foolishness, Harry Lee," said Matilda, settling herself back in the straw and grabbing hold of the wagon. "Here I am without a sun mask for my face. I shall get burned brown as you, and then what will Mother say?"

"I shall tell her, 'I abducted your darling daughter this afternoon, Mrs. Fendall, and I take all the blame for the amazing roses now glowing in her cheeks.' But since I will bring you home again safe and sound in my strong arms, she will forgive me." Harry stuck a piece of straw between his teeth. "She will forgive me anyway, for she dotes on me."

"I declare, Harry Lee, you are the most conceited thing!" Matilda scrambled away from him in the straw.

Harry helped Matilda down from the wagon into a spot of deep shade beside the privet hedge and spread his green tunic on the grass for her to sit on. "Too hot for that wool jacket anyway," he murmured, sprawling beside her.

The sight of the creamy-white skin of his chest at the open neck of his shirt, delicate as a child's and in bold contrast to the brown of his face and neck, gave her a strange feeling, and she looked away.

"What is the matter?" he asked. "Are you upset that I brought you here? I just wanted to be alone with you. I haven't seen you since breakfast, you know."

"I'm not angry." She tossed a persimmon lightly at his boot. "It's just that you sound eager to return to South Carolina, to Greene and the legion. I think you miss your men and the excitement of war."

"It is with me, all the time." He stared into the distance. "War is terrible, Matilda, and it brands one with memories."

"Tell me of your memories, Harry," the girl gently urged.

"Seeing Stratford Hall so strong and beautiful, untouched by war, I am reminded of something that happened last spring on the Congaree River in South Carolina. Francis Marion and I were ordered to take Fort Motte, which had previously been a beautiful South Carolina mansion. The British had confiscated it from the Motte family and fortified it as a supply depot. Mrs. Motte, a widow, was forced to live in an old farmhouse on a nearby hill."

"How terrible," Matilda said with a shiver. "I can't imagine being forced to move out of Stratford Hall."

"Well, Marion and I surrounded the mansion and tried to get the British to surrender, but, aware that reinforcements were on the way, they refused. Finally, we decided the only way to fulfill our orders was to burn them out." Harry looked off at the trees in the distance. "I cannot tell you how I dreaded informing Mrs. Motte of our plans to fire flaming arrows at her beautiful house. But to my great relief, she agreed completely and even gave me a powerful Indian bow with a quiver of iron-tipped arrows, which she thought might well do the job."

"And did it?"

"Aye, the house caught fire with the first three arrows, and before you could snap your fingers the British were hanging out a white flag of surrender. But it was too late to save the manor house. We watched it burn to the ground." Harry looked at Matilda. "She was a lovely lady, Mrs. Motte. The next day she even entertained us for dinner—Marion and myself as well as the captured British officers."

"Harry, you are an impossible romantic," Matilda said suddenly. "You believe in honor and graciousness and bravery. I guess it is what I . . . like most in you."

"You almost said 'love.'"

"I did not!"

"Well, I love you, Matilda Lee." Harry leaned so close that she could almost hear the pounding of his heart . . . or was it her own, beating like thunder in her breast?

He had got to his knees and taken both her hands in his. Suddenly they were standing, his mouth only inches from hers. "Matilda, do you think that you . . . could care for me? That you would say yes if I asked you . . ." Gently his fingers slipped the soft cap from her head and the brown hair came tumbling down between them.

She was drowning in his dark eyes. She pulled her hand from his, gathered up her skirts, and began to run toward the house.

"Have you ever seen such a moon?" Elizabeth Fendall asked her husband. "It is a moon for a harvest ball, and for lovers."

He squeezed her arm. "Look, my dear, what a picture lies before us."

Its posts and nearby trees festooned with streamers and bright-colored lanterns, the Stratford wharf spread deep-purple shadows across the Potomac waters lapping at its pilings. On barges lashed to the dock, a dozen musicians filled the night air with music. Chariots, sedan chairs, and saddled horses lined the wharf road; at the dock was tied the flatboat that had carried the Washington party downriver from Wakefield. It was scarcely seven; already the dance floor, cleared of its barrels and freshly scrubbed, was filling with young people.

Beside the wharf a crew of house and kitchen servants had set up the outdoor supper in the clearing. A fragrant haunch of venison was turning on the spit beside a large roast of pork, and the servants were shucking quantities of oysters to be eaten with sweet butter.

"I cannot believe Matilda was able to raise this crowd on such short notice. There must be forty or so already here, and more to come." Elizabeth's bright eyes swept the dancers. "It is nice to have Richard Henry's boys, Thomas and Ludwell, home again at Chantilly." The two auburn-haired young men had returned from France with their uncle Arthur just over a year ago.

"But where is Matilda?" asked Philip Fendall. "Don't tell me she is still up at the house primping!"

"I saw her dressed an hour ago, her hair all nicely creped." Elizabeth arranged the silk shawl around her shoulders. "She is probably with Harry Lee."

But Matilda was not with Harry. The young soldier stood on the edge of the wharf, deep in conversation with Richard Henry Lee and his brother Arthur.

"Land," Arthur was saying emphatically, "in the long run, it is land upon which our nation's future rests. As a basis for signing a peace treaty with England, the United States must define her borders and gain undisputed title to the western domain. Certainly France is not to be trusted—take it from one who knows! And her closest ally, Spain, has already made claims on our west! I understand the need to share Virginia's northwest territory with the other states, but we must protect ourselves from England's and Europe's claims on our lands. And internally we must protect ourselves where Virginia's rights are concerned! We must not be taken advantage of by the other states in this confederation!"

"I heard, sir, you were recently in Philadelphia with the Shippens. How do they fare? I was very distressed to hear of the court-martial charges brought against Dr. Shippen."

Arthur shook his head. "Politics—in medicine and the military as well as government! It sickens me! Perhaps Will was guilty of some negligence, some attempts to whitewash distressing details. Perhaps there was graft in military stores. But, heavens, the task he undertook was enormous! Drs. Benjamin Rush and John Morgan certainly expended a lot of effort to discredit poor Will. To think that the charges against him were dismissed by a majority of only one vote! Now that he has resigned his position as director of military medical services, they may find out what a thankless job he did for them!"

Richard Henry shifted the subject. "Did you know, Harry, that Nancy Shippen was married this past March? She married Henry Beekman Livingston, the heir to one of the largest fortunes in New York."

Harry stiffened. He had always found Livingston coarse and distasteful, and even worse, an undistinguished soldier! Suddenly he caught sight of Matilda standing at the side of the wharf with Flora and their cousin Ludwell Lee. "If you gentlemen will excuse me," he said with a slight bow.

"Where have you been?" he asked Matilda indignantly as he firmly led her out to dance. "I have been looking everywhere for you!"

"Have you really?" Matilda's tone was flirtatious. "Harry, do you remember the courting game we played the last time you were at Stratford?" She referred to the game in which a sword was placed on a Book of Common Prayer opened to the marriage ceremony. This was held over the player's head just before going to bed. Whoever the person dreamed of that night, he or she would eventually wed. Matilda dimpled. "When we held the Bible and sword over Millie Washington of Bushfield's head, the very next day she told me, secretly of course, that she dreamed of my cousin Thomas of Chantilly."

Harry was looking at her quizzically. "So?"

"Last night he asked her to marry him! Can you believe it?"

"If I recall correctly, Matilda Lee, you, too, played the game that evening. Pray tell, of whom did you dream that night?"

"I can't really remember," she teased airily. The dancing broke into a faster allemande. Matilda lifted her skirts and twirled under his outstretched arm. "I think it was Bobby Carter of Nomini!"

How vexing she was, and how beautiful. "Are you pleased that your cousin Nancy Shippen has married?" He led her to a candlelit table close by the millpond.

"I don't know." Matilda looked at him gravely. "I think Nancy was desperately in love . . . but not with Henry Livingston."

Harry could not suppress a gasp. "Well, why the devil did she marry him? Did her father force her to?"

Matilda twisted the corner of her napkin. "Sometimes a girl doesn't really know what she wants, Harry. Nancy thought she was in love with Louis Otto, a French envoy to Philadelphia. He courted her ardently at teas, balls, and assemblies, and on walks in the park. But he offered no dependable future, and she did not trust her emotions. She was swayed, you see, by the wishes of her father, whom she adores."

"And so she said yes to Livingston and forgot Otto?"

"From Nancy's letters, I gather she had secretly accepted Otto's proposal of marriage and shared the news with her mother, who was quite sympathetic to the match. But Aunt Alice is not well, not well at all." Matilda looked down at her hands. "We could see it during her recent visit here. She is dreamy and lost in her own thoughts, so when Nancy told her father about Otto, her mother was no help. Dr. Shippen then forbade Otto to call at Shippen House for four days while he considered his proposal. But that very night, he overwhelmed Nancy with his arguments to marry Livingston."

"It's hard to believe! I thought Will Shippen such an admirable man!"

"I guess he felt he was saving his daughter from a bad marriage and leading her into a good one," Matilda commented. "At any rate, Nancy married Henry Livingston the next day and left to live with him on his estates in New York."

"Is she happy?" Harry had gently taken one of Matilda's hands in his, and she did not pull away.

"She lives well and she is truly fond of Livingston's mother, who has been kind to her. But in her letters she never speaks of her husband. They are such sad letters."

"I do not wonder. You would not consent to a loveless marriage, would you, Matilda, no matter what the pressures?"

"No." The girl spoke firmly. "I am not of Nancy's easy, abiding nature.

Uncle Frank tells me I am much like my grandmother Hannah Ludwell Lee, the first mistress of Stratford Hall."

Harry pulled Matilda gently to her feet. "Let's stroll," he murmured, capturing her hand more tightly in his and leading her up the steep path toward the quiet millpond.

"You love Stratford Hall very much, don't you?" Harry asked thoughtfully.

"Love it?" Matilda's hand tightened in his. "Why, last spring when the British tried to land gunboats at Stratford Landing, I thought I would die if they harmed one blade of grass! You should have seen Uncle Richard Henry, how he gathered the Westmoreland militia and led them swarming over the low cliffs, to make a stand at the dock to defend this land, our homes. He stayed right at the front, the first to face the British, the last to leave the cliffs. One warship fired its cannon several times, but they soon turned tail and took to the open river. Will West put an exploded mortar shell by the kitchen door for a remembrance. Yes, Harry, I truly love Stratford Hall! I could not imagine living anyplace else." Her eyes widened. "Nor would I ever want to. The man I marry must cherish it as I do."

"Could you love me?" His strong, warm hands encircled her waist.

"Oh, Harry," she whispered, "I have been thinking of nothing else since you began to ask me that the other day."

"Matilda, I love you. I want so much to marry you." The moon shone down through the willows as his mouth very gently sought hers. "Will you marry me, Matilda? Will you be my wife?"

"Yes," she murmured, passionately burying her head in his chest, "my darling Harry, yes."

The Tidewater, 1782

"A nervous bridegroom, are you?" Charles whispered to his older brother, as they waited at one end of the great hall at Stratford. "I swear, Harry, you're as pale as a ghost!"

"No," he whispered back, "but I am reminded of my staff surgeon's answer when asked that question the night before a battle in the Carolinas: 'Not frightened, sir, but damnably alarmed!'"

Charles chuckled. His eyes swept the crowded room, now decked with masses of dogwood, apple blossoms, and lush, sweet bowers of lilacs. Their younger brother, Richard Bland, a student at the College of William and Mary in Williamsburg, was escorting Anne Lee of Chantilly to a silk brocade chair. With child again, was she? How many were there now at Chantilly? Not too many, now that Thomas was married to Millie Washington. Molly Lee was pledged to William Augustine Washington of Wakefield, and Hannah was said to be secretly betrothed to Millie's brother, Corbin Washington. Of late, Lees seemed to marry only Washingtons or other Lees! Young Thomas Lee of Bellevue was supposedly sweet on that pretty Carter girl of Nomini, but then Lees seldom married Carters.

The strains of the harpsichord had faded away, and hushed silence filled the room as every eye turned toward the doors through which the bride would enter. Charles squared his shoulders. Weddings were glorious events! The sacred ceremony, with feast to follow, then all the games and opportunities to dance with visiting belles! Three full days of parties and flirtations and rides to the cliffs! And this wedding was particularly wonderful. Charles sighed enviously. Harry, the golden and gallant hero, and the heiress Matilda, so obviously deeply in love, were perfectly suited for each other.

Now the soft familiar strains of the wedding song began. Matilda Lee stood in the doorway on the arm of her tall, auburn-haired uncle, Richard Henry Lee, titular head of the clan.

There was joy within the family that Stratford Hall would remain a Lee plantation in name as well as blood. To buy out Flora's share of Stratford Hall and to honor Elizabeth Fendall's dower rights, Matilda and Harry each put up twenty thousand pounds. Currency was still desperately scarce, and pledging this bond had taxed Henry Lee of Leesylvania considerably, but the sacrifice was well worth the effort, for Harry would become master of one of the Tidewater's finest plantations.

Matilda moved toward her bridegroom with chin gracefully erect, her carriage regal, befitting the princess of a great house.

The Tidewater, 1784

"We lead the quietest of lives since I retired from politics." Frank Lee studied the shiny red apples he had just plucked from the tree. "Our days are spent reading together and sometimes entertaining a few neighbors. I do some farming, Becky has her handiwork, and with that we are blissfully happy." He looked lovingly at his wife.

"The orchard at Menokin put forth a deliciously sweet crop of apples just for your visit," Becky proudly told Richard Henry and Anne Lee, who had just arrived with their two-year-old, Francis Lightfoot.

Frank gathered his namesake in his arms and hugged him tight. "Can he eat a piece of apple?" he asked Anne. "I'll peel it with my knife and cut it into tiny bites."

"Very tiny bites," Anne admonished as she spread out her skirts to sit beside Becky on the quilt between the apple trees.

Becky hugged her knees in amusement as little Frank, still in his long white dress, played with the pet dogs. "It is so very nice to have you at Menokin! Sometimes I wish . . ." Becky pulled little Frank to her for a kiss. "I told you that William is arriving, didn't I? We've been expecting him since yesterday, but then, he's been feeling poorly, and I expect he travels across the Tidewater more slowly than usual."

"Indeed, at the Assembly in Richmond last June William and I were two crotchety codgers," Richard Henry said with a shake of his head, "I suffering from this miserable gout and he ailing in every bone. What's more disturbing, his eyesight is failing terribly. He was full of enthusiasm when he and his boy arrived home from Europe last year, with a seat waiting for him in the State Assembly and Green Spring to be reopened. But he now finds himself so blind that he has given up the Assembly and put off the refurbishing of Green Spring until Hannah Philippa and the two girls arrive."

"Portia and little Cornelia," Becky said softly, "will be so very European. Whatever will they think of our Virginia?"

Frank answered his wife's questions. "Our nieces will find Virginia beautiful, but Hannah Philippa will discover things are far different from when she left Green Spring. She will soon see Virginia is exhausted from the war; there is no boat-building and little commerce on our rivers. Why, a coin in one's pocket is scarce as hens' teeth!"

"Oh, Frank, we're not that poor!" Becky protested. "Our tables groan with food."

"That, my darling, is because, with no British markets for export, everything we grow goes only to feed ourselves. Damn it all, our whole economy is upside down! Do you realize every state has its own laws, its own currencies? I've said it before, Richard Henry, and I'll say it again, our confederation does not hang together. Something stronger is needed. Every state works only for its own selfish interests and whims."

"But that is as it should be," Richard Henry replied hotly. "Virginia's liberty is the most important consideration! We have fought a long, bloody war to gain it, and I'm not in favor of overthrowing one tyrant to set up another!"

"Richard Henry, there is no way to arbitrate our differences—unless one counts the Congress, and that holds such little power!"

"You and Washington preach the same sermon," Richard Henry said gruffly. "All he writes about is unity. 'The continental scale' is how he puts it—'Think on the continental scale.' Bah, I'm tired of hearing it! I stand with Patrick Henry and, for a change, agree with our good cousin and governor, Ben Harrison. Virginia's interests must always come first."

"I agree." Frank's voice rose in exasperation. "And Virginia is not being served well by these Articles of Confederation. They must be improved upon."

"Just remember that it took five long, painful years to write the articles we then argued and cajoled the states to ratify. Give this agreement time to work, Frank," Richard Henry pleaded. "We must not rush into any modifications that bind the states closer to one another without safeguarding personal and state interests."

"Politics . . . politics," Anne Lee sighed to Becky. "It is Richard Henry's bread and butter. I am about to lose my dear husband again, for he goes in November to represent Virginia in the Confederation Congress at Trenton."

Becky rose to her feet and scooped up little Frank, who was yawning sleepily. "Come, Anne, let us return to the house. Perhaps William will have arrived."

Richard Henry watched his wife and sister-in-law disappear through the trees. It was always a wrench to leave Anne and the children. Politics was his mistress—there was no doubt of that. Politics had so beguiled him, luring him with her siren song, that time after time he found himself in the uncomfortable position of deserting his wife and family for the fickle charms of the Congress. Yet each time he left Chantilly, a bit of his heart remained behind.

"Washington is home at Mount Vernon again," Frank remarked lazily.

"I'm aware of that," replied Richard Henry, "and he is fully enjoying it, I'm sure. He returned last December after saying farewell to his officers at Fraunces Tavern in New York. It is said he cried and embraced them without embarrassment as he took his leave."

"We're all back in Virginia except for Tom Jefferson, who's off to Paris," Frank added. "What the devil has Congress named him—minister plenipotentiary? Well, I wish him, John Adams, and Dr. Franklin well in their attempts to negotiate treaties of commerce for the confederation. Lord knows, our economy can use his skill!"

"Tom has remarkable talents," Richard Henry agreed. "But his life goes badly of late. He needs a place to come out in the sun again."

The war had ravaged Virginia during Jefferson's term as governor, and Virginians had grown disillusioned with the planter from Monticello, who talked of democratic constitutionality and religious freedom while the state reeled from financial to physical disaster. Thomas Nelson, who succeeded, had been better, but the tough, pragmatic Ben Harrison of Berkeley was proving superior to either of his predecessors.

"I hear Jefferson still grieves terribly over the death of his beloved wife." Frank lay back to scan the bright September sky through the lacy limbs of the apple tree. "She died after childbirth, you know." He thought of Becky. There was such gentleness, such abundant love, in his wife's heart that she would have been a wonderful mother. Yet secretly he felt relieved that she had not borne a child. She had never been strong, and even now, when racked with a winter cold or a summer fever, she was forced to spend many days on the couch or in bed.

"Do you realize, Frank, when William arrives, it will be the first time we three brothers have been together for a long time? It is a shame that Arthur cannot join us as well. Has he set forth yet on his . . . great western adventure?"

"Do I detect a shade of sarcasm in your voice, Richard Henry? Do you infer that our Arthur leaps perilously from adventure to adventure?"

"You are absolutely correct!" Richard Henry said with a flourish.

Frank picked up the thread of their conversation as the Lees headed toward the snug Menokin farmhouse. "You know, since he entered Congress two years ago, Arthur has been caught up in controversy. He's fighting to get that peace treaty with England ratified, since it is exactly the one you 'radicals' want." Frank gave Richard Henry a sidelong glance. "He's also battling to settle the Congress permanently in Virginia, at the port of Georgetown. When he's not busy with that, he's attacking Robert Morris for destroying the public credit while grabbing a private fortune during the war."

"Arthur's a fighter, a man of courage," Richard Henry said defensively. "He could have so easily given up in despair, you know. Only now is the proof beginning to appear that Silas Deane and his secretaries were in the pay of the British. Meanwhile, Arthur has suffered humiliation after humiliation. I, for one, am quite proud of him."

"Do you think I am not?" Frank retorted. "Especially now, as he goes off as a commissioner from Congress to secure title from the western Indians to the northwest land. That is a necessity if new states are to be set up in the wilderness territory." He stopped abruptly. From the back kitchen garden, Becky was running toward them, tears streaming down her cheeks.

"Oh, Frank," she cried as he rushed to meet her, "it is William. Just as he was setting out for Menokin, a post rider arrived at Green Spring with a message from his friends in Brussels. Hannah Philippa took ill right before she and the little girls were to sail, and then grew worse. Now word has just arrived that she is dead!"

Mount Vernon, 1785

It seemed remarkable to Richard Henry that George Washington had emerged unscathed from the travails of war and was now visibly enjoying retirement. The two men had absented themselves from a larger group in Mount Vernon's parlor, retiring with a bottle of champagne to the crackling fire of George's private sitting room.

"I hardly know who some of my guests are!" George had joshed as he closed the study door. "My home is like a friendly tavern, always filled with people—children, friends, and strangers—who think nothing of pausing here for a day or a week! I swear, Mrs. Washington and I have not sat down to dinner alone since I returned from the war two years ago!"

The children to whom George referred were the two youngest of Jacky Custis's four children. They had come under Mount Vernon's roof following Jacky's tragic death of the influenza three weeks following the surrender at Yorktown, in 1781.

"The children's mother, Miss Nelly, has her hands full, so I think she is relieved that we have offered our home to little Nell and Washington Custis." George's face broke into a rare wide smile. "He is my namesake— George Washington Parke Custis—and a fat little tub he is!"

How generous George was, Richard Henry thought as he sipped his champagne from the fine-stemmed goblet. Mount Vernon was a haven not only for the many Washington nephews and nieces who leaned on their uncle for guidance and his abiding deep affection, but also for distinguished visitors from here and abroad. As president of the Confederation Congress, Richard Henry was well aware of the master of Mount Vernon's hospitality, for he himself had sent numerous European writers and sculptors with letters of introduction to visit George Washington.

"I do enjoy having guests," George continued as if reading his thoughts, "and none more than you, dear fellow. But to be honest, week upon week of entertaining taxes one's being and . . ."

Richard Henry smiled. "Taxes one's being and one's pocketbook," he finished for his friend. "Congress has received the expenses you submitted for your war years. I am working to see that you are reimbursed, for we are greatly indebted to you!"

George snorted slightly. "My expenses are just part of the cost, and some will begrudge me even that! No one considers the deterioration and neglect of my property, debts and rents uncollected, lost profits from my fields. But then," he said, suddenly gentle, "financial problems are a burden throughout the colonies. Let us talk of other things. I say, you are looking well. I like your breeches! Black satin, what?"

Richard Henry looked down at his handsome, well-fitting breeches. "My nephew Thomas Shippen thought I should be decked out handsomely as the president of the Congress. I told him, 'If it is for the good of the country that I be converted to a young beau, then a beau I shall be.' "

George's smile was wicked. "And a beau you are, if I do say so myself! Perhaps we can make up for lost time and return to being the romantic fools we were in our twenties."

Richard Henry studied his friend. Washington was still firm-bodied and, yes, even a bit lusty; the air of gravity that had often hung about George seemed relaxed. "Do you ever hear from your friends the Fairfaxes? Will they ever return to Virginia?"

"Never," George said firmly. "Our correspondence is rare but valued. I think, on both sides. They will spend the rest of their lives in England."

"You rather grew up at Belvoir, didn't you, George?" Richard Henry persisted.

The full blue eyes fastened upon him. "I candidly say to you, and in private, the happiest moments of my life were spent there!" As usual, George spoke in a slow, firm voice; then with a quick smile, he changed the drift of the conversation. "Did I tell you that I had a letter from my young friend Lafayette?"

"Is he well?"

"Aye. He mentioned recent correspondence with you."

Richard Henry nodded. "We continue a conversation begun when he visited last year. I wrote to suggest we consider a league of nations intent upon protecting the freedom of the individual and of individual states and nations. Perhaps it will one day come to be! My greatest fear, dear Washington, is that the rights and precious liberty of individuals—indeed, the rights of our thirteen sovereign states—will be trampled in compromises, particularly if the avarice of commerce is put before liberty. We have fought hard for freedom. It must be preserved at any cost."

"I do not disagree, nor, I am sure, would Lafayette, who fights oppressive power in his own France." George's expression was tinged with annoyance. "But one must be realistic. As more western states are created and enter our union, more and more problems—commerce being but one of them—will arise. We need a confederation strong and powerful enough to make decisions favorable to all concerned. I tell you, friend, it must be! Virginia must risk losing some of her autonomy for practical reasons. Her future is inexorably bound up with that of Massachusetts, Pennsylvania, and the rest. My God, I fought a war with militias from the thirteen colonies, each with its own chain of command. In the beginning, it was difficult, well nigh impossible, until I was given the authority to override the local commanders. And the powerless Congress, unsupported by the state assemblies, was never able to feed, clothe, and shoe my soldiers adequately!"

Richard Henry slowly shook his head. "I only wish Jefferson were here to argue the point, or Patrick Henry, or Samuel Adams, or Ben Harrison. These men feel as I do. What about your neighbor George Mason? Does he urge a closer, more restrictive union? No, he is fearful of the tyranny too much centralized government can foster!"

The Tidewater, 1785

"Washington and I disagree strongly regarding our new confederation," Richard Henry remarked to Harry Lee a few weeks later as they rode along the cliffs above Stratford Hall. "He says he fears the tyranny of a stronger confederation less than the dissolution of our union. George is not a political philosopher but a pragmatist! I give your general and my friend the highest marks, for he is an extraordinary man, but his mind is occupied with practical things—his wheat fields and his racehorses." Richard Henry struggled for other examples. "On his recent trip west, he searched avidly for a possible link between the upper waters of the Ohio and the Potomac. You know he has formed another trade venture, the Potomac Company, and consented to be president. The company hopes to capture the trade of the new Northwest Territory states through the Potomac before New York can open a route through the Hudson—as if failure of both the Ohio and Mississippi companies has not taught him a lesson!"

"I am well aware." Harry's composed expression did not reveal his own keen enthusiasm for Washington's Potomac Company and the general's idea of a system of canals to connect the rivers of the west to the Potomac. He and Washington had first talked of it when the Society of the Cincinnati had met in Philadelphia in 1783, and again last year, after Washington returned from a trip west and invited Harry and Matilda to Mount Vernon while Lafayette visited. Throughout the reunion, the talk had centered on the western lands. Lafayette, then touring America, had already journeyed to the Ohio to watch the signing of the Indian treaties and waxed enthusiastic, declaring, "It is your west, its acquisition and settlement, that will determine the future of these United States." They were the same sentiments Arthur Lee propounded.

"So, you're soon off to New York to represent Virginia in the Congress." Richard Henry pulled back his horse and looked at Harry. "I can understand your reluctance to leave Matilda and Philip, but you will be of great service there. I am proud of you."

"I only wish you would be there, sir," Harry answered affectionately.

Richard Henry had declined re-election to the Congress. "This damned knee of mine," he told Harry by way of explanation. "But I'm looking forward to spending time at Chantilly, teaching Cassius how to fish and playing with my black-eyed little Frank.

"I did want very much to talk with you, Harry, before you left for New York," Richard Henry continued. "I cannot stress how important it is that the right direction is given to our Confederation of States. I sense apathy in the Congress, a vacuum of leadership. Old men retire and new ones take their places; you take mine in New York, Thomas Jefferson has taken Franklin's in France. It's up to you to make our limited confederation work."

Harry flushed. It seemed better not to admit that he, like George Washington, leaned toward the concept of a powerful central government. "I will do my best, sir, I assure you of that."

They parted at the mill. Richard Henry, heading home to Chantilly, saluted Harry. "Remember my words as you now move into the political sphere: man has innate rights, innate dignity. He need not be burdened with unjust rules and the heavy yoke of unthinking authority. As Thomas Paine says, 'That government is best which governs least.' "

Harry watched until Richard Henry had disappeared over the crest of the hill. He had great affection and respect for the man—indeed, was rather fascinated and awed by him, by the Roman head, the thoughtful eyes, the graceful cadences of his speech. This man, as much as any other, had led the thirteen colonies to their independence. But now came the securing and firming of that liberty. As a soldier, Harry knew the importance of structure and central authority.

He turned his horse homeward through the crisp December air, up past the millpond and docks, then past the outbuildings and the circle of slave cottages. How he loved Stratford. He had poured his heart into the plantation, refurbishing buildings neglected during the war years, experimenting with new crops, purchasing additional acreage to straighten out the plantation's zigzag boundaries. But a term in the State Assembly in Richmond had whetted an appetite for wider involvement in politics, both Virginia's and the nation's.

Harry sighed with satisfaction. The past four years had been happy ones, filled for the most part with love and laughter and many visits from old comrades of the legion on their way home from the Carolinas. Their first son, Nathaniel Greene Lee, died after only a few months of life, but a second, Philip Ludwell, was now a healthy toddler.

As he strode into the great hall, Matilda looked up from the piano. He bent down to nuzzle his face in the crease of her neck.

"Mm . . . cold," she said. "How I shall miss that caress when you go to New York." She closed the keyboard with a sad little gesture and rose to embrace Harry.

Winding her shawl more tightly around her delicate shoulders and enveloping her with his arms, he held her close. "It is only for a few months, my darling. In the spring, the very moment the roads dry and you have put some weight on these fine bones of yours, I shall send for you. I told Will West to give you a milk pudding every day and lots of beef broth."

She wrinkled her nose. "What did he say?"

"He said, 'I been takin' care of Miss Matilda longer than you have. I can figger out what's good for her!'"

Matilda laughed and put her head on Harry's shoulder. "New York! I cannot imagine not being at Stratford. I have never been away from the Neck . . . can you imagine? You are married to a provincial, Harry!"

He ran his finger gently down her forehead and the bridge of her nose, across her lips and chin. "I am married to a lady who enchants and delights me afresh every day, and I cannot truly be happy without you at my side."

Philadelphia, 1786

Nancy Shippen Livingston waited anxiously at the front windows of Shippen House for the Lee carriage to come down Fourth Street. She had been pacing up and down the parlor for so long that old Dr. Shippen, her grandfather, had finally excused himself; the rustle of her striped silk skirt was setting his teeth on edge.

I shall die if they don't come soon, thought Nancy. Ah, there it was! The handsome carriage, bearing the Lee crest of squirrel and acorn, was coming around the corner. Harry Lee was quickly out of the carriage, his small son in his arms. Now Matilda Lee's slender, graceful form emerged. She turned and drew out a little girl with a headful of soft brown ringlets, dressed in a blue velvet cape. "Oh, Lord, thank you, thank you, thank you!" Nancy uttered as she flew out the front door and down the white marble steps to scoop up her beloved five-year-old daughter, Peggy.

"I live for her visits," Nancy told Matilda after dinner as they sat in the parlor by the fire. "You could never know how I suffer when she is taken away from me. I worry constantly whether she is all right. I wonder, what does she wear today, has she grown a bit taller, did she lose another tooth, does she miss me. Matilda, it is as if time stops when she is with the Livingstons."

"My dear Nancy, I truly understand how you suffer! I know my circumstance is entirely different, but I have so dreadfully missed my own Lucy. New York was wonderfully entertaining, and we made many friends, but always in my mind were thoughts of Lucy in Alexandria with my mother. I count the hours until we are reunited."

Nancy's dark eyes welled with tears. "When you arrive, your daughter will again be yours. I can only see Peggy now and then, and she can never be truly mine! A woman has nothing when she leaves her husband, even for just reasons, and, Matilda, I *had* to leave him. He was so awful! You cannot imagine!"

Matilda's heart went out to this cousin whom life had served so cruelly. Nancy spent her days managing the Philadelphia house for her father and brother and visiting her mother, Alice, who, more deeply sunk in melancholia, now lived at a country house in Bethlehem, where she spent her hours alone with her Bible. Henry Livingston had been an abusive husband, so abusive that Nancy had fled the New York estate with her daughter, then seventeen months old. Recognizing that the baby, heiress to the Livingston fortune, must be returned to her father's family, Dr. Shippen had been forced by law to take the little girl from his daughter's arms and return her to her paternal grandmother in New York. Mrs. Livingston had kindly allowed this visit, sternly warning that her son must not find out or he would come and snatch the child away.

Nancy moved to rearrange the firescreen. "I think again and again, Matilda, how it might have been if I had married ... someone else."

"Have you seen your old friend, Louis Otto, since you returned to Philadelphia?" Matilda probed gently.

For a long moment the petite, dark-eyed Nancy did not answer. Then, tearfully, she looked up at Matilda. "Of course. How could we not, since we move in the same society? We talk, sometimes we write letters, but it ends there. Oh, Matilda, I am twenty-three years old and I have nothing to call my own—no husband, no children, no home. Papa is saddled with debts from the war and problems brought on by his trial, and there seems little improvement in Mother."

"You are always welcome at Stratford Hall," Matilda said compassionately. "My Harry is the most generous man in the world, and if he knew you needed a haven, he would insist upon it."

"Here are our lovely ladies." Arthur Lee was the first through the door. How cheering he always is, thought Matilda, throwing a quick smile to her bachelor uncle, who was visiting from New York.

Harry followed, deeply engrossed in conversation with Will Shippen. "What really angers me is that Jemmy Madison has been chosen to take my place in the National Congress. On every issue his feelings are similar to mine, only he has been far more circumspect and careful not to trumpet his opposition to the Mississippi River clause in our treaty with Spain. The Virginia Assembly was shortsighted in insisting that Spain concede navigation rights on the Mississippi. While it will help Virginians in the Kentucky county and other westerners to get their furs and produce to market, it might also encourage them to stand independent and separate themselves from the eastern states' confederation. The thirteen eastern states are financially strapped, and to consolidate trade with the western territories is critically important for the future of the confederation. We need the west if the confederation is to survive." Harry's face flashed with indignation.

"My dear friend, I understand fully—more than most—your resentment at not being reappointed," Will Shippen said wearily, taking a decanter of port and a tray of small glasses from the tall cherry cupboard. "Perhaps it is because we human beings are complex that politics becomes so paradoxical! Consider, for example, my friend and your kinsman, Dr. Arthur Lee, to whom I now offer a glass of the world's finest port." With a flourish he handed Arthur his glass. "Here is a man who initiated the battle for independence against England, then led the fight to ratify the peace treaty with that same country, a man who has always been quick to proclaim his scorn for France's opulent monarchy, yet whose proudest possession is a diamond-encrusted snuffbox presented to him by the King of France!"

Arthur was at the moment holding in the palm of his hand that very snuffbox, a miniature of Louis XVI emblazoned on the gold enameled cover. "*Touché*, my dear Dr. Shippen," he said ruefully, "and for a further paradox, one might point out I am also a man captivated and enchanted by the opposite sex and yet, sad to say, have no damsel to call my own."

"Only because you are so impossibly hard to please," Matilda rejoined spiritedly. "The lady of your dreams is unimaginably beautiful, brilliant in conversation, a good economist, noble in nature, and enchanting in the boudoir! No such creature exists!"

"Not true!" Arthur objected, bending over to kiss her cheek. "They do exist, but alas, they have turned out to be my nieces Matilda and Nancy, whom I adore—but only properly, as an uncle should."

Harry would not be deflected from politics. "Did you know that Virginia—urged on by Madison and Hamilton—calls for a thirteen-state convention, which will offer a forum for settling trade differences, and perhaps revising the Articles of Confederation?"

"It's just Hamilton's clever ruse to try to form a stronger central government!" Arthur exploded.

"Please, hold any objections to the idea!" Harry said quickly. "I know well that your brother Colonel Richard Henry and many others warn that by strengthening the powers of our confederation we risk losing the liberties of the individual states. But it is a risk we must take. I am reminded of Ben Franklin's words before the Revolution: If we don't hang together, surely we shall all hang separately."

"I must agree totally," said Will Shippen.

"I concede the Confederation must be given powers to raise revenue," Arthur allowed. "I serve on the Board of Treasury, and no one knows better than I how empty our national purse is—not that we have ever had it otherwise! Do you realize that when news of the Yorktown victory reached Congress in '81, its members were forced to reach into their own pockets for coinage to pay the messenger? Our national treasury was empty of all but dust!"

Nancy, moving out of the candlelight to sit in the shadows of the sofa, laughed in amusement.

"It is only amusing over a glass of port in the drawing room," Harry said, softening his words with a smile at Nancy. "Our situation becomes desperate when we try to deal and negotiate with other strong nations. Some power must be given to a common commander, if you will, and in my opinion that commander should take the form of a strong legislature. Shays's Rebellion in Massachusetts brings home the ineffectiveness of our Congress. I think my friend Alexander Hamilton puts it very well: 'A want of power in Congress makes the government fit neither for war nor for peace.'"

"Uncle Arthur may be aware of the Confederation's need for revenue," Matilda said later that evening as she handed Harry her silver-backed brush, "but I'll wager he is every bit as fearful of 'rule by few' as is Uncle Richard Henry. They are both Republicans, fearful of the aristocracy."

"Which is yet another paradox," said Harry, brushing out her long brown hair with gentle strokes, "for they are two of the most naturally aristocratic men I have ever known."

The Lee carriage stood ready to depart for Virginia early the next morning while Matilda kissed Nancy good-bye. "I shall think of you and little Peggy often. And give my love to my dear aunt Alice. I hope her spirits rise."

Nancy forced herself to be cheerful. "I shall be sure to tell her about Uncle Richard Henry's being put up for governor last year, then losing to Edmund Randolph, and she will rejoice to hear that William's little girls, Portia and Cornelia, are safe and sound with Becky and Frank at Menokin. News of Virginia will bring a smile to her face."

As their carriage lumbered across the wintry Pennsylvania countryside,

Matilda regarded her husband's strong, sensitive profile. She had never known a man so essentially honorable, so generous to and trusting of those he loved and admired. Harry would give his last coin to a friend—indeed, she had seen him share generously with military companions and friends in need. It was a quality she admired, but one had to keep watch on such generosity for practicality's sake!

The carriage lurched as it rounded a steep turn in the road, and Matilda felt a sharp pain stab her shoulders. She was pregnant again, which both pleased and scared her. With every pregnancy, she grew more vulnerable to dizziness and strange, unaccountable pains.

Dear Lord, she wondered silently, is there any way to stop having babies. "Harry," she whispered to her husband, "take me home as quickly as you can. Please, just take me home as fast as we can safely travel. . . ."

The carriage lumbered on, crossing the icy fords and careening through the stark winter forests of Delaware and Maryland. A recent snowstorm had left the post road barely passable, but the horses managed to flounder through.

"You are trembling. Stay close against my heart, I shall keep you warm," Harry said softly as they passed through the village of Annapolis, its candlelit windows flickering forlornly in the December dusk.

Three long, miserable weeks after leaving Philadelphia, they reached the frozen north banks of the Potomac at midnight. Alexandria lay just across the broad black stretch of water. Should they risk the ferry in the darkness or stay the night in Georgetown, on the Maryland side?

"Please try it, Harry," Matilda begged. "I am so tired of ordinaries. I want to sleep in my mother's house. I want to hold my Lucy in my arms tonight."

He shuddered. The river was thick with treacherous ice floes, its currents swift and deep. He paid the reluctant waterman a double fee to ferry them over. Was this the same crossing where George Mason's father had lost his life? Harry wondered as he stood on the raft, braced against the carriage while the awkward boat slowly surged across the river.

"How does it look, Nat?" he asked anxiously; the black man was moving past him to balance the other side of the raft.

"I trust the Lord," Nat murmured quietly. "We'll sleep tonight in Virginia. I is as set upon it as Miss Matilda."

After four terrifying hours at the mercy of the river, the boat finally bumped into the dark Virginia shoreline. Harry climbed into the coach to reassure an exhausted Matilda. "We are home, my darling. At last we're in Virginia."

The Tidewater, 1787

"I'm both pleased and surprised—honored, in fact," Richard Henry told Anne and Arthur, when he learned he was one of seven Virginians chosen to attend the Philadelphia convention to revise the Articles of Confederation. "Especially considering my reluctance to tamper with them. To be honest, I am reconciled to certain changes. However, I have made up my mind *not* to accept the position offered me in the delegation," Richard Henry informed them. "I've also received an appointment to return to the Congress, and I think it unwise that the same men should review in New York work they did earlier in Philadelphia."

"Rest assured," Arthur interjected, "with George Mason in the delegation, your conservative viewpoint will be well represented in Philadelphia."

The youngest Lee, who had just arrived at Chantilly, was bursting with news. "I journeyed down by way of Gunston Hall and Mount Vernon." He moved restlessly to adjust the weights on the tall walnut long-case clock. "General Washington says Patrick Henry also refuses to join the delegation to Philadelphia, mainly because he fears it is a danger to states' rights. Or, as he so succinctly puts it, 'I smell a rat.'"

Anne looked up from her needlework. "And what of the general? Will he go?"

"He says no." Arthur paced back and forth. "He seemed to suffer rather badly with his rheumatism, and he is depressed over the death of his brother Jack at Bushfield—died from gout of the head, he said."

The death of their good friend and neighbor John Augustine Washington had sorrowed the family at Chantilly. Their daughter Hannah planned to wed Corbin Washington, a son of Bushfield, that summer.

"Is the general not sympathetic with the aims of the convention?" Anne asked.

"Oh, he's sympathetic, all right," Arthur said, looking up quickly. "But his old chief of artillery, Henry Knox, has recommended that he not attend, for the outcome looks quite dubious. Knox says it lacks the support of major political figures."

Richard Henry winced. "Many think I do not sympathize with reforming the Articles, but that is not entirely true. I realize our confederation has become inefficient and ineffectual. Without the common bond of a war, the states simply won't support it. I am reconciled to the idea that our government should be both legislative and executive, with its legislature taking precedence over the state legislatures in certain areas—for example, commerce and trade. And certainly defense," he added dryly.

"Well, I remain ambivalent!" Arthur said ruefully. "I would like to see the Articles of Confederation changed as little as possible. I'm not so certain it's the lack of war that impedes our unity as much as the lack of money. Indeed, I recently suggested to John Wilkes that if England would loan us two million pounds, she would totally redeem herself in many eyes and help us through our present troubled times!"

"Likely chance of that!" said Richard Henry.

"My darling, it has been so lovely having you home these months," Anne murmured later as they walked arm in arm in the garden. "I worry that you will fall again into ill health if you travel north to the Congress. Leave it to Harry Lee to represent our family. I understand he has consented to go back to the Congress in New York to replace Madison, who will attend the Philadelphia convention."

Richard Henry did not answer, only squeezed his wife's arm in reply. While he admired Harry, he was aware of much divergence in their opinions. The young man was bold, expansive in thought, not above taking a risk—in business, in politics, or in government. Perhaps, thought Richard Henry, when one grows as old as I, one learns not to be so ambitious and trusting.

Philadelphia, 1787

Two months later, on the final day of June, Richard Henry sat down and penned a long letter to Anne while stopping over in Philadelphia en route to New York:

My Dearest Anne,

Your prophecy was correct in that I have reached this city much fatigued by the heat and tiresomeness of the journey.

You will be interested in the news of this Constitutional Convention, which meets here in the Pennsylvania State House:

As you may have heard, General Washington changed his mind and decided to attend. His arrival in town was heralded by the firing of cannons and ringing of bells. He was, of course, elected president of the convention, which is closed to the public and whose members are sworn to secrecy concerning its proceedings. I was told that our good George professed his "want of qualifications" upon accepting the presiding chair and spoke with some reserve, but he was, as always, well received. He stays at the handsome, indeed lavish, home of Robert Morris in this city.

The Virginia delegation is, along with Pennsylvania's, the largest and contains, besides General Washington, Governor E. Randolph, James Madison,

George Mason, Judge Blair, George Wythe, and a Mr. McClugg. They have opened the session with fifteen resolves ready to present to the assemblage, some based, no doubt, on the thinking of Mr. Jefferson in Paris, who has sent Mr. Madison no end of books on government. It is my understanding and acceptable to me that a new government will emerge from this meeting—one not unlike that provided by the British Constitution, with an executive and a legislature of two houses. I have come to accept that this departure from simple democracy is necessary if we are to have a stable government in North America —but I pray God that sane heads will prevail and that we have learned from the mistakes of government in the past.

The proceedings are, as I say, held in the strictest secrecy, but James Madison has pledged to keep copious notes.

I am on to New York in the morning, where it is my understanding Harry Lee will join me next week. Please give my love to the family at Stratford and tell Matilda of my relief that she has come through her lying-in without complications. I will present my compliments to the father on the birth of another son when we meet in New York.

To you goes my love and devotion,

Richard Henry Lee

Post Script: It has been raining in Philadelphia since I arrived. I saw old Mr. Franklin carried by his "sedan chair"—an effect he brought from Paris. The bells of Christ Church are ringing. I've no doubt you remember their sweet melody.

New York, 1787

A fine, strapping son, the fourth Henry Lee to be born in the Northern Neck of Virginia, the fourth to bear that name! The thought consoled Harry: this past September his father had died quietly after a brief illness. Henry Lee left a comfortable estate, the majority of which had gone to his younger sons: to Charles, now a lawyer working part-time for George Washington; to Richard Bland, who had graduated from the College of William and Mary and now sat in the Virginia Assembly; and to Edmund and Theodorick, still boys. Harry received only a small portion of the land and slaves, for he was already master of the extensive lands of Stratford Hall and was heir to the family plantation, Lee Hall, the property of his bachelor uncle, Squire Richard.

Settling into familiar New York lodgings, Harry now turned his attention to the Congress. This fall, their main business would be to set up a workable government for the burgeoning Northwest Territory, but even more fascinating was the new Constitution proposed by the Philadelphia Convention. From the beginning he was steadfastly committed to this document, though it was assuredly a patchwork of compromises. Slavery as always was an issue. George Mason had passionately urged that the slave trade be immediately done away with under this new Constitution, but Georgia and the Carolinas, joined by the New England states, successfully defeated his motion, stipulating that the practice could not be prohibited before 1808. Conflict then arose over how to count the slave population in determining the number of congressmen a state would have. In the end, they agreed that three-fifths of the slaves would be counted.

But the real bone of contention, the one that nearly wrecked the convention, was how to protect the interests of both large and small states. Finally, the Virginia Plan, which favored the large states, was melded with the New Jersey Plan, which favored the small, under a brilliant compromise suggested by Roger Sherman of Connecticut. The document was signed by the delegates in September and then sent on to the states for their individual ratification. Once nine states had approved, the new government could be formed. Although Alexander Hamilton had conceived the document and Jemmy Madison had midwifed it with his astute negotiations and compromises, the embryonic Constitution was still a sickly infant, not at all certain to survive.

Harry's military mind was pleased that the new Constitution offered a strong federal government, supreme within a carefully defined sphere. He didn't agree with his friend Hamilton, who, discouraged and too close to the finished product to see its merits, termed it "weak and worthless fabric." Nor did he agree with George Mason and Edmund Randolph, who, disgruntled by the document's lack of a Bill of Rights and the ceding of many states' rights, had departed for Virginia without signing it.

The Tidewater, 1788

In early June, Harry, Matilda, and baby Henry returned to Virginia. Harry had been elected a delegate to the Virginia Convention called to discuss the proposed Constitution, and would soon go to Richmond.

"I am fiercely committed to ratification," he told Matilda as they walked through the rose gardens of Stratford, "though your uncle Richard Henry counsels patience. He would have us call a state convention to propose new amendments, which would then have to be reported back to a new federal convention and woven into a new version. He's trying to negotiate it to death. He wants to weave it into a web, as he calls it!"

"I know," Matilda said with a sigh. "I've heard him declare again and again, 'A web must be produced fit for freemen to wear.' You must admit, Harry, few speak as poetically and eloquently as my uncle."

"I only wish that he were speaking in behalf of ratification rather than against it. Patience! Why, if we wait too long, we may not have any freemen to wear that web!" Harry bent down to cut a rose and, breaking off its thorns, lovingly tucked it into the luxuriant brown sweep of Matilda's hair. "Your uncle was among the first chosen to attend the convention, but he refuses to go, says it's his health, but I think it's principle. Well, it matters not whether he attends! He wields much influence through his letters and pamphlets, which are well read." Harry stared off into the twilight. "Perhaps if I were to talk with him again."

Matilda rested her hand on his arm. "No, don't try," she cautioned softly. "His mind is set. He has not condemned the proposed Constitution. He sees much good in it, but he simply feels without a Bill of Rights it does not preserve the rights of the people."

"There are three positions on this question, Matilda. One group is totally opposed to ratification—that is, until in their eyes the Constitution is made perfect with a Bill of Rights! In that group are George Mason, Patrick Henry, and Uncle Richard Henry. The next sees flaws, but would rather accept it than do without. Jemmy Madison and Alexander Hamilton fall there. And the third group is convinced of the Constitution's excellence, and is strongly for ratification. I join General Washington in that group."

"So you leave me to do political battle in Richmond next month." Matilda leaned her shoulder against his as they walked. "I pray you won't be gone long. I feel so much better, stronger, when we are together."

He bent his head to smell the flower in her hair. "I think of you constantly whenever I am away." Stopping suddenly, he took her chin gently in his hand. "Matilda, something wears on my mind. Perhaps we should not have any more children, at least not for a while. With every birth, your strength ebbs. I live in terror that I might lose you." He pulled her into his arms. "I could not bear it should anything happen to you. I love you so much."

Matilda pulled back from his embrace to look into his eyes. "How kind you are to offer, for my sake, to give up . . . But, could we bear living together, loving each other, and yet not . . . ?"

The scent of roses seemed to be everywhere, flaming his senses. He buried his face in her neck.

Richmond smoldered in the June heat as Harry stabled his horse behind the Swan Tavern and strode down Broad Street toward the new academy on

Shockoe Hill, the meeting place of the 1788 Virginia Convention. As Matilda had predicted, he was ready to do battle!

Easing himself into the back of the wooden building already packed with delegates and spectators, he looked over the heads of the throng and sighted the Convention president, Edmund Pendleton, on his pillow-bolstered chair. The lawyer had been thrown from his horse in 1777, and since that time had been unable to stand or walk without help. But his mind was as keen as ever. Harry was thankful that Pendleton had declared himself an advocate of ratification: he could be an asset. James Madison, discreetly dressed in a dark coat with white ruff, sat quietly in his chair. He had written brilliantly in favor of ratification in *The Federalist*. They and George Wythe, perhaps even John Marshall, would be the major spokesmen for ratification.

Against ratification were posed two strong men of Virginia—the beloved Patrick Henry, his emotional oratory enough to bring tears to any man's eyes; and George Mason, a man capable of splendid logic and impressive presentation. Aligned with them were former Governor Benjamin Harrison, Congressman James Monroe, and, in absentia, Richard Henry Lee.

Harry stirred restlessly in his chair. Were they going to dally all day with these preliminaries? "Mr. President." He was on his feet, speaking clearly but with confidence. Should they not move to the matter of prime importance, the ratification of the Federal Constitution prepared by the Philadelphia Convention?

A quick murmur swept the room, necks strained. Word spread through the crowd: it was Washington's protégé, the young cavalry hero of the Southern Campaign, who spoke.

"Mr. President," George Mason's firm voice cut into the crescendo of excitement, "no man in this Convention is more averse to taking up the time of the Convention than I; but I am equally against hurrying them precipitately into any measure."

Harry turned to meet Mason's gaze. So the strategy was to delay. It was to be a duel of thoughts, of persuasion, to be fought with elaborate punctilio and the courtesy to which they were bred, but nonetheless a duel to the finish.

The lanky, charismatic Patrick Henry informed the crowded hall he would take the proposed Constitution apart, phrase by phrase, beginning with the first sentence: "We the people," he intoned with scorn in his voice. "Why not 'We the states?'"

Once started, Patrick Henry could not be stopped. It was not until the next afternoon that Harry Lee was able to interrupt his oratory and take the floor. "What is the esteemed Mr. Henry so fearful of?" Harry asked. "Why does a man of such admirable talents and reputation envision 'horrors' and speak of 'apprehensions,' instead of looking carefully at the question of ratification based on its merits?"

That evening Harry relaxed with James Madison over a mug of ale at the Swan. "Can you tell me," Harry asked with controlled anger, "why when men are young they are brave and trust the future, but when they are old they are simpering cowards? Where are the firebrands of the Revolution? In particular, where is Richard Henry Lee, once so willing to risk all for independence?"

Madison studied the table, stained with white rings. "You're not being entirely fair, Harry," he remonstrated. "Why, look at Francis Lightfoot. He did not attend the convention, yet he strongly favors ratification. And there is the general watching from the sidelines at Mount Vernon. We are well aware of his enthusiasm for our Constitution. It shall come about, Harry; the Constitution will be ratified. We are ready to take hold of our destiny."

Take hold of one's destiny . . . Harry lay in his narrow bed upstairs in the Swan thinking about Madison's words. Indeed, there was every reason to be optimistic about the future! A nation was being formed, and he was one of its shapers. The nation would surge west—a movement in which he had his own stake. Spurred by General Washington's plans to develop the Potomac Canal from the Great Falls of the Potomac through to the Allegheny Mountains, Harry had already purchased land at the locks of the Great Falls—five hundred acres, bought from the Fairfax estate for four thousand pounds and an annual rent of one hundred and fifty pounds sterling.

Hadn't Thomas Lee, the builder of Stratford Hall, prophesied that a splendid city would one day rise at the fall line of the Potomac? Matilda worried that he had gone too deeply into debt to buy the land at the falls, but someday it would be worth double his investment. Washington was convinced that Lee's plans to establish a town there would meet with outstanding success. It would be a pretty, prosperous town, which he would name Matildaville. Dreaming of its prospects, Harry fell quickly into a deep slumber.

The Virginia debates continued for days. Patrick Henry's oratory roared on, its tide beaten back now and then by voices on the other side, among them the low, almost expressionless one of Jemmy Madison, who rose, his hat in his hand, his notes in his hat, to offer a carefully constructed rebuttal.

Once more, Harry stood to speak with heartfelt emotion, his years as a soldier heavy on his mind: ". . . from the terms in which some of the Northern States were spoken of, one would have thought that the love of an American was in some degree criminal, as being incompatible with a proper degree of affection for a Virginian. The people of America, sir, are one people. I love the people of the north, not because they have adopted the Constitution, but because I fought with them as my countrymen and because I consider them as such. Does it follow that I have forgotten my attachment to my native state? In all local matters I shall be a Virginian; in those of a general nature, I shall not forget that I am an American."

Then the word came. On the afternoon of June 24, nine states had, in one manner or another, ratified the Constitution; it was now binding upon the people of the United States. Tension filled the air as the delegates met to vote whether Virginia would also enter the federal government. Nowhere else had the Constitution been so thoroughly taken apart and debated as in the hot, still air of the academy on Shockoe Hill. Today the tally would be taken. Henry knew in his heart that without Virginia, the new nation could never flourish.

Alexandria, 1789

It seemed to Matilda Lee that she could never quite get hold of her life, filled as it was with enormous happiness rent by jagged pains. Perhaps, she rationalized, her longing to be home again and with her babies made her feel so melancholy. She had been in New York since last fall, while Harry finished out his term in Congress.

She now sat in a pale wash of sunshine in the handsome parlor of the Fendall house, sipping tea with her mother while Harry and Madison inspected the lands at the Great Falls. Inspired by Harry's enthusiasm and with George Washington's tacit approval, Jemmy Madison had recently joined the Potomac enterprise. There was, however, a disturbing problem: though offers to buy lots in Harry's embryonic town of Matildaville were flowing in, they could not be sold. The Great Falls site was part of the ancient Fairfax Proprietary, which had in 1785 been confiscated by the Virginia commonwealth. The ratification of the Constitution last summer had made the unpaid Fairfax quitrents recoverable in the new federal courts. Old Lord Fairfax's heir, Bryan Fairfax (younger brother of George William Fairfax), had forced Harry to abstain from the sale of the five hundred acres he had purchased until the delinquent quitrents—a small fortune—were paid. Harry and Jemmy Madison were not discouraged—"It will all be worked out by the new government," Harry insisted. But Matilda's practical nature told her that it was not going to be that simple, and with so much invested, she was uneasy.

"You look perturbed, my darling." Elizabeth Fendall put down her teacup and looked pensively at her daughter. "Perhaps you are still weary from your long journey from New York."

"No, no." Matilda quickly shook her head. "Actually, I was wondering when we would see our good friends Alexander and Betsy Hamilton again," she continued, recovering her composure. "Rumors are he will join General Washington's government." Matilda's pretty face broke into a smile. "I keep forgetting, I should say 'President' rather than 'General.' "

"Not until he is sworn in next month. Till then, 'tis perfectly proper to say 'General.' Speaking of your friend Mr. Hamilton, is it true . . . ? Well, it is just that I've heard rumors . . ."

Matilda nodded. "It *is* true that Mr. Hamilton was born the bastard son of a wealthy Scottish trader in the West Indies. He's a most handsome man, loaded with charm, and from somewhere, Mother, he inherited a marvelous mind. Harry and I are deeply fond of him."

Elizabeth smiled. "Your father would not have accepted Hamilton's birth, but then, things are becoming so democratic these days." She looked at the mantel clock. "Harry and Mr. Madison will be here for dinner, won't they?" she inquired. "I planned a little music and refreshment tonight. Does that suit you?"

Matilda nodded with pleasure. "They were to meet Harry's younger brother at the Great Falls. Richard Bland is developing the property his father left him, west of the falls. I have a funny story to relate. He tells me he will call his house Sully when it is done. 'What if your wife wished to choose the name?' I asked him. 'Well,' he said with audacity, 'then I shall choose a wife who likes the name Sully.' " She laughed.

"Oh, I do hope that young man will join us for dinner, too. I've always liked Richard Bland, and Charles as well. Charles and Nancy are invited tonight also, along with Flora and Ludwell." Harry's brother Charles had wed Nancy of Chantilly the month before, drawing the family knot tighter still, for Matilda's sister, Flora, had earlier wed Ludwell Lee of Chantilly.

"It seems the whole world wishes to live in Alexandria these days," Elizabeth Fendall sighed. "I wish you and Harry weren't so far away at Stratford Hall. You might consider . . ."

"Leaving Stratford Hall?" Matilda was horrified. "Why, Stratford is our haven, our castle. I cannot imagine living anywhere else. In fact"— Matilda leaned forward in her chair, her taffeta skirt rustling around her— "when I die, I think I shall become a spirit that rides the winds in the treetops at Stratford, or a bright-yellow butterfly dancing in the tall grasses of its meadows, or a sweet-smelling larkspur in my lovely gardens. That would be heaven!"

* * *

Harry rode in at dusk, ruddy-faced and laughing, flanked by his handsome younger brother Richard Bland and Jemmy Madison, both men newly elected to the Congress, the first to meet under the Federal Constitution.

"I rather had my eye on a Senate seat," Madison confided to Matilda when she congratulated him, "but your uncle Richard Henry is far more deserving. He has never failed to serve Virginia with honor!" It was a graceful speech for a pro-constitutionalist to make about an anti-Federalist. Richard Henry Lee was one of the few who had won seats in the new United States Senate, Sam Adams of Massachusetts having been defeated.

"Jemmy is a darling fellow. One just has to get to know him," Matilda admitted in the bedroom as she helped Harry adjust the white ruffles at his neck. "I used to think him terribly dry and somehow old beyond his years, but now that I have got to know him, I like him very very much!"

Harry bent to see himself in the glass as he tied his thick, gold-streaked hair into a queue. "That little sliver of soap is a capital fellow, full of ideas! If indeed we are forced to raise the money for the unpaid Fairfax quitrents, it is his idea that we send drawings of the canal and our prospective town to Tom Jefferson in Paris. Madison is certain Jefferson can find foreign investors who will lend us the money to pay off Fairfax and— Matilda!" Harry reached out and grabbed her arm. "What's the matter? You are trembling again! Dear God, Matilda, let me call your mother."

"No." She reached out a weak hand to stop him. "I'll be fine in a moment. Just let me rest. It is one of my spells . . . all burning and tingling. I've had them a thousand times. It will pass."

An hour later, Matilda sat down at the piano to play a spirited piece by Scarlatti as if nothing had ever occurred. Still, Harry could not help feeling alarmed. He would take her home to Stratford. She would be all right, he was certain of it. He was disappointed they were leaving so soon, for he had hoped to remain in Alexandria until Washington passed through next month on his way north to New York for his inauguration as president. A celebration was planned in the President-elect's honor at Alexandria's Wise's Tavern. Mayor Ramsey had asked Harry to compose the city's farewell address, and he had poured his love and admiration for the general into it. But he would leave it with the mayor to deliver. Nothing mattered as much as getting Matilda home.

The Tidewater, 1789

May turned unseasonably rainy and chillingly cold. Harry instructed Will West to keep the fire burning at all times in the east wing, the parlor, the dining room, the "mother's room," and the nursery. "She's slipping again, Will," he murmured in fright to the old slave. "I don't know what to do but send to Alexandria for her mother."

But a nightmare had begun. Sick herself, Elizabeth Fendall could not travel by coach, so she set sail down the Potomac for Stratford Hall. Scarcely had the boat put in at Baltimore when she died. Matilda was devastated.

The summer of 1789 was disastrous for the plantation. Herds of cattle perished from some unknown malady, and the crops languished and withered in the drought-stricken fields. Harry chafed under his misfortune, for he was not a planter, never had been! He was a soldier, a politician, a thinker.

Secretly Harry yearned to be in New York, to be one of those challenged with reconciling authority with liberty. But nothing would induce him to leave Matilda until she recovered. He had been elected to the Virginia Assembly, and he had his business affairs at Matildaville to straighten out. Those would offer more than enough to absorb his throbbing energies.

He did not tarry long at the fall Assembly session in Richmond, but hurried home, elated to find that Matilda had again rallied. She waited for him in the children's nursery, looking like a beautiful child herself, as the three little ones played around her knees.

"I have missed you with every bone in my body," he murmured as he buried his face in her soft flowing hair. "I have thought of you every hour, every second that I have been away."

"And I thought only of you." She drank in his image, the steady, clear dark eyes that had always transfixed her, the strong, even features, but most of all, his vitality. "I knew I would feel well again by the time you came home!" She twined her arms exuberantly around his neck. "And we shall have the most marvelous Christmas!"

On Christmas afternoon the snow began to fall, and by dusk the world had become a fairyland, hushed and beautiful. When the children, tired from the excitement of the musicians and jugglers, were led off to bed, Harry stood with Matilda in his arms, looking out over the silhouette of trees and the blanket of white that lay on the wide back lawn. "You tremble, darling," he said, tightening his arms about her. "Has today been too much for you?"

"Oh, no." Matilda placed her radiant cheek next to his. "It was just the way I wanted it to be, everyone happy, you and I together at Stratford. I was just wishing time could stand still and that we could always stay like this, frozen somehow in this lovely moment! Sometimes I have this terrible feeling, Harry." She looked frightened.

He hushed her mouth with his.

The Tidewater, 1790

By mid-February, Matilda found she was again pregnant. It was a child conceived in love, and she rejoiced in the thought of giving Harry another son or daughter. If only it weren't for those pains! She let Harry bundle her up for a visit to the medicinal springs in the western part of the state, and then tried to pretend that the waters had helped, but the journey had only exhausted what little strength she had. By May, she had taken to the big bed in the mother's room.

"I need only three thousand pounds to pay off Bryan Fairfax's quitrents for Matildaville." Harry sat by her bed in the cool of a summer evening. "I had put a great measure of hope on Mr. Jefferson to raise the monies in France for the Great Falls venture, but France now rocks with its own revolution. Jefferson has little on his mind but the sorrow of leaving that country, which he has grown to love. Did I tell you he will become Washington's secretary of state?" Harry fanned Matilda with a large dried palmetto leaf. "Hamilton at Treasury and Jefferson at State . . . an interesting pair. They are both brilliant, but can they work together? It is easy to be friends joined in opposition to tyranny, but can friends share power? At any rate"— he changed the subject—"I have been giving a great deal of thought to our project at the Falls, my darling. Everyone who visits becomes as excited as I. Never have I been more certain that it will succeed, particularly now that our nation's capital is to be located on the Potomac."

Matilda watched the intensity flickering in her husband's face. "Is it definite, then?" Harry had told her that there was great pressure in the Congress to have the capital somewhere on the Susquehanna, closer to the commercial centers of Baltimore, New York, and Philadelphia.

"The site has been fixed on the Potomac as a compromise between northern and southern interests. But it is a dear price we pay." A shade of anger tinged his voice. "The keystone of Hamilton's treasury program rests on the national government's assuming the states' war debts, thereby binding state creditors to the national interest. But Virginia has already wiped out the larger part of her state debts." He got to his feet and began to roam around the room. "It seems damned unfair that she can be taxed to assume the debts of the other states! Richard Bland writes me that he was invited to dine with Hamilton and Jefferson, each representing one section of the country. They presented him with a compromise: the southern congressional votes for the Assumption Act would be exchanged for enough northern votes to secure passage of the Residence Act, by which President Washington may choose whatever site he wishes for the permanent seat of government. The deal was made. So you can be certain, my dearest, that spot will be on the Potomac!"

He bent over her bed again to stroke her head gently. "That is why it is so important that we free our land from the Fairfax lien and get on with Matildaville. Bryan Fairfax has consented to our building, so already a warehouse and a storehouse are going up. But lots must be sold, our town established!"

Matilda pulled herself up a little higher in bed. "Wherever will you get the money, Harry? You have already pledged every bit of capital you have, you have sold off land, you've—"

"Hear, hear, I have a marvelous scheme. We can mortgage our lands—all of them, if we have to—Stratford, the lands in Berkeley County, plus the twelve thousand acres of the Sugarland estate in Loudoun and our thousand acres at the Little Falls."

"Mortgage?" Matilda let the word sink in slowly. "Harry, what if the canal to the west should not prove successful? What if your Matildaville should not flourish?"

He stood in the window embrasure and looked out into the gathering dusk. "But it won't fail. It can't! I have every confidence. Matilda, I must do this. Can't you understand?"

For a long time she lay still after he had left the room to hear the children's bedtime prayers. She could understand how a man as farsighted and bold and vigorous as Harry Lee was willing to pledge everything to something he believed in. Caution was never one of Harry's virtues! When he believed in or gave his heart to someone or something, it was fearlessly, without reserve. This was one of the things she loved most about him.

Perhaps it was only the weakness, the pain that never quite left, the feeble movements of the child she carried, that made her apprehensive. She closed her eyes against the heavy white pillow. Oh, God, she didn't want to die! Not yet! Not at twenty-seven, with children to be raised and a husband who was so good, yet so very vulnerable. They needed her!

But mortgage Stratford! This was her heritage and her legacy. No, it was *not* to be mortgaged or sold! Never!

She waited until early August, when Ludwell Lee brought her sister Flora down to help when the baby arrived. Matilda put her hand on the easygoing, kindhearted young lawyer's arm. "I must talk with you alone, Ludwell. When Harry goes out to ride the fields tomorrow, please come in to see me."

She would die with the birth of the child; she had known it from the first. But now she must use whatever energies remained to fight for Stratford Hall. She would have Ludwell draw up papers putting the plantation in trust for the children, with Harry granted the use of it for his lifetime. But he would never be able to mortgage it or sell it. It was Lee land, carved out of the wilderness by her grandfather. Now it was her turn to fight for it. Would Harry be willing to sign such an agreement? He had every legal right not to. Tears ran down her cheeks. Oh, Harry, she wanted to cry out to him, I love you so much, I would give you anything. I would give you my very life. But I cannot rest without knowing Stratford Hall is safe.

"This matters to you a great deal?" Harry stood at the foot of the bed in the mother's room holding the deed of trust that Ludwell had drawn up. "Do you think I would not love and protect Stratford Hall? Do you think I would risk our children's legacy?"

Richard Bland, who had arrived that morning from his half-completed house, Sully, above the Great Falls, closed his hand on his brother's arm. "What Matilda is asking is fair and right, Harry."

The paper shook in Harry's hand as he read it. "All the land and property of Henry Lee and Matilda Lee, his wife, situated lying and being in the County of Westmoreland known by the name of the Stratford tract, the upper and lower Cliffs . . ." The words blurred before his eyes. "To be put in trust for their sons, Philip and Henry."

Harry looked at Ludwell and Flora, who stood in the doorway, then at Richard Bland beside him. But no other opinion mattered. Matilda would have what she asked. He strode to the bedside table and seized the pen. How faintly she breathed! He could have gathered her up in one arm's grasp.

With a breaking heart, Harry knelt beside the bed and laid his anguished face close against hers. "I love you, God knows I love you, Matilda Lee."

The hand of the Almighty works in unfathomed ways, the colonel reflected. Matilda's tragic death, along with that of their newborn son in August 1790, plunged Harry into a whirlpool of despair. She had been his first love, his only love, and it was hard for a man so naturally optimistic and ebullient to cope with the loss of his bright, sparkling wife of eight years.

Returning that fall to the Virginia Assembly at Richmond, Harry channeled his restless energies into bolstering the growing state opposition to the fiscal policies of Secretary of the Treasury Alexander Hamilton. Specifically, he opposed Hamilton's plan to fund the national debt.

As the colonel recalled, Virginians held no real opposition to funding the foreign portion of that debt, for to discharge it was a matter of honor. But to combine and fund the domestic debts of the individual states was a horse of another color, and Virginians had good reason to withhold their support. Hamilton's controversial plan plainly ignored the fact that federal assumption of the individual state debts favored northern interests over those of the south.

Not only had Virginia paid off most of her debt by selling her lands in Kentucky, but the greatest percentage of the proceeds from paying the internal national debt would go to citizens living above the Mason-Dixon line, particularly to money speculators. The bulk of the domestic debt had originated during the war years when certificates of indebtedness were issued by the thirteen colonies. Those who received compensation for military services in this manner had often been forced by hard times and scarce money to sell their certificates to speculators for a fraction of their face value. Thus Hamilton's policy would compensate the speculators for the full value of the certificate while the original holder who made the contribution to his country received nothing: many who had risked their lives in battle, Harry Lee's soldiers among them, would be shortchanged.

Along with James Madison, who eloquently denounced the plan, Harry took a leading role in opposing his friend Hamilton's position. By the time spring of 1791 came around, Harry Lee had established himself as an articulate spokesman on behalf of Virginia and a fierce protector of her rights. Yet he still felt restless and dissatisfied. During the happy years of his marriage, his career as a soldier first and foremost had been sublimated to a contented life at Stratford. Now, at thirty-five, he had lost the wife he cherished and around whom he had built his life. When the Assembly dissolved for the summer, he returned to Stratford Hall and his motherless children still lost in despair.

Fear No Winter

1791–1794

The Tidewater, 1791

A brooding silence lay over Stratford Hall, blanketing the great house like a dark spell and filling the empty fields and wild ravines.

"I don' think I ever see a man what grieves more for a woman than Colonel Harry for Miss Matilda." Nat West stood in the doorway of the kitchen house, looking across the pallid gray of the rain-splashed September afternoon. "The colonel, he stay by hisself all day, day after day. Just sits in that parlor looking out at—"

"That vault," finished the cook, who sat shucking oysters. "Ever since he built that brick grave house in the side garden, he jus' keep starin' out the window or walkin' in the garden beside it, thinkin' about Miss Matilda what's lying inside." The old woman shook her head. "Don't seem like Stratford Hall be the same place it useter, when Miss Matilda and Miss Flora were growin' up."

"It's not the same." Nat's voice broke. Nothing was the same any more. Miss Matilda's death had broken old Will West's heart, too, and the old slave had died just a few months after the young mistress he had helped raise. No, nothing at Stratford was the same. Worn out from tobacco, the land put out little corn or wheat, and in the big, somber house Phil, Lucy, and Henry wandered like little lost souls in the high-ceilinged halls.

"You 'member the good times we used to have?" the cook reminisced. "Parties with horse races, and Old Cricket the fiddler come up from Chantilly to play for the young folks to dance all the night long."

Nat nodded, but his attention was diverted by the sound of carriage wheels on the oyster-shell drive. "Mr. Madison's come visitin'! Now, that's for sure gonna brighten Colonel Harry's spirits today."

James Madison, bundled against the rain in a dark cape, his hay-colored hair covered by a beaver hat, was up the wide stone steps of the west entrance before Nat could reach the big house.

"Whatever has brought you down to the lonely wilds of the Neck!" Harry greeted his old school friend. "I would have thought you were preparing to head north to Congress."

"Soon enough, soon enough!" Madison accepted a glass of port. "I shall be most glad when the capital is firmly situated on the Potomac and I don't have to make any more bone-wearying journeys to New York or to Robert Morris's capital in Philadelphia, where the Congress is to move this fall."

Harry laughed at Madison's caustic comment. At the announcement that the permanent capital was to be located on the Potomac, the financier Robert Morris, now senator from Pennsylvania, had threatened to subtract his state's vote from the Assumption Act unless Hamilton agreed to switch the capital from New York to Philadelphia for the ten years it would take to build the capital city. The Southerners uneasily acquiesced, fearful that the canny Pennsylvanians would use the ten years to convince Congress that their city was the better compromise between New York and Virginia.

Harry settled his friend in a comfortable leather chair. "I hope you have not come to tell me we are having problems with the newspaper!"

For almost a year, Harry and Jemmy Madison had been working to set up an anti-Hamiltonian newspaper to rival the pro-Hamilton *Gazette of the United States*. At Harry's suggestion, Philip Freneau, a renowned poet and Lee and Madison's fellow student at Princeton, had been invited to Philadelphia by Secretary of State Jefferson, ostensibly as a translator, but in truth to set up their newspaper. Freneau had been initially reluctant but was eventually persuaded.

"No, no trouble with Freneau," Madison quickly reassured. "Our *National Gazette* shall make its debut before the first of November and thereby offer an alternative to that Federalist rag that prints only hymns and lauds to Hamilton."

"I do admire and hold the greatest personal fondness for Alexander Hamilton," Harry mused, "but his programs are too nakedly nationalistic to serve the interests of my state."

"You speak much more kindly of him than do most. He and I could have spoken as one voice when we were urging the ratification of the Constitution, but Mr. Hamilton now finds it to his advantage to interpret the Constitution loosely—very loosely indeed." Madison sighed. "Shall I tell you Mr. Jefferson's fear? He predicts Hamilton will pervert the Constitution to strengthen the national government's power and then, by use of financial favors, control a gullible Congress! He claims Hamilton's goal is monarchy, with himself as the heir apparent!"

"How does President Washington look on this?" Harry asked.

Jemmy Madison shrugged. "He is in no way a monarchist, though he is not above allowing a growing amount of pomp and ceremony. I believe he is trying to stay above the struggle for power in his Cabinet between Jefferson and Hamilton." Madison's tone was wry. "Despite the fact that he is a Virginian, the President generally supports Hamilton."

"Incomprehensible," Harry muttered.

"Your Mr. Hamilton is flush with success over his funding schemes and his New National Bank, so he now considers himself indispensable to President Washington." Jemmy Madison eyed Harry over the top of his glass. "And our vice-president, Mr. Adams, having nothing to do but preside from time to time over the Senate, stews in his boredom and publishes essays in the pro-Hamilton gazette offering his forebodings about encouraging the French Revolution."

"I've no doubt that offended our French-loving Jefferson," Harry offered.

Madison leaned forward earnestly. "Jefferson is totally wedded to the concepts of the French Revolution. I tell you, Harry, it is amazing how diverse we have become in our political thinking. We, who banded together to fight the injustices of British tyranny, now find it hard to share the stage of power. To the right we have the aristocratic Hamilton with his pro-British and commercial leanings; in the middle Adams, who walks in his own path; and on the left we have Jefferson, Monroe, you, and me, all sharing more republican and agrarian leanings."

Jemmy Madison's face strained with emotion. "Our beloved Virginia will not be taken advantage of so long as Jefferson serves as secretary of state, your kinsman Richard Henry Lee leads the Senate, and I can rise to my feet in the House of Representatives to voice opposition to Hamilton."

Harry peered out into the September rain. "It is strange that my brother Richard Bland is a Federalist. He knows the provisions of the Constitution are being manipulated by the northern majority, but he says it will all come out right in the end. He has every confidence in the basic integrity of the document."

Madison shrugged. "Hamilton once said this would be a government of checks and balances, but for it to 'all come out right in the end,' we anti-Federalists will have to both check and balance that glory-seeking Hamilton!" Jemmy Madison's nearsighted eyes fastened on Richard the Scholar's portrait over the fireplace. "You know, Harry, your family is most fascinating. Shakespeare might have written of you."

"Perhaps a version of *Romeo and Juliet*, with the Lees and the Carters

cast as the Montagues and the Capulets," Harry said wryly. "Did you hear
that Richard Bland recently asked for the hand of Sarah Carter of Nomini
Hall and was turned down? Can you imagine? Old Rob Carter is staunchly
anti-Federalist and must find Richard Bland too moderate in his politics."
Harry's face relaxed into his old engaging smile. "You see, our feud still
festers."

"As an old philosopher of forty-one years," Jemmy Madison chortled,
"I believe Richard Bland was most fortunate indeed to escape matrimony. I
have yet to meet the member of the fair sex for whom I would exchange
my freedom! I shall tell Richard Bland that I think his rejection to be
disguised good fortune."

Harry's face had taken on color. "Seeing you, Jemmy, does me a world
of good! Stay for dinner. We've ever so much to talk about."

"But not the project at Matildaville. That will only set us both in bad
humor," Madison rejoined.

The venture at the Great Falls was floundering. Washington's canal
project had suffered from a shortage of labor and poor engineering. Harry
had so far not been able to raise the three thousand pounds owed for
quitrents and gain control over the property in order to sell off lots to recoup
his heavy investment.

Jemmy Madison rose to his full height of five feet six inches. "In truth,
my friend, I have come down the Neck today for another reason altogether.
It has come to my attention that the Virginia Assembly will ask you to run
for governor. In my opinion, you are the one rallying point in our beloved
state. It is your honor and duty to take your place at Virginia's helm!"

The Tidewater, 1792

"It's only a levee, not a coronation, Nat," Harry protested as the black man
bustled around him, adjusting his frock coat and giving an extra flick of his
cloth to Harry's twice-polished silver-buckled shoes. "I'm only the new governor, not a Roman emperor, you know!"

And not a very powerful governor at that, Harry told himself as he
negotiated the narrow, uncarpeted staircase of the governor's frame mansion
in Richmond. The State Constitution, designed by George Mason in 1776,
had made certain that the House of Delegates always had the upper hand in
the governing of Virginia. As governor, Harry held no veto, was forced to
operate in conjunction with an eight-member council, and faced re-election
each year. As a member of the House of Delegates, he had found the

arrangement quite satisfactory, but now, some three weeks into the governorship, he found it stifling. Still, his personal influence was not without value. Already the postwar discord seemed to be calming. "Light Horse Harry is leading us." The word had spread throughout the Tidewater.

"The governor!" Madison called out as Harry strode into the small receiving room already crowded with guests. Harry was pleased to see that his brother Congressman Richard Bland Lee had made it down to Richmond, despite the mud-clogged roads from Alexandria.

Harry turned to greet the guest of honor, the secretary of state Thomas Jefferson. He never changes, thought Harry. A sophisticate and natural aristocrat, Jefferson wandered about with a loose, shambling air, wearing a coat that was far too small. Does he play the democratic scholar, or is his appearance simply an unconscious affectation, Harry wondered. Or could it be that Jefferson liked to display himself as the polar opposite of Alexander Hamilton, who was always decked out in the finest bold satins and most expensive laces?

"I am delighted to know that Freneau's *National Gazette* rises fast in reputation," Harry said to Jefferson. "Our Mr. Hamilton likes to say he admires the British system of government, so he should heartily welcome us, his 'loyal opposition'!"

Jefferson smiled warmly. "Mr. Hamilton is indeed pro-British! One evening when Hamilton and Vice-President Adams were dining with me in New York, Mr. Hamilton declared that the British Constitution was the most perfect ever devised by the wit of man, a remark I considered an affront to our own document." Jefferson moved closer. "Then Mr. Hamilton observed three portraits hanging on my wall and asked who they were. 'Francis Bacon,' I said, 'Isaac Newton, and the third is John Locke—my trinity of the three greatest men the world has ever produced.' Mr. Hamilton looked me straight in the eye and replied, 'The greatest man that ever lived was Julius Caesar.' Do you not think that remark to be most revealing?"

Later, Harry remarked to Jemmy Madison, "An interesting man, Jefferson. But I swear his nature eludes me."

"He is brilliant, Harry, believe me—not always likable, but brilliant. And we have him to thank for the design of our new capital city on the north banks of the Potomac—a fine location, thanks to your brother Richard Bland's vote for the Assumption Act. Jefferson convinced Major Pierre Charles L'Enfant, the French engineer, to draw up plans in a classic style, based on the European architecture Jefferson found so inspiring—even sent him the pictures and plans!"

The capital, to be built on marshland and wooded hills that lay on the north side of the Potomac, was to be ten miles square, a diamond on the north-south axis, with the town of Alexandria at its southern tip. Harry winced, thinking of his litigation-locked lands at Great Falls, so close to the new capital. It was still his dream that Matildaville serve as a sister city, and the canal as the commercial gateway to the interior of the continent.

"Governor Lee, it is indeed good to see you again!" Young Thomas Shippen, the bright, articulate son of William and Alice Shippen, stood before him. "I'd like to present my wife, Betsy, and members of her family."

Harry struggled to place the gentle, fair-haired girl who stood before him. Of course! Betsy Shippen was a Carter and a Byrd. Her mother had been the daughter of Will Byrd and his first wife, Eliza Carter of Shirley.

"Governor, may I present my wife's sister, Maria Farley," Thomas went on.

The well-endowed blonde, rustling in a mauve silk dress, swept low in a curtsy that revealed the curve of her rounded bosom. Harry felt all his senses tightening in appreciation. She returned Harry's bow with a smile that carried a hint of teasing.

"You can see, Harry, the dilemma I faced," Tom Shippen said with a laugh, "when I visited my aunt Mary at Westover in past years. I was enchanted by these lovely maids, who were often there, but I was hard put whether to woo Betsy or Maria, or perhaps their pretty cousin, Ann." He reached out to draw another young woman into the circle. "May I have the honor of presenting the daughter of Charles Carter of Shirley Plantation, Miss Ann Hill Carter, better known to those of us who love her as Nancy?"

Ann Carter appeared to be quiet, self-contained, with a poise beyond her eighteen years. Creamy soft olive skin, like a magnolia petal, was Harry's impression, with satiny dark hair and black eyes to match.

"I agree," Harry returned with mock solemnity, "that any man would have found this decision a dilemma."

Later that night when Harry had gone to bed, he could not sleep. The creaky Richmond house, protected only by its modest picket fence, lacked the solid security of Stratford Hall or even of Leesylvania. Still, he would rather be here than at either plantation. Since his mother's death last year, Leesylvania had, like Stratford Hall, become a sad place. Still, it was difficult to live in the city with three small children. The narrow, muddy yard made no playground, and the house itself was barely adequate. But he could not have left them behind at Stratford. Philip, Lucy, Henry, each child carried so much of Matilda.

Restlessly, Harry put his hand over his eyes, recalling Jefferson's scoffing story about Hamilton's avowed admiration for Julius Caesar. To be honest, Harry mused, he had to agree with Hamilton on that one.

Philadelphia, 1792

"Breakfast at Shippen House . . . Philadelphia scrapple and toast with marmalade. This is one of the great pleasures of life!" Richard Henry Lee exclaimed in contentment.

"It is always a delight to have you breakfast with us, for you do so enjoy our Philadelphia specialties, Mr. President!" Will Shippen smiled as he made reference to Richard Henry's recent election to the presidency of the Senate. "What rousing sessions we've spent around this table—you, Patrick Henry and Ben Harrison, Peyton Randolph and Colonel Washington." Shippen sighed nostalgically. "Who would have thought or even dreamed then that someday we would call ourselves Americans!"

Arthur Lee grimaced as he poured too much cream into his coffee. "Nor could I have imagined, while I was leading a cheering procession across London to call on old King George, that someday I would be a farmer back in Virginia, counting my lambs and nursing seedling wheat." ·

Richard Henry laughed gently. "You've never done exactly what anyone expected!" Still, it was a damn shame, he reflected, that Arthur had never received credit for his part in gaining America's independence. That murky Deane scandal, never fully understood or clearly exposed, had placed such a shadow on Arthur's reputation that even the revelation of Deane's complicity with the British government had not removed it. Yet nothing could dampen Arthur Lee! Always a vital man, he now devoted his energies to his farm, named Lansdowne in honor of his old friend the Earl of Shelburne, near the mouth of the Rappahannock.

Richard Henry put down his cup with a sense of sorrow. Shippen was right; they had all seemed indomitable in those revolutionary days. Now only Washington seemed vigorous enough to continue the fight, and even he had had to be coaxed to take this second term. Patrick Henry was retired to his Virginia farm, and Ben Harrison was dead. The old political war-horse had last April risen from the table feeling ill after a festive dinner at Berkeley and died a few days later.

"Is it true Ben Harrison's youngest son, William Henry, is abandoning the study of medicine in Philadelphia to go west as a foot soldier?" Richard Henry asked.

"It is true." The doctor shook his head. "The young man was doing well in his medical studies here, but he did not have the money to continue. He inherited land but little cash from his father's estate, and he was too proud to accept help. William Henry is a very self-reliant eighteen-year-old. President Washington, his unofficial guardian, was at first cold to the idea of a military career for the lad, but seeing that his mind was made up, the President obtained an ensign's commission for him."

"Ho, speaking of the west"—Arthur looked over the rim of his coffee cup—"I hear that our Harry Lee is being considered to succeed General St. Clair."

Indian resistance to the westward push into the Ohio country had grown stronger in recent years. Unexpected raids, brutal killings, and the constant theft of horses and firearms on Virginia's western border and in the northwest territory had last year provoked General Arthur St. Clair, governor of the territory, to lead three thousand men against the western Indians, but he had been ruinously defeated in a battle that left dead or wounded a third of his soldiers. Now there was talk of sending out a fresh army. Light Horse Harry Lee, governor of Virginia, was among those former military officers proposed as commander.

"Harry would undoubtedly welcome the assignment," Richard Henry said, "for the western command is the highest military post in the United States. The problem is that at least seventeen men are being promoted for the position, including Anthony Wayne, Dan Morgan, and Baron von Steuben, many of whom had outranked Harry during the war."

Arthur was now filling in the company on the latest family news. "Poor William! His loss of eyesight takes much of the sweetness from life. No longer able to care for all three children, he is fortunate to have found such a loving home for his little daughters with Frank and Becky at Menokin."

"I would so love to see them." Alice Shippen rested a lace-covered elbow on the arm of her chair. It was good to see Alice with a touch of her old banter and charm. At last she had wandered back from the nightmarish melancholy and depression that had plagued her these past six years.

"Portia and Cornelia are darlings! You should go to visit them, Alice," Arthur urged. "You would find Menokin a perfect Eden! But who is this lovely lady who joins us?" Arthur pushed back his chair and rose to his feet. "I've been waiting for your pretty face, listening for your voice all morning! I thought perhaps you overslept." He kissed the pale cheek of his twenty-eight-year-old niece, Nancy Shippen Livingston, who had quietly entered the dining room.

"Would you like some coffee, dear?" Alice lifted the silver pot to fill her daughter's cup.

Nancy shook her head mutely.

Richard Henry's heart went out to her. Maybe Missy had a point about women deserving equal treatment with men under the law. Surely gentle Nancy had done nothing to deserve a lifetime without hope of remarriage, without income except her father's charity, and, worst of all, without her child. She had considered divorcing Henry Livingston, but little Peggy, now with her paternal grandmother, would then be ordered formally and permanently under the care of her erratic and undependable father.

The worst of it, thought Richard Henry, was that in despair, Nancy had turned against her parents, who had urged her into the wretched marriage to Harry Livingston. She had been much in love with the handsome young diplomat Louis Guilliaume Otto. The Frenchman had been terribly upset at Nancy's marriage and remained close to her even when she returned to Shippen House with little Peggy, but finally he had married and left Philadelphia.

Arthur was trying to cajole a smile from his niece. "Nancy, my love, will you ever forget the hat your brother Thomas sent you from London . . . *that* hat, that charming, glorious, fashionable hat?"

Throwing back his head in laughter, Will Shippen joined in the reminiscence. "It was chosen by young Tom on Bond Street in London and directed to you, Arthur, in New York! Oh, what letters you wrote us when it reached you. You described it so well we could picture it perfectly before it even arrived in Philadelphia. 'The rim of white silk edged in white velvet is less than a yard in diameter,' you wrote, and 'the crown of—' "

" 'Of blue tiffany,' " Alice picked up the story, " 'is *not* above two feet and a half.' "

"I shall never forget *that* hat." Arthur leaned back in his chair. "I said to myself, Helen of Troy must surely have worn such a hat when she enamored Paris, or Cleopatra when she seduced Antony. And now it goes to my Nancy in Philadelphia!"

Even Nancy had begun to smile. "I wore it to every garden party until it became famous, or infamous."

Chuckling, Richard Henry pushed back his chair. "Much as I deplore leaving this good company, I must. John Adams is coming by to give me a ride to the capitol building. He takes pity on my gouty legs!"

"I have grown so cynical, about politicians in particular," Richard Henry remarked as the vice-president's carriage rumbled down Chestnut Street. He shot Adams a sideways glance. "Sometimes I wonder just how you and I ever became so involved in this science of fraud they call politics!"

Adams snorted his agreement. "I think we are all a party of small actors strutting about on this tiny, disagreeable stage of Philadelphia." This was not the first time Adams had alluded to his preference for New York over Philadelphia. As Abigail once caustically remarked, "Two-thirds of the year here we must freeze or melt."

"Consider the players!" John continued in his curious Boston accent.

"There is Jefferson, who dreams of rustic tranquillity throughout the states and a nation composed of *utterly* reasonable, unselfish, and idealistic farmers —which, to be most candid, we are not! And then there is Hamilton, who views corruption as a necessary part of government and considers his own clever dealings and financial manipulations the cement of union, without which the flame of our liberty would flicker! And I, who, it seems, can be friends with neither, I am constantly lambasted by both sides. A pox on both their houses!"

Richard Henry remained silent. It was true that John Adams's role as vice-president was virtually meaningless. "His Rotundity" was the nickname given him in the Congress, where he was more laughed at than admired for the value he placed on form and ceremony. Although a Federalist, he was neither close to Washington nor enthralled with Hamilton's innovative financial measures. Now he seemed to have fallen out with his long-time friend Thomas Jefferson over the French Revolution.

"Well, John," Richard Henry said finally, "perhaps I am overly philosophical. But if I do say so myself, we have done some good, you and I. We have led—yes, led—a nation into independence and shepherded it through the early days of constitutional government. There are many flaws, but when I go home for good at the end of this term, which is my intention, it will be with the knowledge that we have a government and Constitution—amended, thank God, as it is—that bears promise."

"Bears promise." Adams shook his head wearily. "But our infant nation will not stand secure for long if war comes between France and England and Mr. Jefferson, through the fervor of his idealism, is allowed to pull us into the conflict on the side of France."

Richard Henry nodded vigorously. He had to agree with Adams and Hamilton on that. The present booming English trade was necessary to revive the states' economies as they struggled back from wartime difficulties. "I become less enthralled with Mr. Jefferson the longer I observe him, although I greatly admire his intelligence. As long as George Washington stays above the fray and does not ally himself with either Mr. Hamilton or Mr. Jefferson, I shall attempt to do the same." He smiled candidly into the brown eyes of his old friend. "Virginia always comes first with me. I do not have to tell you that, John! But she is welded now into a union whose success will be to Virginia's good, or whose downfall will be her downfall. Why, I do believe I have become almost as pragmatic as George Washington!"

Adams laughed as the carriage pulled to a stop in front of the two-story brick capitol. "You have always been pragmatic, my dear Mr. Lee—proud, fierce, doggedly idealistic, but, in the end, always pragmatic!"

The Tidewater, 1792

The disappointing news that Anthony Wayne was to command the western army came as something of a blow to Harry Lee. He had been General Washington's first choice for the position. The President's letter explained that he had feared officers with greater seniority would not readily serve as Light Horse Harry's subordinates.

Jemmy Madison extended his sympathies. "The disappointment, however, would be more regretted if your present station were less important and particularly to our own country, Virginia, at the present moment."

As it was, Governor Lee had his hands full with Indian problems in his own state. The crisis was worst in the northwestern counties of Monongahela, Harrison, Ohio, and Randolph, which were still receiving the backlash from St. Clair's defeat. Even on Virginia's southwestern frontier, the Cherokees were increasingly active as they tried to stem the white man's encroachments. There was little Harry could do but try to fill the militia regiments and dispatch available arms and ammunition to the threatened counties. More than anything, his own physical presence seemed to calm the situation. In May, he had ridden down to the lower Chesapeake counties and quieted the uneasiness in Norfolk, Hampton, and Portsmouth that had arisen over rumors of a slave insurrection. The servants of French refugees from Santo Domingo, now emigrating into Virginia, brought with them the flames of the revolutionary blaze consuming France. Now, in early June, Harry started west to inspect his line of Indian forts protecting Virginia's frontier.

"You stoppin' again to visit on the James, Colonel Lee?" Nat asked with a gleam in his eyes as he tied Harry's saddlebag. "You want me to put in your dancin' shoes?"

"If you're prying into whether I might be stopping to see Miss Maria Farley, the answer is unfortunately no," Harry retorted. "The James River plantations are not on the route west, my good fellow. I will let you know when I need my dancing slippers! For this trip, an extra pair of boots will suffice."

What a matchmaker old Nat was—just because Harry had gone down to see Maria Farley at Nesting twice this spring and visited again on his return from Norfolk! True, his children did need the attentions of a loving mother, and he hated to leave them. He bent down and gently kissed the impish Lucy and the toddling Henry. And then for a long moment he held close seven-year-old Philip, whose haunting eyes reminded him of his lost love, Matilda.

"Take good care of them for me," he said to Nat, who had followed him to the nursery door.

"Who gonna take care of you, out there in the wilds with Injuns and bears and snakes everywhere?" the tall, slender Nat admonished. "I packed some Jesuit bark in case you gets the fever."

"I promise not to get the fever!"

Actually, Harry felt strong, brimming with vigor, as he set forth with his lieutenant governor for the westward inspection tour. He had Virginia to lead, his children to raise, and somewhere, love waited for him. He felt that down to the marrow of his bones. It would not be the same as it had been with Matilda, but he needed romance in his life again.

As the horses plodded northwest into the tangled green Virginia hills, Harry thought back to Nat's teasing remark. It was true that he had had courting in mind this past May. It had been as if his instincts were telling him to go back to the James, back to the wellspring of his heritage. He had found Westover as beautiful and tranquil as ever, although the Byrd fortune was a thing of the past. The widowed Mary Willing Byrd had never been compensated by the federal government for the looting done by her cousin by marriage, Benedict Arnold. Even after his rampage she was caustically accused of British sympathies because of her dead husband's Tory leanings. Her oldest son, Thomas, had settled in the Shenandoah on land his uncle Charles Carter of Shirley had given him. Because Thomas had espoused the British cause, he could never settle on the family estate, for that would only aggravate his mother's situation. Besides, the plantation's land was worn out. Even Otway, who had sided with the rebel Americans in the Revolution, had been forced west to farm the six thousand acres received for his services as a Continental soldier.

As he dined with Mary Willing Byrd in the shabbily elegant dining room of Westover, he had inquired about her next-door neighbor, young Ben Harrison of Berkeley.

"Like Westover, Berkeley does poorly." Mary's face had mirrored her sadness. "And that young man does not help matters a bit, I can tell you. He is a planter who doesn't plant, a businessman whose interests in Richmond shrivel from neglect. After his Mercer wife died in childbirth, he impulsively married a Randolph from Curles Neck plantation, but the marriage was not at all successful, and his new wife recently fled to her parents' with his dead wife's baby. Now Harrison lives alone in that big house, which he spends all his time and money refurbishing."

A fool, living in a fool's paradise, Harry had thought. Our world has changed, and young Harrison does not know it—or chooses not to accept it.

"I'm looking forward to going on to Shirley tomorrow," Harry had said, deliberately turning to a more pleasant subject, "and then on to Nesting plantation."

"Is it Maria Farley at Nesting or Ann Carter at Shirley you wish to court, my dear Governor?"

Even now, as he picked his way through the rugged Virginia foothills, Harry blushed at her bold question. At Nesting plantation, Maria Farley had bewitched him into dancing the quadrille until one in the morning! An outrageous flirt, Maria was thoroughly spoiled by a throng of admirers. But she *was* desirable, and he had enjoyed the warmth of a woman's cheek against his and the softness of a woman's breast curving against his heart. He needed to have a woman once more in his life and bed.

The tour of the frontier garrisons was far more arduous than Harry had anticipated. Tanned to the color of honey and hardened by days in the saddle, Harry and his lieutenant governor, James Wood, crossed the Blue Ridge and in late August descended into the flatlands that led to Richmond. He returned nervous, filled with an apprehension that he could not explain. The tour was worthwhile, for he had seen for himself where the defense line was weak and had already sent requests back to Secretary of War Henry Knox in Philadelphia, outlining his needs for aid and financial assistance.

As the two horsemen drew closer to the foot of Capitol Hill and the white frame governor's mansion, they saw Nat West standing in the muddy side yard. One look at his sorrowful face and Harry's heart froze. "What's the matter?" Harry asked as he quickly dismounted. "What has happened?"

Nat put his arm around Harry's shoulder. "Come into the house, Colonel Lee. I tell you about it when we be inside."

"Have you heard the tragic news about our governor?" Jemmy Madison wrote from Virginia to his fellow congressman James Monroe in Philadelphia. "It did not suffice that Harry Lee should lose his beloved Matilda, but he now suffers the death of his oldest son, Philip, whom he adored. The boy fell ill with the summer fevers while Harry was away touring the frontier. Apparently he died only a few hours before his father returned to Richmond. Harry has taken the loss very badly."

Philadelphia, 1793

In early January, now re-elected governor for a second term, Harry traveled by horseback to Philadelphia on Virginia business.

"What's more, I'm eager to see you and President Washington," he greeted Madison, "and I want to feel for myself the pulse of government."

"For that you have only to read the newspapers!" Madison said sardonically. "A vitriolic war of words rages between our *National Gazette* and the Federalist press, which delights in portraying us Republicans as self-serving hypocrites!"

Harry frowned. "I cannot say I like the strident tone the *Gazette* has taken where President Washington is concerned. It is one thing to lambaste Hamilton, but another to attack Washington! How can Freneau say that Washington has monarchist leanings? You know as well as I how reluctantly he consented to seek a second term."

"Of course I do!" Madison was all agreement. "He is the only man in this nation that everyone is committed to. Federalists and Republicans alike know that he is the mainstay of all our hopes, for we hold so little else in common." Madison grew defensive. "Freneau simply responds in kind to the vicious attacks the Federalists sling at Jefferson, whom they call an intriguing incendiary. But to be fair, Harry, our Virginian President does enjoy a fair amount of pomp, riding about Philadelphia on a white charger with a gilt-edged leopard-skin saddle. He draws up at the Congress, bedazzling us in his cream-colored coach, adorned with its flowers and cupids, drawn by six cream-colored horses and accompanied by splendidly uniformed outriders."

"Yet Washington has always been the most down-to-earth of men!" Harry protested. "Indulge him his few luxuries. He never has put on affectations or airs."

"It's not that he puts on airs." Jemmy Madison shook his head. "You will see tonight."

Harry dressed for the evening's reception at the President's house with great care. He had not seen the President in months. As a matter of fact, there had been a slight coolness in Washington's letters over the past year, due perhaps to Harry's resistance to the federal assumption of state debts and to his role in setting up the *National Gazette*—though to be sure it had never crossed Harry's mind that Freneau would criticize Washington!

"You see what I mean by ceremony?" Madison whispered as the two men stepped from the carriage in front of the handsome Morris mansion, which served as Washington's residence in Philadelphia. "This is still the finest house in town, despite rumors that Robert Morris suffers financial difficulties. See, liveried servants at the doorway!" Madison continued his low monologue as they ascended the white stone steps. "The President holds two afternoon receptions each week, and this formal evening with the ladies takes place each Friday night. But be prepared to leave at nine sharp, for the President always retires promptly."

Harry looked through the French doors at the collage of familiar faces in the ornate ballroom. There stood the secretary of war, Henry Knox, with his buxom Lucy, and in a small gathering by the marble fireplace Vice-President John Adams was in solemn conversation with Secretary of the Treasury Alexander Hamilton. The rounded torso of the former contrasted with the dapper physique of the latter. How simple and elegant everyone looked! Gone forever were the beauty patches, feathers, and high-heeled shoes, the fashions influenced by Versailles before the Revolution.

With a surge of affection he saw the President and Lady Washington receiving at the end of the room. In his fine dark-brown broadcloth suit, silver-buckled shoes, and dress sword, Washington was no more richly dressed than others in the room, but he still appeared to Harry the most authoritative figure he had ever seen.

"Ceremony be hanged!" Harry left Madison standing in the doorway and strode across the polished floor.

Washington was chatting with his nephew, Bushrod, and did not see Harry approach. But when Harry's hand soundly slapped his back in bold greeting, the tall Virginian stiffened, drew back his shoulders, and turned with a thundering "Sir!"

If Harry had not caught a sparkle of deep affection in the President's eyes as he turned toward him, he would have been shaken to the core by the sternness of the tone. Madison was right! There was a protocol in the national administration, and he had flouted it quite openly!

"I told you," Madison later chided Harry with a laugh at his discomfiture, "John Adams has had some effect on our good Virginian! President Washington wears the mantle of his authority with dignity and with much awareness of his position. He is not·Everyman."

If Washington had been affronted by Harry Lee's familiarity, it was forgotten when he invited the Virginia governor into his private study at the party's close. "I am so very glad to see you, dear fellow, I shall make special exception to my bedtime hour of nine o'clock to have a nightcap." He drew French brandy from his private store. "Here," he said, handing Harry a glass. "This fine bottle was a gift from Lafayette. Let us salute him in his time of travail." The two men held up their glasses in a silent toast.

"My thoughts are often in France," Harry offered. "It is an honorable and desperate struggle to throw off the shackles of a decadent monarchy. But what of Lafayette? Have you any news?"

Washington's eyes betrayed his distress. "I hear that he has been declared a traitor by the French extremists, and that frightens me. Lafayette is like a son to me, one of several young men who are as close as if they were my own blood." The indulgent look the President gave his companion made it clear that Harry was in that select company. With a weary sigh Washington sank into the massive leather chair beside the fire. "No man could know how difficult or how heavy is the burden that lies on my shoulders. You have heard that I agreed to stand for re-election in the spring?"

Harry nodded. "To stand is tantamount to being re-elected. It is our nation's good fortune that you consent to take on the presidency again. You stand unrivaled, unchallenged."

The older man was contemplative. "Our constitution makes no provisions for opposing parties, yet we fast approach the point where we must split and commit ourselves as either Federalist or Republican. Though I value the advice of Mr. Jefferson highly—indeed, so much so that I convinced him not to resign, as he wished to do—I am, however, most often forced to support Mr. Hamilton, for I believe his fiscal policies will bind us into a nation in spite of the penalty our agrarian states must pay." His look was a plea for understanding. "And you must know the pain that causes me, for I know Virginia suffers from it. Even your kinsman Richard Henry Lee now stands with me in support of Federalism. And on the French question, again I feel I must agree with Hamilton." His mouth tightened.

Harry well understood the dilemma the commander in chief faced: Britain and France stood on the precipice of war, and should they take up arms, America would be obliged to take a stand. Federalists and Republicans alike argued for neutrality, each having a different definition of what neutrality meant. The 1778 Treaties of Alliance between France and the United States, which contained provisions for military assistance, were still in effect. Should war break out, Hamilton wanted to suspend the treaties, out of distaste for revolutionary France and the practical realization of the importance of British trade. Jefferson had voiced the opinion that the treaties should be honored, in order to retain French friendship and draw concessions from Britain.

"I have no doubt of your personal regard for the struggle for French liberty and equality, sir, and it is one I share with ardor and personal commitment." Harry's expression was intense in the firelight. "But I see Virginia slowly beginning to regain her vigor. Cargos of corn, lumber, and tobacco are again flowing out of Norfolk, and our shattered economy is beginning to heal. Virginia can never rise again if kept dependent upon tobacco, as she was before the war. But with produce from the west moving through her ports, she is viable. Markets are a necessity, and Britain's favor must on no account be lost. I stand with you, sir. A realistic neutrality is the only answer."

*   *   *

"Thank God, you have begun to see it my way!" Alexander Hamilton exclaimed the next day when Harry joined him for dinner at the Indian Green Tavern. "I thought our friendship was irreparably broken. That grieved me more than I can tell you."

Harry struggled with his response, for much in Hamilton's toadying support of the northern mercantile interests still angered him. But on this question of American neutrality if war broke out between France and England, he agreed with Hamilton's viewpoint. "I must be honest," he began.

"When were you ever not?" Hamilton broke in with a smile.

Harry would not be diverted. "I never did and never will admire the funding system of which you are the author. And other financial actions that you have taken remain anathema to me as well. But we are friends, you and I. You have my word."

Hamilton gave a sigh that mingled appreciation and resignation. "You have always been a man whose loyalty could be depended upon. I've few friends these days, Harry. I'm beset from all sides. You've heard the gossip about me?"

Harry nodded with sympathy, for his old wartime companion was now embroiled in a private scandal that was the talk of Philadelphia. Late in 1792, a jailed embezzler had sent word to several Republican congressmen, James Monroe among them, that he had evidence that could convict Hamilton of fraud. But on closer scrutiny, the crime turned out to involve Hamilton's love life, not his public life.

In the summer of 1791, Betsy Hamilton being out of town, he had begun a love affair with an obscure young woman named Maria Reynolds who had come to the secretary of the treasury's office pleading desertion by her husband and begging for a loan from the government. That night Hamilton delivered some of his own money to her, and an intimate relationship began. In time her husband had returned and, discovering their liaison, promptly blackmailed his wife's paramour, severely draining Hamilton's purse. He had not committed the offense of tapping public funds to subsidize the payments, but he found himself in a most embarrassing position when the blackmailing husband, jailed on another charge, turned to Hamilton for assistance and, rejected, dispatched his damaging charges to the Republican congressmen.

Harry watched Hamilton drain his wineglass with a nervous toss of his head. He remembered watching that proud dark head as Hamilton paraded his troops at Yorktown in full view of British cannons. Brilliance and suicidal bravado seemed curiously combined in the mercurial Hamilton. But then, curious mixtures flow in all our veins, Harry thought, as he idly outlined an empty heart on the white linen tablecloth.

The Tidewater, 1793

On the moss-green lawn that sloped to the quiet banks of the James, nine-teen-year-old Ann Hill Carter strolled aimlessly with her spaniel puppy. Another hour, maybe two, and he would be here! The hours had seemed endless since she heard that Governor Harry Lee was coming again to Shirley. Of course, he was coming to court her cousin Maria Farley, who was spending the spring with her Carter cousins. Still and all, she would see him again. That alone would make her happy. Ann closed her dark eyes dreamily. Just to sit in a corner of the dining room, or hide in a cluster of sisters and friends, and watch Harry Lee move and talk and dance was heaven!

"Here, Ladylove." Her skirts rustled as she sat down in the grass and beckoned the inquisitive black puppy away from the marshy riverbank. "Come here, my little one." Puppy in lap, she settled in the shade of one of the giant oaks that sheltered the wide lawn of Shirley. Except for short visits to Richmond, thirty miles to the north, or to house parties along the James, she had never ventured far from this three-story red brick house. Beneath huge chimneys and a soft-gray sloping roof, many-paned dormer windows looked down on Shirley's brick dependencies, which edged the winding drive to the Richmond road, and the graceful old trees and sweet-smelling shrubs that patterned the expansive lawns. She knew the plantation's every bound-ary, from the broad tidal river to the fields of wheat and beyond, where cattle and riding horses grazed on lush grasses, bordered by a deep forest, its trees draped with honeysuckle, wild grape, and Virginia creeper. She had never ventured far from this house of love and laughter, its roof graced by a huge carved-wood pineapple, the symbol of hospitality.

"There you are, my little Nancy!" Charles Carter, master of Shirley, approached, his footsteps muffled by the thick spring grass. "I have been looking for you." He gave his daughter a smile full of love and tenderness.

Ann scrambled to her feet to receive his embrace. They were very close, father and daughter, and she cherished her time alone with him, for Charles Carter, the most successful planter on the James and father of a lively brood of twenty-one children, was a vital and busy man.

He reached out his hand and drew her into the crook of his arm. This naïve, sweet-natured girl always reminded him of an innocent little Eve playing in the Garden of Eden. "What were you thinking, my darling?" He had noticed Ann's quietness in the last day or so and wondered about its cause. "You and Maria haven't had a quarrel or some such nonsense?"

Maria and Ann were sharing a bedroom at Shirley, and he had noticed that the tempestuous and quick-tongued little cousin often bested his own quiet daughter. "If Maria is too much for you, I'll have her moved in with one of your sisters."

"No, no, Papa." Ann's olive cheeks were now a soft pink. "Maria has not been anything but jolly. I was thinking how especially beautiful Shirley seems this morning."

Carter followed his daughter's gaze back to the big manor house. His father, John, oldest son of Robert "King" Carter, had inherited Corotoman on the banks of the Rappahannock, and through his marriage to Elizabeth Hill, daughter of Sir Edward Hill, an old stander from the days of Jamestown, had added Shirley, a plantation of several thousand acres, to his holdings. Upon the death of his parents, Charles Carter had inherited first Corotoman and later Shirley, which he decided to make his permanent home. He built this fine new house close to the old Hill mansion and moved his family from Corotoman in 1776, when Ann was only three.

He looked down at the slender, finely molded girl leaning against his shoulder. His first marriage had been to his first cousin, Mary Carter of Cleve. When she died in childbirth after twenty years of marriage, he wed Ann Butler Moore, granddaughter of an old governor, Alexander Spotswood. Ann was the first child of that union. Sometimes in the bustle of brothers and sisters, cousins, and kin visiting at Shirley, he found himself looking out protectively for this quiet one. Generally he found her with a smile on her face, perhaps picking a bouquet of the lacy white Queen Anne's lace that grew near the river or content in the pages of a book in the cozy windowseat of his study. She was in many ways the most indomitable of his children, a true Carter, for he never knew her to budge once her heart was set on something.

"Well, I think it is high time you put on a pretty new dress and make yourself noticed," he urged her gently. "The carriages from Cleve and Berkeley and the barges from Turkey Island have already arrived. John Page from Rosewell will be here shortly, and he will certainly be asking after you, as will that young Mr. Tayloe from Mount Airy."

"Papa." Ann scooped up the puppy and walked beside her father toward the manor house. "The governor *is* coming? He did say yes, didn't he?"

"Oh, yes, he will be here." Carter's tone became slightly cynical. "He will be here for certain, charging up on the fastest of horses, looking glossy as a New York dandy."

"You like him, don't you, Papa?"

For a moment Charles Carter considered Harry Lee. He could not help admiring a man who had proved himself so valiant in battle and who was as gracious as he was generous. But still he had reservations about the popular young governor. Harry Lee was rash, impetuous, and he seemed to view himself as a hero. Perhaps it was simply that he was a Lee. And Carters and Lees had never got on really well. The Carters were conservative, cautious. And the Lees! He snorted slightly to himself. The whole lot of them were impulsive, quick to jump—into revolution, into battle, into love. "Of course, I like him." He answered his daughter's question. "I would not be one bit surprised if he asks your cousin Maria to be his wife, and I shall be in favor of the match even though . . ."

"Even though?"

Even though Carters and Lees seldom marry, he thought to himself. "Even though I understand that he considers giving up the governorship to sail off for France and fight alongside his friend Lafayette. I don't quite see how a wife would fit into that picture. But that would be Maria's problem."

It was almost noon before Harry Lee arrived at Shirley. Through her bedroom window, open to the April breezes, Ann observed the young soldier-governor dismount from his black stallion and clasp the hands of a throng of young admiring men who had come out to greet him. He was the handsomest of them all, she thought, broad-shouldered and strongly built, white teeth flashing in a tan face. His brown hair, lightly streaked with gold, was pulled back in a queue, and the brown of his camlet jacket exactly matched the color of his eyes.

But she did not love him just for his comeliness. Love! Ann put her hand to her mouth at the very thought of the word. From the first time she had met him, at the January reception in Richmond she had attended with the Shippens, she had "appreciated" him. She had heard he was a man of honor, a man who lived by his ideals. She had seen him only twice since then, both times at Shirley. He was far too good for that little minx Maria Farley!

A dreadful, unkind thought, Ann chided herself as she came down the wide flying staircase into the great wood-paneled center reception room. To be truthful, Maria was goodhearted and fun to be with, though spoiled. One mustn't judge others, it was not a Christian thing to do.

"Mercy me," Ann gasped aloud, one hand on the banister. Harry Lee was just coming through the doorway. She was not prepared to meet him head-on like this, with no clever words rehearsed, her heart beating a wild storm inside!

"Miss Ann." Harry swept low in a graceful bow before her. "How fine you look today, your cheeks just the shade of wild roses!"

His words were only common Tidewater courtesy, but Ann blushed even more strongly at his compliment.

He did not seem to notice that his young hostess was far too discomfited even to murmur a welcoming word. "You know, I have never before seen the famous scars that my old adversary Banastre Tarleton left on your staircase. Would you be so kind to show them to me?"

"Not *our* staircase." Ann pointed to the banister, which arched gracefully to the second floor without any visible form of support. "It was at Carter's Grove that Tarleton rode right up the staircase, slashing left and right."

He turned to smile at her with bright, teasing eyes. "You were just a child when he marched through Virginia. Banastre Tarleton was a handsome, daring devil with not a grain of mercy in his whole body." Harry grinned. "I shot his hat off once at the 'Spread Eagle Tavern' in Pennsylvania, and it was my greatest desire that he and I meet in one final standoff. But alas, it never occurred." Harry reached out suddenly and clasped her hand in his. "Ann." He paused. "They call you Nancy, don't they? Well, I shall call you Ann, for I think it suits you better! Would you do me the greatest of favors?"

Ann nodded. Anything! Dear God, she would do anything for him!

"Would you find your fair cousin Maria and tell her that I am anxious to see her!"

To tell the honest truth, Maria Farley could never appreciate a man like Harry Lee, Ann concluded that evening as she stood in the shadows of the great center room observing the dancing. She watched the dazzling blonde glide across the floor in the arms of the strong, sure-footed governor. Maria smiled beguilingly over Harry Lee's shoulder at a flirtatious Randolph from Bizarre plantation.

"Here you are, hiding in the shadows. Will a beautiful little maid give her father this dance?" Charles Carter bowed before his daughter and then led a reluctant Ann to the floor. "Are you having a good time, my darling?" His eyes found the answer in her face. Almost roughly, the master of Shirley tightened his grip on his daughter's hand. "Do not dream of knights in white armor! Do not dream of a man who is too bold, too reckless! A man like that could break your heart, and I will not have it, you understand, I will not have it!"

Tears shone in Ann's dark eyes as she pulled her father from the crowded floor. "I cannot help my true feelings, Father," she whispered. "Please understand. They come from deep in the heart."

"So you consider sailing for France as a soldier of fortune?" Charles Carter looked across the candlelit table at his dinner guest. "That would seem a rash step, considering that French affairs are in the highest disorder?" There was more than a touch of challenge in his voice.

Harry had just taken a bite of rockfish. Carefully he wiped his mouth on his white linen napkin. All eyes at the table seemed to be fastened on him. Maria Farley had laid down her fork. "It is a course of action that has some merit, sir. Despite the abuses, the Revolution in France has much in common with our own struggle. And one must remember that many French officers came to our aid then." Harry could not bring himself to say that other, personal, reasons drew him to France. True, if it was not in America's best interests to enter this war, it would be in *his*, offering him a niche, an admirable calling into which he could pour his talents. Lafayette was now a prisoner exiled in Belgium, but a major general's commission awaited Harry in Paris should he wish to take it. And he sought refuge from his grief over Matilda and little Philip.

"And would you, Governor Lee, take a wife to France?" Carter persisted.

Harry suppressed all but a hint of a smile. "I have no wife, Mr. Carter. And if I should take one, that would have to be a decision between us."

"Maria, Maria! How can you?" An hour later Ann Carter faced her cousin angrily in their upstairs bedroom. "Governor Lee has asked for your hand and you refuse. You don't know what you throw away!"

The other girl's eyes were equally stormy. "He is too old for me, Ann, almost thirty-seven. And besides, he is so complex, so overwhelming. I want to have fun, to dance! I don't want to be caught in that whirlpool in Harry Lee's wake." She folded her arms across her breasts. "If you are so much in love with Harry Lee, why don't you go after him yourself? Don't deny it! I have seen your face when he is here at Shirley. I watched you when he helped you carry the punchbowl in the dining room tonight. If you love him so much, Ann Hill Carter, then tell him!"

"I couldn't!" Ann trembled.

"Well, then, he will never know," Maria returned with exasperation.

In the faint moonlight Harry sat, his head in his hands, on a bench at the far end of the garden. She could make out the curve of his back, the bend of his broad shoulders. The scent of the boxwood hedge, mixed with that of lavender and mignonette, suffused the garden with its sweet perfume as Ann slipped close to the bench and, with hesitant fingers, touched him.

He did not look up.

She called forth all her courage and sat down beside him in the spring darkness. "I was thinking of you, Mr. Lee," she began quietly. "I was thinking of your talk at dinner about going to Paris." Her voice faltered, then grew steady. "I was hoping that you will reconsider going. I can only hope that you will seek and weigh the opinions of those you respect before you make your decision."

He stirred beside her. "I have sought out such advice, Ann." His voice was lifeless. "Indeed, I have been advised by several, including the one man I respect more highly than any other, not to make such a move. But at the same time I have nothing to hold me in Virginia—my children are young, content with their nursemaid. I have nothing, Ann, nothing."

Her life, her happiness, were bound up in this moment. "You have me," she offered.

He lifted his head and looked at her in the darkness. "You, little Ann? Whatever do you mean?"

Ann's voice was steady but filled with intensity. "You have my devotion and my complete faith. Indeed, Mr. Lee, you have my very heart."

For a long moment he did not answer but stared at her in the pale glowing light of the moon. Then he reached over and gently took her hand in his.

It was a wedding such as the Tidewater had not seen since the halcyon times before the war. For days, coaches had been driving up the winding avenue to Shirley. By the sultry morning of Tuesday, June 18, the stables were filled with visitors' horses, and at the river dock were moored a dozen bright-sailed barges. Guests wandered on the broad, shaded lawn, carrying cold toddies in pewter tankards clinking with cubes from the ice block brought down to the Chesapeake in the hold of a ship from Maine. By ten in the morning ladies were fanning themselves vigorously with their Spanish fans of woven palm.

Every room in the commodious manor house was filled with family and friends who had come for the wedding. Even the old Hill mansion, which stood behind the new house, and the rooms above the dependencies had been put to use for the occasion of the marriage of Ann Hill, beloved daughter of Charles Carter, to the popular Governor of Virginia.

"I declare," Becky Lee remarked to Frank, "everyone has come to Shirley for Harry's wedding!"

"When a handsome and dashing warrior-governor weds a maiden of beauty and fortune, it stirs everyone's heart," Frank responded. "Have you ever known anyone who didn't respond to a love story?"

Becky finished tying the wide blue sashes of Portia and Cornelia, then stood between them, an arm around each of the girls. "How do we look?"

"Enchanting!"

And indeed they did. The soft new fashions of English cotton, chintz, and light silk were undeniably charming. Becky wore a chemise *à l'anglaise*, the stylish yet simple lines of the ancient Roman republic. But then, Becky had never looked anything but enchanting to him. Frank shepherded his flock of three females before him, directing them down the staircase toward the overflowing lawns.

Glimpsing the bridegroom by the stone portico talking with his brother Richard Bland and James Madison, Frank left Becky and the girls in a circle of chairs and hurried to join them. In Frank's opinion, Madison was one of the most brilliant men in the House of Representatives, always articulate and quick to offer his viewpoint. Despite the contentment Frank felt in his retirement at Menokin, he was always eager to know what was happening with the federal government in which he had been so involved for so many years.

Harry Lee, resplendent in a well-cut frock coat and tight-fitting buff breeches, which displayed to good advantage his taut horseman's hips and legs, accepted Frank's congratulations with affection and jaunty self-confidence.

As Harry and Richard Bland excused themselves to go inside, Frank turned to Jemmy Madison. "I am so happy Harry has chosen matrimony over a return to arms." He shook his head. "He has been dealt bad luck of late; I hope his fortunes will improve and bring him a peaceful and happy future."

Jemmy Madison threw Frank a questioning smile. "Must a life be peaceful to be worthwhile? No, no—I only ask that rhetorically. I, too, hope that marriage will bring him happiness."

"You're still a bachelor, are you not, Mr. Madison?"

With a wistful sigh, Madison placed one hand against the red brick wall. "I have finally reached the time in my life when I would change that unhappy state. But I have yet to discover the young lady who so charms me and is so charmed by me that she would consent to be my life's companion."

Chuckling, Frank walked beside Madison through the rose garden. "Tell me, how fares our great Virginian in Philadelphia? I read the newspaper accounts and the vituperative essays that spew forth from Philadelphia. In particular I read Benjamin Franklin Bache in the Philadelphia *General Advertiser*, who is so bold as to question Washington's personal integrity!

Is the administration so deeply split between the pro-English Federalists and the pro-French Republicans?"

"I wish it were as simple as that," Madison said with a groan. "There is no question that the newspaper war has got out of hand. It greatly disgusts President Washington, who is annoyed, insulted, and often cut to the very quick by the things he reads. On the other hand, the Federalist press is no kinder in its remarks against Mr. Jefferson and, in particular, the emergence of the pro-French Jacobean political clubs. Do you know about them? They are Democratic-Republican societies, which the Federalists believe are attempting to push the United States into the European conflict."

"And Mr. Jefferson?"

"Despite what the press says, Jefferson is in his own way loyal to President Washington. He knows that the discord between himself and Hamilton is painful to all concerned, and more than once he has offered Washington his resignation."

Frank nodded. "I understand that Mr. Hamilton has offered his resignation as well."

"The President refused both, virtually begging them—his two most important cabinet officers—to remain. He desperately needs Hamilton, for more and more the President follows the Federalist line." Madison said the last with some discouragement. "As for Mr. Jefferson, he is the President's main link with the agrarian south and thus necessary to the cohesion of his administration." James Madison looked directly into Frank Lee's eyes. "Tom Jefferson's critics are wrong if they believe he would hamper President Washington's leadership. Though he is ardently pro-French, he supports neutrality in the war between Britain and France."

Frank returned the younger man's steady gaze. "That is easier said than done. Take, for instance, this Citizen Genêt," he said, sneering slightly, "who with Republican endorsement now roams our country representing the new French Republic. Why, if he could, he would fit out French privateers right under Washington's nose! As our governor, Harry must also be alert to this danger."

"Harry will no doubt accept a third term. He is very popular and much needed as governor. As for his politics, I must tell you I am disappointed to see him move away from Republicanism and into the folds of the Federalist camp." Jemmy Madison shook his head. "I understand it, of course. Harry Lee highly esteems George Washington, and he will do nothing that might endanger Washington's position. More and more he aligns himself with the President, or, as you call him, 'our great Virginian.' "

In the paneled parlor of Shirley, Harry stood by the window with two letters in his hand. One, in his possession for several weeks, was from

Charles Carter, bestowing his blessings on this marriage. Harry read again the familiar words. "The only objection we ever had to your connection with our daughter is now entirely done away with. You have declared upon your honor that you have given over all thoughts of going to France, and we rest satisfied with that assurance."

Harry smiled to himself.

That had not been a difficult decision. When George Washington had given his request for counsel a cautious, negative answer, he had immediately begun to lose interest in leaving for Paris. And then, when Ann came to him that night in the garden, his precious Ann! The very thought of the gift of her love made him feel humble and undeserving. Harry's eyes raced to the end of the letter, to the closing lines of Charles Carter's letter: "Mrs. Carter and I are perfectly satisfied that our dear girl will make you a dutiful and loving wife, and we flatter ourselves that you will be to her a most affectionate and tender husband, in full confidence of which I beg leave to subscribe myself, Your very affectionate, Chas. Carter."

The words "and tender" had been inserted as an afterthought. Harry stared at the letter. Did Charles Carter think he would be anything but tender to one as delicate and loving as Ann? The words stung, but then could this marriage overcome the old Lee-Carter conflicts? Harry stared out onto the crowded lawn.

"Mr. Lee." Ann suddenly appeared behind him.

Harry gasped. How beautiful she looked, dark hair and dark eyes shining above the white brocade and tulle of her wedding dress. "My dear, I'm not supposed to see you until—"

"But I wanted to see you," she said softly. "I wanted to see for myself that you were calm and content with this day."

His grin was irresistible. "I am very happy with this day, sweet Ann. And I am more than delighted that you slipped down to see me before the ceremony. Will you wear this for me?" With quick fingers he lifted the top from a small velvet box lying on the table. "It is the President's gift to you. Just arrived. It is a cameo bearing his likeness." His fingers fumbled with its latch. "The note says, 'To my dear Ann from Washington.'" Gently Harry pinned it at the neck of Ann's white wedding dress. "There!" He stepped back and looked admiringly at her. "You are my lovely and beautiful bride. Now, hurry back upstairs; if you are caught consorting with your bridegroom before the ceremony, you shall have to bear all kinds of teasing!"

When she had gone, Harry opened the note addressed to him that had accompanied the cameo: "As we are told that you have exchanged the rugged and dangerous field of Mars for the soft and pleasurable bed of Venus I do in this, as I shall in every thing you may pursue like unto it, good and laudable, wish you all imaginable success and happiness."

Harry felt his old optimism, a feeling of wonderful expectation, rising in him as he thrust the note in his pocket and strode out among the wedding guests on the lawns of Shirley.

It is more than a good marriage, thought Ann Carter Lee as summer gave way to fall. Harry Lee had not disappointed her—he never could! After four days of festivities at Shirley, she had gone with her husband to the governor's house in Richmond. He had apologized for its shabbiness, the smell of goats and horse dung that drifted in through the open windows from the narrow, rutted roads of the capital. But she had known exactly how it would be, and it did not matter in the slightest. All that mattered was the bond growing between them, between man and wife.

His children had been another thing. Dark-eyed and suspicious, the eight-year-old girl and six-year-old boy had looked out at her from behind their nurse's skirts and refused her advances. But that would come in time, for she had always liked children and these two were Harry's and therefore would soon be hers to love and call her own.

In early September, Harry took his family home to Stratford. They traveled by boat, sailing down the James, past Shirley and Berkeley and Westover and Green Spring and Carter's Grove—all the familiar houses of her childhood—then out into the bay, where she stood in the bow of the boat with her hand in her husband's, watching with delight the porpoise at play. They sailed past the narrow opening of the York and the craggy banks of the Rappahannock until the small craft nosed into the wider opening of the Potomac River.

"Don't forget, I was born on the Neck," she reminded Harry when he pointed out the familiar landmarks of Northumberland and Westmoreland counties. "When you're born at Corotoman, you never forget the wild beauty of the north." It was different from the stately elegance of the James, where the trees spread wide, unfettered by underbrush, the Indians having burned it years before to aid in the hunting of deer. Here on the Neck it was all wild and untouched . . . and unbelievably lovely.

"We must go riding," she said in a rush of excitement. "You must take me riding over all your favorite places." And then she blushed, for it struck her that he had been to all those places many times with the pretty Lee cousin who had been his first wife.

Harry only nodded, his mind obviously far away, but she was comforted by the pressure of his strong fingers on hers. What had Matilda Lee been like? "Lovely and spirited as an angel," was how someone at a reception in the first days of her marriage had described her predecessor. It had not bothered her then, but now, at Stratford Hall, Matilda's home . . .

"You shiver. Not cold, are you?" Harry asked solicitously.

"No, just anxious to see Stratford."

"Don't be put off when first we come up the hill from the dock. It is a formidably strong house, without the graceful façade of your Shirley or the charms of Westover or Berkeley. But once you are inside, it will win your heart, for it is a lovely old place, and it resounds with happy memories."

Perhaps she took the words too personally, but they cut her to the heart. Fighting back tears, Ann pulled herself erect and prepared to step ashore on Stratford's dock, where a group of servants and slaves waited respectfully, curious to meet their new mistress.

It was just as Harry had predicted. She recoiled slightly at first sight of the great *H*-shaped house in the meadow. Its windows, reflecting the September sun, seemed to stare back at her as impassively as the eyes of those who had greeted her on the dock. Once she was inside the walls of Stratford Hall, her heart lightened. The gray-columned great hall was filled with the last aromatic summer roses. "These are portraits of all the Lees," Harry said. "But I shall teach you the catechism another day."

"This is no Lee!" She pointed with triumph to a faded canvas of an imperious lady that hung over a sofa. "It is Lady Frances Berkeley of Green Spring."

"Right you are!" Harry knelt on the sofa and straightened the frame. "It was through m'lady Frances that Green Spring passed to the Ludwells and then to the Lees. That does make her an honorary Lee of sorts, don't you think?"

How entrancing he was when he smiled at her like that. It reassured her everything was going to be all right.

The receiving room at the west end and the formal parlor with its Adam mantel were visited in turn. "The man of the house's study," Harry said with mock sternness as he showed her the book-lined room across the hall. "No swishing skirts enter unless invited."

Nat West, who had returned to Stratford ahead of them, had set out a meal in the handsome dining room, with its marble mantel and full-length portrait of Queen Caroline. A tempting late dinner of roast guinea hen and oysters scalloped in green peppers awaited them. "House needs a good cleaning, good polishing," grumbled Nat as he lit the tall candles in the silver holders on the table. "We didn't have time to give it more than a onceover 'fore you and the governor got here."

But it looked very polished and splendid to Ann, who was used to the cluttery confusion of Shirley. She smiled at Nat, whom she had grown to depend on in the few months of her marriage. "Tomorrow you must show me all the rooms on the lower floor, Nat. I shall want a complete tour . . . and the outbuildings, too."

"Just bedrooms on the lower floor," Harry said airily, pouring two glasses of white wine. "Bedrooms and the housekeeping rooms and the plantation office and the wine and root cellars. Unless we have houseguests, you won't need to go downstairs very often. You must set a regular time for the housekeeper to report to you here in the alcove parlor." He indicated the cozy little room adjoining the dining room.

"But the bedroom," she faltered, "the master chamber?"

"Is right across the hall here, on the main floor." Harry smiled at her. "And it is altogether the most agreeable room in the house, I promise."

Ann felt her palms tightening. It was the room where Harry and Matilda Lee had spent their wedding night, where their children had been born, where the beautiful Matilda had drawn her last breath in the arms of her grief-stricken husband. Already Ann had seen from the east doorway the brick mausoleum in the far garden. What if Harry's love for Matilda were so strong that she was shut out?

"You've not tasted a bite!" Harry chided. "Here, let me put some relish on a bit of box bread for you. It will give you an appetite." Harry spread a fine-textured hot roll with cucumber relish and passed it to her.

After dinner, they sat quietly in the alcove parlor, and he chatted knowledgeably of neighbors and family who would soon be calling on her. "The old Washington family house, Wakefield, burned down a few years ago," he said, "and the family is somewhat scattered, but there are Washingtons enough at Bushfield, and your cousins at Nomini Hall and the Lees at Bellevue and Chantilly will come calling at the first opportunity. Also my uncle, Squire Richard of Lee Hall, a delightful old man with a passel of younglings."

How like Harry, thought Ann, not to harbor the slightest resentment. For years his uncle had proclaimed Harry the heir to Lee Hall, but at the age of sixty he married a sixteen-year-old and produced a family of his own, another bit of bad luck for the financially pressed Harry.

"I shall look forward to seeing them all," she answered docilely. "I shall try in every way to please you."

"What is the matter, Ann?" Harry was suddenly on one knee by her chair. "You have seemed like a stone statue all evening. Is it something I have said or done? Don't you like Stratford Hall?"

How troubled he looked. She put her hands on his broad shoulders and felt his hands encircle her waist. "Oh, yes," she confided, her face close to his, "and it is nothing you have said or done. It is only that I am so afraid of disappointing you in some way."

"Disappointing me? You have brought me nothing but joy. Oh, Ann, my dearest, Ann." He buried his face in her breasts. "It is I who am not worthy of you."

With one lithe movement he rose and, gathering her in his arms, carried her across the broad center hall into the shadows of the spacious master bedroom chamber, where the great mahogany bed stood, the curtains drawn back and the covers turned down for the night. "This is your homecoming," he said as he laid her gently on the soft linen sheets.

From that night Ann grew to love Stratford Hall. Insulated by the solitude and serenity of the great plantation, she watched her husband's gratitude and affection for her change daily into something deeper, more urgent. As if she were a new rose, she felt the tight petals that enclosed her innermost self unfurl beneath his eyes, his mouth, his hands. She had never imagined the joy that being his wife, truly his wife, would bring to her. No jealousy remained in her heart about the dead Matilda. Indeed, she felt real sorrow when she gathered the last summer flowers from the garden and placed them at the doorway of the brick vault, before she and Harry departed for Richmond in October. "I pray she rests in peace," she told Nat West, who accompanied her. "I feel certain I, too, would have loved her if we had met."

In Richmond, visitors streamed to the governor's mansion at the foot of Capitol Hill to exchange news of turbulent activity in Philadelphia. Citizen Genêt, the first ambassador from the French Republic, had continued to spread a plague of troubles wherever he traveled in the United States. He insolently commissioned American citizens to arm the vessels he was outfitting and spoke of appealing to the people over the President's head until Washington was white with rage. Even Jefferson privately was calling Genêt's presence "calamitous."

Allying himself with Washington, Hamilton, and the Federalists, Harry strove to keep Virginia completely neutral. Though he was still close friends with Jemmy Madison, he was upset at the Republicans, who had pushed through Congress a series of discriminatory measures against British shipping, supposedly in retaliation for British offenses against neutral American ships. But it was apparent to Harry that the measures were intended to break the United States' dependence on Britain for trade markets and financial credit.

"Do we try to pick a quarrel with England?" he asked Madison crossly when his friend stopped by Richmond a few months later. "I can only say, Thanks be to God, your savior and saint Mr. Jefferson has finally resigned and taken himself back to his mountain home. As long as both he and

Hamilton remained in the Cabinet, there was nothing but tempest-tossed waters for Washington to sail."

Madison shrugged. He was not about to be drawn into an argument. "I understand Patrick Henry refuses to come out of retirement and serve as secretary of state for the President, nor will he be chief justice. He is such a stubborn old codger, but perhaps wiser than I thought." Madison smiled. "Politics is either a quagmire or a rapids. It pulls one down or tosses one about so that there is a question as to which end is up!"

"And so Edmund Randolph becomes secretary of state," Harry said thoughtfully, "another rider of the rapids . . ."

"Of course, politicians have their more ecstatic moments." Madison looked up at Harry from under his eyebrows. "What think you of your brother Richard Bland's wooing of that Philadelphia Quaker miss?"

Harry suddenly was all attention. "You jest!"

"I swear I do not!" Jemmy pulled his chair closer to Harry's. "Eliza Collins is her name, the daughter of a prominent merchant and as pert and charming a young lady as you have ever set eyes on. Why, he has been courting her for several months, and recently she has agreed to become not only his wife but also an Episcopalian! I cannot imagine why he has not told you—perhaps because of the question of religion."

"Richard Bland to marry in June," Harry repeated to Ann that evening. "I can hardly believe it. Just how Jemmy Madison learned all the ins and outs of the love affair I could not imagine until I managed to wring out of him that he was himself courting Eliza Collins's closest friend, a young widow by the name of Dolley Todd. In fact, Eliza introduced them. Despite his most strenuous efforts, Jemmy has not yet managed to win Mrs. Todd's consent and therefore is greatly envious of Richard Bland, who, it appears, succeeded in gaining Miss Collins's heart with much less effort!"

Ann put her hand to her mouth to stifle her laughter. "It's just that I can't imagine your friend Mr. Madison as a suitor—or, even worse, as a lover!"

Gently he pulled her hand away and playfully kissed her nose. "Strange and beautiful are the ways of Cupid."

The Tidewater, 1794

"I knew Eliza would love Virginia and Sully," Richard Bland boasted to Harry and Ann when he had sailed into Stratford with his Philadelphia bride in August. "And she does! She is an uncommonly good manager, and already—in a few weeks—has turned my rough bachelor house into a warm home."

"You're a lucky man. I really like her very much," said Harry.

"And I, as well," added Ann, who had immediately taken to the tall sparkling-eyed Eliza Collins Lee. "I love the stories of her Quaker childhood and life in Philadelphia."

"Good and bad," Richard Bland murmured. "Has she told you about the terrible plague of yellow fever that ravaged the city last year?"

Ann nodded, for Eliza had graphically described the horror in Philadelphia, with vehicles laden with the dead choking the roads, and the stench of death everywhere. Even her best friend Dolley's husband, John Todd, had been taken. "His death nearly broke her heart," Eliza mourned.

"But it will mend soon, I hope," Ann ventured. "My husband's dear friend Mr. Madison has confessed his deepest devotion to Mrs. Todd. It is our understanding that he waits daily and with great desperation for her answer to his suit."

"Oh, when you meet Dolley, you will understand his devotion to her," Eliza answered quickly. "She has the kindest heart and the brightest smile I have ever known. You and she would no doubt quickly come to love each other, just as you and I have."

It was a confirmation of the instant friendship that had sprung between the two sisters-in-law. "I like her, though we are so different!" Ann exclaimed to Harry that night in bed. "Eliza is quick and smart, and I—"

"And you are pure gold, my Ann, pure gold," he murmured, taking her in his arms.

In the dark, still hours of the August night, Harry lay awake, Ann's dark head nestled on his shoulder. His mind raced with the news that Richard Bland had carried from Philadelphia. For one thing, it was rumored there that Harry was to be given overall command of a large federal militia army to march into the back country of Pennsylvania, and perhaps into the western states, to ferret out distillers of whiskey who, by refusing to pay federal taxes on their products, were seeking to "repeal" the tax through their resistance. As governor of Virginia, he had already called on the state militia to put down the rebels in the western part of his state. The step was unpleasant, but necessary if the national tax was to be supported. To command a large military force would be a challenge, and he had little doubt he would accept, even though it would mean leaving Ann for weeks, perhaps even months. He stirred restlessly. Something else was bothering him. Richard Bland had also told him that political talk, particularly the talk among Federalist politicians in Philadelphia, was that Jefferson and Washington had not parted amicably. Richard Bland's revelation had brought to mind a comment a state senator had made to Harry a few weeks earlier in Richmond. The man had been present at a dinner party at Monticello in the late spring and repeated to Harry a contemptuous remark he insisted Jefferson had made about Washington, inferring that Washington would be governed by British influences unless influenced by wise advisers.

Such a slur made Harry burn with anger. The comment insulted the President's integrity and his intelligence. Moving gently so as not to wake Ann, he climbed down from the tall bed and reached for his dressing gown. He lit a candle in his study, then pulled out a clean piece of paper and set it on the desk before him.

Undecided, Harry sat staring at the blank piece of paper. He pictured Tom Jefferson's face, the thin freckled skin pulled taut over the high nose, the cool, judgmental blue-gray eyes. Resolutely Harry dipped his pen into the inkwell. He must report the incident to Washington. He would do it without malice, for his deep loyalty to and love for the President demanded it. He bent his head and began to write.

Upon reflection, the colonel could see that writing to President Washington in the quiet Stratford night was quite in character for Harry Lee, who was a man of candor and completely loyal to the commander in chief, whom he admired and loved. But Harry sometimes acted rashly. That daring and the selfless lack of personal concern for future consequences, so admirable in a soldier, were not always commendable in private and political life. Yet it seemed to the colonel that Lee's impetuosity was always a result of his total integrity of character. Harry Lee did not always care from which side the wind of fortune blew; he could not dissemble. It was, in many ways, his most admirable quality, one which at the same time made the course of his life more difficult.

The President acknowledged Harry's letter without comment. In truth, Washington was facing a year crucial to the federal experiment and to his administration. Among the major problems was the Whiskey Rebellion. In 1791, Congress levied a moderate excise tax on distilleries that was viewed as tyrannical and unjust by the mountain men of western Pennsylvania, for the distilling of surplus corn was a popular means of their livelihood. Pennsylvania

Governor Thomas Mifflin, a Jeffersonian Republican, was dragging his heels in enforcing the tax law, lest it hurt his popularity.

As governor of Virginia, Harry Lee was sympathetic to the views of these Appalachian constituents but acutely aware that Washington and Hamilton had come to view their rebellion as a test of the federal government's ability to enforce its laws within the states. In the fall of 1794, Lee accepted the President's request that he lead an army of fifteen thousand federal militiamen into the Pennsylvania Appalachians. Washington personally inspected the uniformed force at Fort Cumberland before they marched out and Hamilton accompanied the army into the mountains.

When the troops arrived in western Pennsylvania, the rebel leaders vanished and resistance to the tax crumbled. To Lee's credit no lives were lost. A few frightened and unmilitant ringleaders were caught and convicted of treason but later pardoned by the President.

While Jefferson may have scoffed at the incident, Washington and Hamilton expressed great relief. The national government had passed its first severe test in domestic relations, and attention could now be turned back to the stormy international scene. Relations between Great Britain and the United States, never completely restored since the war for independence, had become severely strained. Now at war with France, England was boldly applying her ancient doctrine that enemy property seized on the high seas, even if carried by neutral ships, was fair game. Already a good number of American commerce vessels had been challenged and roughly treated en route to French ports, exasperating even Hamilton.

It would never do for the fledgling nation to become embroiled in another war, so Washington sent Chief Justice John Jay to the English court to try to preserve peace and also secure America's territorial integrity in the Ohio country, for England still stubbornly clung to her military posts in the Northwest Territory.

In March 1795, Jay's treaty arrived in Philadelphia. By its terms, England would overtly replace France as America's most favored ally and thereby reap a plentiful flow of raw materials from the United States to fuel her war efforts against France. In return, Britain promised America respect on the seas and agreed to vacate her forts in the Northwest Territory as well as open the colonial ports in the Indies to American trade.

Jay had won an excellent treaty even though England had held the high cards in the negotiations. But to the Republicans the treaty was distasteful— "a ruinous barge" is how Madison put it. James Monroe, then Washington's Ambassador to France, poured out his anguish in letters to his Republican intimates in the Congress, who fell upon the treaty in a cascade of violent rage.

Thomas Jefferson, retired at Monticello, was not able to lead a Republican fight against ratification, and Edmund Randolph, who had assumed Jefferson's position as secretary of state, found himself in the position of officially supporting Washington's policy while secretly working to defeat it. Despite the vehement opposition and with only a bare majority of the Senate voting to ratify, Washington signed the treaty in June of 1795. It was an act of personal courage on Washington's part, and Harry Lee respected the President for his stand.

When Harry returned to Virginia after quelling the Whiskey Rebellion, he found himself no longer governor. His term was expiring and under state law he could not run again. It was, perhaps, just as well, for statewide Republican sentiment ran high. He was, however, immediately elected to the House of Delegates, where he became one of the strongest voices of Federalism in the south. It was not a popular stance, and Harry antagonized many as he spoke out in support of Washington's government and the Jay Treaty.

Despite worrisome financial problems brought on by the continuing stalemate in his struggle to obtain clear title to the land at Matildaville, Harry remained optimistic and resolute, his happiness increased when Ann bore a son in the spring of 1795.

Renaissance

1796–1810

Mount Vernon, 1796

Reflections of the high noon sun danced so brightly on the waters of the Potomac that Ann Carter Lee had to shade her eyes as she stood on the long veranda—or gallery, as her host termed it—of the Mount Vernon manor house. She and Harry were interrupting an extended stay at Sully for a brief visit with the President and Lady Washington. It seemed to Ann that Mount Vernon crystallized the personalities of Harry's beloved General Washington and his small, blue-eyed wife. All was serene and gracious, never a twig out of place on the entire estate or a moment of confusion in this house, despite the constant stream of relatives and guests. The President kept a sharp eye on his plantation. Not a stalk of wheat ripened in his fields, not a black child outgrew his shoes, not a windowpane cracked in one of the outbuildings, but Washington attended to it. When he was commanding the army, it had been so. And now, as President, he held Mount Vernon ever in his heart.

Ann turned as Lady Washington swept out onto the shady gallery with her granddaughter, pretty Nelly Custis. "I never cease to be amazed at the order and tranquillity of your home." Ann sighed with wonder.

Martha Washington's eyes sparkled as she motioned for the house servant who was following her to place the glass bowl of punch on the gallery table. "Mount Vernon is a soldier's home. Schedule and discipline are the virtues that afford pleasant living. With the heavy burdens the President bears, it is his solace, and my pleasure, to have Mount Vernon run just as he wishes."

Ann almost burst into laughter. Lady Washington now spoke in a rather formal tone about her husband, yet last night, after a glass or two of wine, she had called him "my old man" and on their way to bed had affectionately twisted the gilt buttons on his vest as they stood discussing some household matter in the hall.

Lady Washington smoothed out her full panniered skirts and patted the seat of the chair beside her. "Come, sit beside me, child, and tell me the news of your family and the dear Lees at Sully."

The simple, old-style dress, the dainty white mobcap trimmed in the finest Mechlin lace—she is always dressed just so, thought Ann, but this old-fashioned look becomes her. Eighteen-year-old Nelly, who was languidly dipping glasses into the frosty punch, was dressed, like herself, in a new high-waisted dress of classic lines, and her hair was also unpowdered, falling in a dark cascade of ringlets on her neck.

"Your little son, the one with the charming name, how old is he?" Lady Washington asked Ann as she accepted a glass of punch from her grand-daughter.

"My little fair-haired boy is just over a year old. Algernon Sidney is named for a gallant English soldier and early believer in freedom. He is with us at Sully."

"Dear, dear Sully!" Martha Washington smiled. "I am exceedingly fond of that house and of the family who dwell within!"

Indeed, it was a well-designed wooden farmhouse some fifty miles northwest of Mount Vernon, built by Richard Bland Lee and furnished by Eliza Collins Lee with stylish Philadelphia furniture. "It is lovely and is . . . was" she faltered slightly, "such a happy place."

"What is it, my dear?" Martha had been quick to catch the break in the younger woman's words.

Ann drew a breath. "When Mr. Lee and I arrived at Sully in late May with our little boy, we were greeted by Richard Bland, Eliza, and their baby daughter, Mary, only a month younger than our own baby. How delightful the two babes were as they played with each other! We would sit enchanted on the grass in the garden and watch them toddle about in their puddin caps, like two little blond angels, and, in love and jest, we even joined their little hands on the open Bible and pledged them to each other, hoping that as they grew up they would love each other just as innocently and beautifully." Ann looked down at her hands in her lap. "Only two weeks ago, little Mary took ill with chills, then fever, and before our eyes she died in Eliza's arms." Ann's eyes spilled over with tears. "I know it is God's will. All my life I've seen Him draw babies and little children to Him. It's only that . . ."

Lady Washington reached over to hold Ann's hand. "I understand only too well, my dear. Life is mysterious and not always easy to bear. Children are born, children die. It is so very very difficult to lose a child . . . at any age."

Ann looked up sympathetically. Martha Washington had seen both children from her first marriage die in young adulthood. Now she devoted her affection to her four grandchildren, particularly pretty Nelly and George Washington Parke Custis, who was away in boarding school.

"Life is vinegar mixed with honey." Nell knelt by her grandmother's chair. "Maybe one enjoys the sweetness more because of the sadness that tempers it."

Martha Washington gently touched her granddaughter's glossy dark hair. "I understand the pain you feel for your brother-in-law and his wife, my dear Ann. But at least they had their angel with them for a few precious months. How much more difficult to have never had a child at all."

She means the President, Ann mused. It was obvious that he adored children and young people, and his step-grandchildren and myriad Washington nieces and nephews were always visiting at Mount Vernon. Even those who were not his relations came. The President had always shown a deep, fatherly interest in men like Harry, and Alexander Hamilton, and Lafayette. In fact, Lafayette's young son was now staying at Mount Vernon. It was perhaps the great unhappiness of the President's life that he had no children of his own.

"I didn't mean to sound melancholy," Ann confided. "It is only that I grew up in such a big happy family at Shirley. I was, perhaps, too sheltered."

The sound of voices and heavy footsteps pounding down the hall interrupted her words. The President and Harry, their broad shoulders filling the open doorway, their boots mud-spattered from the long morning's ride, greeted their ladies on the gallery.

Ann rose in deference to the President, her heart leaping as she caught sight of her own handsome husband, a smile flashing across his tanned face, his hat with its blue cockade under one arm.

"I sometimes wonder, Harry, what do our ladies talk of in this quiet hour before dinner?" the President asked with a mocking smile as he accepted a punch glass from Nelly.

Martha had a spirited answer ready for him: "We talk of things in our hearts, and of garden cuttings and gossip."

"And favorite books and the color of ribbons!" added Nelly, linking her arm through her grandfather's.

"I declare," Ann exclaimed to her husband later, as they dressed for three-o'clock dinner, "I have never seen the President look better or seem happier."

"That is because he is home at Mount Vernon for the summer." Harry splashed the foamy lather from his freshly shaved cheeks. "He longs to be done with the presidency and spend his days as a farmer, a fox hunter, a gentleman of books and leisure, sitting under the shade of his own fig and vine again." Wiping his face on a linen towel, Harry crossed the room and took Ann's hand. "How fresh and pretty you look, all in white! Let me pin on your brooch." He took the miniature portrait of the President from her fingers and carefully fastened it to the high collar of her dress.

"You smell of Windsor soap!" She sniffed appreciatively, then grew serious. "But what will happen to the country if the President does not accept another term? There is no one who can take his place!"

Harry nodded soberly. "No one. Pray God Jefferson does not attain the office, for he will surely wreck the delicate balance Washington maintains between England and France. Hamilton is Washington's natural successor, but he has been accused of so much speculation, corruption, and *whatever* that, even now, retired to private life as he has been for over a year, he could not possibly marshal enough votes to win." Harry's fingers played idly with the sash at Ann's waist. "The perfect solution would be to convince Patrick Henry to seek the position. He is not a Federalist, but he does hold Washington's respect and confidence, and Hamilton, who does not like Adams, supports Henry as well. He would surely carry the Federalist vote. Nor is Henry a Republican, for he cannot stand Tom Jefferson, but he is a believer in a strict interpretation of the Constitution and shares many of the Republicans' 'democratic' viewpoints! He therefore would have support from that side, too."

"But would he consent to stand for the office?" Ann asked.

Harry shook his head ruefully. "That is the rub. I have approached him on the President's behalf twice already. Would he serve as Washington's secretary of state when Jefferson resigned? No. Would he serve as chief justice of the United States? No. Nothing will induce him to leave Virginia— not even the prospect of the presidency!"

"What about Jemmy Madison?" Ann stood still as Harry drew a pale-pink rose from the bowl on the dressing table and pinned it in her dark hair.

"Never! He is as controversial as Hamilton. One seems the mirror image of the other." Harry shook his head thoughtfully. "I fear no one remains but John Adams."

"If only President Washington would consent to a third term." Ann sighed and took Harry's hand as they descended the staircase to dinner.

Dinner at Mount Vernon had taken place punctually at three o'clock for as long as Harry could remember. It was the President's favorite meal, a bountiful repast, for he usually took nothing but cold meat and tea in the morning before he rode out on the business of the farm, then cold applejack punch at one o'clock, served outdoors when the weather permitted. Following dinner, the President retired to his study for several hours. He might come out at about six for coffee, but then again, he might not. It was his way of protecting himself from the constant onslaught of family and guests at Mount Vernon.

It seemed that Washington was in a very good mood this afternoon. From the head of the long table in the banquet hall he served leg of boiled pork while Lady Washington presided over the roast chickens at the foot of the table. In between were mutton chops, roast beef, cabbage, hominy, potatoes, fried tripe, green and yellow pickles, white onions—Harry could not count all the dishes.

"Always was my favorite uniform," the President was saying to Ann, who had just expressed admiration for the Peale portrait in which Washington wore his old Virginia militia uniform. The painting, which hung in the hall, captured the wide cheekbones, tight mouth, and strong chin of the man. It was a reflective face, a bit weathered by time, yet with a mildness of expression that did not suggest the emotions rushing beneath.

"And he has captured you so well," Ann continued thoughtfully. "He has depicted a . . . a Roman quality in your face."

By Jove! He does resemble a classic Roman, thought Harry. How clever of Ann to notice. He caught the President's eye. "Did you know, sir, that Gilbert Stuart commented that, when you sat for him, he sensed you have a tremendous temper?" Harry could not resist the bold, teasing question.

Lady Washington's fair cheeks flushed defensively. "Mr. Stuart took a great deal upon himself!" she retorted from the other end of the table.

For a moment a shocked silence surrounded the table before the President finally smiled and said simply, "Mr. Stuart is quite right. I do have a temper!"

Laughter rang through the dining room. "Only you can tease him so, Colonel Lee," Nelly Custis whispered at Harry's side.

Harry took a sip of wine, noting Ann's mock-reproving glance at his remark. He would never have made it, except that he could tell Washington was in an affable mood. There were times in the President's company when one sat in silence for three, five, ten minutes at a stretch. The Mount Vernon planter was not given to small talk, but if one knew him well, one could sense when he was feeling expansive.

The three attending servants brushed the crumbs from the white tablecloth and set out a profusion of tarts, blackberry pies, and cheeses, along with nuts and peaches and raisins. It cost a pretty penny to maintain the standards of this house—of any house!—Harry thought appreciatively. He had grown particularly conscious lately of the high cost of living comfortably. One might be land-rich, but without hard cash, life became a muddle of borrowing to invest in crops and commerce in order to pay back one's loans and, one hoped, make a bit of profit. The Potomac Company's canal had been completed last year, but beset by engineering problems, it was still inoperative. Matildaville, although it boasted an inn, a forge, a gristmill, and a few warehouses, remained all but a ghost town.

Sighing, Harry reached for a brown-sugar tart. His finances were a terrible quagmire. Three years earlier, when it seemed that the Fairfax litigations would soon be resolved, he had gone into partnership with John Marshall, a friend since the dark days of Valley Forge, to purchase some one hundred and sixty thousand additional acres of the Fairfax properties. Marshall contacted his relative through marriage, the Philadelphia financier Robert Morris, who agreed to put up the monies when needed in exchange for a share of the profits. Now the money was due, but Morris was overextended and in great financial difficulty himself. Harry had not told Ann, but he had agreed to loan Morris forty thousand dollars so that partial payment could be made and Morris supported until he could steady his finances. After all, Morris had been the financial wizard behind the Revolution, hadn't he? If anyone could safely pull through these hard times, Morris could. Harry knew his money was safe and in just a little time would be repaid.

"I say, Colonel Lee, shall we walk in the garden after dinner?" The President had turned the full force of his blue eyes in Harry's direction. "It is too nice an evening to sequester myself in my study with newspapers and letters. I would rather continue our conversations."

Harry quickly accepted the invitation. For Washington to break his usual pattern was a compliment. They had already spent the morning together and talked of many things, most of them practical—the prospect of a threshing machine which Washington, who had a great bent for mechanics, was contemplating ordering; the qualities of a new strain of wheat; improvements the President wanted made to his plantation as he contemplated retirement. And they had touched on the disappointment of the canal project at the Great Falls, which gave Harry the opportunity to bring up a financial transaction between them.

In February he had given the President shares in the Bank of Columbia, in partial payment for Washington's holdings in the Great Dismal Swamp Company. He had considered the bank shares to be of par value, and Washington had accepted them with that understanding, but in recent months the shares dropped precipitously in value, and Harry felt himself still in the President's debt. What's more, he realized that Washington felt that way as well. This morning he had explained that he was selling some land to pay off the differential, and Washington had readily agreed.

How fragrant the good earth smelled in the afternoon sun. Harry breathed in its aroma as he followed his host down the neat cultivated rows of currants, strawberries, and gooseberries. Before them lay a shady avenue of towering catalpas and magnolias interspersed with deep-green Scotch pine and pale-green weeping willows.

"Look how well Lee cuttings thrive in Washington soil!" The President took his arm and pointed to a thriving horse chestnut grown from a cutting Harry had once sent from Stratford to Mount Vernon along with an assortment of box plantings. Washington led the way to a wooden bench in the shade of a tulip poplar. "Shall we sit? I am in the mood to reminisce."

"About the war?" Harry settled himself and stretched out his booted legs. "I could do that with you for hours, sir." He sighed nostalgically. "I most often now think of Greene and that drama played out in the Carolinas. What a hero! Next to you, he was the strength of the Revolution."

"My southern commander gave a brilliant and indispensable account of himself, yet I am afraid it went largely unappreciated," Washington said gravely. "No one yet realizes that without the bravery of Greene and Morgan and Lee, the south would have fallen to the British." His eyes flickered to his companion. "And with the toppling of Virginia, the rest of the states would soon have been reswallowed." He shook his head. "I think often of Greene, with his set, stubborn jaw! He and his Kitty were settled on their seaside plantation in Georgia, given to them in gratitude by that state, for such a brief time. I still grieve over his early death." Tears clouded Washington's eyes.

Harry nodded without speaking. Nathaniel Greene, next to Washington, led his pantheon of heroes.

"I think," the President continued, "of those I have known and loved in my life. My first real friend, George William Fairfax, is now dead and buried in England. His widow, Sally, remains there, never to return. And I think from time to time of George Mason. We were bonded in securing Virginia's rights and liberties, only to fall apart over the securing of the Federal Constitution. That our rift never healed saddens me to no end."

"And your friend Richard Henry Lee?" Harry probed.

"He was a most admirable, complex man." Washington pulled a weed from the ground near their feet. "You know, I never did quite understand his nature. He sacrificed everything for this nation and for Virginia, didn't care a bit for money or land—I never really did understand that." His voice drifted away, then came back strongly. "We were friends from boyhood, born only a few miles apart, a few days apart. A part of me died with him two years ago." He looked at Harry. "Richard Henry, Francis Lightfoot,

William, Arthur . . 'a band of valiant brothers,' John Adams admiringly
called them. All the Lees have given everything, risked everything, for that
great undertaking of ours."

Harry looked intently at the older man. "And now, sir, you abandon it
while it still needs you."

"If the nation is worthy, it will stand without me. I have never thought
myself indispensable to its well-being. Other men wait to lead who think it
high time I leave the field—" he looked up at Harry with an enigmatic
expression—"Jefferson, Monroe, even your good friend Madison."

"They love you, sir," Harry said staunchly. "Why can't men rise above
their political viewpoints and keep their affections for each other intact? I
cannot understand that!"

"But it is fact that they cannot!" Washington looked gently at Harry.
"You, who give me and my administration your total support and loyalty, do
so to your own detriment, for Jefferson knows of your animosity to him. It
would be better for you if you stood with the Republican contingent, whose
influence seems to grow daily. I fear there will be no place for you in
politics, either Virginia's or the nation's, should a Republican ever rise to
power."

"I follow my conscience and act from my heart. I cannot do otherwise," Harry replied softly.

"You speak from instinct, Harry. It was always so with me, for I was
never the philosopher setting forth laws or theory of government." He grew
reflective. "Richard Henry Lee, Patrick Henry, Thomas Jefferson, George
Mason, all thought long and hard to define freedoms, create government—
far more than I ever did or could. My role, like yours, was to carry out what
they designated—whether in battle, to win those freedoms they espoused, or
in the execution of government, to make those laws they expounded work. I
could only perform and lead as my instincts and my breeding dictated. I
trust my actions have been acceptable."

"Acceptable!" Harry gasped. "Sir, you must not listen to the vile abuse
the Republicans pour out! Our nation will be sorely tried if you are not at its
helm. And to think we have no one but John Adams to succeed you!"

"He will do well enough. He is completely honest . . . a bit vain and
thin-skinned, but intelligent, cautious, and dependable. He will do the job
nicely." Washington smiled. "Richard Henry Lee would have agreed with
me on that. He and Adams greatly admired each other."

The sun was spreading a purple mantle over the waters of the Potomac.
As the men rose to their feet, Washington put his hand on Harry's arm. "I
leave the burden to Adams without regret. I shall sit on my gallery and
watch the new federal city grow before my eyes, Harry. And when one day I

find I have lived out my life, I shall die and be buried in this red earth I have loved so dearly."

"You are still young, more vital than men half your age," Harry remonstrated.

"I have not got a son, Harry, although I have sons of the heart." He looked affectionately at the younger man.

Sully, 1796

"He talks of death," Harry remarked to Ann as their carriage rumbled toward Sully, "though not in a melancholy way. Look, Ann!" he suddenly cried out. "Can you believe this?" The bend of the road ahead was crowded with wagons lumbering to the market in Alexandria, flocks of bleating sheep and herds of cattle raising swirls of dust as they were driven toward the port city by sunburned hostlers.

"They come far, from the Blue Ridge," Harry explained. "It is this commerce that will bind us as a nation, west to east, east to west. I tell you, Ann, we must not lose faith in the Potomac Canal. You see the future before your eyes. Someday this produce, these animals will be carried by water."

Ann squeezed his hand in support. This winding road, once her great grandfather's, had for years been known as "King Carter's old ox road." Now Harry called it the road west. It was hard to imagine, hard to look so far ahead, as he could.

By late afternoon, they had turned off the pike and started up the lane to Sully, apple trees full of small green fruit on either side. The brown wooden house sat hushed in the hot afternoon sun. Ann gathered her shawl and the basket of jellies Martha Washington had sent to Sully and, with Harry's helping hand, stepped from the carriage, tired but content. Three lovely days with Harry in the serenity of Mount Vernon! Now she wished for nothing but a chance to comb her hair and wash the dust from her hands before holding her little son in her arms.

Richard Bland waited at the door as they climbed the front steps, the servants crowding behind them with canvas portmanteaus and bandboxes. "You must go up quickly, Ann." His voice was anxious. "Your son is sick. Like our Mary, Algernon seems to have the chills and the fever."

The Tidewater, 1798

Harry steeled himself to accept the death of his son and lent his strength to Ann as she watched her baby laid beneath the cool, restful trees of Sully close by the tiny grave of Mary Lee. She had not taken the death with bitterness, and in the months that followed seemed to deal with it in her own head and heart. For that he was grateful.

In the late summer of 1798, she was again pregnant—"The child kicks with the strength of a savage Indian," Harry told James Madison, who had stopped for a short visit at Stratford. "The little Madison," weary of politics, had left his seat in the House of Representatives and now lived "in active retirement," as he put it, on his plantation, Montpelier, in Orange County. His four years of marriage to Dolley Todd of Philadelphia were extremely happy, but as yet childless.

"You are a good father." Madison gave him an affectionate look. "You have the soul of a nurturer, Harry."

"Of children, but not of land. I'm not much of a farmer," Harry confessed. "I have sold a great deal of my acreage in the last few years to meet my debts—perhaps with some relief, for I have no real interest in corn and wheat or even cotton, with which our South Carolina and Georgia neighbors seem to do so well. Stratford I cannot sell, according to the deed of trust I signed before Matilda's death. It will pass to Henry when he is twenty-one. Since the death of Richard Henry and the scattering of his family, I have been forced to sell most of the adjoining land, even the land on which Chantilly stands. You know, old Colonel Phil, Matilda's father, left many large debts unsettled, even with his younger brothers. I have tried to meet those obligations as well as my own. It was a matter of honor."

"You were born to be a soldier, not to grub in the dirt, Harry—" Madison looked up at him with a smile—"or I should say, General Lee; that is your new rank, is it not?"

"It is," Harry said proudly, "but a rank I doubt I shall have an opportunity to carry into battle. I feel Mr. Adams will keep us at peace somehow or other."

Madison scoffed lightly: "Poor old Adams, what a travesty he makes of our government."

John Adams had taken the office of President of the United States on March 4, 1797, with Jefferson, who received the second highest number of votes, becoming his vice-president. "A lukewarm Federalist as president, with an ardent Republican as vice-president," Hamilton had written to Harry. "The lion and the lamb are to lie down together." Adams was not having an easy time of it. Lacking George Washington's charisma, estranged from Jefferson, and put off by Hamilton's audacity, the man from Massachusetts, an uneasy administrator, seemed a lonely, insecure leader.

Over the past months, President Adams had faced serious problems concerning the country's relationship with France. He had been forced to dismiss the ardently pro-French James Monroe as ambassador after a series of disagreements resulting from ratification of the Jay Treaty, and the aggressive, subversive French Directory that now ruled that troubled country refused to accept Monroe's successor. France's attitude toward the United States had in the past year become truculent and threatening, and a three-man delegation sent over by Adams was treated with contempt.

"Adams tries to follow Washington's policy of neutrality despite the efforts of his own party to force him into war with France. You must give him credit for that," Harry insisted. "He walks uncertainly in the footsteps of a hero soldier, always dwarfed by Washington's long shadow."

"So Hamilton remains the dark, changeling heart of the Federalist Party," Madison sneered. "The prospects of war hang heavy over us. Already more than three hundred American ships have been captured by vessels flying French colors. Adams has appointed Washington to be our military commander in chief. And who do we find becomes the chief officer under Washington? Why, none other than that warhawk Federalist Alexander Hamilton!"

"I don't believe we'll go to war," Harry insisted. "We may outfit ourselves for war, building ships like the *Constitution*, but Adams will negotiate, not fight, his way through this. I'm certain of it." He thrust his hands deep in his pockets and looked seriously at Madison. "Again, my reason works against my soldier's heart. While I yearn to lead a battle charge again, in truth I do not want war with France."

His Federalist Party split over the past ten years on the question of supporting the French Revolution, Adams was determined to keep the United States neutral in the war between France and Great Britain. However, under increasing French provocation, Adams had been forced to turn to George Washington to provide military leadership. The new commander in chief's first act was to appoint Hamilton a major general and C. C. Pinckney and Henry Knox, both seasoned veterans of the Revolution, brigadier generals. Knox had refused a position junior to Hamilton's, and Harry Lee, already a brigadier general, was advanced to major general by Washington.

Madison smiled encouragingly. "Harry, you serve as a Federalist in the Republican Virginia Assembly. Why don't you seek greater opportunity? Run for the National Congress."

"But I would argue the opposite viewpoint from yours on most every issue, dear friend, while you, the ardent Republican, would not be there to balance my Federalism. Would you really encourage me in that?"

"Would I? I do, I most surely do!" Madison held out his hand.

Harry hesitated, then smiled. "If war can be averted . . . and our new baby comes safely into this world, then I promise to give your challenge full consideration. I only warn you, be prepared!"

Sully, 1799

"I tell you," Eliza Collins Lee said, "my friend Dolley Madison has come to love your Virginia." She smiled into Ann Carter Lee's dark eyes and affectionately linked arms with her as the two strolled beneath the trees at Sully. "One would think Dolley was born in Orange County and had been mistress of Montpelier plantation all her life!"

Ann smiled. "I am so very anxious to meet your glamorous friend."

"Oh, she's not really glamorous—not even beautiful, like you, my dear Ann. But she is so interesting that in time everyone comes to think she is beautiful! I am anxious to go to Montpelier. Perhaps I shall pay her a short visit."

"Well, if Dolley Madison has really become a Virginian, then you will go for a week and stay for a month!" Ann rejoined. " 'Your horse is lame, you cannot leave today,' your host will claim! 'Your linen dress lies unpressed and I cannot let you go home until all your laundry is done,' your hostess will claim! 'But you must stay and meet Grandmamma, who comes next week,' she'll next plead winningly." Ann dimpled. "You see, as a Virginian, I know all the tricks to hold a welcome guest!"

"Look, Eliza!" Diverted by the pounding of horses' hoofs, Ann stood on tiptoe to look down the winding lane to the pike. "I think I hear our husbands returning home! Can you see them? They are racing each other, riding like the wind!"

Side by side, the horses came pounding up the lane, dust swirling under their hoofs.

"No fair! You won only because you used your spurs!" Richard Bland called out, laughing breathlessly as he drew up his mount beside Harry at the wooden steps of the manor house. "I was leading you for half a mile."

"You gave me a run for my money!" Flushed and exuberant, Harry swung down from the saddle. "You give an old man a hard race," he teased.

Richard Bland snorted, giving the lithe forty-three-year-old Harry a mocking smile. "You, an old man? Never! My dear Eliza, would you be so kind as to send to the wine cellar for some cold cider?"

A short while later, seated under tall willows with glasses of cider at their sides, the brothers regaled their wives with descriptions of the new federal city rising on the banks of the Potomac, which they had visited earlier in the day.

"Such wide mud avenues!" Harry exclaimed. "The President's house is almost complete. It's a nice house, square, made of sandstone, but too close to the swamp for my taste! It's designed after a palace in Dublin."

"There are not many buildings up yet," Richard Bland put in, "a few private homes, mostly built on speculation, and a tavern or two. But the buildings to house the war and navy offices are complete, and there is o lovely wooden bridge over the Potomac. One need not bother with ferries and barges any more."

"A bridge!" Ann marveled. "How extraordinary!"

"But it is still no Philadelphia," Harry warned. "If the governor in moves next year as planned, there will be many down-at-the-mouth faces and complaining wives, I can tell you!"

"Well, I shan't complain," said Ann. "I shall be glad you meet so close to home."

Harry smiled. He still could not believe that he, a Federalist, had been elected to the National Congress for the next session.

As if reading his mind, Richard Bland cuffed his brother's arm. "I would have liked to be at the polls in Montross or Alexandria on April twenty-fourth. Everyone said Mr. Jefferson's candidates would win. To be honest, I would have said so, too."

"My husband counts many friends and honest admirers among the freeholders of Westmoreland County," Ann said loyally. "He is known for his generosity, among other fine qualities. No one ever leaves Stratford without a full meal in his stomach and coins in his pocket . . . or more!" Actually, thought Ann, Harry was sometimes too generous, even giving small tracts of land to men in need. Veterans of the Revolution, in particular, could always win a handout.

"I still say it was something of a miracle. Virginians tend to follow the Republicans under Jefferson, and you spoke out in favor of President Adams's unpopular Alien and Sedition Acts," Richard Bland insisted.

"They are necessary acts! The President needs the right to expel foreigners suspected of exciting Jacobean unrest in this country, and anyhow, that act will expire in two years. As to the other," he said with asperity, "it may go a bit far in providing fines and imprisonment for anyone who defames the President or Congress, but it is necessary. This is a time of violent, even hysterical attacks on a government that is trying to walk a thin line between war and peace."

"It is certain Jemmy Madison does not agree with you." Richard Bland rested his pewter tankard in the grass beside him and loosened his vest. "From his so-called retirement at Montpelier he has written heatedly against the bills."

"Politics creates a rift between us, I grant you that," Harry admitted, "but our friendship remains firm."

"We are so proud to have you in the Congress!" Eliza exclaimed joyfully. "How exciting it will be for you and Ann to go off to Philadelphia again. Were you nervous on polling day that you might not win?"

Harry had not gone to the polls on April 24 but had waited at Stratford for the results. Nat West had been his envoy to Alexandria, surveying the voting throughout the long day and returning the next with a vivid description of the scene. Crowds of men had gathered in the town square, many having left their farms and plantations before daybreak so as not to miss any of the election-day excitement. The long wooden plank table stood in the grass by the courthouse steps, with officials with quills and sheets of paper sitting behind it, staring up expectantly as each newcomer pushed through the crowd, registered, and loudly proclaimed his vote to a roar of approval or disapproval from the candidates' supporters. At noon, out came a barrel of whiskey—"Put there by some 'publicans,' " Nat had reported with a snort, "and it was drunk down like rainwater!" The tension and political disagreements grew fierce as the afternoon progressed, men rolling up their sleeves and falling into fistfights, their curses ringing in the air. By three o'clock the balloting was even between the Republican, Dr. Jones, and the Federalist, Harry Lee.

"But then," Nat had explained, "just like the Lord walkin' on the water, a man rides up on a big white horse. Everybody what saw him fell silent, just like lighten' done struck 'em. He hitches his horse to the rail and walks right up to the tables. He gives his name and thunders out, 'I vote for General Lee!' " Nat had sat back with a look of enormous pride. "It was President Washington! He voted for you for the Congress and your brother Richard Bland for the Assembly!"

Harry still felt incredibly grateful for Washington's support. He looked at his sister-in-law. "Was I frightened, Eliza? Nervous?" His face broke into a wide smile. "Not at all, but I admit to being mighty alarmed!"

Philadelphia, 1799

How exciting, invigorating, to be back in Philadelphia! Harry strode down the familiar streets of the old port city, barely warmed by the pale December-morning sun. Thank God for his greatcoat! With his son Henry at the College of William and Mary, he had settled Ann, thirteen-year-old Lucy, and little Carter with a corps of Stratford servants in a comfortable house on Franklin Court near Washington Square, decidedly the most fashionable section of the city. He could barely afford the extravagance. His finances were now more tangled than usual, since Robert Morris had gone bankrupt and now sat in debtors' prison unable to meet his obligations. So much for Harry's loan of forty thousand dollars to Morris. The thought of the prestigious, once highly respected financier languishing in prison was an unpleasant specter, and Harry turned his thoughts to Ann's happy face. She and Lucy, never before close despite Ann's patient efforts to win her stepdaughter's affection, were now having a wonderful time in the city, their days busy with social calls and shopping for new silk dresses, slippers, and bonnets.

He turned to walk by Shippen House, sadly deserted, the windows boarded shut. The doctor was away, and young Thomas lived in South Carolina. Alice Shippen and Nancy, estranged from each other, lived separately in small lodgings in other parts of the city. Poor little Nancy! They had been unable to call on her, for she had become a recluse, a far cry from the sparkling belle once courted by Bushrod Washington when he was studying law in the city, her elegant French diplomat, Louis Otto, and the prominent but despicable Livingston.

How remarkable were the threads that bound a man and a woman, for better or worse, in marriage. What would his life be without Ann? Some would scoff and say that he was being dramatic, but Harry knew of the powers of love. Why, two years ago, in 1797, Francis Lightfoot and his beloved Becky died just days apart. Harry could not imagine one without the other.

Stepping off the curb to allow a full-skirted elderly lady to pass, Harry noticed a gathering on the corner. Curious, he quickened his steps.

Suddenly a man burst from the crowd and stumbled toward him, tears running down his cheeks, and answered the question on Harry's lips. "The President... George Washington is dead."

Washington? Dead? Harry would not believe it! He forced his way through the people grouped around a coach. "A week ago it was," the coach passenger wearily repeated. "Came back from his daily horseback ride on a cold, rainy morning and was soon down with a sore throat. Doctor did all he could to save him, even bled him twice—took a cup of blood, they say! Died of inflammatory quinsy... died peacefully, they say."

Pushing his way out of the crowd, Harry turned homeward. He could not go on to the Congress this morning, could not face anyone.

Ann was out, and he hurried up the stairs to their bedroom, ignoring the happy sounds of his little Carter laughing with his nurse, to be alone with his grief, to control himself. He reached for a piece of paper, for writing always seemed to help him vent his emotions. An hour later, he looked down at what he had scrawled. It was a set of resolutions to present to the Congress the next day, resolutions for the man who had done so much, meant so much. They would help set the precedent for the death of a United States president; the nation's tragedy must be marked with honor. Harry read over the words he had written:

The House of Representatives of the United States, having received intelligence of the death of their highly-valued fellow-citizen GEORGE WASHINGTON, General of the Armies of the United States, and sharing the universal grief this event must produce, *unanimously resolve:*

1. That this House will wait on the President of the United States, in condolence of this national calamity.

2. That the Speaker's chair be shrouded with black, and that the members and officers of the House wear mourning during the session.

3. That a joint committee of both Houses be appointed to report measures suitable to the occasion, and expressive of the profound sorrow with which Congress is penetrated on the loss of a citizen first in war, first in peace, and first in the hearts of his countrymen.

Harry stared at the words, his eyes brimming with tears. He could not contain his sorrow, and, putting his head down on the desk, he cried like a child.

The next day in Congress, Harry listened while his tall, lanky friend and fellow Virginia congressman John Marshall read the resolutions. Marshall had been on the floor of the House when news of Washington's death arrived and moved that the Congress adjourn for the day. By protocol, Marshall then had the right to propose any resolution offered for the observance of the former President's passing, and he had gratefully accepted Lee's.

"It was just as well that Marshall read them," Harry told Ann later that night. "I am not sure I had my emotions well enough in check to say the words myself."

She wrapped her arms about his neck consolingly. "And how were they received?"

"They passed unanimously. Washington's death would seem to be the only thing that draws the Federalists and the Republicans together," he said sadly.

A week later, as Harry sat by the fire on Christmas Eve dandling Carter on his knee, a knock sounded at the front door.

He handed the baby to Ann and greeted the speaker of the House, Mr.

Sedgewick of Connecticut, and the Senate president pro tempore, Mr. Livermore of Massachusetts, as they brushed the newly fallen snow from their hats.

"No, do not leave, Mrs. Lee," Sedgewick said to Ann, who had risen to excuse herself. "Forgive our intrusion on this hallowed eve. We have come to deliver a sad honor to your husband." He paused to look at Livermore. "It is the opinion of the House and the Senate that the funeral oration of our departed president should be delivered by one who knew and loved him well, someone respected by all." With a slight smile, he looked at Harry. "There are many in our Congress whom that description fits, but none quite so well as General Lee. It is our agreement, House and Senate concurring, that the spokesman be you, sir."

"How wise and appropriate of Congress to have chosen you," Ann whispered later after their guests departed, having lingered only for a small glass of holiday wine. "You are the perfect choice, my dear. The President would have liked that."

Throughout that night and all Christmas day, he labored over the eulogy, which he presented at noon on December 26 in the spacious German Lutheran church. The sanctuary was packed to the rafters; even before the solemn firing of the cannon in the early morning, country people had been flocking into the city to join the fashionably dressed somber Philadelphians who thronged the squares and congregated in hushed silence outside the church. Shortly before noon, the Congress had marched, flanked by uniformed soldiers, in solemn procession through the mud- and snow-spotted streets to fill the front pews of the church.

"Your father looks so magnificent," Ann whispered to Lucy as Harry, in his well-cut black frock coat, took the pulpit. It was a long speech, an emotional speech. "Will you go with me to the banks of the Monongahela?" the eulogy began. The soldier-statesman was praised and mourned, but Harry could not refrain from expressing the sweeping, almost compelling sense of nationalism, of continental unity, that Washington had inspired in him. But it was Harry's love for his general that dominated the eulogy. He drew his oration to a close by repeating the simple words he had written in his resolutions: "First in war, first in peace, and first in the hearts of his countrymen . . ."

Philadelphia, 1800

"I've dinner with President Adams tonight!" Harry announced as he entered the Franklin Street house, taking the steps two at a time. "One would think," he told Ann as he dressed for dinner, "that this sixth Congress could unite in our respect for Washington, that his death could narrow the gulf between Federalists and Republicans. But no! The Republicans become more strident, and the Federalists now divide into the 'high party,' led by Hamilton, and the more moderate faction loyal to Adams, of which I am conceived to be a part." He looked at her wryly. "It's funny what ambition and jealousy do to men. I think Hamilton resents the fact that he was not able to lead our army to glory against France—this, although Bonaparte, the same Napoleon Bonaparte who dismissed the Directory and proclaimed himself first consul, turns out to be most agreeable to deal with and, more important, sympathetic to America. Why, he has ordered the cannons of France's army draped with crepe in respect for Washington!"

"Does it matter what Hamilton thinks about the French situation? President Adams had kept us from war quite nicely," Ann said flippantly. "Does it matter that the 'high Federalists,' as you call them, are disturbed, that they omit you from their political maneuverings?"

"Of course it matters, for it more deeply divides the party." Harry was clearly despondent. "Although we rarely see each other, I have written to Hamilton and he to me expressing our continued friendship, but politically we are continents apart. He would seek to have someone other than Adams, preferably a 'high Federalist,' elected president. So Adams retaliates by dismissing from his Cabinet those members who are Hamiltonian Federalists. And since neither side can win without the other, the door is opened for our wily Vice-President Jefferson." Harry frowned in disgust. "The gift of the presidency will be thrust in his lap!"

"You never have liked him, particularly since he delayed his return to Philadelphia this winter to avoid the period of congressional mourning for General Washington, have you?" Ann asked gently.

"Ann, I won't be drawn into it. I do not dismiss Jefferson's brilliance or many of his arguments," Harry said evenly. "To be honest, he dislikes me as much as I him, for he discovered that I wrote Washington about his criticisms. Madison tells me he has given me some rather unpleasant labels—in private, you understand."

"But Mr. Madison would defend you, wouldn't he?" Ann was shocked.

"As a friend, he would defend me, but politically he is bound to Jefferson, for Jemmy's as ardent a believer in states' rights above national interests as any Republican! He stands by his beliefs as I stand by mine, the difference being that he and I respect the beliefs of the other, a posture few in politics find possible" He reached out and pulled her close. "Now, don't look so concerned. Everything will right itself. It always does. Come now, lie on the sofa with your book until I return." He led her to the damask sofa, lighting a candle on the side table. "Think good thoughts . . . think of the joy we shall feel seeing Stratford next week, think of the baby on the way." He bent and kissed her longingly. "Think of me trying to make conversation with Adams tonight. Why he has invited me to dinner I can't imagine! I have stood by his decisions, yes, but we have never been friends."

As Harry's carriage rumbled across the cobblestone streets to the Morris mansion, he considered his last remark to Ann. He and Adams were not friends, in part because Adams had no friends! The solemn-faced little President spent much of his time with his family at his farm in Quincy, Massachusetts. It was rumored he and Abigail Adams disliked Philadelphia, for they had never been well received in the city. Perhaps they would prefer the swamps and thickets and wide, lonely dirt streets of the new federal city! Harry smiled to himself in the darkness of the carriage. Somehow he doubted it.

The President's mansion on Market Street was dimly lit. Harry gave his hat to the black-coated servant and waited in the front hall. Abigail and the rest of the President's family had gone home to summer in Quincy, the President had explained in his note. They would be joining him in the new federal city when the government moved to the banks of the Potomac in the fall; already the handsome crimson damask furniture and Wilton carpet had been removed from the formal receiving room at the front of the house. Harry peered into the empty chamber, then spun on his heel in surprise as John Adams himself came down the hall.

Adams greeted him nervously. "Glad to see you, always glad to see you, General Lee. We've much to talk about. Just a small dinner, another guest has joined us! There will be just three of us."

The President looked tired and agitated as he led his guest into the family sitting room, putting Harry in mind of a remark Benjamin Franklin had made about Adams: "always honest, often great, but sometimes mad."

Harry strode into the sitting room beside the President; to his astonishment, there waited the vice-president, Thomas Jefferson.

It was, he told Ann later that night, a disastrous evening. "John Adams is so fearful of Hamilton, so incensed by Hamilton's lack of loyalty to his administration, that he has turned for support to his archenemy, Thomas Jefferson!" Harry pounded the tabletop with his fist. "I had to sit there, Ann, choking on my dinner, while Adams poured out his heart and Jefferson listened sympathetically. Sympathetic like a fox who is about to consume a jack rabbit!"

"How awful." Ann's eyes were filled with consternation.

Harry loosened his ruffles and tore off his jacket. "When Jefferson had gone, I tried to tell Adams how foolish he was to trust Jefferson. I told him that Jefferson was after the presidency himself!"

"And?"

"And he grew testy with me, replying with some heat that he considered Jefferson less an enemy than many who professed to be his friends. He probably had in mind those two Federalists, McHenry and Pickering, whom he recently dismissed from his Cabinet. Furthermore, he stated that it was his opinion that Mr. Jefferson aspires to no higher station than the vice-presidency!"

"Oh, Harry, I fear you may have alienated Adams. Don't you see? You will have no party unless . . ."

"Unless I keep quiet, hold my tongue." He shook his head. "No, Ann, I must say what I think, what I feel. It is the only honorable thing to do."

The Federal City, 1801

"The winter rains have turned our new federal city into a miserable swamp, a mudhole almost equal to the great Serbonian bog," one of the newly arrived senators had complained miserably the night before, over his ale in Alexandria's Gadsby's Tavern.

I hate having to wade through it myself every morning, Harry thought, a splatter of mud having just broken before his horse's hoofs.

Pennsylvania Avenue, tree-lined and handsome in L'Enfant's drawings, presented itself only as a deep morass of fresh tree stumps and bushes as Harry picked his way alongside horses, carriages, pigs, muddied pedestrians, and a multitude of dogs, all of which were slowly making their way between Georgetown and the new Capitol, three miles away on Jenkin's Heights.

Perhaps, thought Harry, turning his collar up against the freezing rain, he should move from the rooms he had taken above the tailor's shop in Georgetown to one of the new boardinghouses on New Jersey Avenue. Most of the congressmen were staying there, for the avenue was the only main road besides Pennsylvania Avenue convenient to the Capitol. "Capitol" sounded much too impressive to describe the small north wing now completed and occupied by the Senate. A foundation had been laid for the central dome of the building, but the House, lacking quarters, was meeting in a cramped temporary annex—the so-called oven, for it was hot and windowless.

No, he would stay where he was in Georgetown, he told himself. The rooms were cheaper, and money was scarce as hens' teeth these days. God knows, he had sold and mortgaged every bit of land he could over the last few years. But with his Great Falls lands still tied up in litigation, he had little money coming in. At least Ann and the children were safe and warm at

Stratford, with plenty of food in the cellars and the meat house. How brave and beautiful Ann had looked, waving him off in late November, their new baby daughter, Ann, in her arms!

Actually, what I'd like to do, Harry thought, is build a townhouse here in the federal city. John Tayloe III of Mount Airy had already contracted to build a handsome octagon-shaped dwelling nearby on New York Avenue. That showed faith in the new city—although, to be honest, Tayloe was more interested in the racecourse going in on K and 21st Streets than in politics!

As he trotted past the boggy meadow called the President's Square, Harry bought an apple, a hot bun, and sausages from a peddler's cart. The square had become the market for the struggling little city, which to date boasted only a few taverns, an oyster house, one washing woman, and a shoemaker.

He looked at the far end of the meadow, where the President's big sandstone house sat. It looked mournful, desolate, raw against the elements, for there were still no lawns or fences or gardens, only a few ramshackle workmen's shacks and the pits from abandoned brick kilns.

Adams had been living in the President's House for a few months but would have to leave in March. Embarrassing, downright humiliating for the Federalists that he had lost his bid for a second term!

When the Sixth Congress reconvened in the new federal city this past November, the presidential contest between John Adams and Thomas Jefferson had seemed evenly balanced. The campaign leading up to the election had been unusually vicious, the candidates remaining discreetly silent, making no speeches, no charges—indeed, on amicable terms with each other—while their friends and the newspapers did the mudslinging. Adams was linked with militarism and monarchy, while Jefferson was accused of everything from cowardice and egotism to licentious behavior—everything, it seemed, short of murder!

As early December rolled around, Adams appeared to be holding New England solidly in his camp, and New Jersey and Delaware as well. Jefferson was expected to take all the southern states except South Carolina. It was anticipated that South Carolina's eight votes would go to Adams, since the Federalist vice-presidential candidate was that state's venerable soldier C. C. Pinckney.

But they did not. South Carolina had obviously been swayed by the vicious charges and slanders hurled by the Republicans. On December 12, the *National Intelligencer* announced that South Carolina had rejected its native son, Pinckney, along with Adams, and would cast its electoral votes for Jefferson and his running partner, New Yorker Aaron Burr.

Thus Adams would pack up and go home in bitterness to Quincy. But who would serve as president? That question was still unresolved. Jefferson and Burr had received seventy-three electoral votes each, and, according to the election rules, the presidency would go to the man with the larger number of votes, no matter the office for which he had originally announced. The decision therefore, was thrown into the House of Representatives. Today, February 5, would bring the crucial vote.

Exhilarated, Harry tightened his grip on the reins. Early on, Madison had written Richard Bland a scenario of how he thought Aaron Burr would bow to the "obvious intent" of the people and gracefully excuse himself from the presidential contest to accept the vice-presidency, but Burr had not followed this script. What a coup it would be if the Federalists in the House, still the majority, could gain valuable concessions from Burr by promising him their votes, and then elect·him to the presidency!

A strange fellow, this dapper Colonel Burr. An ambitious, volatile politician, Burr had been a fellow student of Harry's at Princeton and an officer in the Revolution, but Harry had never known him well. Odd how Alexander Hamilton hated Burr so, privately describing his fellow New Yorker as unprincipled and corrupt!

Hated him so much that he had sent Harry an urgent letter arguing that, as a member of the House, Harry should throw his vote to Jefferson. At least the Virginian was a man "of some integrity," Hamilton insisted.

But was Aaron Burr truly a blackhearted scoundrel, or was it simply that the egotistical Hamilton could not bear to see the man with whom he had often bitterly sparred years before, in the arena of New York politics, gain the presidency?

The rain seemed to be turning to snow as Harry wended his way through the straggly trees up to the Capitol. If a heavy snowstorm came, they might well have to remain indeterminately on this ragged hill above the river.

The hall was smoky, for the oil lamps were already lit against the winter gloom. As Harry took off his cloak, he felt the expectancy and tension in every face. Quickly he counted. Everyone appeared to be present, even the desperately ill Congressman Nicholas of Maryland, who must have been carried in by servants and now lay on a litter in the corner. Since the winning candidate must have a majority of two-thirds of the Congress, every vote carried heavy weight.

Harry waited quietly, stifling his anxiety as the House settled down and Speaker Sedgewick called the session to order. Ironic, thought Harry: had the new peace treaty that Adams's commissioners signed with Napoleon arrived but a few days earlier, the President would probably have won the election, and this tug-of-war between Jefferson and Burr would be unnecessary. But then, one couldn't dwell on might-have-beens.

The vote was called. Ballots had to be written and dropped into the box. Could Jefferson be beaten? Harry felt himself sweating. The Federalists had caucused moments before, and he knew Burr had won the support of the six states with Federalist-controlled delegations, while Jefferson would hold the eight states with Republican-controlled delegations. The other two states, evenly divided, would cancel each other out. If the votes fell as he predicted, nine states to seven, neither candidate would hold a two-thirds majority. They would be stalemated until some in their midst knuckled and broke under pressure, changing their votes to give one or the other a clear majority.

"It snows hard out there, a veritable blizzard" a latecomer murmured to Harry. "Pray to God the first ballot vote is decisive so we can get off this damnable icy hill before we're snowed in. Any place with a warm fire will do."

Sully, 1801

"Marooned together on a snowbanked hill," Harry later told Richard Bland, "twelve days and thirty-five ballots. What an impasse! But I would have stood firm for a hundred days and a thousand ballots. Nothing could have induced me to change my vote to Jefferson. Congressman Samuel Smith of Maryland wooed every Federalist with assurances that Jefferson would maintain some of the Federalist aims, such as keeping a strong navy and upholding the nation's credit. I would still have no part of it, but there were those who were sold and came over." Harry stared gloomily out of the dining-room window at Sully. "Congressman Bayard of Delaware was one. Some arrangements were made, and on the thirty-sixth ballot, one member absented himself from the room, another dropped a blank vote into the box, and thus Mr. Jefferson was elected, ten states to four."

"Well, it is over!" his dark-eyed brother said. "I am not so convinced that our nation will collapse with Tom Jefferson as president. Granted, he will want a small, frugal national government, but the threat of war has passed. And Jefferson's ideas will benefit Virginia, for he believes in an agrarian society. Moreover, with John Marshall as chief justice—" he laughed, for appointment of Marshall to the top post in the judiciary had been one of John Adams's last presidential acts—"and with Jemmy Madison racing down from Montpelier to serve as secretary of state, I believe we are safe. You trust and admire both Madison and Marshall, do you not?"

Harry did not answer at once. He was staring out at the grove of trees. "My usefulness in Congresss is over, Richard Bland. I have no place in a Republican Congress. I shall go home to Stratford to try to make some sense of my life and my fortunes—for both our sakes. I feel badly about the Great Falls, you do know that."

"Don't blame yourself," Richard Bland said quickly. "I joined the Matildaville venture with my eyes open, and as for the money I lent you, I know you will repay me when you have it."

Heavily, Harry moved from his chair toward the door. "I do leave the Congress with one deep regret. I so wanted to raise a marble monument in the federal city to commemorate Washington. Strange, isn't it? I was easily able to convince my fellow congressmen to commemorate Nathaniel Greene with a statue, but unable to move them to so honor Washington. 'A waste of money,' the Republicans cried! 'Money better spent on the education of the poor,' they said!"

The Tidewater, 1803

Stratford was enveloped by that quiet peace peculiar to winter. Ann Carter Lee, lulled by the warmth of a cozy fire in the alcove parlor, daydreamed as she attempted to finish a letter to Eliza Lee at Sully. What to say? How could she sum up all that had happened in the past six months? She leaned back against the soft chair, relieved to be momentarily distracted by the muted sounds of Carter and little black-eyed Ann, who were playing with their toys in the nursery across the hall. Beside them, in the mother's room, their new baby brother, Smith, slumbered quietly.

Even six months ago, when she, Harry, and the children had stopped at Sully for a few days before beginning their "tour" to Philadelphia and New York, Eliza Lee had noticed the change in Harry. She had said nothing, but Ann had seen her sister-in-law watching with concern as he paced up and down the checkered Wilton carpet in the dining room.

"I've made many loans to friends in the northern states over the past years. To date, most have not been able to repay me—not that I've called directly for the money, you understand!" Harry's tone had been feverish, his eyes flashing with anxiety. "But now I must call my loans. Times are so very hard, and I've need of the monies due me. While this trip north is a pleasure jaunt for Ann and the children, for me it is an important business trip to collect some of what I'm owed."

Eliza had understood that it was not really a pleasure jaunt for Ann, who had been again expecting. (In fact, the baby had come while they were traveling through New Jersey. Sydney Smith Lee was named after the kind gentleman who opened his home to the family.) No, it was a trip planned from desperation. Bless Eliza, she had not even objected when Richard Bland made yet another small loan to Harry to help finance the journey north. Ann blushed now in remembering it. The Lees of Sully were as critically strapped as they, for Richard Bland had enthusiastically supported almost every venture his older brother had entered. These had been many, and far too few succeeded.

Although the trip had held some happy moments, it had been unsuccessful; Harry had not been able to collect one red cent of the money owed him. Nor was Robert Morris able to replay his loan. He was now out of debtors' prison, but without a dollar to his name.

Ann looked up as Nat came into the parlor to stir the fire. "Has my husband returned from the courthouse in Montross yet?"

"No'm." He knelt by the hearth and vigorously stirred the slumbering logs until they crackled afresh. "But they gonna be people awaitin' you soon."

She smiled. When Nat said people, he meant the servants, slaves, and tenant farmers with their families. Harry might spend his days scurrying about the countryside selling land, seeking to hold off his creditors, but life at Stratford must go on as ordained; hospitality to be dispensed to callers from Bushfield, Nomini, and Mount Airy, her children nurtured, the plantation managed, and the needs of its people met. She regularly took her place in the chintz-covered chair beside the fire in the mother's room to listen attentively to accounts of new babies on the tenant farms and miseries in the quarters that called for the medicines and herbs kept in her corner cabinet.

Distracted, Ann laid down her quill pen and paper and, wrapping a wool shawl around her shoulders, wandered on quick, silk-slippered feet into the great hall. She loved this room best of all—better than the new parlor in the west wing, which Harry had enlarged some ten years before, refurbishing it in the newest style and hanging a handsome portrait of his friend Lafayette. No, the great hall was clearly her favorite room. Warmed by the morning sunlight streaming in through the tall windows, its soft gray pilasters gleaming against the light wall, the room seemed an oasis of calm beckoning her in.

Was the piano-forte still in tune? She moved back the mahogany cover and ran her fingers lightly over the keys. She had not played in weeks, months. What was the song she used to sing as a child when she practiced on he spinet at Shirley? "The Despairing Shepherd." How her father used to chuckle when she sang its melancholy words: "Ah, welladay . . . must I endure this pain . . . ?"

"What a sad song you sing!" Harry, his face reddened from his morning ride, boots muddied by the winter roads, stood in the doorway behind her.

"I didn't hear you!" Ann blushed and quickly closed the piano-forte, then looked up at him. "I missed you," she said softly. "You were gone before I woke."

"Aye." His mouth compressed into a hard line. "I was off to the courthouse before first light. Do you realize, Ann, last spring I paid taxes on two thousand and forty-nine acres in Westmoreland County and on more than a hundred acres in Henrico County? This spring I shall pay taxes on little more than two hundred acres—total. I hated to sacrifice the Richmond property . . . rich land that sold for far less than its value. Why, I've hardly enough land left to provide work for my field hands!"

"I am so sorry. If there were only something I could do to help you," Ann answered.

He hardly seemed to hear her. "I've a debt coming due in July, to Alexander Spotswood, for land I bought from him and have since sold. I owe him fifteen thousand dollars, Ann, a fortune. I am trying to put him off, but . . ." His eyes moved restlessly about the room.

Ann stepped close and nestled sympathetically against his shoulder. "Don't despair," she whispered. "We still have each other, the children, and Stratford."

The Tidewater, 1806

Last night she again dreamed of Shirley. Why did she dream so often of her girlhood home? Ann walked through days as if she were asleep, scarcely noticing the passage of hours, months, seasons. Repairs to Stratford had long ago ceased. And the beautiful gardens had become tangled jungles of vines and wild roses. Was this some kind of nightmare that would never end? She woke sobbing in the stifling heat of a June night. "I must go home to Shirley. Please, take me home to Shirley for just a little while. . . . Please Harry."

He turned over and held her passively, listlessly. She could feel his eyes open and stare up in the darkness at the ceiling. "Of course you can go home to Shirley. But you must go without me, Ann. With this summer drought . . ."

It was as if a Biblical plague had withered the lands of the Northern Neck. As the shabby old Stratford carriage, shining and tight in the days of Colonel Phil, pulled slowly down the dusty drive, Ann looked back at the great red brick house with despair. The giant beeches that sheltered the east wing were stark with shriveled yellow leaves, the boxwood by the garden wall was burned and blighted. Horses and cattle in the fields, the new corn, everything thirsted. Would the drought never end?

Ann bit her lip until the blood came. She would go home to Shirley, home to her father's smile. And when she came back to Stratford in the fall, Harry would have somehow resolved his debts and put an end to the almost insane rage of the past weeks. An acquaintance had told him that President Jefferson had implied that Harry had offered a farm for sale without authority to do so. This had so infuriated her husband that he could not eat or sleep. When she came back, he would be calm, light-hearted, and again, she told herself, the grass would be green in the Neck.

Ann almost held her breath until they had safely crossed the splashing rapids of the Rappahannock and the threatening depths of the York. As they pressed on through the James River Valley, the effects of the summer drought seemed to abate. Landmarks familiar to her from childhood raised her spirits until finally, when the tired horses made the last turn up the familiar drive to the manor house at Shirley, Ann was almost exultant. She tied her little daughter's sunbonnet in a perky bow under her chin, combed little Charles Carter's curls and Smith's wisp of dark hair, then sat erect on the worn cushion of the wagon. All her senses rose to the beauty of her childhood home, the excitement of the long-awaited reunion with her father.

But Charles Carter, master of Corotoman and Shirley, was not among those who gathered to greet her. In his seventieth year, the grandson of old King Carter had passed away in his sleep a few days before Ann and her children reached Shirley. Shattered by the news, she stood numbly in the front hall of the house, oblivious of her brother Robert's embrace, too shocked to cry.

"Be consoled that he was so happy these past weeks knowing that you were coming, Ann. He was marking off the days on his almanac until you, his heart's darling, were beneath his roof again."

Woodenly, she went about meeting the needs of her children and the two servants who had accompanied her from Stratford. She sat by her grieving mother's bed. Oh, Papa, dear, dear Papa. Her father had been her strength, Shirley her nesting rock. Was there no sanctuary for her anyplace on earth?

One afternoon, she sought the still, quiet waters lapping against the moss-covered bank of the James, where a covey of ducks were diving tail over head searching for their evening repast in the shadowy reeds. A wave of nausea and light-headedness rolled over her as she bent to loosen a briar's hold on her skirt, her nose pinched from it's force. Dear Lord, no! Ann stood up quickly. She could not be pregnant again! She looked up at the big manor house outlined in the twilight. How sturdy and serene it looked, the burnished wooden pineapple on its sloping roof a beacon of friendship, an open hand. She was just exhausted from the trip. And she was still a Carter, with strengths in her that flowed back through the generations. She must handle this loss, absorb it, and go back to Stratford, to Harry, darling Harry, who needed her, depended on her. Ann pressed her fingers to the locket at her neck. She must be strong for his sake.

"I have written to my husband," Ann told her brother a few days later. "I shall not stay as long as I had intended. As soon as Mr. Lee can send another carriage for me . . ." She flushed slightly. "I fear the one I came in will not make the long journey back across the Tidewater."

Young Robert Carter looked up from his paperwork in dismay. "Don't go back so soon, dear Ann. Please say at Shirley as long as you would like."

She held her head high. Her father's will had been read the night before. By its terms, her portion of the estate was to be held in trust for her and her heirs, its income available for her use. This had been Charles Carter's canny way of protecting her inheritance against Harry and his creditors, and for this she was grateful. Yet it made her all the more determined to return quickly to her beleaguered husband's side.

The long months of the summer passed into fall with no answer to her letters. Perhaps Harry had not been able to repair the other carriage, the last one in the coach house; or—God forbid—had he taken ill? Ann continued through the quiet days at Shirley, outwardly calm but with a breaking heart.

In November, a vehicle arrived from Stratford to carry Ann and the children home. Nat West surveyed it, arms akimbo. "You not goin' home in no open carriage, Miss Ann. I don't care if it's the last thing what has wheels to roll, I not takin' you home in this!" He looked at her intently. "Yo' brother offer to let you take one of his carriages. Why not say, 'Thank you,' and be grateful?"

Ann shook her head firmly. "Pack up our things, Nat. This coach will serve our needs most adequately. I would have us start for Stratford tomorrow."

For a moment, he hesitated as if he might argue the point further; then, seeing the steel in her face, he shrugged and went off to do his mistress's bidding.

A patrician of Virginia, a child of the fabled Tidewater, Ann was now unable to appreciate the land's beauty or draw comfort from the kindness of friends who opened their houses to her wherever the miserable little wooden carriage stopped. Once life had been lush and ripe with potential. Where had it all gone? Look at poor Alexander Hamilton, once so brilliant, so promising. The first secretary of the treasury, leader of the Federalist party, now lay dead, killed in a duel with Aaron Burr two years before.

One had to accept life, and not swim against the tides. What was she fighting? What was it she was trying to avoid, going on with her head held high as if nothing was amiss? She wrapped her children more tightly in the blankets Nat had put in the carriage, pushed back her bonnet, and set her face to the cold November winds.

"We almost home, Miss Ann." Nat shook her out of a cramped slumber as the carriage limped into the shadowy drive to Stratford. How somber and winterswept the scenery, how dark the towering house in the meadow. No one was there but Harry and the servants. Her stepchildren were grown —young Henry in college at William and Mary, the temperamental Lucy now married to Ann's younger brother. She looked anxiously for Harry. How she longed to see him come out to meet her, full of his old grace and vitality. How she longed to hear that somehow, miraculously, one of his investments had proved itself, and that the hard times were behind them. But it didn't matter. Nothing mattered except that she loved him more than life itself and wanted to be with him. She had come home.

Nat West had brought Ann Carter Lee safely home. But Stratford was his home even more certainly than hers, for he had been born here, had spent all his life here. He was a slave. God knows he had railed enough about that fact in his youth, and he had been supported in his anger by his boyhood friends William and Arthur Lee. For one man to belong to another, body and soul, was wrong, an evil, Arthur had said, and Nat had observed its terrible effects on peoples' lives, black and white, all his life. But when General Lee offered to give him his freedom the year he became governor, Nat had hesitated. He was not young any more. If he had been, he would have accepted the offer outright, without a second thought. But his home was Stratford, his people were Stratford people. If he accepted his freedom, he would have to leave, for General Lee had no cash to pay wages. In the act of choosing to stay, he had become free—at least that was how he saw it. And he now gave of his love and his devotion just as he gave his labor, out of his own free choice.

"Why didn't anyone tell me, write me, she was carrying another baby?" General Lee asked, his frustration barely contained. "I would have come myself. . . . I would have somehow got a closed wagon."

"Miss Ann, she don' tell nobody she gonna have another baby. Peoples at Shirley so busy, so upset 'bout the old man dying, they don' notice. But I notice." Nat looked directly into Harry's eyes. "I says to myself, if Miss Ann don't want to talk about it, thas all right with me, but I takes good care of her. I done stopped that carriage every time she look tired and let her rest at somebody's house, kin or not."

"Thank you." Harry struggled to hold his emotions in check. "Now, Nat, we must go on taking care of her until this baby is born. Keep strong fires burning at all times in the mother's room, the nursery, and across the hall in the dining room and alcove parlor. We'll close off the rest of the house . . . the west wing and the lower floor . . . except"—he smiled sadly—"the great hall. It's Mrs. Lee's favorite room."

Harry started from the room, then turned and said with effort, "I've been forced to let the overseer and his family go, Nat. I've not the money to pay. We'll struggle to get through this winter, but I am hoping in the spring . . ." The words trailed off as Harry walked out

The Tidewater, 1807

"I just finished writing to James Monroe, who is now our American minister in England," Harry told Ann hopefully in early January. "If he would intercede on my behalf, introduce a petition to the English courts to settle some land disputes involving my interests, I'm sure I could recoup some of my investments." He sat down beside her on the sofa. "I am miserable seeing you in want," he said in despair.

"I am not in want." Ann's smile was steady, her love constant in her dark eyes. Now in her early thirties, she had a refined, mature beauty that made her more lovely than she had been at twenty. "We are warm and comfortable. Good food graces our table."

"Your dress is old," he argued, touching with gentle fingers the soft wine-colored folds of wool.

"I choose to wear it so often only because I thought it was one of your favorites." She took his hand and linked her fingers in his. "When spring comes and I am strong again, we shall ride to the cliffs, you and I, and watch the eagles build their nests."

"Yes," he said quickly. "And I have been thinking. We all suffer so from flus and agues and colds. Let us go away—perhaps to Bermuda, where an old friend offers me a house, or to South America. They tell me it is warm and sunny there. In fact," he said thoughtfully, "it crossed my mind that I could write to Jemmy Madison. As secretary of state, he could recommend that I be made consul to Brazil. Would you like that, my love?"

She nodded faintly, leaning her head back against the brocade cushion of the sofa. "I would be happy to be anywhere, just as long as I've you and the children."

Their fifth child was born in the quiet of a January night in the mother's room.

"Here he is!" Harry came out to show Nat, who had been waiting impatiently in the hall. "A big, fine, strong boy. I was so afraid that his mother might not . . ." He looked down at the blanket-wrapped baby, already sucking its fingers in the curve of his arm. "But when I laid him beside her, her smile was like that of a Madonna, Nat." There were tears in Harry Lee's eyes. "I could tell she loved him from the first moment she saw him."

How could she help loving him, this baby she had named for her two favorite brothers, Robert and Edward? He was a beautiful baby, an angel baby, fair and golden, with great wondering, dark eyes.

"An embargo!" Harry exploded upon receiving an answer from Jemmy Madison. "We cannot go to Bermuda or to South America, because Jefferson has persuaded the Congress to put an embargo on all seagoing vessels, Ann."

It was an embargo that might have been expected, for Britain, still warring with Napoleon, had been detaining American vessels on the high seas to search the crews for deserters from the British Navy. These desertions were not unusual; the pay of American seamen was much higher than that of the British. In June of 1807, the British frigate *Leopard* attacked the American cruiser *Chesapeake* some ten miles off Cape Henry. Three Americans were killed and eighteen wounded as the *Chesapeake* lowered her colors in defeat.

Reaction to the incident had been quick and furious. President Jefferson, fearing war with England, urged the economic embargo on a receptive Congress, which passed it without so much as a day's deliberation. American frigates were to be put in dry dock, all exports from America prohibited, and America's coastline was to be defended by only a handful of gunboats.

"Jefferson has made a mistake this time," Harry said bitterly. "I do not like the man, I grant you that. But I have supported many of his efforts. The purchase of the Louisiana Territory from France was masterful, even though I also suspect it was a cloak to hide aid to Jefferson's beloved France. He sent James Monroe to Paris to help our minister Robert Livingston buy the port city of New Orleans. And what does Napoleon do? He impetuously offers to sell the whole confounded Louisiana Territory, from the Mississippi to the Rockies. Monroe and Livingston were easily able to persuade Jefferson that it was a worthwhile bargain—and constitutional, to boot!" Harry smiled. "Even our play-by-the-rules Jefferson can apply some Hamilton-style 'loose construction' when he chooses! Where does the Constitution authorize acquisition of territory? But, then, he has always been a practical man where land is concerned. He told the Congress that the constitutional treaty-making power *implied* the right to acquire new territory as well. I can see Hamilton rolling over in his grave! I think the expedition Jefferson sent west under Meriwether Lewis and William Clark was admirable . . . more than admirable. But he is wrong if he thinks an embargo, which in substance bans all foreign trade for this nation, will solve our problems. There will be smuggling and hardships for planters and merchants alike." He shook his head. "And worst of all, my darling, it means that we must stay on at Stratford. And I must face up to my debts, for I cannot go on like this."

The Tidewater, 1809

The sheriffs of Westmoreland and Spotsylvania Counties were searching for him, armed with court orders demanding his arrest. He was besieged by demands from all sides.

Chains on the door of Stratford could not keep Harry's creditors away. Ann Lee or Nat West might say, "No, the general is not at home today," but it did no good. The collectors only returned on the following day. Some Harry could put off with his enormous charm and earnestness, but not all. Finally, on a brisk April day in 1809, he surrendered himself at the courthouse in Montross to enter prison.

"Do not tell Mrs. Lee any more than you have to," he cautioned Nat West, who had accompanied him into town. "Tell your mistress that I am comfortably situated and that she must not worry."

Nat looked around skeptically at the cramped iron-barred cell, the foul-smelling dinner on a battered tin plate that had been carelessly left on the rough plank table. How, he wondered, would the fastidious General Lee bear this.

When Nat left, Harry walked to the small window and closed his fists around the iron bars. God knows, he had done everything he could, turned everywhere he could, to find the money. To think of the thousands of dollars paid from his family's purse to buy arms, uniforms, horses, and provisions for his first cavalry troop! He shook his head. No, he couldn't begrudge that. It had been freely given.

The heaviest burden was the knowledge that others suffered because of his rash actions—Ann and the children, his people at Stratford, his younger brother, Richard Bland, and his family at Sully. He had tried to idemnify Richard Bland for the losses sustained in his behalf by turning over several parcels of land, one of them the sixteen-hundred-acre Langley tract near the Great Falls. Please God, he prayed, make it be enough to save Sully!

Harry looked around in despair. Could he bear this place? Would he go mad on this filthy cot, in this dank, dark spot with nothing to occupy his mind but his own thoughts? He pressed his face against the stone wall and prayed for his own salvation.

"Well, he'll not eat their rotten food!" Ann cried when Nat, broken down by her questions, described the wretched tin plate. "Pack up a parcel of clean sheets and blankets. I shall see to it that he has a good nourishing meal carried every day from Stratford. And I shall go with you myself, Nat! No, don't look like that. . . . I mean what I say! Though you must *not* say I came with you . . . Oh, and paper . . . and a supply of quill pens!" Her fertile imagination took hold as she searched the house for things that might make her husband's incarceration easier. Harry had always said he wanted to write an honest and true account of Nathaniel Greene and the Southern Campaign. Now he must begin his memoirs. She would goad him into it! He must not sit idle. his brilliance wasted.

The Tidewater, 1810

He had begun to write. Ann could tolerate the days and nights of loneliness by turning her thoughts to that. Page after page of foolscap were piling up, Nat said, all filled with the general's small, neat handwriting. This was the flame in her heart that kept her warm as the long year passed. She read to her children, played with them like a young girl in the tangled gardens. One spring morning in early 1810, when the hawthorne and wild peach and azalea were blooming, she planted a horse-chestnut tree in a clearing at the end of the garden near the row of mossy-cup oaks that Tom Lee, it was said, had brought back from Pennsylvania when he negotiated with the Indians in 1748.

Her youngest child, the sturdy dark-eyed Robert, leaned against her knees and asked why she planted the seedling. "Because . . . just because," she answered. "A tree continues life. It will stay here on the good earth of Stratford even after we are gone."

"Gone?" Carter wondered. "But where would we go? I would not want to live anywhere but Stratford Hall, Mother."

She followed his gaze up to the strong red brick house, its interior shabbiness hidden by the solidity of its thick outer walls. "The time may come when we shall have to leave Stratford. Your father will be coming home to us soon with plans and dreams for the future."

"But Father says Lees have always lived at Stratford," Carter insisted. "I don't want to go away."

"Stratford," Robert repeated solemnly, as he stacked a pile of pine cones in the grass by her knee.

Ann looked at her children, then out toward the bright horizon where the Potomac sparkled blue in the spring sunshine. "Wherever you go, whatever you do, Stratford will always be part of you, just us Shirley will always be part of me."

Oh, glorious day! Ann stood in the great hall, its floors polished to a glossy shine, waiting for the wagon to appear in the turn of the lane, bringing her husband home from prison. A year of their lives was gone, but all of Harry's debts and obligations had finally been met or dismissed. Poor as the mice at the Glebe they were, but they would put life together and face the future with strengthened hearts.

Oh, to stand in the moonlight and to feel his strong, sensitive hands tremble as they unfastened the pearl buttons of her dress, the press of his arms as they closed around her, his mouth seeking hers, hot, wooing, insistent, to lose herself in that first kiss, and then to feel him draw in his breath from the pure joy of their embrace . . . it was worth anything, everything! No wait was too long, no hardship too much to bear when there were moments like this in one's life.

"My darling?" His dark eyes seemed to search hers for reassurance as he came up the steps.

"Oh, Harry, I've counted the hours till this moment." She flew into his arms.

Their lovemaking was gentle that night, full of discovery and passion that could not be spent. When finally they lay content in each other's arms, it was not to sleep, but to hold each other and talk into the dawn.

"It was only the book, the writing of it, that kept me sane, kept me alive." Harry admitted. "I thought first to write a comprehensive life of

Greene, but I had little firsthand knowledge of his early life, so I compressed that period and spent my efforts on the Southern Campaign." His arms tightened around her. "Oh, Ann, my darling Ann, who urged me to begin it. Many old companions in arms, even their sons, wrote me their impressions, and I buried myself in the task day after day. It is not yet finished, but by the year's end, it will be." He paused. "If it is all right with you, I thought I would turn the rights to the book over to Richard Bland; perhaps he can make a nice profit out of it."

"A most admirable idea." Ann nestled against her husband's heart. She would not tell him just yet that any profit for Richard Bland would probably come too late. Sully and the vast Langley acreage were now mortgaged to Judge Bushrod Washington of Mount Vernon. Eliza Lee had written that they would probably soon have to sell Sully and move into Alexandria.

"I want to talk to you, my darling, quietly and sensibly about our future," she said sleepily. "Your Henry is twenty-two, and though you have life tenancy at Stratford, it is by rights his inheritance. I want you to consider the possibility of our—you, the younger children, and I—moving to Alexandria. There are schools there for the children."

"Leave the Neck?" Harry sighed.

"I know." She rose up on one elbow and faced him in the darkness. "We were born in the Neck. But the winds of time blow, Harry. Nothing stays the same. Think on it, my darling."

It took Harry some months to realize that Ann was right, but then he accepted it and began to yield to a sense of optimism about their future in the handsome port city so close to the nation's capital. His old friend James Madison was now President of the United States, James Monroe the secretary of state. No, it would not be easy to leave Stratford, but young Henry would be marrying Anne McCarty soon, and the Lee heritage would live on here.

One hazy fall morning, Harry and his three small sons walked through the fields and meadows around Stratford Hall. He was very close to his sons—always had been, by God, and always would be! They were his legacy.

"An Englishman named John Smith sailed up that river almost two hundred years ago, with the wind to his back," he began. "He brought with him English ways, English rights. The man who built this house, the men and women who have lived in it through the years, always gave the best of themselves to Virginia. I pray God that you will always do the same." He told them the tales of Tom Lee and his vision that looked west, all the way to the golden sea of California, and he told them of the gallant band of brothers, who lived by ideals of integrity and valiantly fought for freedom.

Ann was waving to them from the stone steps. "Nat says everything is loaded on the wagons," she called out. "We must be off if we are to reach Bellevue by nightfall."

Hand in hand they walked through the rooms of the old house. How it resounded with memories—the parlors, the study, the mother's room, the great hall. "Richard Henry Lee once told me of a ball here in this room," Harry said slowly as he looked around the handsome ballroom at the center of the house, "an anniversary dance for his mother and father, held when he was just a boy. Indians and wild bears and wolves still prowled in the forest then, and pirates and highwaymen threatened travelers on sea and road. Old Councilor Tom Lee had positioned men with muskets on the roof to guard his guests that night—although no one was aware. And they danced the night away—brave and dauntless councilors dressed in their silks and satins and powdered wigs, as English songs rang through the rooms. The windows were thrown open to the Virginia night and"—Harry's eyes grew misty— "George Washington, just a shy, awkward boy, danced his first formal dance with my mother that night, or so old Chantilly Lee later claimed!"

"The wagon's done been ready for an hour." Nat West stood in the ballroom doorway, his impatience evident. "Time we be goin' to Alexandria now."

They followed him out to the waiting wagons. When Ann was comfortably settled with a cushion at her back, Harry gave her a quick, reassuring smile. She had told him last night that she expected another baby in the spring, a prospect that pleased them. Life lay open and clear ahead.

"Carter will ride in front with you, Nat, and Smith, too, if room allows. But where is Robert?" Harry asked.

Ann saw his consternation. "He is still in the house. I am sure of it. We have simply missed him in the bustle." She held out a hand so that Harry could help her down. "Let me go back with you to find him."

Fall leaves swirled through the open doorway of the great hall. Ann ran ahead of Harry, who called for Robert down the echoing passages.

He was there, in his nursery, kneeling by the small time-blackened hearth. "I'm here, Father," he said. "I just came to kiss my angels good-bye." The little boy crept into the shallow fireplace and gently kissed each of the cherubs on the old fireback designed by Hannah Ludwell Lee. Then he turned to his mother and father. "Now we can go."

Epilogue

San Antonio, February 17, 1861

It was almost dawn, a faint pink-rimmed Texas dawn, when the colonel woke from his troubled half-sleep. He felt surprisingly refreshed and calmed, having drawn new strength and a feeling of resolution from the images and remembrances that had flooded his mind and heart during the long night. Had all this once happened?

He had gleaned these impressions from the vivid stories and legends told and retold by his father and mother in the soft cadences of their Tidewater accents. Old Westy, an aged black man dozing by the kitchen fire when the colonel was growing up in Alexandria, had filled in the gaps, making the distant past vivid and real to an impressionable boy. Some of it he had read in his father's book.

But Stratford Hall was no dream, no myth, though it had not belonged to him for very long. He had felt the rough red brick of the garden wall beneath his fingers, seen the sunlight mirrored on the blue waters beyond the cliffs, smelled the scent of rose potpourri that had always permeated the alcove parlor.

The colonel left the Read House that morning in February 1861 and returned to Arlington, his home in Virginia, arriving on March 1. A few days later, Abraham Lincoln was inaugurated president.

On April 13, the rift between the northern and southern states deepened irrevocably with the firing on Fort Sumter in the harbor of Charleston, South Carolina. Four days later, the Virginia Convention, meeting in secret session in Richmond, voted to secede from the union and join the other southern states in a confederacy.

The following morning, April 18, 1861, the colonel rode across the wooden bridge from Arlington into the city of Washington to the home of a Washington power broker, Mr. Francis Preston Blair, on Pennsylvania Avenue. There, on instructions from President Lincoln, he was offered command of the new federal army being called to move against the seceding southern states.

The colonel's answer was courteous and brief. He was, he explained to Mr. Blair, completely opposed to secession; he despised slavery and could anticipate no greater calamity than the dissolution of the union. He fervently believed in the government of Washington, Hamilton, Jefferson, Madison, and the other patriots of the Revolution and for twenty-five years had given all the energies and abilities he possessed to its service. But he was a Virginian first and foremost, born and bred to the land. Save in defense of his native state, he never again desired to draw his sword.

Two days later, Colonel Robert E. Lee, with the greatest regret but with complete resolve, resigned his commission in the United States Army.

Notes

The words by which Thomas Sorrell turned over The Cliffs plantation to Tom Lee (p. 31) are based on a memorandum in the Westmoreland County records quoted in *Stratford Hall: The Great House of the Lees,* by Ethel Armes (Richmond: Garrett and Massie, 1936, p. 33).

The *Maryland Gazette* account of the fire at Matchotique (p. 51) was published on 4 February 1729.

The account of the Lancaster meeting (pp. 87–88) is based on *Indian Treaties,* by Benjamin Franklin (reprinted by the Philadelphia Historical Society, 1935).

The brief account of Bacon's Rebellion (pp. 100–01) is based on that given in *The Far Frontier,* by David Horowitz (New York: Simon & Schuster, 1978, pp. 104–27). Thomas Lee's call to Williamsburg to serve as council president (p. 107) is documented in *Executive Journals, Council of Colonial Virginia,* (p. 299).

The French commander's response to Dinwiddie's letter (p. 122) is quoted in *A Williamsburg Galaxy,* by Burke Davis (Williamsburg: Colonial Williamsburg, 1968, p. 68). The King's reply to George Washington's remark about the sound of whistling bullets (p. 123) is also found in *A Williamsburg Galaxy* (p. 117). Quotes from Richard Henry Lee's speech in the House of Burgesses (p. 138) are to be found in the *Society of Lees Magazine* (Vol. 9, no. 1, pp. 18–19).

The letter from Arthur Lee (pp. 147–48) is a collation of two authentic ones in *Arthur Lee: Diplomat,* by Marguerite du Pont Lee (Washington: Privately printed, 1936, pp. 5–7). The account of Patrick Henry's speech before the House of Burgesses and the quotations and resolutions (pp. 165–67) are based on *Patrick Henry: A Biography,* by Richard Beeman (New York: McGraw-Hill, 1974, pp. 35–38). Thomas Lee's note about the Leedstown meeting (pp. 171–72) is taken from *Stratford Hall* (p. 139). The proceedings at Leedstown and the quotation from the Resolves (pp. 172–73) are based on *George Washington,* Volume 4, by Douglas Southall Freeman (New York: Charles Scribner's Sons, 1951, pp. 153–55).

Quotes from the Townshend-Grenville interchange (p. 191) are from *The Oxford History of the American People,* by Samuel Eliot Morison (New York: Oxford University Press, 1965, p. 190). The quotation from John Dickinson (pp. 196–97) also comes from *The Oxford History of the American People* (p. 191). The account of Governor Botetourt's dissolution of the House of Burgesses (p. 209) is taken from *A Williamsburg Galaxy* (p. 90).

Patrick Henry's words to the Convention (p. 227) are taken from *Patrick Henry* (p. 60). Galloway's view of the Convention's support for Massachusetts (p. 229) is quoted in *The Oxford History of the American People* (p. 201). Pitt's view of the American Congress, as related to Benjamin Franklin (p. 232), is based on *Benjamin Franklin and a Rising People,* edited by Oscar Handlin (Boston: Little, Brown, 1954, p. 152) The quote of Pitt's speech to the Lords' Chamber (p. 233) is found in *The Oxford History of the American People* (p. 209). The words from

Patrick Henry's speech against the Stamp Act (p. 240) are from *Patrick Henry* (p. 66).

The dialogue between Ethan Allen and the commander of Fort Ticonderoga (p. 252) is found in *The American Revolution*, by Hugh Rankin (New York: Capricorn Books, 1964, p. 39). The Congressional resolution for a day of fasting (p. 254) is quoted in Freeman's *George Washington*, Volume 3 (p. 432). George Washington's comment regarding his appointment as commander-in-chief, made to Patrick Henry (p. 256), is recorded in *Virginia: The New Dominion*, by Virginius Dabney (New York: Doubleday, 1971, p. 129). Governor Dunmore's letter to the House of Burgesses (p. 257) comes from *A Williamsburg Galaxy* (p. 108). Pendleton's resolution (p. 273) is recorded in *Virginia: The New Dominion* (p. 135). Richard Henry Lee's resolution for independence (p. 274) is found in *Stratford Hall* (p. 156).

An account of the award given to Harry Lee (p. 306) is found in *Lee of Virginia*, by Edmund Jennings Lee (Philadelphia: Franklin Printing Company, 1895, p. 332).

The quotation from Patrick Henry's speech to the Virginia Convention (p. 341) is from *Light Horse Harry Lee*, by Thomas Boyd (New York: Charles Scribner's Sons, 1931, p. 171), as are Harry Lee's words (pp. 342–43) at the Virginia Convention (p. 175). The deed of trust signed by Harry Lee for his wife Matilda (p. 349) can be found in *Stratford Hall* (p. 259).

James Madison extended his sympathies to Harry Lee (p. 361) in a letter quoted in "Henry 'Light-Horse Harry' Lee," a thesis by Thomas Templin (University of Kentucky, 1976, p. 336). Charles Carter's letter to Harry giving his consent for him to marry Ann Carter (p. 376) is found in *Lee*, by Clifford Dowdey (Boston: Little, Brown, 1965, p. 14). George Washington's letter to Harry (p. 376) is found in *Stratford Hall* (p. 277).

Harry Lee's resolutions on the death of President Washington (p. 401) are taken from *Light Horse Harry Lee* (pp. 255–56). Quotations from Harry Lee's eulogy of President Washington (p. 402) also come from *Light Horse Harry Lee* (p. 260).

Bibliography

The following special collections proved invaluable in the preparation of *Tidewater Dynasty*: the Library of Congress, Division of Manuscripts (Henry Lee papers, Richard Bland papers, Shippen papers), Washington, D.C.; the personal library of Frances N. Shively, Director of the Lee-Fendall House, the Special Collection at the Lloyd House, and the Archives of the Society of the Lees of Virginia, all in Alexandria, Virginia; the Virginia Historical Society (Ludwell-Lee papers), in Richmond, Virginia; the Alderman Library (Lee papers) of the University of Virginia, in Charlottesville, Virginia; the Library of the College of William and Mary and the Archives of the Williamsburg Colonial Foundation, in Williamsburg, Virginia; the Archives of the Robert E. Lee Memorial Association, Inc., in Stratford, Virginia; the Archives of the Westmoreland County Courthouse, in Montross, Virginia; the Pennsylvania Historical Society, in Philadelphia, Pennsylvania; the Guildhall and the London Museum Archives, in London, England, and the Ben Franklin Library of the United States Embassy, in Paris, France.

Manuscripts and pamphlets

Alexander, Louise L. "Restless Hero: A Biography of General Henry Lee," unpublished.

Commetti, Elizabeth. *Social Life in Virginia.* Virginia Independence Bicentennial Commission, Williamsburg, 1978.

Dill, Alonzo T. *Francis Lightfoot Lee: The Incomparable Signer.* Virginia Independence Bicentennial Commission, Williamsburg, 1977.

Dill, Alonzo T. *William Lee: Militia Diplomat.* Virginia Independence Bicentennial Commission, Williamsburg, 1976.

Dill, Alonzo T., and Cheek, M. T. *A Visit to Stratford and the Story of the Lees* (A Stratford handbook). Stratford, Va., 1976.

Hudson, J. Paul. *This Was Green Spring.* The Jamestown Foundation, Jamestown, Va.

Kilmer, Denton, and Sweig, Donald. *The Fairfax Family in Fairfax County.* Fairfax County Office, Fairfax, Va., 1975.

Matthews, John Carter. *Richard Henry Lee.* Virginia Independence Bicentennial Commission, Williamsburg, 1978.

O'Toole, Dennis, and Strick, Lisa. *In the Minds and Hearts of the People: Five American Patriots and the Road to Revolution.* National Portrait Gallery, Washington.

Riggs, A. R. *The Nine Lives of Arthur Lee: Virginia Patriot.* Virginia Independence Bicentennial Commission, Williamsburg, 1976.

Rouse, Parke, Jr. *America's First Legislature.* The Jamestown Foundation, Jamestown, Va.

Rouse, Parke, Jr. *Planters and Pioneers.* The Jamestown Foundation, Jamestown, Va.

Rouse, Parke, Jr. *Virginia's Three Capitals: Jamestown, Williamsburg and Richmond.* The Jamestown Foundation, Jamestown, Va.

Rouse, Parke, Jr. *Traveling the Roads and Waterways of Early Virginia.* The Jamestown Foundation, Jamestown, Va.

Selby, John E. *A Chronology of Virginia and the War of Independence 1763–1783.* Virginia Independence Bicentennial Commission, Williamsburg, 1973.

Smith, Howard W. *Benjamin Harrison and the American Revolution.* Virginia Independence Bicentennial Commission, Williamsburg, 1978.

Templin, Thomas E. " 'Light Horse Harry' Lee, Federalist." Thesis presented to the graduate faculty of the University of Virginia, 1967.

Templin, Thomas E. "Henry 'Light Horse Harry' Lee." Doctoral thesis. University of Kentucky, 1975.

"William Lee Letterbooks." Archives of the Society of Lees of Virginia, Lee-Fendall House, Alexandria, Virginia.

General References

Calendar of Virginia State Papers and Other Manuscripts, vols. I–XI, 1875–93.

Commemoration Ceremony in Honor of the First Continental Congress, U.S. House of Representatives, September 25, 1974, U.S. Government Printing Office.

Hening's Statutes at Large, vols. I–XIII.

Indian Treaties—Ben Franklin, 1935, Historical Society of Pennsylvania.

Minutes of the Provincial Council of Pennsylvania, vol. IV, 1851.

Northern Virginia Heritage Magazine.

Pennsylvania Magazine of History and Biography, vols. I–II.

Society of Lees Magazine, December 1922–February 1939.

The American Legion of Honor Society Magazine, Autumn, 1944.

The Virginia Quarterly Review.

Tredyffrin Eastown History Club Quarterly, vol. XVII, no. 1.

Tyler's Quarterly Historical and Genealogical Magazine, vols. I–X, 1919–1928.

Virginia Cavalcade Magazine.

Virginia Magazine of History and Biography.

William and Mary College Quarterly Historical Magazine.

Books

Akers, Charles W. *Abigail Adams: An American Woman.* Boston: Little, Brown & Co., 1980.

Alden, John Richard. *The American Revolution.* The New American Nation Series. New York: Harper & Row, 1954.

Alderman, Clifford Lindsey. *The War We Could Have Lost.* New York: Four Winds Press, 1974.

Alexander, Frederick Warren. *Stratford and the Lees Connected with Its History.* Oakgrove, Va.: private, 1912.

American Heritage Publishing Co., Inc. *The Light of the Past.* New York, 1959.

Amherst College, Dept. of American Studies. *Problems in American Civilization: The Declaration of Independence and the Constitution.* Boston: D. C. Heath & Co., 1956.

Armes, Ethel (compiler and editor). *Nancy Shippen: Her Journal Book.* Philadelphia: J. B. Lippincott Co., 1935.

Armes, Ethel. *Stratford Hall: The Great House of the Lees.* Richmond: Garrett and Massie, 1936.

Ayling, Stanley. *George the Third.* New York: Alfred A. Knopf, 1972.

Ballagh, James C. (editor). *The Letters of Richard Henry Lee,* Vols. I & II. New York: The Macmillan Co., 1914.

Banner, James M., Jr., Hackney, Sheldon, and Bernstein, Barton J. (editors). *Understanding the American Experience: Recent Interpretations.* New York: Harcourt Brace Jovanovich, Inc., 1973.

Beeman, Richard R. *Patrick Henry: A Biography.* New York: McGraw-Hill Book Co., 1974.

Beitzell, Edwin W. *Life on the Potomac River.* Abell, Maryland: private, 1968.

Bell, Whitfield J., Jr. *The Colonial Physician and Other Essays.* New York: Science History Publications, 1975.

Bemis, Samuel Flass. *The Diplomacy of the American Revolution.* Bloomington, Ind.: Indiana Univ. Press, 1967.

Bendiner, Elmer. *The Virgin Diplomats.* New York: Alfred A. Knopf, 1976.

Beverly, Robert. *History and Present State of Virginia.* 1705, revised 1722. Chapel Hill, N.C.: Univ. of North Carolina Press, 1947.

Billias, George A. *George Washington's Generals.* New York: William Morrow & Co., 1964.

Blair, Carvel Hall, and Ansel, Willas Dyer. *Chesapeake Bay: Notes and Sketches.* Cambridge, Md.: Tidewater Publishers, 1970.

Blanton, M.D., Wyndham B. *Medicine in Virginia in the 18th Century.* Richmond: Garrett & Massie, Inc., 1931.

Boatner, Mark M., III. *Encyclopedia of the American Revolution.* New York: David McKay, 1966.

Boorstin, Daniel J. *The Americans.* New York: Random House, 1965.

Boorstin, Daniel J. *Landmark History of the American People.* New York: Random House, 1968.

Boting, Douglas, and the Editors, Time Life Books. *The Pirates.* Alexandria, Va., 1978.

Bowen, Catherine Drinker. *Miracle at Philadelphia* (The Story of the Constitutional Convention. May to September 1787). Boston: Little, Brown & Co., 1966.

Bowers, Claude G. *Jefferson and Hamilton.* Boston, Mass.: Houghton Mifflin Co., 1925.

Boyd, Thomas. *Light Horse Harry Lee.* New York & London: Charles Scribner's Sons, 1931.

Bridenbaugh, Carl. *Seat of Empire* (The Political Role of Eighteenth Century Williamsburg). Williamsburg: Colonial Williamsburg, Inc., 1950.

Brock, R. A. (editor). *Robert Edward Lee.* Richmond, Va.: Royal Publishing Co., 1897.

Brodie, Fawn M. *Thomas Jefferson. An Intimate History.* New York: W. W. Norton & Co., 1974.

Brown, Robert E., and Brown, Katherine B. *Virginia 1705–1786: Democracy or Aristocracy.* East Lansing, Mich.: Michigan State Univ. Press, 1964.

Bryant, Irving. *James Madison 1751–1780.* Indianapolis, Ind.: Bobbs Merrill Co., 1941.

Burton, Elizabeth. *The Pageant of Georgian England.* New York: Charles Scribner's Sons, 1967.

Butterfield, L. H. (editor). *Letters of Benjamin Rush,* Vols. I & II. Princeton, N.J.: Princeton University Press, 1951.

Canfield, Cass. *Sam Adams' Revolution.* New York: Harper & Row, 1976.

Cappon, Lester J. (editor). *The Adams-Jefferson Letters, I & II.* Chapel Hill, N.C.: The University of North Carolina Press, 1959.

Carson, Gerald. *The Polite Americans.* New York: William Morrow & Co., 1966.

Cash, W. J. *The Mind of the South.* New York: Vintage Books, 1941.

Catton, Bruce, and Catton, William B. *The Bold and Magnificent Dream.* New York: Doubleday & Co., Inc., 1978.

Chitwood, Oliver Perry. *Richard Henry Lee.* Morgantown, W. Va.: West Virginia University Library, 1967.

Churchill, Winston S. *A History of the English-Speaking People,* Vols. I–IV. New York: Dodd Mead & Co., 1959.

Clark, Kenneth. *Civilization.* New York: Harper & Row, 1969.

Clayton and Leftwich. *The Pageant of Tower Hill.* London: Longman, Green & Co., 1933.

The Colonial Williamsburg Foundation. *The Williamsburg Collection of Antique Furnishings,* 1973.

Cooke, John E. *Virginia: A History of the People;* Vol. I, *American Commonwealths.* New York: AMS Press, Inc., 1973.

Corner, Betsy Coppins. *William Shippen, Jr.: Pioneer in American Medical Education.* Philadelphia, Pa.: American Philosophical Society, 1951.

Cox, Marian Buckley. *Glimpse of Glory.* Richmond, Va.: Garrett & Massie, Inc., 1954.

Cunliffe, Marcus. *George Washington: Man and Monument.* Boston, Mass.: Little, Brown & Co., 1958.

Dabbs, James McBride. *Haunted by God.* Richmond, Va.: John Knox Press, 1972.

Dabney, Virginius. *Virginia: The New Dominion.* New York: Doubleday & Co., Inc., 1971.

Daniels, Jonathan. *The Randolphs of Virginia.* New York: Doubleday & Co., Inc., 1972.

Davis, Deering, Dorsey, Stephen P., and Hall, Ralph C. *Georgetown Houses of the Federalist Period.* New York: Bonanza Books, 1954.

De La Fuye, Maurice, and Babeau, Emile (Edward Hyams, translator). *The Apostle of Liberty: A Life of LaFayette.* London: Thames & Hudson, 1956.

Dickinson, Josiah Look. *The Fairfax Proprietary.* Front Royal, Va.: Warren Press, 1959.

Diprose, John. *Some Account of the Parish of Saint Clement Danes.* London: Diprose and Bateman, 1868.

Dowdey, Clifford. *The Great Plantation.* New York: Rinehart & Co., Inc., 1957

Dowdey, Clifford. *Lee.* Boston, Mass.: Little, Brown & Co., 1965.

Dowdey, Clifford. *The Virginia Dynasties.* Boston, Mass.: Little, Brown & Co., 1969.

Dunan, Marcel (editor). *Larousse Encyclopedia of Modern History from 1500.* Paris: Paul Hamlyn, 1972.

Durant, Will, and Durant, Ariel. *The Story of Civilization,* Vols. VIII, IX, X. New York: Simon and Schuster, 1963.

Earle, Alice Morse. *Home Life in Colonial Days.* New York: The Macmillan Co., 1926.

Emery, Noemie. *Washington: A Biography.* New York: G. P. Putnams Sons, 1976.

Evans, Elizabeth. *Weathering the Storm: Women of the American Revolution.* New York: Charles Scribner's Sons, 1975.

Farish, Hunter Dickinson. *The Journal and Letters of Philip Vickers Fithan.* Colonial Williamsburg, Inc., 1965.

Farrar, Emmie Ferguson. *The Virginia Houses Along the James.* New York: Bonanza Books, 1957.

Fishwick, Marshall W. *Virginia: A New Look at the Old Dominion.* New York: Harper & Brothers, 1959.

Fitzpatrick, John C. (editor). *George Washington's Diaries 1748–1799.* Boston: Houghton Mifflin Co., 1925.

Fleming, Thomas. *The Man from Monticello.* New York: William Morrow & Co., 1969.

Fleming, Thomas (editor). *Affectionately Yours, George Washington.* New York: W. W. Norton & Co., 1967.

Flexner, James Thomas. *Doctors on Horseback.* New York: Garden City Publishing, 1939.

Flexner, James Thomas. *George Washington,* 4 vols. Boston: Little, Brown & Co., 1967.

Flexner, James Thomas. *Washington: The Indispensable Man.* Boston, Mass.: Little, Brown & Co., 1969.

Ford, Paul Leicester. *The True George Washington.* Philadelphia, Pa.: J. B. Lippincott Co., 1907.

Freeman, Douglas Southall. *Lee of Virginia.* New York: Charles Scribner's Sons, 1958.

Freeman, Douglas Southall. *George Washington,* Vols. I–VII. New York: Charles Scribner's Sons, 1951.

Freeman, Douglas Southall. *R. E. Lee, A Biography.* New York: Charles Scribner's Sons, 1935.

Furnas, J. C. *The Americans: A Social History of the United States 1587–1914.* New York: G. P. Putnam's Sons, 1969.

Gamble, Robert S. *Sully: Biography of a House.* Sully Foundation Limited, 1973.

Gerson, Noel B. *Light Horse Harry.* New York: Doubleday & Co., 1966.

Gibson, James E. *Dr. Bodo Otto and the Medical Background of the American Revolution.* Baltimore, Md.: Charles C. Thomas, 1937.

Gipson, Lawrence H. *The Triumphant Empire: The Rumbling of the Coming Storm 1766–1770.* New York: Alfred A. Knopf, 1965.

Gipson, Lawrence H. *The Triumphant Empire: Britain Sails into the Storm 1770–1776.* New York: Alfred A. Knopf, 1965.

Gutheim, Frederick. *The Potomac.* New York: Grosset & Dunlap, 1968.

Handlin, Oscar (editor). *Benjamin Franklin and a Rising People.* Boston, Mass.: Little, Brown & Co., 1954.

Hatch, Alden. *The Byrds of Virginia.* New York: Holt, Rinehart & Winston, 1969.

Hatton, Ragnhild. *Europe in the Age of Louis XIV (1648–1721).* History of European Civilization Library. New York: Harcourt, Brace & World, Inc., 1969.

Haynie, Miriam. *The Stronghold: A Story of the Historic Northern Neck of Virginia and Its People.* Richmond, Va.: Dietz Press, 1959.

Hendrick, Burton J. *The Lees of Virginia.* Boston: Little, Brown & Co., 1935.

Hess, Stephen. *America's Political Dynasties from Adams to Kennedy.* New York: Doubleday & Co., Inc., 1966.

Hofstadter, Richard. *America at 1750: A Social Portrait.* New York: Vintage Books, 1973.

Horowitz, David. *The First Frontier.* New York: Simon and Schuster, 1978.

Hummel, Orvin, Jr. *The Virginia House of Burgesses 1689–1750.*

Jefferson, Thomas. *Notes on the State of Virginia.* New York: Harper & Row, 1964.

Junior League of Washington (editors). *The City of Washington: An Illustrated History.* New York: Alfred A. Knopf, 1977.

Kerr, Sophie. *Sound of Petticoats: Eastern Shore, Maryland.* New York: Rinehart and Co., Inc., 1948.

Ketcham, Ralph. *James Madison.* New York: The Macmillan Co., 1970.

Koch, Adrienne, and Peden, William (editors). *The Life and Writings of Thomas Jefferson.* New York: The Modern Library, 1944.

Langdon, William C. *Everyday Things in American Life.* New York: Charles Scribner's Sons, 1937.

Lee, Cazenove G., Jr., and Parker, Dorothy M. (editors). *Lee Chronicle: Studies of the Early Generations of the Lees of Virginia.* New York: New York University Press, 1957.

Lee, Edmund Jennings. *Lee of Virginia: The Descendants of Colonel Lee.* Philadelphia, Pa., 1895.

Lee, Lucinda. *Journal of a Young Lady of Virginia, 1787.* Stratford, Va.: Robert E. Lee Memorial Association, Inc., 1976.

Lee, R. H. *Memoir of the Life of Richard Henry Lee and His Correspondence.* Philadelphia, Pa.: H. C. Carey & Lea, 1825.

Lewis, W. S. *Three Tours Through London in the Years 1748, 1776, 1797.* New Haven, Conn.: Yale University Press, 1941.

Malone, Dumas, Milhollen, Hirt, and, Kaplan, Milton. *The Story of the Declaration of Independence.* New York: Oxford University Press, 1975.

Mason, George C. *Tobacco Coast.* Newport News, Va.: The Mariners Museum, 1953.

McIlwaine, H. R. (editor). *Executive Journals: Council of Colonial Virginia VIII, May 1, 1705–October 23, 1721.* Richmond, Va.: Virginia State Library, 1928.

Miller, Helen Hill. *George Mason: Gentleman Revolutionary.* Chapel Hill, N. C.: University of North Carolina Press, 1975.

Miller, John C. *The Federalist Era.* The New American Nation Series. New York: Harper & Row, 1962.

Mitchell, Broadus. *Alexander Hamilton: The Revolutionary Years.* New York: Thomas Y. Crowell Co., 1970.

Mitchell, R. J., and Leys, M. D. R. *A History of London Life.* Baltimore, Md.: Penguin Books, 1958.

Moore, Virginia. *The Madisons: A Biography.* New York: McGraw-Hill Book Co., 1979.

Morgan, Edmund S. *American Slavery: American Freedom.* New York: W. W. Norton & Co., Inc., 1975.

Morgan, Edmund S. *The Meaning of Independence.* New York: W. W. Norton & Co., Inc., 1976.

Morgan, Edmund S. *Virginians at Home: Family Life in the 18th Century.* Colonial Williamsburg, 1952.

Morison, S. E., and Commager, H. S. *The Growth of the American Republic,* Vol. I. New York: Oxford University Press, 1950.

Morison, Samuel Eliot. *The Oxford History of the American People.* New York: Oxford University Press, 1965.

Morpurgo, J. E. *Treason at West Point: The Arnold-André Conspiracy.* New York: Mason-Charter, 1975.

Morris, Richard B. *The American Revolution Reconsidered.* New York: Harper & Row, 1967.

Morris, Richard B. *Seven Who Shaped Our Destiny: The Founding Fathers as Revolutionaries.* New York: Harper & Row, 1973.

Morris, Richard B., and Woodress, James. *Voices From America's Past,* Vol. I. New York: E. P. Dutton & Co., Inc., 1961.

Morton, Louis. *Robert Carter of Nomini Hall.* Colonial Williamsburg, 1941.

Notestein, Wallace. *The English People on the Eve of Colonization.* The New American Nation Series. New York: Harper & Row, 1962.

Osborne, J. A. *Williamsburg in Colonial Times.* Port Washington, N. Y.: Kennikat Press, 1972.

Paine, Thomas. *Age of Reason.* New York: Peter Eckler, 1794.

Peterson, Merrill D. (editor). *James Madison.* New York: Harper & Row, 1974.

Phillips, Ulrich B. *Life and Labor in the Old South.* Boston, Mass.: Little, Brown & Co., 1929.

Pratt, Dorothy, and Pratt, Richard. *A Guide to Early American Homes South.* New York: Bonanza Books, 1956.

Rankin, Hugh F. *The American Revolution.* New York: Capricorn Books, 1964.

The Readers Digest Association, Inc. *The Story of America.* Pleasantville, N.Y., 1975.

Reardon, John J. *Edmund Randolph.* New York: Macmillan Publishing Co., 1974.

Robins, Sally N. *Love Stories of Famous Virginians.* Richmond, Va.: Dietz Printing, 1925.

Rogers, Frances, and Beard, Alice. *The Birth of a Nation: July 1776.* Philadelphia, Pa. and New York: J. B. Lippincott Co., 1945.

Rossiter, Clinton. *Seedtime of the Republic: The Origin of the American Tradition of Political Liberty.* New York: Harcourt, Brace & Co., 1953.

Rouse, Parke, Jr. *Planters and Pioneers: Life in Colonial Virginia.* New York: Hastings House, 1968

Rouse, Parke, Jr. *Tidewater Virginia.* New York: Hastings House, 1968.

Runes, Dagobert D. (editor). *The Selected Writings of Benjamin Rush*. New York: Philosophical Library, 1947.

Rutland, Robert A. *The Papers of George Mason*, Vol. I, 1749–1778. Chapel Hill, N.C.: University of North Carolina Press, 1970.

Sayre, Robert F. *The Examined Self: Benjamin Franklin*. Princeton, N.J.: Princeton University Press, 1964.

Shepherd, Jack. *The Adams Chronicles*. Boston, Mass.: Little, Brown & Co., 1975.

Silverman, Kenneth. *A Cultural History of the American Revolution*. New York: Thomas Y. Crowell Co., 1976.

Singleton, Esther (editor). *Historic Buildings of America*. New York: Dodd Mead & Co., 1906.

Smelser, Marshall. *The Democratic Republic*. The New American Nation Series. New York: Harper & Row, 1962.

Smith, Howard W. *Benjamin Harrison and the American Revolution*. Virginia Independence Bicentennial Commission, 1978.

Smith, Page. *John Adams*, Vols. I and II. Garden City, N.Y.: Doubleday & Co., Inc., 1962.

Spenser, Alfred (editor). *Memoirs of William Hickey*. London: Hurst and Blackett, 1948.

Starkey, Marion L. *Land Where Our Fathers Died: The Settling of the Eastern Shore 1607–1735*. Garden City, N.Y.: Doubleday & Co., Inc., 1962.

Stern, Philip Van Doren. *Robert E. Lee: The Man and the Soldier*. New York: McGraw-Hill, 1963.

Stetson, Charles W. *Washington and His Neighbors*. Richmond, Va.: Garrett and Massie, 1956.

Sydnor, Charles S. *American Revolution in the Making*. New York: Macmillan Publishing Co., 1952.

Talpalar, Morris. *The Sociology of Colonial Williamsburg*. New York: Philosophical Library, 1960.

Templeman, Eleanor Lee. *Virginia Homes of the Lees* Arlington, Va.: private, 1975.

Thane, Elswyth. *The Fighting Quaker: Nathaniel Greene*. New York: Hawthorn Books, Inc., 1972.

Thane, Elswyth. *Potomac Squire*. New York: Duell, Sloan & Pearce, 1963.

Thorp, Willard. *A Southern Reader*. New York: Alfred A. Knopf, 1955.

Tilp, Frederick. *This Was Potomac River*. Alexandria, Va.: private, 1978.

Tinling, Marion (editor). *The Correspondence of the Three William Byrds of Westover*, Vols. I and II. Charlottesville Va.: University of Virginia Press, 1977.

Toynbee, Arnold. *A Study of History*. New York: Oxford University Press, 1947.

Treloar, William Purdie. *Wilkes and the City*. London: John Murray, 1917.

Trudell, Clyde F. *Colonial Yorktown* Old Greenwich, Conn.: The Chatham Press, Inc., 1938–1971.

Van Doren, Carl (editor). *Indian Treaties Printed by Benjamin Franklin*. Pennsylvania Historical Society.

Van Schreeven, Schriber. *Revolutionary Virginia: A Documentary Road*. Charlottesville, Va.: University Press of Virginia, 1973.

Walsh, Richard, and Fox, William Lloyd. *Maryland: A History*. Baltimore, Md.: Maryland Historical Society, 1974.

Warner, Charles Willard Hoskins. *The Road to Revolution*. Richmond, Va.: Ganett & Massie, 1961.

Wartel, Harry R., Gabriel, Ralph H., and Williams, Stanley T. (editors). *The American Mind*, Vol. I. New York: American Book Co., 1947.

Wertenbaker, Thomas J. *Patrician and Plebeian in Virginia*. New York: Russell and Russell, 1959.

Wilcox, R. Turner. *Five Centuries of American Costume*. New York: Charles Scribner's Sons, 1963.

Williams, Henry L., and Williams, Ottaliek. *Great Houses of America*. New York: G. P. Putnam's Sons, 1969.

Williams, Lloyd H. *Pirates of Colonial Virginia*. Richmond, Va.: Dietz Press, 1937.

Willison, George F. *Behold Virginia!* Harcourt, Brace & Co., 1952.

Wilstach, Paul. *Mount Vernon*. Indianapolis: The Bobbs Merrill Co., 1930.

Wilstach, Paul. *Tidewater Virginia*. Indianapolis: The Bobbs Merrill Co., 1929.

Winchester, Alice (editor). *The Antiques Book*. New York: Bonanza Books, 1950.

Wister, Owen. *The Seven Ages of Washington*. Garden City, N. Y.: Garden City Publishing Co., 1907.

Woman's Auxiliary of Olivet Episcopal Church. *Virginia Cookery Past and Present*. Franconia, Virginia, 1957.

Wright, Louis B. *The Cultural Life of the American Colonies*. The New American Nation Series. New York: Harper & Row, 1962.

Wright, Louis B. *The First Gentlemen of Virginia: Intellectual Qualities of the Early Colonial Ruling Class*. San Marino, Cal.: The Huntington Library, 1940.

Wright, Louis B. (editor). *Letters of Robert Carter (1720–1727)*. Westport, Conn.: Greenwood Press, 1940.

Wright, Louis B., and Tinling, Marion (editors). *The Secret Diary of William Byrd of Westover (1709–1712)*. New York: G. P. Putnam's Sons, 1963.

Wright, Louis B., and Tinling, Marion (editors). *The Life of William Byrd of Virginia (1717–1721)*. New York: Oxford University Press, 1958.